# THE VICEROYS
## I VICERÈ

# THE
# VICEROYS

FEDERICO DE ROBERTO

*Translated from the Italian by Archibald Colquhoun*
*with an introduction by the translator*

VERSO
London • New York

This edition published by Verso 2016
First published by MacGibbon & Kee Ltd 1962
Originally published as *I vicerè*
© Aldo Garzanti, editore, Milan 1959
Translation © Archibald Colquhoun 1962, 2016

1 3 5 7 9 10 8 6 4 2

**Verso**
UK: 6 Meard Street, London W1F 0EG
US: 20 Jay Street, Suite 1010, Brooklyn, NY 11201
www.versobooks.com

Verso is the imprint of New Left Books

ISBN-13: 978-1-78478-256-6 (PB)
eISBN-13: 978-1-78478-257-3 (US)
eISBN-13: 978-1-78478-258-0 (UK)

**British Library Cataloguing in Publication Data**
A catalogue record for this book is available from the British Library

**Library of Congress Cataloging-in-Publication Data**
A catalog record for this book is available from the Library of Congress

Printed in the US by Maple Press

# CONTENTS

# FOREWORD

## Franco Moretti

In the late nineteenth century, the European novel discovered a new protagonist: the family. Unified yet proliferating, fictional families allowed writers to explore large social and geographical expanses (France in Zola's Rougon-Maquart cycle, remote reaches of the Hapsburg empire in Roth's *Radetzky March*), and to follow the course of history across several generations—from the bourgeois stability of Mann's Lübeck, to the hundred tumultuous years of Garcia Marquéz's Buendía saga.

Federico De Roberto's Uzeda are part of this constellation: a microcosm of Sicily—its 'viceroys', no less—in the decades of the *Risorgimento* and the Italian unification. Seldom, however, has a crowded novelistic family so thoroughly coincided with a single social class—and one sliding irreparably towards its ruin. The result is a unique combination of naturalistic lucidity over the fate of impoverished aristocracies, and a Goya-like inventiveness in extracting from social disintegration a whole gallery of grotesques and monstrosities, culminating in the desperate scurrility of the sadistic and promiscuous monk Don Blasco.

Readers who have encountered nineteenth-century Sicily through Lampedusa's *Leopard* (and, possibly, Visconti's silky reworking for the big screen) will find *The Viceroys* familiar, yet strangely uncanny. Though the overall arc of the story is roughly the same, Tancredi's seductive liveliness, or the Prince's civilized intelligence, are nowhere in sight; all the Uzeda have to show is sickness onto death, impotent greed, and outright imbecility. *The Viceroys* is a superb lesson in how coarse and rancid the collapse of a ruling class actually is.

# INTRODUCTION

CATANIA is one of those places that have a pervasive effect on all who live there. Cyclops were the first inhabitants of the area, and the province is scattered with place-names beginning with ' Aci ', from a local shepherd whose rivalry with a Cyclop was sung by Theocritus; at Acireale, beneath Etna, craggy islets just off the coast are called *I Ciclopi*. These legends may refer to a time when a crater of the volcano looked like some glaring eye, linked by mariners with mysterious troglodytes who lived hereabouts, the ancient Siculians. Even now there is something improbable, obsessed, about this part under Etna; slopes twist into grim shapes, houses perch on jagged residues of lava-flows, and against a prevailing colour-tone of dark grey the vegetation is all strident pinks and greens.

In atmosphere it is far removed from the serenities of Syracuse, a few miles to the south. Yet all these shores face across to the Aegean; and some underlying harmony in contrast, a creative tension emanating from these Greek parts of Sicily has combined to produce hereabouts the island's best minds, from Archimedes to Pirandello. The birthplaces of nearly every Sicilian writer, ancient and modern, are along the eastern coastline from Messina to Pachino, or at Agrigento and Caltanisetta; in comparison the Phoenician and Arab west has had speculative or scientific minds, an eighteenth-century dialect poet, and now the Prince of Lampedusa. The last great period of Palermo as a Mediterranean centre of culture dates back to Frederick II. For the last hundred years or so, the literary capital of Sicily has been half-way down the east coast, at Catania. There, towards the end of the last century, appeared a small group of writers who have gone down to Italian literary history as the *Veristi* or ' Realists '. One, Giovanni Verga, has long been considered a genius. His life-long friend and pupil, Federico De Roberto, is only being generally appreciated in Italy now, thirty-four years after his death. All were closely linked to their environment.

Volcanoes, to those who live under them, are symbols of un-predictable or sinister power, and no city in Europe is closer to one than Catania. In certain lights or under rain, the place has a brooding quality; its huge buildings, lava-grey chequered with grimy white, ooze as if from bombing in the last war. Here the volcano's influence is everywhere. A few years before the great earthquake that destroyed the town in 1693, a lava-flow had submerged and reshaped whole districts, cutting off, for instance, Castell 'Ursino from the sea which had been its outlet since medieval days. Thus the architect Vaccarini had a free hand to produce his town-planning scheme on a vast scale. The briefest tour shows how masterly was his grouping. The plan hinges brilliantly on one main artery, Via Etnea, running straight through the entire city towards the volcano. This street is an epitome of Catania's character and history. It emerges first from under the Uzeda gate, down by the old seashore where even now can be found professional story-tellers, *cantastorie*, declaim-ing tales of Roland and Excalibur. Next it passes the great steps of the cathedral, with its image of the local patron-saint, St Agata, winged and hieratic as the goddess Isis whose cult once centred here. On a fountain opposite perches the city's symbol, an elephant in lava with an obelisk on its back. From there Via Etnea sweeps on past huge churches in ' exasperated ' baroque with tiled domes glittering in the sun, past endlessly parading throngs (the street is Catania's open-air club), past gardens and monuments to another presiding genius, the com-poser Bellini; on up to where new districts spring up almost nightly in the present east-coast boom. Over it all, so near that the Cyclops should have found it easy to fling down either lava or snow, hangs the white cone, vast, aloof, of the volcano.

Etna is not mentioned much by local writers, perhaps because it is so much part of the texture of their minds. References to the volcano are oblique, as to a deity which needs propitiating. In *I vicerè*, for instance, the slopes of the volcano are merely referred to as useful boltholes from invasion or cholera. The name Uzeda is taken from a Duque de Uceda (a town, in the province of Madrid, the Spanish ' c ' changing into Sicilian 'z '), a Vice-roy of Sicily at the end of the seventeenth century, said to be partly responsible for rebuilding Catania after the earthquake of

1693. Against their setting and period the chronicles of De Roberto's Uzeda come into focus; with Etna an ever-present monster brooding over landscape, climate and architecture, this family of monsters looks less grotesque. To the inhabitants of Catania they are based on recognisable originals, accepted as part of the highly charged pattern of local life. To us they might seem provincial oddities were it not for that quality in Sicily which transforms island peculiarities into reflections of the universal, and which may be connected with its geographical position in the centre of the Mediterranean. What more universal and corroding than the pride which recurs in variations throughout *I vicerè*?

This sort of novel seldom has a hero, and the real protagonist is the Year of Unification, *dies irae, 1860* itself. Stresses of local nature combine here with exasperations of a period tense from social and economic changes centuries overdue. Garibaldi's sweep that year from Marsala across the island and up through southern Italy to beyond Naples, all in a few summer months, was one of those events with an exhilarating sense of recasting the map of history. It was the fuse-point (retarded as it turned out) of modern Sicily, politically, economically, socially, even in a way religiously. That summer Garibaldi was not only the bogey-man of the nobles, but a symbol to Sicilians who have never quite absorbed their pagan past and hailed the hero in a red shirt on a white horse as kinsman of the patroness of Palermo, Santa Rosalìa, blood-brother to the knights of the puppet-theatres, paladin in the struggle of Charlemagne and Roland against the Moors, of good against evil. There were even pictures of him wearing a crown of thorns. Surely after this apparition of the ' Knight of Humanity ' nothing would ever be the same again (though a glimpse into the interior today might make anyone wonder what all the excitement was about). But the Campaign of the Thousand—the very name rings of some antique feat—left a mark all over the south. No disillusion has quite affected it, even when Garibaldi's deputy stamped out a peasant's revolt in the (British-owned) Bronte estates, and at Aspromonte two years later he himself was attacked by troops of the Italian state he had helped to create. Whether or not Garibaldi could ever have solved Sicilian dearth, there is no doubt about the ' moment-of-truth ' quality of 1860 in the south; this explains why all major Sicilian writers, dramatists and composers have been obsessed with that year ever since, why Verga and Pirandello, De Roberto and now Lampedusa, wrote novels about the impact of change, the technique of accommodation, the effects of opportunism, in the Year of Unification. Of them all the vastest picture in size, detail and historical scope was De Roberto's.

*I viceré* is about the Risorgimento betrayed. Until recent years the aims and results of that movement have been blurred by official rhetoric and a process of falsification which began in the north of Italy and was at first due to the rôle of Piedmont and its dynasty. The piazzas of Italy are still cluttered with some of the less harmful results, those bewhiskered and gesticulating statues of the first King of United Italy, Victor Emmanuel of Savoy. Amid the confusion of motives, nationalism, dynastic aggrandisement, social aspiration, it was the south that came off worst. Seen from there the posturing and rhetoric looked suspiciously like cover for failed promises; in time this even became linked with Mussolini's rodomontades about ' eight million bayonets '. The age-old distrust of rulers throughout the south spread next to ' those in Rome '. Subsequent waves of immigration from the depressed areas of Sicily and Calabria brought with them the Mafia and Camorra, to spread all over the Americas; and, less obvious but more damaging, the diffusion from Soho throughout the world of that most inadequate and adhesive of national images, the Italian organ-grinder with a monkey on a stick.

A preoccupation of Manzoni when writing the first Italian novel *I Promessi Sposi* (' The Betrothed ') had been ' the millions whom history ignores '. In the pages of Verga we glimpse for the first time the southern worker, sober, toiling, undemonstrative, bitter sometimes at hopes deferred. Manzoni's Lombard peasants of fifty years before had been irradiated by Providence; the Furies dog Verga's fisherfolk at Acitrezza and peasant proprietors in the hinterland. All the Catanian so-called *Veristi* (' *Verismo, verismo, verità, io dico!*', exclaimed Verga) were haunted by this bitter aftermath of a Risorgimento that in Sicily during the decades after 1860 looked almost a mockery. This spirit pervades

*I vicerè*, though its protagonists were nobles and its plot the end of Sicilian feudalism (or, according to a modern historian, ' the feudalising of the Sicilian Risorgimento '). Its pages almost vibrate at times with an indignation about cant that must have affected most sensitive inhabitants of the island then, and has left traces today. They show in that very different book with a similar plot, *Il Gattopardo* ('The Leopard '); but De Roberto was nearer to the facts and less involved than the Prince of Lampedusa, not watching the ruin of his own class on its way later but noting in detail the moves used by the old order to preserve itself at the time. On a deeper level the oriental fatalism prevalent in western Sicily scarcely touched these writers of the east, who with all their disillusion (a modern critic has even accused Verga of ' narcissism of defeat '), kept alive something of the dynamism of the Risorgimento.

One result of the sweeping away of ancient state barriers was a sudden awareness of local cultural roots. In Sicily, with its unimaginable riches of untapped image and legend, there was no danger of artificial ' folklore ', and a dialect breakaway was avoided by Verga's insistence on using an Italian modified by local speech rhythms; ' By listening, listening, one learns to write ', he would say. Another major influence was literary theory from France, then prevalent in northern Europe. The French realists' advocacy of close ' objective ' study of physical and psychological detail, in effect usually turned into fixation on the drabber aspects of middle-class life around them. Since Attic days, Sicily has been a forcing-house for ideas from outside and the Catanian *Veristi*, working directly on the Sicilian themes they found around them, brought off a grafting process which made them more vital, and eventually more influential, than their French teachers.

Verga was born at Vizzini, one of those remote places in the interior whose roofs lie like leaves around a church, and whose male inhabitants appear to spend their days in the streets, cloaked and silent, staring into space. Capuana's birth-place, Mineo, is a primeval hill-town behind Catania. But De Roberto was only half-Sicilian by blood, and born in Naples, in 1861, over twenty years after either of his masters. His father was a Neapolitan who, on service in Catania as a regular officer in the Bourbon army during the last years of the Kingdom of the Two Sicilies, married the daughter of a local family, the Asmundo. Colonel De Roberto, according to family tradition, was the officer who personally consigned Naples to Garibaldi on the latter's historic entry in September, 1860. On the colonel's death his only son, aged ten, was sent for education down to his mother's family at Catania. There Federico De Roberto made his home, never to return to Naples except for an occasional visit to such family property as was there.

The Asmundo were a vast involuted tribe, of Spanish origin as the name implies (so was Verga), ruled by an aged and autocratic grandparent, chief charity commissioner for the city. Systems of life centuries behind the times have a way of being preserved in Sicily; the Asmundo were more patriarchal than feudal, and memories of the family set-up must have been at the back of De Roberto's mind when he started *I vicerè*. Not that the Asmundo, though of ancient Spanish stock, were grandees on any such scale as the book's Uzeda. One catches a glimpse, in De Roberto's background, of something far rarer, particularly in the south; the old professional upper middle-cum-minor-landowning class whose standards have helped to give fibre to the south since the Renaissance; the class to which, in Naples, belonged many of the promoters of the Parthenopean Republic and later the opposition to King ' Bomba ', and in more recent days De Sanctis, founder of Italian literary criticism, and the late Benedetto Croce. Rare on Sicily's east coast, it is almost non-existent in the west; at Palermo, even today, such standards as there are (outside the Church, the Communists, and the followers of Danilo Dolci) have devolved, for the arts at least, on to sprigs of the nobility, who take a serious part in the Regional Government's various ' Assessorates ' for the encouragement of opera, music, even tourism. Catanians have always prided themselves on energy and thrust, and life there, however provincial and enclosed, has less social rigidity. Verga, for instance, in spite of his radical views, spent most of the last twenty afternoons of his life dozing away beneath the springing arches of Palazzo Càrcaci, the Nobles' Club in Via Etnea. For De Roberto this place was merely a waste of his maestro's time. He himself had an early ' salon period ' (there is an agreeable glimpse in an early story of a duchess on her *venitiènne* in a remote darkened boudoir toying with a tortoiseshell papercutter over the pages of Bourget); but he kept away from most Catania society, which was far more flourishing at the time than it is now. No volumes of his inscribed to local great ladies survive, as they do of Verga, Capuana, and even of the ' anarchist ' poet Rapisardi. Detachment from his characters' lives gives an oddly transposable air to *I vicerè*, as if it might be in another medium, music or even dance, heard or seen through a door. Perhaps it was this quality that made the Prince of Lampedusa consider *I vicerè* as a ' picture of the Sicilian aristocracy seen from the servants' hall '. The introspective poetry of *Il Gattopardo* which gives that book its effulgence was a sign of its author's lingering involvement, while De Roberto changes key and presses on almost obsessively.

Whatever De Roberto's preferences in the way of company, he was anything but a recluse most of his life, and must have taken an active part in literary life in Florence and then in Milan, where he was established by the late 'eighties. For he followed a pattern common to Sicilians of all classes, who long to escape from their island, sometimes do and always yearn to return. In northern Italy De Roberto had no difficulty in finding his feet as critic and literary journalist; Milan had been an intellectual centre since the first Italian Encyclopedists and the ' Società del Café ' at the end of the eighteenth century. In the ferment of those years after the Unification, it was the liveliest place in the peninsula, with writers and aspirants from all over Italy, Giacosa, the two Boitos, young D'Annunzio, young Fogazzaro, congregating in the cafés around the Scala. There De Roberto first met his fellow-townsman Verga, already an established writer and just plunging into the great creative period of his life. Capuana joined them, and it is pleasant to think that the meeting of these three Sicilians amid the Lombard mists helped to bring about a renovation of Italian letters.

Cosmopolitan though Milanese literary life may have seemed then, with its pervading influences from Zola, Flaubert and Bourget, most Italian writers of the time were as provincial in their habits and interests as they are today. De Roberto cast one of the widest nets among literati of his time; he translated

Baudelaire, wrote essays on Tolstoy, Maeterlinck, Nietzsche, and through the pages of the new *Corriere della Sera* of Milan, (while Capuana did the same through *La Nazione* of Florence), became a major diffuser of French, English, German and Russian literature in the peninsula. Through forty years and in thirty volumes he ranged from psychological stories, tales of peasant life (early efforts, in imitation of Verga, though one may have been the original plot of *Cavalleria Rusticana*), realist studies, the earliest psychological thriller in the language, to works on art and antiquities, and a series of volumes on a hybrid science, very popular at the time and fitting somewhere between Lombroso and Havelock Ellis, ' the psychology of love '. At times he had hardly finished a book in one style before he was busy on something totally different, and the very breadth of his interests has tended to defy docketing and to confuse his reputation. Restless, searching, diffusing throughout his life a kind of intimate disquiet, he was an example of that strange island ill which Sicilians are apt to illude themselves preoccupies us all, *la tensione siciliana*.

He began writing early, first published some scientific papers at the age of nineteen, and in spite of the tacking of his talent remained a dedicated writer all his life. A cool eye for the vagaries of human conduct and of daily reality combined with technical control to avoid literary attitudes. According to Brancati and Pirandello he was already at his best in his very first book of stories of Catania life, *Processi Verbali*. Soon, in his first novel, *Ermanno Raeli* (1889), came influences from France, particularly of Bourget; this is an uneven book about a young Sicilian of half-German extraction and his troubles in integrating a double nature into Sicilian life. ' Happiness is a chimera ' is the opening line, and one might dismiss this book as full of woozy adolescent self-pity were there not glimpses of an adult and original mind, some good talk on a local baroque painter who is still too little known, Pietro Novelli il Monrealese, and well-observed details of a Palermo winter season in the 'eighties, when for the locals ' all foreigners were English '. Tension and disquiet show again, more clearly, in his second novel, *L'Illusione* (1891), whose theme was a bold one for the period, a woman's search for true love from one affair to another. Poor

Donna Teresa may have some affiliations with that other self-destroying charmer, La Pisana of Nievo's *Confessions*; but she is more obviously a victim; her provenance is from Flaubert and she is a Sicilian Bovary. *L'Illusione* also turns out to be a crab-like approach to *I vicerè*, for the heroine is an Uzeda, daughter of two main characters in the later novel, the selfish charmer Don Raimondo and his hapless first wife. De Roberto's correspondence has not yet been properly sifted and we do not know if he already had the vast novel in view when he wrote *L'Illusione*. Or did an attempt to explain Donna Teresa in terms of heredity draw him into an ever-spreading family chronicle, hoping to find somewhere an answer to the nag of his life, the meaning of love?

*I vicerè*, published in 1894, seems to have been written very fast, though it may have been partly in his head already, for its structure suggests careful planning. The manuscript, unlike the tortured pages of Manzoni's *I Promessi Sposi*, shows few erasions for a first draft. The idea of the book must have been with him ever since the time when, a youth just out of school, he had spent a period as librarian in the new civic reading-rooms, once the great library of the monastery of San Nicolò l'Arena in Catania. No-one could work there now without being affected by past splendours, for the monastery, according to De Roberto's own later computation, was the biggest in Europe except for Mafra; it now houses not only the huge municipal library, but four day-schools, an art-school, a gymnasium, a barracks and an observatory, the whole with its orchards and outhouses covering in its day a district of the town. In this improbable building were set some of the most fascinating scenes in the book. The vast luxurious monastery becomes a twin pivot, with the palace of the Uzeda in the town below, for pride, corruption and greed. The facts may be coloured, but there is no doubt about their accuracy. At the time of the sequestration in 1862, when church property was sold off at what turned out to have been mainly rigged auctions, the monastery drew an income from fifty-two estates, for the benefit of some fifty choir-monks and their dependants, of about the modern equivalent of £100,000, or $280,000, a year (untaxed). The Sicilian Church, until 1860, had become progressively more prosperous ever since the allocation to it by the Norman Kings of a third of the island's land and many privileges. Both at San Nicolò and at their other great house, Monreale outside Palermo, the Benedictines in Sicily had become powerful and lax. Though their Order's ancient tradition of distinction in science and letters was still very important to island life, and their vast rentals were so extensively used for the relief of the needy that no-one has yet filled the gap (facts never mentioned by De Roberto), yet their discipline was loose; power and riches had brought pride, and there was an insistence on noble blood which is certainly not to be found anywhere in the Rule of St Benedict.* Annals show how tense their relations often were with the local archdiocese, and even with the Papacy itself, while their public contribution to the religious life of Catania was limited to one sumptuous procession on Corpus Christi Day. Like most Italian writers during the last hundred years, De Roberto was anti-clerical. The local combination of paternalism, outward splendour, squalor, insistence on the letter to the detriment of the spirit, must have driven hard such faith as he had. San Nicolò, to him, represented the worst side of religion in Sicily, and his prejudices were apt to run away with him, although he was generally scrupulous about his documentation. The weak Abbot who makes an occasional semi-imbecile appearance in *I vicerè* can only be based on a very different figure, who tried to reform both Monreale and then San Nicolò at this time: the saintly and shrewd Cardinal Dusmet, revered in Catania as ' friend of the poor ' and now under process for sanctification. But the relations of love-hate, attraction and repulsion between modern Sicilian writers and their Church would make a fascinating, though rather macabre, study in itself.

Identifying characters in such a local novel can be a stimulating entry into Catanian life, and so an effective if roundabout help to appreciation. Though the family of Uzeda have as much basis in reality as Proust's Guermantes, only the Paternò Castello clan in its various branches held an analogous position at the time. Don Blasco, for instance, an improbable figure to us outside the pages of some biased account of

---

* *cf.* the causes of relaxation of monastic discipline in the ninth century, at the times of the reforms of St Benedict of Aneane ; these according to Mabillon, were undue severity or indulgence by superiors, greed for property, and consequent law-suits and quarrels.

monastic life before the French Revolution, turns out to be *una cosa naturalissima* in Catania, possibly based in part on a Father Paternò Castello who was famous in the town fifty years ago and is still remembered for his private life and public bluster. There, opposite the great monastery façade (for the Italian State Monopoly rarely changes sites) is still the tobacconist's where reigned his mistress, the 'Cigar-woman'. To create these macabre grandees, near-brigands or near-saints De Roberto had to combine traits of feudal families all over Sicily, and his Uzeda stand out like Goyas, exceptional beings demanding exceptional treatment. For such a conception gentler sides have to be played down. The Princes of Bìscari, Paternò Castello, were Maecenases of the arts with a liberal tradition since their ancestor corresponded with Voltaire and befriended Goethe; the Dukes of Càrcaci, Paternò Castello, still have the most civilised manners in town ('Wherever there is a Càrcaci one can *breathe*!' says a young American resident). A more obvious model was the late nineteenth-century Marchese di San Giuliano, Paternò Castello, who became Foreign Minister of Italy under Giolitti, and whose character and career are freely sketched into the young Prince Consalvo. Palazzo San Giuliano may well be the original of the Francalanza palace of the book, for it fills a whole side of its own square on Via Etnea and is so vast and imposing that, with its entrance covered in commemorative plaques of royal visits, it is often mistaken for the town-hall opposite. Although now housing a bank, numerous shops and businesses and a large hotel, high on its main façade can still be seen two shuttered windows on rooms which are never opened, due to some tragedy, rumour has it, or perhaps some monster . . . In Catania the monstrous and improbable are never very far away, particularly among the established classes. Even poor old Don Eugenio, the only Uzeda who was perhaps an artist manqué, had a prototype, an old beggar often seen within living memory around the smarter cafés, who would take alms only from nobles of rank equal to himself.

Later, Vitaliano Brancati extended this panorama to the middle classes, whose predicament between the two wars was brilliantly and terrifyingly caught by his novels, *Il Bell' Antonio* and *Don Giovanni in Sicilia*.

Since the late 'nineties De Roberto had spent part of each year at Catania, and eventually ill-health decided him to settle definitely in his beloved city. This return to origins did not have the psychic effect on him that it did on Verga, whose displacement home from cosy Milan brought about one of those mysterious crises of Sicilian inertia, so that he never wrote more than an odd chapter or so of his great planned cycle about *I Vinti* ('The Defeated'). De Roberto, as well as directing the city's museums and antiquities, kept up a flow of varied productions; studies, short stories, plays, essays, they appeared regularly, uneven, original, all stamped somewhere with a directness, at times an acrid immediacy, that was becoming increasingly rare in Italian letters as D'Annunzio's influence grew. Occasionally he produced something outstanding, such as his tales of military life during the first world war; one short story written at this time, *La Paura*, about a soldier's fear, treated battle so frankly that it was not published until after his death. Such writing has only been appreciated in Italy during the last few years, partly through the influence of Hemingway, who might have written these stories himself.

Sometimes De Roberto's choice of plots make an unconscious pattern; an old lady gambles away her last cent with her chaplain; a confessor is tempted by his penitent; an anarchist prince murders his mistress; love natural and supernatural is found and lost and twisted. Among his most impressive stories are *Il Rosario*, about an old woman reciting her rosary as she refuses to pardon a dying daughter; *Il Sogno*, a successful piece of experimental writing, on a man's thoughts to the rhythm of the train in which he is escaping from wife to mistress; *La Messa di Nozze* (1911), a short novel whose plot turns on a moving and elaborately treated crisis of conscience by a woman during her marriage service. Fascination with the Church, horror of unctuousness, terror of love ' *soif de l'absolu* ' perhaps unacknowledged . . . no wonder his fiction and his ' scientific ' and even his historical studies, emanate a tense, sometimes brusque disquiet; even at the Feast of the Assumption at Randazzo the decorated float reminded him of the chariot of Vishnu or Moloch.

Neither Verga nor De Roberto ever married, both having theories about a writer being wedded to his work. This did not prevent Verga from keeping secret mistresses with whom he would vanish for long jaunts in northern Europe, unknown to all till after his death. De Roberto stayed at home with his mother, locked in one of those relationships which are inexplicably both closer and less neurotic in the south. Love betrayed recurs so often in his writing that he must have set up some embittering pattern of his own, driven perhaps too by that sexual rhetoric of Catania for which Brancati found a new word, based on the image of a strutting cock, *gallismo*. With all De Roberto's clarity and energy his writing is full of the strange Sicilian character, its subdued fervour and sadness, its solitude beyond the smiles. Is its only cause, as some historians insist, a social structure too ill-balanced to release local energies? Or is there some deeper anguish in Pirandello's comment ' Intelligence is a terrible thing because it destroys the beauty of life ', or in the title of his last ' Notes on my involuntary sojourn on earth '? A remark which De Roberto put into the mouth of Mme de Maintenon, ' Nothing is more able than irreproachable conduct ', calls up one of those silently screaming cardinals by Francis Bacon. Sicily now is one of the few places where Stendhal would still find his ' *sombre Italie* '.

De Roberto's last years were spent either tending at his mother's bedside or looking after Verga's literary interests, and at his death in 1927 he left behind a mass of unfinished manuscripts; a history of Malta, a biography of Verga, the complete first part of a novel, *L'Imperio*, which continued the story of the last Uzeda, Prince Consalvo, in Rome. Such fame as he had outside Sicily dated back to the 'nineties, his writing was not the kind to appeal to Fascism, his books were allowed to fall out of print while in public demand, and within a few years he was almost forgotten except by specialists; though it is pleasant to record that Edith Wharton was an enthusiast about *I vicerè*, and, through her, Bernard Berenson. Now Italians are probably closer to his spirit than ever before. There is a growing realisation of the odd and important place that Sicily occupies in their modern literature, of, for instance, De Roberto's influence on the narrative style of Moravia, of the *Veristi's* direct perception as part of that chain in Italian art which links Giotto to realist films. De Roberto's work is likely to be reassessed against a wider background. 'God concedes to every artist one hour that is truly great ', he once told an admirer, but never said which he thought to be his.

We catch a glimpse of him through contemporary eyes, out on his stroll at *l'ora del gelato* ('ice-cream-time ') in Via Etnea; Cavaliere Roberto, he was known as, one of the city's major personalities; a spry figure, with a quizzical look behind his eye-glass and above a high stiff collar and white waistcoat. He passes among the parading carriages, the jostling carts, the barrel-organs playing *Casta Diva*, under the all-seeing eye of Etna. If it were the Feast of St Agata there would be tall constructions of gilt and baroque quivering down Via Etnea among squibs and shouts and fervour, as they do every year. Even now, feudalism has its trappings and some descendants of the old Spanish viceroys flourish, for during the feast the image is still greeted by a flow of splendid liveries in the palace on Via Etnea of the Prince of Roccaromana (Paternò Castello). As the afternoon light fades great balloon figures, floating spread against the sky, diffuse an odd sense of timelessness, so that De Roberto and the carriages might still be there. On one such afternoon he must have scribbled the lines found on his desk after his death: ' Among all human constructions the only ones that avoid the dissolving hands of time are castles in the air.'

ARCHIBALD COLQUHOUN

*Allington, Kent.*
*July, 1961.*

# TRANSLATOR'S NOTE

T H E first publication of *I vicerè* was in 1894, and its earliest translation, into Polish, in 1905. In 1954 it was translated into French by Henriette Valot, with an introduction by Marcel Brion (Club Bibliophile de France), and in 1959 into German (Nymphenburger Verlagshandlung, Munich). This is the first book by Federico De Roberto to appear in English. The Italian prose flows very fast, as if under pressure, and is full of racy idiom, Sicilian and otherwise. Without the numerous, meticulous and very valuable suggestions of Mr John D. Christie, Lecturer in Humanity at Glasgow University, I should often have gone astray. I am also grateful to Mr Anthony Pensabene for translating the verses, to Signora Natalia Baldini (Natalia Ginzburg) for drafting some difficult pages, to Professor Ermanno Scudèri of Catania for many informative and agreeable conversations about De Roberto, and to Dott. Andrea Cavadi and the staffs of the Biblioteca Universitaria, Catania, and of The Italian Institute, London, particularly Signor Camillo Pennati, for invaluable help. The author's niece, Donna Marianna Paola De Roberto of Catania, owner of most of his manuscripts and letters, among other kindnesses, showed me her uncle's library and the original manuscript of *I vicerè*.

This text is complete, and based on the Garzanti edition of 1959, edited by Luigi Russo. In the same edition are to be found the other works by De Roberto now in print, *La Messa di Nozze*, *Il Rosario*, and *La Paura*.

A.C.

# The
# VICEROYS

# PRINCIPAL CHARACTERS

*The Uzeda family*
The late Donna Teresa Uzeda and Risà, Princess of Francalanza

*Her children*
Donna Angiolina (Sister Maria of the Cross), Nun of San Placido
Don Giacomo XIV, Prince of Francalanza
  First wife:    Margherita (*née* Grazzeri)
  Children:     Consalvo, Prince of Mirabella (*later* Prince of
                Francalanza)
                Teresa, *later* Duchess Radalì
  Second wife:  Donna Graziella (Carvano)
Don Lodovico, Prior of San Nicola (a Benedictine monk, *later*
           Cardinal)
Don Raimondo, Count of Lumera
  First wife:    Donna Matilde
  Second wife:  Donna Isabella (Fersa)
Donna Chiara, Marchesa of Villardita
  Her husband: Federico, Marchese of Villardita
Don Ferdinando, of Pietra dell'Ovo
Donna Lucrezia, *later married* to Benedetto Giulente

*Her in-laws:* the brothers and sisters of her late husband
              Don Gaspare, Duke of Oragua
              Don Blasco (a Benedictine monk)
              Cavaliere Don Eugenio
              Donna Ferdinanda (spinster)

Land in Sicily was measured by SALMA, equivalent to just under an acre. The main weight measurement was a ROTOLO, equivalent to about 2lb: these terms became officially disused after 1860.

# BOOK I

# 1

GIUSEPPE was standing in front of the gates, dandling his baby, showing it the marble coat-of-arms on top of the arch, the arms-rack nailed to the vestibule wall where the prince's men hung their pikes in olden times, when there came the sound, quickly growing louder, of a vehicle arriving at full tilt; and even before he had time to turn round, into the courtyard with a deafening clatter drove a curricle so dusty it looked as if it had been snowed on, its horse afroth with sweat. From the arch to the inner courtyard peered faces of servants and retainers; Baldassarre the major-domo opened a window on the second-floor loggia as Salvatore Cerra jumped from the vehicle with a letter in his hand.

'Don Salvatore? . . . What's up? . . . What's new?'

But the other gave a wave of despair and rushed up the stairs four at a time.

Giuseppe stood there in amazement, not understanding, the baby still round his neck. But his wife and Baldassarre's wife, and the washerwoman, and lots of other servants were already surrounding the carriage, and crossing themselves as they heard the coachman say between sobs: 'The princess . . . dead of a stroke . . . This morning as I was washing the carriage . . .'

'Jesus! . . . Jesus! . . .'

'Orders to harness . . . Signor Marco rushing round . . . the Vicar-General and neighbours . . . Just time to get there . . .'

'Jesus! Jesus! . . . But how? . . . Wasn't she better? And Signor Marco? . . . No warning from him? . . .'

'How should I know? . . . I've seen nothing; they called me . . . She was said to be well last night . . .'

'Without one of her children! . . . In the hands of strangers!
. . . Ill, yes she was ill; even so, all so suddenly! . . .'
A shout from the top of the stairs interrupted the chatter.
'Pasquale! . . . Pasquale! . . .'
'Ehi, Baldassarre?'
'A fresh horse, right away!'
'At once.'
While coachmen and henchmen worked to unharness the
sweating, panting horse and put in another, all the other ser-
vants gathered in the courtyard, commenting on the news, pass-
ing it on to the clerks in the administrative offices leaning out
of the first-floor windows, or even coming right down them-
selves.
'How terrible! . . . Just can't believe it! . . . Whoever'd
thought it, like this . . .'
The women were lamenting most:
'Without a single child by her! . . . Without even time to
call her children . . .'
'The gates? . . . Why don't you shut the gates,' suggested
Salemi, his pen still behind his ear.
But the porter, having handed the baby over to his wife at
last, and now beginning to understand something of what was
going on, looked around at the others.
'Should I? . . . What about Don Baldassarre?'
'Ssh! . . . Ssh! . . .'
'What's up?'
Talk died away again and all stiffened and took off their caps
and lowered their pipes, for the prince in person was descending
the stairs between Baldassarre and Salvatore. He had not even
changed his clothes! He was leaving in the same suit, to reach
his dead mother's bedside as soon as possible! And he was white
as a sheet, glancing impatiently at the ostlers not yet ready, and
whispering orders meanwhile to Baldassarre, who bowed his bare
gleaming head at each of his master's words: 'Yes, Excellency!
Yes, Excellency!' The coachman was still fixing the girths as his
master jumped into the carriage with Salvatore on the box.
Baldassarre hung on to the carriage door, still listening to orders,
then ran beside the curricle beyond the gate to catch last instructions: 'Yes, Excellency! Yes, Excellency!'

'Baldassarre! . . . Don Baldassarre! . . .' All besieged the major-domo now as, having finally left the carriage, which raced off, he re-entered the courtyard. ' Baldassarre, what about it? . . . What do we do now? . . . Don Baldassarre, shall I shut up? . . .'

But, with the serious air of solemn occasions, he was hurrying towards the stairs, freeing himself from the importunate with a gesture of the arm and an impatient ' Coming!'

The gates stayed wide open; a few passers-by, noticing the unusual movement in the courtyard, were asking the porter for news; the cabinet-maker, the baker, the vintner and the watch-maker, who had shops on the east front, also came to put in their heads, hear news of the great disaster, comment on the prince's sudden departure:

' And people said the master didn't love his mother! . . . He looked like Christ down from the Cross, poor boy! . . .'

The women were now thinking of Signorina Lucrezia and of the young princess; did they know nothing, or had the news been kept from them? . . . And Baldassarre, what the devil did Baldassarre think he was doing, not giving orders to shut all up? Don Gaspare, the head coachman, looking green as garlic, shrugged his shoulders:

' Everything's upside-down here.'

But Pasqualino Riso, the second coachman, spat out right in his face:

' Don't worry, you won't have to put up with it long.'

Back came the other with:

' You're all right, being the master's pimp!'

Out came Pasqualino, quick as a flash, with:

' As you were the young count's . . .'

On they went till Salemi, on his way back to the offices, called out:

' You ought to be ashamed of yourselves!'

But Don Gaspare was so sure of losing his job that he had lost control of himself, and went on:

' Ashamed? Of being in a house where mother and children are at each other's throats!'

And now many voices called out:

' Silence!'

But those who had sided too openly with the princess were feeling very small, sure as they were of being dismissed by her son. Giuseppe did not know what to do in all that confusion; he was longing to shut the gates for his mistress's death, as seemed proper. Why ever didn't Don Baldassarre give the order? And without Don Baldassarre's order not a thing could be done. Why, not even the shutters were closed on the main floor. And as time passed and no order came, some down in the court began fearing or hoping that maybe the mistress wasn't dead. 'Who said she was dead? . . . The coachman! . . . But he never saw her! . . . He might have misunderstood! . . .' Other arguments were produced in support of this idea: the prince would not have left in such a rush if she were dead, as there would have been nothing for him to do up there . . . And for some the doubt began to be a certainty; there must have been a misunderstanding, the princess was only on her deathbed . . .

But eventually Baldassarre put his head out from above the loggia and shouted:

'Giuseppe, the gates! You haven't shut the gates! And close the stable and coachhouse windows. And tell 'em to shut the shops. Shut everything!'

'No hurry!' murmured Don Gaspare.

And as, pushed by Giuseppe, the great gates turned at last on their hinges, passers-by began gathering in little groups. 'Who's dead? . . . The princess? . . . At the Belvedere? . . .' Giuseppe, now quite beside himself, shrugged his shoulders. But questions and answers crossed confusedly in the crowd, 'Was she in the country? . . . Ill for at least a year . . . Alone? . . . With none of her children! . . .' The better informed explained, 'She wanted no one with her, except her agent . . . she couldn't bear them . . .' Said an old man, shaking his head, 'A mad lot, these Francalanza!'

Meanwhile the retainers were barring up windows of stables and coachhouses; baker, vintner, cabinet-maker and watch-maker also put up their shutters. Another group of curious passers-by had gathered by the service gates, which were still open, and looked at the confused coming and going of domestics in the courtyard, while from up on the loggia, like a ship's captain, Baldassarre imparted order after order.

Pasqualino, go to the Signora Marchesa and to the Benedictines . . . But give the news to the Signor Marchese and to Father Don Blasco, d'you understand? . . . Not to the Prior! . . . Now you, Filippo, go to Donna Ferdinanda's . . . Donna Vincenza? Where's Donna Vincenza? . . . Take your shawl and go off to the convent . . . Ask the Mother Abbess to prepare the nun for the news . . . Just a minute! First come up and see the princess, who wants a word with you . . . Salemi? . . . Giuseppe, only let in close relatives . . . Has Salemi come? . . . Drop everything. The prince and Signor Marco are expecting you up there, as they need help. Natale, you go to Donna Graziella and the duchess. Agostino, these wires to the Telegraph Office . . . and pass by the tailor's . . .'

As they got their commissions, the servants left and made their way through the crowd outside. They passed with the hurried air of military aides-de-camp, amid bystanders' comments: 'They're off to tell the relatives . . . the sons and daughters, the in-laws, nieces and nephews, the dead woman's cousins . . .' The whole nobility would be in mourning, all the gates of noble palaces were now being closed or half closed according to degree of kinship. And the cabinet-maker explained:

'Seven children, let's count 'em; the Prince Giacomo and the Signorina Lucrezia, who lives at home with him, that's two. The Prior of San Nicola and the nun of San Placido, that's four. Donna Chiara, married to the Marchese of Villardita, that's five. The Cavaliere Ferdinando up at Pietra dell'Ovo, six. And finally the young Count Raimondo, who married Baron Palmi's daughter . . . Then come her four in-laws; the Duke of Oragua, the last prince's brother; Don Blasco, also a Benedictine monk; the Cavaliere Don Eugenio; and Donna Ferdinanda the spinster . . .'

Every time the wicket-gate opened to let a servant through, the watchers tried to look inside the courtyard. Giuseppe lost patience and exclaimed:

'Away from here! What the devil d'you want? Waiting for lottery numbers?'

But the crowd did not move and stared up at the windows, now shut, just as if they were waiting for the appearance of numbers on placards.

31

The news was racing from mouth to mouth, like that of a public event. 'Donna Teresa Uzeda is dead . . .' the populace pronounced it ' Auzeda ', ' the Princess of Francalanza . . . She died this morning at dawn . . . Her son the prince was there . . . No, he left an hour ago.' Meanwhile the cabinet-maker, amid a group of listeners as attentive as if he were telling legends from old chronicles, went on enumerating the other relations. ' There's the Duke Don Mario Radalì, a loony, with two sons, Michele and Giovannino, by Donna Caterina Bonello; he belongs to a collateral branch, Radalì Uzeda; the Signora Donna Graziella, daughter of the princess's dead sister and wife of the Cavaliere Carvano, and so a first cousin of all the dead woman's children; the Baron Grazzeri, the young princess's uncle with all their relations; then the more distant relatives, and connections, almost all the city nobility; the Costante, the Raimonti, the Cùrcuma, the Cugnò . . .' Suddenly he interrupted himself to say :

' Aha ! Here come the parasites arriving before anyone else !'

Don Mariano Grispo and Don Giacinto Costantino were arriving, as they did every day at lunch-time, to pay court to 'the prince, and knew nothing. On noticing the crowd, and the shut gate, they stopped in their tracks.

' Holy Faith ! Good God of Love ! . . .'

Suddenly they increased their pace, and went in, questioning in consternation the porter as he gave them the first news. ' It can't be true ! . . . A thunderbolt from a clear sky ! . . .' Then they went upstairs with Baldassarre, who was also just going up from the court, and moved before them murmuring :

' Poor princess ! . . . It was too much for her . . . And the Signor Prince left at once !'

As they passed through a row of antechambers with gilt doors but almost bare of furniture, Don Giacinto exclaimed in a low voice, as if in church :

' 'Tis a disaster indeed ! . . . A bigger one for this family than for any other . . .'

And Don Mariano confirmed in as low a voice, with a shake of the head :

32

' She led 'em all, kept the whole thing going! . . .'

On entering the Yellow Drawing-room they stopped after a few steps, unable to make anything out in the dark. But they were guided by the Princess Margherita's voice:

' Don Mariano . . . Don Giacinto . . .'

' Princess! . . . Ah, dear lady . . . How are you bearing up? And Lucrezia? . . . Consalvo? . . . The girl?'

The little prince, sitting on a stool, with his legs dangling, was swinging them to and fro, staring in the air with his mouth open. In the corner of a sofa, apart, Lucrezia was crouched, dry-eyed.

' But how did it happen, all so suddenly?' Don Mariano kept on asking.

The princess flung out her arms and said:

' I don't know . . . I don't understand . . . Salvatore just came from the Belvedere with a note from Signor Marco . . . there on that table, look at it . . . Giacomino left at once.' Then in a low voice, turning to Don Mariano as the other read the note, she added, ' Lucrezia wanted to go too, but her brother said no . . . What could she have done there?'

' Just made more confusion! . . . the prince was right . . .'

' Not a thing!' announced Don Giacinto, after reading the note, ' it doesn't explain a thing! Have the others been told? . . . Cables been sent? . . .'

' I don't know . . . Baldassarre . . .'

' What a death, all alone, without a child or relation near her!' exclaimed Don Mariano, unable to take it all in; but Don Giacinto continued:

' It's not their fault, poor things! . . . They've clear con-sciences.'

' If she'd wanted us . . .' began the princess timidly, in a lower voice. Then, almost as if frightened, she did not end the phrase.

Don Mariano drew a sad sigh and went up to the girl.

' Poor Lucrezia! What a tragedy! . . . You're right! . . . But take heart! Courage! . . .'

She, who was sitting staring at the floor and tapping a foot, raised her head with a bemused look as if not understanding. Then, a clatter was heard of carriages entering the courtyard, and Don Mariano and Don Giacinto began exclaiming in turns:

' What an irreparable disaster!'

In came the Marchesa Chiara with her husband, and also Cousin Graziella.

' Lucrezia, your mama! . . . sister! . . . cousin! . . .'

On their heels was Aunt Ferdinanda, whose hands the women kissed, murmuring:

' Excellency! . . . You've heard? . . .'

The gaunt old spinster nodded. Sobbing, Chiara embraced Lucrezia, the marchese gave the two hangers-on a subdued greeting; but Donna Graziella was most moved of all:

' It just doesn't seem true! . . . I just couldn't believe it! To die like that! . . . What about poor Giacomo? They say he rushed straight off up there? . . . Poor cousin! . . . If only he'd been in time to close her eyes! . . . What sorrow for him not to have been in time to see her again! . . .' Hearing Chiara sobbing on her sister Lucrezia's bosom, she exclaimed, ' That's right, let yourself go, my poor child! One has only one mother! . . .'

So sorrow-struck did she seem by her cousins' tragedy as even to forget that the dead woman was her own mother's sister. Proffering help to the princess, she drew her aside and said:

' D'you need anything? . . . Would you like me to give a hand? . . . How's my goddaughter? . . . What message did my cousin leave? . . .'

' I don't know . . . He gave Baldassarre orders . . .'

Baldassarre in fact was rushing up and down, sending more messengers, seeing those returning from their commissions. All the relations were now told; only the messenger sent to the Benedictines came to say that Father Don Lodovico was about to arrive, but that Father Don Blasco was not in the monastery.

' Go to the Cigar-woman's . . . he'll be with her at this time of day . . . Hurry up, tell 'im his sister-in-law's dead.'

Don Lodovico arrived in the San Nicola carriage. In the Yellow Drawing-room all rose at the appearance of the Prior. Chiara and Lucrezia went towards him, each took one of his hands, and the marchesa fell on her knees and burst out with:

' Lodovico! . . . Lodovico! . . . Our poor mama.'

All were silent, looking at that group. Cousin Graziella with red eyes was murmuring:

' It tears the heart-strings!'

The Prior bent over his sister, raised her without looking her in the face, and in the general silence broken by short repressed sobs, said, raising dry eyes to heaven:

' The Lord has called her to Him. Let us bow our heads before the decrees of Divine Providence . . .' And as Chiara tried to kiss his hand, he withdrew it.

' No, no, sister . . .' And he drew her to his breast and kissed her on the forehead.

' 'Tis our lot! . . .' Don Giacinto exclaimed sadly in Don Mariano's ear, but the latter shook his head and moved forward with a resolute air:

' Enough now, please! . . . The dead are dead, and no weeping will bring them to life . . . Consider your health now, that's the important thing . . .'

' Yes, take courage, you poor dears!' added Cousin Graziella, taking her cousins by the hand, and lovingly forcing them to sit down. Meanwhile the marchese was kissing his wife on the forehead, drying her eyes, whispering in her ear, and Donna Ferdinanda, not much given to scenes of pathos, took the little prince on her knees.

Signor Marco's note passed from hand to hand. The Prior now announced his intention of leaving for the Belvedere too, but the two hangers-on protested.

' What for? . . . Torture yourself for no purpose? . . . If there were any help to be given . . .'

' Let me go!' added Cousin Graziella.

' Let's just wait,' proposed the marchese. ' Giacomo is bound to send some news . . .'

The arrival of another carriage made people think that someone had in fact arrived from the Belvedere. But it was the Duchess Radalì. As her husband was mad and she never paid visits, her prompt arrival drew more tenderness than ever from Cousin Graziella, who called her ' aunt ' though there was no relationship between them. But Donna Vincenza's return from San Placido brought emotion to its climax. The serving-woman could find no words to express the nun's sorrow, and clasped her hands with pity:

' Poor girl! Poor dear girl! . . . Like a mad woman she is,

just like a mad woman . . . And calling out, "Sisters! Sisters!" . . .'

Now Lucrezia also was weeping, Chiara said between her sobs:

'I'm going to the convent . . .'

'Your Excellency would be doing holy work . . . The Mother Abbess too was sobbing, "the poor princess! a worthy servant of God!"'

Cousin Graziella offered to accompany her; then seeing the princess did not know where to turn:

'I'd better stay and help Margherita,' she said to Chiara, and the latter got up, while everyone gave messages:

'Give her a kiss from me . . . And from me . . . Tell her I'll come to see her tomorrow . . .' And Don Giacinto called out, 'Marchese, marchese . . . Accompany your wife . . .'

Amid this confusion, while the marchesa was going off with her husband, Don Blasco at last appeared, his big face gleaming with sweat, and a tricorn on his head. He came in without a greeting to anyone, and exclaiming:

'I said it, didn't I? . . . It was bound to end like this!'

No one replied. The Prior lowered his eyes to the floor as if looking for something. Donna Ferdinanda did not even seem to have noticed her brother's arrival. The monk began to walk from one end of the room to the other, mopping the sweat on his neck and still talking to himself:

'Pig-headed! . . . pig-headed! To the very last! . . . To go and die in that twister's hands. I foretold it, eh? . . . Where is he? Hasn't he come? And to think he's master here!'

As no one breathed a word, Cousin Graziella took it on herself to observe:

'Uncle, at such a moment . . .'

'What's that mean, at such a moment?' replied the monk caught on the raw. 'She's dead, may God glorify her! . . . But what's to be said about it? That she's done something wonderful? . . . And what about Giacomo? . . . Has he gone? . . . Has he gone alone? . . . Why does no one else go? . . . Has he forbidden others to go? . . .'

'No, Excellency . . .' replied the princess timidly. 'He left as soon as he heard the news.'

' I wanted to go with him . . .' said Lucrezia, whereupon the Benedictine pounced on her :

' You? What for? Always you women interfering! D'you think you are the only ones who can settle things? . . . Where's Ferdinando . . . Hasn't he come yet?'

At that moment arrived the Cavaliere Don Eugenio, and Don Cono Canalà, another of the hangers-on. Don Cono entered on tiptoe, as if afraid of breaking something, and stopping in front of the princess, waving his arms, exclaimed:

' Immense calamity! . . . Immeasurable catastrophe! . . . Words die on lips . . .' while the Cavaliere read Signor Marco's note.

Meanwhile Don Blasco was wandering round like a spinning-top, stopping by doors, looking down the row of rooms, seeming to sniff the air as he muttered:

' Such haste! . . . Such devotion!' and other, incomprehensible, words.

Within the group of relatives each was now giving his own opinion. The Prior, next to the duchess and to his Aunt Ferdinanda, was talking in a low voice about his mother's ' unfortunate obstinacy ', but every now and then, as if afraid of doing wrong by discussing the dead woman's wishes, however respectfully, he would interrupt himself and bow his head. Cousin Graziella was worrying about the lack of news from the Belvedere:

' Giacomo could have sent someone down! . . .'

At this Don Eugenio offered to go up if a carriage was harnessed for him; then the princess, embarrassed and confused, did not know what to do, and observed in her cousin's ear:

' I don't know . . . Giacomo may not like it . . .'

Then Donna Graziella intervened:

' Let's wait a little longer; maybe Cousin Giacomo will return himself.'

The Prior and the duchess were now asking again:

' What about Ferdinando? Why isn't he here?'

The hangers-on hurried off to question Baldassarre. The major-domo replied:

' I did not send anyone to the Cavaliere Ferdinando, as the Signor Prince told me that he would pass by there himself.'

'He may have gone to the Belvedere too . . . Or he'd be here by now.'

Anyway it took some time to reach the Pietra dell'Ovo; and in fact the marchesa returned first from the convent, having been given by her sister, the nun, a habit for the dead woman to wear.

'Touching sign of filial piety!' murmured Don Cono to Don Eugenio.

No one else spoke in those moments of emotion; only Cousin Graziella, drying her red eyes, suggested into the princess's ear:

'I'd like to take advantage of this moment to induce Uncle Blasco to make it up with Aunt Ferdinanda and Don Lodovico. What d'you say, Margherita?'

'As you think . . . if you think . . . you do . . .'

And Cousin Graziella went to look for the monk. She could not find him, he had vanished. Baldassarre, told to track him down, discovered him at the other end of the house, before a locked door leading to the dead woman's apartments. Hearing footsteps, the monk swung round.

'Who's there?'

'They are awaiting Your Paternity in the Yellow Drawing-room.'

The Benedictine turned back with a snort. Cousin Graziella came to meet him with a mysterious air and said:

'Excellency, come and embrace your sister . . . and let Lodovico kiss your hand . . .' He turned his back and exclaimed out loud so that all could hear him even down in the courtyard:

'Let's cut out the charades!'

Donna Graziella shrugged her shoulders, with a gesture of sad resignation.

The monk, noticing the marchese, who had returned with his wife from the convent, went up to him, seized him by an arm and pulled him into the Portrait Gallery.

'What are you doing here? . . . Why haven't you left? The other one's gone . . .'

'What for, Excellency?'

'Will you always be a ninny? That other has gone there! By now he'll have made a clean sweep . . .'

' Excellency!' protested his nephew, scandalised.

Don Blasco looked him in the whites of the eyes as if wanting to eat him. But then, as Baldassarre rushed by, he turned on his heels booming:

' Ah, no? Go stew in your own juice, the lot of you . . .'

After giving all his orders to the servants, Baldassarre was now in a great rush, as messages began to arrive from more distant relatives, friends, and acquaintances who were sending to express their condolences and get news of the survivors. The major-domo received the more respectable messengers in the ante-chamber of the administrative offices, leaving servants to the porter; but many among these were bearers of funeral gifts: trays of cakes, jellies and chocolates, crystallised fruit, sponge cakes, bottles of muscatel and rosolio wine. Baldassarre went rushing round arranging these things, and announcing the gifts to the family, and thanking the givers, and giving audience to new arrivals. Cousin Graziella, with cupboard keys at her waist, was acting as mistress of the house, to save the princess. The Cavaliere Don Eugenio was also giving a hand, and although the hangers-on were working like domestics and protesting, ' Leave things to us,' he was emptying trays to be returned, carrying their contents into the dining-room and every now and again thrusting a handful of sweets into his pocket.

In place of the Duchess Radali, who had left, being unable to leave her husband alone for long, another ten visitors arrived: the Baron Vita, the Prince of Roccasciano, the Giliforte and Grazzeri families, and Don Carlo Carvona, Cousin Graziella's husband. As the day wore on letters and notes of condolence poured in from all sides. The Royal Intendant sent to express his sorrow at the mourning of a family so devoted to the King and the good cause; the Bishop participated in his dear children's sorrow; from the Uzeda orphanage, the old folks' home, and the other charitable institutes founded or supported by the Francalanza family came rectors and chaplains, many a black cassock, or poor tenants themselves, but these were not allowed to go upstairs and had to express their regrets to the porter or the under-coachman. The Garrison Commander, the President of the High Court, all the authorities, the entire city came to

39

condole with the family. Groups of beggars waited in the hope of alms being distributed. Many people asked insistently for Signor Marco. Hearing that he had not yet come from the Belvedere, some went off to come back later; others began walking up and down in front of the palace, patiently waiting to catch him as he passed.

The two courtyards looked like a fairground, with so many carriages lined up in the shade. Horses, with heads inside fly-bags, ruminated and every now and again grated at the cobbles with their hoofs. One by one, as dusk came on, servants of the relatives arrived, to await their masters and mistresses, and make lively chat, all about the event and its consequences. The women, seeing the confusion, and the coming and going and processions of messengers and letters, were all compassion for the young princess: 'Poor lady! At this hour she must be in tortures . . .' In fact she suffered from a kind of nervous disease by which she could not bear to be in a crowd or touch things handled by others. Luckily her cousin was there to help. And others were reflecting philosophically: 'Now if the prince's mother had died six years ago instead of today, that cousin, instead of helping the mistress, would be mistress here herself.' But the old princess had forbidden the marriage. The prince had obeyed his mother and married Donna Margherita Grazzeri. It must be said, though, that Donna Graziella had behaved very well. Married to the Cavaliere Carvano, she had been most affectionate to the aunt who had refused her as daughter-in-law, and treated her former lover's wife like a real sister. 'And what about the prince? Maybe he remembers having loved her that way? . . .' But there were also many praising what the dead woman had done; she had turned out right in opposing that marriage, since the two former lovers had set their hearts at rest. 'A great woman, the princess! After all, she did pull the family together when it was already bankrupt!' And all asked, 'Who'll she leave things to? . . .' But who could know, as she had never confided in anyone at all, even her own children? . . . 'If young Count Raimondo had been here, though! . . .'

Then the prince's partisans came out flatly with, 'It should all go to the master, if that mad woman hasn't played another of her tricks! . . .' For she had loathed her eldest son and made

40

a favourite of young Count Raimondo, and the young count, though called again and again by his mother as she felt her end near, had not moved from Florence . . .

At the arrival of Fra' Carmelo, sent by the Abbot of San Nicola for news of Don Lodovico and Don Blasco, the conversation took another turn. Fra' Carmelo knew the palace well, as he had often accompanied Don Lodovico there when he was a novice, and all the servants loved him, he was so good, with his big face which looked as if it was about to burst, and its rolls of fat down the nape of the neck.

' The poor princess! . . . What a tragedy!'

He praised the dead woman and recalled the days of Father Lodovico's novitiate, when, taking the boy home on leave, he would bring her little presents of fruit which the good lady had deigned to accept.

' So easy-going! . . . So warmhearted! . . . Poor Father Lodovico! How he must have wept!'

The women exclaimed:

' Imagine! A saint like him! . . .'

And Fra' Carmelo:

' A saint indeed! There are no other monks like him. It's not for nothing he was made Prior at thirty!'

' His Uncle Don Blasco is not like him, is he? . . .' said the head coachman suddenly, with a wink.

' He's different. People can't all be alike, can they? But he's good too! . . . A gentleman too! . . .'

The conversation had just reached this point, when the distant jingle of harness bells made them all quiet. Giuseppe peered through the wicket and flung open the gates. The curricle of that morning entered at full tilt and from it alit the prince and Signor Marco, who was holding a valise, while all doffed hats and Don Blasco peered from the first-floor loggia.

The reappearance of the head of the family in the Yellow Drawing-room produced renewed emotion: sighs, sobs, mute handshakes. The prince was still pale and spoke with an effort, making sweeping gestures of distress.

' Too late! . . . Nothing more to be done! . . . Till last night she was quite well, in fact ate a couple of eggs and drank a cup of milk with appetite . . . At dawn this morning, suddenly she

41

called out and . . .' he fell silent, as if unable to continue.

Signor Marco, having put the valise down, added:

'The catastrophe was impossible to foresee . . . In the first moments, I hoped it was only a stroke . . . But alas, the sad truth . . .'

Chiara and Cousin Graziella wept. The Prior was deploring in particular that no priest had been present at her last moments, but Signor Marco assured him that she had confessed two days before and that the Vicar-General Ragusa had arrived in time to give her absolution. Meanwhile the prince on his side was saying:

'We've improvised a mortuary chapel . . . All the flowers in the villa sent in from every side . . .'

'What about Ferdinando?' asked Chiara.

'Hasn't he come? . . . Ah!' he suddenly struck his forehead, 'I was to go past and warn him . . . I quite forgot . . . Baldassarre! . . . Baldassarre!'

But in the middle of this Don Blasco, who had been eyeing the valise as if it contained contraband, pulled him by a sleeve and asked:

'What about the Will?'

The prince's reply was in quite a different tone, no longer sorrowful, but very precise and scrupulous.

'Signor Marco here,' he said, 'has informed me that our mother's last wishes are deposited with the Notary Rubino. We will await, if you agree, the arrival of Raimondo and our uncle the duke. Meanwhile we have sealed up all that was to be found so as to render a strict account, at the proper time, to whoever it is due . . . But Signor Marco has a document about the funeral in his possession. I think this should be read out at once . . .'

And Signor Marco drew a piece of paper from his pocket and read out amidst deep silence:

'On this day, the nineteenth of May 1855, being in health of mind and not of body, I the undersigned, Teresa Uzeda Princess of Francalanza, recommend my soul to God and dispose as follows. The day that it will please the Lord to call me to Him, I order that my body be handed over to the Reverend Capuchin Fathers that it may be embalmed by them and kept in the necropolis of their friary church. I desire the funeral to be celebrated with ceremonial proper to our family in the church of the said Fathers, in sign of my devotion to the Blessed Ximena, our glorious forebear, whose body is venerated in the same church. During the funeral and after my body has been embalmed, I desire, order and command that it be robed in the habit of a nun of San Placido, and that from the girdle be hung the most holy Rosary given me by my beloved daughter Sister Maria of the Cross on the day when she took her vows, and that on my breast be placed the ivory crucifix, given me by my beloved consort Prince Consalvo of Francalanza. In sign of particular penitence and humility, I expressly impose that my head be supported upon a simple and bare tile; such are my wishes and no others. For my tomb in the Capuchin church I order to be constructed a glass coffin, inside which my body will be placed, robed as above: it will have a lock with three keys, one of which will be given to my son Raimondo Count of Lumera, the second, in sign of particular benevolence for the services he has rendered me, to Signor Marco Roscitano, my procurator and general administrator, and the third to the Reverend Father Guardian of the said Friary of Capuchins. In case, however, of the said Signor Roscitano ceasing to administer my household, I order his key be passed to my other son Lodovico, Prior in the Monastery of San Nicola dell'Arena. Such are my wishes and no other.

TERESA UZEDA.'

Signor Marco, who had bowed respectfully at the passage relating to himself, lowered the sheet of paper. The prince, looking round at those present, said:

'Our mother's wish is law to us. All will be done as she has laid down.'

'In full and without exception . . .' confirmed the Prior, bowing his head.

Don Blasco was puffing like a bellows, and did not even wait for the meeting to break up. Seizing the marchese by an over-coat button, he exclaimed:

'More charades? . . . To the very last? . . . Making herself a figure of fun . . .'

Signor Marco had scarcely gone up to the administrative offices near his own little rooms, to give dependants appropriate orders, when persons waiting to see him appeared. The chandler of San Francesco came to offer him candles of the finest quality, worked in the Venetian mode, at six *tarì*; the music master Mascione brought a letter from Lawyer Spedalotti, begging Signor Marco to have the young composer's *Requiem* sung; Brusa, the painter, asked for the contract for decorations at the prin-cess's solemn funeral.

'How d'you know there'll be a solemn funeral?'

'For a lady like the princess!'

'Come back tomorrow . . .'

And Baldassarre called:

'Signor Marco! Signor Marco! . . . The prince . . .'

But new petitioners arrived. No-one had yet said so, but it was known that the Princess of Francalanza could not go into the next world without much pomp and much spending of money, and all were hoping to earn some of it. Raciti, the first violin of the Municipal Orchestra, offered a funeral Mass com-posed by his son; on hearing that Mascione had a letter from Spedalotti he had rushed off to request a more weighty recom-mendation from Baron Vita; Santo Ferro, who was in charge of upkeep of the public gardens, hoped to be given charge of the floral decorations for the lying-in-state; but Baldassarre, from the courtyard, was calling out again:

'Signor Marco! Signor Marco! . . . The prince! . . .' Signor Marco broke brusquely away from the petitioners:

'Oh go to hell . . . I've other things to do now!'

On Saturday morning the Capuchin Church was like an ant-heap, with more people there than came to visit the Sepulchre even on Maundy Thursday. All night a din of hammers, axes and saws had come from the church and the windows had been blocked since the day before. Very early, in view of the curious crowds milling on terrace and steps, there had been nailed over the great doors a huge draped curtain of black velvet with silver fringes, on which could be read in gilt lettering:

FOR THE SOUL

OF

DONNA TERESA UZEDA AND RISA

PRINCESS OF FRANCALANZA

OBSEQUIES

About ten o'clock, Don Cono Canalà, under the door, with nose in air, was explaining to the Prince of Roccasciano, amid elbowings of people constantly entering.

'On the exterior you see, I didn't think it proper . . . to say too much . . . Greatest simplicity. *For the Soul . . . Obsequies* . . . I think that in its concision . . . quite by chance . . .'

But the shoves, kicks, cries of the sightseeing crowd did not allow him any consecutive speech. People were pouring torrentially all around, pushing into the church, overturning the beggars crouched down beside doors and gates who had come to make some money.

'Just the name . . . it occurred to me quite by chance . . .'

Eventually Don Cono decided to enter too, but, separated from his companion, he was drawn, like a coffee bean in a grinder, by the human turbine squeezing into the church through the narrow entry.

It was dark, because of the veiled windows and the black drapery covering walls, hanging in the chapel arches and swathed along cornices. On a platform raised six or seven steps above the floor and surrounded by a treble row of candles, rose the catafalque; the four sides a truncated pyramid draped with ivy and myrtle, and bearing in the centre, designed in fresh flowers, four great coats-of-arms of the Francalanza House. On top of the pyramid two silver angels kneeling on one leg were waiting to bear the coffin. At the lower corners of the catafalque, on silver tripods, were set four torches as thick as poles, with escutcheons in cardboard tied halfway up. Six lackeys in eighteenth-century liveries, red, black and gold, motionless as statues, with freshly shaved faces, were each bearing one of the

45

ancient standards of alliance. After the lackeys came twelve professional mourners, dressed in black cloaks and with disordered hair, standing all around the catafalque holding handkerchiefs to dry their tears. But it needed a lot of elbowing and walking on neighbours' toes and bruising ribs and kicking heels and sweating shirts to reach all this, around which a crowd of workmen, servants and women were standing ecstatically admiring as they waited for the funeral procession, the platform's false marble, the cardboard urns propped on the steps, the silver paper tears dropping from black veils.

' A fine job! . . . Never seen a better! . . . Real lords they are! . . . They know how to do things! . . . Twelve professional mourners! . . . Not even for the Pope's funeral! . . . The body's already at the embalmers!' And Vito Rosa, the prince's barber, explained, ' As soon as it was brought down from the Belvedere it was taken to the palace and carried round the apartments for the last time, as the custom is. The bier was born on shoulders without poles . . . and all the relations behind, servants with lit torches, like a procession! . . .' And the waiting women exclaimed, 'A tile under her head . . . As if she had any lack of velvet cushions? . . . Ah, that's for greater penance, to go with the habit of San Placido, don't you see?'

But people pressed in behind them and all talk was interrupted. First arrivals had to give up their places and move to beneath the musicians' gallery, set up by the organ. It had four rows of benches and the necks of double-basses could be seen jutting from the highest, but the seats were still empty. Or they went round the other way, towards the chapel of the Blessed Uzeda, resplendent with votive lamps. And there they stopped, once out of the crush, to look at the hollow altar where could be seen, through glass, an ancient leather-covered coffin enclosing the saintly woman's body. Then they tried to go back towards the middle of the church to read the inscriptions attached to the other altars, but the crowd was now compact as a wall. Don Cono Canalà, after glancing over the whole pyre, had made three or four attempts on his own to approach one of the epigraphs, but had not succeeded in pushing far enough ahead to read them. With his head back, his hat dented with all the shoving, his feet trampled, his shirt asweat, he was

tacking like a boat in a storm. By politeness, and by saying
'Please! . . . I beg you! . . . Excuse me!' he finally got within
sight of the first placard, where he read:

BENEATH A WOMAN'S MORTAL REMAINS

BEAT

A VALIANT AND COMPASSIONATE HEART

AN ELECT AND GENEROUS SOUL

AN ALERT AND FERTILE SPIRIT

EVERY WHIT WORTHY

OF THE HIGH-MINDED RACE

WHICH SHE MADE HER OWN

'Every whit? . . .' said Baron Carcaretta, who found himself
beside Don Cono. 'Why " whit "?'
' " Wholly " or " entirely ". " Every whit worthy of the
race . . ." How d'you like the concept? . . .'
'Oh, it's all right; I don't understand why people go out of
their way to find difficult words!'
'You see . . .' Don Cono then explained, insinuatingly,
'epigraphic style must rise to the highest flights of sustained
nobility . . . I could not use . . .'
'Oh you wrote it, did you?'
'Yes, sir . . . but not alone, actually. In collaboration with
the Cavaliere Don Eugenio . . . My particular care was the
form . . . I should like to see the others, as I fear some slip in
copying . . .'
But the church was so crammed that they could scarcely
advance two paces in a quarter of an hour, and all round people
who could not move back or forward or see anything but the
top of the pyramid were whiling away their impatience by
chatting and saying whatever came into their heads about the
princess. 'Now her children can breathe at last! She held them
in an iron fist . . .' ' Her children? Which? . . .' ' She forced Don
Lodovico, the second son, to become a monk when his due was
the title of duke. The eldest daughter she shut into a convent! . . . If she'd still lived, she'd have put the other in too . . .
She married Chiara off because the girl didn't want to . . . And
all for love of just one of them, young Count Raimondo . . .'

47

'What about the father? . . .' 'The father, in his day, never counted a fig. The princess held him and her brother-in-law in her grip!'

But all recognised that had it not been for her there would have been nothing left by that time. 'An ignorant woman, yes, but a shrewd, calculating one!'

'Is it true she couldn't read or write?'

'She could only read her prayer-book and her account-book!'

Meanwhile Don Cono was nearing, at snail's pace, the second inscription.

DEPRIVED

OF THY FAITHFUL CONSORT

IN THIS MORTAL PILGRIMAGE

PROXY THOU STOOD

TO THY CHILDREN

FOR THEIR FATHER

Even before making out the letters, Don Cono, who knew it by memory, was reciting the epigraph to the baron, pausing a little at each word, and longer at each line, waving a hand as if scattering holy water in order to underline the salient passages:

'I wonder if you approve of the concept, "deprived . . . proxy thou stood . . ."'

But new waves of the crowd divided him from his companion once again. From terrace and steps now came a great hiss as strokes of the death-bell at last announced the procession's departure from the palace.

Round the Francalanza home it was still like a fairground, with all the waiting carriages and people quivering with impatience. Through the half-shut gates could be seen another crowd gathered in both courtyards, a swarm of domestics in black liveries coming and going, the major-domo, hatless, panting around giving orders, the state carriage with four horses to be used as funeral car. When finally the heavy doors turned on their hinges, every head turned, every person rose on tiptoe. Ahead came a row of Capuchin friars bearing a cross, then the funeral car, with the coffin covered in red velvet, flanked by all the servants bearing torches; then the inmates of the Uzeda old folks' home, all bare-headed; then the girls of the Orphanage with blue veils hanging to the ground; then the family carriages; two more four-horsed carriages, five two-horsed carriages, then on foot another group of forty men or so, most of them bearded, with black velvet jerkins, and also bearing wax candles.

'Who are they? . . . where've they sprung from? . . .'

They were the Oleastro sulphur workers, called on purpose from Caltanissetta to accompany their mistress, and this last accessory really did astound all. Never had such a thing been seen before! . . . But the carriages advancing from all sides to get into line were pressing back the crowd, four-horsed ones coming to take first places, two-horsed ones backing amid a pawing, and a crack of whips, the curious, at risk of being crushed under the animals' feet, recognised their owners by the coats-of-arms on doors and also by the coachmen.

'The Duke Radalì . . . the Prince of Roccasciano . . . the Baron Grazzeri . . . the Cùrcuma . . . the Constante . . . every one is here . . .'

Suddenly all turned at distant shouting.

'What is it? . . . what's up? . . . The Trigona carriage! . . . The coachman won't go at the end, the others don't give way . . . He's right . . . It's an abuse . . .'

The Marchese Trigona's coachman, in fact, though driving a rickety equipage drawn by two old nags, had refused to go at the end of the queue where there were finer carriages belonging to people who were not noble. Baldassarre, all asweat from his efforts at ordering the procession and getting precedence respected, advanced to back up the coachman, scarcely managing to cleave a way through the crowd, cuffing urchins getting in his way and begging, 'Make way . . . make way . . .' while a good half of the procession had already started.

From every church in the city rang a death-knell, calling people from all sides as the procession passed; the great bell of the Cathedral brought out particularly big crowds. It rang death-knells only for the noble and the learned, and its grave and solemn *nton, nton,* cost four *onze** each, so that people on

* A Sicilian gold coin of the period.

hearing the great bronze boom would say 'Some big-wig has died! . . .'

Quite a number of carriages, after the Trigona's, were still waiting to get started when the head of the procession had already stopped at the Capuchins.

It was impossible to bring the coffin into the church by the main steps. Not that it weighed much, for in fact it was empty, but the press on the stairs was growing, no one could go back or forward, and only a cannon-ball could have made room. They would have to take a different route, open a way among the throngs in the alleys of Santo Carcere and San Domenico and take the coffin through the monastery and sacristy. Nearly an hour went by before it was finally put on the catafalque.

The musicians had already taken their places in the gallery and unwrapped their instruments; friars with long poles were lighting the candles on the High Altar. The curious crammed in the church went on talking about the dead woman, asking each other one insistent question again and again: 'Who'll be heir? . . .' Nobles and plebs, rich and poor, all wanted to know what would be in the Will, as if the dead woman could have left something to every one of her fellow-citizens. At the palace they were awaiting the arrival of the young count from Florence and of the duke from Palermo before reading the princess's last wishes, and opinions amid the public were diametrically opposite. Some maintained that all would go to the young count, but although the dead woman had loathed her eldest son, could she really disinherit him? 'No, sir; it'll all go to the eldest son. It's true she could not endure him, but he's the head of the family, the heir to the princedom! . . .'

A new pushing and shoving suddenly cut off talk, and thickened the crowd at the end of the church. In came the orphan girls of the Sacred Heart with green dresses and white shawls. Baldassarre, all dressed in black, directed them towards the High Altar, calling out:

'Make way, make way, ladies and gentlemen . . .'

A child, half suffocated by the press, began to scream. A beggar who had managed to enter, stumbled against an altar step and fell to the ground.

GRANTING

TO THE DESTITUTE

THE MITE OF CHARITY

THOU HAST FOUND

IT

RETURNED AN HUNDREDFOLD

IN EXPIATORY PRAYERS

In a low voice Don Cono was proclaiming the other inscription to Canon Sortini, whom he had bumped into amid the crowd:

' To conciliate imagery and beauty of form that is the great problem of the epigraphic style . . . " the mite . . . a hundredfold " . . . if I'm not mistaken . . .'

Now the High Altar was all aflame with candles, the movement of friars and sacristans was growing, instruments were being tuned in the musicians' gallery, a clarinet sighed, violins squeaked, a double-bass boomed, and Baldassarre, helped by lackeys of all the relations, also dressed in black, was arranging rows of chairs for the old folk and the orphans. The chairs they held high above the crowd seemed to navigate on a sea of heads, and as new people kept on pushing in, the press was awful. People's breath, the smell of candle grease, the midday heat, made the little church into an inferno. Some women had already fainted, in two or three places quarrels had broken out between those who wanted to push on and those who refused to pull back. But no one decided to leave, and in corners, along walls, before altars, gossips and idlers milled over the story of the dead woman and her family, and commented on all the extravagance.

' A coffin with three keys! . . . All the more difficult to return to this world! . . . A habit and a rosary . . . Enough penance for a queen's funeral! . . .'

In a low voice evil tongues added:

' After her gay life . . .'

Beside the holy water stoup, amid a little group of envious and penniless petty nobles, Don Casimiro Scaglisi was announcing:

' D'you know about the prince? About what the prince did?

As soon as he got the news of his mother's death, off he rushed to the Belvedere without even having his gates shut, to gain time and be in the villa alone, and never warning Ferdinando at the Pietra dell'Ovo . . .'

Some protested; Don Casimiro confirmed:

' But it's true, I tell you! . . . So he could have time to arrange things, and lay hands on papers and money.'

All around shook their heads. Don Casimiro was talking thus from pique, for he had been a hanger-on of the Francalanza till three days before, but since the princess had gone to the country the prince had refused to see him, thinking he had the Evil Eye.

' Anyway, excuse me,' they observed. ' Why ever did the prince need to keep Ferdinando away?'

' Yes, sir, he lives a Robinson Crusoe's life at the Pietra dell'Ovo, doesn't bother about business and in the family they call him the Booby, the nickname given him by his mother. But that doesn't matter! Booby or not, the prince didn't want any of his family interfering! . . . I tell you I know it for sure!'

Another observed:

' Don't talk ill of Ferdinando. With all his manias he never does any harm; he's the best of the whole family.'

' So much so he mightn't be of the same stock . . .' replied Don Casimiro.

' Sssh, sssh! we're in church,' they adjured him.

' Don Cono's passing.'

Don Cono was now crossing the church to read the inscription set above the holy water stoup. When he neared the group they stopped him.

' Don Cono! . . . Don Cono! . . . you have long sight. What does it say up there?'

And Don Cono read out:

IN THIS TEMPLE

WHICH HARBOURS THE MORTAL REMAINS

OF THE BLESSED UZEDA

GRANTED BE

HER KINSWOMAN'S

INTERCESSORY PRAYERS

'Fine! Excellent! . . . I like that "intercessory" ', they exclaimed in chorus, but a prolonged ' sssh!' suddenly passed from mouth to mouth. The Maestro Mascione, perched at the top of the orchestra gallery, had given three taps on his lectern, and conversation died, all heads turned towards the players. Amid the general attention Don Casimiro suddenly nudged his neighbours and exclaimed in a low voice:

'Look! look!'

Just then, protected against the crowd by a servant, entered old Don Alessandro Tagliavia. In spite of his age he still held his tall figure erect, and his fine white and pink head, with its clear aquamarine eyes and moustaches yellowed with tobacco, dominated the crowd. Being unable to advance, he gazed from afar at the catafalque, the musicians' gallery, the placards of inscriptions, and meanwhile, in the silence which had fallen as if by magic, the orchestra intoned the prelude. A long groan, broken sounds of short sobs in cadenza spread throughout the church, and the professional mourners started to cry again, while the friars before the altar began their genuflections. Many heads bent, and the buzz of chat was followed by deep concentration.

'Look! . . .' repeated Don Casimiro, in the group next to the holy water stoup, ' he's come to say his last farewell!'

All their eyes were fixed on the old man. The dismissed courtier went on, interrupting himself when the orchestra quietened:

'And I remember him crying like a child . . . like one in despair . . . when the dead woman left him for Felice Cùrcuma . . . after all there'd been between them! . . . Now it's she who's rotting away . . . And he'll live another twenty years; an iron constitution . . .' and in a lower voice, as trumpets suddenly blared and voices sang *Requiem aeternam dona eis,* he added, ' and he keeps a girl of his own too in a little place in the suburbs . . . Every evening he spends with her!'

The old man made another attempt at getting near one of the inscriptions, but as Mass had begun, no one moved, and he turned back. On reaching the church door, when the fresh air hit his forehead, he thrust his hat on his head before he was even outside.

' *Sic transit gloria mundi!*'

But when the first effect of the music was past, conversations again started up here and there. Raciti, the first violin of the Municipal Orchestra, muttered away among unknowns:

'A fine show, no doubt of that, a fine ceremony! . . . The point is, who'll pay up!'

He was furious, as Signor Marco had preferred Mascione's Mass to his son's, and was consoling himself by talking against the family: there was no one as sticky in paying, and Titta Caruso, the box-office manager at the theatre, knew something of that, forced as he was every year to go up and down the palace stairs a hundred times before getting them to pay for their box. One day the prince wasn't in, another the princess, another time Signor Marco was out, or they were all in the country . . .

'Why, my son Salvatore wouldn't offer them his Mass! Better have it played gratis for the souls in purgatory. At least there's some earning for the soul!'

And he turned his back furiously, to leave as the music struck up a *Tuba mirum* filched from Palestrina . . . Like him, all those were in church who had rushed to the palace to offer their services in the first moments, but those who had left empty handed were now spreading round tales of the avarice and petty meanness of this family whose luxury was only on the surface: had the princess not once sued her shoemaker for the price of an unsatisfactory pair of shoes? And in the kitchen hadn't the cook orders to drain off the oil still in the saucepan after frying, and hand it back to his mistress?

' The richer they are, those swine, the meaner they get!'

An imperious ' sssh ' stopped all the chatter. The orchestra was intoning the *Quid sum miser tunc dicturus?* and the people who were listening to the music did not want it disturbed. But conversations started up again a moment later. Some groups of Liberals were vaunting the patriotism of the Duke Gaspare, but in low voices, and looking round for fear some spy might hear.

'They get it both ways!' exclaimed Don Casimiro, next the stoup. 'In this family some play the revolutionary and some the pro-Bourbon; so they are sure to be all right whatever happens! Isn't the girl Lucrezia playing the Liberal for love of that ass Benedetto Giulente . . .?'

Baron Carcaretta, joining the evil tongues, protested:
'Surely they'll never give an Uzeda to a Giulente?'
And Don Casimiro:
'That's why I say Giulente's an ass . . .'
'Silence, there they are!'
In fact the young man entered that moment with his uncle
Don Lorenzo, a celebrated Liberal satellite of the duke's.
'Well?' asked Don Casimiro. 'When will you be having
this revolution of yours?'
'We won't be telling you, in any case!' replied Benedetto
with a smile.
The other then turned to the uncle:
'What about your friend the duke? His sister-in-law is dead,
his nieces and nephews awaiting him, why didn't he leave at
once? What's he cooking up there?'
'What does it matter to you?'
'To me? Not a fig! I'm no one's dish-washer!'
'Dish-washers, let me tell you,' replied Don Lorenzo, 'I've
always kept to my kitchen . . .'
'Silence, we're in church.'
The hieratic prayer was at *inter oves locum praesta*. But Don
Casimiro refused to recognise that his resentment at no longer
enjoying the Uzeda's intimacy was animating him against them.
'Fools!' he exclaimed as the two Giulente moved away. 'I'd
just like to see how those swine treat 'em in the end!'
The Prince of Roccasciano, who had been round the church,
tossed about by the crowd, was now pushed into the middle of
the group. His whole person, so small and thin that it seemed
an economy model, expressed amazement:
'My dear sirs, what a funeral! What an expense! . . . There
must be at least a hundred *onze's* worth of wax! And all the
decorations! And the sung Mass! I may say that for my father's
funeral, God rest his soul, I spent sixty-eight *onze* and thirteen *tarì*, and what did they do? . . . Nothing! . . . Here, I tell
you, there's a hundred spent on lights alone . . .'
'Ssssssh! . . . The *Lux aeterna* . . .'
Every new part of the Mass produced a reshuffle in the crowd.
Some tried to leave, most changed their places, moved round the
catafalque, went to read the inscriptions. Don Cono had one

still to check. Don Casimiro stuck to his side, followed by various others of the group.

AH, HARSH DEATH!

NOT EVEN

THE WEEPING

OF AN ILLUSTRIOUS STOCK

AND

OF AN ENTIRE PEOPLE

COULD TURN AWAY

THINE ARM

'Excellent!' exclaimed Don Casimiro. 'The stock is illustrious indeed; they descend direct from Anchises. People weep, d'you see their tears?' And he pointed to the silver tears scattered over the funeral draperies. 'Even the orphanage girls are weeping . . . thinking they'll now end as maidservants to the illustrious prince . . .'

'It seems unbecoming . . .' objected Don Cono.

'I can assure you they're all in despair at this death, in the family who all love each other so much! Poh! Not a day can they let pass without embracing and kissing each other . . .'

'It seems unbecoming . . .'

'Prudence, my dear sirs, we're in church!'

Just then the repeat of the *Dies irae* deafened them all. The friars came down towards the catafalque and blessed it; the music intoned the *Libera me*, took up the phrases of the start, implored at the *Requiem.* 'Is it over? . . . God willing! . . .' There was a general movement. Those who had been stuck far from catafalque and inscriptions started towards them; many, who from exhaustion could no longer stand, moved towards the doors. But there the confusion started up again worse than ever, for all the people who had stayed outside thinking that it would be easy to enter when Mass was over were crowding round tumultuously, knocking against those wanting to come out, stumbling over the halt, blind and maimed who were again risking an outstretched hand to passers-by. 'Careful! My feet! . . . What behaviour! . . .' and dominating that buzz of voices from the square came an incessant clatter of horses: the car-

56

riages of the funeral procession filing off one after the other.

The Prince of Roccasciano, as he came out on to the terrace, began enumerating them:

'Seven four-horsed carriages, sixty-three private carriages, twelve hired,' said he when the last passed. Then he totted them up. 'At twelve *tarì* each, apart from the private ones, that makes thirty-four *onze*! . . .'

Then the crowd of spectators began to disperse. The poor who had stayed crouched along the walls could drag themselves to their places at last, but now no one passed.

2

T O W A R D S dusk, as the servants gathered in the courtyard, still commenting on the funeral's magnificence, from the Messina road arrived Count Raimondo with the Countess Matilde. Baldassarre, hearing the tinkle of harness bells, rushed down the main stairs and reached the carriage just at the moment when it stopped and its master jumped out.

'Who's here?' asked the young count, abruptly cutting short Baldassarre's ceremonious greetings and pointing to the carriages lined up in the court.

'Visitors for the Signor Prince, Excellency . . .' and the major-domo at once took on the sad and grave air suitable to the mournful circumstances.

The count moved off up the great stairs without bothering about wife or baggage. Baldassarre, with bent head, offered his elbow to the countess, but she alighted without his support.

'Lovelier than ever!' judged the women, drawing respectfully near her. 'Though maybe a little thinner . . .' The porter's wife also observed, 'She looks sadder than the young count . . .' And how sweet was her voice as she asked them to bring up the trunks and night bags, and answered the 'Welcome, Excellency' of the servants, finding out about their health, and asking Giuseppe if his child was well and Donna Mena if her daughter had married . . .

Upstairs in the antechambers, the prince and Lucrezia came to meet their brother and sister-in-law. Raimondo let himself be kissed by his sister and shook the hand which Giacomo held out to him, then entered the Yellow Drawing-room, crowded with people as was the Red one; for now that entry was no longer refused to any but close relations, processions of fourth and fifth cousins, of connections and friends were coming to condole on the tragedy. All, at the appearance of the Countess Matilde, rose to their feet except Don Blasco and Donna Ferdinanda. The latter, as her niece kissed her hand, stuttered out a very cold, 'Good evening.' As for Don Blasco, he did not even reply. He was shouting, amid gesticulations:

'So they want more, do they? Ah, they want more, do they? If they want more all they have to do is ask for it . . .'

The meeting between the Prior and Raimondo was observed by all. The Prior, who was sitting next to Monsignor the Bishop with the Vicar-General and various canons, at the sight of his brother, got up and opened his arms. Raimondo allowed himself to be embraced once more, but these demonstrations of affection plainly bored him. Then the prince led him away and all returned to their places and interrupted conversations.

In a group of bigwigs, including among others the President of the High Court, the General and some city counsellors, Don Blasco was continuing to breathe fire and sword against the revolutionaries and men of '48 who were threatening to raise their heads. Had that lesson given them by Satriano not been enough? Did they want more? Then they'd have it at once!

'But whose fault d'you think it is most, the revolutionaries' or that man Cavour's? It's those ruffians', who with their positions ought to be supporting the Government instead of throwing in their lot with beggars!'

He was particularly furious at his brother the duke, who had got it into his head to act the Liberal, he, the second son of a Prince of Francalanza! The Marchese of Villardita was nodding approvingly, judging though that the revolutionaries, with or without the help of certain gentry, would lie low for another half-century at least; the city still bore the signs of the terrible repression of April '49; traces of arson and sacking had not altogether vanished, and half the population was still mourning those dead, condemned to life imprisonment, or exiled.

The Prior, having sat down next to the Bishop again in the group of black cassocks, was also deploring, in a low voice, the iniquities of the times in the shape of the Piedmontese laws against religious Orders, while Don Blasco, in the group opposite, was shouting:

'Now they're going to war without money! By robbing the Church of Christ! That man D'Azeglio! Have you read his effusion? . . .'

In the women's place, the princess sat in a corner, a little apart, to avoid contacts. Donna Ferdinanda, sitting by the Prince of Roccasciano, was talking to him of business, crops, the price of victuals, while the Princess of Roccasciano was describing to the Baroness Cùrcuma how her mother had appeared to her in a dream with three lottery numbers in her hand—6, 39 and 70— on which she had put 12 *tarì*, without her husband knowing. The Mortara and Costante girls, friends of Lucrezia, were talking to the latter about clothes to distract her, although she was not listening and replied distractedly as was her habit. But Cousin Graziella kept the conversation going brightly all by herself, turning to all and each, passing from one room to another, chatting about clothes, dressmakers, the Crimea, Piedmont, the war and the cholera. The Countess Matilde, tired from her journey, spoke little, waiting to retire to her rooms. Don Cono, who had come to sit by her, was reciting all the epigraphs he had composed for the funeral. 'A variation has occurred to me. I should much value the countess's opinion . . .' and the Cavaliere Don Eugenio was saying how poor modern funerals were compared to those of yore. 'In 1692 there was even a decree to prevent excessive show in ceremonies for the dead!'

All rose to their feet at the appearance of Donna Isabella Fersa, with her husband Don Mario and Father Gerbini. The Benedictine was gallantly carrying one of the lady's veils on his arm. She kissed all the Uzeda women, except the princess, who drew back and introduced:

'My sister-in-law Matilde . . .'

Donna Isabella warmly shook the countess's hand and sat down beside her with a sigh.

'What a tragedy! . . . But God's will be done! . . . You've been in Florence? . . . We were there last year too . . . but you were both at Milazzo then . . . Only one child so far? . . . The count will be hoping for a boy, of course. Lucky you to have a daughter. I envy you, you know, countess.'

Father Gerbini was meanwhile doing the round of the ladies, talking at length with the youngest and prettiest, saying gallant and forbidden things. He took their soft white hands, held them a little in his equally white and beringed ones, and kissed them. When he saw the prince re-enter the room with his brother, he left the ladies to lead Raimondo up to Donna Isabella.

'The Count of Lumera . . . Donna Isabella Fersa . . . the loveliest lady in the realm . . .'

'Don't you believe it, he says that to everyone,' claimed she with a smile. 'I am sorry to be meeting you,' she went on in another tone and squeezing his hand, 'in these sad circumstances . . .' She sighed a little, then began again:

'The countess was just telling me that you've come from Florence . . .'

'Directly. We scarcely stopped at Messina . . .'

'To leave the child with your father-in-law. You were quite right! What is this place Milazzo like?'

'Don't talk of it.'

Luckily, he went on, he was there as little as possible, being always drawn to Florence where he had so many friends. As he quoted the great names of Tuscany, Donna Isabella repeatedly nodded approval. 'The Morsini, of course . . . the Realmonte . . .'

The countess was giving her husband begging looks, almost as if saying 'Take me away . . .' but Raimondo never stopped talking of his favourite theme. Fersa came up to him a moment to shake his hand and express his own regret.

'Is your uncle the duke arriving tomorrow?'

'So Giacomo told me.'

'What about the Will?'

'Nothing is known yet.'

Amid the talk of politics, fashions and travel, that question, murmured curiously here and there, always obtained the same reply. The President of the High Court, witness of the handing over of the secret Will made by the princess to the notary the year before, knew nothing about the contents of the document whose envelope he had signed, and the dead woman's children were even more in the dark than strangers. Perhaps, had Raimondo come in time, when his mother had called him so insistently, he might have been told something, but the count, amusing himself in Florence, had turned a deaf ear, as if they were not his own interests involved. Was it possible, then, that the princess had confided in no one at all? In none of her brothers-in-law? In some man of business at least? Suddenly Don Blasco, leaving Cavour and Russia in peace, exclaimed:

'Well, why didn't she? It's what anyone who reasons would do . . . But logic's different in this family! . . . No one must know a thing! All must be done according to *their* whims; always *hidden*, always *mysterious*, as if they were *forging* the money!'

The President gave an amiable nod to quieten the fiery monk, but the latter went on:

'D'you want to know what the Will says? Ask her confessor! Yes, sir, her confessor! . . . You talk to your confessor about sin, don't you? About matters of conscience? . . . Business, of course, you leave to lawyers and notaries and relations, don't you? . . . But here, on the other hand, it's the confessor who wrote the Will. Maybe the notary imparts Absolution?'

Some smiled at this sally, and suppositions had free rein. The President was sure, whatever was said to the contrary, that the heir would be the prince, with a big legacy to the count, and the General confirmed, 'Of course, the heir to the name!' But the Baron Grazzeri shook his head, 'They never got on, did they?' Don Mario Fersa was whispering his opinion to the Cavaliere Carvano, according to which the heir would be Raimondo. Perhaps the latter's behaviour during his mother's illness, his constant refusal to come and see her, might have done him a little harm, but the princess's predilection for that son had been too great for its effects all to be scattered in a moment. 'Don't let us forget,' commented the Cavaliere Pezzino, 'that the poor lady, may she rest in peace, always refused to ask for the Right of Primogeniture, so as to be free to do what she liked.' Would such an enormity be seen as the head of the family disinherited? Raimondo, who had no son, made heir? The prince, who already had a successor in little Consalvo, disinherited? . . . The family courtiers, as being in the dead woman's confidence, were asked for their opinions, but these who knew less than others replied evasively so as not to disagree with anyone.

'What about the other sons? Ferdinando? The women? . . .'
Curiosity, though contained and expressed in whispers, was very
lively. Had her confessor, that Father Camillo, not spoken? 'He's
not here, he's been in Rome for some months, and even if he
were, he wouldn't talk. He's far too clever . . .' And all eyes
naturally turned to Giacomo and Raimondo. The latter was
still chatting to Donna Isabella, and his mother's will seemed
the very last thing in his thoughts; indeed he might never have
heard of his mother's death. The prince, on the other hand, had
a graver air than usual, as suitable to the melancholy of those
days. He was receiving with expressions of gratitude the
reiterated condolences of those leaving. Some of these, however,
could not succeed in finding him, and went off unable to bid
farewell, and familiars gave each other understanding looks out
of the corners of their eyes. He was terrified of the Evil Eye, and
attributed that dreadful power to a great number of individuals.
In their presence he was in tortures, and avoided greeting them
by keeping his hands in his pockets.

But the President of the High Court, as he got to his feet,
found the prince beside him.

'If my uncle comes tomorrow, President, shall we fix the
reading for the day after?'

'Whenever you think fit, Prince! I am at your disposal!'

'In truth . . .' he added, lowering his voice, 'I would not
wish it to be so hurried . . . in fact it seems to show a lack of
proper respect for our mother's memory . . . But you know what
happens when so many people have to be taken into consideration . . .' and as his brother the Prior was also leaving with the
Bishop, he warned them both, Monsignor being another
witness.

'Do arrange things as you like . . .' said the Prior without
interest. 'What need have you of me?'

But Giacomo protested:

'No, no, not at all! Things must be done properly, to everyone's satisfaction . . .'

As it was getting dark, many were leaving. Father Gerbini,
although the Prior had given the example, stayed a little longer,
chatting to the ladies, then he went off too. There remained,
inveighing against the revolutionaries and his dead sister-in-law,

63

Don Blasco, always the last to re-enter the monastery.

Now servants were lighting the lamps, and with the windows shut, the heat in the room was getting intolerable. The Countess Matilde felt herself on the point of swooning, and had lost sight of her husband, who had followed Donna Isabella into the Red Drawing-room, and was now discoursing about Paris. Once again she found herself beside her uncle Eugenio and Don Cono, who were still disembowelling the old city chronicles and quoting flowery Latin.

'The funeral rites for Charles V took place in the presence of the Viceroy Uzeda . . .'

'The royal chapel was set up in our cathedral, where was erected a high pyramid ornamented with busts and allegorical figures, among which those of Italy, Spain, Germany and India . . .'

'Exactly, and the epigraph went like this:
    *India moesta sedet Caroli post funera Quinti* . . .'

'And what about the opening of the favourite horse's veins?'

'For our grandfather's funeral, the very last time! When the prince our grandfather died, his saddle-horse had a vein cut . . .'

'A barbaric custom, surely. The noble steed spattering the street with blood till it fell and breathed its last . . .'

Suddenly Don Cono exclaimed:

'Countess, great God!'

All rushed to her. She was pale and cold, her eyes turned up and her lips parted. Her husband, hurrying in with Donna Isabella, said:

'It's nothing . . . just tiredness from the journey . . .' And in a low voice, almost to himself, as they carried her away, 'The usual nonsense! . . .'

What days of constant novelty those were! Next day, as expected, the duke arrived. He had been away for five years, and at first the servants and even relatives scarcely recognised him. When he had left Palermo he had a fine wreath of whiskers in the Bourbon style, but now he had grown a small pointed beard, which gave his face a completely different character. All his nephews and nieces kissed his hand. He enquired about the tragedy and excused himself for not having come sooner. He also excused himself for the disturbance he was causing to the prince, who had ordered the third-floor rooms prepared for him which he had occupied before leaving his family home. But his nephew protested:

'Your Excellency is not disturbing, but helping me . . . and at this moment I greatly need your advice . . .'

'Heard anything?'

'Not a thing!'

'I hope your mother hasn't had one of her crazy whims . . .'

'Whatever my mother has done will be well done!'

So the reading of the Will was arranged for next day at noon, and Signor Marco had orders to warn notary, judge, and witnesses to hold themselves in readiness. Meanwhile the news of the duke's arrival had immediately spread through the city, and his first visitors were announced before he had even rested from his journey. All sorts of people came, many of whom no one had ever heard of. Donna Ferdinanda, hearing their names announced by Baldassarre—Raspinato, Zappaglione—opened her eyes wide. Don Blasco, on his side, was puffing like a bellows. But the worst was towards evening, when there began a real procession, 'all the starving down-and-outs in town', as the monk cried to the marchese, 'that have squeezed or want to squeeze money out of that pig of a brother of mine!' While the duke was giving audience to his friends, the Royal Intendant Ramondino came to make his visit of condolence to the prince, who received him in the Red Drawing-room, together with the Marchese of Villardita and Don Blasco. The latter, forgetting that the gates were on the point of shutting at San Nicola, let out a terrific diatribe against the agitations of the revolutionary party; but the representative of the Government shrugged his shoulders and seemed to give no importance to the symptoms about which the monk was holding forth: yes, they had actually arrested a few agitators at Palermo; but when in prison hot heads would cool off.

'Why don't you call for more troops? Make an example? . . . The stick is what's needed; a few floggings!'

The monk seemed frenzied; but the head of the province shrugged his shoulders; the troops of the garrison were enough; there was no fear of anything! Anyway the Government put its trust in the moral influence of the *well-disposed* more than in bayonets. This praise was directed to the prince, who took the point, but Don Blasco swivelled his staring eyes as if something he'd eaten had gone down the wrong way, and he was making violent efforts either to swallow it altogether or vomit it out.

'What about the defunct lady's Will, may God rest her soul!' asked the Intendant, as curious as the rest of the city.

'It will be opened tomorrow . . .'

At this point the duke entered, shook hands with the Intendant and sat down by him. Don Blasco then got up noisily to go away. In the antechamber he shouted to the marchese accompanying him:

'You see? All day with the down-and-outs and now making up to authority! It turns my stomach! . . . I'll never set foot in this house again!'

In the princess's work-room, where the rest of the family and some of the hangers-on were gathered, Donna Ferdinanda was also breathing fire and sword against the traitor; but when Baldassarre, thinking that the duke was there, announced at the door:

'Don Lorenzo Giulente and his nephew ask for the Signor Duke . . .'

'This is too much!' burst out the spinster, flushing to the whites of her eyes. 'It's a scandal! The police should see to it!'

Don Mariano, with an air of consternation, exclaimed:

'The boy too now . . . It's really most disagreeable! One can overlook the uncle, who's penniless; but the nephew . . .'

'The nephew? . . .' shrieked the spinster. 'Don't you know that when the fox couldn't reach the grapes it said they were sour?'

Lucrezia had gone pale and kept her eyes down, picking at the fringe on her chair. The little prince Consalvo, sitting near to his aunt, asked:

'Why grapes?'

'Why? . . . because they wanted royal consent to institute primogeniture. Not having got it, they've flung in their lot with the down-and-outs . . . the Royal consent! As if article 948 of the Civil Code isn't quite clear! . . .' and still turning to the boy, who was looking at her with his eyes popping out of his head, she recited in sing-song, gesticulating with a finger:

'The institution of an entail may be requested by those whose names are found inscribed either in the *Golden Book* or in other registers of nobility, by all those in the legitimate possession of titles granted at some time in the past, and finally by *those persons who belong to families of known* NOBI-LI-TY in the kingdom of the two Sicilies . . .'

'I believe the Giulente are noble,' said Lucrezia, before her aunt had finished, and without raising her eyes.

'I on the other hand believe they're ignoble,' rebutted Donna Ferdaninda dryly. 'If they possessed documents to prove it they'd have obtained the royal consent.'

'Nobles of Syracuse . . .' began Don Mariano.

'Syracuse or Caropepe, if they had titles they wouldn't be refused inscription in the *Red Book*!'

'The *Red Book* stopped publication in 1813,' announced Don Eugenio in the tone of one with grave news.

Lucrezia had remained with head down, looking at the floor. When her aunt thought she had reduced her to silence, the girl began again:

'The Giulente are nobles of the robe.'

The spinster's reply was a subtle little laugh; 'Only dolts think the nobility of the robe equal to that of the sword! . . . What difference was there among the six judges of the Royal Patrimony, Don Mariano? The three with short cloaks were noble—*noble*! . . . and the three with long cloaks were *attorneys* . . . ATTORNEYS ! . . . D'you know how things are now? . . . Every notary thinks himself a prince! . . . Once there were ten-*scudi* barons, now there are ten-cent ones . . .'

The girl got up and left. Donna Ferdinanda went on smiling subtly, looking at the Countess Matilde.

Meanwhile Signor Marco was arranging the Portrait Gallery for the reading of the Will. The prince had been a little hesitant in choosing the place for the ceremony; the Red Drawing-room was decently furnished but held very few people; the Hall of the Chandeliers was vast but empty except for the old lamps hanging from the ceiling and the mirrors let into the walls. But the Portrait Gallery combined size with splendour, for it was as big as two drawing-rooms put together and furnished with sofas, stools, side-tables and gilt tripods, and the generations of ancestors hanging in effigy on the walls also made it worthier of the solemn occasion for which their descendants were gathering. In the middle of that kind of vast corridor, the general administrator set a big table covered with an antique carpet and provided with a monumental silver inkstand. Around the table twelve big armchairs awaited witnesses and interested parties. The prince's was highest, with its back to the great central portrait of the Viceroy Lopez Ximenes Uzeda, on horseback and in the act of reining in his animal with his left hand and of pointing his right forefinger to the ground as if to say ' Here I give the orders . . .' All around, high and low, along the whole length of the walls, along the width of the spaces between the windows, were multitudes of ancestors: men and women, monks and warriors, bishops and doctors, ladies and abbesses, ambassadors and viceroys; in full-face, profile and three-quarters view; dressed in armour, velvet, ermine; their heads crowned with laurel, or shut into helmets, or covered with hoods; carrying sceptres and books and croziers and swords and maces and fans.

On the day arranged, before the arrival of notary, judge, witnesses or other relations, appeared Don Blasco, chewing his nails. On entering, he began wandering round the house, looking at everything, his ears alert as a cat's, his nostrils open as if sniffing for prey. Immediately after, appeared Donna Ferdinanda, and down in the court the servants began observing that the dead woman's relations by marriage, for whom the Will had no interest, were more impatient to hear it than her own children. But now curiosity was making everyone tense and almost irritable. The hangers-on, as they arrived to help the prince receive, were exchanging exclamations of ' Now for it! In half an hour or so . . .' The Prior came with Monsignor the Bishop, protesting again that his presence was useless, while the prince repeated that he wanted all there. The judge arrived with Rubino the notary at the same time as the marchese with his wife and Don Eugenio. Then came the President of the High Court with the Prince of Roccasciano, other witnesses, then Cousin Graziella with her husband, then the Duchess Radalì, then more distant relatives, the Grazzeri, the Costante, and finally the last witness,

Marchese Motta. But Ferdinando had not yet appeared. And Don Blasco, taking the marchese by an overcoat button, said to him: 'What d'you bet they forgot to warn him again?'

There was a painful wait. No one spoke of the Will again, but all looks were turned to the notary's brief-case. Most indifferent of all, however, seemed Count Raimondo, who was chatting with the ladies, and the prince, who was talking to the President of the High Court about a law case connected with his wife's dowry. But whereas the younger brother was hopping carelessly from subject to subject, the prince was making long pauses, during which his eyes were fixed in a frown and worry veiled his forehead.

When finally Ferdinando did appear, with his eyes staring, looking stunned as if fallen from the clouds, there was a scandal. With even the servants dressed in black, he was still wearing a coloured suit, and when Don Blasco said to him, 'What the devil d'you think you're doing?' he stuttered out in reply, 'Oh excuse me . . . excuse me . . . I wasn't thinking . . .'

At the prince's invitation all passed into the Gallery. The prince, the duke, the count, the marchese, the cavaliere, Signor Marco, the judge with the notary and four witnesses took places at the table. The others sat on sofas all around, the princess apart in a corner, Donna Ferdinanda with Chiara and Cousin Graziella on one side, Lucrezia with the duchess and the Countess Matilde on another. The Prior sat on a stool, crossed his hands in his lap and raised his eyes to the ceiling with an air of resigned indifference. Don Blasco, leaning against the mullion of the central window, dominated the meeting like a sceptical onlooker at a display of conjuring.

'Will your Excellency allow me?' asked the notary, and at the prince's gesture of assent he took from the brief-case an envelope on which all eyes settled. Having ascertained that the seals were unbroken, and verified the signatures, he opened the envelope and took out two or three sheets bound together. After a short exchange of ceremonies with the judge, the latter, amid a religious silence, finally began the reading:

'I, TERESA UZEDA, born Risà, Princess of Francalanza and Mirabella, widow of Consalvo VII, Prince of Francalanza and Mirabella, Duke of Oragua, Count of Venerata and Lumera, Baron of La Motta Reale, Gibilfemi and Alcamuro, Lord of the lands of Bugliarello, Malfermo, Martorana and Caltasipala, Chamberlain to His Majesty the King, (whom may God ever bless).

' On this day, the 19th of March, in the year of Grace 1854, feeling healthy in mind but not in body, I commend my soul to Our Lord Jesus Christ, the Blessed Virgin Mary, and all the glorious saints of Paradise, and dispose as follows:

' My beloved children are not unaware that on the day in which I entered the Francalanza House and assumed the administration of the family property, so many mortgages were outstanding on my husband's fortune that it could be considered to be, and actually was, destroyed and on the verge of dismemberment among his numerous creditors. Urged meanwhile by maternal affection to sacrifice myself for the good of my beloved children, I set myself from that day onwards to restoring this fortune, a labour which has lasted my whole life. Assisted by the prudent councils of good friends and relatives, supported by the intelligent labours of Signor Marco Roscitano, my administrator and general agent, today, with the help of Divine Providence to which I render all my heart-felt thanks, I find myself in the position not only of having saved but even increased the family fortunes . . .'

At the passage referring to him Signor Marco had respectfully bowed his head. Don Blasco, still standing, changed his position; he left the window and went and stood behind the judge, in such a way that he could not only hear better but verify the true fidelity of the reading with his own eyes. The prince kept his arms crossed on his chest and his head a little bent. Raimondo was tapping a foot, and looking about with a bored air.

' The whole of this fortune belongs only and exclusively to me: both in the part representing my dowry invested in it, and also because the remainder is from my own jointure and labours, as is proved amply and fully by the Will of

70

my beloved spouse, Consalvo VII, which goes thus . . .'

The judge paused a moment to observe:
' I think we can skip this part . . .'
' Quite . . . it's useless . . .' replied many voices.
But the prince unfolded his arms and protested, looking around: ' No, no, I wish all things to be done in full order . . . Do read everything, please.'

'. . . which goes thus. "On the point of rendering my soul to God, having nothing to leave my children because, as they will know one day, our ancestral patrimony was destroyed by family misfortunes, I leave them this precious advice; always to obey their mother, my beloved wife, Teresa Uzeda, Princess of Francalanza, who, ever hitherto inspired by the good of our House, will thus continue in the future to have no other aim but that of assuring along with the glory of the family, the future of our beloved children. May the Lord preserve her for a thousand years yet, and on the day when the Almighty is pleased to grant me her company again in a better life, may my children faithfully carry out her wishes, as ones which could be directed only to their good and their fortune."

' Therefore,' went on the princess's Will, ' my dear children can give no better proof of their affection and respect towards the memory of their father and towards mine, but scrupulously to respect the dispositions which I am about to dictate and the wishes which I shall express.

' I therefore name . . .'

All eyes were set on the reader, Don Blasco bent farther down to see the writing better,

' as universal heirs . . .'

the prince's lips suddenly imperceptibly contracted,

' of all my possessions, excluding those which I intend shall be distributed in the manner herein contained, my two sons Giacomo XIV, Prince of Francalanza, and Raimondo, Count of Lumera . . .'

The judge made a brief pause, during which the Bishop
and the President nodded and looked at each other with
amazed approval. The prince recrossed his arms, and put on
his sphinx-like air again; he was only a little pale; Raimondo
did not seem to notice the smiles of congratulation given him;
Donna Ferdinanda, with her lips tight-set, was passing in
review the ancestors hanging on the walls.

' I instruct, however,' went on the reader, ' that in the
division between the two said brothers there be assigned to
Prince Giacomo the Uzeda family estates ransomed by me,
and to Raimondo, Count of Lumera, the Risà properties and
those acquired by me in the course of time. The family
palace goes to the eldest son; but my other son Raimondo
will have the use, during his lifetime, of the apartments
facing south, with their attached stables and coach-houses.'

By repeated nods of the head the President and the Bishop
went on expressing their approval; and the marchese was
also heard murmuring, ' Very proper.' Cousin Graziella, who
had been silent for a quarter of an hour, glanced rapidly
from one to another, as if not knowing what attitude to take.
The reading went on :

' Next, using my right to make legacies to my other legitimate children and wishing to give each of them a proof of
my particular affection, I assign to each legacies superior
to the quota assigned to them by their legitimate rights of
law, in the following manner:
' I except, first of all, those who have entered Holy
Orders, for whom I repeat, confirm and complete the dispositions made by me at the time of their profession, which
are:
' First; in favour of my beloved son Lodovico, in religion
a Benedictine Father of the Cassinese Congregation, a
deacon in the Monastery of San Nicola dell'Arena in
Catania, the income of 36 (thirty-six) onze yearly, assigned
by the Act of 12 November, 1844.
' Secondly; in favour of my eldest daughter Angiolina,
in religion Sister Maria of the Cross, nun in the Convent

of San Placido in Catania, as sign of my particular satisfaction and pleasure at the obedience shown by her in
agreeing to my desire to see her embrace the religious life,
I complete my disposition of 7 March 1852, ordering that
from the total of my possessions be deducted the sum of
2,000 (two thousand) *onze*, the value of the property
named La Timpa situated in the Etna Woods in the Belvedere district, ordering that with the income from this there
be celebrated three Masses daily in the Church of the said
convent of San Placido, and precisely at the Altar of the
Cross, such celebrations to begin after the death of my
beloved daughter Sister Maria of the Cross, intending that
during her lifetime the income should go to her by right
of perpetual lease as a life annuity. On my daughter
departing this life, I order that the administration be entrusted to the Mother Abbess *pro-tempore* of the said convent, on which Superior and on no others I intend to be
conferred the faculty of selecting the celebrating priests.

' Next I come to my other children, and in accordance
with the legitimate division, I leave to my well-beloved
Ferdinando . . .'

And Ferdinando, who had been following the flight of flies,
finally turned towards the reader,

' . . . the full and absolute ownership of the estate called
Le Ghiande, situated near Pietra dell'Ovo, in the territory
of Catania, as I know the particular affection in which he
holds this property, granted to him by lease by an Act of
2 March 1847. And that my said son may have special
proof of my maternal affection, I wish to condone, and
hereby do condone, all past rentals due by him to me
on the aforesaid estate in virtue of the above-quoted Act,
whatever sum these past rentals may total at the moment
of succession.'

Witnesses and courtiers, in gestures, looks and whispered
words, expressed ever-growing admiration.

' Thus there remain my two beloved daughters, Chiara,
Marchesa of Villardita, and Lucrezia; to each of whom,

in order that the real estate be left to their brothers and my male heirs, I desire should be paid, always as part of their legal share, the sum of 10,000 (ten thousand) *onze* . . .'

Almost all now turned towards the women with expressions of pleasure,

'. . . three years after succession and with interest, from the day of succession, of five per cent; it being of course understood that my daughter Chiara should take her grant of two hundred *onze* a year from the capital of her marriage dowry. Furthermore as token of my pleasure at the marriage contracted by her with the Marchese Federico Riolo of Villardita, I leave to her all the jewels brought by myself into the Uzeda family, to be found listed and described apart; I desire that the ancestral jewels of the Francalanza, ransomed by me from the hands of creditors, should remain to my beloved daughter Lucrezia during her lifetime; but as she well knows the state of marriage to be neither conducive to her health nor suitable to her character, I wish them to go to her as a life interest and at her death to be divided in equal portions between Prince Giacomo and Count Raimondo, my universal heirs as above.

'Having thus provided for the future of my beloved children, I pass to the assignation of the following alms and pious legacies to be paid by my above heirs, as follows :

'To Monsignor the most Reverend Bishop Patti, five hundred *onze*, in outright gift, for him to distribute to the poor of the city or to cause Masses to be said by needy priests of the diocese, according as may seem proper to his great judgement . . .'

The Bishop began nodding in sign of gratitude, admiration, regret and modesty all at once; but above all of admiration as the judge read out the pious bequests of the following paragraphs :

'To the Chapel of the Blessed Ximena Uzeda, in the

Church of the Capuchins in Catania, fifty *onze* a year, for a perpetual votive lamp and a weekly Mass to be celebrated for the repose of my soul. To the Church of the Dominican Fathers in Catania, twenty *onze* a year for alms and to celebrate another weekly Mass as above. To the Church of Saint Mary of All Graces in Paternò, twenty *onze* as above. And to the Church of the Convent of Saint Mary of the Holy Light at the Belvedere, twenty *onze* as above.

' I also desire my heirs to see that the following legacies are carried out in favour of dependants who have served me faithfully and assisted me during the course of my illness, as follows :

' I except before all else my administrator and general procurator, Signor Marco Roscitano, whose excellent services, bearing no comparison to those of a domestic, are not to be bought with money.'

Signor Marco had gone as red as a tomato, either at the words of praise or at getting nothing but words.

' I leave him therefore all the golden objects, snuff-boxes, brooches and watches which came into my possession by inheritance from my maternal uncle the Cavaliere Risà, a list of which will be found among my papers; and I make it an obligation for my heirs to continue to avail themselves of his help, there being no one with more knowledge of the state of our affairs and of pending law-cases, or who has greater influence for their success.'

The prince still seemed not to be hearing, with his arms crossed and his look blank.

' Among my servants, I leave to my footman Salvatore Cerra two *tarì* a day as a life-annuity; and the same to my maid Anna Lauro. The sum of a hundred *onze*, in one payment, to my major-domo Baldassarre Crimi, and fifty *onze* to my head coachman Gaspare Gambino, and thirty *onze* to the cook Salvatore Briguccia.

' I also destine small mementoes to my friends as follows :

' The large watch set with miniatures and jewels belonging to my late consort, to Prince Giuseppe of Roccasciano; my defunct father-in-law's carbine to Don Giacinto Costantino; the stick with an engraved gold handle to Don Cono Canalà; my three emerald rings to each of the three witnesses of the present solemn testament, excluding the Prince of Roccasciano as above.

'To all my relatives, relatives-in-law, nieces and nephews, cousins, etc. in general, ten *onze* each for mourning expenses.

'Given at the Belvedere, written by a person in my trust to my dictation, read, approved and signed by me.

TERESA UZEDA OF FRANCALANZA.'

A few minutes before the judge lowered the document, Don Blasco, by moving from the chair-back, had already given signs that the reading was about to end. At the final passages, the gestures of admiration and approval, the nods of gratitude had been general, but as soon as the voice of the reader stopped, the silence was, for an instant, so deep that a fly could have been heard on the wing. Suddenly the prince pushed back his chair.

'Thanks to you all, gentlemen, friends; thank you from the bottom of my heart . . .' he began, but did not end, for the witnesses, getting up too, surrounded him, shaking his hand, shaking Raimondo's hand, congratulating all and sundry.

'There was really no need to read it! . . . We all knew that the dear departed would never . . . A model of a Will! . . . What wisdom! . . . What a brain! . . .'

The Bishop was particularly approving 'She has forgotten no one! All should be content . . .'

And Ferdinando, Chiara, Lucrezia, each and all received their share of congratulations, while the notary and the judge were going through the formalities. But Don Blasco, who as soon as the reading ended had gone back to chewing his nails again more hungrily than ever and meandering around like a bumble-bee, seized Ferdinando as the President was shaking his hand and drew him into the vane of a window.

'Stripped! Stripped! You've been stripped! Stripped like a wood! . . . Reject the Will. Ask for what's your due!'

'Why?' said the young man, astounded.

'Why?' burst out Don Blasco, looking him in the whites of the eyes as if wanting to eat him alive, as if finding it difficult to believe anyone could be so silly, so outrageously ingenuous as his nephew.

'This is why!' and out came a swear word fit to make his painted ancestors blush; then he turned his back on that wretch of a booby and rushed after the marchese.

'Ruined, stripped! Tied in a sack!' he spluttered, nearly thrusting a finger into the other's eyes. 'Legitimate division? How does she make that out? . . . If you accept this Will, you're the last . . .' and out came another swear word. 'I'll make out the accounts in a second! There's money due to you you won't have! And not a word about the Caltagirone legacy! Declare you refuse it, now, on the spot!'

The marchese, astounded by all this fury, stuttered out: 'Excellency, really . . .'

'What's really or unreally to do with it? . . . Or d'you think I get anything out of it myself? . . . I say it in your own interests, you prize idiot!'

'I'll talk to my wife,' replied the marchese, but the monk stared hard at him for a moment, then sent him packing like that other booby and made for the marchesa.

The latter was with all the other ladies, who were standing around Donna Ferdinanda. The old spinster was not expressing her own opinion, not answering the remarks of those around her:

'How just! . . . All treated well! . . . A model of a Will . . .' And Cousin Graziella was saying to the princess, 'And to think evil tongues were hinting that my aunt would disinherit your husband! As if her love for Raimondo could prevent her recognising Giacomo as head of the family, heir to the title!' The Duchess Radalì, on the other hand, part in amazement and part in consternation, was confessing to Don Mariano, 'I'd never have believed it! Co-heirs? What about the primogeniture then? Are families to come to an end then?' But the princess looked acutely embarrassed and did not dare reply, did not take her eyes off the prince. The latter, among the group of men who were repeating ceaselessly, 'What wisdom! what foresight!' was declaring in grave tones, 'Whatever our mother did is well done . . .' While the Prior kept on repeating to the Bishop, 'The dear departed's Will must be a law unto us all . . .' and only Raimondo seemed bored with congratulations and sick of congratulatory handshakes. But now Baldassarre, flinging wide the doors at the end of the room, entered ahead of two footmen carrying two great trays of iced drinks and cakes and biscuits. The prince began serving the witnesses; the major-domo moved towards the ladies.

'Robbed of what is yours! Stripped! Reduced to your shirt-tails!' Don Blasco was saying meanwhile to his niece Chiara, whom he had managed to corner. 'To favour that good-for-nothing who never even bothered to come and see her before she died! And that bumpkin of a wife of his too, who's come and put her nose in here!' The monk launched furious glances towards the Countess Matilde. 'Will you let yourself be robbed like this? Here you must act at once, let people know clear and frankly that you refuse the Will, that you ask for your due . . .'

'I don't know, uncle . . .'

'How d'you mean " you don't know "? . . .'

'I'll talk to Federico . . .'

Then the monk quite lost control of himself:

'Oh, go and . . . yourselves, you, Federico, the lot of you, and me too, silliest of all for worrying about it! . . . Here you!' he ordered Baldassarre, who was on his way to serve Matilde, took an iced drink and drank it at one draught to temper the bile rising in his throat.

His brother Don Eugenio, very quietly, was slipping cakes and biscuits into his pockets, over-eating himself, drinking up glasses of Marsala, like someone uncertain of his luncheon. In spite of this he was giving deep nods of approval at Monsignor the Bishop, who, seeing the Prior Don Lodovico refusing to take refreshments because it was the vigil of a fast, was declaring to the President, 'An angel! No worldly interest has ever touched him! A living example of evangelical virtue . . .' And the President, with his mouth full, confirmed, 'An exemplary family! . . . the old kind . . . Where's that excellent prince gone off to?' For the prince had finally got into a window recess with his uncle the duke:

'Did Your Excellency hear? . . .' he said, with a bitter laugh.

78

' What seemed impossible is true! . . . My family is ruined . . .'

' I couldn't believe it either! . . .' exclaimed the duke. ' His having a privileged position among the heirs, that I can see; but co-heir?'

' Even apartments in the house here . . . just to annoy me! The home of our ancestors to house a Palmi . . .'

' How pleased she must be!' Cousin Graziella was just saying to the duchess. ' Her husband co-heir! . . . Poor Giacomo having to halve with his brother! . . . I'm sorry about that intruder, who'll get even more above herself! . . .'

On the Countess Matilde were weighing the angry or severe looks of Don Blasco, of Cousin Graziella, of the prince. Every time that Baldassarre went towards her to serve her, someone made signs to the major-domo to serve some other male or female guest. Now she was the last unserved; but Donna Ferdinanda beckoned to the young prince Consalvo, sat him on her knee and called out:

' Here, Baldassarre . . .'

## 3

FROM that day Don Blasco could find no peace. Whether the inheritance was divided one way rather than another did not affect him personally in the very slightest, but since entering the monastery he had constantly occupied himself, having no affairs of his own, by putting his nose into those of others.

As a boy he had seen the hey-day of the House of Uzeda, when his father, Prince Giacomo XIII, spent and scattered money everywhere, with twenty horses in the stables, a swarm of servants and a whole court of hangers-on taking seats at tables set day and night. Then the future monk had heard constant talk of his father's extraordinary riches, his vast estates, the revenues he drew from half Sicily; and he had naturally acquired a mania for enjoyment, a greed for pleasures, which he himself was still unable to define precisely. Then one fine day he was put into the novitiate of San Nicola, and later made to pronounce the Vows. All those riches were to go to the eldest brother; to him would come nothing but the grant of thirty-six *onze* a year which was indispensable to enter the rich and noble abbey! . . .

Life, actually, was very comfortable at San Nicola, maybe even more than at the Francalanza palace. The monastery, vast and sumptuous, ranked with royal palaces, in token of which chains were hung in front of the gates; and its income, of about 70,000 *onze* a year, was barely enough for fifty inmates, monks, lay-brothers and novices. The excellent food, good living and almost complete liberty to do what he liked, did not dissipate the monk's soreness at the forcing of his will; particularly as the other younger brothers, the second son, Gaspare, Duke of Oragua and even Eugenio, had stayed in the world, with, it was true, very little money, but at least the chance of acquiring it; at all events they were entirely free and able to dress according to the fashion, and not forced to wear the habit which weighed more on Don Blasco than livery on a servant.

The monk's acrimony, regret for riches lost, envy of his brothers, rancour against his father, found an outlet in the daily exercise of bitter unrelenting criticism of all his relations. He found a wider field for this when the day of reckoning came, his father's fortune was destroyed in a very short time, and the young prince, Consalvo VII, was married off to that Teresa Risà, who now entered the Uzeda household as its mistress. According to family traditions, in order to ensure the continuation of the line through the eldest son and also, in those special circumstances, to restore the shattered family finances by a large dowry, Consalvo was married off at the age of nineteen, when Don Blasco had not yet pronounced his vows. But since that moment the novice had conceived for his sister-in-law a particular aversion which began showing itself later, at every moment, and in everything that she did and did not do.

The Baron of Risà, father of the bride, had come to Catania from Niscèmi in the interior of the island in order to find a husband for his only children, two daughters, between whom he had at first intended to divide his great riches equally. But when the elder, Teresa, was suggested for the young Prince of Mirabella, future Prince of Francalanza, the Uzeda family let it be understood that, although ruined, they would not give Consalvo VII to the daughter of a simple rustic baron if the latter did not fill with money the gap separating her from a descendant of Viceroys. Both the baron and the girl recognised this to be just, but when the father gave 400,000 onze, that is, nearly all, to Teresa, and despoiled his younger daughter Filomena, who just managed to find herself a husband in the Cavaliere Vita and was for ever after on cold terms with her sister, he insisted, by agreement with his daughter, that the marriage contract should stipulate a community of property with the wife in control.

The bride was nearly thirty; ten years older than Consalvo VII. She was born in 1795 and had been unable to find a suitable match for a long time. Her character, already strong, had been toughened by the long wait for matrimony, and the great riches and almost feudal power exercised by her father in his native parts had given her a need of command, of authority, of supremacy which she wanted to use in her new home. Prince Giacomo XIII had to bow to these hard conditions in order to avoid ruin and bankruptcy, and so both he and his son were forced to leave the reins in the hands of wife and daughter-in-law. Donna Teresa did in fact save the family fortunes, but she wielded a tyrannical power to which all bowed, from first to last, except Don Blasco. Fearing neither God nor Devil, the monk made her the constant target of his most violent opposition. If she drew in on certain expenses he accused her of dishonouring the family by meanness; if she went on spending as before he accused her of trying to bring them all to final ruin; if she listened to others' advice she was an idiot, incapable of using her own brain; if she acted on her own she was more of an idiot than ever, coupling presumption to idiocy.

That money she'd brought as dowry? A mere pittance! But when that pittance propped and fortified the tottering family it became the price for which she bought the title of princess. Her nobility was fifth-class, not only incapable of any comparison to the sublime nobility of the Uzeda, but not even worthy of one of their hangers-on, of those starving petty nobles who lived by acting as quasi-servants to great nobles. She could not order a dress at the dressmakers or buy a hat or pair of gloves without the monk criticising expense, quality, and choice of shop. But Don Blasco did not spare other relations either; not his father, who having swallowed up a fortune was now reduced to living on his daughter-in-law's bounty, not his brother, who allowed his wife to wear the trousers while he just wore . . . 'Holy Prudence! Holy Prudence, help me . . .' he would then exclaim, thrusting a hand over his mouth and saying more by this reticence than by a long speech, thus confirming the scattered gossip about his sister-in-law; and when both princes, father and son, died in the same year and the princess was left alone and much freer than before (which had always been free enough) the monk positively spat out the name he considered suitable for her.

She let him have his say. No cries from the monk could prevent her doing whatever she wanted whenever she liked. And Don Blasco went on tormenting himself as he saw her excesses and follies. Was the eldest son in every family in the world not the favourite? Here, though, he was hated! Who was the favourite? The third son! For centuries the title of Count of Lumera had gone together with all the others to the head of the house. Now from pure caprice, from mad folly, it had been given to that boy Raimondo, who had been brought up like a ' pig '! And the second son, whom even the King could not deprive of his title for life of Duke of Oragua, had been shut up in San Nicola . . .

Don Lodovico's story was very like Don Blasco's but with this difference: while Don Blasco was a third son, Lodovico had only the prince before him, and as Duke of Oragua he could have hoped, if not from his mother at least from some uncle, for the money necessary to bear that title with decorum. It was understood that another Uzeda in that generation was to enter San Nicola, and reason and tradition pointed to the third son, Raimondo. But Donna Teresa, in order to make her own will prevail over all human and divine laws, inverted the natural order and took to protecting Raimondo above all the other brothers, left him a layman with the title of count and began working on the young Duke Lodovico to sense a vocation. Thus no one in her presence could call the boy by the title which was his due.

He had been dressed in the black Benedictine habit since childhood. As toys he had nothing but little altars, pyxes, holy water sprinklers and every other kind of sacred object. When his mother asked him, ' What do you want to become?' the boy was trained to answer, ' A monk of San Nicola.' At this reply he would get caresses and promises of pocket-money, amusements, carriage-drives. And if at times he dared reply, ' I don't know . . .' Donna Teresa would pinch his arm hard enough to make him cry until she had torn the desired answer from him. Her confessor meanwhile, Father Camillo, a Dominican, was also working towards this result by educating the boy to blind obedience to the clergy, mortifying his senses and imagination in every way, rousing in him the fear of hell, making him sense the joys of Paradise. In order to succeed in her intention better, the princess did not place the boy in the novitiate early. She kept him at home until he was fifteen.

Those were the times of rigid economies, of creditors crowding in the administrative offices, of debts paid off bit by bit, so that while Don Blasco had heard constant talk of the treasures which had in part melted under his very eyes, Lodovico heard nothing but complaints, threats from people demanding money, and his mother's eternal refrain exaggerating their condition on purpose, 'We're ruined! What are we to do? There'll be nothing left!' In the Francalanza palace the princess introduced strict thrift and made open show of the poverty to which they were reduced, collecting match-ends to relight them, selling off old clothes before getting a new dress; and she would describe to Lodovico the Benedictine monastery as a place of eternal delights where life passed without cares of today or fears of tomorrow, amid delicious meals, sumptuous ceremonies, sprightly conversation and jolly outings. And when eventually Lodovico entered San Nicola as a novice he realised that his mother had told the truth, for the cornucopia of abundance seemed to spill continually over the monastery and life flowed easy and pleasant there.

The youth, coming from the iron tutelage of the princess and her confessor, appreciated particularly the liberty, almost the licence, which he saw reigning in the monastery. So he was persuaded of the suitability, instilled in him since childhood, of entering that Order. Even so, before pronouncing his vows he hesitated for a time, realising, at the moment of carrying it out, the gravity of the sacrifice being imposed on him, while Don Blasco tried to open his eyes to his mother's intrigues. But apart from paying little heed to the monk's opinion, whose implacable criticism he knew, it was actually that very severity of his mother's which he was so anxious to escape and which made him renounce, in terror, any attempt at open rebellion.

Too late, Father Don Lodovico had realised the trick of which he had been a victim, when he saw that the poverty so lamented by his mother was a lie, and that the place which he had been made to renounce had passed to his brother Raimondo. But it

84

was now too late to turn back; hood and scapular were to weigh on his shoulders until death.

The rebellion, fury and hatred that burst into his mind were even more violent than his uncle's, as he was incapable, from long habit of pretence and self-mortification, of exploding into words recklessly like Don Blasco. Nothing appeared of the feelings that were aboil in his heart. Before his mother he remained as reverent and submissive as before, and as prodigal of demonstrations of fraternal affection to that Raimondo who was enjoying the place usurped from him. He confirmed, by exemplary life, his vocation for the monastic state. While Don Blasco, gross, ignorant, greedy for material pleasures, revelled with the worst of the monks, playing the lottery to enrich himself and carrying a knife under his habit, Don Lodovico, subtler, better educated and above all shrewder and more self-controlled, was pointed out as a rare example of ascetic virtue, a pillar of theological doctrine. While the uncle, to revenge himself for his lost worldly power, tried to dominate the monastery, grumbling against abbot, prior, deacons and cellarers, cursing Saint Nicholas and Saint Benedict and all their celestial companions, the nephew seemed to take every care to keep apart, to nourish no other ambition but study . . .

In his heart he was longing for revenge. Finding himself for ever shut in there he wanted to reach the highest ranks quickly and before anyone else. Among the Benedictines, indeed, there was a kingdom to be conquered; the Abbot was a power in the land, with any number of feudal titles and a fabulous fortune to control; the ancient Constitution of Sicily gave him the right to a seat among the peers of the realm.

Don Lodovico wanted to reach that position in as short a time as possible. Once he realised the line to take he never deviated from it a hairsbreadth; nobody could ever reprove him for the slightest trespass, no-one ever draw him into any of the many factions in which the monks were divided. Living apart, usually shut into the library, he gained sympathy by the humility of his bearing, the obedience he lent to his elders and his equals too, his strict observance of the Rule, and a reputation for learning which he had soon acquired. So he had been elected Deacon at the age of twenty-seven. But, praised to the skies by the Abbot and most of the monks, he drew on himself his uncle's ever harsher and more violent hatred.

Thirsty for power, Don Blasco also wanted to be Prior and Abbot, but his scandalous life, his violent character, his supine ignorance made the achievement of this ambition if not impossible at least very difficult. Consequently he had not been made Deacon before the age of forty. Thus the sight of his nephew 'scarcely out of swaddling-clothes' in that position made him quite beside himself. And on the death of the Prior Raimo, early in 1855 a tremendous battle broke out. That one of the Uzeda, whose ancestors had been such benefactors of the monastery, should occupy the vacant chair, was beyond discussion, but Don Blasco expected the dignity for himself, nor did he think that 'Jesuit' of a nephew of his could dream of barring his way. When he heard that that 'pig' was competing with him and daring to put himself on a par with his uncle, he very nearly had a stroke. The things he said against Lodovico were enough to draw lightning on the dome of San Nicola and burn the monastery with all its inhabitants to ashes; the least he called him was 'pimp of the Chapter, Abbot's pot-emptier, son of I don't know who . . .'

Don Lodovico let him have his say, and edified the whole monastery by the humility with which he treated his uncle's violence. He was quite sure of himself; the election of the ignorant and overbearing Don Blasco, who had sown the whole quarter with his children and kept three or four mistresses, among them the famous Cigar-woman, was judged impossible by all. Age was the one advantage he had over his nephew, but that was not enough to compensate for his vast number of defects. Don Lodovico was elected by an overwhelming majority, and from that day Don Blasco became an implacable enemy of the 'filthy Jesuit' and of that '. . . . . .' of a princess, on whom he naturally blamed this latest and most unforgivable kick from her 'mule' of a son.

Nor had the other nieces and nephews, whom the monk defended out of hatred of the dead woman, and incited to reject the Will, ever been in his good graces. It was enough that they should be children of the woman whom he considered as a personal enemy; but then in his eyes each and all of them had particular faults, beginning with Chiara and her husband.

The latter's great fault consisted in having been chosen by the princess as a son-in-law and of having loved Chiara in spite of the aversion shown by the girl herself. That was just why Don Blasco had given him a good spattering, being able all in one go to have at him for trying ' to force his way ' into the Uzeda family, at the princess for trying ' to violate ' her daughter's Will, and at his niece for being ' silly and mad ' enough to refuse a match ' like that '. By resisting her mother Chiara should really have gained her uncle the monk's praise and encouragement, but Don Blasco was made in such a way that when someone agreed with him he changed his opinions so as to put them in the wrong. And so the engagement had meant one long violent quarrel between brother-in-law and sister-in-law, between uncle and niece and also between mother and daughter, since the princess had played one of her tricks there too.

For her, as for all heads of great families, the only really desirable and lovable children were male; females did nothing but eat their heads off and bear away family property if they took a husband. This Salic idea, deep-rooted in her, did actually admit of some exceptions—her own self for example—but not with her own progeny. Even among the males, though, she had not treated two alike. In her lifetime she had almost hated her eldest son and idolised Raimondo. But the one she hated was heir to the title, future head of the house, and her favourite, in spite of sacrificing Lodovico, was simply a younger son. So she had compromised between respect for feudal tradition and satisfaction of her personal wishes by deciding, without telling anyone, to divide her riches between the two brothers, that is by defrauding the eldest son, who should have had everything and favour the other, who should have had nothing. Of the other two, Lodovico had been more or less suppressed so as to give a place to Raimondo, whilst Ferdinando had been able to live his own free life up to a point. Towards the women on the other hand she had nursed a deeper, uniform repulsion and almost contempt, and done all she could to prevent them ' robbing ' their brothers. Angiolina, the eldest, had been condemned to the life of the cloister from birth, for the unpardonable fault she had committed of coming

A year after marriage Donna Teresa, when about to give birth, had expected a son, an eldest one, a little Prince of Mirabella, a future Prince of Francalanza. She not only expected him but she was determined he would appear. Instead of which a daughter was born; and the mother never forgave her. From the moment she took off her swaddling-clothes she dressed her up as a little nun; before the child could even talk she was taken to the Convent of San Placido every day. At the age of six she was shut in there 'for education' and at sixteen the gentle and simple creature, ignorant of the world, subdued by her mother's will and also by the impenetrable walls of the convent, felt herself truly called by God; and so Angiolina Uzeda died, and Sister Maria of the Cross remained.

Chiara, who had come immediately afterwards and stayed at home, felt the maternal rigour even more. The princess had not left her in the lay state for fear of any criticism of what people might consider the sacrifice of two daughters, but so that she herself could exercise over the girl a vigilance and authority firmer and more severe than that which the Abbess exercised in a convent. 'But from a crazy woman like my sister-in-law,' Don Blasco would say, ' and a swine like my brother, what would you expect to come out? A super-crazy swine, of course!'

And what happened? What happened was that as long as the mother held her in a grip of iron, this daughter had always bowed her head, respectful and obedient. Then on the day when the princess, having found that ass of a Marchese of Villardita offering to marry the girl for nothing, decided to marry her off, she had said no, no, and no! Unbelievable! . . . The marchese, having seen the girl every now and then under veils in church, had fallen in love with her, and the princess, determined to give him her daughter, had admitted him to the house. But, discouraged by Chiara's cold greeting and stubborn repulses, persuaded by relatives and friends that he was mad to marry against her will a girl who did not want him, he would have retired in good order, had Donna Teresa, who when she made a decision would not be deviated even by the Devil, not ordered him to stay at his post. So when he saw the girl again, sitting in a corner, her head bowed, handkerchief in hand, he felt like weeping too. 'Silly calf!' said Don Blasco, ' so soft as to fall in love with that long-faced niece of mine!' Chiara, in fact, was no beauty, and her mother, first to dissuade her from marriage and then to induce her to accept this match, would repeat every day, ' Take a look at yourself in the mirror! Don't you see how ugly you are? Who d'you expect to take you? . . .' but Chiara replied, ' No one, all the better! Your Excellency didn't want me to marry, did you? Let me stay at home! . . .'

Reacting at first sight, like all the Uzeda, Chiara had refused to consider this proposed fiancé for the one and only reason that he was rather fat, but once she had taken that line the stubbornness which was much more of an Uzeda hereditary trait than sensibility had been the most powerful cause of the resistance she put up to her mother. Till the very last moment, tenacious, stubborn, inflexible, she said that never, never, never would she marry that barrel of a man; and in vain her brothers and uncles, her Father Confessor explained that though the marchese was not thin he had a heart of gold and was marrying her without a dowry for the love he bore her, and that she could queen it over his home as he was all alone and very rich, and that if she let this match slip her mother might go back to her first idea of not marrying her off at all, of letting her grow into an old maid. Her back to the wall, she had still replied no, no and no again.

The princess had at first refused to speak to her, then cursed her like a servant, then locked her up in a dark little room with no clothes and little food; then she had begun to hit her with hard knobbly hands, hurting her, swearing she would let her starve to death if she did not give in. To the marchese, who, overcome by scruples, came to take back his word, she said, ' No, sir. Marry you she must, because I wish it so. If she is an Uzeda, I am a Risà! You'll see she'll change . . .' She knew what they were like, all those Uzeda; when they got an idea into their heads it could not be moved, even if their heads were broken in two: they came from Viceroys, so their will should be law! But from one day to the next, when it was least expected, for no reason, they would suddenly change. Where first they had said white they then affirmed black. If, say, they wanted to kill a man, the latter would suddenly become their best friend . . . Till the very last moment Chiara had not changed.

Before the altar, with two rangers each side of her, brigand faces sought out by her mother on purpose to instil terror in her, she had fainted, and the priest only heard a ' yes ' of his own good will; but the day after the marriage, when the family went to visit the bride and groom, what did they find but them embracing and holding hands? . . . ' It really takes one aback!' cried Don Blasco.

Servants, retainers and friends jested for a time among themselves about the means used by the marchese to domesticate his wife, but the fact remained that from that day Chiara was all one with her husband, to the point that he could not be a quarter of an hour late home without her sending all the servants after him, to the point of being jealous of his very thoughts. And she no longer had an opinion differing from her husband's, in any circumstances big or small. If she was asked something, before giving a reply she would interrogate him with her eyes as if fearful of not saying what he was thinking himself. Her only great sorrow was not having had a child by him after three years of marriage, and being in such haste she had announced her own pregnancy four or five times; but even this showed her love for her Federico.

The princess had given her to him for many reasons. First of all because she had borne a third daughter after the four boys, and so had reasoned—or ' unreasoned ' as Don Blasco put it— like this: of the three girls the first a nun, the second a wife, the last at home. Now the marchese on falling in love with the girl not only promised to take her without a dowry but even to lend himself to a little play-acting. Though her firm intention as a mother was for the family fortune to be untouched by the females, her pride as Princess of Francalanza could not allow people to praise her son-in-law's generosity for taking Chiara without a cent, as if from a foundlings' home. So in the marriage contract she had granted her daughter an income of two hundred *onze* a year; so said the contract registered by Rubino the notary, and so everyone was told; but then the marchese handed over to her a receipt for the entire capital of four thousand *onze*, not a cent of which had he ever seen!

Now Don Blasco, who had already set himself against the marchese for his marriage to Chiara and against Chiara for her sudden conversion from hatred to love of her husband, had blamed both of them for the fiction to which they had lent themselves in order to obey that mad sister-in-law of his who ought to be in an asylum. What he blamed them for even more, and found even more unforgivable, was their not insisting on their rights to the paternal inheritance.

In fact, according to the Benedictine, the Uzeda fortunes were not entirely destroyed when Donna Teresa entered the family; and in any case, as the income from the properties had been paid even in the very worst times, the princess should have taken them into account, as she could scarcely pretend they all went in daily expenses. They had helped, on the other hand, to pay off the debts and save the estates, then had all been fused with the newly reconstructed family fortune and were put down in the general assets of Prince Consalvo VII. The latter, like the idiot he had always been, had gone and crowned his short and stupid life with that clownish Will, imposed and dictated by his wife; by this, in declaring the whole of his family fortune as destroyed from ' family disasters ' he had left his children ' enough to make a dog retch . . .', their mother's affection; but now the children —if they weren't even more idiotic than their father—ought to demand accounts down to the very last cent.

With this aim the monk had gone assiduously round his nieces and nephews, except for Raimondo, to whom he had not said a word for years and years just because he had been his mother's favourite, and incited them to stand up for their rights; but no one, in the princess's lifetime, had dared breathe a word; and he had reluctantly excused them in view of the pressure to which she had subjected them. But this marchese who was only a son-in-law and so should not be afraid of her, and who had already been tricked once in that matter of the capital, was considered by Don Blasco the worst of cowards for deciding not to speak out. Why? Please why? Because of his declaring he had married Chiara for the love he bore her and not for the money that she could bring him . . .! Such was the monk's fury that it brought on an attack of bile, but in time he had shut his mouth and waited for his sister-in-law's death before sallying into battle again. Now she had finally died and that bestial Will of hers had been read out, the furious monk forgot Federico

91

and Chiara's stupidity and attacked them once again to get them to take action. The dead woman, instead of declaring 'honestly' how much was her husband's part and dividing it 'equally' among all her children, was now disposing of the entire family fortune as if it was her own! Not content with that, she was defrauding the legitimate heirs by pretending to assign them a quota higher than the law, but in reality giving them 'nothing at all'. Chiara in particular had been 'stripped like a wood', as the Will never mentioned Canon Risà's legacy. This was another of Donna Teresa's little arrangements some time before.

Among other arguments used to conquer Chiara's resistance and induce her to marry the marchese, the princess had used money too, but in order not to open her own purse strings she had recourse to an uncle of hers, Canon Risà of Caltagirone, who promised a legacy of five thousand *onze* to his grandniece if the girl would marry the Marchese of Villardita. Donna Teresa had countersigned the document to guarantee this payment on condition that this sum really existed in the property left by the Canon, who promised to leave everything to her. Instead of which when the Canon died two years before leaving his property half to his old housekeeper and half to the princess, she had refused to recognise the pact made; nor did the marchese, from respect and disinterest, think of asking for it to be carried out.

Don Blasco now, as his sister-in-law had not even remembered that obligation in her Will and even arranged 'with her infernal art' that other little matter of the four thousand *onze* which Chiara had never received, and which she was to contribute as if she had already received them, visited the marchese every day to turn him against the dead woman and the co-heirs, inciting him to demand: firstly the legal division; secondly the money of the marriage contract with all its back interest; thirdly the part due to Chiara from her father; fourthly the Canon's legacy: and he would show in a flash that not only ten thousand *onze* assigned her in the Will was due to her, but three times as much at least. The marchese, though he listened and nodded to all that the monk said, for discussion was impossible with this blessed Benedictine, told his wife that he had no wish to cause any family quarrel and would wait and see what the others did. And Chiara fell in with that as with all her husband's other opinions. In her heart though she agreed with her uncle, and wanted to be given what was due to her, for in her vying devotion she was sorry that Federico should have to sustain the whole weight of their household expenses alone; but the marchese, on his side, protested, ' I took you for yourself and not for your money! Even if you had nothing it wouldn't matter to me . . . And anyway it doesn't mean we'll renounce our rights. Let's leave it to Lucrezia and Ferdinanda to act first. I don't want to be the one to start a law case in your family . . .'

This disinterest and respect which he showed for the Uzeda family increased Chiara's devotion and admiration and she agreed with him the more eagerly, as in those very days, after making a vow, by the Abbess of San Placido's advice, to the miraculous San Francesco di Paola, she had new hope of being pregnant. And so in order to defend her husband from that horse-fly of a Don Blasco she faced her uncle herself and said to him :

' Yes, indeed; your Excellency's right, and only talking from love of us; but our respect for the wishes of our mother . . ."

' Your mother was an animal,' shouted the monk. ' Even more than you are! . . . What was it your mother wanted? To ruin you all for love of Raimondo and hatred of Giacomo! You're as mad as she was! A bunch of madmen, the lot of you . . .' And more and more enraged by the endless love-play between husband and wife, particularly during mealtimes when they would serve each other as if in mid-honeymoon and coo away like two doves, the monk burst out, ' I don't really know which of you two is more of an animal . . .'

At this Chiara once took him aside and protested :

' Your Excellency can say what you like to me, but don't touch on Federico. I won't allow you to speak badly of him . . .'

' What the hell do I care what you allow!' burst out the monk in reply. ' Or d'you think people have forgotten that first you didn't even want him as pigs' food and threatened to let yourself die rather than marry that water melon . . .?'

The niece turned her back on her uncle; the latter sent his niece to stew in her own juice, vowing never to set foot in her home again, and loudly calling himself a triple-dyed idiot for the stupid interest he had taken in that pair of animals. But those were mere sailors' vows; he could not resign himself to being silent and was set on preventing the dead woman's Will being carried out. And so, while awaiting a chance to return to the charge, he began to work on Ferdinando.

Whatever hour he went to see him, up at Pietra dell'Ovo, he found him always alone, with plane or saw or hoe in hand, intent on working as carpenter or gardener, in his shirtsleeves, like a workman or peasant. He had been like that since childhood, had Ferdinando; taciturn, timid, half-wild because of the little care his mother had taken of him, forced to amuse himself as best he could, for he never got a present even of the poorest toy. He had more or less brought himself up, used his own ingenuity to get what he needed and to look after himself. When others went out for amusement he stayed in the house, tearing up wooden or cardboard boxes to make little theatres or altars or huts which he would then give to whoever asked for them, particularly to Lucrezia, of whom he felt very fond as his companion in destiny; and if at times they came to look for him because he had visitors, or some relation wanted to see him, he would run off and hide in holes where no one could manage to find him, or take refuge in the shop of a watchmaker, a close friend who was teaching him his craft.

One day, on St Ferdinand's Day, Don Cono Canalà gave him a copy of *Robinson Crusoe*. He devoured it from cover to cover and was overwhelmed as if by a revelation. From that moment his taste for the savage life grew; his one and constant desire was to be shipwrecked on a desert island and sustain himself. Then he began to try out experiments in the garden and terrace of the villa, and acquired a taste for country life which the princess encouraged. She had given him the nickname of 'The Booby', because of his crazy manias, but, realising that these favoured her own plans, she let him run wild at the Pietra dell'Ovo, first amid the shrubbery and cacti, then in time, maturing her plan for general spoilage in favour of her eldest son and of Raimondo, over the whole estate, insisting, however, on a contract in full legal order, by which her son had to pay her

94

five hundred *onze* a year on the takings with the residue to him.

The contract was a bargain to Donna Teresa, for it saved her thirty-six *onze* a year for the agent, as Ferdinando went straight off to settle there so as to cultivate on his own the *island* which he had acquired; and then it ensured her an income which the estate did not yield. The Booby relied on improvements to pay the five hundred *onze* for his mother, leaving the rest for himself, and as soon as he entered into possession he began digging, scooping out wells, tearing down almond trees to plant lemons, stripping vineyards to replant almond trees, going his own sweet way, in a word, as he had dreamt. His pleasure, actually, would have been far greater had he been able to do all by himself; but, forced to call in labourers and gardeners, he himself worked with them, tearing out weeds, carrying off basketfuls of stones, lopping trees, and acting as carpenter, builder and decorator too, for one of his first occupations had been to enlarge and embellish the agent's old house. He was happy leading the life of the hero who had excited his imagination as if he really were on a desert island a thousand miles from the world. He slept on a kind of sailor's bunk, made tables and chairs by himself, and the house was like a workshop, littered with saws, planes, drills, pulleys, spades and picks; there was also an assortment of stakes and beams, and sacks of flour to make bread, and supplies of gunpowder, a shelf of books, all the things which a wrecked man would save from a ship before it broke up.

From the very first year, though, he had been unable to pay the whole of the rent promised to his mother; there still remained a good half to give her which the princess noted regularly as a debt from him. Then by changing plantations, putting into action novelties he heard talk of or read about in treatises on agriculture or thought up for himself, he succeeded in diminishing the yield from the estate each year. It was the fault of hired labourers who did not carry his orders out properly, he would say, or of the confused weather, but his mother would jeer at him on purpose to encourage him in his mania, and succeeded wonderfully well. And the yield got less and less, and did not even reach a hundred *onze*, in spite of the fact that apart from his tools and a book or two he never spent a thing on himself and subsisted frugally on the products of his garden and shooting; and the few times when he did appear at the palace he scandalised even the servants, he was so ragged and dirty and down at heel in very old clothes.

But the princess, though deriding him, let him be, and noted down one after the other in her book of rents all the money which he failed to give her every year. This already amounted to quite a considerable sum which the Booby did not know where to lay hands on. His continual fear was that his mother, tired of finding she was never paid, would take the estate away from him; and indeed the princess did threaten this more than once. Thus a master-stroke in her Will was assigning the property at Pietra dell'Ovo to Ferdinando. That property was worth more to him than a great estate: if he were to exchange it for the whole of his elder brother's heritage he feared to lose on the deal. As if that was not enough there was also the con-donation of past rents which now totalled nearly one thousand five hundred *onze*; so that, quite beside himself with delight, he thought himself very well treated indeed, beyond his every hope, and to Don Blasco trying to induce him to rebel he would say, candidly, stopping work, his digging or his pruning:

'What? Isn't what I've got enough?'

'But you should have had at least three times as much! You've been tricked with all the others! Your father's part is due to you in equal proportion to all the others, and now's the moment to claim it! And don't you know that Giacomo didn't even send for you on the day of your mother's death?'

'That's impossible!' replied Ferdinando scandalised. 'But why?'

'So he could lay hands on certain papers and valuables! He rushed up there and began turning the whole villa upside down. That's known! And then he went through all that act of putting on seals! You'll realise that when you see the inventory, my little virgin soul!'

The monk was in a frenzy of impatience for this inventory, but the prince on the other hand seemed in no hurry to know what there was in the house, never spoke of business to any of his brothers or sisters, not even to his co-heir Raimondo, to whom it never even occurred to ask for any account. In spite of mourning the latter was always out at the Nobles' Club, chatting about Florence to old friends, having his game of cards, or commenting on the carriages that filed past at the evening parade. And Don Blasco made Ferdinando's ears hum with his invective against his brother. 'A scandal, a lack of respect to the dead woman whose body is still warm,' was the conduct of this good-for-nothing who thought only of amusement, who had not come to 'close his mother's eyes' even for love of the money which she wanted to give him *brevi manu*, 'stolen from the others! . . .' Then on the day when the inventory was finally made out and it showed that cash in hand had been only five *onze* and two *tarì* in ready money, and a security of a hundred ducats, the monk rushed off to Ferdinando like a madman.

'D'you see? D'you see? D'you see? . . . What did I say? Five *onze*! Your mother never had less than a thousand! And securities! Securities! I knew of up to five thousand ducats' worth! . . . D'you understand now? D'you see how your dear brother has robbed you? That thief of a Signor Marco there held the sack open for him! Robbed! Robbed! If you don't complain, if you don't make yourself heard, you deserve to have 'em spitting in your face!'

On and on he went about this new deception to his nephew, who was stunned by all the shouting. Why, for instance, had Giacomo left Signor Marco in his job, when he had thrown out all the servants whom his mother had protected, the head coachman, the cook, all those to whom she had left something? That 'pig' Signor Marco, 'the evil genius' of the dead woman, should have got a 'kick in the backside' as soon as his protectress had closed her eyes; instead of which why ever was he still in service after two months? Just because as soon as his former mistress died he had flung himself 'vilely' at the new master's feet, handed everything over to him, let him 'steal' the valuables which were to go 'to all' or at least 'to the co-heir . . .'

And here was this fool Ferdinando acting the simpleton, refusing to believe all this chicanery and declaring himself grateful to his mother for letting him off that fifteen hundred *onze*! As if that contract between mother and son had not been all wrong in itself, as if the princess had not on purpose settled for a sum higher than the yield from the property so as to get him into

97

her clutches all the more . . .! Yet by dint of preaching to him that he should have more money, that he could be more than twice, more than three times as rich, the monk might have managed to shake his nephew, had he not, as he had with Chiara by speaking ill of her husband, committed a grave imprudence with Ferdinando too. Ferdinando feared that if he refused the Will and asked for the legal division, Pietra dell'Ovo might pass into the hands of others, or that at least he would have to divide it with his brothers. One day Don Blasco, when showing him the chance of keeping all for himself, cried out:

'And anyway if you do lose this place, you'll get another in exchange worth a hundred times more . . .'

'No, Excellency,' replied Ferdinando. 'There's no other place like this in our family.'

'Like this?' the monk burst out then. 'Just about good enough to fling a herd of pigs on? What's there here apart from acorns? Particularly now that you've completely ruined it with your mad experiments?'

Ferdinando, hearing his own land and work run down, was struck dumb and flushed like a tomato. Then, recovering his voice, he declared:

'Excellency, you know the proverb? " A madman knows more of his own home than a wise man of others ".'

Then the monk, gurking curses at this ill-mannered nephew, never went up to his ' pigsty ' again and was reduced to laying siege to Lucrezia. He had kept her to the last because, with all his instinctive loathing for each of his nieces and nephews, it was her he loathed most.

Like Chiara and Ferdinando, Lucrezia could not remember her mother ever giving her a caress; but whereas Chiara from the beginning had the relative merit in the monk's eyes of resisting the princess in the matter of her marriage, and Ferdinando that of having been sent away from home, his youngest niece had nothing but demerits, one worse than the other. Under Donna Teresa's lash, treated with particular harshness for having been born when her mother expected no more children, considered an intruder come to steal part of the money destined to the two males, Lucrezia had grown up, said the Benedictine, like a ' marmot ': backward, taciturn, savage as Ferdinando, and always so distracted that her answers aroused laughter from everyone except her uncle Blasco, who could have eaten her alive.

In her subjugation and ill-treatment of her daughter, the princess never forgot her principal aim; that of keeping her at home, a spinster. So, assiduously, daily she had shown Lucrezia that marriage was not for her; firstly because of her bad health —but the girl was perfectly well; then because the good of the family required it—and she pointed to the example of Donna Ferdinanda; then because with no money she would never be able to find a suitable match—and the exception of the Marchese Federico confirmed the rule; and finally, in case all this was not enough, because she was ugly too—and there she told the truth. When the mother saw her looking in a mirror, or on the rare occasions when the girl was present at visits Donna Teresa would exclaim, 'How ugly you are, my girl! . . . What a misfortune it is to have such an ugly daughter, is it not?' The most persuasive argument even so was that of poverty; the money belonged to the 'males'. When her agents brought in sackloads of coin she would say to Lucrezia, 'D'you see these? They're all for the men . . .' And if the girl raised her eyes to the maps of their estates hanging in the antechambers, her mother would repeat, 'What are you looking at? They're all property of the men!'

When the conversation fell on marriage in her daughter's presence, Donna Teresa would warn, 'Be careful what you say in front of girls!' and when they were alone she would tell her that thinking of marriage was a mortal sin, to be confessed. Her confessor Father Camillo confirmed Lucrezia in these ideas. Then the princess would repeat again and again, 'Anyway you've got nothing, so you'll be forced to stay at home; who'll want to marry you without any money?' Chiara had been another matter; she had found someone willing to take her in nothing but her shift, as he knew she was wise, God fearing, and obedient to her mother. Sweetening the pill, the princess let fall now and again, 'If you behave like your sister, I'll make it up to you in some other way!'

So Lucrezia had grown up; constantly mortified and humiliated, more segregated from the world than in a convent, invisible to her elder brothers and even to her uncles, tyrannised a little even by Chiara who, being five years older, acted as a grown-up; loved and protected only by Ferdinando, with whose character hers was so much in accord. The Booby had to think of himself, not disposing of much goodwill in the family, but he showed Lucrezia as well as he could the love he had for her.

Older only by a year or so, he played with her and gave her toys he had made himself. Later on, when he got some notion of letters and taught himself to draw and do various little crafts, he passed on his knowledge to his sister, for whom the expense of a tutor had been spared. Besides Ferdinando's company and protection was not all Lucrezia had; she had also Donna Vanna's, one of the women-servants. And the princess, always wary and alert, did not see the danger from that direction.

The Francalanza servants were paid little and accustomed to trembling before their mistress. In spite of this it was rare for any of them to leave unless dismissed, as all found a means of recouping morally and materially for bad treatment. The means consisted in secretly taking sides with one of the children or in-laws against their mistress, in fomenting rebellions and acting as spies. For this reason there were as many factions down in the courtyard as there were heads up in the palace wanting to get their own way. Now Donna Vanna was one of the 'young ladies' faction: as before she had encouraged Chiara's desperate resistance to the marriage imposed on her, so later she would tell Lucrezia her sister's story in order to show her the harshness and quirkiness of her mother; and she put the idea into the girl's head of getting married too, and gave her a consciousness of her own rights and qualities. It was not true that she was poor; the princess could only dispose of half of her own fortune, the other half had to be equally divided among all her children. 'She must do that, as it's written in the law; that's why a part is called " legitimate " . . .' And Lucrezia listened to her open-mouthed, trying to understand. She understood more easily the praises of the maid, who found recondite beauties in the person of her little mistress as she dressed and combed her. 'How straight Your Excellency is! . . . Like a palm-tree . . .

And these tresses! Like boat ropes!' Then she would conclude, 'We must find a man to enjoy them.'

So it happened that, when the Giulente family came to live opposite the Francalanza palace, Donna Vanna said to her young mistress, 'Has Your Excellency seen the Signorino Benedetto? What a handsome lad!' Lucrezia began watching him from her window, and agreed with the maid. 'Hasn't Your Excellency noticed how he looks at you?' Lucrezia went redder than a poppy and from that day her eyes often strayed to the young man's balcony. But as long as the princess was in good health things went no further than that and nobody suspected her. Then one day Donna Teresa, already poorly, woke with a pain in her side which at first she took no notice of, but which a year later was to take her to the tomb. When the mistress's illness grew worse, and particularly when she went off alone to the Belvedere for a change of air, as Raimondo, her favourite, was in Florence and her other children were all more or less abhorred by her, then Donna Vanna, freer to favour her young mistress's love more and more, talked to the young man, bore, first, greetings from one side to another, then messages, and finally letters. This was noticed in the family, and all turned on Lucrezia.

The Giulente, who had come to Catania almost a century before from Syracuse, belonged to a dubious class that was no longer 'middle' or bourgeois but had not yet acquired true and proper nobility. Nobles they thought and vaunted themselves to be, but they could not succeed in spreading this conviction to others. For a number of generations they had intermarried with families of the true 'old stock', but only among those short of money, for a girl who was both noble and rich would never have married a Giulente. In order to play at being the equals of authentic barons they had adopted all the baronial habits; only one son among them, the eldest, could marry; the others had to remain bachelors. The abolition of entails had pleased them, as there was none in their family; when the majority law was instituted, they had tried to get it applied to them, but without success. In spite of that everything was left to the eldest son. Don Paolo, Benedetto's father, was very rich while his brother Don Lorenzo did not have a cent; that was the reason, maybe, why he intrigued with revolutionaries. Benedetto, partly from his uncle's example, partly from the air of the times, was also a Liberal. He was very proud of his birth, but much against the arrogance of the nobility—'When the fox can't reach the grapes!' cried Donna Ferdinanda—and because of these sentiments, though all his father's fortune would one day come to him, he was studying for a lawyer's degree. Hence Don Blasco's anger against his niece for falling in love without asking his permission; and who with? A Giulente, a Liberal, a lawyer!

Now, after the reading of the Will, after the opposition put up to his suggestions by Chiara, the marchese, and Ferdinando, the monk turned to Lucrezia. He had greater hope of succeeding with her as her love of Giulente gave her a reason for rebelling against the family. It was true that for the moment he would have either to help or at least pretend to ignore his niece's love affair, but as long as he could plot and put his finger in things, and get himself noticed, Don Blasco was willing to pass over greater difficulties than that. So he began to show Lucrezia how wrongly she had been treated, and what was to be deduced from it, and how Giacomo had robbed them all as soon as his mother was dead; and he went over the accounts with her again and encouraged her to come to an agreement with Ferdinando, on whom she alone could have an influence, in order to put up a united front against their elder brother.

At her family's opposition Lucrezia had gone stubborn, like every Uzeda when contradicted, and sworn to Donna Vanna that she would marry Giulente at all costs; now, on hearing the monk talk of her rights, show her that she was richer than she thought, and instigate her to make her own will felt, she listened, though diffidently and suspecting a trick. At night she took counsel with the maid and, Donna Vanna encouraging her to follow the monk's reasoning, she came to recognise that her mother had indeed sacrificed her like all the others for the sake of two sons, and she bowed her head to the arguments repeated to her by Don Blasco. But when she was just about to promise that she would speak out to Giacomo, fear held her back. She had grown up with the idea that he was of a different mould, a finer nature; while all her brothers and sisters used the familiar *tu* among themselves, the eldest son was always addressed by the formal *voi*. And the prince, who had always kept her at a distance and looked down on her from a height, now, after the reading of the Will, seemed even more withdrawn to all, particularly to her. Prepared to put up a fight for Giulente's love, she wanted to reserve her strength for the right moment and not waste it on an aim which to her seemed secondary. Benedetto had let her know that as soon as he had his degree, which would be in a couple of years, he would ask for her hand, and that the Duke of Oragua, being such a close friend of his uncle Lorenzo's, would be sure to support them; but meanwhile they must be patient and prudent, try not to arouse the Uzedas' animosity. When consulted on the question of the Will he repeated his advice about doing nothing against the prince, partly for the old reasons, partly lest he should seem avid for her to have a bigger dowry. ' You see, Your Exellency?' commented the maid, hearing these letters read out by her mistress. ' You see, Your Excellency, how good he is? He loves Your Excellency, not your money! Anyone out for the dowry would have replied differently and said " let's fight it out!" . . .' He was in fact a good, studious young man, with a head rather in the clouds, inflamed by his uncle's Liberal doctrines and burning with love for Italy; to Lucrezia he wrote that he had three passions : her, his mother and their country to be redeemed.

So Lucrezia, after listening to Don Blasco's instigations, did nothing of what her uncle wanted either. In fact once when he was being particularly insistent, she replied :

' Why doesn't Your Excellency talk to Giacomo yourself?'

At this remark the monk went purple and seemed on the point of suffocating.

' So I'm to talk to him, am I? You little idiot! You'd like me to pull the chestnuts out of the fire with cat's paws, wouldn't you? Ah, so you want me to talk to him! . . . What the devil d'you think I care if he takes everything from you, if he eats you all up, you mob of madmen, Jesuits and imbeciles, eh? . . .'

To talk to Giacomo, to take the side of those other nephews and nieces against him, really was impossible for Don Blasco. It would have meant his involving himself definitely, coming down on one side, never being able to disagree with those he had agreed with before and vice versa; and that was something he just had to be free to do. Thus, for example, the prince had been the only one of the whole 'bad lot' (as the Benedictine called his family in moments of exasperation, that is almost always) to behave obediently and submissively to him and support the monk in his struggle against the princess; now Don Blasco was turning his brothers and sisters against him in exchange. But the monk did not think he was doing wrong in this. Sceptical and suspicious as he was, he knew that Giacomo had supported him not from any affection or respect but from simple self-interest.

Prince Giacomo did, in fact, have his own reasons. His mother, as if unable to forgive him for his not being born just when she expected or wanted him, had never shown affection for her eldest son, who had also endangered her life by his birth. Instead of loving him the more for his having cost her so much, Donna Teresa had loved him less. At Lodovico's birth she had been even more vexed and indifferent; it was Raimondo who suddenly touched her maternal instincts. And so, while all the other relations who were not 'mad' like her, or mad in a different way, had given Giacomo the idea that he was above them as eldest son, as heir to the title, the princess had given all her love, a blind, exclusive, unreasonable love, to Raimondo. And the mother's protection was a good deal more useful than the father's or uncles', for while these gave only vain words to Giacomo, who was avid for money and yearning for authority, Raimondo was showered with gifts, bossed everyone and made his whims law.

So began the split between the two brothers; Raimondo, who was younger, took some knocks, but when the princess saw her favourite appear in tears she let Giacomo feel the strength of those terrible hands of hers, which left bruises wherever they fell. The boy went obstinately on, until the mother's coldness changed to definite hatred. Then he realised he was taking a wrong turning and changed tactics, played the hypocrite, became a spy for Don Blasco, and enjoyed his revenge by seeing the monk hit Raimondo out of hatred for the princess. But those were mediocre and short-lived satisfactions; as the years passed the princess shut her second son up in San Nicola, and gave

Raimondo the title of Count. Mean, almost miserly with others, she was generous only with her favourite; Giacomo never had a coin on him, and went about in rags while the other was dressed up like a tailor's dummy. If Raimondo expressed an opinion, it was at once supported, or at least not derided; Giacomo could get nothing done. For years he had nursed a longing to act as master and change the palace about in his own way; his mother did not allow him to move a chair. She herself had done a lot to change the architecture of the place, which seemed composed of four or five different buildings put together; for each ancestor had amused himself blocking windows in here and piercing balconies through there, or raising floors on one side and dismantling them on another, or changing the colour of a wash or design of a cornice.

Inside, the disorder was greater; sealed up doors, stairs going nowhere, rooms partitioned into two down the middle, walls torn down to make one room out of two. The ' mad lot ', as Don Blasco called even his forebears, had built and dismembered in their own way one after the other. The biggest changes had been made by his father, Prince Giacomo XIII, when flinging money about in all directions; then that 'pumpkinhead' of a Donna Teresa, instead of thinking of economy, had gone and amused herself by wasting more money in other ill-considered novelties! . . . Giacomo wanted to change about the plan of the house too, but his mother would not even let him put in a nail. And the Benedictine was particularly furious to find that the son who had always been overruled was in fact just like his mother, hectoring, greedy, hard, scheming; while that goose of a woman preferred Raimondo, who did not know the value of money, wasted all he had, despised business, and liked and sought only amusement and pleasure . . .

The two brothers, though having the same family air, did not even resemble each other physically; Raimondo was very handsome, Giacomo very ugly. The two types could be seen in the Portrait Gallery. More distant forebears had that mixture of strength and grace which gave the young count his charm. Gradually, as the centuries passed, features began to alter, faces lengthened, noses grew, skin darkened; extreme fatness like Don Blasco's, or extreme thinness like Don Eugenio's, disfigured the portraits. Changes were most obvious among the women. Chiara and Lucrezia, though both of them fresh and young, were so hideous they scarcely looked like women at all. Aunt Ferdinanda, in male attire, would have been taken for a moneylender or a sacristan. And there were other harsh, mannish faces to be seen among feminine portraits of recent date, while in older ones the strange head-dresses and extravagant costumes, the huge Flemish collars, which made heads look as if they were on a basin, the ample robes enfolding the body like tortoiseshells could not quite hide slimness of form or alter pure lineaments of features. Now and again among the degenerate faces in more recent generations could be seen one or two reminiscent of the earliest; thus, as if by a kind of recrudescence of the old cells of noble blood, Raimondo was like the purest ancient type. The princess's eyes would laugh with pleasure when she saw his graceful and elegant figure riding or driving or fencing. Her eldest son on the other hand she called by as many nicknames as she found defects in his person: ' dancing bear ' because of his awkwardness; ' Pulcinella ' because of the long nose; and ' dwarf ' because of his short stature.

Thus Giacomo's grudge against his mother and brother was always alive; it grew out of all proportion when Donna Teresa filled the cup to the brim and found Raimondo a wife. Family tradition, maintained until 1812 by the law of entail, forbade any son except the eldest to take a wife; in fact in the generation before neither the duke nor Don Eugenio had married. But the princess, as always, waived rules and found Raimondo a wife even before she had found one for Giacomo. At her death, because she would leave her fortune to both, the financial condition of the two brothers would become equal; but in her lifetime she was unwilling to deprive herself of anything; Giacomo would of course have to marry in order to hand on the title and could be set up on his wife's dowry, while Raimondo, if he remained a bachelor, would have nothing.

Having decided that her favourite also must be given a wife she hesitated a long time even so before putting her resolve into practice, not because she felt any scruple at breaking tradition and creating in the Uzeda family a twisted branch which might compete with the straight one, but because of her very love for the youth; the idea of another woman with him night and day threw her into blind jealousy. So when she did finally decide, she could not bear to give him any girl from Catania or its province, but began looking about for a match in Messina, Palermo, even farther, on the mainland, with certain criteria of her own, one of which was that the bride's mother should be dead. She looked for a number of years and no one suited her. Finally through one of the Benedictine monks, a colleague of Don Blasco's, Father Dilenna from Milazzo, she fixed her choice on the daughter of Baron Palmi, the Benedictine's cousin. Then, as even she thought it too much for Raimondo to marry before Giacomo (still a bachelor at twenty-five, a unique case in the family history), she arranged to get both brothers married at the same time, and chose for her eldest son the daughter of the Marchese Grazzeri.

Quarrels on that occasion were violent. Strong as was Giacomo's rancour at his brother getting married and founding another Uzeda family which would bear off part of his own inheritance, it was no less strong about his own marriage. Violent, grasping and arid though he was, he had for long been in love with his cousin Graziella, daughter of his mother's sister, and determined to marry her, though her dowry was far less than that of the Grazzeri; but the princess, partly because of the latter's greater riches, partly because she had never got on well with her sister, whom she had in fact always kept at a distance, and above all from a desire to go against her son's inclination, made him marry the Grazzeri girl.

Giacomo was no longer a boy to obey his mother for fear of punishment or blows, but she held a more powerful weapon: that of controlling the money and threatening to disinherit him. ' Not a cent . . .' she would say to him coldly, flicking her thumbnail against her teeth, ' not a cent will you get!' And the scant sympathy she had shown him, her passion for Raimondo, and the latter's imminent marriage confirmed the threat and made him suspect that she would carry it out. The prince, who till that point had never wholly succeeded in adopting the policy of pretence, after this last and violent quarrel, bowed to her in resignation and gave her his blind obedience even in things useless and ridiculous, with much talk of fraternal love, unity, and respect for elders. Inside he chafed, and while waiting to gather the fruits of his conduct, showed his vexation and exercised his own tyrannical sway only with his wife. From the first day of marriage she was treated worse than a servant, forbidden to express not only wishes, but even opinions, and trained to obey a simple movement of the prince's eyes. When she needed a roll of cotton or a bit of ribbon, she had to ask him for the necessary coins—after bringing him a dowry of a hundred thousand *onze*. Her job was to give her husband an heir, to perpetuate the Viceroys; having done that, she was considered a useless mouth to feed, worse than a hanger-on; for the hangers-on did at least pay court to the family, and if need be give the major-domo a helping hand, while Donna Margherita could do nothing and, with her mania for cleanliness and obsession about contagion, thought of nothing but avoiding contact with others. Anyway she was a mild creature without will-power, soft wax which the prince moulded as he wished. Her mother-in-law, the princess, more than once took up her defence from dislike of her own son, not from any love for her; then she suffered all the more, as Giacomo, yielding outwardly, afterwards made her pay harshly for that protection.

If the prince's marriage went so badly, Raimondo's went much worse. Giacomo did not want the Grazzeri girl since he loved his cousin; but Raimondo wanted no-one and had decided not to marry at all. His mother's caresses and favouritism had roused in him an insatiable appetite for pleasure and freedom; but the princess's protection weighed almost as much as her aversion, so despotic was she in all things. Her favourite had to do what she wanted, repay her by meeker obedience for the privileges she granted him. Yet these privileges, extraordinary in comparison to the subjection in which the other children were held, were not enough for Raimondo; they merely aroused his desires without satisfying them. He alone, for instance, was given money to fling about as he liked, but the princess gave it in fits and starts, and the young man, who was not only spending constantly on clothes and women but also had a passion for gambling, would throw away in a night what his mother gave him in a year. He was the only one allowed to go as far away as Florence, but that quick trip gave the young man a taste for travel and long sojourns in countries finer and richer than his own, which he could not follow up.

So, though treated so differently, both brothers were awaiting their mother's death with equal impatience; Giacomo to exercise his own authority as head of the house, revenge himself for the ill-treatment he had suffered, lay hands on the property; Raimondo to pay the debts he had secretly contracted, fling money about in the satisfaction of his own whims, appease his great yearning to leave Sicily, see Milan and Turin, live in Florence or Paris.

So at the first announcement of his marriage he rebelled openly against his mother, being the only one among them all able to say 'I won't!' to her face. Marriage was a chain round his neck, slavery, rejection of the life he had dreamt of; and he refused to accept it at any cost. The princess, who treated her other children with sharp sarcasm, harsh punishments and extreme threats, appealed to him by persuasion. Did he want to have his fun, lots of money to spend, do as he liked? A dowry would allow him all that at once! The jealous mother, prepared to see him married as a necessity, not wanting a local daughter-in-law and seeking a bride for him from a distance, refused to admit the possibility of her son loving that other woman, being faithful or considering himself seriously bound to her. 'You silly boy!' she would say then. 'Marry her now; then when you get tired of her just drop her!' And only by such language and arguments was the young man induced to say yes, convinced that in this way he would at once be rich and at the same time get away from his mother's oppressive protection.

Don Blasco, on hearing of Giacomo's marriage, really let himself go and belched out curses against this nephew who had wanted to marry his cousin Graziella, daughter of another Risà! And against the sister-in-law who 'forced him' to take a Grazzeri instead! But Raimondo's marriage was the real limit! . . . Let another son marry? Create a second family? Break family tradition? Was there ever such a raving mad woman? . . . Don Blasco did not bother about any contradiction between the respect he claimed they should have for traditions and his own insatiable rancour at having been sacrificed to the same traditions himself; to be in opposition, give vent to his feelings in some way, he ignored much bigger obstacles. What particularly affronted him, in Raimondo's marriage, was the choice of the bride. Among so many matches offered, which had been that preferred by his sister-in-law? The one suggested by Father Dilenna, Don Blasco's personal enemy!

Among the many factions dividing the monks at the Benedictine monastery, the fiercest were political; Don Blasco, of course, was an out-and-out pro-Bourbon and Father Dilenna had thrown his hand in with the other Liberals in 1848 to get rid of Ferdinand II. Don Blasco had his revenge next year; but Dilenna had made him eat garlic later when, foreseeing the office of Prior being vacant, he supported Lodovico Uzeda, though Don Blasco was aspiring to that office himself! So to choose for Raimondo a wife proposed by Dilenna, the man's own cousin in fact, was the last straw.

It would take too long to describe what Don Blasco did and said at the palace, the chairs he overturned, the fists he banged on furniture, the curses and swear words that poured from his mouth; things got to such a point that the princess, who had let him shout on before and put up only passive resistance, now declared to his face that she had always done what she liked in her own house and that even her husband had never dared to say a word to her about it; ' So just let me tell you! Be good enough not to come here again!' Back Don Blasco flashed with, ' You tell me not to come here, do you? Don't you know the honour I've done you every time I set foot in this place? Don't you know I don't care a rap about you and all yours? Oh, go and . . . . yourselves, the lot of you, and cursed be my own silly feet for bringing me here!' Off he went and said things against his sister-in-law among his colleagues that should have brought the roof down.

For more than a year he did not set foot in the palace, though his yearning for a good rant nearly made him ill; so that when the young prince Consalvo VIII was born, and Giacomo, breathing peace and love, suggested to his mother that their uncle should be invited to the baptism and she agreed, the Benedictine reappeared in his sister-in-law's house, and after a short period of apparent calm, started shouting around worse than before.

So the princess, to marry off Raimondo, had a struggle, grim and violent at times, not only with her eldest son and Don Blasco, but with the very son whose future she wanted to ensure and even with herself. On that occasion she also had another and no less terrible opponent: Donna Ferdinanda.

The spinster was then aged thirty-eight but looked fifty; nor had she when younger ever possessed the graces of her sex. Destined to remain unmarried in order not to diminish the patrimony reserved to her brother the prince, she might have been shut up for precaution in a convent had her ugliness and her natural and sincere aversion to the married state not re-assured her parents against the dangers of temptation more than the cloister. She had never seemed female, either in body or mind. When as a child her companions talked of clothes and amusements she would list the Francalanza estates; she under-stood nothing about the cost of stuffs, ribbons and fashionable objects, but knew as well as any dealer the price of crops, wines and vegetables; she had at her fingers' ends all the complicated system of measuring solids, liquids and money; she knew how many *tarì*, how many *carlini*, how many *grani* went to an *onza*, into how many *tumoli* was divided a heap of grain or soil, how many *rotoli* and how many *coppi* formed a barrel of oil . . .

Just as, physically, the Uzeda were divided into two great categories, the handsome and the ugly, so morally they were either unbridled pleasure-lovers and wasters like Prince Giacomo XIII and Count Raimondo, or self-interested, miserly, capable of selling their souls for a coin, like Prince Giacomo XIV and Donna Ferdinanda.

Donna Ferdinanda's father had left her a pittance, a so-called *piatto*, enough to ensure daily fare, which was the meagre provision made for younger children by the entail-system. With this pittance she had sworn to achieve wealth. All her thoughts day and night were directed to translating her dream into action. As soon as she got her miserable sixty *onze* a year she began to negotiate it, to lend it out against mortgages or security according to the debtor's solvency, dealing in I.O.U.'s, making loans on valuables and goods, doing every sort of ghetto banking operation, since the meagreness of her income obliged her to deal with the poor, with petty merchants, shopkeepers, foremen builders, old-clothes dealers, small vintners and even the family servants. She never touched any of the capital and risked only its income; this she redoubled and tripled, such was her natural talent for business and so sharp and inexorable was she at getting back her money and its interest, which she would demand till the very last cent, deaf to any prayers and sobs of women or children. And she was more expert, more quibbling than any lawyer if she had to go to law. She was also miserly, not spending on herself more than two *tarì* a day, which she handed over to the princess in exchange for the food and service assured her by the latter. As lodging she still had the little room on the third floor under the roof which she had occupied as a child, and as clothes she bought her sister-in-law's cast-off dresses. Gradually she had extended the circle of her business and put together a little hoard which she then began circulating among people of higher standing, wholesale merchants, speculators, embarrassed landowners.

As her money grew, in the minds of the princess and of Don Blasco there also grew a blind jealousy against sister-in-law and sister. By different methods, Donna Ferdinanda was working towards an aim similar to Donna Teresa's. The latter's was to salvage and increase the Uzeda fortune, the former's to create a fortune on her own. Now, as Donna Ferdinanda had started from nothing, her glory would be all the greater and would obscure Donna Teresa's; hence came the princess's blind antipathy, the sarcasms she would aim at her sister-in-law's avarice, while her own was of course legitimate and admirable. As for Don Blasco, his resentment at having had to renounce the world grew more bitter every time any of his relatives acquired fame, power and money; so when he saw his sister doing what he would have done himself had he stayed in the world, and doing it so unexpectedly and speedily, his blood boiled, his temper worsened, envy poisoned him.

Donna Ferdinanda seemed insensible to the sarcasms and sharp comments of her sister-in-law and brother. It suited her at that moment to be silent, as she was and wished to continue to be the princess's guest until she had enough money for a home of her own. Every day her relations and friends advised her to take her little fortune out of such dangerous circulation, and acquire solid property. She shook her head, affirmed that her money ran no risk at all, for only ' he who lends without security loses money, friend or wit '. Really she was waiting until she had enough to make a good purchase.

In '42, ten years after entering into possession of her meagre pittance, she astounded all her relations by acquiring, at public auction for five thousand *onze*, the Carrubo property, a fine piece of land worth ten thousand. She was fortunate, or rather shrewd, there too, in taking advantage of a superb opportunity. All had known that she possessed a tiny capital, but no one imagined that in ten years she had put together a small fortune. Her sister-in-law and brother were more biting than ever, particularly on seeing that she did.not spend a cent more on herself. She let them have their say and went on speculating with the four hundred *onze* of income that she now had. She made it yield as much as possible, never lost a cent, and when the I.O.U.'s fell in, her notary, agent or lawyer, brought her due in fine gleaming and clinking coin. Lawyer, notary and agent were her friends. Among the frequenters of the Francalanza palace she had chosen and made friends with the sharpest and cleverest, those who, like her, had a bent and passion for business, to whom she could look for information and suggestions. Her preferred adviser was the Prince of Roccasciano, as noble as any Uzeda but with little money, which he was multiplying patiently, prudently and with none of her meanness and harshness.

In '49, when she least expected it, a chance came to buy herself a house. She had given a thousand *onze* or so to the Cavaliere Calasaro, whose son was involved in the revolution, and forced to go into exile. The father, who had stripped himself and exhausted his credit so that his son should lack for nothing, could not satisfy Donna Ferdinanda when the I.O.U.'s fell due. Sniffing the wind, she demanded to be paid at once, threatened him with expropriation and sent him a first writ. The debtor came to fling himself at her feet, his head in his hands, to prevent final ruin, and offered whatever she liked of all his property. Donna Ferdinanda spurned the lot as heavily encumbered and capable of bringing down only a deluge of stamped paper, and when the other insisted and offered her a house clear of mortgage, the spinster wrinkled her nose and said, 'We'll see.' But she wanted it for her thousand one hundred *onze*, plus interest and expenses, without adding another cent, while the owner valued it at two thousand *onze* at least and claimed the balance. The matter was not settled; Donna Ferdinanda pushed on with her case. The other, with the water at his neck and his son still demanding money from Turin and the Government at him because of the young exile, finally yielded. 'Pay at least for the expenses of the Deed', he sent to say, but Donna Ferdinanda's answer was 'A thousand one hundred *onze*, that's my last word!' So she got the house. It was small, of course, for that price; two shops flanked the entrance and there was only one floor above, with a large balcony and two small ones on the front; but it had an inestimable value in Donna Ferdinanda's eyes; it was situated in the Crociferi, the old quarter of the city nobles, and was itself a noble house, having belonged for a long time to the Calasaro, nobles of 'the old stock'.

In fact as well as a passion for money the spinster had one for nobility. All the Uzeda were vainglorious of their family's origins; Donna Ferdinanda was positively sick with the pride of it. When she talked of 'Don Ramon de Uzeda y de Zuellos, who was Señor of Esterel' and came from Spain with King Pedro of Aragon to 'settle' in Sicily; when she enumerated all her ancestors and their descendants 'promoted to the highest offices in the Kingdom': Don Jaime I, 'who served the King don Ferdinando, son of the Emperor don Alfonso, against the Moors of Cordova, on the battlefield of Calatrava'; Gagliardetto, '*caballero de mucha qualitad*'; Attardo, 'a spirited knight, and armigerous'; the great Consalvo, 'Vicar of the White Queen'; the even greater Lopez Ximenes, 'Viceroy of the unvanquished Charles V'; then her eyes would glitter more brightly than newly-minted coin, and her pale, hollow cheeks flush. Indifferent to all but her money, incapable of emotion about any event, sad or gay, she found one passionate excitement, the memory of her ancestors' splendours.

At the time of her grandfather there had been a fine library in the palace, but when Prince Giacomo XIII began getting into deep water, it was the first thing to be sold. She saved a copy of the famous Mugnòs' '*Teatro genologico di Sicilia*' where the longest chapter was on the Uzeda family, occupying not less than thirty big pages. And those dry and yellow pages, exhaling the must of old paper, printed in clumsy, dim characters and fantastic orthography, that emphatic spavined seventeenth-century Sicilian-Spanish, was her favourite reading, the only pasture of her imagination; for her it was romance, it was the gospel which she used in order to recognise wheat from chaff, and select the true nobles from among the mob of ignobles and the ' weeds ' of false nobles. ' Outſtanding amid the genealogies from Spain ſhines one of the moſt ancient and ſublime families of the Kingdom of Valencia and Aragon, the family of Vzeda, acknowledged by all to be thus benamed from an eſtate known as the Barony of Vzeda, granted by the aforeſaid kings in recompenſe for their ſervices in contributing to the royal and perennial military glories forever refounding in the Supreme Heavens.'

For Donna Ferdinanda, this style was of supreme elegance and magnificence, and she read such words as ' perennial ' quite literally. As it was considered ' low ' for women of her class at the beginning of the century to be lettered, she had learnt to read on her own as a necessity for her speculations.

And now to flout the spinster's infatuation for her own origins and for the institution of nobility in general, here was the princess thinking of giving Raimondo as wife—whom if you please—a Palmi from Milazzo, daughter of a worthless baron of whom Mugnòs did not and could not make the very least mention! He gloried, did this so-called Baron Palmi, in certain privileges granted 150 years before; but what were 150 years compared with the centuries of Uzeda nobility? Without taking into account that these privileges were not even mentioned by the Marchese of Villabianca, an author flourishing only a century after Mugnòs! . . .

The princess, who felt almost if not quite as strongly about nobility as did Donna Ferdinanda, had judged those 150 years of the Palmi family as sufficient, and more simply because, wanting her Raimondo's wife to be as lowly to her husband as a slave-girl to her master, one whom he could treat loftily and do what he liked with, she had even for a moment thought of choosing him the humble daughter of a rich farmer . . . The disagreement was bitter.

By then Donna Ferdinanda, having acquired the Calasaro house, had left the Francalanza palace and set up house on her own, continuing to pinch and scrape but paying for the luxury of a private carriage. These were a couple of rickety old vehicles bought for a few ducats but decorated with the Uzeda coat-of-arms; and the horses, two thin nags which she had fed with a little straw from the Carrubo land, a handful of bran and rotted vegetables. The coachman, as well as serving stable and coach-house, acted as cook and butler. The princess's sarcasms had of course become sharper at all this, now the spinster was holding her head as high as her sister-in-law. Being rich in money, and as she thought in sense, Donna Ferdinanda expected to be paid court and held in account; while before, when living with her relations, she had been indifferent to their affairs, she now tried to put her nose into all family matters from a distance. But the princess would tolerate neither patronage nor imposition; hence daily quarrels.

On the other hand, Don Blasco, exasperated by his sister's rising fortunes, was now maddened at seeing her rival him in his position as niggling critic and infallible judge. The spinster in return frankly expressed her opinion of his scandalous life. Once, when a nurse had to be engaged for the young prince and Donna Ferdinanda thought the woman's milk suspect, Don Blasco declared it to be of first quality (evil tongues said he had reason to know); and brother and sister almost came to blows. Calmed with difficulty by their nephew Giacomo, they never spoke to each other again. The odd thing was that though never talking, and avoiding each other like the plague, they were the only ones in the family to see things in the same way and express the same opinions about everything. As Don Blasco spat flame and fire against Raimondo's marriage, so Donna Ferdinanda became viperish. Not only was that sister-in-law of hers protecting the third son just because she loathed the heir to the title, not only was she trampling on the ' law ' which looked only to the continuation of the direct line; but she was giving him who? Who, good God? A Palmi from Milazzo! . . . Palmi? Donna Ferdinanda never called her by that name; but at times Palma, at others Palmo, and gave her as coat-of-arms either the four palms' length of bamboo which haberdashers used for measuring cotton, or a couple of small, shaggy palms, 'like the peasants they were'. The two sisters-in-law became so sarcastic and quarrelsome that they nearly got to tearing out each other's hair. Like Don Blasco, the spinster announced she would never set foot in the Francalanza palace again but, like her brother, she could not bear to be away from it for long and returned at the first opportunity.

The other two brothers-in-law, the Duke Gaspare and the Cavaliere Don Eugenio, had not given much bother to Donna Teresa.

The Cavaliere Don Eugenio, at the time of those quarrels, was not in Sicily. At first destined also for the Benedictine Order like his brother Don Blasco, he had saved himself by adducing an inclination for a military career. It was his first lie, to avoid the monastery; he could not feel any calling to a profession almost unknown in Sicily, where there was no conscription and a popular motto went 'better swine than soldier'. Thus not even the nobility went in for soldiering. But Don Eugenio wanted to be free and gain himself a place in the world. After remaining for education at the Novitiate of San Nicola till almost eighteen, on coming out of the monastery he went off to Naples and was enrolled in the noble corps of Royal Bodyguards, sure of rising to the highest ranks at once. But after ten years he was still a cornet.

Infatuated with his nobility like all the Uzeda, he looked down on his companions and even a little on his superiors, and boasted not only of sublime birth but of vast wealth. When it came to the point, however, the young Neapolitan lordlings would bring out their money while the boastful Sicilian younger son drew back, or worse, made debts which he did not pay.

Treated as a braggart, he was almost outlawed by his companions; anyway he himself realised that he had not reached his aim, though to his family he wrote that his lack of success was due to envy and injustice; and one fine day he decided to resign. He stayed on, however, in Naples, whence he wrote that the richest and noblest houses were open to him as if they were his own, and that the Duke This and the Prince of That wanted him to marry their daughters. None of these matches, constantly bruited as certain, ever came off.

Meanwhile, in great need of money, he had applied for a post at Court, and in spite of his unpromising past, yet for political reasons, as the Bourbons were eager to keep on good terms with great Sicilian families, he was named Gentleman of the Bedchamber, with functions. In 1852, he returned home, an unexpected guest. He said that he had been passed from active to honorary service because the climate of Naples did not agree with him; there was an insistent rumour, however, of certain squalid little arrangements with one of the suppliers for the Royal Family . . .

The ex-Royal Bodyguard and Gentleman of the Bedchamber returned from Naples with a new vocation, archaeology, numismatics, and fine arts. With him he brought a quantity of rubbish coming, so he said, from Pompeii, Herculaneum and Paestum, and of enormous value; enough canvasses to rig out a sailing ship; 'all from famous hands: Raphael, Titian, Tintoretto'. With all this material he filled a little apartment he had rented —for the princess would not hear of his living at home again— and began dealing in antiques. Giacomo had been married for two years and already had the expected heir; Raimondo was in Florence with his wife, where she had borne a little girl.

The Duke Gaspare had not been at home either at the time of the marriage but, though from afar, he was the only one to approve his sister-in-law's arrangements, drawing on himself of course by this approval, and even more by the motive which dictated it, the thunderbolts of Donna Ferdinanda and Don Blasco. This reason was entirely of a political nature. Baron Palmi, Matilde's father, a Liberal of long standing, had played such an active part in the revolution of '48 that after the Restoration he had taken refuge in Malta with a capital charge on his head; and without very special protection and solemn promises not to do it again his exile would have lasted a lifetime instead of a few months. Even so, when pardoned and admonished, he began directing the movement against the Bourbons in his own part of the country and throughout most of Sicily. Now it was these political opinions and this authority over the still very active Liberal Party that were the reasons why the duke was so benevolently inclined towards the marriage of the baron's daughter with Raimondo.

Until 1848, the duke, like all the Uzeda, had been an out-and-out pro-Bourbon. But although, as second son and Duke of Oragua, he had drawn rather more than the meagre pittance of the others, and maternal uncles had helped to enlarge his substance, he was still envious of the eldest son, and longed to get rich and make himself a greater place in the world than his brothers; his portion had awakened but not appeased his appetite. While the entail-system lasted the younger sons had put up with their wretched condition in resignation, being unable to go against the law, but now that eldest sons were only preferred by what, in the light of new ideas, seemed mere prejudice, envy gnawed them. This reaction, which drove Don Blasco to behave like one possessed and fanned Don Eugenio's cupidity, made the duke lend an ear to the flattery of the revolutionaries, who were eager to draw on their side a person of importance like the Duke of Oragua, second son of a Prince of Francalanza. He did not cease at the same time to pay his usual court to the Royal Intendant, so as to prepare a safety-exit for himself in case of possible reverses; he joined the Reading-Circle which was a nest of Liberals, without leaving the Nobles' Club, which was the headquarters of the purists, and in fact trained himself to steer between the two currents.

At the first outbreak of the revolution fear overwhelmed him: to his new friends he declared that the movement was unprepared, inopportune, and certainly destined to fail. And while the people armed and fought he retreated into the country, letting the chiefs of the Royalist Party know that he was waiting for the end of that 'carnival'. But the 'carnival' looked like lasting; the Neapolitan troops evacuated Sicily and although their return was announced every day no news of them came whatsoever, and the provisional Government was settling in. The duke, seeing his skin in no danger, returned to town and lent an ear to the flattery of the party in power, which promised him whatever he wanted in order to get him on their side. He waited and watched a bit longer, dallied, advised prudence, talked of the good of the country and of possible dangers and traps, thus playing with both sides.

Being short-sighted as well as presumptuous, just as things were taking a turn for the worse he judged that the moment had come for him to throw himself into the Liberals' arms. When he was about to burn his boats and already tasting the first fruits of popularity, one fine day the Prince of Satriano landed at Messina with twelve thousand men to put things back to where they were before. The duke thought himself lost; and panic made him commit a folly he was later to repent. While the city was making ready to resist, he signed with other faithful pro-Bourbons and Liberal traitors a document invoking the early restoration of legitimate government.

At the beginning of April the companies of Sicilian militia garrisoned at Taormina evacuated at the appearance of the royalist troops and returned to Catania. On the 7th, Satriano, after a bloody battle, entered the city. All the Uzeda had escaped to the country; the duke had barricaded himself in at Pietra dell'Ovo, because the general opinion was that the Neapolitans would appear on the opposite side, that is by the Messina road. Instead of which they came springing down from the Etna woods and captured, after short skirmishes, the block posts at Ravanuso and Barriera. On reaching Pietra dell'Ovo the Bourbon general and his staff entered the Uzeda estates, where he was greeted by the duke as master, saviour and god. Meanwhile guns swept the Via Etnea in Catania; the royalist troops were counter-attacked at the Aci Gate by a desperate battalion of Corsicans. Decimated by dagger thrusts from that handful of desperate men in the grim light of dusk, they went wild, slaughtered a thousand or so to the last man, then vented their wrath on the defenceless city . . .

Friend of Satriano, protected by the signature he had put to that act of submission which Liberals were now calling the *Black Book*, protected even more by his own name—since it was thought impossible for an Uzeda to have been serious about throwing in his lot with revolutionaries—the duke was never once troubled during the reaction and was even courted. But on the other hand there was a great ferment against him among the defeated. He was blamed for that odious signature, but even more for his welcome to Satriano at Pietra dell'Ovo. The matter of the signature was known to few, to the leaders only; the tale of what happened at Pietra dell'Ovo was spread among the rank and file and went round everywhere; each added a bit more, and people got to the point of saying that when the city was in its death agony the duke was actually watching through Satriano's telescope; that at the conqueror's entry into the city he had ridden by the general's side.

Don Lorenzo Giulente, who had remained his friend, had a difficult time defending him, denying exaggerations, asserting that the duke, alone and helpless as he was, could not very well send packing a general and an entire army. Minds embittered by disappointment demanded a scapegoat, and as Mieroslawski, the Polish commander of police, had been accused of treason, popular rancour turned against the duke although thousands deserved it more and were more to blame than he. After all the duke had accepted no rank or money or decorations from the revolution; he had just looked on and awaited the outcome; while many others, after playing hell, had flung themselves at the Intendant's feet and swept the ground with their hats when naming His Majesty Ferdinand II, 'whom may God always preserve!' That was what the duke wanted to say in his own defence; and that was what Giulente did say. But they were talking to the deaf; and the duke found himself pointed at, branded with the name of traitor, insulted, and even threatened by anonymous letters.

One day his friend Don Lorenzo advised him to leave; only distance and time could make that hatred simmer down. The duke did not wait to be told twice and made off to Palermo. There, the Party of Action, though also defeated, was less depressed even so; hopes were either not dead or beginning to rise again. Once he had got over the fear given him by recent events, his ambitions mortified and unappeased, the duke again lent an ear to the Liberals' wiles, partly to show his dear fellow-citizens that he did not deserve their contempt. And although he did not stray far from his usual prudence, and went to revolutionary meetings as well as to the Royal Lieutenant-General's receptions, and was playing, in fact, the same old game as before, the rumour even so reached Catania that he was in the action committees and corresponding with exiles, and giving money for the good cause and helping persecuted patriots. With this rumour also came money sent by him to local committees; for he now realised finally that such was the right way to set about things, and that one like him, lacking faith or courage, could only get anywhere by paying cash down. Meanwhile, as minds calmed and events were seen more clearly people realised who were most to blame and turned against them their former hatred of the duke.

Then came Raimondo's marriage with a Palmi to ensure him new graces. He had met the baron at Palermo through agitators whom the latter, unknown to the authorities and on pretext of business, came to visit from Milazzo. When the duke heard of the marriage designed by the princess he hastened not only to approve it but also to offer himself as mediator, making much of his friendship with the baron. He felt that this alliance between his own nephew and the old Liberal's daughter could not but favour him and help him to reacquire credit with the party he had betrayed. As to the princess, pro-Bourbon like all the Uzeda, the liberalism of the Palmi family, rather than being an obstacle, was yet another reason in favour of the marriage. She was pro-Bourbon by instinct before all else, but took no part in politics, having other things to think about; and just as she had wanted a bride who could not vaunt outstanding nobility, so she was quite pleased at the girl's family being persecuted by the Government, as it meant that Raimondo would be able to impose his will better in all ways on his wife and her family.

For his nephew's marriage the duke returned home. It was scarcely two years since the incidents which had brought the hatred of his fellow-citizens down on him, and he could already see the effects of his being away, of his new policy, and of his friendship with Baron Palmi and his support of Raimondo's marriage. While Don Blasco and Donna Ferdinanda, in their war-to-the-death with the princess, also took him to task for his support of his sister-in-law and the policy which had dictated that attitude, cursing him and almost denouncing him to the authorities for Liberalism, then laughing at him and almost throwing in his face the betrayal of 1849, his signing of the *Black Book*, his friendship with Satriano; while his brother and sister were at this, many of those who had cut him before, now came up and shook his hand; other peace overtures were quickly sealed through Giulente; and everyone seemed to have forgotten those tales of the past. Even so the duke left again and returned to Palermo, partly because he had begun to like being there, but also in order to confirm these good dispositions.

When he came home now for his sister-in-law's death he was received almost in triumph, and people flocked to greet him. Not only did no one ever mention those incidents of 1849, now six years old, not only was he considered to be one of the hopes of the party, but his long sojourn in the capital, his frequenting of Palermo notables, unexpectedly conferred on him a great reputation for knowledge. He quoted the opinions of So-and-So, ' my friends ' the celebrated patriots—just as Don Eugenio had as friends the chief grandees of Naples. He larded his remarks with erudite quotations, second- or third-hand, and explained over again in his own way, as if he had thought of them himself, the economic and political theories which he had heard discussed at meetings in Palermo. People stared at him open-mouthed.

This patriot, it was true, did receive visits from the Intendant and repaid them, and had no scruples about showing himself in company of fervent pro-Bourbons, but that was not held against him; he had to wear a mask with the authorities to avoid arousing suspicion and to learn his opponents' moves. He gave money, and never let anyone go empty-handed who asked for his help. Don Blasco and Donna Ferdinanda abused him, each on their own, more violently than ever; he let them have their say, and continued to gamble on liberty, as the monk did on lottery numbers and the spinster on people's credit. Just as he kept on good terms with all in politics, so at home he never took sides for one more than another. He watched Don Blasco's manoeuvring to arouse the defrauded nieces and nephews, and knew the reasons for it, but he also watched the prince's frowning brow, and heard his bitter complaints at his mother's ' betrayal '. And so he sat on the fence, agreeing a little with all; with the prince who was offering him hospitality and treating him deferentially, with Lucrezia who by loving and marrying a nephew of the conspirator Giulente would help him to enter further into the Liberals' good graces.

4

'DON'T we eat today?'

The young prince was famished. Dinner was always being put off nowadays; either the duke was out, or Raimondo, or the prince himself. That day all three were out, as well as Lucrezia and Matilde. And the boy was the desperation of the whole household; up and down he ran from kitchen to stables, from coachhouse to gardens, disturbing old and new servants intent on their work. As Don Blasco had foretold to the Booby, all servants protected by the princess had been dismissed by Giacomo; but the disinherited, those who by favouring the son had incurred the mother's aversion, had been reconfirmed in their jobs.

The prince had made only two exceptions: one in favour of Baldassarre and another of Signor Marco. Baldassarre, son of a former maidservant, brought up in the palace and put into the job of major-domo very young, knew from childhood the family weaknesses, rivalries, aversions and manias, and so concentrated entirely on his own duties, praising every master and mistress whatever they did or said, checking his dependants who dared to murmur against either. Both mother and son had liked him, and the princess's legacy did not procure him the prince's dismissal. As for Signor Marco, the dead woman's broken lance, they were astounded that the son, head of the family now for two months, had not cast him off yet. Actually, since the princess had fallen ill, the administrator had changed tactics and treated the prince most respectfully, foreseeing that he would soon have to serve him; if he had not actually let the prince steal the petty cash on his mother's death, as Don Blasco said,

124

he certainly bowed to him in every way. Anyway an agent like him, who had been with the family for fifteen years and knew the condition of the property and the state of pending law cases, could not be supplanted from one moment to the other.

'Don't we eat any more? . . . What are you doing? . . . I want to see! . . . Why not serve up? . . . For me!'

In the kitchen the young prince snatched from Luciano the butler a knife that the man was sharpening, and went on with the operation himself.

'What's Your Excellency up to?' said the new cook, *Monsù* Martino, not knowing how to take this. 'Please go upstairs and let us work.'

'Stand back! I want to do it!'

He had to be allowed his own way. If they denied him at all he became a fury, ground his teeth, shouted like one obsessed, upset whatever he could lay hands on. Actually, the prince was bringing up his son severely and did not let him get away with much; but on the other hand he rebuked servants who, with backs to the wall, lost patience and answered their young master rudely. And now after the princess's death the post of cook in the Francalanza household had become more important than before.

Giacomo was even more distrustful and watchful than his mother; he had all provisions put under lock and key, kept check on petty items such as left-overs and crusts of bread. But even so, the daily expenses, not counting any increase for guests, were considerable, and food more lavish. They now ate four dishes; in the mother's time three were made for her and for Don Raimondo, while others had to put up on ordinary days with a *minestra* and a little fish or meat. Even when Giacomo became rich from his wife's dowry and the princess made her son pay his part of the expenses, she went on ordering food in her own way, while the prince, in his determination to show himself obedient, had remained silent. So too he had been unable to carry out long-planned alterations in the palace; on Donna Teresa's death he had at last got the reins of the household in hand and was now turning everything upside-down.

The picks of workmen and the squeaks of pulleys drawing up

materials from the courtyard to the floor above could be heard even in the kitchen; and scullions, busy peeling potatoes and beating eggs, exchanged observations on these works.

' They're taking out the stairs to the offices to gain space! . . .'

' I'd not have shut in a part of the terrace.'

' The master has to account to his brother too, as they're both heirs.'

' But the palace belongs to the prince. The count only has an apartment . . .'

The young prince did not lose a word of what was said.

' The count will soon make off . . . He's not one to stay here . . .'

Work on sauces quietened them every now and again. After a time Luciano, with a wink, said to his companion:

' Starting again, is he?'

' Let him! He's a real lord, he is!' And Luciano bowed his head in sign of admiring approval. In the kitchen they were all for the count, as they were in the antechambers and stables, for the young man was quite unlike his older brother; he was so gentle with his orders and so generous too.

' A real lord indeed, in his ways and thoughts . . . not like the *friend* . . .'

' The *friend*'s an old fox . . . so was *she* . . .'

' What's that?' asked the young prince.

' Nothing, Excellency!' replied the cook; and he turned to his dependants. ' Now get to work!' he ordered. ' And not so much chatter . . .'

' You don't want to tell me, do you?'

' What, Excellency? We were just talking in the air.'

' So you don't want to tell me?'

Suddenly there was the sound of a carriage entering the courtyard, and Consalvo ran to look.

It was his Aunts Lucrezia and Matilde back at last from the Convent of San Placido. The boy, forgetting kitchen and cook, ran to join them upstairs in his mother's apartments, to see if they had brought him anything.

Donna Matilde did, in fact, give him a parcel of cakes, but his Aunt Lucrezia took no notice of him, she was talking with such animation to the princess.

' She was crying, you know? . . . We talked to the Abbess, who confirmed everything. That's true, isn't it, Matilde? . . . What a thing to do! . . . Our mother's Masses! . . .'

' Sssh! . . .'

The princess signed to her sister-in-law to be silent because of the boy.

' Mama, don't we eat today?' he asked her.

' But your father hasn't come in yet! . . . Go, go and see if he's arrived.'

The young prince realised he was being sent away. At the age of six he was even more curious than Don Blasco. The machinations of his uncle the monk, the constant intriguing in that house, had aroused his attention very early. After his grandmother's death he had noticed, from his relations' behaviour and the servants' talk, that they were opposed to his father for one reason or another, but no one dared attack him directly. He realised a lot of other things too; that his Aunt Ferdinanda could not endure his Aunt Matilde; that there was discord between the latter and her husband; he realised all this and kept silent, pretending to notice nothing lest he arouse someone's anger. In fact his uncle Don Blasco gave him a resounding slap or two and his Aunt Lucrezia would pinch his arm, particularly after he'd gone rummaging in her room, but his father was always gruff, and when he hit made him smart. Anyway, the boy had little talk with his father, though he could not keep away from his mother.

Donna Ferdinanda, indeed, showed much preference for him, but no-one would excuse the boy's defects like the princess. Quivering and apt to go into convulsions if anyone came too near her, she overcame her mania for isolation only out of love of her children, and hugged Consalvo to her breast and kissed him even when he was not too clean, the more fervently as she thus defended herself from all other contact. For some time, since his little sister Teresa was born, her caresses had not gone only to him; even so the princess was the only person who could get anything out of Consalvo by treating him well, by affection.

' Go, off with you now and see if Papa's back . . .'

Prince Giacomo re-entered at that moment. He was frowning even more than usual, and never said a word of greeting on entering; at sight of him Lucrezia fell silent. He asked if the duke had come home and, on hearing that he had not, gave orders for the meal to be served as soon as the duke appeared. Then he went off and shut himself in his study with Signor Marco. Consalvo sat there for a time without knowing what to do, hesitating between returning to the kitchen and watching the workmen. Instead of which, seeing his Aunt Lucrezia deep in conversation with his mother again, he went up to her room. He had been forbidden to enter it because she was now studying water-colour painting and wanted none of her things touched, particularly in case anyone found Benedetto Giulente's letters; but the pans of colour, the boards to be primed, the brushes and rubbers, fascinated the boy.

No warning or threat from Lucrezia could keep him away; if she complained, she was more abused than ever by her brother, who had become intractable since the reading of the Will, so that the boy, when he got a chance, did what he liked in his aunt's room. Going up at that hour when he was sure not to be surprised, the young prince began to rummage on the table, among sketches, papers, drawers. Where were those painting materials hidden? Perhaps in the highest drawer of that tallboy, where he could not reach. Meanwhile from the courtyard came a bell announcing the duke's arrival. The boy continued to look round, to search feverishly under the bed, under the chest of drawers, in the mirror-table. This was a little table covered with embroidered cloth; he raised a corner and uncovered a small drawer. In there, amid old combs and empty tins of marzipan, was a bundle of papers tied with a red ribbon. Consalvo undid the knot and spread out the letters. Suddenly Lucrezia appeared at the door.

'Aha! . . .' she screamed, flinging herself on her nephew and giving him a great slap.

The boy let out as sharp a shriek as if he were being murdered.

'I've told you a thousand times not to touch my things! I can't keep a single thing to myself any more! I might as well be in the street . . .'

At those desperate shrieks, in rushed Vanna the maid, but she had scarcely begun, 'Signorina . . . let him go . . .' when the prince appeared.

' How dare you raise a hand to my son!'

' He just won't obey! . . . I can't keep even a pin to myself . . .'

He raised Consalvo from the floor, took him by the hand and said slowly, staring hard at her:

' Another time, if you dare touch my son I'll hit you; d'you understand?'

She stood there for a moment, stunned. When her brother left, she rushed to the door, shut it by banging it violently, and did not answer any of the servants who came to call her for dinner. The duke had to come up and beg her to open the door.

At the duke's remonstrances and warnings, she finally burst out:

' Patience? Why, he's been treating me like this for two months! . . . What has he against me? Something to do with our mother's Will? Is this part of playing his cards? Was Don Blasco right then? . . . Have you heard, has Your Excellency heard what he's just done?'

' What's he just done?'

' He's refused to recognise the legacy to the Convent of San Placido! . . . We found Angiolina sobbing and the Abbess breathing fire and flame . . . he wants to deal all cards himself, and treats us in this high and mighty way, to degrade us all . . .'

' Quiet! . . . Enough for the moment . . .' The duke begged her once more for the love of peace, ' Enough! . . . come and dine now . . . I promise you I'll talk to him later . . .'

Raimondo had not yet returned when the whole family, with Don Mariano, sat down to table. Lucrezia's eyes were still red, her head was bowed, she did not say a word. But the prince now looked quite serene and chatted courteously with the duke. Every day it was like this; after long hours of sulks, silence, turning his back on his brothers and sisters and even more on his sister-in-law Matilde, at table he put off his frowning mien to be polite to his uncle. It was not the first time that the dinner started without Raimondo, and Lucrezia's ill-humour was reflected that day by a shadow on Matilde's brow.

They were not very nice to her in that house. The prince, Donna Ferdinanda, Don Blasco, and to some extent even Cousin Graziella must have found unpardonable faults in her, because they were so constantly criticising her or being very off-hand in their treatment of her. But she forgave all their rudenesses to her; what she could not endure was rudeness to her husband. Perhaps that was her great fault, the love she had for Raimondo! . . . She had loved him ever since she had seen him, even before; since when, affianced by letter to that Count of Lumera whom her father, proud of becoming connected to the Viceroys, praised endlessly, she had let her imagination represent him as handsome, noble, generous, and knightly, as a hero of Tasso or Ariosto. And the reality had been superior to anything she had imagined. How fine he was, her husband, how graceful and comely and splendid, and she who had never known other men closely, who had fed only on dreams, poetry, on fantasy high and pure, had given him her whole self for ever; she had loved him even in those dear to him, and idolised him in the daughter born from him. She had no other idea of life than that expressed in her own simple and even existence, spent with her sister Carlotta, with their mother, that sweet sad memory, and her father, a man of violent passions, friend or enemy till death of other men, but blind and crazy in his love for his daughters . . .

Now, as she turned again and again to look at the door, anxiously waiting for Raimondo's arrival, the scene before her reminded her of another, in lively contrast, indelibly etched on her mind. Memory conjured up for her the family board in the big dining-room of her father's house in Milazzo; her mother, her sister, she herself, intent on her father's stories, smiling with him, sad or sorrowing with him; her father, his every thought and action concentrated wholly on them; a constant almost superstitious respect for ancient habits, patriarchal peace, reciprocal love, absolute confidence. If she looked round now, what did she see? The princess, timid and fearful before her husband; the boy trembling at a glance from his father, but proud of the humiliation inflicted on his aunt; Lucrezia and her brother still cold and suspicious with each other; the prince making an ostentatious play of good humour with the duke after a day of frowning silence.

She had not even suspected the passions dividing this family, on the day she had entered it as another family of her own; with what amazement and sorrow had she noticed the grim resentment with which they repaid her! They considered, of course, that she was unworthy of Raimondo because inferior to him. No one put him higher than herself, but she had not been helped by feeling and being humble before him and them; their rancour had not been placated. Then she had begun to realise the separate passions which, apart from pride, animated each of these hard, violent Uzeda . . . Raimondo's mother, idolising her son to the point of being jealous of his wife; so after getting him married and ensuring his dowry she humiliated her daughter-in-law, using an iron hand from the very first day to enforce true subjection to her favourite. But the wife's idolising submission and blind devotion took away any pretext for cruelty, threw new fuel on the flames of maternal jealousy, and made Donna Teresa implacable. The elder brother, unable to forgive Raimondo's privileges or to resign himself at having Raimondo's family competing with his own, turned his rancour against his sister-in-law. All the others had been pitiless against the intruder, either from hatred at the princess, who had brought her into the family, or from hatred of Raimondo, whom the mother protected.

Thus she found herself the target of these relations to whom she had come with confident soul and warm heart, and the discovery that their hatred was as bitter against her as against Raimondo instead of lessening her suffering had sharpened it; for being deeply in love with her husband she suffered and enjoyed through him and for him . . . Whenever the prince seemed not to see his sister-in-law or, turning in her direction he suddenly put off his jovial air and showed her a face grimmer than if she were a stranger, it was not so much that ostentatious coldness which made her suffer as the indifference shown by all towards her husband.

Dinner progressed as if he would no longer be coming; no-one asked after him, Lucrezia still kept her head bent over her place, the princess tended her son, the prince talked about the condition of the estates, the price of produce, and the dangers of cholera, the duke discoursed on the war in the East, and it was only the stranger, Don Mariano, who said now and again:

' Where's Raimondo? . . . Isn't he coming? . . . What can have happened to him?'

Then that question resounded in her thoughts, as if by an

echo, ' Isn't he coming? . . . What can have happened to him? . . .' Why was he so late? Why did he leave her alone among all those hostile or indifferent strangers?

' The Russians are still holding out . . . a hard nut to crack . . . Napoleon knew a thing or two about that . . .'

Absorbed again in graver and more disturbing thoughts, she heard snatches of phrases, words whose sense she could not catch. How long he had left her alone, Raimondo! How long, how long! . . . She remembered only too well the first pain he had inflicted on her, long ago. Good to her just after their marriage, during the honeymoon and their stay at Catania; as soon as they reached Milazzo, where they had gone on business to see her father and sister, he declared that he had not married to live in that hovel, to fall under his father-in-law's tutelage after having got away from his mother's . . . Of course she saw that life in her little native town could be no fun for him. Of course she would follow him wherever he cared to take her. Yet that brusque judgement about things and people dear to her heart had given her a pang of unforgettable anguish. He wanted to leave Sicily for ever, to go and live in Florence; his mother's disapproval had been no obstacle. To his wife, who, to avoid being moved too far from her own family, exhorted him to obey, he answered brusquely, ' Let me do things in my own way!' And yes, she had realised his reasons. Sicily, Tuscany, any part of the world where they would be happy together, was it not all one to her? Could her mother-in-law's despotic veto weigh more with her than her husband's wishes? And were those wishes of his not legitimate maybe? Was her Raimondo not one made to figure in the exclusive society of a great city? Young and rich, would they not be the envy of all no matter where they went? . . . And she had not persevered in her efforts at resistance for another, more serious, reason too.

Raimondo, whose rather brusque ways she forgave or rather tried to ignore, his dislike of contradiction, all the little defects of a spoilt son, showed his real self to his father-in-law. The latter's character being very strong, a quarrel might break out from one moment to the other. At first the baron had gone out of his way to treat his son-in-law well, as if he were the princess herself, charmed too by the young man's exquisite grace and

proud of his good fortune in being connected with the Francalanza, but Raimondo had replied to all this zeal and affectionate care by a show of discontent with everything in that
house by repeating every quarter of an hour:

' How on earth can people live here? . . .'

The baron had got from him a Power-of-Attorney to
administer the property given to his daughter, and he intended
to follow old methods whose worth he knew. Raimondo, on the
other hand, to occupy his spare time in Milazzo, when he did
not spend the whole day gambling at the Casino with good-for-
nothings quickly met, insisted on his father-in-law rendering an
account of all his dealings in order to criticise them and suggest
ones which in his opinion should be adopted. In such matters
he showed an absolute ignorance of affairs, an irresponsibility
very similar to his brother Ferdinando's; the baron laughed at
him and he took it badly. But the tables were turned when the
baron asked him how he had placed the capital of the dowry;
then he criticised certain ill-considered operations of his son-in-
law, and the latter declared that his father-in-law understood
nothing. Often, in those discussions, at Raimondo's lively re-
joinders, the baron had to make a visible effort to control himself
lest he lose his temper. Then Matilde would intervene, change
the subject of conversation, making up the petty disagreement
with many a smile bestowed equally on the two people whom
she loved most in the world.

Thus, to her great sorrow, she realised that if she wanted to
see them at peace, she must avoid their spending any time
together. So she decided to support her husband's wishes
and follow him to Florence. But this last decision of Raimondo's
had been the cause of the most lively opposition from the baron,
who wanted his daughter near him and judged an establishment
in a great city to be too costly, advising short trips to the mainland instead. Raimondo had replied shortly that this was silly
advice, because trips would cost a fortune, and turning his back
on his father-in-law, he declared to his wife in crude, over-harsh
and unjust words that he could no longer endure the other's
interference in his private affairs. Then, to win over her father's
opposition she had had to fall back on the expedient she had
used so many times as a child: to tell him that the plan to live

partly in Tuscany was dear to herself, and beg him to please her . . .

' Waste of money and lives . . . A war so far away ! . . .'

While the duke was still disembowelling the Eastern Question and suggesting diplomatic combinations, all turned towards the entrance door. The countess gave a start, hoping it was her husband; instead of which Don Cono Canalà advanced ceremoniously : ' Good day to each one of you ! . . . But I don't see the count?' Yes, in Florence too, a city where she not only had no relations but, at first, not even an acquaintance, she had spent long hours, day after day, awaiting him in vain. There she had wept her first tears on finding herself neglected; there she had hidden herself to sob, as he either derided her for her ' silly ' devotion or declared that he did not want to be ' bored ' . . .

Their ways of seeing life were radically different; while she put above all her love for her husband and her family's happiness and wished only to prolong, by Raimondo's side, in other settings, the ineffable domestic joys she had felt as a girl, the young man, spoilt by his mother and away from her iron bondage at last, aspired only to freedom and pleasure. Telling herself that he had a right to amuse himself, that he was doing no harm or wrong, that people had different tastes by nature, she had repressed her own sorrow and convinced herself of being in the wrong. As a reward for her resignation she had finally been granted the joys of motherhood; then as if by enchantment the happy days of the honeymoon seemed to return, either because Raimondo really did improve, or because she herself, absorbed in sweet thoughts and detailed cares, dwelt less on his life. To her father when he visited her on that occasion she was able to show a radiant face; in his joy at her happiness the baron entirely forgot his squabbles with his son-in-law, and became as fond of him again as in the early days . . . All were expecting a boy, except herself who, had she dared go against anyone else's wishes and make a distinction between one child and another, would have preferred a girl. A girl in fact was born; and when it came to baptising her, although Matilde and her father wanted to call the child by the name of her dead mother and his dear wife, they acknowledged even so the suitability of giving her the princess's name. Did the happy mother remember her own rough treatment by her mother-in-law and her husband's relatives? Was this not a little angel come to tighten the knot uniting her with Raimondo, to dissipate the clouds threatening her clear sky, bringing only peace and love? . . . But alas! Sooner than she could have thought possible, she had realised her own deception. Ever since their arrival in Florence her mother-in-law had not written to her or answered her letters or mentioned her in letters to her son. The silence continued during her pregnancy and, after the birth, included the baby too.

When Teresina was weaned, Raimondo thought of paying a visit to Sicily; and from that journey she promised herself the end of the princess's incomprehensible rancour. Instead of which she began to weep once more . . . Donna Teresa Uzeda, being unable to blame Raimondo for moving to remote Tuscany, had put all the blame on her daughter-in-law; her jealousy and hatred had doubled, and Matilde was even criticised for the baby's birth . . . How could she show that harsh woman she was wrong? How persuade her that her son, against everyone's wishes, had been determined to do what he wanted himself? Had not the baron in his simplicity said that Raimondo had gone to Florence to please Matilde? . . . Thus without realising it she had given her mother-in-law a new weapon; in trying to bring her husband and father together she had loosed that fury against herself . . .

'Your Excellency's aunt!'

Announced by the major-domo, as dinner was about to end, Donna Ferdinanda entered. Except for the duke, all stood up, the countess with the others, but the spinster greeted all except her. A few minutes later appeared Don Blasco, whose only greeting was, 'Still at table?' He did not even seem to notice Matilde . . . What, thought she, was being ignored by these compared to the war waged against her years ago by the princess? Retirement had not helped then, nor had never expressing a wish, desire, or opinion of her own; hatred had always found an outlet. The pretext then was the innocent baby who had the double fault of belonging to the despised sex and of being born from that mother; and as the mother was resigned personally to this treatment though bleeding at the slights to her child, the princess had begun persecuting her little granddaughter with special ferocity. Raimondo had appeared to notice nothing and left her alone longer than in Florence, not considering that she was alone as long as she stayed 'in the family', and in a short time the torment of that life had become so acute that she had begun yearning for the moment of returning to the solitude, calm at least, of her home in Florence . . .

'Where's that other one? . . .' suddenly asked Don Blasco, snorting at his brother the duke's political lucubrations.

'That other one' could only be Raimondo; all understood so and answered that they had not seen him and that perhaps he had stayed out to dine with a friend.

'He could have warned . . .' observed the prince.

And although that observation, made in a severe tone with no regard for the presence of his wife, wounded Matilde, there was another voice inside her saying, 'It's true! He's right!' Had she herself not thought just that, back in Florence, in the refuge which had once seemed so full of peace and felicity, during those long waits, day and night, for the return of Raimondo, who left her nearly always alone, when she had felt overwhelmed by anguish and fear at not knowing what had happened to him, always fearing dangers and disasters in her sick imagination? Her husband, on the other hand, refused to tell her anything of his life, as if he were still a bachelor, as if she had no rights over him, as if their child did not exist! That child who was to have brought them closer together, who should at least have been a refuge for the mother in times of sorrow, not only seemed to say nothing to Raimondo's heart, but could not even comfort her; now she could no longer excuse her husband's ever wilder conduct as she had at first, now she could no longer ignore his neglecting her for other women, and now this discovery made her feel a sudden stab of jealousy . . .

Once more her past sufferings seemed nothing compared to her present ones. She loved Raimondo more than ever, for the very defects which she had forgiven him, for all that he had cost her; and the new, brusquer remarks with which he rejected her prayers and derided her tears and almost blamed her for loving him, drew her ever closer to him. No, the child was not enough, the little creature could not console her, no one in the world could console her, she even had to hide her agonies from her father and write him that she was happy and content, in case he came and asked Raimondo to account for his behaviour, in case the two men had an open quarrel! Once more she had pinned her hopes on a return to Sicily; the terrible Uzeda home seemed an oasis, since there at least she had been free of the suspicion that gnawed like a canker. When from Catania they wrote to Raimondo asking him to return soon, when his dying mother called him, she did all she could to induce him to leave; but seeing him deaf to the dying woman's voice, deaf even to self-interest, and remaining in Florence, her anguish had been exacerbated, so powerful did she think must be the reasons, the links which held him back . . . And in those very days her body was aquiver for another reason: she was to be a mother again— a cold, bad mother if she did not rejoice at this discovery. But how could she, when the father of her child caused her so much distress; when at the announcement of his being a father again he was indifferent and almost bored, as if it were just another bother? . . . When the telegram came announcing the princess's death, as they suddenly left she had drawn breath freely, asking the Lord to forgive her for feeling joy at a death. But the implacable aversion of his relations afflicted her once again as a sign of the unsuspected depths of human malice, and now that Raimondo, with no respect for his mother's memory, was making the whole town gossip about his wild life, she asked herself agonisingly, ' When, where, will I have peace? . . .'

Dinner was already over and Lucrezia, the princess and Consalvo had already got up from table, when Raimondo appeared. He seemed very gay and had an excellent appetite. At a question from the duke he replied that he had been delayed by friends and had not noticed the late hour.

' Anyway you dine appallingly early here! In civilised countries one doesn't go to table before the Angelus!'

The prince did not reply. He got up as his brother began devouring the *minestra* which had been kept hot for him, said to the duke, ' Uncle, would you come with me a moment?' and led him into his study.

Very much on his dignity, as if negotiating a treaty, he locked the door of the antechamber, offered his uncle an armchair, remaining on his feet himself, and began:

'Your Excellency must excuse me for disturbing you after dinner, but having to talk about important matters and not wanting to waste your time . . .'

'Not at all! . . .' exclaimed the duke, interrupting this preamble. 'You're not disturbing me at all . . . Go on, do say . . .' and he lit a cigar.

'Your Excellency can see every day the life Raimondo is leading,' went on the prince, 'and how instead of giving me a hand in arranging matters of succession he thinks of nothing but amusement and leaves everything on my shoulders. To talk to him of his interests is useless; either he won't listen or doesn't understand . . . or he pretends not to.'

The duke approved with a nod of the head. Privately he thought rather strange such complaints by his nephew, who should surely not be very upset at his brother taking no hand in matters of the inheritance and thus leaving him free to do as he liked. And if Raimondo showed small eagerness to take part in such matters, had his elder brother not shown even less to render any account to co-heir and legatees? Was this not the first time, maybe, that he was talking in such terms to any of the family?

'Now,' Giacomo was going on meanwhile, 'I think it first of all proper, in the common interest, for the division to take place as soon as possible. In the second place all should know what I've only just learnt . . .'

'What's that?'

'A fine thing!' exclaimed the prince with a bitter little smile. And after a short pause, as if preparing his uncle's mind for the sad news, he said, 'Our mother's inheritance is full of debts . . .'

The duke took the cigar from his mouth in surprise.

'Your Excellency doesn't believe it? Who ever could have thought such a thing? After hearing such praise all round for the admirable way my mother had put our family on its feet again! Instead of which it's a positive abyss! . . . Until the other day I suspected nothing. It's true that in the first days after the tragedy I was warned of a few small I.O.U.'s signed by our mother, whose holders had patiently held them during her illness beyond their time of falling due, but I naturally thought that they were for small sums, the sort of petty debts which all of us, even the wealthiest, have to contract at times. What was my surprise to find instead that they come to many thousands of *onze* and that a new creditor appears every day. If things go on like this most of the inheritance will vanish in smoke . . .'

' But Signor Marco . . .'

' Signor Marco,' went on the prince, without giving his uncle time to formulate his objection, ' knew less of it than I did, and is even more astounded than Your Excellency. Your Excellency well knows my mother's character, God rest her soul, and how she did whatever came into her head, hiding it not only from those who should have been her natural confidantes but even from those to whom she had given her trust . . . Signor Marco has not noted in his debit columns a tenth of the sums we owe now. I don't know what else will turn up. Just imagine, there are I.O.U.'s which fell due three, or four years ago, and even five! . . . I confess that at first I thought myself a victim, with all the others, of some ghastly fraud, of dealing with a group of forgers. But I had to think again; the signatures are there, quite genuine. So I was forced to suppose that the system of having recourse to credit, for which my mother so blamed our grandfather, was not so alien to herself. And the worst of it is one can't know how far the rot goes! This is the administration we've heard so praised! . . . But they say one shouldn't talk ill of the dead . . . so that's enough! . . . Now I wished to inform Your Excellency, firstly as it was my duty, and secondly so that Your Excellency could say a word to Raimondo. If these debts are to be paid, and alas there's little hope of avoiding that, each will have to take on their part. I would also like to ask Your Excellency to tell the others that their legacies too will be debited in proportion . . .'

The duke began nodding his head again, but with a different expression. The legatees were complaining of having had too little; now they were to be told they had even less!

' Why don't you tell them yourself?' he suggested to his nephew.

'Why?' went on the prince, with the slight irritation of one asked a tiresome question, 'doesn't Your Excellency know what the family's like? Secretive, suspicious, mistrusting? Does Your Excellency think I've not noticed certain intrigues, not heard of underhand accusations being bandied about? They all seem against me, particularly that crackbrained Lucrezia! . . . Didn't she make another scene today? . . .'

'No, no . . .' interrupted the duke, 'quite the contrary, I assure you. She was complaining that you were against her and never said a word to her . . .'

'Me? Why should I be against her? . . . I've not spoken much these last days, it's true, but can Your Excellency expect anyone to want to talk with this fine piece of news on his mind? Why should I be against her or the others? I've always thought and said that the chief thing in families is peace, union, concord! . . . Is it my fault that wasn't possible while our mother was alive? Your Excellency knows how I was treated . . . Better, much better, not talk of it! . . . Now, however much I've been stripped, have they heard me make a single complaint? I've been the first to say, "Our mother's wishes must be our laws!" Instead of which, what do I see? Sour looks to right and left, Raimondo refusing to take any interest in our affairs, as if punishing me for taking away half his inheritance . . .'

'No, just amusing himself . . .' corrected the duke.

'My uncle Don Blasco,' went on the prince, as if not hearing the observation, 'whom I've always treated with respect and deference like all the others, instigates the legatees against me . . .'

'He's merely off his head!'

'Are the others sages, would your Excellency say? What do they want, what do they expect? What do they accuse me of? Why don't they come and tell me their reasons? Lucrezia talked to Your Excellency today; let's hear what she said . . .'

Although he had resolved not to keep the promise made to his niece a few hours before, the duke was forced by this question to reply, giving a little smile to temper what could only be unwelcome words:

'You complain of being stripped, and that's what they think they have been . . .'

The prince replied with an even bitterer smile than before.

'Do they indeed? And how may that be?'

'By getting less than their due . . . as there's your father's part . . .'

Giacomo frowned a minute, then burst out with ill-contained violence:

'Then why do they accept the Will? Why don't they demand the accounts? They'd do me a pleasure! They'd do me a service!'

'All the better then . . .'

'What do they think our mother's inheritance was anyway? Let's make up the accounts. Yessir! Let's make them up to-morrow, today! Or rather why don't they go to law then?'

'What's that to do with it?'

'Let 'em sue me! Let's set the whole city talking, let's give this fine example of fraternal love! Let Raimondo join 'em, and all accuse me of twisting the Will . . . ah! ah! ah! . . . They're capable of thinking that! I know them, yes, I know them! This is the result of their upbringing here, of the example they were given, of distrust and Jesuitry erected into a system.'

He was really excited, talked violently, and had quite lost the solemn composure of his preamble. The duke, throwing away his cigar-end, went on nodding as if recognising that when all was said and done he was not so far out in those last remarks. But, rising from his chair, he put a hand on his nephew's shoulder.

'Keep calm now!' he exclaimed. 'Don't let's exaggerate on either side. The papers are there . . .'

'No one'll touch them!'

'They want to make up the accounts, you're ready to hand them over . . .'

'Now, this very minute . . .'

'Then you're bound to come to an agreement. Make up these accounts, see if your mother's division is just or not; arrange everything in a friendly way.'

'Now, this instant!' repeated the prince, following his uncle, who was moving off. 'Why didn't they talk before? I'm not the

Holy Ghost to guess what's milling in those unbalanced heads of theirs!'

'There's time! There's time!' repeated the duke in a conciliatory tone, without pointing out to his nephew the contradiction into which he was now falling after asserting before that he knew of their plots. 'Don't get so excited about it! I'll talk to Raimondo, then to the others; the papers are there; there won't be any questions, you'll see . . . Oh, by the by,' he exclaimed, turning back at the door, 'what about that matter of the convent?'

'What matter? . . .' replied the prince in surprise.

'The legacy for Masses . . . The thousand *onze* that you won't give Angiolina . . .'

'Thousand *onze*? I won't give her them? . . .' exclaimed Giacomo then. 'Can't Your Excellency see what cheats and liars they all are? I won't give her them? Why, our mother's legacy is null as it means the institution of a benefice, and no institution of a benefice is valid without royal approval!'

In the Yellow Drawing-room Don Blasco was chewing his nails, knowing that brother of his was in confabulation with his nephew and not being able to hear what they were discussing. In his frustration he was snorting and pacing up and down, not even listening to what was being said around him.

Cousin Graziella had arrived and was chatting with the princess, Lucrezia and Donna Ferdinanda; less with Matilde, in order to show she participated in the feelings of the Uzeda towards the intruder. Once she had thought that she herself, Cousin Graziella, could enter the Francalanza family too, could take first place there in fact, as Prince Giacomo's wife, but her Aunt Teresà's opposition had triumphed over both her and the young man. Instead of 'Princess' she was now called simply 'Signora Carvano'. But although her cousin had taken the wife his mother chose for him, put his heart at rest and even seemed to have forgotten that there had once been tender words between the two of them, she had continued to make love, if not with him, with his family. She came to the house assiduously, made close friends with Princess Margherita, induced her husband to go and pay court to the Uzeda too, held Teresina at the

142

baptismal font, and showed in every way and on all occasions that her old failed hopes could not weaken her affection for all her cousins.

During Donna Teresa's illness, and particularly after her death, Donna Graziella had almost become a member of the family; every day and evening she came to get news, lavish sympathy, suggest advice, and make herself useful in word and deed. The princess had no reason for being jealous of her, as Giacomo appeared so indifferent towards his cousin that at certain times he scarcely said a word to her, dropped the *tu* and called her by the cold *voi*. But Margherita was incapable of jealousy or any other feeling for her or anyone else, so much did her natural listlessness and need of isolation and the subjection in which she was held by her husband render her indifferent to everyone and everything apart from her own children.

That afternoon in fact, after dinner, the nurse had come to tell her that the baby was coughing a little. Nothing serious, of course, but she had been worried, and her cousin on hearing the news made much show of medical knowledge, advised decoctions for her goddaughter, assuring her, however, that the illness was not serious, yet scolding even so the nurse who must have left the balcony window open.

Raimondo, who usually escaped as soon as he had snatched a mouthful to eat, seemed to want to stay at home for his own pleasure, and Matilde, reassured, suddenly forgot her sadness of an hour before and followed him round with radiant looks. She was so made that a word, a mere nothing, could disturb or reassure her, and she asked so little to be happy! If only he were always like that, if he dedicated a part of his time to his family, if he were as prodigal of caresses to his own baby as he was that evening to little Prince Consalvo . . . The latter, amid the group of men, was repeating his declensions to the Cavaliere Don Eugenio, who had appointed himself tutor, amid the applause of the parasites, who were dazzled by his every reply; but he was beginning to get confused and make mistakes.

'Don't torment him any more, poor child! . . .' exclaimed Donna Ferdinanda. 'Here, come to auntie . . . They're making

your head fuzzy with all these stories, eh? You just reply,
" I'm not going to be a writing-master, am I?" '

Don Eugenio, hearing *belles-lettres* despised, replied:

' He must study, though! . . . A man's worth as much as he
knows. And then you must also honour the name you bear;
among your ancestors is Don Ferrante Uzeda, glory of
Sicily!'

' Don Ferrante?' exclaimed the old spinster, ' what did Don
Ferrante do?'

' What did he do? Why, he translated Ovid from Latin, he
wrote a commentary on Plutarch, he described our island
antiquities: temples, coins, medals . . .'

' Ha, ha . . . ha! ha! . . .' Donna Ferdinanda broke into roars
of laughter, which spattered everyone around with saliva. The
cavaliere was open-mouthed, Don Cono did not know where
to look.

' Ha, ha! . . . aha! . . .' Donna Ferdinanda went on laughing.
' Don Ferrante! Ha, ha! . . . Ferrante, d'you know what he
did? . . .' she explained eventually, turning to her nephew. ' He
had four writing-masters, paid at the rate of two *tarì* a day,
working for him. Then when they'd written his books for him,
Don Ferrante had his own name printed on them! . . . Ha,
ha! . . . I've grave doubts if he even knew how to read! . . .'

Then a great discussion started up. Don Cono and the cavaliere each sustained on his own that if this ancestor had not
in fact written his own books, he had at least dictated the contents; so much so that the academies of Palermo, Naples and
Rome had enrolled him among their members. But the old
spinster interrupted, ' Oh, come on now . . .' while Cousin
Graziella, shaking her head, affirmed that in truth study had
not been a strong point with the old nobility.

' Strong point?' exclaimed the old spinster. ' But till my own
times learning to read and write was considered shameful.
People only studied to become priests. Our mother couldn't
write her own signature . . .'

' And was that a good thing?' objected Don Eugenio.

' Now don't you begin talking to me about progress too!'
burst out Donna Ferdinanda. ' Progress means the boy has to
fuzz his head with books like a notary! In my day young men

learnt fencing and went out riding and shooting as their fathers and grandfathers had done!'

As Don Mariano approved with a nod of the head, the spinster went into a paean of praise of her grandfather, Prince Consalvo VI, the most accomplished cavalier of his day. He had had such a passion for horses that every winter he had a covered passage built down the middle of the public streets, so that his noble animals should always keep dry.

'Could other people go along it too?' asked the little prince.

'They could when it wasn't the time for the prince's ride,' replied Donna Ferdinanda. 'If he came out, all drew aside! . . . Once when the Captain of Justice dared to pass with his own carriage, d'you know what my grandfather did? He waited for his return, ordered his coachman to set the horses at him, broke up his carriage and horse-whipped him! . . . Ah, the gentry made themselves respected in those days . . . Not like now, when they agree with every ragamuffin! . . .'

This shaft was directed at the duke, who was at that moment re-entering the Yellow Drawing-room together with the prince. Don Blasco, ceasing at last to pace up and down, stared at his brother and nephew.

'What the devil have you been up to?' he said to the prince.

'Nothing . . . there were some things I wanted to ask our uncle . . .'

At that moment Chiara and the marchese appeared. Lucrezia, still sulky, saluted her sister coldly, but the latter noticed nothing, being on tenterhooks and full of a secret idea.

'Margherita,' she whispered to her sister-in-law confidentially, 'this time I think it really is . . .!' Were those the symptoms? Could she be making a mistake? So often had she hoped and celebrated the event in vain, that now she did not dare announce her pregnancy openly if it was not confirmed first. Then, leaving the princess, she took Matilde aside and began saying to her, 'The midwife is certain! What d'you feel? . . . How did you realise? . . .'

Matilde did not hear her. Now that Don Blasco was no longer marching from one end of the room to the other, Raimondo had caught his uncle's restlessness and was not still a moment, continually asking what time it was. Did he want to go out? Was

he waiting for someone? His restlessness made her restless . . .
Meanwhile new visitors arrived: the Duchess Radalì and the
Prince of Roccasciano, Donna Isabella Fersa with her husband.
The latter's entry put the whole company topsy-turvy; the
prince, not usually very gallant with ladies, went to meet her in
the antechamber; Raimondo too was one of the first to greet her.
As always, she wore a brand-new dress, which Lucrezia
examined from the corner of her eye, and the princess, Chiara,
all the other women, judged in one voice to be of the highest
elegance.

'Made in Florence, isn't it, Donna Isabella?' asked Raimondo.

'One can see your husband understands these things,
countess!' she replied indirectly, turning to Matilde.

Don Mariano was talking of the parade for the Queen's birth-
day that day, Fersa of the cholera, the ten days' quarantine
just decreed against anyone arriving from Malta, about the
putting-off of the Noto Fair, and the danger to Sicily again;
and Don Blasco's boom replied:

'It's all due to the Crimea! A present from our Piedmontese
brethren, d'you see?'

The duke, as if not realising that the allusion was aimed at
him, went on with his speech on the war interrupted at table,
saying that Cavour had made a mistake. The right way was
different: to keep quiet and calm, lick the wounds of '48. With
the State in debt to the eyes how could it make new debts? 'It's
a principle of political economy . . .' And then, in the tone of
authority he had brought from Palermo, he began a long speech
which made Don Blasco positively swallow barrel-loads of
poison, larded as it was with quotations from newspapers and
parliament, and tainted with liberalising theories. The prince,
hearing Fersa express once more a great fear of the cholera,
shook his head.

'If they've ordered it to be distributed from Naples again . . .'

Just as he believed in the Evil Eye so he was unshakable in
his opinion that the cholera was an evil spell, an expedient on
the Government's part to scatter the population and inculcate
a healthy fear in the survivors. Before his uncle the duke, who he
knew had a contrary and more 'progressive' opinion (that the
plague came through atmospheric currents), he was prudently

silent, but with Fersa he could let himself go, deride the quarantine and all the other petty restrictions put on to throw dust in people's eyes.

'Don't listen to all this gloom!' Raimondo was meanwhile saying to Donna Isabella, beside whom he had taken a seat. 'Are you going to the gala night?'

'Yes, count; we have a box.'

'What are they doing?' asked the princess.

'Holbein's *Elvira*, and Dumanoir's *An Inheritance in Corsica*. A pity you can't hear Domeniconi, princess. What an artist! And what a company!'

Don Eugenio too was expressing his regret at not being able to go to the Muncipal Theatre and so show that in his capacity as Gentleman of the Bedchamber he had been invited to the Intendant's box. But he had some business to do that night; the sale of some 'very important' terra-cottas on which he would make a fine profit. In fact he was waiting to talk about it to the Prince of Roccasciano, also a knowledgeable amateur of antiquities.

'It's all very well, fifteen thousand men,' the duke was making his peroration in his turn. 'But suppose the war lasts another year? another two, another three years? It means more troops being sent, more expenses made, the growth of the deficit . . .'

'At Messina they're expecting the Archduke Maximilian.'

'Will he come to us here?'

At this question of Don Mariano's, Raimondo jumped up as if stung by a wasp.

'What d'you expect him to come and do here? Visit the elephant in the cathedral square? You people have got it into your heads that this is a city, and you won't understand that it's just a wretched little place ignored by the rest of the world. Donna Isabella, you say. Have you ever heard it even named outside here?'

'It's true, it's true!'

She was waving a mother-of-pearl and lace fan in a gracefully languid manner and agreeing with Raimondo's opinions against his native town. And the Countess Matilde did not know why the sight of that woman, her words, her gestures, inspired her with secret antipathy. Was it maybe because she heard her

approving of a sentiment by Raimondo that she forgave in
her husband but blamed in others? Or because she noted in all
Donna Isabella's person, in the showy richness of her clothes, the
affected elegance of her attitudes, something studied and false?
Or because all the men gathered round her and she looked at
them in a certain way, over-boldly, almost provocatively? Or
maybe because once Raimondo was beside her he never moved,
seemed no longer to want to leave or to be waiting for anyone? . . .

Once launched on his favourite theme, he was now steaming
along, enumerating all the advantages of life in big cities, interrupting himself every now and again to ask Donna Isabella,
'It's true, isn't it?' or, 'You tell them; you've been there!'
And describing again the high society, the sumptuous shows,
the rich and noble pleasures. Donna Isabella was nodding her
head and adding other arguments:

'When shall we see any races here, for example?'

Just at that moment Don Giacinto entered the room. He was
looking so flustered and was so obviously the bearer of bad
news that everyone was silenced.

'D'you know what?'

'What? Tell us . . .'

'Cholera's broken out in Syracuse . . .'

All surrounded him.

'What? Who told you?'

'Half an hour ago, at Dimenza the chemist's . . . Sure news,
it comes from the Intendant's . . . Real cholera this time; like
lightning!'

All at once, as if the announcer had the disease himself, the
gathering broke up amid terrified comments and laments;
Raimondo accompanied Donna Isabella down to her carriage,
giving her his arm; half-way down the stairs, under the nose
of the duke going to verify the story, Don Blasco boomed:

'It's a present from the *brethren*! . . . Ah, Radetsky, where
art thou! . . . Ah, for another '49 . . .'

# 5

B E F O R E the universal disquiet about public health all other interests faded as if by magic; for the news brought by Don Giacinto, denied at first, then confirmed, could no longer be doubted when, a few days later, it was not just a matter of suspected cases in Syracuse, but of the disease breaking out in Noto.

The duke, who was considering a return to Palermo before things got worse and the roads were closed, obstinately resisted the invitations of the prince, who was preparing to leave for the Belvedere at the first case announced in the city. The year before, as in '37, the Uzeda had escaped to their villa on the slopes of Etna where cholera never reached. Suddenly the prince put aside his scowl and talked of accord and union, wanted the whole family safe with him, all aunts and uncles, brothers and sisters. Although it was no time for business, yet to show his nephew that he had taken his interest to heart, the duke before leaving repeated to Raimondo the conversation about the I.O.U.'s and exhorted him to come to an agreement with his brother. Raimondo listened distractedly and replied almost irritably, ' All right, all right; we'll see about it later . . .'

He too had changed, but, contrary to Giacomo, for the worse; he had become nervous, irascible and verbose, and was good-humoured only when Donna Isabella came to the palace. The two Fersa did not know yet where to flee the cholera. The prince advised them to take a house at the Belvedere, and be near them. This idea much attracted Donna Isabella, though her mother-in-law preferred to take refuge at Leonforte like the year before.

'And you, where are you going?' she asked Raimondo. And the young man, who was always by her side, said:

'Wherever you go yourself!'

She lowered her eyes with a severe look of censure, as if offended.

'And what about your wife and daughter?'

'Let's change the subject!'

In spite of alarm at the epidemic, relations between the two families became even closer in those days. Fersa, who had always been proud and glad to come to the Francalanza palace, now enjoyed being received there with signs of particular approval; not only Raimondo, but also and perhaps more Giacomo, seemed much to enjoy his company and that of Donna Isabella. When the princess went out for the first time after their mourning, he told her to pay them a visit; the countess, by her husband's wish, accompanied her sister-in-law.

By herself Matilde might never have gone to that woman's house. She did not want to call it jealousy, the feeling with which the other inspired her. If Raimondo, gallant with all the ladies, was for ever hanging around this one who was surrounded by every man in sight, that was no surprise; did she herself not receive continual protestations of warm friendship? And yet every time that Donna Isabella embraced and kissed her she had to make an effort not to shrink from those demonstrations of affection. She did not know how to account for the almost instinctive revulsion which she felt more strongly every day. When she tried to explain it to herself she attributed it mainly to a radical difference in character, to the lightness, affectation, lack of simplicity which she seemed to notice in the other. Had she not even heard her complain, in veiled hints, about her husband's relatives and her husband himself? Yet Matilde could observe, and almost envied, Fersa's devotion for her, and heard people say that her mother-in-law treated her better than a daughter! When she went to pay her a visit with the princess, had she not noticed this with her own eyes?

Donna Mara Fersa was of the old school, quite uneducated and even rather coarse mannered; but very shrewd and direct, and easy-going as any good housewife. She had hoped to marry her son off in her own way, but he had once gone to Palermo, seen Isabella Pinto, an orphan, fallen violently in love and immediately asked her hand of her maternal uncle who had brought her up. She was of very noble stock but without a dowry, though she had received an excellent education in her rich uncle's house. The Fersa, on the other hand, though admitted among gentry, were of mediocre birth; Donna Ferdinanda, an admirer and friend of Donna Isabella, nicknamed them ' Farce '—*laughable farce*—but they had a mass of money.

Donna Mara had at first tried to oppose that marriage; but as her son was head over heels in love with Isabella, who seemed even more so with him, the mother had finally agreed. And so the daughter-in-law from Palermo, elegant, educated, and noble, came to set the household upside-down; this Donna Mara took in very good part for love of her son, realising that one cannot oppose the tastes or whims of the young. Donna Isabella, though calling her ' Mama ' and showing her the respect which was her due, seemed discontented with her, ashamed of her ignorance and simplicity. This attitude was so subtle that Matilde almost blamed herself for ill-will in noticing a kind of condescending pity for the mother-in-law's opinions, as if they were those of a child or an inferior, an imperceptible exaggeration of obedience, a vague air of sacrifice which seemed intended to arouse pity in others but was particularly distasteful to Matilde.

Anyway it seemed certain that she would not have to endure her company for long. The only thing keeping Raimondo in Sicily could be the need to settle his interests; but he might hasten his departure to escape the cholera. Already at the first rumours of an epidemic, worried at being so far from her father and child, she had asked what he wanted to do; but her husband had not yet decided. The year before, in Tuscany, on hearing the news of the carnage in Sicily, of the terror reigning in the island, of the collapse of all civil organisation, he had expressed his satisfaction at being far away from his ' savage ' native land, where, said he, he would take good care not to find himself in times of epidemic; so she was almost sure that they would cross over to the mainland, picking up the baby on the way.

Raimondo, on the other hand, seemed hesitant. He did complain of the evil star which had got him caught by the plague in an island trap, but said they could not travel because of her pregnancy now that the disease had broken out. Meanwhile Matilde's father was writing for them to join him at Milazzo, as the cholera was coming from the south, and leave Catania soon, not wait till panic-stricken locals barricaded all roads. And so, as the news got worse, as her father's letters became more pressing, as the danger of being cut off from her child grew graver, her heart was assailed with terror and anxiety as if she were about to lose her dear ones for ever; she exhorted Raimondo more warmly to come to some decision and leave at once.

'Let's get away! . . . let's go to my home for a time! I don't want to leave Teresina alone . . . We'll also be farther from the plague's hot-bed.'

'Why should I shut myself up in a seaside village in time of cholera? And die like a dog? You must be mad! No, write to your father and sister to bring the child here.'

But the baron replied at once that he would on no account do anything so silly, as the cholera was at the gates of Catania, and he adjured his daughter not to lose time and even to leave Raimondo alone if he refused to come with her . . . Then she no longer knew what to do or whom to heed, frenzied at the idea of staying apart from her daughter and father, and unable to face the idea of leaving Raimondo, feeling she could live away from neither at such a time. The day that the duke packed his bags and left for Palermo she felt lost . . .

Till the last moment the prince had pressed his uncle to come with him to the Belvedere. The duke continued to refuse, adducing his affairs calling him to the capital and the greater safety there.

'Don't give me a thought,' he said to his nieces and nephews, 'I'll run no risk; but get to safety yourselves.'

'Your Excellency need not worry about me; I have all ready to leave at the first alarm,' replied Giacomo. Turning to his brother, whom he had already invited once, he repeated in Matilde's presence:

'If you care to come too, I'd be pleased.'

152

Raimondo did not reply. Did he really want to stay apart from his daughter? Could he live so calmly far away from her in the terrible days coming? Matilde sobbed, begging him not to do such a thing. He replied testily:

'I don't know yet what I'll do. One thing's sure, I'm not going to Milazzo.'

'Are we to leave that poor child alone then? Suppose they close the ferry, suppose we can't see her any more?'

'First of all your daughter is not abandoned in the middle of a road but is with her grandfather and aunt. Then if that stiffneck of a father of yours had listened to me by now he'd have brought her here and we'd be ready to go off all together to the Belvedere, where there isn't a shadow of danger . . . Anyway, I'm not going to Milazzo; there's already talk of suspected cases in Messina. Go alone, if you wish.'

And all the Uzeda, as if enjoying her anguish, as if not wanting to let her out of their clutches, approved and said that now everyone must stay where they were. Her father reproved her harshly for stubbornness and selfishness, while she thought she was going mad; dreaming every night ghastly dreams about slow death agonies, final separations, grisly tortures; weeping as if her child were dead and the new creature moving in her womb too; seeing her father and Raimondo hurl themselves at each other . . . And one terrible nightmarish day the prince came to say that the first case had appeared in the city, that the roads were being blocked, that they must leave for the Belvedere at once—where the two Fersa would be coming also . . .

Villa Francalanza at the Belvedere was still in the same state as three months before at the moment of the princess's death. There, with their suites of servants, met the families of the prince and his guests, Chiara and the marchese, Donna Ferdinanda, the Cavaliere Don Eugenio, Raimondo and his wife. Ferdinando had refused to hear of leaving his own place; he had stayed there for the cholera of the year before; he would stay for this year's too, declaring that no place offered better guarantees of immunity. Don Blasco and the Prior Don Lodovico had already made off, with all the San Nicola monks, for Nicolosi.

The Uzeda country mansion was big enough to house a regiment of soldiers as well as the prince's guests but, like the palace in town, it had been through so many modifications and successive remodellings that it seemed made up of various layers of building stuck together haphazardly; there were not two windows of the same design or two façades of the same colour. The internal lay-out looked like the work of a lunatic, so often had it been altered. The same had happened with the surrounding land. Once upon a time, under Prince Giacomo XIII, this had been nearly all noble gardens. The prince, a lover of flowers, had spent on these some of the sums which had brought about his ruin; he had caused a well to be dug for water through the centuries-old lava of Mongibello, to a depth of 100 *canne*. The whole work was done by hand, with picks, and took about three years. When the water was finally found and drawn up by a chain-pump, he considered that viticulture could advantageously be exchanged for orchards, so he tore up all the vines in the land not yet transformed into a garden, to plant oranges and lemons. Thus the money laid out by his grandfather to build vats and cellar was lost.

But on Donna Teresa's advent, all was thrown upside-down once more. Flowers being things 'which one can't eat', roses and carnations were uprooted, pillars reduced to bricks, hot-houses transformed into stalls for mules, and as wine fetched a higher price than fruit, the fine orange and lemon trees which had been tended so carefully were sacrificed for vines. There were now only a few acres of garden left between the gates and the house, and just enough fruit-trees for lemonade in summer-time. So all the money was truly flung down the well.

Now as soon as he arrived the prince began renovating too, as he had at the palace. The land he did not touch, judging, like his mother, that the bedraggled roses clambering over the iron gates and walls of the villa were enough for the pleasure of sight and smell, and that cabbages, lettuces and onions were much better in the old flower-beds; but he called in workmen and told them to pull down walls and divide up rooms and block in doors and pierce new windows. He was in excellent mood and treated his guests well; he paid devoted court to his Aunt Ferdinanda, was all courtesy to his brother and sisters, his brother-in-law the marchese, and his sister-in-law Matilde. Of course, considering the time of year, no one spoke of business. Lucrezia was even more content than he, for the Giulente, who had no house of their own in town, owned one of the pleasantest villas at the Belvedere, and Benedetto, having come up there with his family at the first rumour of cholera, passed to and fro at any hour by the Francalanza gates.

The marchese was also very pleased, and Chiara quite beside herself with delight as her symptoms of pregnancy were confirmed; the husband and wife's only worry was inability to prepare baby clothes. Even Donna Ferdinanda seemed more approachable, domesticated by the prince's hospitality, pleased at saving the expense of taking a villa—though not of food, for each of the guests paid his own share.

But most pleased of all was the young prince. Morning and evening he was out in vineyards and garden, digging, carrying earth, building mud-houses. When tired of these occupations he would gallop to and fro astride a donkey or a mule, and if lackey or factor or other guide did not let him go where he wanted, he gave the man the whipping which he would have given his mount. Only the sight of his father could rein him in, for the prince had brought him up to tremble at a glance, though all his other relatives let him do what he liked. The princess agreed with him at a sign; his Aunt Ferdinanda also helped to spoil him, as heir to the princedom; only Don Eugenio vexed him now with lessons worse than in town. The boy would understand everything when attentive, but the difficulty was to make him keep quiet.

'Study now or your father will send you to college!' his uncle warned him; and in fact the prince had more than once expressed the intention of sending his son away from home and putting him either at the Cutelli College, founded to educate the nobility 'in the Spanish mode', or in the Benedictine novitiate, where youths who did not want to make vows received an education equally noble. Consalvo did not want to go to either place, and the threat was enough for him to decide to practise his handwriting and recite declensions. As a reward Don Eugenio took the boy with him around the countryside of Mompileri, where, a few days after his arrival at the Belvedere, he had begun to make certain mysterious trips.

155

About two centuries before, in 1669, the Etna lava had covered a little village near there called Massa Annunziata, and later on a few remains of its houses had been found. Now Don Eugenio, who had not earned much from trafficking in pots and was always brooding over some great coup which would enrich him, had conceived the plan of starting a series of excavations, like those he had seen at Herculaneum or Pompeii, to uncover the buried village and enrich himself with the money and objects which would certainly be found there. Secrecy was necessary so that others should not filch his idea. And that was why, alone or accompanied by the boy, who would go off on his own to hunt for lizards and butterflies, the cavaliere wandered amid the gorse and cactus lying below Mompileri with old books in his hand, getting his bearings from the spires of Nicolosi and Torre Del Grifo, studying the land, taking measurements, and risking arrest as an evil spirit by muleteers and shepherds who noticed him in those suspicious attitudes. But keeping the secrecy of the idea was not enough; to put it into action a great deal of money was also needed. So one day Don Eugenio called the prince aside, and with an air of great mystery informed him of the plan and asked him to lend enough money to pay for excavations.

'Is Your Excellency joking or really serious? Excavate the mountain and find what? A few cooking-pots and bits of copper? You must be mad . . .'

Indirectly the prince was applying the word 'mad' to himself by that reply, which he would never have dreamt of making to the duke or Donna Ferdinanda. But Don Eugenio had little prestige in the family because of his follies in Naples, and in particular because of his utter lack of money . . . The cavaliere never mentioned the idea to him again. He changed his line and wondered whether to write to the government to do the excavations at public expense in the hope they would make him director. The young prince breathed freely as lessons were interrupted; after dinner Don Eugenio would shut himself up in his room to work on his memorandum and was not to be seen again for the whole evening, while the others gossiped or gambled.

Gradually quite a considerable society gathered at the villa;

all the gentry in refuge at the Belvedere, all the local notabilities came to Villa Francalanza, where the prince held court and regaled them on anise and water. Half Catania was at the Belvedere, and the Uzeda, who were very exclusive in town, now made concessions because of the place and season, receiving people of small or even no nobility, all those whom Donna Ferdinanda derided or despised, whose names she would twist or to whom she would assign clownish coats-of-arms; the Maurigne for instance, who called themselves 'cavalieri', dubbed by the old aunt 'foot cavaliers'; or the Mongiolino, who being descended from enriched brick-makers ought to have had tiles and bricks on their shields. Of that dubious class only the Giulente did not come to the villa because of Benedetto, but when the prince met Benedetto or his father or uncle at the public casino he was most affable, and the young man, who had not interrupted his correspondence with Lucrezia, would pass this on to her, delighted with such amiability. The girl's joy increased her distraction of mind instead of decreasing it: she asked widowers for news of their dead wives, mistook one person for another, forgot everything. One evening she made everyone laugh by asking the Belvedere chemist, who had a sister in a convent:

'And who is your sister the nun married to? . . .'

The thread running through all talk was of course news from town, where the cholera was spreading, though slowly and not raging with the terrifying force of the year before. Each exchanged news of relations and friends who had taken refuge in various parts of the Etna Woods; Cousin Graziella, who was at La Zafferana, sent notes and messages by carters almost every day to ask after her cousins, give news of herself and her husband, send warm greetings with presents of fruit and wine; the Duchess Radalì-Uzeda did not write from La Tardaria because in the stress of unexpected departure, her husband had gone raving mad: madness was hereditary in the Radalì branch of the family; the Duke Radalì had suffered his first fits three years before at the birth of his second son Giovannino.

Since then the duchess, finding the responsibility for the whole household on her shoulders, had renounced the world to take the father's place with her children. She loved them both, but preferred the young Duke Michele. Not content with instituting primogeniture she worked to improve the property, and led a life of economy and sacrifice so as to leave him even richer. She gave no umbrage to any of the Uzeda; even Donna Ferdinanda, who thought herself the only balanced mind, approved of her. At the Belvedere, in spite of the cholera, the old spinster took an interest in business, drawing apart the men who understood it, talking of loans, mortgages, credits to be granted, failures to be feared; and while the Prince of Roccasciano was explaining to the old speculator the laborious plans on which he was slowly and patiently building up his own fortune, his wife the princess, unbeknown to him, was gambling away with Raimondo and other passionate card-players all the money she had on her. Giacomo could sometimes be seen playing without ever producing a coin, but most of the time he spent chatting with people from the village.

There came to pay him court the doctor, the chemist, the landowners, when he found their aspect pleasant, for those among his mother's familiars whom he thought to have the Evil Eye had been refused the door. The parish priest, the canon, and all the clerics in the village came. As in town, the Uzeda home was frequented here by all the regular and secular clergy, because of its reputation for devoutness and the good it had always done to the Church. The prince's refusal to recognise the legacy to the Convent of San Placido did not prejudice him with these; it was human and natural for him to try to keep most of the property for himself; his mother had done so too. On dying he would be generous with the Church for the good of his soul.

As head of the family he also had the faculty of nominating priests celebrating Mass in all chapels and benefices founded by his ancestors; there at the Belvedere, particularly, was a very prosperous one, that of the Holy Light. One Silvio Uzeda, a dotty creature, who lived a century and a half before, had always been surrounded by priests and friars, and the monks of the monastery of Saint Mary of the Holy Light had persuaded him that the Madonna wanted to marry him. At this he was beside himself with joy. Tradition said that the ceremony had been carried out with all formalities. The bridegroom, after Confes-

158

sion and Communion, had been led, dressed in gala clothes, before the statue of the Blessed Virgin, where the priest asked him according to the formula if he wished to marry Her. 'Yes!' Uzeda had replied. Then the same question was asked of the Queen of Heaven, and, through the mouth of the Father Guardian of the Monastery, she too had replied 'Yes'. Then rings had been exchanged; the statue still had on its finger that of the bridegroom who had of course left all his goods to his Consort. A long legal battle had followed, as the natural heirs refused to recognise the madman's Will. Finally they had come to terms; as a result half the property had been used to found at the monastery a lay chaplaincy over which the Uzeda had patronage.

So all the monks came in the evenings to pay court to the prince and discuss the affairs of the monastery with him. Among all these he acted the grandee, was treated like a pope and listened to like a god. He would forget the rest of the society, the ladies and gentlemen gambling at tombola or playing at charades or arranging excursions on the mountainside and spending their time so gaily that, had it not been for the news of the cholera and for the armed peasants keeping fugitives away later, no one could have thought those were times of pestilence.

The only one who failed to hide her own sorrow amid these general distractions was the Countess Matilde. She had come away from town almost in a frenzy, so strong had been the trials to which she had been put. Terror-struck, she had realised when just on the point of leaving for the country that the pain she could bear least was not separation from her child but Raimondo's betrayal. How could she doubt that any more? Had the truth of that not been suddenly made clear at his announcement that he was going to the Belvedere, where Donna Isabella Fersa was going? Why ever had he, who so hated living in Sicily, refused to leave for the mainland unless it was because he wanted to keep near that other woman? He had pretended that he couldn't decide, so as to wait and see what she decided! And he had thought up pretexts and accused his father-in-law and temporised so well that when the pestilence broke out he had done just what he wanted!

In those pretences and lies of his she no longer saw confirmation of the bad sides of his character; the fact that he was capable of them did not hurt her. Her one torture was the thought that he had used them for love of that other woman. That he had no love for his daughter, that he was unjust to his father-in-law, and bullying, capricious and rude, did not bother her at all; she did not want him to belong to any other! In Florence her jealousy had had no definite object, or had continually changed its object, for he paid court to all the women he met. She herself had also felt reassured up to a point, as, though he was gallant in speech with ladies, his changeableness and impatience made him prefer those others—paid women . . . How shameful it had been to find herself reduced to the point of rejoicing at that! Yet now she envied her past sufferings, finding it intolerable that he should be so full of another woman as to keep away from his own daughter in such terrible days in order to be near her!

Her anguish grew as she realised how fast he was advancing along the road of betrayal. In Florence, Raimondo's intrigues had a certain shame about them; he even tried then to gain her forgiveness by being nice to her at times. Now he was doing it all so openly she was forced to be spectator of his infamy! This wounded her most; that they should be so shameless as to make such a rendezvous, under her very eyes, while hearts all round were trembling at the thought of death!

What a day was that of their flight to the Belvedere, through streets roasting in the sun, amidst clouds of hot, suffocating dust! She shared a carriage with Chiara, Lucrezia and the marchese, and the sight of the latter being so attentive to his wife made her suffering the more acute. Raimondo had refused to travel with her, left her alone in that rush through villages where armed men stopped every person and vehicle, barring the way: but she understood nothing of all that! She saw nothing on the road! All she saw, in her mind's eye, was Raimondo smiling and happy beside that woman, as she had seen him so often in reality without her innate trust suspecting anything! Now, however, all the things that she had been unable to explain acquired an obvious meaning; Raimondo's long absences, his impatient waiting, the pleasure which could be read in his eyes as soon as that woman entered, even the mysterious instinct of revulsion which that woman had aroused in her from the first moment.

What a false and evil creature she must be, to call her by the tender name of friend and embrace her and kiss her while taking away her husband! Was he himself not just as false? How many lies! He had even used her pregnancy as a reason for not leaving Sicily, quite disregarding the fact that he was thereby risking the life of the creature she bore in her womb!

What a terrible day! In the furnace-hot carriage, its windows peered through by suspicious faces of brutish peasants, its air full of the nauseating smell of camphor which Chiara and Lucrezia were holding to their nostrils against infection, she felt her breath fail. She did not know where she was or where she was going; she yearned to shout out to coachman and travelling companions, 'Turn back . . . I don't want to come!' She longed to confront her husband, fling his betrayal in his face, adjure him not to take her near that woman, not to kill her, to save the creature moving in her womb, restore peace to her heart, air to her breast . . . Long before arriving at the Belvedere she had quite lost her senses, and could not even remember how and when she entered the villa.

There began for her a life of constant trepidation. Every instant she expected to find the Fersa woman there before her. Every time Raimondo went out she thought, 'Now he's with her . . .' and not seeing her, and not hearing her spoken of, increased her panic, darkened it, gave her all kinds of horrible suspicions of conspiracy against her by everyone around. Incredibly, she managed to find the strength to hide her feelings lest she arouse her husband's suspicions, lest she play into her enemies' hands, but the silence she imposed on herself made her torment more acute by depriving her of means to learn what was going on. Why did no one ever name that woman? Why did she never come to the villa, with all the prince's other visitors? Where was she living?

And intent on mulling over the thousand terrifying ideas suggested by her restless fancy, she forgot the cholera, scarcely thought of her far-away daughter or noticed her father's silence. He must be thinking that she had forgotten her child amid all the pleasures of the Belvedere! Why did she always find that

161

whatever she did unwillingly and in obedience to others was blamed on her by all as culpable caprice? Was she not one of those unfortunate people who never succeed in doing anything well and are destined to be disliked by all?

But she did not weep; she did not even weep when not her father but her sister Carlotta wrcte to tell her that Teresina was well and that they were all safe. She did not weep, but she felt overcome by a gloom she could not hide. Raimondo himself noticed it and asked her:

'What does your sister write?'

'Nothing . . . that they're all well, that they're in no danger.'

'D'you see? What did I tell you? . . .' and he turned his back on her.

Two weeks had gone by since their arrival and she had still heard no one speak of the Fersa. On the evening of that day, as guests began arriving, she shut herself into her room. She felt ill, not only in spirit but physically; the long period of agitation was finally affecting her body too. She had flung herself on the bed and been lying there some time, her eyes and mind fixed on sad visions of the past and alarming previsions of the future, when there was a knock at the door.

'Sister-in-law? . . .' It was the prince's voice. 'What are you doing? Why not come down? There are numbers of people here tonight . . . They're gambling . . .'

She got up, arranged her tumbled hair with a trembling hand and went downstairs. She was sure that other woman had come at last! She was quite certain that Raimondo was beside her! They were calling her down so that she could watch that sight and enjoy her agony! She glanced quickly round the crowded drawing-room; the woman was not there. But scarcely had she taken a seat next to her sisters-in-law, when she heard her name. Someone was saying:

'. . . the little villa rented to Donna Isabella . . .'

'A box of a place,' replied another. 'The Mongiolino are squashed in there like anchovies in a barrel.'

She did not understand.

'Where have the Fersa gone then?'

Was that really Raimondo asking this question? Did he really not know where that woman was?

' To their country place at Leonforte; Donna Mara preferred that.'

Suddenly she understood; her throat constricted. She slipped away without saying anything, crossed the house with swelling eyes and heart in tumult. When she reached her room she fell at the feet of the Virgin's statue and broke into floods of tears; tears of joy, of gratitude, and also of remorse; for she had suspected the innocent.

She seemed to have returned from death to life. With her suspicions ceased her pains, both of mind and of body, she took part in family life, and finally enjoyed the sweet taste of repose. Nor did the news of the cholera arouse her fear for her distant dear ones. After the slaughter of the year before, the pestilence seemed to have exhausted itself and meandered vaguely around without strength.

Life was as gay as ever at Villa Francalanza, with nightly receptions and card parties. No-one frequented the green tables more than Raimondo. When he took up the cards, stakes rose, risks grew. Many would get up and go, as they had come there for amusement and not to leave with empty purses.

The Princess of Roccasciano on the other hand asked for nothing better and often stayed on alone with the young count playing bezique at twelve *tarì* a hand. She had to hide from her husband, who, like all misers, disliked all forms of gambling. Complaisant friends would be on the look-out to tip them off as soon as he approached; then she and her accomplice would spirit away the counters, interrupt the game, and let themselves be surprised intent on an innocent game of *scopa*. Raimondo enjoyed this, incited the princess to high play, drew her off to an out-of-the-way room where they gambled for long hours, deceiving the suspicious prince with the help of all the other guests. Matilde would also smile at these comedy scenes, though considering that her husband did wrong to encourage the princess's vice; but she had not the heart to reprove him, so indulgent did her reborn faith in him make her. As long as he did not betray her, what did anything else matter? Raimondo seemed to have no eye for any of the ladies who came to the villa. He spent little time in their company and dedicated him-

163

self entirely to gambling, in daytime at the Casino, in the evening at home. Not only did she not blame him, but felt almost like urging him farther along a road which drew him away from that other which was infinitely more painful to her. In her heart she would have liked him without vices, loving only her, her family and her home, but she took him as he was, or rather as he had become, for she attributed whatever was least good in him to his mother's over-indulgence and blind love.

When away from cards, Raimondo was bored. If he could not arrange a good game he inveighed against the tedium of country life, the conversation of the country folk, the silly amusements of tombola, the donkey excursions. She could have said, ' Why complain? Didn't you yourself want to come?' But she was silent lest he should take such words as a reproof. Instead when seeing him in a bad humour she would ask him gently what was wrong.

' I'm bored, don't you know that?' was his reply.

' What can we do? . . . As soon as the cholera stops we'll go back to Florence . . . Why not go to the Casino?'

Off he went before she had time to repeat the suggestion. Gradually his gambling became wilder and wilder; in the course of a few hours, hundreds of gold *onze* would change hands. No one at home said a thing to Raimondo; the prince, friendlier with all, seemed carefully to avoid being a spoil-sport with his brother. One day the latter asked him for a few hundred *onze* as advance of the income he had inherited, since money was late in coming from Milazzo because of the cholera, and the prince put his purse at his brother's disposal; an offer taken up on several occasions. Of course, until the cholera ended, nothing could be done to order the inheritance. Even so the prince now spoke of it directly to his co-heir and told him his own plans.

The legatees, said he, had been given to understand that they had been treated badly by their mother, but it would be easy to show the contrary. Anyway neither Ferdinando nor Chiara had listened to these whispers, and Lucrezia would soon be convinced she was wrong. And so, for love of peace, to make it all clear, although there was still plenty of time for paying their sisters, would it not be better to get that weight off their shoulders as soon as possible? They would need to save a little to put together the sixteen thousand *onze* needed, for if ten thousand was due to Lucrezia, Chiara was to have only six after the subtraction of the four 'paid' when she married. First, however, creditors must be paid and all put in the clear. And meanwhile they could both gain time and make their own arrangements about the division. Raimondo found nothing to object to in any of these arguments of his brother. 'Fine, fine,' was his reply.

Amid this peace suddenly one day appeared Don Blasco from Nicolosi, astride a huge Pantellerìa donkey. Since his escape with the other monks he had not put a nose outside in the first weeks for fear of catching cholera from the air he breathed. But seeing men and animals flourishing in the countryside he felt reassured about the danger of contagion, and when he finally heard of all the fun going on at the Belvedere, he longed to get on the move. He arrived between luncheon and dinner, announced by loud yells as no-one opened the gates. On seeing the young prince coming towards him carrying a riding-crop that terrified his mount, he yelled at the boy as if wanting to eat him alive, 'Stand still now, devil take you!' And he finally entered the villa exclaiming, 'Isn't there anyone here? . . Where are you all? . . .' To the prince, who tried to kiss his hand, he spat out, 'Drop all that nonsense now . . .' and without greeting anyone took him by a button on his coat, drew him aside and asked point-blank:

'Is it true that your brother is gambling away the shirt on his back? How can you allow such a thing?'

'Does Your Excellency not know Raimondo?' replied the prince with a shrug. 'Who can say a word to him? Why does Your Excellency not try and persuade him? . . .'

'Me? Me, eh?—I don't care a cabbage for him or any of the others! This is the result of the upbringing he was given! And what about that other good-for-nothing, his wife? Scratching at her stomach all day, what? And your sister? And those madmen? And your son? . . .'

He spared no-one. Chiara's and the marchese's chatter about baby clothes for the new birth put him in a huff, the news about the Giulente infuriated him; but what really sent him into a frenzy was reading the Catania newspaper brought up by the

165

Prince of Roccasciano in the afternoon, when the first visitors began arriving. Immediately after the cholera bulletin, came:

' It was to be foreseen that our chief patricians would be generous in such calamitous times and come to the help of the unfortunate. The most illustrious Don Gaspare Uzeda, Duke of Oragua, though far away from his fellow-citizens, has sent our senate the sum of 100 ducats to be distributed in help of the most needy . . .'

' A hundred ducats thrown away to help the needy?' shrieked Don Blasco. ' To buy himself popularity rather! A hundred ducats thrown into the sea! It's not as if the swine had money to squander! With all this generosity one fine day he'll find himself on the rocks, as he deserves for his stupidity! Pig, swine, three times swine!' So beside himself was the monk that when Roccasciano asked for news of his nephew Don Lodovico, he turned on him like a fury:

' What's all this nephew stuff? I deny all knowledge of him! I deny the lot of you!' And taking the other one also by a coat button, he shouted in his ear, ' D'you see what they're up to? . . . Not three months since they lost their mother and now they're gadding about without a thought in the world . . .'

Some days later came a visit from the Prior. He arrived in a carriage, rested and serene. He greeted and embraced all, asked to visit the room where the princess had died, talked of the pestilence and attributed it to the Lord's concern at the wickedness of the times. All complained of the stubborn drought, for in three months of torrid summer not a drop of water had fallen. He said that he had arranged for a triduum and procession at Nicolosi to beg for rain, and advised them to do the same at the Belvedere.

' One must never tire of begging the Almighty. Only prayer and penance can induce the Divine Clemency to forgive sinners.'

Then he announced that their cousin Radalì had written to tell him that as soon as the cholera was over she wanted to put her second son Giovannino in the novitiate; a praiseworthy arrangement, as with her husband in that state the poor duchess could not see to the education of both her sons. The prince said that he might do the same with Consalvo. The princess

166

lowered her eyes to the ground, not daring to reply but unable to endure the thought of separation from her child.

So uncle and nephew resumed their visits, each on his own and on different days, like cat and dog incapable of being together. But all realised that the fault was Don Blasco's; Don Lodovico, with his angelic nature, would ask for nothing better than to make peace, but the other could not forgive him yet for his assumption of the office of prior. Anyway the schism was unpleasant; family friends, familiars of the monastery, spoke of it with sorrow. Fra' Carmelo did not mention it at all when he also came up to visit the princess and bring her the first walnuts and chestnuts. He did not want to talk of the ill-feeling between uncle and nephew from love of the monastery's good name and respect for the monks who, in his judgement, were all equally good and fine men; but particularly from his veneration for the two Uzeda. These feelings of his included their whole family. When the princess, in exchange for the fruit he brought her, had a little meal set before him, the monk as he cleared the board would praise the nobility of the family, grandees second to none. And the princess liked him for his affectionate ways with little Consalvo, the caresses he gave him, the special little presents he brought him, and particularly because, when he described the novitiate of his uncles Don Lodovico and Don Blasco, he would say to the boy:

'Ah, there have been so many Uzeda at San Nicola! But we won't have Your Excellency! Your Excellency is an only son, and certainly won't be put into the monastery . . .'

All the relations, on the other hand, except for Chiara, who if she had a son would have sewn him to her skirts, agreed with the prince that it was good for the boy's education and instruction to send him away from home. Don Blasco, at his grand-nephew's little sallies and the princess's indulgence, would cry out, 'Now he's growing, the jackanapes! . . . He's not getting much education here! . . .' Donna Ferdinanda, though she considered all instruction to be unnecessary, yet recognised too that to put the boy in a noble institution would accord with family tradition; both the Cutelli college and the Benedictine novitiate had seen many of those ancestors she read about, whose stories she told her nephew. When Consalvo was tired of bothering the servants and animals, he would come to see his aunt and say: 'Auntie, can we have a look at the " escutcheons "?'

The ' escutcheons ' were the work of Mugnòs, illustrated with the coats-of-arms of families mentioned in the text; and Donna Ferdinanda would spend entire days reading this out and commenting on it to her nephew.

She had already put him through a little course of heraldic grammar, and explained what was meant by *per pale* and *per fess*, by *quartering* and by *inescutcheon,* and she would always put a knobbly finger on the branch ho!ding the Uzeda family shield, describing it to him each time so that he would learn it by heart.

' Quarterly, first and fourth or and eagle sable, langued and armed gules, impaling fusilly azure and argent; second and third per fess azure and sable, in chief a comet argent, in base a chevron or; on an inescutcheon or four pallets gules, for Aragon. Behind the shield six banners of alliance.'

Then she explained the symbolism. The comet meant fame or glory; the chevron represented a knight's spurs. The small shield in the middle of the big one was that of the Aragonese Kings; the Uzeda had obtained a right to it, a pale at a time, the first pale at the time of Don Blasco II.

' Having served,' the spinster read out ' at the request of King Don Jaime, in the war being waged against Count Uguetto of Narbonne and against the Moors for possession of Majorca, he received no reward of any kind for his services, and so withdrew from the Royal Service and returned with his men to his own estates; there he heard that the King was sending a great sum of money to the Queen; so with 200 knights he lay in wait in a narrow pass, seized the royal baggage wagons, and took the money and whatever else they bore; then he sent a message to the King that his first obligation was to pay for personal services, then to satisfy the Queen's wishes; but the King, much incensed at this action, waged a great war against Blasco, which was peacefully settled by the intervention of many barons; he obtained the barony of Almeira, as well as the privilege of superimposing on his Arms a pale gules of Aragon.' The spinster loved reading out that story, and after reading it would repeat it to her nephew in simpler language, so that he could get the sense better. 'A fine King, he was, eh? Making use of his barons and then not giving them a thing! But Don Blasco Uzeda's idea was a grand one, wasn't it? " Oho, so you're not giving me a thing after I've fought for you, and sending presents to the Queen instead, eh? I'll just see to that!" . . .' Her voice trembled with excitement as she repeated the story of the ambush, and her eyes flashed with the centuries' old cupidity of the ancient Spanish race, the Viceroys who had despoiled Sicily.

'What about the other pales on the shield?' asked the little prince, who was hanging on his aunt's lips even more than if she were telling fairy-tales from *Betta pelosa* or *Mamma Draga*.

The old woman quickly turned over the pages of the book, and found the passage she wanted.

'Because of this it happened that the aforesaid Consalvo de Uzeda, being an excellent huntsman, was invited by King Carlo to go ahunting in his woods, which invitation was accepted by Consalvo; and while everyone including the King himself were endeavouring to pursue deer, boar and hare, the King attacked a big boar all alone; craftily it turned on him, but the King's horse rushed at it wildly, and as it passed fell to the ground with the King, who remained with a leg under the horse; seeing this the boar rushed on the King to kill him, and the Monarch would have been unable to defend himself, having only a dagger, and would undoubtedly have been killed on the spot, had not the said Consalvo noticed his King's danger and hastened to his assistance; at the first onslaught he killed the boar; then he got off his horse and helped the King to mount his own horse; and the King thanked him, praised him, and called him " My good son!" which was why ever afterwards the Uzeda had the title of " relatives " to the Sicilian kings, and bore on their escutcheon the Royal Arms of Aragon and all its powers, as in effect to this very day they explain to the present author, and as also says the chronicler of Madrid : " *Los feruicios de los Vzedas fveron tantos, y tan buenos que por merced de los Reyes de Aragona hazian la mefmas armas que ellos . . .*" '

Once Donna Ferdinanda had started on this, there was no stopping her. She had never had a more attentive audience than the boy, and that made her affectionate to him, as her other relatives would only listen distractedly, either thinking of nothing but their own 'silly business', or working away to dim the family splendour like that fox the duke flirting with republicans, like that crazy Lucrezia for ever out on her balcony waiting for Giulente to pass . . .

Don Eugenio, when not working at his memorandum on the disinterment of his new Pompeii, was the only one to listen to the reading of Mugnòs, and also 'other historians of the family'. Then brother and sister would pass in review their long line of ancestors, and recite tales of their deeds and of their efforts, centuries ago, to seize and maintain fortunes; the betrayals, rebellions, terrorism, never-ending quarrels, described by the writers in veiled ways, and all made to sound magnificent. Artale di Uzeda 'daily issuing with his armed retainers from his castle dominating the whole countryside around'; Giacomo, living in the time of King Lodovico, and 'ruling Nicosia, was eventually removed for the many taxes he imposed'; Don Ferrante, 'nicknamed *Sconza,* which in Sicilian dialect means the same as "Ruined"', who lost all his estates 'due to disobedience to his King. Later he obtained a pardon, but even so did not remain loyal, since for his own reasons he disobeyed the King once again, was condemned to death and saved his head only by Royal Grace and Favour.' Don Filippo was celebrated 'for showing such valour in support of his King, Don Ferdinando, against the King of Portugal, that on banishment from Court for murder he was freed and taken back into the Favour of his King'; Giacomo V, 'having sold his estates to Errico di Chiaramonte, then attempted to recover them by force'; Don Livio, 'delighted in taking harsh revenge for insults offered him'; etc., etc. Such, for Donna Ferdinanda, were deeds of valour and proofs of shrewdness. Nor had the Uzeda quarrelled only with their sovereigns and rivals, but also among themselves. Don Giuseppe, in 1684, 'married Donna Aldonza Alcarosso, by whom he had Don Giovanni and Don Errico, who on their father's death before their grandfather claimed the latter's estates and sued him for many years before the Royal Courts'; Don Paolo 'had long and most criminal contests with his stepfather'; Consalvo, Conte della Venerata 'at the death of his father was despoiled by his uncle, and on repudiating his infertile wife quarrelled for many years with his brother-in-law'; Giacomo VI, 'nicknamed *Sciarra*, which means Quarrel in Tuscan idiom, had many a difference with his father'; Consalvo III, 'nicknamed Head of St John the Baptist, suffered for the crime of his sons who followed Frederigo Count of Luna, bastard of King Martin'; but most terrible of all was the first Viceroy, the great Lopez Ximenes 'who lost the esteem of his subjects because of the excesses of a bastard son of overbearing ways and loose habits; his father, on finding him to be an incorrigible criminal, treated him with the greatest severity and condemned him to death, a sentence which would have been carried out had King Don Ferdinando, who happened to be in Sicily, not ordered it to be suspended . . .'

Now and again Don Eugenio considered it proper to make some moral comments for the boy's edification. Donna Ferdinanda, on the other hand, praised all, admired all. In time the aggressive race had been weakened by exercise of power; the second Viceroy, challenged to a duel by a rebel baron, 'prudently refused to listen to the invitation of that ill-advised young man'. The shameful conduct of this ancestor was found as praiseworthy by the old spinster as that of all the others who had quarrelled with everyone within sight for no reason. And as to duels, what about that famous decree of Lopez Ximenes?

'He had put out proclamation after proclamation to forbid duels,' narrated the spinster to her little nephew, 'but he might have been speaking to the wall. No one took any notice! Oh, so they won't, eh? Then he gets a notion; he waits for the very next duel, which happened to be between Arrigo Ventimiglia Count of Geraci and Pietro Cardona Count of Golisano, and confiscated all their property; he took the lot away from them, d'you understand?'

'And who got it?'

'It went back to the King,' explained Don Eugenio, 'but then matters were arranged. Ventimiglia left the kingdom and Cardona presented the Viceroy with his castle at La Roccella, to obtain pardon . . .'

So many such 'notions' did the Viceroy have that he got himself loathed by all. So much so that Parliament sent deputations to Spain for the Sovereign to remove him. That was done by envious and rascally barons—in the spinster's eyes—but he was cleverer than the lot of them, for what did he do? He offered the King a gift of thirty thousand *scudi* and so remained at his post; not, however, for long. Obviously he was so unpopular because he was much richer and nobler and more powerful than others. Before that there had been many other governors of Sicily taking the King's place, but they were Presidents of the Kingdom, or Viceroys without full powers, and had to consult His Majesty before electing anyone to the offices of Chief Justice or High Admiral or Grand Seneschal . . . And they were unable to grant estates to nobles or burgesses with a larger income than two hundred Castilian *onze*, or sums of money superior to two thousand Florentine florins. They were also forbidden to nominate Governors of Palermo, Catania, Mozia, Malta, etc., etc.; while Uzeda exercised the very same powers as the King, being able, as his mandate said, 'to emanate lasting decrees *at his pleasure*, condone death sentences, confer dignities, to do *all that the King himself would have done*, carry out all actions *reserved to the supreme power and to the Royal dignity*, for which he would otherwise have to acquire *special* or *very special* permission . . .' So who could be compared to him? What had they to envy the noblest families of Naples and Spain? Why, they even gloried in a saint in heaven : the Blessed Ximena. She had lived three and a half centuries before. Married off by her father against her will to the Count Guagliardetto, a terrible enemy of God and man, she had obtained her guilty husband's conversion and done great miracles during her life and after her death; her body, miraculously incorrupt, was preserved in a chapel of the Capuchin Church! And turning over the leaves to see the other escutcheons, those of the Radalì, of the Torriani, the boy asked his aunt why his Aunt Palmi's was not there; at which the spinster replied dryly :

'The printer forgot to put it in; but it's this : her father, with a spade in his hand, planting a palm-shoot . . .'

Towards the end of September the cholera intensified. The bulletin of the 25th named thirty deaths, but there were said to be more and over a hundred cases of infection as well as scattered cases disturbing the countryside. Now came a new onrush of people escaping. Up at the Belvedere vigilance was continuous lest refugees enter from places under suspicion. Peasants and villagers, armed with shotguns, carbines and pistols, guarded all roads leading to the village, acting as a kind of arbitrary unnamed police; and as scenes, part-comic and part-tragic, took place at every passage of refugees, Raimondo, to overcome his boredom—now that gambling was suspended because of the new terror—would often wander among the guard-posts. One day news came that there were people with cholera at Màscali, and carriages and carts coming from there were not allowed to pass. While the men of the Belvedere were calling about-turn with muskets at the ready and the emigrants were arguing, showing certificates and imploring, threatening and shouting, Raimondo, who was enjoying all this, suddenly heard himself called, ' Don Raimondo . . . Count! Count! . . .' and looking around, he saw two women making desperate signs to him from the door of a dusty carriage.

' Donna Clorinda! . . . you here?'

Donna Clorinda was the widow of the notary Limarra. She was famous for her gay life in youth, and, now this was near its end, for the beauty of her daughter Agatina who, following in her mother's footsteps, had flirted in her girlhood with all the young men rubbing up against her skirts; later she married the barrister Galano, for whom she got all kinds of clients. Donna Clorinda had a weakness for young men of the nobility, and more than ten years before had been Raimondo's first conquest. On leaving the mother he had made up to the daughter, without much result actually as she was then searching for a husband. Then he himself had married, left Sicily, and lost sight of them. Now the two women, and also the husband, crouching more dead than alive in the depths of the carriage, put themselves under his protection to obtain refuge at the Belvedere. Thanks to him, they were allowed to enter; their difficulties began immediately afterwards, for, with refugees invading every corner, there was nowhere but the stables to put new arrivals.

Nevertheless, for Donna Clorinda and Agatina, who met a new friend at every step, the whole Belvedere was set into motion until they were found two little rooms on a ground floor, a little out of the way, but with a small garden. As soon as they were settled in, they arranged one of those little rooms as a drawing-room, and there at once began a coming and going of all those from town, in a flutter at this arrival.

Donna Clorinda had not yet given up, and granted audience to all and sundry; but the place next to her daughter was reserved for Raimondo. Because of the freedom of the little household and the good humour of the two women, even those left penniless spent a better evening than at the Casino, playing cards, gossiping, and singing. And Raimondo put off his boredom and long face and no longer came home; once again he was awaited hour upon hour by his wife, sad and restless at the renewed danger of plague, at the suspicions evoked in her by that sudden change, and tortured later by the allusions with which Donna Ferdinanda, the prince, even the servants revealed her husband's old love. Could she believe in a new intrigue now with the daughter of his former mistress? Was that not a mortal sin, a monstrosity which her mind refused to conceive? Should she not believe, rather, that the family's grudge against Raimondo and herself had started this malicious accusation?

Brusquely torn from her peace, she began to torture herself once more, to struggle with herself against the suspicions which re-assailed her as soon as they were brushed off, to spend the long autumn nights trembling as she awaited his return, weeping at his rough answers to her questions.

'Why d'you stay out so late? I'm afraid for your health . . .'

'Aren't I free any longer to stay out as long as I like?'

'Indeed you're free . . . but not to go to that house, among people whom your brother is ashamed to receive.'

'Where do I go? Among what people? It's to the Casino I go. D'you want to spy over me too?'

No, she believed him; she wanted and had to believe him. But why was she so conscious of part-ironical and part-pitying looks from all the family and servants? Why did the conversation die in people's mouths when she drew near them?

One night, after four months of drought, a terrible storm broke out; the dark sky was seared by flashes like swords, the roads suddenly changed into muddy torrents, the hail crashed on panes and roofs. She had hoped to see Raimondo return at the first signs of the storm, and awaited him trembling with fear. Not a sound, not a footstep. The storm stopped after an hour, and Raimondo was not yet back . . . It was not the malice of others, it was he himself who was lying and incestuous; could she doubt it any longer? Had not she too, that shameless creature, stared her challengingly in the face as if saying to her, 'I'm prettier than you, that's why he prefers me! . . .' And it was true. Her jealousy was all the more humiliating as she realised that she no longer attracted her husband, particularly now she was also deformed by pregnancy. But was he really trying to kill off the creature she bore in her womb by inflicting torture after torture on her, by leaving her thus on a dark tempestuous night, with horror at his new sin, at his new betrayal, with her soul all pain and shame and terror? . . . He returned at midnight, soaked, his clothes as muddy as if he'd been rolling in the ditch.

'Holy Mary! . . .' she exclaimed, wringing her hands. 'How did you get in that state?'

'It was raining. Are you deaf? Didn't you hear water?'

'But the rain's been over some time . . .'

'I got soaked before . . .' he almost yelled. 'Must I listen to you now too?'

Suddenly she felt her own suspicions confirmed; he replied like that and reacted violently to reason when caught in the wrong; then he cut off discussion with shouts . . . Leaning her forehead against a pane of glass on which a fine drizzle was now drawing damp lines, she began silently to weep. Then the love she had for him, the obedience she showed him, the submissive devotion she gave proof of every day, were not enough. All was useless! He escaped from her, betrayed her, for whom? And he had made her leave her own child, exposed her to her father's rebukes for this! . . . for this! One sorrow after the other, always, always, even now when she should have been sacred to him because such agonies could kill the creature about to be born!

Raimondo's voice, hoarsely calling for his valet, suddenly aroused her the following dawn. He had gone to bed; his teeth were chattering with fever. Then she dried her tears and rushed to his help. For three days she never left his bedside a moment, acted as nurse and maid, forgetting her own anguished state from terror lest that illness should turn into pestilence, remaining alone with him when the family, suspicious, refused, any of them, to enter the room again. Trembling at the idea of contagion, they were all afraid of catching it, Raimondo more than any, in spite of the doctor's comforting laughs, in spite of her assurances.

On recovering from his chill he had nothing else wrong with him, but before he was yet quite set up he wanted to go out.

'Please, for our sakes!' implored Matilde, clasping her hands, 'for our daughter! Do not expose yourself to another germ . . .'

She had not said anything to him about her suspicions so as not to irritate him while he was ill, but now she threw her arms around his neck and said to him, looking him in the eyes and passing a hand over his hair:

'Where do you want to go? Why leave me? Stay with me!'

'I want to take a little walk; I feel quite well . . .' he replied, touched by those caresses, by that submission like a faithful dog's.

'We'll take one together in the vineyard . . . there's no need to go outside . . . if it's true that you love me, me alone . . . and don't think of others . . .'

'Who should I be thinking of? . . .' exclaimed Raimondo, with a fatuous smile.

'Of no other woman, none at all . . . not even of her?'

'Who d'you mean?'

'The Galano girl? . . .' the name burnt her lips.

'Me?' replied he in a tone of protest. 'I wouldn't dream of it! . . . Whoever put such ideas into your head, I wonder!'

'No one. I fear them, because I love you, because I'm jealous . . .'

He laughed heartily, and reassured her.

'But no, what ideas you get hold of! . . . and then, little Agatina . . . A girl who goes with anyone who wants her! . . .'

'Is that true? Is that true? . . . then why d'you visit her?'

'I visit her because it amuses me, it's like going to the café or the club . . .'

'What about that night you caught your chill?'

' I got soaked because the rain caught me at La Ravanusa. You can ask anyone, if you don't believe me!'

Yes, she would have believed him had the gentleness with which he treated her not been a new undeniable proof that he had done something to be forgiven . . . Well, what did it matter if that was the reason? Whatever the feeling which dictated those words to him they were good words, they took away her anguish, at least for a time. And with a mind reopening to hope, she heard him suggest:

' Anyway, now the cholera's nearly over, we'll all be leaving. When I've arranged this division with Giacomo we'll return to Florence. But for now, if you like, we can make a trip to Milazzo. Your child can be born at your own home. How'd you like that?'

6

'*Abbas! Abbas!* . . .' said the lay-brother porter with a bow.

'What does that mean?' Consalvo asked his uncle the Prior, who was leading him along by the hand.

'It means that the Abbot is in the monastery,' explained His Paternity.

Up the great staircase, all marble, the boy looked at walls hung with huge bas-reliefs of white stucco on a pale-blue ground; Saint Nicholas of Bari, the martyrdom of San Placido, the Baptism of the Redeemer, surrounded by swarms of angels, crowns, swags and palm branches, all over the ceiling. The stairs led on to the east corridor, before great windows opening on to the terrace of the first cloister.

'There he is,' said the Prior, bowing towards a black shadow passing behind the glass.

From outside the Abbot brought his face close up to the window, and on recognising the visitors exclaimed with a wave:

'Open, open up, Ludovì . . .'

The Prior turned the sash-bolt, then took his superior's hand and gave it a respectful kiss; the prince and his son followed this example.

'Blessings on you, my children, blessings on you! . . . So here's our little monk then, is it? Ah yes, a fine little monk we hope to make of him! . . . Consalvo, eh?' he turned to the prince, then back to the boy. 'Consalvo, are you pleased to be with us, eh? . . .'

'Answer . . . answer His Paternity.'

Looking him in the face, the boy said:

'Yes.'

'That's right! . . . what a handsome lad . . . what eyes . . . you'll stay here with your uncle and grow up good and holy like him, what, eh? . . .' and he put an affable hand on the Prior's shoulders, who murmured with a blush:

'Abbot!'

The latter moved off, leaning on his stick, the Prior on his right, the prince on his left. Consalvo went to the grille and stared down into the cloister. This was surrounded by an arcade supporting a terrace full of statues, and had basins of tinkling water, seats set amid symmetrical flower-beds, and a pavilion in the middle of Gothic style, with four arches, its roof of gleaming tiles mirroring the sun. The boy was still staring curiously round when his father called him. The group moved towards the Abbot's apartment, next door to the Royal one in the southern corridor, where the doors were surmounted by great pictures representing lives of saints. On reaching his door the Abbot gave some orders to his servant, then all moved towards the Novitiate, through the Clock corridor more than two hundred yards long, so that the great window at the end looked small as a bull's-eye. First they passed through the second cloister, which had an arcade up to the first floor with a terrace above like the other. That too was cultivated; on it grew a grove of oranges and dark-leaved cedars against which the golden fruit stood out. Then they passed the Night Choir with another staircase rising from it, then the clock; and still the corridor went on. Between the prince and the Prior the Abbot was chatting away volubly, scattering his sentences with 'what, eh? . . .'—syllables which apparently required no reply. The monks they met stopped three paces before the group, bowing heads and folding hands across their breasts as their superiors passed. At the door to the Novitiate stood Fra' Carmelo, who on seeing the boy opened both arms with a joyous air and exclaimed:

'You've come . . . you've come!'

Father Raffaele Cùrcuma, novice master, approached the Abbot then led them to the classroom where the boys were all gathered, among them Giovannino Radalì, who had been in San Nicola for six months.

'Here's our new little monk,' explained His Paternity, 'embrace your cousin now! . . . Your room is ready, we'll be going there in a minute. Now you put aside your old name, and we call you Serafino. Your little cousin is Angelico, isn't he? And this is Placido, and this Luigi . . .'

Meanwhile arrived two lackeys bearing trays full of cakes, greeted with cries of delight by the novices.

' You'll see how nice it is here,' said the novice master to the new arrival, stroking him. ' You'll have all these companions to play with . . .'

Consalvo bowed his head and let them have their say. Now the curiosity of the first moments had passed he felt a longing to cry, but in spite of this he looked everyone in the face almost challengingly, so as not to appear defeated before his father, who had been determined to thrust him in there. Fra' Carmelo was amazed by his mien; all other boys on their first day there had red eyes, said they did not want to stay and were sure to sob when the barber cut off their hair and when they laid aside lay clothes for black habits. Instead of this the young prince, when his father left after a final admonition, let them do whatever they liked, watched his hair fall under the scissors without a word, put on a habit as if he had worn it from birth.

' That's the way ! . . . Always content like this ! . . . You'll just see what games and fun . . .'

The boy answered harshly :

' I am Prince of Francalanza, I won't be here for ever.'

' For ever? Who said such a thing? . . . You'll be here a year or two until you're learned. It's your uncles are here for ever . . . now, now, we will go to visit Father Don Blasco . . .'

And taking him by the hand he led him back the way they had come as far as the Deacon's room in the southern corridor, with a picture of St John of the Golden Mouth over the door.

' *Deo gratias?* . . .'

' Who's there?' replied the monk's loud voice.

The door opened a little and he appeared in trousers and shirt-sleeves, with a pipe in his mouth, standing in a room as messy as a worked field.

' Here is Your Paternity's young nephew, come to kiss Your Paternity's hand.'

' Ah, so you're here, are you? . . .' exclaimed the monk, wiping his lips with the back of a hand. ' Good, very glad !'

he added without touching him. Then he turned to the lay-brother and said, ' Take him out into the monks' garden, will you?'

After bewailing his grand-nephew's ignorance and uncouthness the monk had been furious when the prince decided to put him in San Nicola. So they were putting him there to educate him, were they? That meant that they weren't capable of educating him at home! Wasn't he right, then, in saying they gave the boy a fine example? But Giacomo also wanted to put his son in San Nicola to study. As if the Uzeda had ever known more than to sign their names! Was it so difficult to find a tutor if they were so determined to turn him into a literary man? Schoolmasters, though, have to be paid something, big or small, and the only real reason for the decision was to save money, for not only did they pay nothing at the Benedictines', but the families of students even made something from it!

The rooms of the Novitiate opened on to a garden set aside for the boys' amusement. It was full of flowers and fruit-trees, orange, lemon, mandarin, apricot, Japanese medlars, and in the morning novices were awakened by a great fluttering of sparrows, even before Fra' Carmelo came to call them for their devotions in the chapel. After prayers they all returned to their rooms, had a frugal breakfast because luncheon was at midday, and went through their lessons so as to be ready for the arrival of masters who taught them Italian, Latin, and arithmetic, and on Sundays calligraphy and plain chant. At the third hour, after lessons, came Mass, which they attended in the church. This was the biggest in Sicily, all marble and stucco, white and light with its dome piercing the sky, and Donato del Piano's organ which had taken thirteen years to make and cost ten thousand *onze*.

Immediately after Mass the novices went to the refectory, sometimes to the big one together with the Fathers, sometimes by themselves in a smaller one as the Rule prescribed; recreation began later, after their meal, when they scattered in the gardens, where they would play at hide-and-seek, skittles, or castles, or garden and each tend his own tree, or send up kites and balloons. Beyond the surrounding wall stretched uncultivated land, all lava and scrub, as far as the Flora, the big garden set aside for the monks' recreation. The boys would sometimes go there to run up and down the great alleys, and the young prince, who had quickly got into the monastery ways and was the liveliest of the lot, would often clamber on to the wall, try to climb over it and get into the wilds. But then he would be warned by the monk in charge and by Fra' Carmelo.

' Don't pass there . . . don't risk the other side, or the spirits will lay hands on you; if they get you they'll take you away with them . . .'

' Have you seen these spirits?' Consalvo once asked Giovannino Radalì.

' No, I haven't; they come at night, they say.'

At night they could not look there because after their evening walk down in the town, they went in after supper for evening studies and prayers.

Fra' Carmelo kept them company, saw they had all they wanted, and when there was nothing to do amused them by telling stories of former novices who were now either choir-monks or back home; or by repeating old tales such as the famous theft of wax during the Night of the Holy Nail; or of the 1848 Revolution when San Nicola had served as headquarters for Mieroslawski; or the coming of King Ferdinand and his Queen in 1834. But he was at his most expansive on things to do with the monastery.

It was not quite certain who had founded it at the very beginning, but in 1136 some devout Benedictine monks had withdrawn to meditate and do penance in the Etna woods, and there with the help of Count Errico they had built the first monastery of San Leo. San Leo was one of the many extinct craters of the Mongibello, covered with woods and mantled with snow for six months of the year; a true solitude adapted to their holy purposes.

In winter the north wind whistled round their poor hut, cut into their faces, chapped their hands, froze everything; so severe was it that many of the monks caught serious illnesses, being unable to stand up to such rigours. And so permission had been got to send the sick ones lower down, to a hospice built in the wood of San Nicola; and there, as it was less uncomfortable, some of the healthy monks also began to go. At San Leo, on top of the cold came another trial when the mountain erupted,

182

vomiting fire and burning cinders; earthquakes shook the building, lava destroyed trees and dried up wells, red-hot cinders burnt up every bit of green. 'How could the poor Fathers endure so many disasters?' Meditation was all very well, but when the ground itself began dancing a tarantella, how could they concentrate and pray? Penance was even better, but with such mortifications penitents might go straight to the next world before getting a chance to purge their sins. In consequence they decided to ask permission to settle definitely at San Nicola, around which soon grew a village called Nicolosi, after the saint. There a monastery was built with more space, bigger than the old one, and there for many years the monks stayed.

Nicolosi was no joke either though. The snow may not have lain for six months, but it fell thick in winter, and the cold was still piercing, so much so that sick monks had to be sent to another infirmary built lower down, at the gates of Catania. The countryside was also infested by robbers. Of course the monks, with their vow of poverty, should not have feared them, for 'not a hundred thieves', says the proverb, 'can despoil a naked man'. But kings, queens, viceroys and barons had begun to make gifts to the monastery, and soon there were so many legacies that the monks found themselves possessed of a large fortune. Now were all those riches to be left to the mice to enjoy? And so in 1550 the Benedictines decided to establish themselves in the city, and laid the foundation stone of a superb building in the presence of the Viceroy Medinaceli.

Some suggested that St Benedict must be suffering agonies at his sons leaving the woods and coming to settle like gentry in the city, but this was surely belied by the fact that when the monastery was finished it was preserved by the glorious founder of the Order from the volcano's fire; the lava from Monti Rossi, which had got as far as Catania and was moving straight towards the monastery, on reaching the façade turned west and plunged straight into the sea without doing it any harm. It is true that an earthquake in 1693 razed the building to the ground, but this punishment was inflicted not only on the monks but on half Sicily as well, which collapsed like a house of cards. So finally the buildings to be admired now were begun, on plans too grandiose to be carried out completely; by 1735 only half was done. The wealth of the monks was then at its height: seventy thousand *onze* a year, and some of their estates were so vast that none had ever got round them!

When Fra' Carmelo talked of these things he would go on and on, for he had spent more than fifty years amid those walls, and loved the monks, the novices, the pictures in the church and the trees in the park as if they were all part of his own family. He knew their estates, lands, and farms better than all the country Procurators to each of whom was assigned only one property to look after, and if something had to be remembered such as the date of a distant event or the extent of an old crop, everyone would have recourse to him.

The young prince was now his great joy; he kept him by as much as he could, gave him sweets and toys, praised him to the Abbot, to the master of the novices, to his uncles and to all. The boy was in truth rather too lively, apt to bully his companions and quarrel with them. Fra' Carmelo, ever patient and indulgent, would excuse him with the novice master if he committed some little fault, and recommend forbearance to other lay-brothers if they had to pay the penalty for these escapades.

' One must let them be, these lads. Remember they're gentry, and it's for us to obey them.'

The lay-brothers, in fact, were there to do the heavy work. They served the Fathers in the refectory and ate at a second sitting, and when the monks said office in Choir they only recited the Rosary in a corner. Those who entered into the novitiate and became monks had to be noble, and Fra' Carmelo, as enthusiastic about such matters as Donna Ferdinanda, would exult over all the nobility at San Nicola. There in fact were members of the leading families, not only in the Val di Noto but the whole of Sicily, because in the rest of Sicily there was only one other monastery of Cassinese monks, at Palermo, and that was so inferior in size, wealth and importance that re-calcitrant monks were sent there from Catania as a punishment. The Abbot was a Neapolitan grandee, second son of the Duke of Cosenzano; Father Borgia, a Roman, of the family which had given a Pope to Christendom, had come from Monte Cassino; and then among islanders there were the Gerbini, descended from King Manfred in the female line; the Salvo, who had come to Sicily with the Swabians; the Toledo, the Requense, the Melina, the Currera, of Spanish origin like the Uzeda; the Cùrcuma and the Sangonti, of Lombard nobility; the Grazzeri, who had come from Germany; the Corvitini, who were Flemish; the Carvano, the Costante, who were French; and the Emanuele, who belonged to a branch of the Paleologhi, Emperors of the East.

'Just being with the Benedictines, as monk or novice, means a man's noble,' explained Don Carmelo to the young prince. 'Here only enter those from top families like Your Paternity.'

The boys were called 'Your Paternity', and 'Don' like the monks, and every time that a Father or a novice passed in front of lay-brothers the latter were supposed to bow very low with arms crossed on their chest; if they were sitting, to get to their feet in greeting. One of these lay-brothers, Fra' Liberato, who was very old, almost a centenarian and quite incapable by then, used to come out of his room to tremble in the sun on an arm-chair. One day the young prince passed by him and the old man did not get up. The boy reported this to the novice master, who gave the old lay-brother a great wigging.

'He's ga-ga, poor old boy,' said Fra' Carmelo in excuse. 'When we get old we're worse than when we were children!'

So Consalvo received the same lessons as those given him by Donna Ferdinanda, and absorbed far more easily than others those in Latin and arithmetic. They gave him an extraordinary idea of his own worth but also got him into trouble with his companions, particularly those older than himself, because of the contempt with which he treated them. Michele Rocca also gloried in having a Viceroy among his ancestors, but Consalvo corrected him, 'A Viceroy? Just a President of the King-dom! . . .' and when the other said, 'No, Viceroy . . .' Consalvo said, 'No, President . . .' until Michelino rushed at him in fury. Then, rather than come to blows, he shouted for help and Fra' Carmelo had to make up the quarrel. But he would start again with others, causing squabble after squabble.

Most of those baronial families had a nickname, often deroga-tory, by which they were better known in the city than by their own names. The Fiammona were called the *Kegs*, because they were gross as half-barrels; the San Bernardo the *Beaneaters*, an allusion to the poverty to which they were reduced; the Currera were called the *Scabby* because all had heads as bald as billiard-balls; the Salvo were called the *Saliva-eaters,* and others worse. The young prince, when short of insults, would yell to his companions, 'Oh, you *Bran-bellies*! . . . Oh, you *Pork-skins*! . . .' and they, being unable to give as good as they got, since the nickname of the Uzeda, 'the Viceroys', showed that family's former power, would jump on him when they could lay hold of him and give him a good hiding. Fra' Carmelo then rushed up with hands on high to free his protégé and preach peace, mutual love and attention to study.

During lessons, when he took the trouble to be attentive, Consalvo understood all and got praise and prizes, but there were no punishments anyway, for the masters, who were all priests of low-class origin, did not even dare call their pupils 'donkey'. The Prior, to show his satisfaction at the novice master's good reports, came to visit his nephew at the Novitiate sometimes, bringing presents of sweets and holy books; Don Blasco, in the refectory, gave him an occasional slap in sign of caress; and the first time Fra' Carmelo brought him to the palace on half-a-day's holiday, the whole family, all united for the occasion, made a great fuss of him.

'What a fine little monk! . . . what a fine little monk!'

The princess, sad at having him no longer with her but resigned as always to her husband's wishes, devoured him with kisses, embracing him the more tightly because of her repulsion for others; Donna Ferdinanda, who had come on purpose to the palace, was also full of caresses for him; Lucrezia, placated now that there was no danger of finding him in her room, gave him sweets and biscuits; the prince praised obedient children, though without laying aside his habitual severity. Don Eugenio made a speech about the benefits of education, and even his Uncle Ferdinando came down from the country to be present at this visit. Only his Aunt Chiara and the marchese were not there; sure they were about to have the son long-awaited and desired, one sad day they had found the pregnancy gone, and from that day were mourning for their lost hope. But there was a six-year-old girl who looked at the little monk with big, curious eyes, and a nurse holding a baby-in-arms.

'There are your cousins, Uncle Raimondo's daughters,' explained the princess.

'Where's Aunt Matilde?'

'She isn't very well . . .'

But Donna Ferdinanda cut short this empty talk and began questioning her young nephew about his companions, life in the monastery and how he spent his day, while Fra' Carmelo praised the boy to his mother.

'Would you like to be a monk?' asked the prince as a joke. 'And be in the monastery for always?'

'Yes,' replied he, so as to hold his end up. 'It's fine at San Nicola . . .'

The monks, in fact, had a high old time: eating, drinking, and amusing themselves. On getting up in the morning they each went to say their Mass down in the church, often behind closed doors so as not to be disturbed by the faithful. Then they withdrew to their apartments, to eat something while awaiting luncheon, at which, in kitchens as spacious as barracks, worked no fewer than eight cooks, apart from kitchen-hands. Every day the cooks got four loads of oak charcoal from Nicolosi to keep the ovens always hot, and for frying alone the kitchen Cellarer would consign to them every day four bladders of lard of two *rotoli* each, and two *cafissi* of oil; enough for six months at the prince's. The pots and pans were big enough to boil a whole calf's haunch and roast a swordfish complete; two kitchen-hands would each grasp half a great cheese and spend an hour grating it; the chopping-block was an oak trunk which no two men could get their arms round; and every week a carpenter, paid four *tarì* and half a barrel of wine for this service, had to saw off a couple of inches or it became unserviceable from so much chopping.

The Benedictines' kitchen had become a proverb in town. The macaroni pie with its crust of short pastry, the rice-balls each big as a melon, the stuffed olives and honey-cakes, were dishes which no other cook could make; and for their ices and fruit-drinks and frozen *cassate*, the Fathers had called specially from Naples, Don Tino, from the Benvenuto café. All this was made in such quantities that it was sent round as presents to monks' and novices' families, and the servitors would sell the remains and get four, and some six, *tarì* each for them daily.

The servitors looked after the monks' apartments, bore messages for them in town, accompanied them to Choir holding their cowls, served them in their rooms if their Paternities were unwell or did not feel like coming down to the refectory. There laybrothers served. At midday, when all were gathered in the vast hall with its frescoed ceiling, lit by twenty-four windows big as front doors, the Reader for the week would get up on the rostrum and begin mumbling at the first forkful of macaroni, after the *Benedicite*. The rota for reading went from the youngest novices to the oldest monks by order of age, but once it reached the newly-ordained it went back and began again in order to avoid the bother for the older Fathers, who sat comfortably at tables arranged along the walls above a kind of wide pavement. In the centre of the big horseshoe the Abbot had a table to himself. The lay-brothers took round the dishes, eight at a time, on a tray called a ' porter ' which they bore on their shoulders. There was a distinction between dinners and suppers, the latter composed of five courses, the former of seven on feastdays. And as a confused clatter of crockery and gurgling of drink and tinkling of silver rose from the tables, the Reader mumbled, from high on his rostrum, the Rule of St Benedict. '. . . 34th Commandment, be not proud; 35th, give not yourself to wine; 36th, eat not too much; 37th Commandment, sleep not too much; 38th Commandment, be not lazy . . .'

The Rule was actually read in Latin, but while the young prince and other novices were learning to understand it in that language, once a month this was explained in Italian translation. St Benedict, in the chapter on *Moderation in feeding*, had ordered that the daily meal should consist of no more than two cooked dishes and one pound of bread; ' If there is need of supper, the Cellarer is to reserve a third part of the said pound to give at supper.' But this was one of the many ' antiquities '— as Fra' Carmelo called them—of the Rule. Were Their Paternities to eat hard bread then? And at night the bread was a second baking's, smoking hot like that of the morning.

The Rule also said, ' All except the weak and infirm are to abstain from eating the flesh of four-footed animals ', but every day half a calf was bought as well as chickens, sausages, salami, and the rest. On abstinence days the head cook earmarked the best fish as soon as the catch was disembarked and before it reached the fish-market. In truth there were many other ' antiquities' in the Rule. St Benedict, for instance, made no distinction between noble Fathers and plebeian lay-brothers; he wanted all of them to do some manual work or other, he threatened monks and novices who did not carry out their duty with penance, excommunication and even beating. In fact he said a great deal of ' nonsense ', as Don Blasco defined it.

As to wine, the founder of the Order prescribed that a modicum every day was enough; ' but let it be said that those to whom God gives the grace of abstaining will receive particular recompense '. The cellars of San Nicola however were well provided and highly reputed, and if the monks drank deep they had good reason, for the wine from the vineyards of Cavaliere, Bordonaro, from the San Basile estate, would have roused the dead. Father Currera, known as one of the most valiant trenchermen, used to rise from table every day half-tipsy, and on returning to his apartment, give a shake at his heavy paunch, eyes gleaming behind gold-rimmed spectacles on his rubicund nose, and get down to a flask which he kept day and night under his bed in place of a chamber-pot.

The other monks would leave the monastery immediately after dinner and scatter around the neighbourhood among families, each of which had its Father protector. Father Gerbini, whose room was full of fans and sunshades given him by ladies to mend, began his round of visits. Father Galvagno went to the Baronessa Lisi, Father Broggi to the Signora Caldara, other monks to various other ladies and friends. They would return at Angelus time, and go into church. But those who came a little late or had a headache went straight up to their rooms; not to sleep however, for in the evening and until midnight, when the gates were locked, visits were made by relatives and friends, receptions were held, and many Fathers had games of cards. At one time, due to Father Agatino Renda, a great gambler, there had been very high play; in one evening alone Raimondo Uzeda lost 500 onze and more than one head of a family had been ruined; so much so that the superiors of the Order, after shutting an eye to many peccadilloes, had finally had to step in.

Then Father Francesco Cosenzano from Monte Cassino came as Abbot; and for a short time, with the authority of his new nomination and the help of the good monks—for there were some—the fine old man had managed to control the worst; then, as time went by, quietly and gradually the latter had returned to their former habits: gambling, tippling, populating the local district with their mistresses, getting their bastards into the monastery as lay-brothers (of the Fathers—a new kind of relationship). The Abbot's timid attempts at resistance now loosed a violent opposition against him. Don Blasco was one of the worst. He kept three women in the San Nicola district: Donna Concetta, Donna Rosa and Donna Lucia the Cigar-woman, with half a dozen children. And the Abbot let him be, in spite of the scandal of all his women and bastards coming to attend the same monk's Holy Mass. Every morning he would go down to the kitchen and order the best cuts to be sent off to his mistresses, and on abstinence days he stood at the gates waiting for the cook to arrive with the fish, of which he made his choice, ordering: 'Cut a piece off this *cernia* and take it to Donna Lucia!' And the Abbot let things be.

Then finally one day because of this woman things came to a head. The monastery owned a good half of the district immediately surrounding it; the three buildings in the semi-circular space in front of the church and a number of one-storey houses all around the walls. These buildings only yielded a meagre income, partly because they were let at special rents to old tradesmen or retired sacristans, and partly because some were granted free to the unfortunate, such as noble families fallen on evil days. Now Don Blasco with his very particular affection for Donna Lucia Garino, the Cigar-woman, had arranged for her to be granted a fine apartment in the southern-most building, with a shop beneath where her husband sold tobacco.

The Abbot, hearing that this Donna Lucia was neither indigent nor a noblewoman in decay, and that her only title for having the house while so many other wretches had nowhere to lay their heads was her scandalous friendship with Don Blasco, decided to order her either to pay a regular rent for the apartment and shop, or quit it.

Don Blasco, already so irritated by the moralistic behaviour of the new Abbot that he was only waiting for a chance to open fire, when told by his sobbing mistress, became like an animal but for holy baptism, and went shouting outrageously up and down the corridors of the monastery under the Deacons' noses and behind the Abbot's door, that whoever dared turn out the Cigar-woman or ask her for a cent would have him to deal with. Having cowed the still uncertain and hesitant opposition and gathered round him the scum of the monastery, the other recalcitrant monks, who bore ill their superior's austere warnings and the end of all their fun and games, he became not only the terror of the Chapter but its scourge. From love of peace the poor Abbot had to rescind his order, but the elder Uzeda was not placated by this, and wherever he could find a reason to stir up strife and complaints he gave his 'enemy' no rest. This was when the Abbot, in admiration for the austere habits and wisdom of Don Lodovico, had begun to protect him, even to sustain him for the office of Prior; so now Don Blasco, who had also had an eye on that post, coupled his nephew and his superior together in savage and inextinguishable hatred.

There had always been many differing groups at San Nicola; for, as there was a huge patrimony to administer, and great amounts of money to be dealt with, and large sums to be distributed in alms, and work to be given to many, and free houses as well as free places in the Novitiate to be granted, and in fact a notable influence to be exercised throughout the city and estates, each did his best to bring grist to his own mill; but at the time of the young prince's admission quarrels were daily and violent.

First of all the Abbot had his partisans, but not all the good monks were on his side for they did not like supreme power being in the hands of a *foreigner*. Don Blasco tried to draw these monks into his group, yelling that they must send home that 'macaroni-eating Neapolitan'; but although the opposition was agreed on that, it was divided again on the matter of a successor. And there was of course a party of those who declared they had no party. And Don Lodovico, a model of this kind, by keeping apart and doing some under-water navigation, had managed to obtain the office of Prior. Many maintained that after all he was the only one worthy of aspiring to the dignity of abbot, but his uncle, to avoid that 'slimy pig' placing the mitre on his head, almost came to support Abbot Cosenzano. Lodovico himself did not allow anyone to mention promotion; if anyone did, he would protest:

'At the moment His Paternity is Abbot, and I must obey him before all others.'

Then the Abbot in person, tired of the situation, confided to him that he wanted to retire and hand over office to him; even if he himself had not thought of retirement, said he, surely sooner or later death would think of it for him? At which the Prior exclaimed:

'Your Paternity must not talk of such things now! . . . They sadden the heart of a devoted son, Reverend Father.'

The old man then took him into his confidence and complained of the little respect the monks bore him, and the scandal that many still gave by their libertine lives. The Prior shook his head sorrowfully.

'Our glorious founder, the father of monks, teaches us the remedy against errors of those that stray: the prayer of the good, so that Our Lord, who can do all things, may give health back to our infirm brethren . . .'

And meanwhile he reproved no one, did nothing about the complaints which were often brought him, let each stew in his own juice. Among those thirty or so inmates there was never a moment of peace or agreement. If the question of personalities divided the monastery in one way, this grouping was thrown into confusion by politics, which brought monks together in quite different order. There were Liberals, those who had been for the provisional Government in '48, and given hospitality to the Revolution in the person of its soldiers; and there were the pro-Bourbons, whom the Liberals called 'rats'. Don Blasco captained the latter, among whom were many friends of the Prior; the Liberals, who on the questions of internal order were nearly all on the side of the actual Abbot (himself very pro-Bourbon), in politics obeyed the honorary Abbot Ramira, of 1848. So if the raised voices of monks were often heard cursing lay-brothers and sending waiters to hell, yells rose as soon as any discussion began on political events in the shade of the arcades or by the front gate.

Liberals and pro-Bourbons almost came to blows about the end of the Crimean War, the Congress of Paris, and the part played in these by Piedmont. Don Blasco was violent against that 'polenta-eating Piedmontese' Cavour, and covered him with insults, recalling the tale of the frog and the ox, and prophesying that he would burst from puffing himself up. He was even worse against the constitutional system which the Liberals so longed for, exclaiming that Ferdinand II's best action had been on the 15th of May, when he ordered a bayonet-attack on the 'buffoons and pimps' of Palazzo Gravina. When the Liberals said that they would get rid of the King again, he yelled:

'Send him away then if you can; I'd like to see you try, with those bellies of yours!'

When he heard praises of the young King of Sardinia he would raise his arms to his head and shake his hands like bats' wings in a gesture of desperate horror, 'Savoy passes! . . . Savoy passes! . . .' In 1713, when Victor Amedeo of Savoy, having assumed the crown of Sicily, came to the island in pomp and crossed it from end to end, the new sovereign's passage had been followed by one of the worst years for crops in living memory, and that saying: 'Savoy passes! Savoy passes!' had stuck in the minds of the terrified and poverty-stricken population as a proverb, a symptom of disaster, a scourge of God.

'And then, as if the first wasn't enough they wanted another of those in '48! To get us into a worse state than they are in Piedmont, where they're so down-and-out they despoil monasteries!'

There were political parties among the novices: Liberals, revolutionaries, Piedmontese; and pro-Bourbons, Neapolitans, 'rats'; but though the two camps were almost equally divided there the Liberals were in a majority.

'They're all down-and-outs,' explained Don Blasco to the young prince, 'who haven't enough to eat at home, and despise the good things God sends and all these lovely *lasagne* dropping all ready-cooked into their mouths!'

This was not at all true, for the Liberal novices were captained by Giovannino Radalì-Uzeda, who belonged to a family that in nobility and wealth came immediately after the Uzeda

193

of the direct line; although a second son, had he remained a lay-man he would have the life title of baron. But the young prince followed the opinions of his uncle Don Blasco and his aunt Donna Ferdinanda; though a friend and gambling companion of his cousin he was an adversary in politics, and when the revolutionaries spoke among themselves, when they plotted to raise the convent and issue forth with a tricolour paper flag, he would watch out and question the most ingenuous and then repeat what he learnt to his uncle to be passed on to the Abbot. Consequently Don Blasco soon acquired a new consideration for his grand-nephew.

'The little runt is not such a fool as he looks . . . yes, yes . . .' he would say approvingly, praising Consalvo's espionage. 'He listens to what they say and then comes and tells me.'

Politics caused quarrels and enmity among lay-brothers too. The wiliest did not bother about Cavour or Del Carretto and thought only of fattening their families with gleanings from the monastery, but a number also took sides either for government or revolution.

One in particular, Fra' Cola, a revolutionary leader, was always talking of beginning where they left off in '48. The Liberal novices would get him to tell the story of that time, and as he served them at table, as he took round water or wine in a great crystal decanter in his right hand, with the fore and middle finger of his left hand he would secretly make the sign of cutting scissors. One day the young prince asked Giovannino what it meant. His cousin replied:

'It means we must cut off the "rats" tails!'

Consalvo reported this to his uncle, and Fra' Cola, as punishment, was sent to the malarial Licodia house. Fra' Carmelo, though, never bothered about politics, and when asked if he was a Liberal or pro-Bourbon made the sign of the Cross.

'Stop, please, for the Lord's sake! What do I know about these things! They're the Devil's works!'

For him there was no world outside San Nicola, no other power outside that of Abbot, Prior and Deacons. He would list all the Abbot's eighteen titles, naming the Kings, Queens, royal princes, viceroys and barons who had endowed the monastery. Every Sunday, in Chapter, the Abbot would read out a litany of those royal and princely donors for whose souls so many daily Masses were said. But often one only was said for the lot; it helped the dead just as much and did not take up so much time of the living.

In general the Fathers were in a hurry to get such things over and on with their own affairs. In order not to go down into church for matins when it was chilly, they had built, many years before, another choir, called the Night Choir, in the middle of the monastery. It was all in carved walnut and cost a number of thousands of *onze*, but now the Fathers did not get up even to go there, a few steps away; they stayed between their sheets till broad daylight and had their matins said for them by the Capuchins, for payment. But on great religious feast-days, Christmas, Easter, or the Feast of the Holy Nail, all took part in ceremonies whose magnificence dazzled the city.

The first ceremonies at which the young prince was present were those of Holy Week. For a month the church was upside-down for the construction of the Sepulchre at the end of the left-hand nave. Enclosed in great scaffolding, with windows blocked out, decorated with crystal candelabra glittering like diamonds and vases of wheat grown in the dark so that it was colourless, populated with statues representing the Holy Family and the Apostles, it was quite unrecognisable. On Thursday at Terce, the whole monastery went down into the church for Pontifical High Mass, led by the Abbot, his staff, mitre and ring borne by novices and his train by pages. The colour-scheme was like the White Queen's, all red brocade embroidered in gold, and to Donato del Piano's majestic organ tenors, basses and baritones specially hired for the occasion sang the Passion, which the massed crowd followed as if in a theatre.

Opposite the Abbot's dais, in the best places, were all the Uzeda; the prince and count with their wives, Donna Ferdinanda, Lucrezia, Chiara with her husband. They, noticing Consalvo, made him signs with their heads, particularly his mother and the old spinster, admiring his white cotta starched in a thousand tiny folds, special work of the nuns of San Giuliano. Through the whole church, when the powerful organ stopped, could be heard a buzz like a beehive, a scraping of

195

chairs, a stamping of feet. There was a glitter from rifles and sabres of soldiers lined in front of the three doors and along the naves to clear the way for the procession later on. Meanwhile, twelve paupers, representing the twelve Apostles, had entered the choir. The Abbot on his knees washed their feet. It was a second washing, the first having already taken place in the sacristy lest His Paternity dirty his hands.

At that moment a murmur came from the end of the church. Consalvo turned round from the High Altar and saw that his uncle Raimondo had left his place and was making his way through the crowd towards a lady. It was Donna Isabella Fersa. Like all the other ladies she was dressed in black mourning for the Passion, but her dress was so rich, so covered with frills and lace, that it looked like a ball dress. Having arrived late, she could not find a good place. Raimondo, on reaching her, gave her his arm and led her amid a double row of curious spectators to his own chair next to his wife's. Countess Matilde, out for the first time that day since her illness, was very white-faced, and her black wool dress made her look even paler. Then, at that point, Jesus died; the church suddenly went dark, the lay-brothers turned the candelabra over on the altars, took off the white altar cloths and substituted violet, veiled the Cross; and the monks also set aside their festive vestments and put on those of mourning. In the darkness the candles shone with a brighter flame, and the Holy Sepulchre was like a monstrance with all its torches, lamps, reflections of crystal and gold. Donna Isabella looked at the spectacle through her lorgnette, while the count, bowing over her, named monks and novices one by one.

'Is that one there not your young nephew? . . . what a fine little cleric, countess . . .'

Matilde made an ambiguous gesture of the head. The organ was intoning the *Miserere,* and the sad music was full of sighs and laments which echoed in every corner of the dark church, of wails which made the air tremble, of groans like winter wind. It seemed that the world was about to end, that there was no more hope for anyone; Jesus was dead, the Saviour of the world was dead; and the monks, two by two, the Abbot at their head, went down into the apse and moved round the vast church between two rows of soldiers holding back the crowds and presenting reversed arms. Then the Abbot deposited the Sacred Host in the Sepulchre. Kneeling with her head bowed over her chair and her face hidden in her handkerchief, the Countess Matilde was quietly sobbing. Donna Isabella exclaimed:

'How touching this ceremony is! . . .'

She too had slightly red eyes, but when the count gave her his arm again to lead her into the sacristy she leant against him languidly.

'By rights I shouldn't come,' she protested. 'Only relations are allowed in . . .'

'Oh nonsense! . . . you're with us! We'll say we're cousins.'

In the sacristy splendid refreshments were being offered to relatives of the monks and novices; trays full of cups of smoking chocolate were circulating, with iced drinks and sweets and sponge-cakes. Consalvo, between his mother and Donna Isabella, was receiving caresses and compliments for the exemplary way in which he had taken part in the ceremony; Father Gerbini, without having yet taken off his mourning vestments, was greeting the ladies and inviting them to the ceremony next day.

On Friday the Uzeda arrived with the Fersa; the count gave his arm to Donna Isabella, who wore another black dress, even more elegant than the first. The sacristans had reserved them the same places, guarding them amid the milling throng. But the soldiers were holding it back, and as the organ accompanied the dirge of Three Hours of Agony there was deep silence; only Raimondo, sitting next to Donna Isabella, was saying things in her ear that made her smile. Meanwhile the Abbot was carrying out the ceremony of the Deposition from the Cross. Taking the veiled Crucifix, he put it on the floor on one of the altar steps, where a velvet cushion embroidered all over in gold had been set. The monks went off, the Sepulchre remained empty for a moment. Suddenly, while the organ started its lamentations again more sadly than ever, all of them reappeared from the sacristy in procession, two by two, with their Superior at their head. They were shoeless, with feet in black silk socks, for the Adoration of the Cross.

Kneeling at every step, between the hedges of soldiers, they came down to the main door, went back as far as the altar, and there one by one threw themselves on the ground before the cushion with the dead Christ, and kissed it. The crowd got up on chairs to see better; Donna Isabella and Raimondo passed each other opera glasses, while Matilde, on her knees, sobbed and prayed. At the end of the ceremony there were more refreshments in the sacristy. The young prince, now caressed by all, saw that his relatives were served first; his uncle Don Eugenio was drinking chocolate as if it were water, stuffing into his pockets cakes he could not eat, but his Aunt Matilde took nothing.

On Holy Saturday, Consalvo did not see her in church for the ceremony of the Resurrection, but his Uncle Raimondo was still giving an arm to the Signora Fersa.

# 7

E v e r y evening the countess watched till late by her child's
cot, holding a little hand white and cold as wax, making no
movement with her own stiffened arm lest she wake the sleeping child. Late at night the gates were locked, and no sound
was heard in the sleeping house except the faint snoring of
the nurse sleeping by Teresina's cot in the room next door.
Raimondo did not return. Laid out on the night table in rows
were bottles of medicine, pots of ointment, the whole chemist's
shop prescribed by the doctor for the sick little girl. She was
suffering from shingles, they said; bad blood came out in skin
eruptions and glandular obstructions, all reassuring symptoms,
as they meant that the poison was being expelled by the
organism.

She had made a vow to Our Lady of Graces, promised to
wear Her habit until Lauretta recovered. Deep in her heart
she had asked Our Lady for another grace; to illuminate
Raimondo, reawaken his affection as husband and father.

Since they had been to Milazzo, according to the promise
made at the Belvedere after the cholera, he had begun to fret
again, to show himself bored and restless, declare that he could
not stay long so far from home because of the property-division.
And she had scarcely given birth and was still between life and
death after a very difficult delivery, when he alleged a call from
his brother and left. He stayed away only a few days, but it
was the first time that he had left her, at the very moment when
his company and help were most necessary to her. This new
sorrow certainly did not help her towards recovery; but a
greater one awaited her, and her premonitions all came true,

for the creature she had borne in her womb while in such mental agony had come into the world so weak and wan that it seemed about to die at any moment.

And so many long months had passed, almost a whole year, without her being able to leave her father's roof or the baby's bedside. During that year Raimondo had come and gone, left and returned a number of times, and she had gradually become accustomed to those absences, being unable either to follow him or to oppose the business reasons which he adduced. When the doctors ordered a change of air for the convalescent baby, he wanted to take them all off to Catania. The baron too was leaving Milazzo and going to Palermo with his other daughter, Carlotta, so Teresina, who could not be left alone, went with her father.

Matilde was delighted to find Raimondo taking so much interest in his daughters, and almost blessed her own sufferings, if indeed they had brought this respite. But as soon as she arrived at the Uzeda home she found her daughter in relapse and Raimondo neglecting her, leaving her alone amid those 'relations' who were again looking at her askance, and, crueller still to a mother's heart, hurting her through her children. They derided the sufferings and predicted the death of her youngest, but their greatest hostility was to Teresina. She was a vivacious, curious, restless child, who was often naughty, spoilt things at her games and shouted gaily as she ran through the rooms. Then she would be reproved and sent off; the prince would say he had put Consalvo with the Benedictines so as to have a quiet house and instead of that it was now resounding with shrieks, even more than before.

With his own daughter, the other Teresina, he was more indulgent, and the whole family and even the servants treated the two little cousins differently, giving first place to the young princess. Even Princess Margherita, the only one to be good and sweet to the other, could not hide her preference for her own daughter, and Matilde, though realising they were right, suffered at this disparity of treatment.

Her Teresina, at the age of six, was vain as a maiden; she would gaze at herself for long in the glass, watch and stare as her mother's hair was dressed; and she loved ribbons, brooches, bits of jewellery. The old spinster would often criticise her for coquetry, shake her head and predict ill for the future, making Matilde sob at this kind of evil spell put on the innocent child. Now they had another reason for getting at her, for the purpose of the baron's journey to Palermo was to arrange the marriage of his other daughter, Carlotta. The latter, they contended, should not marry, and they urged Matilde to oppose her father's plans and her sister's happiness so that all their father's fortune should go to herself. And because such calculations never occurred to her they looked at her askance and punished her through her children, as if she had stolen something from them.

Raimondo, in truth, did not himself seem at all put out by the marriage plans, but he was beginning to neglect her again, to hurry out immediately after luncheon, to return as dinner was ending and go out again till late at night. When she saw her two daughters ill-treated, tears came to Matilde's eyes and she shut herself in her room with Teresina, told her to behave herself and tried to keep her there as long as possible. When Raimondo came home she did not accuse his relations to him, lest she annoy him and make them all say she was sowing discord in the family; she merely begged him not to leave her always alone . . .

The Uzedas' hostility towards her, the rebukes and sneers at her children, were as nothing to the jealousy gnawing at her once more. He had begun courting the Fersa woman again, went to visit her at home, every Sunday in church they met at the same Mass. And Matilde could no longer pray when she saw that woman in front of her and realised that he had not got her out of his mind, was again being drawn by her elegance, her languorous attitudes, the studiously graceful gestures with which she raised her scented handkerchief to her lips or waved her feather-fan, as she looked around or bent her head over a prayer-book without ever turning a page . . . In church! In the house of God! . . . That she could not understand, to her it seemed a continual and appalling sacrilege. Why, to San Nicola, for the ceremonies of the Passion, she had come dressed up as if for the theatre, making people turn round by her unsuitable appearance! Why must Raimondo put her so near him and make obvious an assiduity that was already giving rise to comment! On Easter Sunday, weeping with sorrow and tenderness, Matilde broke down at the baby's bedside and begged her husband:

'By this solemn day, by your love for this innocent baby, swear you will not make me suffer any more.' He had asked her, 'What harm am I doing you? What are you accusing me of?'

'You leave me alone, you neglect your children, you don't think of us, you don't love us any more.'

Shaking his head, Don Raimondo exclaimed:

'Your usual fixations, your usual fantasies! . . . I neglect you? How do I neglect you? When, why, for whom do I neglect you? . . .'

For whom? For whom? . . . And he had gone on with gathering warmth, 'Yes, for whom? You're not starting again with that silly jealousy of yours are you? Have you got some other whim into your head? . . . About Donna Isabella, eh? . . .' He had named her! 'I see! Just because I gave up my chair for her, because I invited her to join us? . . . but that was just good manners, my dear. It's only in this wretched hole one would get blamed for such a thing!'

In that summer of '57 he was seen around assiduously with both the Fersa; at the theatre, where he went every night to a stage-box, he would often go up to their box when it was their subscription night; he would also meet them at his Aunt Ferdinanda's, which Donna Isabella very often visited; at the Nobles' Club he was always gambling with her husband, whom he let win every day. Although he had the use of his brother's carriage he had bought a magnificent pair of thoroughbreds and a brand-new phaeton with which he followed the Fersa's carriage. When there was music on the marine parade he would get down, leave the reins to a coachman, and go and stand at their carriage door, chatting with Donna Isabella, her mother-in-law and husband. He was dressing with greater care than usual and was never at home except, by lucky coincidence, when they came to visit the princess. His conversation was always about Florence, life in big cities, the elegance and wealth of other places. He would settle down next to Donna Isabella, exclaiming, 'You're the only one who understands me!' and bewail the fate which had got him born in that hole and was holding him there, when he never wanted to set foot in it again, never again. 'Must I really leave my bones here? I don't think so! It's not possible!'

And hearing him speak in that way, Matilde asked herself why he did not leave and keep the other part of the promise he had made a year and a half before of returning to their house in Florence? Because of business? But although Raimondo never talked of such matters to her, she knew that the division had not yet been discussed and would not be for some time.

First the cholera, then its residue of worries, then his brother's departure had been the prince's reasons for not discussing the division yet. Raimondo's new luxuries were costing a lot; he was constantly asking his brother for advances, and the latter never let him ask twice, while hinting that it was time they settled their heritage definitely. But Raimondo found it convenient to take money without ever having to add up bills, cite bad payers, or involve himself in all the bothers, big and small, of administration. When his brother mentioned some doubt or asked for his opinion about prolonging a lease or concluding a sale, he would reply, 'You do whatever you think fit . . .' The important thing for him was to have money. Sometimes, when he asked too frequently, the prince would say:

'Actually our agents haven't paid us yet. We've had a lot of expenses, but if you like I can lend you whatever you need . . .' and Raimondo would take the money as an advance or a loan. His one preoccupation, in fact, was to spend money, with a blind faith in his brother which made Don Blasco furious. Already the monk, on hearing of the I.O.U.'s, had spat fire and flames at the prince, declaring him capable of forging his mother's signature, as 'that bitch of a sister-in-law of mine was a numbskull I know, but not to the point of making debts on one side and hoarding money on the other'. And he now began to rouse the other nieces and nephews against 'that crook', urging them to impugn the validity of those I.O.U.'s, for if they were not entirely false they must have been old I.O.U.'s paid up by the princess, found by Giacomo among her papers, and tinkered up to look new! But since those silly creatures Chiara and the marchese and Ferdinando and Lucrezia refused to listen—as if it were not all in their own interests!—the monk almost got to the point of forgetting his former aversion for Raimondo and going to open his eyes to the secret malpractices of his co-heir and brother, to shout at him:

'Open your eyes, if not he'll truss you up and devour you! . . .'

Now, seeing that they were all the same about this, he was grinding his teeth night and day. Then another fact had come to enrage him and make him inveigh against those ' mad swine ', in the monastery, around chemist-shops, even in the street with the first person he ran into. In their Oleastro sulphur mines the Uzeda had dug so far that they had passed underground beyond the boundaries of their property on the surface; so the owners of this surface sued them.

Raimondo, bored even by putting a simple signature on receipts and contracts, on that occasion showed Signor Marco, who came to read him out documents of the case, his annoyance at all this continual ' bother '. Then Signor Marco suggested, ' Why doesn't Your Excellency make a power-of-attorney with the prince? Then you'll avoid a lot of bother and things will go much faster until the time comes when, after Your Excellency's sisters have been paid, we can get on to the division . . .' Raimondo accepted this at once, and signed a deed giving the prince power-of-attorney to administer the inheritance in the name of the co-heir too.

Matilde, having heard of this accord, asked herself why Raimondo still wanted to stay in Sicily now? If he no longer took part in business affairs, what other interest held him there? And she began again to torture herself with jealousy, seeing him with that woman once more, unable to endure having to treat her as a friend while warned by an inner voice not to trust her. Sick in heart and mind, her nerves agitated by her constant sorrows, she now had gloomy presentiments and feared and suspected everything. In the happy simplicity of other days she would never have entertained the suspicion that the prince was letting Raimondo do what he liked most, almost encouraging his vices, inciting him to gamble and finding him occasions to see that woman, so as to distract him from business matters and get the sole management of them into his own hands. Such a suspicion would never even have passed through her head when she thought them all good and sincere. Now, terrified by others and by herself, she could not put it out of her mind . . . How could she, as the prince seemed to be making every effort to get Donna Isabella to the palace while her mother-in-law, Donna Mara Fersa, was beginning to show some fear that this relationship might become too intimate?

Donna Mara Fersa had tolerated much in her daughter-in-law from Palermo; the upset household, the ill-concealed condescension with which she was treated, the costly tastes and bold opinions; and although she closed both eyes on her own suffering she did not intend to close one if her son was involved. This friendship with the Uzeda was fine and she was greatly pleased about it, but why should Raimondo always be at Isabella's side, at his own home or hers, in church, at the play or the parade? It might be a smart custom in Florence, but one which she, in her old-fashioned way, could not understand. Anyway she did not like it and did not intend that it should continue. Without giving reasons, lest she put the cart before the horse, she hinted to her son and daughter-in-law that they could be good friends with the Uzeda without sharing every moment of the day and night with them. But she preached to deaf ears; Mario Fersa was more infatuated than ever by the prince and the count, Donna Isabella was always with the princess, Lucrezia and Donna Ferdinanda.

Then, on seeing her exhortations disregarded, and being unused to finding herself disobeyed and unheeded in a matter which a daughter-in-law should be first to understand, Donna Mara, incapable of hiding what was in her mind, became acrid and ironical towards her daughter-in-law, while at the same time telling her son openly the reason for her disquiet. Even so she was not too precise and kept to generalities, saying that leading a life in common like that was dangerous, and that the Uzeda house was not only frequented by numbers of men but also had two young men, the prince and the count, with whom Isabella should not be so continuously seen . . . But her son cut her short. 'The prince? Raimondo? My best friends? . . .' From indignation he went to laughter. 'Suspect them? Two excellent family men? . . .' Nor did his mother's insistent reasoning draw any other reply.

Meanwhile, Donna Isabella, at her mother-in-law's sudden change to severe looks and brusque ways from a former attitude of prudent but pained resignation, now assumed the airs of a real victim. To Raimondo, when he chattered of the boredom and misery of provincial life, she would nod her head approvingly, but add that one could be happy in country or desert as long as one felt surrounded by care and affection . . . and saw around people dear to one . . . who were capable of understanding and appreciating one . . . Donna Mara, seeing none of her moves succeed, finally decided to try more energetic means of putting an end to this ' comedy '.

Fersa on his side still noticed nothing, for he would have denied the light of day before suspecting his wife and Raimondo, with whom he shared most of his life and spent all day and every evening chatting or gambling at the club or in a stage-box at the opera. He was more than ever proud of the friendship shown him by the prince, the long monologues the latter made him while Raimondo and Isabella chattered in a corner; and it was a shock to him when his mother came up and said brusquely, ' Let's go, it's late! . . .'

One fine day Raimondo, on going to pay a visit to the Fersas' and after seeing Donna Isabella behind the shutters, heard the servant reply that there was no one in. At first he was amazed; he very nearly gave the door a push to get in by force, but he just managed to contain himself, and went downstairs and out into the street scarlet in the face as if he had caught sunstroke. He at once realised whence the blow came, having already noticed Donna Mara's coldness, and at the idea of obstacle and opposition the blood boiled in his veins, mounted to his head, dimmed his sight.

Till that moment he had sought Donna Isabella's company because she seemed one of the few women he could talk to, because she reminded him of society outside, and also because he liked her personally, not greatly though, not enough to set his heart on conquering her. It was not the chance of ruining her, not her husband's friendship, that deterred him; Fersa in fact, with his adoration for his wife and his blind faith in her and in him, seemed fated for the usual disaster; and Donna Isabella, with that martyred air of hers, with her instinctive coquetry, with her eternal talks about soul-mates, was presumably yearning to be understood. He had always laughed at love and passion, which was just why his wife bored him, and he had never sought anything but easy pleasures, ready and safe; a presentiment of the trouble which an affair with Donna Isabella could bring had prevented him pushing things too far. At the Belvedere, during the cholera, when Donna Isabella was to come and failed to do so, he had been almost pleased at their not meeting as arranged, and amused himself with Agatina Galano as if forgetting the distant Donna Isabella. When he saw her again, temptation had revived; then his wife's moping made it stronger, and Donna Mara's opposition put new fuel on the fire. He had the sort of character that is excited by obstacles, which made him frenzied and restive as a foal at a bit. Even so he had contained himself still, thinking of the future, of sure troubles and possible dangers. Now finding himself forbidden to set foot in her house suddenly gave him a great longing to break down that front door and bear the woman off. The bloodthirsty instinct of the old predatory Uzeda threw him into a passion; had he been able he would have done something wild, like his grandfather driving his horses at the Captain of Justice. Now not so much times as circumstances were different; he could not make a scandal, so he had to dissimulate and fall back on craft . . .

On reaching home, he wrote to Donna Isabella to say that he had realised what were ' the unjust suspicions ' of her relations, and went on to complain that ' in this hateful city ' it was impossible to make and keep ' friendly associations '. The letter was sent by means of Pasqualino Riso, the prince's coachman, to Donna Isabella's coachman, who was a crony of his. Donna Isabella replied at once by the same means, complaining of the ' slavery ' in which she was held, of the evil suspicion with which she was treated, thanking him meanwhile for his ' delicate ' sentiments, for the ' friendship ' of which he gave proof and which she returned ' with all her heart ', but begging him to ' renounce ever seeing her again ' lest she hurt the susceptibilities of ' certain persons '. This was the same as saying ' do your best to triumph over their opposition.'

207

The two coachmen cronies saw each other again every day to pass on verbal messages. Pasqualino, on the look-out at a corner by the Fersas' home, would hurry off to the Nobles' Club to warn his master, who had set up headquarters there, when Donna Isabella left the house.

Meanwhile Raimondo followed her about everywhere just the same. He even went up to her carriage still and visited her box at the theatre, on the rare occasions when the mother-in-law was not there. And the husband, deaf to maternal warnings, smarting at unjust suspicions, behaved the same to him as before, in fact made an even greater show of friendship, as if excusing himself for his mother's conduct, and was an assiduous visitor to the palace.

The Uzeda all seemed to have passed some mutual message about protecting and shielding the pair. As they spoke to each other in a corner the prince or Donna Ferdinanda would be chattering to Fersa, and leading him into another room; the spinster drove around with Donna Isabella, and when she met her nephew stopped the carriage to give him a chance of being with her; or she invited her to her home more often, and Raimondo would soon arrive. They also saw each other at the houses of other Francalanza relatives, the Duchess Radalì's, the Grazzeri's, most often at Cousin Graziella's, who had become a great friend of Donna Isabella.

All conspired to prevent Matilde noticing anything, but she was warned by a kind of sixth sense, realised that her husband was slipping away from her, and wept with the agony of it. Now that her child was better and she should have been able to breathe calmly, that thought tortured her all the time. She knew that if anyone opposed him Raimondo had a habit of sticking all the more to his whims, and that the only way, if any, of getting him back, was to let him have his head. But how could she resign herself to knowing that head was full of another woman, to being looked at by the part-curious and part-pitying eye of Lucrezia, the marchese, strangers, even servants? So she would sidle up to him timidly and imploringly, tell him of her jealousy, beg him not to make her suffer if he was really not thinking of that woman . . .

'This cursed country!' exclaimed her husband excitedly.

'Who ever invented such foul nonsense? You yourself? You've been putting round your silly suspicions, now tell the truth, haven't you?'

'Me? . . . Me? . . .'

'D'you want to ruin her, d'you want to get me killed by her husband?'

Then another terror froze her; suppose Fersa had noticed something too? And wanted revenge? . . . Suddenly she saw her husband lying dead in the middle of a road, with a bullet in his forehead or a dagger in his side. Every time he was late in coming home she wrung her hands and pressed her heart, almost hearing the cries of terrified servants at the sudden arrival of his lifeless corpse; then she would caress her children and sob over them as if they were already orphans. What particularly distressed her was having no one with whom to let herself go, no one to comfort her at least with a kind word. She could say nothing to her father, and the Uzeda seemed to protect that other woman; those of them who did not go as far as that in their rancour against the 'intruder' remained neutral and did not even notice her.

Don Eugenio had now finished and despatched to Naples his memorandum on Massa Annunziata. Its title was: '*Anent the propriety—of excavating—the Sicilian Pompeii—otherwise called Massa Annunziata—in the ancient Mongibello—buried in the year of Grace 1669—by the belching lava of that fiery volcano —together with all the riches it contained—Memorandum submitted to the Royal Government of the Two Sicilies—by Don Eugenio Uzeda of Francalanza and Mirabella—Gentleman of the Bedchamber of His Majesty (with functions).*' In the evening he would read out to the assembled company from his rough copy. This was written in a strange style which was the fruit of grammatical reforms thought up by him, with his own emphasis and expressions.

Don Cono was the only one to listen to these verbal reforms and solemnly discussed whether ' solemn ' should have one or two ' l's '; everyone else turned their backs on this idiot, who after losing two appointments by his own idiocy now expected to be appointed a director of excavations; Don Blasco and Donna

Ferdinanda, among others, though each on his own, jeered mercilessly at him to his face, but they were singing to the deaf, as the cavaliere was quite sure that this time he had seized fortune by the forelock.

The marchese and Chiara, who came to the palace every day, might not have been there at all, for while people spoke of one thing or another they thought of nothing but their own progeny. At a certain period every month Chiara really seemed in the clouds; she did not reply or replied vaguely to questions she was asked; then she drew all the ladies apart one after another and muttered certain questions in their ears. So when Don Blasco went to her house and inveighed again against the prince and Raimondo, she did not bother to listen, so rapt was she in constant and intense expectation.

As for Ferdinando, he let his uncle the monk say what he liked. Delighted to be absolute master at Pietra dell'Ovo, he had indulged his whims to his heart's content. Gradually however the place was falling into ruin, and he realised it. He had tried all the things that he found in books of agriculture; having read, for instance, that in every tree branches can act as roots and roots as branches, he began trying out the truth of this by pulling up the tall flourishing orange trees to replant them upside down. One by one all the trees died. But this would not have made him decide to stop these experiments had he not thought of others of a different kind. Among the many books he bought were some on mechanics; then, remembering his former love for watchmaking he hired a bailiff to take over the estate, and begun to make wheels and springs. Why did water in suction pumps never rise farther than five *canne*? Because of atmospheric pressure. Was there no way of counter-balancing it? So he had built a machine with a gadget worked by a handle whereby the water did not rise even an inch, far less five *canne*. This was all the fault of the workmen, who had not understood his orders. Now he was studying a much vaster problem: perpetual motion . . .

What happened in the house, what others did never bothered him, and his visits to the palace became rarer and rarer; had it not been for Lucrezia, he would never have gone at all. But his sister was busy making signals to Benedetto Giulente, and only seldom came down into the drawing-rooms. The flirtation was going stronger than ever; in each letter the young man told her that the time for him to ask the question was drawing nearer and that in a year they would plight their vows. Even now that the little devil Consalvo was no longer there to search about amid her things, Lucrezia would still lock up her room when she went down to the floor below, and the prince said nothing to her about the resulting inconvenience.

And so none of the legatees bothered about the division of property. As for Raimondo, he was more than ever intent on his gay life and on following Donna Isabella over sky and sea. Pasqualino Riso scarcely did any other service nowadays, busy as he was in watching Donna Isabella's movements and carrying letters and messages. There was even jealousy of him among the other servants, the under-coachman particularly, who was now left all the work, and the footman Matteo. They spoke through set teeth of their colleague's good luck, saying that they could not understand how the prince could go on paying him just like before and leaving him at his brother's disposal. So disgusted were they that they nearly changed allegiance, for from being against the Countess Matilde before, now they felt sorry for her and said she did not deserve such unfaithfulness and ill-treatment . . .

The Uzedas' harshness towards Donna Matilde was really becoming excessive, particularly towards her daughters, for ill-treatment of them hurt Matilde more than any directed personally at herself. There were terrible days, when Donna Ferdinanda had raised her hand to Teresina, which Matilde spent sobbing like a child, drinking in her tears so they should not fall on the letters that she wrote to her father to hide her sorrow from him and give him to understand that she was happy.

At the beginning of September, when the time drew near for going to the country, the baron arrived from Milazzo to see his little grand-daughters and take them all with him to his estates, where Carlotta's fiancé had gone too; the wedding was to take place in a year. The prince asked the baron to stay at the palace, and all the others who were so harsh to his daughter greeted him with politeness, as if to prevent him suspecting their ill-grace towards her . . . Nor did he read her long sufferings in her face; proud of the kinship and of the family's nobility, he even felt confirmed in his idea of having ensured Matilde's happiness. She, on her father's arrival, at the announcement that he had come to take them all away, began trembling again for another reason, the old fear of a quarrel breaking out between her father and her husband. Would not Raimondo refuse to follow his father-in-law? . . . Instead of which a ray of sun shone suddenly in her long sadness; Raimondo replied to the baron's invitation by ordering preparations for a journey. That consent was nothing really; it could not reassure her, as no one would be staying in town at that season and Donna Isabella Fersa was leaving as in other years for Leonforte. And yet, in the anguish to which she was reduced, the idea of leaving the Uzeda household, of returning to her father's by consent and in company of Raimondo, made her breathe freely.

The prince invited the whole family to the Belvedere. But things did not go too smoothly there, and the first to provoke friction were Chiara and the Marchese Federico. Beginning to lose hope of the child they had so much expected, almost ashamed at their constant announcement of a pregnancy which was never confirmed, husband and wife were now overcome by a melancholy which gradually turned to irritability, to latent rancour with no definite object.

Chiara in particular was unable to resign herself to her failure at maternity, and blamed herself as if it were her own fault. So, to get her husband to forgive her, while before she had awaited his every word as an oracle's, she now forestalled his judgements and guessed his every wish. He had not time to turn round, for example, at the faint draught from an open window, before Chiara was calling servants to shut everything up and threatening to get them all dismissed if they were ever so careless again. When someone in conversation described a fact or suggested an idea she would read in her husband's eyes if he disagreed and then reply vigorously before he had opened his mouth.

Federico was not to be outdone and showed the same disposition as she, so that all the quarrels avoided between themselves they started up with other people. Now the start of the one with the prince, whose guests they were, was that matter of the legacy to the Convent of San Placido. As Giacomo was still determined to consider it void for lack of royal approval, the Mother Abbess had called the convent's lawyers, who had declared unanimously that the prince's reasons were not worth a button and that the late lamented princess had not instituted a benefice at all, but left a legacy *cum onere missarum*; hence there was no need whatsoever of the royal approval, hence the prince must pay out the two thousand *onze*. But the latter stuck to the other interpretation and his poor Sister of the Cross wept morning and night. In a moment of ill-humour, seeing that friendly dealings were getting nowhere, the Abbess had confided to the marchese and Chiara another of the prince's tricks; the late lamented Donna Teresa, before departing for the Belvedere from which she was never to return, had left a box full of gold coins and precious objects to be kept in the convent treasury and later handed over to Signor Marco, who was then to pass it to Raimondo. As soon as his mother was dead, Giacomo had presented himself to withdraw this deposit, and as she made some objections, he had returned with Signor Marco, whom she had been unable to refuse.

For a time husband and wife were scandalised, but they would have taken no action if the Abbess, to get them on her side, had not told them that the glorious Saint Francesco di Paola had prevented their marriage being fruitful and made Chiara's first pregnancy fail because they had allowed a sacrilege against the convent. With this bee in their bonnets they both turned against the prince, Chiara in particular persuading her husband of the brother's roguery. The marchese bowed to his wife's reasoning, and gradually from the legacy for Masses and the vanished deposit they went on to other questions concerning the inheritance, to the arbitrary division, the subtraction of ready cash, the refusal to present accounts, the demand that the pretended handing over of capital should appear as a payment already made, to all the accusations of Don Blasco, who came over on purpose from Nicolosi to fan the flames.

Within seven months the three years would be up since their mother's death. After this the women could draw their portions, which the prince, in spite of his promise to pay in advance, still kept to himself; all these things must be put clearly and their real due established. But although both were sure that if they did not complain Giacomo would cheat them, neither wife nor husband dared complain directly to brother and brother-in-law.

Chiara, wishing to show her zeal, began instigating Lucrezia to try to get Ferdinando on their side too. She shut herself up with her sister, or drew her into a corner to pass on all the remarks of her uncle the monk, adding that she, Lucrezia, was the most victimised of them all, for Giacomo would continue his mother's policy and not let her marry or postpone marriage for her as late as possible, in order to remain master of her dowry. Lucrezia, understanding nothing of business, let her run on and replied, 'We'll see! . . . I'll have my say too! . . .' She did not confide her love for Benedetto Giulente to her sister, and would not have listened to her instigations, as she did not to her uncle the monk's, had the prince, noticing these secret confabulations, these attempts at plotting under his roof while enjoying his hospitality, not become colder to his sisters and refused to greet Giulente. Lucrezia, having heard this, and after consulting with her maid, who said that if the prince was now behaving badly to the 'Signorino' too it was time to make herself felt, decided to listen to Chiara's reasoning. The hostility between brother and sisters grew harsher on return from the Belvedere, when Lucrezia began to complain to Ferdinando in order to draw him into their league. Then onto the scene came Father Camillo, the confessor.

On returning from Rome after the princess's death the Dominican had remained, to everyone's amazement, the prince's confessor as he had been his mother's. Giacomo not only went to confession every month but called his spiritual adviser into his home and took his advice as had Donna Teresa. Don Blasco breathed fire and sword against 'this turn-coat Jesuit' who after acting as spy for his mother was now acting as spy for the son, which was why 'that thief' Giacomo had not 'kicked him in the backside'. But Father Camillo, all sweetness and light, never even heard the Benedictine's diatribes.

One day he took Lucrezia apart and began a long speech to tell her that a declaration of discontent with her mother's Will was as bad a sin as disobeying her mother in life. The princess, like a wise just mother, had divided her fortune 'with scales', for to a mother's heart all her children should be 'equally dear'.

Certainly the prince and the count had obtained a privileged part, but they were the head of the house and heir to the title, and the count was another son with a family to maintain with decorum. For the others the late lamented princess had arranged equal parts 'to the last cent'. Were these suggesting that she should have had land instead of money? He quoted the past Wills of defunct Princes of Francalanza, the institution of primogeniture and Salic laws, quoting as examples what had happened in the previous generation.

Had Donna Ferdinanda been given any property? She had some now, yes, but that was because, gifted with that spirit of shrewd prudence traditional to the family, she had multiplied the capital left by her father by investing it later in houses and land. But apart from that, who among all those sons had married? None of them! Don Blasco, with his 'exemplary' vocation, had renounced the lures of the world to take the habit. The eldest daughter had shut herself up in San Placido, neither the duke nor Don Eugenio had taken wives, nor had Donna Ferdinanda a husband. Why? Because they considered themselves as mere depositories of their part of the family fortune! In the present generation there had been two exceptions to this rule: the count, who had married Donna Matilde, Chiara who had become Marchesa of Villardita. But here there shone the princess's zealous maternal love. Not everyone is made in the same way; what may seem redundant or useless to one is convenient for others; some are content with the single state and others suffer from it. But the late lamented princess had realised that marriage was necessary to Raimondo's happiness, so she had given him a wife without looking to the sacrifice involved.

As for Chiara, a propitious occasion had presented itself and in order to ensure this daughter's happiness the princess had even forced her hand; time now showed who had been right! As for her, Lucrezia, God had allowed her mother to die before the time for thinking of her future, but disaster though this was, her future was just as close to her elder brother's heart. It was strange for him to talk to a girl about certain matters, but necessity forced him. Her late lamented mother's wish, a reasonable wish, founded on positive arguments and not on whims, was that she should remain at home, but if on the contrary she had

215

decided for her own good to do otherwise, had it ever been suggested that if she did want to marry, the prince would oppose her? When a chance came of her marrying well, with the decorum suitable to her name, the prince would not let it pass. But she must trust him and be sure that he wished only his sister's good and considered himself invested with a kind of moral tutelage. And she must not give an example of family dissension, a scandal in this world and a cause of great bitterness to her late lamented mother in the next . . .

While the confessor was making this speech to Lucrezia, the prince was making a slightly different one to Donna Ferdinanda. The spinster, though inveighing against the Giulente, had in time resigned herself to their pretensions; with that pig of a duke no longer there to help on the love affair, she had thought it entirely over. But one day, when they were talking about the responsibility of heads of families with marriageable girls at home, Giacomo told his aunt that Lucrezia should get married too and that he for his part would leave her free to choose whom she liked best, particularly as she seemed to have made her choice already . . .

The spinster turned on him like an asp:

' Chosen? Chosen? And who's she chosen?'

' Who? Oh, Giulente of course . . .'

She went scarlet as if about to suffocate.

' Ah, yes? . . . Still? . . . And you let it go on?'

' Your Excellency knows our family,' replied the prince with a smile. ' When we get something into our heads it's difficult to induce us to change our minds . . .'

' Ah, it's difficult, is it? I'll show you if it's difficult or easy! . . .'

From that moment the spinster became viper-like to her niece. Her railing, for any reason or excuse, could be heard even down in the stables; her ironical allusions to petty love affairs poured out acidly and pungently. Insults against the Giulente family followed in endless variety. She said terrible things about them, accused them of every kind of filth, even crimes. She no longer merely said they were common, but affirmed that old Giulente's grandfather had first made his money as a vintner at Syracuse, his son had robbed the municipality, his grandson the Govern-

216

ment, and all the women of the family had been so many strumpets . . .

Lucrezia let her have her say. They did not realise that the more they abused Giulente the better she thought of him, that all talk intended to loosen her intention merely drew it tighter. 'I'll marry Benedetto or no-one,' she would say to the maid after those outbursts. 'Let them go on shouting; when the time comes I'll marry him.'

Meanwhile the prince, having decided to let up on this particular matter, treated her less harshly. One day when the woman was bringing a letter to her young mistress from Giulente, he took the missive from her hand, read the address and handed it back. Donna Vanna rushed to Lucrezia and said, panting:

'Be of good heart, Your Excellency! This means that he's pleased, he's finally agreed . . .' He had also achieved his aim of breaking up the league against him, for the Marchese Federico, as fanatical about nobility as any Uzeda, on hearing that his young sister-in-law had got it into her head to marry Giulente, showed his own disapproval of this match. Then his wife took sides with her aunt against her sister, calling her eccentric and accusing her of madness. Lucrezia, on the other hand, when she let herself go with Vanna, would remember the frenzies, sobs, swoonings of Chiara when forced to marry the marchese. 'And now she's with those who want to force me! I don't care about her opposition! A mad-woman like her! A rag in the wind! Now she's all one with the husband whom she wouldn't even hear mentioned before. She'll change once again tomorrow; you'll see!'

In the midst of this strife Raimondo returned from Milazzo without his family. He did not even spend a quarter of an hour with his relations; as soon as he arrived he shut himself up with Pasqualino and next day was seen following Donna Isabella Fersa into church. Once again began murmurs by servants, by the curious, by idlers at the Nobles' Club. He had told his wife that he would be away a week on business, but two months later he had not yet announced his return. To her letters he either replied asking for time or did not reply at all. At carnival-

217

time Matilde joined him, with her father. He greeted her with four words, pronounced icily:

'Why did you come?'

He had arranged a series of entertainments with the help of friends; on Shrove Tuesday he passed and repassed beneath Donna Isabella's house, in a cart rigged as a ship with all on it dressed as sailors, each time throwing flowers and confetti for a quarter of an hour up at her balconies; on Saturday, at a subscription ball in the Town Hall, he danced with her the whole evening; and again on Monday at the Opera ball.

And Matilde, all alone, as her father had gone to rejoin the children, would repeat to herself his question, the only words with which he had answered her solicitude, 'Why did I come?' To watch this! . . . So he was still pretending, lying, deceiving her, or rather not even bothering to do that! Soon after his arrival at Milazzo he had railed like one demented against life in that 'hole of a place', tortured her with complaints, rebukes, with daily discontent and constant ill-humour, until he managed to escape. Injustice, rudeness, violence, she would have forgiven all, so much did she still love him; she even forgave him his indifference to his daughters, innocent creatures of his own flesh and blood! But to find him escaping far away, to know him given over to another woman, to smell on him the scent of that other woman's dresses, hands, and hair. No, that she could not endure!

'You aren't at it again, are you? You haven't come to bother me again?' he would answer her attempts at remonstrance, her timid reproval. 'Why didn't you stay with your father, then?'

'Because I ought to be with you, because my place is by your side, because you should not leave me either!'

'Who's leaving you? If I wanted to leave you, d'you think it would be difficult? I'd have already packed my bags by now and gone off to Florence, Paris or the Devil!'

'Let's go away together! Why don't we return to Florence? We have our house there.'

'Just now I'm busy here!'

'But now you've given to your brother that power-of-attorney . . .'

'I gave the power-of-attorney for day-to-day business ad-

218

ministration! Now we must get to the division and to paying my sisters, as the three years are now up since the succession. D'you see that? Or would you like me to add it up? My mother died in May '55 and it's now March '58 . . . That's three years, isn't it? Is there anything else you want to know?'

'Why d'you talk to me like that? I've said nothing wrong, have I?'

'Nothing! Nothing! Nothing! But d'you think it's fun for me to hear these continual complaints and suspicions of yours?'

'No, no. I won't do it any more . . . I won't say another thing to you . . .'

He was capable of putting his threat into practice, of leaving her, of leaving his daughters! So she hid her own sorrow, seeing that he was worse than before, as if her every remonstrance was an incitement. But she said to herself that Fersa was finally listening to his mother, opening his eyes and showing the count that he did not like all that assiduity. And in fact he no longer brought his wife to the Uzeda palace, nor was Raimondo seen with Donna Isabella in public any more, though he still followed the Fersa carriage with his own everywhere, as if in pursuit. In church, at the theatre, he would sit right opposite and not take his eyes off her.

One day Cousin Graziella came to the palace to ask for the prince, and shut herself up with him to say:

'Cousin, there's something very serious I must talk to you about.' For many years, since Giacomo had married, they had used the formal *voi* to each other. 'Donna Mara Fersa sent me a message through a friend, about this matter of Raimondo!'

'What matter?' asked the prince, as if he did not understand.

'Don't you know what people are saying? . . . Raimondo has got it into his head to pester Donna Isabella. And everyone has noticed, to tell the truth . . .'

'I have noticed nothing.'

'Well, it's true, cousin, I can assure you . . . The thing is not right and I don't like it . . . At one time they used often to meet at my home, and I received them with open arms. How could I have suspected any harm in it? Or I would never have lent myself to such a thing! Raimondo is a father, Donna

219

Isabella has a husband too; what do they want to do? . . . An open quarrel has broken out in the Fersa family between daughter-in-law and mother-in-law. Cousin Raimondo must really be persuaded to stop it once and for all.'

'And why do you tell it to me?' replied Giacomo, with a shrug.

'Why? Because I'm not on very close terms with Raimondo . . . and anyway it would be better if you talked to him; you are head of the family and can . . .'

'You're mistaken. I can do nothing; here each one of us does just what he or she likes. Head indeed! Try and realise that I'm very nearly the tail!'

Cousin Graziella went on invoking Giacomo's authority and the prince complaining about the lack of accord in the family whereas he would have liked to see them all united, mutually affectionate, disposed to help and advise each other.

'You want me to talk to my brother, do you? He's quite capable of replying, "What are you putting your nose into?" It wouldn't be the first reply of the kind . . . My dear cousin, you know how obstinate we all are! . . . No, no, believe me, it would be useless, if not worse.'

His cousin, delighted at having a finger in the pie, began on the same subject with the princess.

'Can it really be true? . . .' exclaimed Donna Margherita, who had noticed nothing. 'Poor Matilde! . . . She doesn't deserve such treatment!'

'That's what I say! With such a charming wife I can't understand why Raimondo looks for distractions elsewhere . . . But who can understand men? I'm really sorry, I am indeed! Two families disturbed while they could have been together in peace and harmony! Anyway, my cousin should be persuaded to leave Donna Isabella in peace. As for me, I'd have no difficulty in saying so to his face; I'm not afraid of his eating me up! But you know how these things are. We're cousins, it's true. But I'd not like it said that I was trying to put my nose into other people's business and stirring up strife! While God alone knows how sorry I am!'

The princess nodded, sincerely sorry, all the more as she could do nothing. Had her husband not warned her to mind her own business, under pain of his displeasure? . . . And now Cousin Graziella began to manœuvre around Matilde herself, having decided to say everything to her. Was she not the wife? Who more than she had a right to talk to Raimondo and an interest in detaching him from that intrigue? . . . One evening she happened to meet her alone in the Red Drawing-room and began to ask news of the baron, of her sister's marriage, and of the children's health.

'Will they be coming here, or will you go and join them?'

'I don't know,' replied Matilde in embarrassment. 'I don't know what Raimondo will decide.'

'I understand!' replied Graziella with a sigh. 'Men want to do whatever they get into their heads . . . One thing today, another tomorrow . . . You, of course, would like to go to your family home with your father. It's all very well, a husband's family, yes, yes, but one never forgets one's own! Cousin Raimondo should also decide to leave here . . . it would be much better . . . for him too . . .'

Matilde bowed her head and avoided looking at her, pressing her hands together. Graziella went on:

'For him too . . . He'd get away from temptations . . . and have only his family to think of! . . . You're right to be restless, you poor thing, I do understand . . . You don't deserve to be treated like this . . . But you ought to tell him so! . . . You're his wife after all, and mother of his children . . . You can talk out . . . Make him stop it once and for all.'

The blood had rushed to Matilde's forehead, and her eyes were shut. Then she felt herself go icy. Suddenly she brought both hands up to her face and burst into sobs.

'Oh, Lord God! . . . Cousin! . . . What's wrong with you? . . . Holy God! . . . Cousin, don't do that!'

'I! . . . I! . . .' stuttered Matilde, her lips twisted with emotion, 'I have been crying over it for two years . . . I who no longer have daughters . . . I who have prayed as well as I could . . .'

'Divine goodness! . . . You're right! But quiet now, do not sob like that . . . My dear cousin . . . take courage. It's only death there's no remedy for! Anyway I don't think anything actually wrong has been done. Just gossip by the evil-minded.

Raimondo is a little out of hand, but not that! No, I can't believe that! The fault, I swear, is the other's . . . She may like being courted, particularly by the Count of Lumera! Pure vanity, you can be quite sure! But don't weep! How these things hurt one, Holy God! . . . With such a lovely family where there should be the peace of angels, with two little cherubs who might have come straight from heaven! But your husband ought to know it; you see he'll understand . . . Why not call your father? It's for him to help you.'

The baron, on the other hand, was writing her reproving letters for abandoning her daughters, accusing her of loving her husband more than her children, and calling her home for her sister's wedding. She tried for a little longer to hide from him the tempest broken over her head, the torture to which she was put by those accusations. But suddenly in the autumn he came to see her alone.

' What's up? Are you ill? What's wrong with your husband? Why haven't you written to me? Why haven't you come?'

She protested that nothing was happening, that she did not feel very well, and that was why she had been unable to come to him. The imminent explanation between her father and Raimondo terrified her. Knowing the overbearing character and contemptuous manners of her husband, and the outbursts of rage her father was capable of, she lived in suspense, forgetting her sorrows in order to avoid an outburst, the more so as the baron did not seem to believe in her protestations and showed a frowning brow in that house where before he had always been so proud to set foot. Now he was out most of the time and came back more frowning than ever, without saying a word to Raimondo. One evening he shut himself in her room and said:

' Will you talk to me finally now? Don't deny, it's useless; I know the whole story.'

She trembled all over and stuttered out:

' What d'you know? I don't understand . . . I don't know . . .'

' I know that your husband is leading a gay life and showing you his great love,' exclaimed the baron in a voice heavy with menace. ' I got an anonymous letter; that's why I came. There's never a lack of good folk of that kind! But as you don't talk . . . as you don't confide in your father! . . . Now you must put cards on the table, d'you understand?' He banged one hand hard against the other.

'Yes, yes, don't worry yourself . . .'

She did not now know from whence came that superhuman calm, that strength to deny the reason for her long agony.

'Don't worry yourself, darling daddy. Can't you see how calm I am . . . I swear to you, I know nothing. They must be calumnies . . . There are so many bad people about. An anonymous letter! D'you take seriously what is in an anonymous letter?'

The baron walked up and down the room, clicking his thumb and forefinger, and looking round with a frown.

'All the better! All the better! But this continual coming and going must end! You must decide to stay at some place permanently, in your own home, with your children, like all other human beings.'

'That's what we are saying too. D'you think that we're not sure of that? Raimondo wants to return to Florence. We'd be there now if it weren't for this business of division and payment to my sisters-in-law . . .' And she added with a smile, 'Are the children a burden, perhaps?'

'Don't be silly. You can't take me in, you know!'

From every word of her father's, from that impetuosity of his, reined in with difficulty, she felt that he knew with certainty of Raimondo's betrayal and of something more serious still; and her heart shut up as in a vice, and strength abandoned her, and a quiver began to run over her whole body. Suddenly she started. Raimondo was knocking at the door, calling her.

'What are you doing?' he asked as he came in, glancing at them with curiosity.

'Oh, nothing . . .'

'Nothing,' repeated the baron. 'We were talking about the decision you must take . . . D'you want to continue homeless, and pay for that place in Florence just to keep it shut?'

'Me?' replied Raimondo in a tone of amazement, as if falling from the clouds. 'If I could,' he burst out, 'I'd already have got out of this filthy place even on foot. Do you think I enjoy it here among these dolts, presumptuous, ignorant, stinking, envious, ill-mannered?' Nothing could hold him back, never had he launched out so violently against his fellow-citizens. Gesticulating wildly, as if he were being contradicted, he went through a whole litany of recriminations, including in his disgust the whole of Sicily, the Neapolitan kingdom, the entire south.

'Then when have you decided to leave?' interrupted the baron sharply.

'When?' replied Raimondo, looking at him a moment. 'You know I'm chained here by business, don't you?'

'Business can be hurried through in a week if one wants to.'

Raimondo was silent a little, then exclaimed with a shrug of the shoulders:

'All right then, you hurry it through if you can.'

The baron was just about to reply, but the words stayed in his throat. Raimondo, slim, graceful, elegant, with his contempt-uous looks and the subtly ironical expression of his delicate white face dominated his father-in-law's strong vigorous figure with its square shoulders, knotty wrists, bronzed visage. They looked at each other an instant, while Matilde stood there pale, her teeth chattering as if from fever. Then the baron glanced at his daughter, saw her dazed eyes turned to him, and bowing his head murmured:

'All right . . . all right . . . Just try to be quick. My daughter's getting married in a few days; I shall expect you then.'

He left next day. When just about to start he told Matilde to get ready, so determined was he to take her with him, even alone, so as to make his son-in-law join them later. She bowed her head and agreed, throwing her arms round his neck in gratitude, for she realised that he had let himself be dominated for love of her and to spare her the pain of a scene. But the baron had scarcely left when Raimondo said to her:

'He's very odd, your father. Does he think we must all do what he likes? Or that I'm married to *him*? . . . I want to see to my own family business myself, d'you understand? And go where I like whenever I like!'

She agreed, subdued as ever by his will, merely murmuring as excuse for her absent father his love for them both.

They went to Milazzo for Carlotta's wedding; then, when bride and groom and the baron left for Palermo, they returned to

Catania, or rather to the Belvedere, where all the Uzeda were. There she had some months of truce; with the Fersa couple not there the Uzeda family seemed to have become amiable again. Her father wrote sometimes from Palermo, sometimes from Milazzo, sometimes from Messina; then he went to Naples too. Finally he returned in April, together with the Duke of Oragua. The latter said he had come on business and had put forward his departure so as to travel with the baron, but he talked a lot about public events, the war in Lombardy, the illness of Ferdinand II. In the duke's company the baron seemed a different man; the intimacy between them, which had grown closer during the journey, soothed him. Even so he repeated to his daughter the offer to take her away with him; but as Raimondo had declared to her that he could not move yet, her reply was:

'No, papa . . . we'll all come . . . soon, in a few days.'

8

STANDING with arms raised, red as a tomato, Don Blasco looked as if he'd like to eat his opponents alive.

'Is that what you call winning? With the help of the strongest, eh? Why did they call for help in that case? Why didn't they fight alone if they had the guts? Is this what you call a victory? Two against one?'

'No, sir,' protested Father Rocca, 'they were twenty thousand less . . .'

'A hundred and sixty thousand Austrians against a hundred and forty thousand Allies,' added Father Dilenna.

'And the Piedmontese fought alone! . . .' affirmed Father Grazzeri.

'What? Where? When?' yelled Don Blasco. 'What are you trying to put across me?'

'Read the papers if you don't know!' exclaimed the others in chorus.

He went pale then, as if mortally insulted.

'Read the papers? . . . Read your newspapers?' He stuttered as if looking for words. 'D'you know what I'd use your newspapers for? . . . Ah, no? You prefer not to understand, eh? . . . This is how I'd use them, this . . .' and he made the gesture of cleaning his backside.

The lay-brother porter put his head over the staircase wall; from the terrace appeared the face of Father Pedantoni peering down into the cloister where the quarrel was growing fiercer.

'That's no sort of answer! Who gives you news, then? Have you a private information service of your own, then, if you don't read newspapers?'

'This . . .' Don Blasco was still gesticulating away, beside himself with rage. 'You dare talk to me about your dirty paper? To me, who'd have the lot of you roped up, you and whoever brings 'em here?'

'Go and denounce us, then. You're capable of it . . .'

'I'd be doing my duty!'

'You'd be doing the spy!'

'Me?'

Father Massei, who was enjoying all this from a seat, suddenly exclaimed, seeing Don Blasco make a gesture to loosen his leather belt:

'Ssh . . . Ssh . . . The Abbot's coming . . .'

But Don Blasco boomed, 'To hell with the Abbot, the Prior and the whole Chapter! Come on then, whoever thinks he's a better man than me! Call me a spy, will you, ye carrion!'

Seeing that he was serious, Father Dilenna moved towards him with a frown. Then Father Pedantoni was forced to get between to separate them.

'Oh, come along, do stop it. What a way . . .'

For some time discussions had ended like that, with yells, insults and threats. Don Blasco had become a fanatic since the Liberals raised their crests after events in Lombardy, the chasing of the Grand Duke from Florence and the growing agitation all over Italy. 'This time it's really true! It's zero hour at last . . .' they would say, and he would launch out first against Napoleon III, that 'son of a who-knows-who', not content with his own manger he comes to scratch about in that of others; then he boomed that Francis II would make them keep a straight plough. 'Just because he's a boy? Just because his father's dead? . . . He'll have you all tied up, the lot of you! You'll see! . . .'

He burst into his greatest fury when the Liberals, after prophesying imminent changes in Sicily and talking of the revolutionary movements that were all ready to break out, produced as proof the return of his brother, the Duke of Oragua, from Palmero. 'That fellow ought to be in prison, tied hand and foot; the imbecile, madman, brigand and traitor! . . .' Then he laughed at himself and vilified his brother in different terms, 'He dangerous? That rabbit? He plot? He's come to hide from the storm! . . . Palermo's all very well for fun, but in time of

227

trouble one's own place is best, where one can shut oneself up and get well under cover . . . If all the mob are like him, Francis will reign another hundred years.'

These remarks he would repeat outside the monastery, before strangers, particularly at the Cigar-woman's where he went every day on leaving the refectory. At the canonical hour Donna Lucia would shut up shop and settle down at her window to watch him leave the monastery gates and enter those of the house where she lived; then she would go to meet him, half-way downstairs, with her daughters and husband. The girls, who were now ten and twelve years of age, looked exactly like Don Blasco, fat and gross as barrels, and they would kiss his hand and call him ' Your Excellency '. Garino, too, did all he could to serve him, pushing out the most comfortable armchair and offering him the biscuits and Rosalìo wine given them by the monk at San Nicola's expense. That was Don Blasco's public visit to his mistress, for later there was a second one when Garino took the girls out for a walk and the two of them remained alone.

Sometimes there was a third meeting at the tobacconist's shop. Apart from tobacco, Garino also kept a café and had two tables with six coffee-cups each for the use of passers-by, most of them police spies and constables and police agents, for he exercised a third profession, that of informer. And so amid this public of faithfuls Don Blasco would have his say about revolutionaries in general and his brother in particular, and learn news at first hand about the traitor's movements. Actually Garino professed great respect for the Duke of Oragua, uncle of the Prince of Francalanza, member of one of the leading families in the kingdom, and when listening to Don Blasco's curses he shook his head a little. But, if one thought it over, was His Paternity so entirely mistaken? The duke did wrong to frequent Don Lorenzo Giulente so much, who was an out-and-out Liberal—of course not being a real noble—and who by means of the British Consul —the police knew everything!—got newspapers, proclamations and other prohibited matter. Don Lorenzo in fact had been visited by police inspectors at home, but they did not go to the duke from respect for the Uzeda family . . . That was just what Don Blasco found intolerable; that he should enjoy immunity, be spoken of as a revolutionary leader without running any kind of risk. The monk would have liked to see him treated like others, shackled even more tightly.

'They're all mad dogs! What's needed is a stick! What's needed is a muzzle!' Garino shook his head; the Royal Intendant Fitalia would never allow the Duke of Oragua to be molested unless of course he went too far. But this much was certain, that a grandee like him had everything to lose and nothing to gain by getting on the side of the 'disestablishment' and the agitators; the Intendant had told him so face to face! ... Then, on hearing that his brother was received by the representative of the Government, Don Blasco abused him in different terms:

'The fox! The chameleon! The turn-coat! ... How can they trust him? He just goes with the winning party! He tricks the lot! He'd betray the father who created him!'

And on leaving the Cigar-woman's he would repeat all these remarks in public at Timpa's pharmacy, which was the head-quarters of the loyalists, while the revolutionaries met at Cardarella's. If any one of them, scandalised by the monk's violence, suggested that he ought not to talk in such a way to strangers about his own brother, 'Brother?' he would protest. 'I've no brothers! I've no relations! I've no-one; how could I praise 'em?'

He was particularly enraged because nothing at the palace went as he wanted. The year before, at the moment when the dates arranged by the princess for payment to her daughters fell due, Chiara and Lucrezia had not been in agreement. The marchese, critical of the girl's love for Giulente, had again made friends with the prince, who had also gone out of his way to be friendly in return in order to propitiate him. Ferdinando, intent on putting together a museum of natural history, did not even know what was happening. And so, not only had the legatees never asked for accounts, but the prince, adducing lack of money, had got powers from the marchese to put off payment until the following year.

The date came when it was due and still Giacomo did not pay, with the excuse of public disquiet, hold-up in business, scarcity of crops and impossibility of marketing them. And Don Blasco was infuriated to hear that his nieces and nephews, forgetting any reasons, had even accepted the constant delays and the prince's canny excuses. That potty Federico and his wife in particular now refused to listen to anyone, being in the seventh heaven with hope for a child—as if the Messiah himself was to come from Chiara's belly!—and that booby Ferdinando was reducing his garden to a stinking charnel-house from a sudden mania for embalming animals—without realising that he himself was the most animal of the lot! Then that other wretch Lucrezia was living in the clouds, sillier than ever, going pale at the mention of Giulente, a beardless, complaining youth who also chattered away about constitution and liberty! Finally there was this business about Raimondo not wanting to move and his wife longing to go; Don Blasco, from hatred for the intruder, took the side of the nephew he most loathed.

'Leave? To go where? What about the earthquake in Florence? These aren't times to leave one's own parts!'

Raimondo adduced the same reason, and the others repeated it; Matilde felt a plot tightening ever more closely around her. She had to be content now with going to and from Milazzo every month to see her daughters, as she could no longer endure the Uzedas' ill-treatment of them. Her father seemed to have forgotten about Raimondo and was going round Sicily on pretence of business, but actually on work against the Government. Don Blasco and Donna Ferdinanda would amuse themselves by predicting he would be thrown into prison any day, as that made the *intruder* weep. The duke, on the other hand, spoke well of the baron, and had long interviews with him when he passed through Catania. Now he was exalting the genius of Cavour and the triumph of his policy; when his old criticisms about the Crimea expedition were brought up, he denied having ever made them. Francis II's line of conduct he considered mistaken; the king should have made an alliance with Piedmont, not with Austria, granted a constitution and avoided stirring up the patriots, for Napoleon had said clearly, 'Italy must be free from the Alps to the Adriatic . . .' Hearing such opinions made Don Blasco want to vomit, and he would champ with rage, unable to attack his eldest brother directly. But the day that the news came of the peace of Villafranca he nearly had a stroke from delight. Along the corridors of San Nicola, before the monks of the other party quietly tucking their tails between their legs, he went shouting triumphantly:

'Oho, so what about the great Cavour? And the great Piedmont? Where are they now? Why don't they go on with the war alone? What about the Adriatic? And the Tyrrhenian? And that fellow who was always making pronouncements and for ever shouting N A B B O L E O N E! As if Napoleon would ever have told him what he wanted to do! They thought they'd got him right in their pocket, Napoleon! . . .'

'But aren't you against him for not keeping to his own manger?'

'What? When? Nonsense! The spree's over! . . . What a king, Francis II! What a king! A worthy son of his father! . . .'

He could not have been more arrogant or looked down on people more if they had made him king himself. And he let himself go at the palace too, seeing his brother shaking his head and murmuring that the last word was not yet said.

'Last word indeed! The great C A V U R R E can shut up shop! The legitimate princes are all coming back! You've backed the wrong horse, can't you see?'

Every day he would ask if the duke had made any preparations for departure; that brother of his weighed on him like a stone in the belly, and he longed for him to return to Palermo, as if there could be no peace in town until he had gone. At the monastery he insulted those who still dared to contradict him and discussions nearly ended in blows. Even the Abbot had to ask Fathers Dilenna and Rocca to let him have his say so as to avoid a scene. The Prior, on the other hand, kept away from such matters; no one knew what way he thought. If anyone talked to him of politics he would listen, shake his head and reply, 'Such matters do not concern me . . . Render unto Caesar the things which are Caesar's . . .'

In the Novitiate, strife between the two parties was sharpening. The young prince, on Don Blasco's passing the word, now also took on an air of triumph, jeering at Giovannino Radalì, head of the revolutionaries, calling him a 'baron without a barony' and a 'loony's son'. The Duke Radalì had in fact died in raving delirium, and so his widowed duchess had arranged for the second son Giovannino to take the vows. This was another argument used by Consalvo to crush his cousin, 'I'll leave, and you'll always stay here . . .' Giovannino, in spite of their differing political ideas, liked him and put up with his jeers. But sometimes he went into a dangerous frenzy too; blood would rush to his head, his eyes flash. Flinging himself on his cousin, he would knock him down and hit him hard until Fra' Carmelo ran up with hands on high.

'For the love of God . . . What ways are these? . . . Can't you keep quiet? Think of some other amusement!'

When the two boys made it up they did amuse themselves. The cousins were yearning to smoke. Giovannino had obtained a few tobacco seeds from Fra' Cola in great secrecy, and planted them in a corner of the garden; the plants were growing fast and soon they could make cigars from them. Meanwhile they played from morn till night, with a few minutes of study sandwiched in between and a few hours of religious ceremonies.

For the Feast of St Agatha in August they were free all day and watched the procession, the sung Mass in Piazza degli Studi, and with more pleasure the race of barbary horses, called by Raimondo *barbarian*. This they did along the Corso, between two living hedges of spectators, on whom the horses often flung themselves, distributing kicks and bruising ribs. The winning horses then returned down the street at walking pace, preceded by grooms calling out every now and again to the balconies:

> '*Come out, oh princes and barons,*
> '*Tis the King of Beasts who passes.*'

And from the crowds came 'Olè . . .'

Consalvo's attention was riveted by the Spanish ceremonial of such festivals. The city Senate, in a state coach as big as a house, preceded by outriders and standard-bearers and catapans playing drums, passed on its way to fetch the Royal Intendant, who was waiting at his gates. The youngest senator then had to put a foot on the step as if about to alight, but the representative of the Government came forward, with arms outstretched to prevent him touching the ground. These were prerogatives of the city. The Senate had long contests with other authorities about positions to be occupied in the cathedral during great religious functions; to avoid more dissension a line of marble which no one could cross had been set in the floor.

When the Feast of St Agatha was over, novices and lay-brothers at San Nicola prepared for that of the Holy Nail, awaited every year with high anticipation.

King Martin had always worn that relic round his neck, and presented it to the monks in 1393; it was one of the nails with a piece of wood of the True Cross. On the 14th of September the golden orb encrusted with jewels containing the sacred relic was exposed to the adoration of the faithful, while the Abbot, surrounded by all the monks in cowls, celebrated pontifical High Mass to the accompaniment of the great organ.

But the real festival took place that night, when the big open space in front of San Nicola seemed transformed into a drawing-room, with torches everywhere, and chairs arranged for ladies who came in carriages from the Trinità and the Crociferi to watch the procession. This issued to the sound of bells and a band, between two rows of soldiers, from the main door of the church which seemed aflame with light. The Abbot held the gold reliquary, followed by a long procession which returned inside again after making the round outside. Then began the fireworks —rockets, catherine-wheels, luminous fountains, and a great final display which changed shape and colour four times and ended with a stunning crackle of continuous fireworks while hundreds of shining snakes uncoiled in the dark air . . .

The young prince, next to his parents, had no time to watch them all, so busy was he, acting host, because the people in the square and throughout the district were guests of the Benedictines. The whole city had turned up there, the ladies in pretty summer dresses, which they were wearing for the last time, as this celebration marked the end of the season. Donna Mara Fersa, with her daughter-in-law and the latter's relatives from Palermo, were on the opposite side of the square to the Uzeda; Don Mario was in the country. Now they scarcely greeted each other before the eyes of the world; Donna Isabella had been forbidden to go to Donna Ferdinanda's any longer, or to any other of the count's relations. People had gradually stopped gossiping on that subject. Even Raimondo seemed resigned; he was no longer to be seen rushing after Donna Isabella, and she was not quarrelling any more with her mother-in-law or playing the victim as she had before. That evening she was wearing such a sumptuous robe and so many jewels that all eyes were on her. When the crowd began to thin out, Father Gerbini, always gallant, accompanied her to a carriage and, as by chance, the Fersa and the Francalanza coachmen had put their carriages alongside each other, Raimondo and the prince as they drove off took their hats off to the ladies, to which only Donna Isabella and her uncle from Palermo replied.

The very next day after that festa, from mouth to mouth throughout the city ran an amazing, an astounding, an incredible piece of news: Donna Mara Fersa had thrust her daughter-in-law from the house! . . . Was it true? Surely not! . . . Had they not been together the night before at San Nicola? . . . What? Why? Everything had seemed over! . . . But the well-informed said it was not over at all and that the bomb had burst that very night because of Don Mario's absence. Donna Mara, after having driven her daughter-in-law's relations to their hotel, returned home and fallen asleep, had heard a sound in Donna Isabella's room. On entering it she found her daughter-in-law half-naked, with a window open and a man's hat on the floor. Had she been a moment earlier she would have caught them in the act, but he had escaped in a flash by the balcony giving on to the stable roofs. Without any need to name names, all understood that *he* was the count . . . Donna Isabella went pale as a corpse, they said, when her mother-in-law cried hoarsely, ' Get out of my house! . . .' just like that, as she was! In slippers, without giving her time to put on a pair of shoes! She had gone, with her maid holding a bag, to the hotel of that uncle who had providentially come from Palermo. ' Suppose he hadn't been there? Where would she have gone? What about the husband, Don Mario? . . .'

Don Mario arrived at dawn at breakneck speed, called by express message. And how he sobbed! Like a child! How devoted he'd been to his wife! And to the count too! That was his mistake! Not his mother's though; the friendship of the Uzeda had not gone to her head. Since the very beginning she realised the turn things were taking. Had it not been for her the crisis would have happened a long time before, and Raimondo need not have taken so many precautions. For he was risking his life every time. Whenever Fersa went off to the country the count entered Donna Isabella's room, having bribed all the servants; but from the stable gates, which the coachman opened, he had to get up on to the coachhouse roof, climb over the balcony and enter his mistress's room from there . . . It was a miracle that he had not been caught before! The last night, as he was escaping without a hat, he had met the nightwatchmen, who were about to arrest him; but hearing that he was the Count Uzeda, they let him go.

The incredulous and curious went so far as to ask the police, but were sent packing. And that very day everyone saw young Count Raimondo at the Nobles' Club gambling and chattering away the same as ever. Could he really flout public opinion to that point? Or was the story going around to be doubted? Already versions favourable to Donna Isabella were circulating. Her being up at midnight? She had been unable to sleep! And the open window? Because of the great heat. And the hat on the floor? An old one of the coachman's, which she had been amusing herself throwing about that afternoon! . . . If all these things had not been made clear at once, it was due to that old harridan Donna Mara. She loathed her daughter-in-law, everyone knew how she had ill-treated her! Who had even mentioned the count? What had the count to do with it? Who had seen him? He was in his own home, where he had returned immediately after the procession of the Holy Nail; the prince, the princess, the whole family, all the servants could attest that! Perhaps it was because he had paid Donna Isabella a few visits some time ago? But he had soon stopped, seeing how such an innocent friendship was being taken in ill stead! How right he was to want to leave Catania, to rebel against the malice of his own fellow-citizens . . . Gradually those voices acquired credit; it was even said that Fersa had quarrelled with his mother for not having given the accused woman time to prove her innocence.

The whole town discussed, commented, weighed every piece of news about this affair, got more worked up about it than about a kingdom's fall. Some were on the count's side, protesting that a family man like him would never upset another family; some judged him capable of this or that, to satisfy a whim. Had he not led a wild life as a bachelor? And when a married man had he not made his poor wife suffer a lot? Luckily when all this happened she was away with her father in Milazzo.

Three days later Raimondo's defenders triumphed; he left for Milazzo to join his wife and daughters. Donna Isabella, meanwhile, had left with her uncle for Palermo. Who dared still affirm there had been anything wrong between them? That fool of a Donna Mara Fersa had put her foot in it! . . . The incredulous went to the Francalanza palace and the hotel to see if the departures were true. They were; Donna Isabella and Raimondo had left, one for Milazzo and the other for Palermo; the prince was making ready to go off to the Belvedere; Fersa with his mother was already at Leonforte.

During that autumn in the country the story was discussed ceaselessly.

There was much talk of it at Nicolosi among the Benedictine fathers. Father Gerbini among others was a paladin of Donna Isabella's innocence, encouraged in this by the fact that Raimondo had gone from Milazzo to Florence, where he was now settled with his family. Don Blasco, though, did not open his mouth on this subject. He seemed to have forgotten about his relations' affairs, busy as he was breathing fire at the news of public events, the votes by Romagna and Emilia for annexation to Piedmont, Farini's dictatorship, and particularly the Treaty of Zürich, which kept him on the rampage for the whole autumn and winter. With the Liberal monks he would plunge into tempestuous discussions which threatened to end in blows, about Cavour's return to office, the plebiscites of central Italy and all the symptoms of radical change. But when Nice and Savoy were ceded to France he was as delighted as if they'd been given to him; after the abortive attempt at revolt in Palermo on 4th April he crowed victory, shouting:

'Aha, you're done, can't you see? Down with those hands now! Talk and shout and bawl as much as you like, but you don't break anything! Who breaks pays, and the plates aren't yours!'

'It's you who can't see! You can't see it's not like '48 now!'

'Eh? Ah? Oh? Why not? What's so new then?'

236

'What's new is that Piedmont is strong . . . That France is helping her secretly . . . that England . . . that Garibaldi . . .'

'Who? . . . When? . . . France? . . . Fine help! Garibaldi? Who's Garibaldi? Never heard of him . . .'

He heard of him on the 13th of May, when the news of the landing at Marsala burst like a bomb. But this time he did not shout, or spit curses; he merely shrugged his shoulders and affirmed that at the first shot from the Neapolitans, the 'brigands' would disperse. The Murat, Bandiera, Pisacane affairs, were proof of that.

'It's another tune now!' said Father Rocca in his face after the defeat of Calatafimi.

Don Blasco burst out:

'But, you bunch of cadgers, why on earth are you rubbing your hands so? Have you had a win on the lottery? Or d'you think that Garibaldi will come and make Popes of you all? Don't you see, ye cretins, that you've a lot to lose and nothing to gain?'

He was beside himself; the Garibaldini's victorious advance exasperated him; the formation of rebel squads, the ferment reigning in the city and country infuriated him. But his rage was most violent against the duke, who was now definitely siding with the revolutionaries and leaving the sinking ship. The monk said things against his brother which would have made a cavalryman blush, called all the authorities traitors because, instead of repressing the movement, they waited, scratching their bellies, to see if Garibaldi entered Palermo or not.

'Palermo? Lanza'll fling him out! There are twenty thousand troops in Palermo! But examples must be made! Raise the gibbet in the Fortress square!'

Instead of which the rebel squads all linked up around the city, Liberals talked out loud, the police pretended not to hear, and 'decent folk' had to go into hiding! And that swine General Clary, with three thousand men under his orders, would not leave the Ursino castle and make a clean sweep, he just let the 'decent folk's' panic increase. On the night of the 27th, amid ill-concealed jubilation by the revolutionaries, arrived news of Garibaldi's entry into Palermo; the bands threatened to come down into Catania and attack Clary's troops. But the duke recommended calm and assured all that the Neapolitans would leave without firing a shot. Giacomo, in spite of the imposing and protective air he now put on with the family, as if he controlled wind and rain, decided, just in case of trouble, to make arrangements for their safety at the Belvedere. Lucrezia, seeing those preparations for departure, fretted at the idea of leaving Giulente, who wrote to her, 'The hour of trial is at hand: I rush to the post where duty calls me, with Italy's name and yours on my lips!' But at the news that all procrastination was over and the squads were about to enter the city the prince went to San Nicola to put his son in the care of the Abbot, the Prior and Don Blasco, had his carriages harnessed and left with his whole party except Ferdinando, who would not leave his own place even for plague or revolution. Then the duke, so as not to remain alone in the deserted palace, went and stayed at the monastery where his nephew the Prior gave him a room in the guest wing. Don Blasco on seeing him in there thought he was a ghost; at first he could not bring out a word, then rushed among the monks of his set, shouting:

'The hero! The hero! The hero! The great hero! . . . The thunderbolt of war! . . . He's got in here from fright! Using the excuse of there being no-one at home! His cheeks are awobble with terror . . .'

The monastery was beginning to fill up with timid folk, fugitive priests, Bourbon spies, people in the Liberals' bad books; even the castle was not considered so safe. For the novices, those not taken off by worried parents, it was a holiday; new faces everywhere, an incessant coming and going, constant anticipation of no one knew quite what. The Liberal boys had also got together a band like the ones encamped outside the city. Its leader was Giovannino Radalì, who was nurturing a plot to raise the monastery, go into the streets and join the adult rebels. But they had no flags, and with the excuse of decorating a small altar sent a servant out to buy papers of various colours. The man brought white and red, but blue instead of green; a mistake which caused a day's delay.

The young prince, to whom, as he was considered a spy, the

revolutionaries had of course said nothing, had even so sniffed something in the air and decided to find out what it was. An unusual circumstance helped him. The tobacco he and his cousin had planted was ripe. The leaves, torn off, set for a few days in the sun, were already beginning to shrivel; they just had to be rolled up to make three or four cigars, and these Giovannino considered ready to be smoked. Then, hidden together in a corner of the garden, for they were friends apart from politics, they lit matches and began drawing the first puffs. Out came an acrid, pestilential smoke which burnt eyes and throat. Giovannino was very pale and breathing in gasps, but went on drawing as Consalvo was declaring:

'They're excellent! . . . Real tobacco through and through . . . Don't you like them?'

'Yes . . . a glass of water . . . my head's going round . . .'

Suddenly he went white as paper, his eyes rolled and he began to mutter deliriously:

'The master . . . water . . . the flags.'

Consalvo, on whom the poison was working more slowly, asked:

'What flags? . . . Where are they? . . .'

'Under the bed . . . the revolution . . . Oh dear! . . . I'm going to be sick! . . .'

The young prince flung away his cigar and went indoors. He too felt nausea coming over him, his feet were unsteady and his sight rather misty, but he dragged himself as far as the master.

'They've made flags . . . for the revolution . . . under the bed . . .'

'Who? . . .'

'Them . . . Giovannino . . . the plot . . .'

Nausea was rising, rising, clutching at his throat; his hands were freezing, everything was swirling vertiginously around him.

'What plot? . . . And what's the matter with you?'

'Giovan . . . the rev . . .'

He put his hands out and fell to the ground like a corpse. When he came to his senses he found himself in bed, with Fra' Carmelo watching over him. The light was dim, it was impossible to tell if it was dawn or dusk. No voice or sound of footsteps could be heard in the monastery; only the chirping of sparrows on the orange blossom.

'How do you feel?' asked the lay-brother, tenderly.

'All right . . . What's happened? What time is it?'

'The sun's just risen! . . . You did give us a fright! Don't you recall?'

Then, confusedly, he remembered the cigars, nausea, his denunciation. Had a whole night passed then? What about Giovannino?

'He too! He's better now . . . The master searched in all the rooms, under the beds . . . he found lots of flags . . . His Paternity blamed me . . . as if I knew anything about these devilries!'

The plotters, finding themselves discovered, were desperate, not knowing whence the blow had fallen. But Giovannino, then also recovered, had just got up and was walking among his consternated comrades.

'How did it happen? Was it you?'

'Me? . . . Ah, that Judas of a cousin of mine! . . .' And the blood rushed to his head with a wild impetus of rage, like a true 'loony's son'. 'Wait! Wait!'

They hid and waited for Consalvo to come out, then surrounded him in the garden. Giovannino went up to him and asked:

'Was it you, you dirty little spy, who told the master?'

Consalvo understood. Pale, trembling, he began protesting:

'By the Most Holy Mary! The master . . . It wasn't me . . .'

But the circle grew closer round him.

'So you deny it too, do you? Have you only the guts to lie, you filthy spy!'

'I swear to you . . .'

'Oh, you stinking spy, you . . .' and the first blow fell on his shoulders. Then they were all on top of him; he began yelling, but no-one heard his cries, for suddenly, at that unusual hour, all the bells of San Nicola began ringing out, so unexpectedly and strangely that the boys stopped hitting the informer and looked at each other, flustered. Suddenly Giovannino exclaimed:

'The revolution! . . .' and rushed indoors.

The rebel squads had finally entered the city, to attack the

Neapolitan troops. All the monks locked themselves in. The Abbot had the gates chained after a terrified mob came clamouring for refuge inside the monastery. Only the bell-tower remained open to those in revolt, who continued to ring wildly as the thunder of the first cannons were heard from the Ursino castle.

Don Blasco, in spite of the dagger he wore under his habit, was green with bile and terror and came to take refuge, together with the most suspected pro-Bourbons, in the Novitiate, as a safer corner which no one would be likely to enter because of the young people. Even so he spat out a string of insults against that coward of a brother of his who had stayed inside with the excuse of the gates being shut, while still plotting with that other ' swine ' Lorenzo Giulente.

'Why doesn't he get out into the streets? Why doesn't he go out and fight? I'll open the gates myself if he wants! . . . The rotter! The traitor!'

Actually the duke, who was in confabulation with the Abbot and his nephew the Prior, disapproved of the attack and was repeating General Clary's view as wise and prudent.

'Clary said to me yesterday, "Let's wait to see what Garibaldi does; if he stays in Palermo I'll embark with my soldiers and go; if not, you people must all be patient; I'll be staying." He was quite right, it seems to me! What need was there of attacking him? The fate of Sicily will not be decided here! But they won't listen to me! What can I do about it? I wash my hands of it!'

'They won't listen to him!' stormed Don Blasco, ' after he's gone and loosed them? . . . And now he acts the Jesuit? To stay on good terms with Clary if the mob gets the worst of it?'

Cannon boomed occasionally; people coming from the Botte dell' Acqua seeking a refuge said that the heaviest skirmishing was at the Quattro Cantoni, but elsewhere the rebels were only sniping at the troops from behind corners of houses or terraces. Bourbon agents, pale and terrified, hurried in to take refuge in the lay-brothers' cells. Garino, one of the first to shut himself up in San Nicola, stuck to Don Blasco's habit and seemed quite out of his mind. The young prince too kept close to his uncle,

not daring even to complain about the beating-up he had
received, while Giovannino Radalì and the other Liberals among
the boys surrounded Fra' Carmelo and said to him:

'Now Garibaldi's coming! . . . We'll all be leaving! . . .
We'll never be returning! . . .'

Before evening the bell-ringing and cannonades stopped. Don
Blasco, who had gone to question passers-by from the walls
of the flower-garden, returned waving his arms and roaring with
delight:

'The great revolution's over! . . . The Lancers came out and
cleared the streets . . . Hurray! . . . Hurray! . . .'

This news was confirmed from all sides, but the duke, for the
moment, prudently remained inside. Don Blasco's joy, however,
was of short duration. Next day, on orders from Naples, Clary
prepared for departure, and, handing over the city to a provisional junta, embarked the day after with all his troops.

Don Lorenzo Giulente with his nephew went up to San Nicola
and invited the duke to the Town Hall, where leading citizens
were trying to control the revolution. Already, after the troops'
departure, in the first excitement of liberation, the first impulse
to vengeance, a group of workmen had chased one of the worst
and most hated police 'rats', killed him, and carried his head
around the town. The duke's heart was aquiver at the thought
of leaving the safe refuge of the monastery and going into the
city in its ferment, but the two Giulente assured him that all
was quiet now and that he was expected by friends. So together
they crossed streets more deserted than in time of plague, with
all shops and windows barred up and a terrifying silence.

Don Gaspare Uzeda, in spite of the Giulentes' assurances,
and the proofs of his popularity newly acquired among Liberals,
was afraid that someone might blame him for his lurking in
San Nicola on the day of battle, or that the revolutionaries of
'48 would remember old tales. His legs trembled as he entered
the Town Hall, crossed the crowded courtyard, went up to the
room where they were deliberating; but gradually a smile came
out on his pale closed lips, blood began circulating freely in his
veins again, as he found himself saluted respectfully and cordi-
ally on all sides. Workers bowed to him, friends shook his hand

and exclaimed, 'At last! . . . It's come! . . . We're free! . . . At last we're our own masters! . . .'

The most urgent matter to be dealt with was arranging some kind of service of public order, a militia to act until the formation of a National Guard. Money was needed to arm this militia and Guard. A subscription was opened to collect funds, and the duke offered three hundred *onze*. No one had given so much, the sum produced a sensation. When the meeting broke up, Don Gaspare was accompanied back to San Nicola by some dozens of people.

Next morning he added another hundred *onze* to buy ammunition. His popularity was growing by leaps and bounds. There was a dearth of work, as the city was still more or less a desert; he let no-one of those who turned to him for help go away empty-handed. He plucked up courage and went every day to the Reading Room, where Liberals commented jubilantly on news of the revolution's progress. He put himself at the head of demonstrators going to fetch the band from the Charity Home, and went round town to the sound of the 'Garibaldi Anthem'. Gradually, as he felt more and more reassured, he became quite at home in the Town Hall where his advice was always being asked. While all were talking of liberty and equality, no-one thought of doing anything to show how times had changed and privileges been destroyed and all citizens become really and truly equal. He suggested and had passed a decree for the abolition of superfine bread. This made him a great hero.

Don Blasco, lying low in the monastery, fumed away; not so much perhaps at the ruin of his party and the triumph of heresy, as at the news of his brother being suddenly considered a champion of liberty. The Governor would do nothing without the duke's consent and put him on every commission, a group of admirers accompanied him to the Francalanza palace, which he had reopened and was now living in lest its closing be imputed to the family's pro-Bourbonism; and petty shopkeepers and workers, all those who did not know what would happen next, were converted to the new party on hearing that a grandee like the Duke of Oragua, a Francalanza, was in it. Day and night as many patriotic demonstrations with music and torches and flags took place beneath the palace windows as beneath those of old Liberals who had been in prison or returned from exile.

Now everyone talked in the squares, from balconies, to stir people up or discuss what action to take in the political clubs being formed. But the duke, incapable of saying two consecutive words in public, terrified at the idea of having to speak before a crowd, would come down and meet them at the gates and get out of it by shouting with them, 'Long live Garibaldi! Long live Victor Emmanuel! Long live liberty! . . .' by taking Garibaldi volunteers to a café, paying for their ices, cigars and liqueurs. On the formation of the National Guard he was made a major in it. Every day he sent round to the guard on duty bottles of wine, cakes, packets of cigars, presents of all kinds. And his reputation grew and grew; in demonstrations the cry of 'Long live Oracqua!'—as most pronounced it—was as frequent as 'Long live Garibaldi!' or 'Victor Emmanuel! . . .' All these enormities reduced Don Blasco to grim silence more terrible than any shouts. But the monk was not at the end of his trials. For where should the exiles, the brigands enrolling to follow the anti-Christ, be lodged? At San Nicola! . . .

At the announcement that Nino Bixio's and Menotti Garibaldi's column was coming to Catania, the Governor had sent a messenger to tell the Abbot that he had arranged for the soldiers of liberty to be put up at the monastery of the Benedictine Fathers. The Abbot, pro-Bourbon to the eyebrows, tried to make difficulties, but the Prior Don Lodovico persuaded him that it was best not to put up opposition.

On the 27th July the National Guard marched out to meet, just outside the gates, the column entering the city amid hurricanes of applause, and the volunteers were quartered at San Nicola, along the first floor and Clock corridors. Straw scattered over the floors, arms racks, rifles, cartridge cases, bayonets, pipestems, reduced the monastery to a state of siege. To reach the refectory Don Blasco had to cross this inferno twice a day. He would pass by, mute, pale, fretting, while the soldiers shouted 'Hurrahs!' to the Prior Don Lodovico, who had wine and cakes distributed.

All day long the men trained down in the outer courtyard.

Bixio watched, whip in hand; occasionally he laid it across the shoulders of the most recalcitrant . . . 'All in the name of liberty! All to get rid of age-old tyranny!' the pro-Bourbon monks exclaimed to Don Blasco, but the latter did not even reply. Nothing seemed to interest him any longer, as if the world were about to end.

Bixio and Menotti were lodged in the guest wing. The Abbot avoided them, but the Prior—from prudence he said—treated his guests with all respect, enquired solicitously if there was anything they needed, and put the flower-garden at the disposal of the son of anti-Christ, who spent his leisure moments cultivating roses. One day, the novices, who were much reduced in number because many families had withdrawn their sons during the upset, were in a state of great expectation; Menotti was to come among them. Giovannino Radalì, Pedantoni, all the Liberals gazed at him with wide eyes as if he'd dropped from the moon, without bringing out a word, while he patted their heads. But Giovannino ran into the garden to pick the best rose and offered it to him calling him 'General! . . .' Consalvo was standing apart, frowning like his uncle Don Blasco, very downcast.

'Not acting the spy " rat " any more,' said his companions, when Menotti left. 'Are you afraid of your tail being cut off?'

He did not reply. One day his father, reassured by the way public events were going, came down to see him.

'I don't want to stay here any more,' the boy told him. 'So many boys have left . . .'

'*Want?* . . .' replied the prince in a harsh tone, 'Who taught you to use the word " *want* " . . .? You have to stay here for the moment.'

The duke not only approved of that decision but induced his nephew to bring his family back to town, as there was no danger, and such prolonged keeping apart, such signs of fear, might be taken ill by people. They all arrived a few days later, the marchese and the marchesa alone, beside themselves with delight in a carriage moving at foot's pace out of regard for Chiara's pregnancy, now finally confirmed as being in its sixth month. Every time the carriage stopped at blockposts Lucrezia put her head out of the window, thinking she recognised Giulente in every soldier.

But Benedetto was no longer in Sicily. In the first days he had helped his uncle Lorenzo and the duke to bring some order into the revolution, haranguing the crowds, speaking in the clubs with an eloquence admired by all, writing articles in a paper called *Italia risorta* founded by his uncle to urge annexation to Piedmont. Then in spite of his father and mother's opposition, he had volunteered as a Garibaldino in a regiment of Scouts, and left for the mainland. On arrival in town, Lucrezia found a letter from the young man announcing that he was going to join Garibaldi to carry out his duty towards his country, and recommending her not to weep should the great fate befall him of dying for Italy. She began reading every newspaper and every bulletin to learn what had happened to him, but understood less than ever, as she was quite incapable of making out the southern army's movements.

Don Blasco, at his relations' arrival, finally let out the bile that had been accumulating for three months. Every day, on coming to the palace, he spewed out curses against his brother and heaped the prince himself with insults for allowing the hated tricolour flag to hang from the central balcony, for putting out lights to greet that 'brigand's' victories.

The prince looked humble and agreed, exclaiming, 'But what can I do about it? He's my uncle! Can I send him away?' He was careful, however, not to make any remonstrances to the duke, very glad that the great patriot's popularity should guarantee him his person and his home. But he made safety doubly sure; he talked against the duke to Don Blasco, against Don Blasco to the duke, certain of not being found out, as those two avoided each other like the plague. He also had to keep at bay Donna Ferdinanda, who had become a termagant after the fall of the legitimate Government, was for ever invoking its return and even went so far as to promise Saint Barbara a votive lamp if she threw all her thunderbolts against the betrayers. She demanded that the young prince be taken away from a monastery so infested by revolutionaries, and she adjured her little nephew, when the latter came to see her on holiday, 'Don't risk talking to those enemies of God or I'll never look you in the face again!' Consalvo's reply was, 'Yes, Excellency!' as it was to the duke when the latter said to him, 'Fine soldiers, those Garibaldini, eh? . . .'

The boy's shoulders were still smarting from that beating for spying; now he was following the example of his uncle the Prior, who enjoyed the confidence of the out-and-out pro-Bourbon Abbot and was meanwhile very popular with the revolutionaries . . . What did the young prince care about Bourbon or Savoy? He wanted to get away from the Novitiate; that was why he had a secret rancour against his father, who had not allowed him to do so.

Anyway, even with the revolution and liberty and Victor Emmanuel and abolition of superfine bread, at San Nicola there was no joking about privileges. In those very days the Giulente family had recommended to the Abbot a distant cousin of theirs, a young man who had been orphaned at Syracuse and come to Catania to become a Benedictine. This Luigi was a complete contrast to his cousin Benedetto. Not only was he against the revolution, but he had true fear of God and a great vocation for the monastic state. The Abbot, considering the nobility of his family proved, had taken him under his own protection and entered him in the Novitiate. There his noble companions, without distinction of party, made fun of him, jeered at him, played all sorts of tricks on him, considering him unworthy of being among them. And the monks, even the liberal Fathers, turned up their noses; Victor Emmanuel was all right; annexation and constitution even better; but to renounce their privileges and be quite indiscriminate, that was really a bit too much!

The annexation question and how to vote on it was agitating public opinion then; some wanted to confide the mandate to an elected assembly, others were for direct suffrage. Every day with the Governor of the city and Don Lorenzo Giulente and the Liberal leaders, the duke upheld a plebiscite. 'The people must be left free to pronounce. Their own fate is in question! You see what's been done in the rest of Italy! . . .' This advice increased his popularity a thousandfold, but drew on him, more violently than ever, Don Blasco and Donna Ferdinanda's hatred and even Don Eugenio's criticism.

The cavaliere, having lost hope of excavating Massa Annunziata, had thought up a new idea: to get himself nominated university professor. Were there not a number of nobles in such posts, which were both decorous and gentlemanly? He had his eye particularly on the chair of history. His archaeological knowledge, his little work on *A Sicilian Pompeii*, were surely titles enough. To have an even better one, he was now writing: *A Chronological History of the Uzeda Viceroys, Lieutenants-General of the Aragonese Kings in the Trinacria*. Being a Gentleman of the Bedchamber, he did not show himself around much, but, sure that the revolution would be crushed at any moment, he too inveighed against the duke.

'What's all this about the people! If only the Viceroys could return from the next world! If they heard these heresies, saw one of their descendants join the mob!'

Don Cono, Don Giacinto, Don Mariano, all the parasites shook their heads in sorrow at such a degeneration, but they also tried to placate the just anger of purists by suggesting that the duke's liberalism was just for show, a political necessity of the moment; it was impossible that, in his heart, a son of a Prince of Francalanza, one of those Uzeda, who owed everything to legitimate dynasties, should support anarchy and usurpation!

'So much the worse!' screamed Don Blasco. 'I can understand a resolute turn-coat, one who has the courage of his convictions! But if the Neapolitans return he'll go and kiss their arses! You'll see when they return! . . .'

But they did not return. Instead there arrived the news, in rapid succession, of Francis II's departure from Naples, Garibaldi's triumphal entry, the Piedmontese advance to meet the volunteers. At the Belvedere, where the prince returned at the end of September for his autumn visit, Lucrezia read bulletins of the Volturno battle mentioning Benedetto Giulente among the wounded. She did not cry, but shut herself in her room refusing food, deaf to the comforts of Vanna, who promised her that she would try to get news from his family. But the Governor had already applied to the army command and the Director of the Military Hospital at Naples, and the reply, which came before any more bulletins, was made public in a communiqué put up on the Town Hall: Volunteer Giulente was wounded by steel in the right leg and was in Caserta Hospital; his state was satisfactory and his recovery assured.

He arrived a fortnight later, on the eve of the plebiscite, with other Sicilian volunteers from the Volturno. His uncle Lorenzo, the Duke of Oragua, the Governor and the National Guard went to meet them. The young man was leaning on a stick, and waving a handkerchief with his left hand in reply to the greetings of the crowd. His father and mother wept with emotion; the duke gently violated their wishes and took the wounded man into his own carriage, which moved off towards the Town Hall amid waves of popular acclamation. From the balcony of the Town Hall, crowded with National Guards, returned exiles, patriots, notabilities, Benedetto glanced down over the square where not a grain of millet could have fallen, then raised his left hand. He already had an established fame as an orator; at that gesture they were silent.

'Citizens!' he began in a clear, firm voice, 'we cannot and we should not thank you for this trumphal greeting, knowing that your applause is not directed to our persons, but to the sublime ideal which guided the Dictator from Quarto to Marsala.' A hurricane of applause broke out, in the midst of which the orator's voice was lost '. . . dream of Dante and Machiavelli, yearning of Petrarch and Leopardi, throb of twenty centuries . . . to her, to our great common land . . . to our re-born nation . . . to united Italy . . . go the hurrahs, the applause, the triumph . . .' At his every phrase rose a great clamour from the square; those on the balcony waved their handkerchiefs, the duke exclaimed in his neighbours' ears, 'How well he talks! . . . What a brilliant young man! . . .'

'We have done our duty,' went on the orator, 'as you have done yours. 'Tis not a few drops of blood but life itself we should have liked to offer for the great cause . . . worthy of envy, but not of regret, are those who can say as they die " The life which thou my native land gavest me I render back to thee . . ." Honour to the strong who fell! . . . With you lies no less proud a duty: to give admiring Europe the example of a people which, having broken its chains and being left to its own devices, is already showing itself worthy of those free institutions which were its ancient heritage . . . which an abhorred and perjured power dared to cancel . . . and which will now be more resplendent than ever! . . . Citizens! Applaud yourselves . . . Applaud your rulers . . . Applaud these warlike brethren who were unable to bare the sword as their duty was to look after your interests at home . . . Applaud this noble patrician who has added to the glories of his ancestral name that of the purest of patriots! . . .'

He pointed to the duke, majestic and martial in his major's uniform. But the latter, at the idea of having to reply, suddenly felt his tongue go dry, saw the square transformed into a terrible swirling sea with waves all darting looks up at him; such was his spasm of terror that he had to hold tight to the balustrade. But Giulente swept on into his final peroration, amid stunning applause. 'Citizens! Prodigious is the road we have covered in five months; but a last step remains to us . . . The enthusiasm with which I see you animated gives me confidence that it will be done . . . The sun of tomorrow greets Sicily united for ever to the constitutional monarchy of Victor Emmanuel!'

Already ' Yes ' was traced in huge letters on walls, doors, ground; at the palace gates the duke had had a colossal ' Yes ' written up in chalk; next day, in city and countryside, clusters of people wore it in their hats, printed on cardboard of every size and colour. At the Belvedere, Donna Ferdinanda noticed peasants had put the letters upside down being unable to read and exclaimed:

' Yes, yes,' pronouncing it *chis*, *chis*, the sound people made to chase cats away, and commented:

' They're not saying " Yes, yes "; they say " *chis*! *chis*! . . . Out, *chis*!" '

Lucrezia was in high excitement at the news of Giulente's triumph, impatient to return to town in order to see him again, irritated by her aunt's sallies.

The prince had also ordered a big ' Yes ' to be traced on the wall of the villa as a precaution, and the crowd of peasants on strike in the lanes clapped hands and cried, ' Long live the Prince of Francalanza! . . .' while inside Don Eugenio was demonstrating how throughout history Sicily was one nation and

Italy another; and Donna Ferdinanda shouted herself hoarse with:

' Ah, if Francis gets back!'

' Aunt, he won't get back . . .' Lucrezia exclaimed eventually.

The old spinster looked as if she was going to eat her up alive.

' You too, you silly little thing? Listen to who's talking now! Don't you know the name you bear, you little idiot? Do you also believe these jailbirds are heroes? Or vulgar chattering ragamuffins?'

This last remark was directed against Giulente; Lucrezia got up and went out, banging the doors. But Donna Ferdinanda's fury passed all bounds when, on going to the window at a louder burst of applause, she saw Benedictine novices from Nicolosi pass by astride donkeys, each with a big ' Yes ' on their tricorns. So loud were her shouts at this outrage that the prince hurried towards her.

' Aunt, please! D'you want to get us all killed?'

' It's that Jesuit Lodovico!' breathed the spinster, through clenched teeth as if biting him. ' The boys too! Consalvo too!' And when the young prince came up for a moment to greet his family she pulled the piece of paper out of his hat and tore it into a thousand pieces. ' Like this! . . .'

9

'LOVELY! . . . Lovely! How pretty these bibs are! Tiny socks and shoes; you've thought of everything!'

Piece by piece, under Chiara and the marchese's eyes, Cousin Graziella was examining the layette for the baby's birth; six big baskets full of enough clothes for an entire hospice of new-born babes. She had words of admiration for all the diapers, all the bonnets, all the little vests, but every now and again she stopped, drew in her breath sharply and passed her tongue over her lips, also pregnant with something she wanted to say but which neither the marchese nor Chiara seemed to be asking her.

'The little frocks now, you've not seen those yet, have you? Look, do just look at them!'

'Oh, how lovely! . . . Where *did* you find that lace? . . . Lovely, all of them, lovely! . . . Particularly the white one with those little blue ribbons! Adorable! . . . Did Lucrezia work on them?'

'No, no-one; I wanted to do it all with my own hands.'

'What you must have spent! . . . May the Lord bless you! . . . You have waited a long time, and now that your happiness is assured . . . You do love each other so much! . . . Such a delight for me to see a family so united . . . That's how I'd like to see Lucrezia. Don't you know?'

'What?'

She lowered her voice a little, to say with an air of mystery:

'Giulente has asked the duke for her hand!'

But Chiara went on folding the baby-linen on her knees, as if she had not heard or understood that this concerned her sister. Only the marchese asked, distractedly, as he put things carefully back into their baskets:

' Who told you?'

At this Cousin Graziella let herself go:

' My husband told me last night; it's sure and certain as we are here! The matter was brought up by Don Lorenzo in a friendly way. The duke wants to be a deputy, and the young man is supporting his election by writing in *Italia risorta* and making speeches every night at the National Club in his favour, as he's now got his lawyer's degree. The group *Nazione Italiana* are putting forward against him Bernardella the lawyer, who's been in prison; what we're reduced to! . . . But Giulente fights like a lion . . . for his future uncle . . . D'you see? . . . Lucrezia is beside herself with delight but Don Blasco and Donna Ferdinanda and Don Eugenio will make trouble . . . and Cousin Giacomo too . . . A Giulente to marry an Uzeda? It takes a revolution and a world upside down for such a thing to happen! Our uncle the duke, I am sorry to say, has quite lost his head ever since he went into politics; his brothers are right! . . . What do you think of it all?'

Chiara went on handling the pretty white, fine and scented baby things, and the marchese, fearing this movement might exhaust her if she went on too long, said:

' That's enough now . . . leave it to me . . . Well, cousin, what can I say? There's nothing I can say; such things don't concern me. My brother-in-law is free to give his sister to whomever he likes . . . I don't meddle in other people's affairs.'

' If Lucrezia wants him,' chimed in Chiara, ' let her take him! After all it's not us who are marrying him, is it?' she asked Federico with a laugh.

' Of course not! . . . I, my dear cousin, have always respected my wife's family, as you know. If they say yes and Lucrezia's content that's all right with me! For myself, I thank the Lord that I am finally to be granted such a great joy; for the rest, let them do whatever they want . . .'

Cousin Graziella looked quite put out, having banked on an outbreak of indignation. Twisting her mouth as if to swallow down a bitter mouthful, she exclaimed:

' Of course! Such matters regard his conscience only! And

Lucrezia's too! As long as she is pleased! That's just what I say!'

There was nothing else to be got out of those two, both living in another world because of their child's birth, now very close. Their cousin, who never failed to show a ceaseless interest in the Uzeda, hurried straight to the prince's. At the gates she met a group of ten or twelve people, among them the two Giulente, uncle and nephew, asking for the duke. She stopped, smiled at Don Lorenzo and Benedetto, and beckoned them with a hand.

'What are you plotting, all you revolutionaries? To set fire to the palace?'

'We've come to offer candidature to the duke,' replied Don Lorenzo, ' in the name of our patriotic societies.'

'Bravo! Congratulations on your choice!'

The commission was about to mount the great stairs when Baldassarre appeared from the second courtyard. He let Donna Graziella through, then warned, ' No, sirs . . . Please come this way . . .'

The prince, in fact, while approving his uncle's liberalism and enjoying the advantages of his popularity, could not allow all the scarecrows surrounding him to enter the great reception rooms, the Yellow and Red Drawing-rooms, so he had set apart two rooms in the estate offices to the right of the entrance for the duke to receive his boot-lickers if he felt like it. Thus while the delegates were going around by the stables, Donna Graziella pompously mounted the grandiose stairs and was introduced into the princess's room. The prince was with his wife and shouting something at her, but at his cousin's appearance fell silent at once.

'Don't you know there are visitors?' said she as she entered. ' A commission from the patriotic societies . . . to offer candidature to the duke . . . just play-acting, as it was all arranged beforehand . . . The Giulente are the only ones I've ever seen before; the rest of them . . . such faces! . . .'

'My uncle is free to receive whomever he likes,' replied the prince. ' Times have changed now and one can't make so many difficulties. That's what I was just saying to my wife . . .' and turning on his heels he was about to go when the voice of Donna Ferdinanda, arriving, made him stop. The spinster was yellower in the face than usual, exuding gall, with a harsh frowning look that was really terrifying.

'So it's true?' she asked through set teeth, without even noticing Donna Graziella.

'He told me so himself,' replied the prince. 'We can talk it over before our cousin . . . He thinks it an excellent thing, an advantageous match, a windfall . . .'

'And you said nothing?'

'Me? I told him our mother would turn in her grave at hearing such a thing! And at seeing what happens in this house! And how her wishes are respected! That's what I told him; but I might as well have been talking to the wall. Your Excellency knows how we are in the family . . . But it's not our uncle's fault. Had Lucrezia not listened to that ragamuffin, does Your Excellency believe that things would have got to such a pitch? But the Giulente have always been presumptuous, have always had a mania for acting as everyone's equals; even so such an idea as this would never have entered their heads without my sister's fixation . . .'

The princess did not breathe a word. Donna Graziella did not speak either, but kept looking now at the prince or at Donna Ferdinanda then shaking her head as if to say that was just the way it was, just so indeed. The spinster chewed her thin lips, twisting her snout and sniffing the air through flaring nostrils.

'If my sister were not quite wild,' went on the prince, 'she would not think of marrying, with her health as it is. She would not listen to that young nuisance who says he loves her out of pure vanity, while playing the republican. If she, on the other hand, respected our mother's advice she would not be giving us reason for worry and preparing so many disappointments for herself . . . And so let us hope that she comes to herself, and that our uncle will change his mind, for if this marriage does take place, the first to suffer would be her! . . . Does she think she will find in those people's house what she has in her own? Do you think they can ever agree, with so much difference in their upbringing and their . . .'

At that moment Lucrezia appeared. The prince was silent as by magic; the princess made herself still smaller in her chair, Cousin Graziella kept eyes and ears even wider open.

'Good day, aunt . . .' began the girl, but Donna Ferdinanda got up from her chair, took her by the hand and said shortly: 'Come with me.'

She went into the next room and shut the door. Cousin Graziella, who had been following them with her gaze, when she turned saw that the prince had vanished in another direction. Then as she sat there alone with the princess, she began wriggling in her chair. She would have gone to listen at the keyhole if she could, had she dared suggest it; instead of which she had to contain herself and chatter away, while now and then Donna Ferdinanda's voice rose so much that she could make out entire words, "*I* want? *I* want? You'll die first! . . . A lawyer? . . . You'll die first! . . .'

'Oh, dear God, I'm so sorry about this . . . 'Tis something, cousin, that . . .'

'We'll just see, I tell you!' shouted Donna Ferdinanda. Immediately after this her voice stopped, and Cousin Graziella went on:

'Lucrezia should think . . . should listen to those who talk to her for her own . . .'

'Then you won't listen, you little bitch?' These words were shouted so loud that cousin and. princess both pricked up their ears. A few minutes of deep silence followed; suddenly came the sound of a chair being turned over and immediately afterwards the sharp sound of a violent slap. The princess jumped to her feet with joined hands; her cousin ran to the door to listen. No more; neither voices nor sobs. Donna Ferdinanda reappeared alone, and came and sat down calmly next to her niece, rubbing the palm of a reddened hand. She talked of indifferent matters, asked what they had for dinner and for news of Teresina, who that day was at San Placido with her aunt the nun. Then she rose to leave; and the cousin went with her.

Meanwhile down in the estate-offices the delegates of the patriotic societies had been admitted into the duke's presence and invited by him to sit down. Giulente the younger, speaking in his quality as orator, was saying:

'My lord duke, in the name of the patriotic societies comprising the National Club, the Civic Union, the Workers' League,

Italy's Redemption, the Sons of the Nation, whose representatives I present . . . we are here to bring you the mandate confided to us, to ask you to accept candidature to the parliament of Italy. Our city well knows it is asking a sacrifice of you, and no light one; but the patriotism of which you have given so many and such splendid proofs makes us hope that once again you will respond to your country's call . . .'

The three or four working-men sat holding their caps tight in both hands as if someone wanted to take them away; uncle Giulente was looking at the floor. When the young man's little speech was over the duke replied, seeking for words one after the other, his voice strangled:

' Citizens, I am confused . . . and I thank you, truly I do . . . I have been happy . . . proud I should say . . . to have been able to contribute as much as I could to our national redemption . . . and to the great work of unifying the nation . . . But truly what you ask of me . . . is above my poor powers . . . it is a mandate . . . Allow me!' He added in another tone of voice seeing them making gestures of denial, ' which I should not know how to carry out . . . which calls for special talents that I do not possess . . . There is no lack of patriots who would do far better than me . . . being responsible for the interest . . . the tutelage of the interests . . . of our country! . . .'

' Excuse me,' came the young man's reply, ' we appreciate the delicate sentiment which makes you speak so; your modesty could dictate no other reply. But your capacity must be judged— forgive me—by the country itself. Had you other reasons for refusing, private or business, we would bow to them, being unable to allow your sacrifice to go too far. As your only objection is your incapacity, allow us to say that it is not for you to know whether you are capable or not!'

As Giulente was silent, Bellia, a tailor, of the Sons of the Nation, said, ' Duke, the workers want Your Excellency . . . there are many who are canvassing for our votes, but in them we have no confidence. We want a good patriot and a gentleman like Your Excellency.'

Then turning to his companions the uncle Giulente said in a tone of jesting amiability, stroking his beard:

' Don't worry; the duke just wants to be entreated.'

'To be entreated?' exclaimed the candidate laughing. 'What d'you take me for, an amateur pianist?'

All smiled and the ice was broken. Putting aside the grave dignity and flowery language of an official mission, everyone gave his own opinion, in dialect, in his own way, so as to induce the duke to accept. They were all agreed on his name; if he refused, their votes would be squandered among three or four people, and as that was the first election Sicily had ever had, a unanimous affirmation of the will of the constituency was necessary. This could only be obtained by the duke's acceptance; for him all others would withdraw; his refusal would produce a pullulation of petty ambitious eleventh-hour patriots. At this insistence the duke exclaimed:

'Gentlemen! You confuse me! You're too good! . . . I do not know what to answer.'

'Answer yes! . . . Accept . . . Is it so difficult? . . . We want it!'

'But I'm not suitable . . . I feel the gravity of the responsibility towards the electorate . . . It's no joking matter! It's one thing to give some advice in the Town Hall, with all you supporters round me! It's another thing to sit among representatives of Parliament!'

'Gentlemen,' suddenly exclaimed uncle Giulente, putting an end to this courteous squabbling, 'D'you know what I say? Our commission has been done! The duke knows what all our wishes are; for the moment he does not say yes or no; let us leave him to sleep on it. Tomorrow, the day after tomorrow, when he's thought it over and taken advice from friends he will give us an answer, and let us hope it will be the desired one . . .'

'Just so! Thank you, just so! . . .' replied the duke, 'Excellent! I promise you I'll think it over and will do all I can . . . Meanwhile thank you all! Thank the workers' societies for me; I will be going there to do my duty all the same . . .'

He kept them a little longer, talking of the news of the day, interesting himself in matters of public moment, touching passingly on what suggestions would have to be pressed with the Turin Government for the city's good, and the better adjustment of the new régime. From a drawer in his desk he took a box of cigars, Havana cigars, golden-coloured, sweet and scented, and distributed them widely, shaking everyone's hands, those of the two Giulente hardest of all.

Next morning *Italia risorta* bore a leading article by Benedetto on the imminent elections, which ran:

' There are only two criteria to inspire voters; their choice's fearless patriotism—which is an earnest of his truly Italian feelings; and his social prominence—which will allow him to carry out his mission with an independence that guarantees disinterest and sincerity. Now, when our city has the good fortune to possess a man responding to the name of Duke GASPARE UZEDA of ORAGUA, we think that all discussion is pointless, and that the votes of all citizens who have the public good at heart should concentrate on the name of that illustrious patrician!'

The great majority of the electorate were for him and in the chorus of consent discordant voices were stilled. Most fervent of all were the populace, the workers, the National Guard, the lowest orders which did not enjoy the vote but drew voters with them. If anyone put up arguments against that candidature, he was at once reduced to silence. The Uzeda were all pro-Bourbon to the eyebrows, were they? The more merit to the duke for having embraced Liberalism in spite of them! He hadn't taken any part in '48? But he had not betrayed as had so many others! ...

Those voices had seemed more or less reduced to silence when they suddenly blew up again more insistently. Ever since that summer after the Neapolitans left there had been found now and then, stuck at street corners and circulating in cafés and chemists, anonymous leaflets with nasty bits of news, disquieting judgements and obscure threats. These had become rarer but now began circulating again, and contained, apart from gloomy prophecies on the future of the revolution, malicious allusions to persons in public view, particularly the duke. There were not many words about him, and usually in the form of questions, but someone always turned up to explain them. What had the Patriot done on the day of 31st May? He had hidden in San

Nicola, said the comment. And what about that telescope in '48? The one through which he had enjoyed gazing at the attack and the fire while surrounded by soldiers of Ferdinand II! And his visits to the Royal Intendant? To ensure he was on the winning side if the revolution was swept away in a whiff of grape-shot! . . .

The duke, from whom the Giulente had kept these attacks, even ordering the National Guard not to hand the leaflets over to their major when they took them off walls, now began to ask about them and to insist on seeing them. At reading his own name he went rather pale and glanced quickly over the phrases where he was mentioned, but said nothing.

' Not to know from whose hand they come!' exclaimed Benedetto. ' Not to give the rascals a good lesson!'

' Oh, there's nothing we can do about it!' replied the offended party then. ' They're just the little inconveniences of revolution and liberty. But liberty corrects itself. Don't give them another thought . . .'

As soon as the two had gone away, however, he put on his hat and went straight to San Nicola, where he asked for the Prior Don Lodovico.

' Let me tell you,' said he calmly, ' that your uncle is playing a dirty game. The anonymous leaflets come from him and his gang. His attacking me is no matter; that only helps me by drawing more sympathy to me. But if he continues attacking everyone, scattering suspicions and lying news, he will get into trouble. I warn you because you who are close to him can pass it on. In the end everything comes out . . . Let him take care!'

To Don Blasco himself the Prior did not breathe a word, but reported the whole matter to the Abbot, for him to have a word with one of the monk's friends. Father Galvagno was charged with the commission. On hearing the subject mentioned Don Blasco changed colour.

' What's this you're saying?' he exclaimed. ' You're mad, you and those who sent you. Let me tell you that if I want to say what I think, I say it right out in people's faces, even if necessary in Francis II's, whom God preserve! . . .' and he gave a deep bow. ' So imagine if I'm afraid of this gang of brigands and scavengers . . .' and here he began rolling out an even worse litany than usual.

But from that day on the anonymous leaflets became rarer and gradually ceased. Don Blasco, the bile almost squirting from his eyes, let himself go at the prince's—when the duke wasn't there—saying appalling things against his brother, insulting him, defaming him, hurling brand-new epithets at him, compared to which the exchanges between porters and prostitutes were sweet complimentary nothings. His rage also had a closer and more direct target in his niece Lucrezia. The little bitch was still daring to think of that little rotter, was she? Had she been brought up to bite the hand that fed her, to filthy the name of Uzeda and make a mockery of it by marrying that little swine?

' Oh, the putrid filthy race! Ah, pig of a Viceroy who created it . . . It would have been better . . .' (to bring bastards into the world, was the idea expressed in his next unprintable words) ' rather than generate this stinking crew . . .'

Those were fearful days for Lucrezia. Everyone was against her; either they did not say a word to her or loaded her with insults; Donna Ferdinanda seized her arm and gave her pinches that tore the skin off; one day Don Blasco nearly knocked her down. Pale and silent, she let the storm blow over, with eyes lowered. She did not weep, did not complain, confided in no-one, asked no help of the duke, whom she knew to be Benedetto's friend and in favour of the match, said no word of her torments to Ferdinando, who came to the palace only to see her, leaving those animals of his that were either stuffed or waiting to be stuffed. Only when she shut herself in her room with Vanna to read the young man's letters, did she say, with a faint cold smile:

' It's useless! I'll marry him! . . .'

He, meanwhile, was continuing to support the duke's election by speaking in clubs, writing in *Italia risorta,* and in leaflets with such titles as, *Who is the Duke of Oragua?, A Patrician Patriot,* and so on. ' Since 1848 the distinguished gentleman has sided against the Government of King Bomba, with all the more merit as he had no wrongs against himself or his family to redress, but against the whole people of Sicily . . . During the long period of preparation we find him at Palermo, intimate with the most outstanding patriots and intent on contributing his activity and his substance to the national cause. No sooner has the movement for liberation started than he hurries home in order to participate in the sorrows and joys of his beloved fellow-citizens. Here he is generous with precious help to the Liberals, and the representatives of the execrated Bourbon already hear his condemning voice. He contributes to the formation of voluntary squads, subsidises those persecuted Liberals that are in want. When Francis' minions retire, he is among the first to help regulate the city's government and joins the ranks of the national militia, bulwark of liberty; for it he buys uniforms, ammunition and many a weapon. He opens his ancestral home to Bixio and Menotti and renders the honours of the city to the liberators. When asked to represent the first constituency in Parliament he modestly declines the offer, wishing to be first in sacrifice and last in honours. But his country wants him. Our sister Palermo envies us him. One bearing the name of DUKE OF ORAGUA cannot disappoint his country's wishes. He will be our Deputy!'

On his part the duke spoke to the prince again about Lucrezia's marriage, praised the young man and asserted that it was a match not to be missed, for the Giulente had that son only and to him would go all their fortune.

'It is suitable for another reason too,' he explained to his nephew, 'they won't worry about a dowry . . .'

'Whether they worry or not it doesn't affect me,' replied the prince. 'Lucrezia has her own money: does your Excellency think I wish to deny it to her?'

'Whoever said such a thing? All I say is that they would be content with what she has.'

'The matter has nothing to do with me. It would be odd for me to prevent my sister doing what she likes at her age! Maybe our mother's wishes were for her to remain at home, but our mother is in the next world, and even if she were alive . . .' He went on in this tone, repeating that his sister was free to take Giulente; but the words seemed to drop from his mouth, and he broke off as if there were other things he could say and was only keeping silent from prudence and propriety, in order not to appear stubborn. So much so that the duke one day asked him:

'Talk clearly, can't you! Are you against this marriage?'

'Me? . . . If Your Excellency approves?'

'Don't you like Giulente?'

'Must I like him? . . . He's a decent young man; it's enough to know him to be Your Excellency's friend . . . Not badly off, either. . . I haven't Aunt Ferdinanda's and Don Blasco's prejudices, times have changed . . . Your Excellency must know that if Lucrezia thinks she can be happy with him, I will not oppose it . . . But it's only right that she should not seek a quarrel with me either!'

'Why ever should she do that?'

'Why? . . . Why? . . . Your Excellency knows nothing of it all, being in Palermo at that time! . . .' And then he told of the pain caused him by his sister plotting with Chiara and the marchese and Ferdinando, by laying claims and interpreting the law in her own way, even accusing him of wanting to despoil her and all the others. 'Now if she marries, she must put an end to all that once and for ever . . . Otherwise your Excellency will see that they will begin all over again!'

'No, sir,' replied the duke firmly, 'the marriage will take place, but I guarantee that you will not be molested.'

Father Camillo had already talked in the same vein to the girl. He began by telling her that the union was opposed by the entire family not because they expected her to remain a spinster—not at all!—but because it was not a suitable match. Birth was certainly a matter of some importance; not so much for its own sake, as because of the upbringing, the moral and religious principles involved.

Giulente might well be an excellent young man—he did not wish to defame without knowing him—but he professed dangerous doctrines and sided with the enemies of social order, legitimate power, and Holy Church; and he did so not only in words but in action too. And would an Uzeda, 'descendant of Blessed Ximena, daughter of a Prince of Francalanza,' marry such a man as that? What basis of understanding could they have? Could love and accord reign between them? And then apart from that could Giulente, though prosperous, maintain her in the style to which she had been accustomed? Had he any notion of noble habits?

Thus the family was not opposed from caprice but for grave and valid reasons. But, said he, she herself must be the best judge of all that; maybe she felt herself animated with love enough to cope with the material disadvantages of such an existence and hope enough to convert the young man too. Most praiseworthy and admirable; but the chief and only question really was that without the approval, acceptance, blessing of those representing her late lamented father and mother, she could have no hope of prosperity and peace.

So far Lucrezia had not said a syllable.

When the confessor was silent she said, 'What must I do to have their permission to marry him? Let them say what it is; I will do whatever they like.'

'I was sure of that!' exclaimed the Dominican in a tone of joyful triumph, 'I was sure that a good girl like you would give no other reply. And the prince, who loves you, will support you! Agree, and always keep together; such is your mutual interest and the joy of those looking down on you from above.'

And so when the duke, who had not yet mentioned Giulente's request to his niece, told her of it and said at the same time that Giacomo, before giving a reply, wanted to come to a settlement with her, Lucrezia declared herself ready. The prince, who had been holding many a confabulation with Signor Marco and spent days shut up in his study, now asked, in his brother the co-heir's name too, that this settlement be based on the division made by his mother, demonstrating the justice of this with great heaps of documents and figures; these also showed that their father's part had never existed outside the imagination of their uncle Don Blasco. There were, though, the I.O.U.'s that he had paid; his sister must pay her proportionate part in these.

When all this was settled not more than 8,000 *onze* would be due to her. Lucrezia accepted this sum. Her mother's Will laid down that the prince should pay her five per cent interest; but then in the five years since their mother's death had he not maintained his sister entirely, providing her with home, food, service, clothes, use of carriage, etc. etc.? Was he to sustain all these expenses himself? Had his sister been in need, he would of course have kept her in his home from affection for her and because she was of the same blood. But she had her own money; so it was not right for her brother to keep her for five years nor could she herself allow it. When the accounts were gone over again it was found that the interest of the 8,000 onze represented exactly the expenses of maintenance; so all that was due to her was the capital. Again Lucrezia said yes. So everything seemed arranged; but at the last moment the prince put up a new condition to his uncle the duke:

'I wish to regulate the situation of the other legatees also. Either they are all right or they are all wrong; does that not seem logical and just to Your Excellency? As we have to make out a legal document, let us get it all over and done in one. Why does Your Excellency not talk to the others and get them to agree?'

Chiara and the marchese did not have the same reasons for bowing their heads to the prince's conditions, but it was a propitious moment to try to induce those to the transaction too, as they lived only in expectation of their child and their joy at the imminent event was such that it must dispose them to pass over all other interests. And so when the duke told them that Lucrezia was to marry and had come to a settlement, they approved, considering only that to keep the interest back as compensation for maintenance did the prince little honour. But if she was happy about that then they all were.

'And now you too must settle things up! . . .' added the duke, in a tone of affectionate insistence allowed him not so much in his position as uncle as from having accepted the holding of the new-born child at the font.

The marchese exchanged glances with his wife and replied:

'If Your Excellency so wishes . . .'

'Chiara's account is of course the same as Lucrezia's but there is no question about the interest with her and Giacomo will pay it to the last.'

'I took my dear Chiara for the love I bear her and not for money . . .' and bowing over his wife, Federico kissed her on the forehead.

'But what about my uncle the Canon's legacy? And the

265

dowry?' she reminded him, to prevent her generous husband being swindled.

'Giacomo does not intend to recognise them, and I do not know if he is right or wrong . . . But anyway this must be settled now once and for all! A few thousand *onze* makes no difference to you for the moment; I will make up for them to my godson in time . . .'

So that was decided, to the great joy of husband and wife. There remained Ferdinando, from whom the prince demanded 2,000 *onze* of debt. Lucrezia was the only one with any influence over the Booby, but instead of talking to her brother she took to her bed and refused to see anyone, alleging mysterious sufferings. The Booby, on hearing of his sister's illness, came to visit her every day, but Lucrezia seemed to be particularly averse to seeing him. Her maid had told her, and she herself realised, that Giacomo was squeezing her; but in order to triumph over her relatives she would have ignored much more. Now she felt the harm she was herself doing her younger brother, the only one who loved her, by inducing him to strip himself of part of his meagre inheritance, the least of all the portions. But in her head the parts were inverted; the fault was Ferdinando's for not taking an interest in her, not asking her what was wrong, not removing the last obstacle to the conclusion of the marriage.

Ferdinando on the other hand knew nothing about anything and was open-mouthed when the duke, to get this last little sacrificial lamb over and done with, told him:

'There is a chance of a good match for your sister . . . Benedetto Giulente, you know, that intelligent young man who's done so well . . .'

'Oh, yes! Fine, I'm pleased . . .'

'But of course first Giacomo wants to arrange all your various interests and conclude the division which is still unsettled. Lucrezia has agreed and Chiara too; now your brother wants to arrange matters pending with you, since it's all the same question . . . That is what Lucrezia's illness is . . .'

'Why didn't she mention it to me before?'

He hurried to his sick sister's bedside and said to her:

'Silly girl! You aren't worried about that, are you? Our uncle

266

told me all . . . if you agree, aren't I right to agree too? We must tell him so at once! Does that please you?'

The day of the election drew near. The two Giulente, particularly Benedetto, had wormed out every elector and gone through all the formalities of registration. Morning and night people came to visit the duke and declare they would vote for him; the two Giulente were always present. On the eve of the voting, while the candidate was giving audience to his supporters, a servant came hurrying over from the marchese to call the prince and princess, as Chiara was about to give birth. When Giacomo and Margherita reached her home they found Federico in a frenzy of anxiety, unable to be with the suffering woman, but every instant calling the maid or Cousin Graziella or one of the three midwives who were taking turns at the future mother's bedside. The prince stayed with him while the princess entered Chiara's room. In spite of the agonies of labour she had a serene air and, smiling between her spasms, asked them to reassure her husband.

'Tell him I'm not suffering . . . You go yourself . . . Margherita . . . Ah . . . Poor man . . . he's on tenterhooks . . .'

The desire of all those years, her most ardent longing, was now about to be realised! At this idea the pains decreased; at the thought of her husband's distress she scarcely suffered any more . . . When the princess returned to the room, the midwife exclaimed:

'We're there! . . . We're there! . . .'

'Is it showing its head?' asked Cousin Graziella, holding the marchesa by the shoulders in her final spasm.

'I don't know . . . Courage, signora marchesa . . . What is it?'

Suddenly the midwife went pale, seeing her hopes of rich tips vanish; from the bleeding womb came a piece of formless flesh, an unnameable thing, a beaked fish, a featherless bird; this sexless monster had one eye, three things like paws, and was still alive.

'Jesus! Jesus! Jesus!'

Chiara, luckily, had fainted as soon as she was freed. The princess, who had been wandering round the room without touching a thing, incapable of giving the suffering woman any help, now turned away her head in disgust at the sight. And the midwives, Graziella and the maids looked at each other in consternation exclaiming:

' Who will give her husband the news?'

Just then the marchese, hearing no sound, called out:

' Cousin! . . . Donna Agata! . . . How's it going? Cousin! Is no one coming?'

Donna Graziella had to go out to him and prepare him for the blow:

' Cousin, be of good heart . . . Chiara is freed . . .'

' Is it a boy? Is it a girl? . . . Cousin! . . . why don't you speak?'

' Courage! . . . The Lord has not wished . . . Chiara is well; that is the important thing . . .'

The prince, entering to see the abortion whose single eye was now lifeless, tried to prevent his frenzied brother-in-law from entering the room too, but he could not succeed. Before the monster which the appalled midwives had put on a heap of baby-clothes the marchese stood rooted to the ground, his hands in his hair. Meanwhile his wife was coming to and, looking around at those standing by.

' Federico! Is it a boy? . . .' were the first words she gasped out.

' Stay quiet now!' enjoined the women together, moving in front of the abortion so as to prevent her noticing it. ' Let's not say anything to her for the moment . . .'

' Federico!' exclaimed the mother.

' Chiara! . . . How are you?' exclaimed the marchese, running up to her. ' Have you suffered much? Are you still suffering?'

' No, nothing . . . Our son?'

' Chiara, be comforted! It's a little girl,' announced her cousin hurrying up to her, ' What does it matter! . . . She's so pretty!'

' A pity!' sighed she. ' Are you sorry?' she asked her husband then, seeing his gloomy face.

' No! No! . . . All children are just as dear.'

' Where is she? . . . Bring her here! . . .' she exclaimed with another sigh.

At that point a maid, on the princess's orders, was taking

away the foetus wrapped in a cloth, trying not to be noticed.

'There! . . .' exclaimed Chiara. 'I want to see her.'

All were speechless with confusion. Federico, stroking her hands and kissing her forehead, said to her:

'Courage, my dear . . . You must be brave . . . I'm resigned too you see! The Lord does not wish it.'

'Is she dead? . . .' asked she, going pale.

'No . . . it was born dead . . . Courage, my poor dear . . . As long as you're all right . . . the rest is nothing. May the Lord's will be done!'

'I want to see her.'

Everyone surrounded her, trying to dissuade her; it was dead after all! Why torture herself by the sight? She must take care of herself; the important thing now was her own health!

'I want to see her,' she answered sharply.

There was nothing for it but to do what she wanted. She did not cry, she showed no disgust at examining that abomination. She said to her husband:

'He was your son! . . .' and ordered it not be taken away for the moment. Meanwhile other relatives were arriving; Don Eugenio, Donna Ferdinanda, the Duchess Radalì, the marchese's cousins. All condoled but wished them better luck next time. Towards evening the duke also arrived to express his regrets, but he remained only a short time, as the Giulente were awaiting him below to tell him the latest news about the electorate's dispositions. Benedetto was like Garibaldi saying to Bixio, 'Nino, tomorrow we'll be in Palermo! . . .'

Next day in fact he rushed all round the constituency, into voters' houses, urging the erection of voting-booths, interpreting an electoral law new to all, inciting people to place the name of Oragua in the urns. Meanwhile in Chiara's house, as if in sign of protest against this last madness of the duke's, were met all the pro-Bourbon Uzeda except for Don Blasco, who since the transactions by his nephews and nieces and the arrangement of Lucrezia's wedding and his brother's candidature, seemed to have gone really quite off his head.

Chiara was more or less re-established in health and taking her misfortune with some resignation. The marchese never left his wife's bedside and would lean over to talk in her ear. Neither of the two listened to Donna Ferdinanda's ferocious remarks against her brother, or the cavaliere's historico-critical discourses to the young prince, who also came to visit his aunt together with the Prior and Fra' Carmelo. Chiara had sent for Ferdinando and was awaiting him impatiently. When he appeared she called him to her bedside and talked to him in a whisper for a long time. Then she called her maid, took a bunch of keys from beneath her pillow and gave them to him, ordering him amid the clatter of conversation :

' You know the glass jar for lard in the store cupboard? . . . The big one? . . . Get it, empty it and wash it out . . . carefully, now. Better use hot water.'

When the jar was ready, Ferdinando went to see her.

' All right,' he said. ' Now we need spirit.'

Chiara ordered someone to go out and buy it. Then amid a circle of astounded relatives, the foetus, yellow like wax, was brought out, washed, dried and then introduced by Ferdinando into the glass jar which he filled with spirit and then corked up.

' Is there some tallow . . . or clay?'

' There's my ointment, if that's any use . . . said the marchese.

With the ointment, whose stink filled the room, Ferdinando stuck down the edges of the cork so that no air should enter the jar. Chiara followed the operation attentively. Consalvo, with eyes starting out of his head, looked at that piece of fat swimming in spirit. Suddenly he said to Don Lodovico:

' Uncle, doesn't it look like the goat in the museum?'

In the Benedictines' museum there was another abortion, an animal's, a lump of flesh with paws, like a ghostly bladder with limbs; but Chiara's creature was more horrible still.

Don Lodovico did not answer; after a short visit to his sister he left. The others gradually went off too, leaving Chiara alone with her husband gazing almost contentedly at that lump of anatomy, latest product of the Viceroy's race.

The prince was in a hurry to get back to his uncle the duke and in order to please him took his son along, though it was the usual time for the boy to return to the monastery. Scarcely had the family reached the palace than confused sounds were heard in the distance; claps, shouts, trumpet-calls and bangs on a big drum. A citizens' demonstration of all classes with banners and music, headed by the two Giulente, was on its way to acclaim the first deputy for the constituency, the notable patriot, Don Gaspare. The porter, seeing a yelling crowd drawing near, made to close the gates, but Baldassarre, sent down by the duke, told him to leave them wide open. The crowd was crying, ' Long live the Duke of Oragua! Long live our deputy!' while the band played Garibaldi's Anthem and urchins did somersaults to the music. The Giulente, the Mayor, and another eight or ten of the most important citizens were parleying with Baldassarre and asking to go up and compliment the people's choice.

The duke was upstairs in the Yellow Drawing-room and there the major-domo led them. As soon as Benedetto Giulente entered he saw Lucrezia standing by the princess, still with her hat on. The duke came towards his fellow-citizens and shook everyone's hand, prodigal with thanks, while from the street came the din of shouts and applause. The prince, seeing a man with the reputation of the Evil Eye in the group, went pale and muttered, ' Save us! Save us!' The newly elected deputy, meanwhile, was presenting Giulente to his nieces and nephews. The young man bowed and exclaimed, radiant:

' Signora, princess, signorina, I am indeed happy and proud to present to you for the first time my homage on this happy day, which is an occasion of rejoicing for your family as it is for the entire city.'

' Hurrah for Oragua! . . . Out with the duke! . . . Hurrah for the deputy! . . .' they were yelling below.

Benedetto flung open the balcony as if he were in his own house. Then the duke went even paler than his nephew; now he would have to talk to the crowd, finally open his mouth, say something. Clinging to Benedetto he stuttered:

' What is it? . . . What shall I say? . . . Help me, I'm all confused . . .'

' Say that you thank the people for this flattering demonstration . . . that you feel the responsibility of their mandate, that you will concentrate all your strength on carrying it out . . . animated by the trust, upheld by the . . .' Then as the shouts redoubled he pushed him towards the balcony.

As soon as the deputy appeared, a louder clamour than ever rose from the antshill of heads in the street. They were waving

hats, handkerchiefs, flags, and shouting 'Evviva! Evviva! . . .'
Yellow as a corpse, hanging on to the balustrade with both
hands, grim-faced, rigid all over, the Honourable Member
began:

'Citizens . . .'

But his voice was lost in the vast and incessant tumult, the
stunning chorus of applause; from the deputy's attitude they did
not realise that he was about to talk. Benedetto raised an arm.
And as if by magic obtained silence.

'Citizens!' began the young man. 'In the name of you all, in
the name of the sovereign people, I have informed the illustrious patriot . . .' ('Hurrah for Oracqua! . . . Hurrah for the
duke! . . .') 'of the superb, the unanimous affirmation of the
whole constituency . . . To the many proofs of his self-sacrifice
for his native city . . .' ('Hurrah! Hurrah! . . .') 'the Duke of
Oragua now adds this: once again he bows to the wish of his
fellow-citizens to represent them in that august assembly where
for the first time there will meet the sons . . .'

But he could not finish. Acclamations and applause drowned
his words. They were shouting, 'Hurrah for Italian unity! Long
live Victor Emmanuel! Long live Oracqua! Long live Garibaldi! . . .' Others added 'Long live Giulente! Hurrah for the
wounded hero of the Volturno!'

'The enthusiasm which I see animating you,' he went on, 'is
the finest confirmation of the voting-urns' response . . . Those
urns from which once more comes liberty . . . the sovereign will
of a people who are now their own masters . . . Citizens! On
the 18th February 1861, amid the representatives of our newly-
arisen nation we shall have the supreme good-fortune of seeing
the Duke of Oragua take his seat. Hurrah for our deputy!
Hurrah for Italy!'

Out thundered a final crash of applause, and the crowd began
to disperse. A second time, in a hoarse voice, with no gesture or
movement, the duke began, 'Citizens! . . .', but they did not
hear him, did not understand he was about to speak. Then,
turning towards those crowding the balcony, he said:

'I just wanted to add a few words . . . but they're leaving . . .
We can go inside . . .'

He was smiling, drawing breath at last, as if freed from a

nightmare, shaking everyone's hands, Benedetto's particularly hard as if trying to break it off.

'Thanks! . . . Thanks! . . . I shall never forget this day . . .'

He guided the young man into the next room to make his farewells to the ladies, and then accompanied all to the top of the stairs. When he returned, the prince, also freed of the incubus of the Evil Eye, began complimenting him again and pointing him out to his son as an example.

'D'you see? D'you see how much they respect your uncle? How the whole city is for him?'

The boy, stunned slightly by the din, asked:

'What does "deputy" mean?'

'Deputies,' explained his father, 'are those who make laws in Parliament.'

'Doesn't the King do that?'

'The King and the deputies together. The King can't do everything, can he? D'you see what an honour your uncle is to the family? When there were Viceroys, we were Viceroys; now there is a Parliament, our uncle is a deputy!'

# BOOK II

# 1

W H E N it was known in town that Count Raimondo had suddenly arrived at the Uzeda palace from Florence, unexpected, alone, baggage-less, with a grip in which he had just thrust a change of linen for the journey, the muttering and exchanging of comments and suppositions, of curious and insistent questions were enough for a grave public event. First mouth-to-mouth news said that the count had deserted his wife once and for all. The well-informed knew that after the revolution Donna Isabella Fersa had gone to Florence from Palermo. Was not that fact alone enough to explain all? The only doubt was if she had joined the count on her own initiative or by arrangement. Some said that she had gone on the mainland to amuse herself, and forgotten all about young Uzeda; but then why choose the very city where he was? She had very little to lose herself. What hope had she of being taken back by her husband after two years of separation? That was quite impossible while her mother-in-law was alive. Don Mario might of course be weak enough to forgive, as he still loved his wife and mourned her night and day more than if she were dead; but his mother was watching him.

So Donna Isabella risked nothing; in fact being so young and so unable to resist temptation it suited her better to return to her first lover rather than look for new ones: one mistake would be so much more easily forgiven . . . But for Raimondo things were different. There were his children, two innocent babes to be considered! And people pitied the countess, so gentle, so sweet, so devoted to her husband, yet condemned—such is the world! —to a life of anguish.

The servants in the Francalanza palace could talk of nothing else; they even forgot Benedetto Giulente's engagement to the Signorina Lucrezia. This event, although foreseen and long discussed, had already stirred up again the factions into which the prince's familiars were divided; and while Giuseppe the porter would doff his cap and bow at Benedetto's arrival, as if the master of the house, no less, were entering, Pasqualino Riso did not even touch his cap from under the arch of the second courtyard where he was lounging, and scarcely deigned to lower his pipe and turn aside if he felt like spitting.

Baldassarre alone kept his usual fine impartiality, did his job and treated the Signorina's future husband as he saw the prince treat him: very politely but aloofly. 'Masters are masters,' the major-domo would say, and if he heard the lower orders of servants discuss too warmly their young mistress's choice he would send ostlers back to the stables and scullions to the kitchens with, 'Suppose she was your own sister, animal?' What business was it of theirs if Donna Ferdinanda and Don Blasco, in agreement as always in spite of their mutual dislike, no longer came to the palace because they disapproved of the marriage?

Actually an Uzeda marrying a *lawyer* did rather worry Baldassarre, though the young man had studied for his own pleasure and not to carry on a profession. And although not a grandee he had been brought up a gentleman and called his father and mother 'Excellency'; also on first coming to his bride's home he had tipped the servants in a proper manner. Perhaps his father and mother were a bit coarse, but the young couple would not have to share a house with them after all. For all these reasons Baldassarre would not allow his dependants to chatter criticisms, but gossip went on and only the young count's arrival turned it in another direction.

To the servants it was obvious that their young master Raimondo had not come on business as some tried to suggest; if he had he would have brought at least a trunk, not just that grip with a couple of shirts and pairs of socks and pants; nor would he have looked so preoccupied, he who was always in such good humour when away from his wife! Anyway if there had been business it would have been with his brother the prince; instead of which every day he visited his aunt Donna

Ferdinanda, who had served as cover in the early days of his relationship with Donna Isabella. And Donna Ferdinanda told everyone her own opinion frankly: things being as they were, considering the incompatibility of the husband and wife's characters, there was nothing for it but separation by agreement; put the girls in college, marry them off as soon as possible, and thereafter each go their own way.

The prince, on the other hand, never mentioned wife or children to his brother, never even asked if they were alive or dead. On his side Raimondo seemed to have left his tongue at home, and if he did open his mouth spoke distractedly whatever the topic, taking less interest than ever in family affairs. He had not said a word about the agreement with the legatees, or about Lucrezia's marriage, as things of no interest to him or about which he had already shown his own opinion. And he scarcely noticed his future brother-in-law Giulente at all.

Lucrezia was triumphant; Benedetto came to pay her court every evening; in six months he would be her husband. The transaction forced on her, the sacrifice made by herself and almost imposed on the others, she did not even remember. The young man had scarcely let her say a word about money, as he wanted her and not her dowry, and such were the conditions under which he had obtained the prince's consent. Yet this consent was so cold that it might have been forced. And now Don Blasco and Donna Ferdinanda no longer came to the palace, and even Don Eugenio put on a forbidding look when he saw his future nephew.

But the more her relations seemed to take against the marriage, the more affectionate Lucrezia was to Benedetto, 'Don't bother about them; they're all mad! They hate you without reason now, and one day they'll all make it up without reason . . .' And she would describe their various foibles, suggest ways of disarming them, of taking them at their weakest spot.

The young man had no need of her advice; he was doing all he could to get himself accepted by his future relatives, well aware that, though he might have made a better marriage financially, he would never have made a nobler. And the Giulente had a mania about being nobles, or at least ennobled by the number of judges in the family; their greatest grief was the abolition of primogeniture. Meanwhile they carefully preserved diplomas and portraits of all the doctors, magistrates and judges from whom they descended, and boasted of noble alliances contracted, particularly in the most recent generations.

In the eyes of the undiscerning they were considered as nobles, and as untitled nobles were called *Cavaliere*. But purists kept them at a certain distance. In such conditions Benedetto's marriage with the Prince of Francalanza's sister was a real stroke of fortune, and was considered as such by Don Paolo and his wife Donna Eleonora. So proud were they of having brought it off that they never even noticed the coldness and hostility of the Uzeda, or attributed that to Benedetto's liberalism. The young man, vain as they but less dazzled, did notice and set himself to overcome it.

The princess's sympathy he captured at once by avoiding shaking hands and by praising Teresina's beauty and grace. It was not very difficult to conquer Don Eugenio, who had affected not to notice him at first. Put up to it by Lucrezia, the young man had begun to talk of historical and artistic matters and about the Uzeda Viceroys, and listened open-mouthed to the cavaliere's opinions. Then he begged the old man to show him his art collection, and went into paeans of praise at the sight of all the pots and daubs, laying on superlatives before Titians and Tintorettos which he declared superior to all pictures by the same painters in the Naples Museum.

On Raimondo's arrival, though, Benedetto often found himself between two fires, for when Don Eugenio and Don Cono praised the city's glories and buildings Raimondo broke his silence only to denigrate them. Then Giulente would try to agree with both, not knowing quite how to set about that as they never agreed between themselves. Such was Raimondo's admiration for all that was not Sicilian that he almost despised the nobility of his own family, while Don Eugenio was hard at work on his *Chronological History*. As this title did not seem sufficiently impressive, he had changed it to—*Historico-Chronological Disceptation*. And when Don Cono sustained that a ' disceptation ' was not the same as a ' dissertation ' the pair of them would start discussions even longer and more vivacious than those about whether to write the word ' solemn ' with one or with two ' l's '. Asked for his opinion, Benedetto, thinking less about words than about the cold way he was being treated, and the open war declared by the monk and the spinster, replied:

' I think they must be synonymous . . .'

' Did you hear, you stubborn head?' Don Eugenio then said triumphantly to Don Cono. ' Will you surrender at last?'

The prince on the other hand made different use of his future brother-in-law. In May 1861 the Sardinian Code of Law had been substituted for the Neapolitan, and judges, lawyers and litigants were now going into frenzies over those new laws. Benedetto, partly from love of study, partly from patriotic zeal, had mastered them with his tutor. So, discoursing of this and that, the prince would get the young man to make comparisons between the two codes, show where they differed and agreed. Sometimes, as if he were talking generally about imaginary cases of no interest to himself, he would take what amounted to legal consultations. One day he asked what the other thought of the legacy to the convent.

Giulente, although he actually thought the opposite, replied it was a doubtful case and that the nullity of the deed might easily be sustained. To ingratiate himself with all these Uzeda he supported and encouraged their pretensions, but from pride at frequenting their home and joy at becoming a relation he accepted that rôle and came to espouse the causes of his future relations quite sincerely; the cavaliere's *Disceptation* seemed to him a genuinely useful work; the prince's reasoning genuinely plausible. His father's vanity about aristocracy and his uncle's infatuation with the Liberals were now linked in him, so that, glorying in his descent from Giolenti, Master of Law, he maintained, in connection with the Duke of Oragua's election, that the government of the country should be taken over by ' us ', by, that is, ' an aristocracy capable, like the English, of understanding and satisfying the nation's needs . . .' But at this point he lost the thread, for the prince and the cavaliere were smiling, not so much from contempt for Liberal theories as at hearing him use that ' us ', at seeing a Giulente take seriously his own nobility.

When the young man talked of his ancestors, of the honours they had gained, of his family's noble traditions, of their coat-of-arms, the prince would stroke his whiskers, Don Eugenio look into the air, the princess lower her eyes, and the hangers-on wink at each other; even Lucrezia would look glum at this sudden chill in the atmosphere, and agree by a nod but not dare to by word.

One evening he was talking of a Canon Giulente who had flourished the century before and been celebrated for works on ecclesiastical law, particularly for a great treaty *On Marriage*. Raimondo, who was present, seemed interested in this subject.

' The treatment is new,' Benedetto was saying, ' in the chapter about impediments, impedients and diriments. I've had many a work on this subject through my hands, but the development, richness of quotation and comment of that are really admirable.'

' Yes, yes . . .' the cavaliere confirmed this time. ' I've read it too.'

' What did you say?' asked Raimondo. ' Impediments?'

' Impedients and diriments.'

' To me, though,' observed Don Eugenio, ' impediment and impedient seem the same thing.'

' Yes, Excellency ' (he already called his future uncle that), ' but I said " impediment " to distinguish it from " diriment "; in other words, obstacles which impede the celebration and obstacles . . .'

' Excuse me!' interrupted the Gentleman of the Bedchamber. ' An impediment that impedes must be nonsense—isn't it? Surely no impediment can be a help?'

Very patiently Benedetto went over his demonstration again, but the cavaliere kept on repeating obstinately that the ' wording ' was confused, and only stopped when Raimondo exclaimed irritably:

' Uncle, go and tell that to the canonists! If that's the right legal expression! And what *are* the diriments?' he asked Giulente.

' The diriment impediments are those which annul a marriage after it has already been contracted.'

' Such as?'

' Eh? . . . There are over a dozen of them . . . fourteen to be exact. Before there were twelve, then the Council of Trent added two . . . It's some time since I studied them. Nowadays,' he added turning towards Lucrezia, 'rather than the impediments I ought to be studying the reasons contained in the *sacramento magno.*'

'The Blessed Sacrament . . .?' exclaimed Lucrezia, who was quite in the clouds . . . 'It's exposed in the cathedral.'

Everyone smiled and the subject was dropped for that evening. But a day or two later Raimondo asked his future brother-in-law again:

'So you haven't remembered what the diriment impediments are?'

'Yes . . . but not all of them,' replied Benedetto, who did not want to explain certain things in the presence of his future wife. So he said them in Latin.

'*Error, conditio, votum, cognatio, crimen . . .*'

'Enough! Enough! It's useless, I don't understand . . .' Raimondo turned his back on him.

But before leaving Benedetto called him aside:

'I couldn't explain in front of the women. The impediments are these,' and he then enumerated and explained them all in Italian.


A few days after this discussion the servants down in the courtyard were all a-chatter. A rumour was going round the town that the duke was coming back from Turin for the sole purpose of arranging the young count's affairs. Baldassarre, when asked if the news was true, shrugged his shoulders.

'Why should I know! Wait till the duke comes, can't you?' But the news was true; it was repeated by Giulente, by his uncle Don Lorenzo, and by all the deputy's political friends who even talked of going out to meet him if he came by land, and giving him a demonstration of welcome. He arrived by sea and was not alone; Baron Palmi, nominated Senator after the revolution, was with him. The latter, instead of going to the palace as at other times, put up at the hotel. Things seemed very grave. Did this mean a complete break between the count and his wife? That it was now a question of separation? Then what about the duke? Why had he come back too?

In the town the deputy's arrival caused great excitement, and visitors began pouring in on him at once. Don Lorenzo Giulente and his nephew were the very first, then came authorities, representatives of many political societies, then numbers of citizens of all classes, notabilities, old friends, and new patriots coming to pay their respects to the Honourable Member and thank him for the great things he had done in Turin, and while they were there ask for news of the particular matters with which they had entrusted him. These he received downstairs in the estate offices as at the time of his election, thanked them for their thanks, made a great show of modesty. When questioned, though, by admirers, he would describe the sittings of Parliament, the audience with King Victor Emmanuel and 'poor' Cavour, the political life of the capital; and all listened rapt. He had not opened his mouth in Parliament to say either yes or no, but in this room he was not alarmed by his audience, composed as it was of more or less familiar people who were standing deferently before him, and he enjoyed his triumph, chatty as an old magpie, the fatigues of his journey quite forgotten.

Cavour had promised him the earth: what a pity the great minister had died! But the new Government was just as well disposed towards Sicily; soon work would start on railways, ports, great public schemes. To keep watch on these promises being carried out he should not have left the capital at that period, but he had had to come rushing down about grave family affairs . . . to settle certain matters . . . His lips remained sealed, but everyone knew what he meant all the same. Visits followed till right on into the evening; those wanting to talk to him privately stayed and seemed determined to sleep there. When he had enough he gave a sign to Don Lorenzo, who led them all away.

But the Honourable Member did not go to bed. Raimondo, warned by Baldassarre that his uncle wanted to talk to him, was awaiting him in great agitation in his room.

' What d'you want to do?' began the duke, without bothering about preamble.

' About what?' replied his nephew, as if he did not understand.

' About your wife and family! . . . Your father-in-law is here, don't you know?'

' I know nothing.'

'After escaping like a fugitive! After not showing your face there for two months! Now I think it's time this little matter was wound up . . .' He was talking in a grave tone of authority, walking up and down the room with hands clasped behind his back; Raimondo was sitting staring at the floor, like a boy frightened by the threat of a rebuke.

'What have you to say against your wife?' Don Gaspare suddenly asked, stopping in front of him.

'Me? Nothing.'

'That I knew quite well! I just wanted to hear it confirmed from your own mouth. I ask because your conduct could only be explained if you had any complaints against Matilde! Well, why ever did you leave her?'

'I haven't left her.'

'What? You've been here two months, you haven't written her a line, you haven't done a thing about your family, as if none of them existed? And now you say . . .'

'I came because I'd things to do. I can't be sewn to my wife's skirts, can I?' And he looked the other in the face.

'Well, there's no question of your being sewn now!' replied the duke. 'But no-one who is leaving on business or pleasure or any other reason, just rushes off as you did, leaves his home for a hotel.'

'That's not true!'

'Your father-in-law told me . . . I've heard everybody repeat it.'

'It's a lie!' his nephew cried again loudly, almost stridently. Then the duke beat a retreat.

'If it's a lie all the better. Anyway that's not the important thing . . . what's done is done . . . now we've the future to think of. If it's not true you've left your wife, you ought to have no difficulty in going back to her.'

'I haven't,' replied Raimondo, getting up.

His uncle stood looking at him for a moment, as if not sure he had heard properly, then repeated:

'You're ready to take her back?'

'I'm ready to do anything provided they stop all this fuss.'

'Better still . . . They must have exaggerated, misinformed me. All the better! Can your father-in-law come tomorrow?'

'Tomorrow or whenever he feels like it! What I want to know is why he went and stayed at the hotel? He could have stayed at home instead of putting on this silly act, causing all this gossip by behaving so idiotically!' He was talking harshly now, between set teeth, with red eyes. And the duke also changed his tone and exclaimed in agreement:

'Yes, indeed . . . How right you are . . . I did all I could to dissuade him! But the dear man is made like that. Anyway it doesn't matter; we can say he didn't want to bother Giacomo . . . we'll find a reason. And you, do try to realise that one must take people as they are, be a bit circumspect. Have your fun,' he added with a meaning little smile, 'but without making it obvious, saving appearances. It's unfortunate enough there was that bit of trouble earlier . . .'

'Has Your Excellency anything else to tell me?' asked Raimondo, interrupting him brusquely. 'If not, I'll bid you good night.'

Next day towards midday when the baron was expected and a palace carriage had gone to fetch him, suddenly Donna Ferdinanda appeared. It was over six months since she had been up the palace stairs, since in fact the day when Giulente entered. Till the last moment she had hoped to prevent the monstrous thing, but since slaps and pinches no longer had an effect on Lucrezia, as if she had been turned to stucco, and Giacomo was defending himself by throwing the blame on his uncle the duke, the Booby and on his own sister, the old spinster had finally gone off with a great banging of doors, shouting, 'He'll laugh best who'll laugh last!' As soon as she reached home she called her maid, cook and stable boy, taken a piece of paper from a cupboard and torn it into little pieces 'Not one cent . . .'

She expected her nieces and nephews to obey and submit to her because of the money which, having no children, she would be leaving them. The punishment for their rebellion was destruction of her Will in the presence of servants. The prince had been silent at first, to let the storm blow over, then he sent Fra' Carmelo with his son to visit his aunt, so that the sight of her favourite grand-nephew would placate her fury. Then he had gone to visit her himself and accepted, humble and mute, the hail of reproval flung at him by the old spinster. And gradually, from a need to feel courted, from being unable to renounce putting her nose into her nephews' and nieces' affairs, she had been placated, though without going to visit them; the home of her ancestors was profaned, contaminated by the presence of that beggar, that bandit, that assassin who called himself Benedetto Giulente, *lawyer*, L A W Y E R!

Not even Raimondo's arrival had changed her determination; anyway her nephew came assiduously to her for advice. In her hatred for 'the Palma woman' and in order to destroy that marriage which had taken place against her own wish, she urged the young man to make a definite break. Like Giulente, 'the Palma woman' was a blot on the Uzeda house; she did not want her to set foot in there again. And she defended Donna Isabella against the accusations made against her; she too had been sacrificed to that ignoble *Fersa*, that farce of a man; nothing more natural than for that ill-assorted marriage to end badly; had they given the Pinto girl to Raimondo, ah, then!

Suddenly, close on each other, had come the news of the duke and baron's arrival, and of an imminent reconciliation between her nephew and his father-in-law. Raimondo had not put in an appearance; the thing was about to happen unknown to her! It was time to get her horses harnessed and go straight off to the palace.

When she entered the Yellow Drawing-room she found there the prince and princess, Don Eugenio, the duke, Lucrezia with her fiancé, Chiara with her marchese, and Raimondo walking up and down like a caged lion. As soon as Benedetto Giulente saw her enter, he got up respectfully. She passed him by as if he were one of the pieces of furniture scattered round the room. She answered no one's greeting except that of Raimondo, whom she drew apart towards a window.

'Mad old bitch!' said Lucrezia to her fiancé, her face suddenly flushing.

He shook his head with an indulgent smile, but the duke now came up to the couple, as if to make up for his sister's rudeness.

'The baron should be here by now,' he said, looking at his watch. 'I'd have gone to fetch him myself if I hadn't feared giving too much importance to something which should have none . . .'

'Your Excellency did very well,' replied Benedetto. 'There'd have been more gossip than ever . . . Not,' he added, 'that it in any way reduces Your Excellency's merit for having brought peace back to a family which . . .'

'Petty misunderstandings! Young folk have hot heads!' exclaimed the Honourable Member with a smile partly of indulgence and partly of pleasure.

Meanwhile Raimondo had stopped talking to his aunt and begun walking up and down again. He was green in the face and chewing his moustaches, twisting his lips, with hands in pockets.

Donna Ferdinanda now sat down next to the marchesa, who was in seventh heaven at being seven months with child. After two miscarriages in spite of following all the doctors' prescriptions, all the midwives' suggestions and all the old wives' tales she could find, she had at last changed her system completely and was doing just whatever she liked, going out driving or walking, running up and down stairs, swallowing all the mixtures which she imagined must help her. She was declaring to her sister-in-law that never had she been so well as now.

'Those idiots! Those impostors . . . And the midwives are no better. Why the other day Donna Anna had the courage to come and see me. I took her by the shoulders and said, "My dear Donna Anna, if you'd like you can come and see me three months after I've had the child. It'd be a pleasure, but for the moment you can go, for I don't need you . . ."'

Everyone around was talking in whispers as if in a sick room, but at the sound of a carriage entering the courtyard all speech ceased. The duke moved into the antechamber to meet his friend; but there instead was Cousin Graziella.

'How is Your Excellency? I heard of your arrival and said to myself—I must go and kiss my uncle's hand. My husband wanted to come too, but he's been suddenly called to the Courts about some boring case. He'll be coming later to do his duty . . .'

At sight of her, Raimondo sniffed louder than ever and exclaimed to his uncle, 'Now this gossiping bitch too? Must the whole city be here? . . . Can't Your Excellency see what a ridiculous scene . . .'

'Patience . . . patience . . .' began the duke. But now another carriage was entering the courtyard. He passed out of the room and shortly afterwards reappeared with the senator. The latter was very pale and his jaws could be seen nervously clenching under his cheeks.

'Raimondo,' exclaimed the deputy in a careless and conciliating tone, 'here's your father-in-law . . .'

The count stopped. Without taking his hands from his pockets he gave a nod of greeting and said:

'How are you?'

Palmi replied, 'Well, and you?' and turned to greet the others.

No-one breathed a word, every eye was on the baron. His hands too were trembling a little and he did not look his son-in-law in the face.

'Please be seated, Don Gaetano,' went on the duke, taking him by the arm and urging him in a friendly way. Then Palmi sat down between the princess and the marchesa. Donna Ferdinanda sat stiffly upright, her chin in her neck like an old chicken.

'Is Matilde well?' asked the princess.

'Well, thank you.'

'And the children?'

'Very well.'

Raimondo was standing in the middle of the room, nervously snapping his fingers. The duke coughed a little, as if he were starting a sore throat, then asked him:

'When are you going back to your wife?'

He replied shortly and briefly: 'Tomorrow if need be.'

'We'd like to have Matilde here a little,' went on his uncle, looking at the other relations as if asking for their assent; but no one said a word. 'Well,' he went on then, 'why not do this; go and fetch her and then you can all return together. What d'you think of that, baron?'

'As you think best,' replied Palmi.

Suddenly for the third time there was the sound of a carriage entering the courtyard, and all eyes turned towards the door. Who could it be? Ferdinando? The duchess?

In bounced Don Blasco.

Like his sister, the monk had not set foot inside the palace since the day of Lucrezia's engagement; like Donna Ferdinanda he had blamed it all on the prince, and had been so stubbornly deaf to all justifications that the latter had finally tired of insisting, having no legacy to hope for from him as he had from the other. Then, finding himself isolated, unable to take part in family affairs, forced to hear news of them at second or third hand through the Marchese Federico or strangers, the monk felt quite lost. Squabbles at the monastery kept him busy up to a point, but shouts and curses at Liberals, though redoubled as the new order became more established, were not enough, had no flavour unless made to his own relations in the very place where that renegade brother of his had his triumph, where that adventurer Giulente was sure to be spewing heresies. So, puffing frenziedly, he had been on the point more than once of going to visit the prince, but on getting half-way he had thought better of it, not wanting to give his nephew the satisfaction of seeing him yield first. At the news of the duke's and the baron's arrival, of the peace about to be made between father-in-law and son-in-law, he felt it was time for him to come to a decision.

The prince went towards him to kiss his hand. Lucrezia and Giulente, sitting together, were nearest the entrance doors. As the monk passed the young man got up as he had for the spinster, but Don Blasco went straight on towards the middle of the room. At this second affront Lucrezia became redder than ever and made her fiancé sit down.

'They'll pay for it, you'll see!' she said. 'They'll pay for it . . . Never will I set foot in this house again! . . . Never so much as look them in the face! . . .'

The duke did not seem to notice his brother's arrival. To revive the languishing conversation and overcome the chill entrammelling all, and make herself useful, Cousin Graziella began asking about his journey through Italy, and the deputy now talked away at top speed:

'What a confusion in Naples, eh? Such a place! You'd think that once the Court and Ministers and all the movement of a capital had gone it ought to lose population, reduce itself to a provincial town; instead of which every day it grows more animated than before. Turin is full of life too, but in a different way . . .'

'In a different way . . .' repeated the baron in a condescending tone, as if to avoid being silent.

'Is it true that it's rather like Catania?' asked the marchese.

Raimondo broke out of his dumbness to say ironically:

'Exactly like it! Two drops of water . . .'

'The streets are said to be designed in the same way.'

'Yes! Yes, indeed . . . Why not admit it! Turin is uglier, smaller, poorer, dirtier.'

Chiara then leapt to her husband's defence:

'This mania for criticising one's own home town I've never understood.'

'Excuse me,' protested the duke, 'no-one's criticising here.'

'One can't really compare them,' said Benedetto conciliatingly.

Donna Ferdinanda slowly raised her eyes and turned them in the direction whence the voice had come, but when she had them half-way there she switched them over to the window where Don Blasco was listening to his nephew's account of developments.

'He says he'll join his wife and then they'll both come here. Our uncle the duke arranged everything. As far as I'm concerned they can do just whatever they like. But they'll begin all over again, you'll see. I hope I'm mistaken, but we're only at the start . . .'

'Why did that old swine do it? Hasn't he enough bees in his bonnet? Must he put his nose into this too? But I know the reason . . . Yes, I know . . . I know the reason . . .'

He was about to go on and have his full say when Baldassarre entered, grave and dignified as the solemnity of the occasion demanded.

'Excellency,' he said to the duke, 'the representatives of various organisations are asking to pay Your Excellency their respects.'

Before the deputy had time to reply the baron had got to his feet.

'Duke, do go, I leave you free.'

'But no, stay, do . . . I'll be back in a moment . . .'

'I have a lot to do too. Many thanks!'

'Won't you at least come back to lunch with us?'

'Thank you, no; I'm leaving today. I've arranged a special coach.'

It was useless to insist; the baron always put up a polite but cold refusal. He said goodbye to everyone and left accompanied by the duke, who was going downstairs to see his electors, while Raimondo went off to his own rooms. The three had scarcely vanished when a general murmur went up in the Yellow Drawing-room.

'What a way of behaving!' exclaimed Donna Ferdinanda. 'He's not said a dozen words in half an hour!' said Cousin Graziella. 'What's wrong with him? What have they done to him?' And the marchese said:

'If one's in that sort of mood one shouldn't visit people.'

'And how haughty he was!' added his wife.

From his place Benedetto Giulente observed:

'His departure seems an excuse . . . to refuse . . .'

Then Don Blasco, without turning to the young man, as if answering the idea just put forward by him, boomed out:

'The swine, idiot, and buffoon in this case is the one who invited him here!'

Benedetto, though the monk was not looking at him, made a gesture of the head that seemed part assent at what was said and part excuse of the duke's insistence.

'He might have been granting us a special grace, honouring us by his presence!' Donna Ferdinanda was continuing meanwhile. 'As if it had not been in his own interests! As if the fault for what's happened weren't his! And to make things worse that swine begging round him and agreeing with him! Just to make him all the more presumptuous and stuck-up . . .'

Benedetto, who was sitting almost opposite her, went on giving continual and regular nods of the head like an automaton, and as Cousin Graziella was chattering in a low voice with Chiara, and Don Blasco had drawn the marchese aside and was letting himself go, and the prince was sitting there silent, and the princess even more silent, that gesture of assent and approval eventually drew the spinster's eyes.

'While Raimondo is in the right,' she went on, 'in not wanting to be spied on in his own home, in refusing to tolerate his father-in-law's continual interference in every little family affair . . .'

Seeing she had glanced at him one or twice, Benedetto, still nodding approval, agreed:

' Yes, the baron really has a very difficult character . . .'

Donna Ferdinanda made no reply, partly because at that moment the marchese rose and Chiara with him. But as she went off with her niece and nephew she gave a slight bow in reply to a new, deeper, ever more respectful one from the young man.

Meanwhile down in the steward's rooms the duke was receiving delegations and great numbers of influential electors, while a procession of admirers of all classes came to pay him their homage. It was the same scene as the night before, but on a bigger scale. Gradually the whole town seemed to be filing past the deputy; for two people who went away, four arrived; and there being no more places to sit everyone else stood, hat in hand, waiting for the handshake which the duke was distributing all around. A few improvised orators, people whom he did not even know, spoke in the name of their companions, affirming in reply to his expressions of modesty that the town would never forget what it owed to the Signor Duke. All the others listened open-mouthed, religiously intent on gathering the Honourable Member's words; when compliments stopped, he talked of public events, promised them Venice, had Rome in his pocket, assured them that as well as political revival, the country would have moral, agricultural, industrial and commercial revival too.

' That was Cavour's programme. What a head that man had! He used to talk of Sicily as if he'd been born here. He knew the price of our crops and our sulphur better than one of our own merchants . . .' The Government had promised him many things for the island, although they had so much to think of; from education of youth to work for labourers. Little by little, with peace and amity, public and private prosperity would be achieved. He almost made them feel it within their grasp, and those come to hear what had happened about their requests for a small post or a subsidy or a pension went off praising him to the skies as if he had filled their pockets, and spread throughout

293

the town the news of the reconciliation between the count and his wife; all due to the duke, who had made the sacrifice of leaving the capital at a moment like this simply in order to induce his nephew to see reason. Paeans of praise for the deputy could be heard everywhere. From the palace courtyard to the Reading Club all were agreed that this had been both good and dutiful work on his part; only Don Blasco, at the pro-Bourbon chemist's, yelled like one obsessed:

' Ah, that's what you think, is it? . . . Why d'you think he did it? To satisfy the mob! To have it said he's defending morality . . . And for yet another reason . . . to ingratiate himself with that other rascally friend of the lazy scum . . . That fellow who kept harping on *my* faults! That baron with seven pairs of b . . .!'

W H E N the Countess Matilde returned to her husband's family after two years' absence, they themselves did not recognise her at first. She had always been pale and thin, now she was wan and emaciated. Her chest was hollow, as if she were being eaten away by some slow relentless disease, her shoulders bent as if by weight of years, and her sunken eyes, in livid surrounds, glinting with fever, told of torturing thought, frenzied worry, mortal fear.

'Poor Matilde! Have you been ill?' the princess asked her, in spite of her husband's injunctions not to take sides.

'A little . . .' replied her sister-in-law, shaking her head with a sweet sad smile, 'it's over now . . .'

In fact she felt reborn. Her father had refused to accompany her to that house or to let her bring the children. Yet forgetting all she had suffered there she entered it with a sense of relief, almost of confidence. The recent tempest had been so violent and harsh that she even thought with regret of former sorrows; they had seemed intolerable then, when she did not know how slowly and surely they would grow till they began to contend even with her hope of any kind of return to peace. How her heart had shut at the first disillusionment, at seeing that her love was not enough for Raimondo, that his mind was different from hers, that he found happiness in things which had no value for her! And yet at that time he had not betrayed her! But then betrayals had come, and she had forgiven because all men did such things, so it was said, though she herself suffered silently at them in the depths of her heart. What could she have done anyway? What could she have done before this greater danger, this more dreadful threat? Leave him? He himself had left her! . . .

When she thought over those two years spent in Tuscany, of all she had suffered watching the building up of final ruin, unable to do anything to prevent it, she felt a need to kneel down and thank God, so miraculous seemed Raimondo's reform. Could she now hope it would last? How often had he seemed to recover his senses, and then behaved worse than ever? Two years ago, before the Fersa scandal broke, had she not thought all was over for her? At the news of that woman being thrust out by her own mother-in-law she had sensed that the apparent break between her and Raimondo was mere play-acting and foresaw quite lucidly what was to happen later . . . Even so the departure for the mainland had deceived her again. Distance, time, worldly pleasures for which he was always avid, would they not destroy the memory of that other woman in Raimondo's heart? But she, that other one, must have sworn to steal him from her at all costs, for she had followed him to Florence, and appeared far and near, in streets and in society, everywhere, tempting him, even in front of Matilde herself! She did not blame Raimondo now, did not suspect that he was in collusion with that other, that he had pretended to run away so as to find her the more surely. Matilde's suspicions and jealous accusations only fell on that woman; to Raimondo she merely addressed indulgent requests, humble petitions to spare her new sorrows. He grew furious, denied it all as at other times, blamed her for wanting to create embarrassments and dangers, and reduced her to silence with words which still rang in her ears: 'That woman is the very last person in my thoughts; but if you don't stop vexing me I'll do something mad, you'll see!' She had not been able to tell then how far he was sincere . . .

Raimondo's fancy for Donna Isabella, in truth, had been calmed as soon as satisfied. The fuss about separation, the fear of finding some heavy material responsibility on his shoulders, had flung a good deal of water on the flame of his desires. In Florence, where they had arranged to meet, he wondered how to break in some way the chain he felt growing tighter; what he longed for was a gay and varied life which was above all free. But as news spread of the domestic drama in which he had been the hero he found himself higher in the estimation of his reckless Tuscan friends, whose judgment meant more to him than anything else; the conquest of a genuine lady of quality like Donna Isabella Fersa brought smiles of rather envious pleasure from the dare-devils he took as models. So he became a little less indifferent to Donna Isabella. But his wife's jealousy eventually tightened this link to a point which he found almost burdensome.

Every time Matilde made a begging remonstrance to him he felt it his duty, as a kind of compensation, to increase his demonstrations of affection to his mistress; the more submissively his wife begged him not to leave her too much to herself, the stronger was his craving to rush out of the house. She knew what he was like, how intolerant he was of every obstacle, of any contradiction, of any comment by her; but could she keep silent, pretend to ignore what was happening? Could she, without a sob at least, allow him to leave her alone for long days and longer nights, to abandon his children, so as to go off with that other woman, to show himself publicly in her company, to take his friends to the other's house as if it were another of his homes? And when she had once burst out not against him but against that other woman, Raimondo ordered her to be silent, in a loud voice, with an evil look and raised hand . . .

This wretched scene had taken place on the day before her father was to pass through Florence on his way to Turin. Terror of the two men clashing had made her be silent, and as her father, who was beginning to suspect Raimondo again, had suddenly switched with his usual violence from warm affection for his son-in-law to suspicion and watchful coldness, she had to gulp down her own tears, cancel traces of them, and look gay and pleased, to prevent the two attacking each other. So she had consumed herself, suffering in silence, forcing down bitter draft after bitter draft, invoking God for strength to continue pretending, deluding herself to believe that no serious danger was threatening.

But it was already too late. All that his wife in her jealousy said against his mistress urged Raimondo more and more into the latter's arms; as Matilde spoke badly of her, she must be the very first among women. This idea became the deeper rooted in his head since Donna Isabella on her side never said a word against the countess; at most she hinted a mild complaint at his wife's dislike for her.

'When she meets me she turns her back on me . . . She talks against me. What have I done to her?' Or she would suggest they break off their relationship, offering herself in sacrifice to ensure peace in his family.

'Don't worry about me! I'll go off, I'll live alone, as God wills . . . I'll go and fling myself at my husband's feet; maybe he'll forgive me . . .' Then in return he would insist on doing things which she herself did not want him to do; if he had not hidden their friendship before, he now made an open display of it; if he had been seldom enough at home before, he now would let whole weeks go by without setting foot in his home, without seeing his own children; at the theatre he spent the entire evening, from beginning to end of the show, in his mistress's box; at the parade, if he was with friends, he would not answer his wife's greeting when they met; and while the countess dissolved in tears at the back of her carriage, he would go and lounge at Donna Isabella's carriage door.

Early that summer, at Livorno, the scandal had grown to such a point that a few good friends of Raimondo, his landlord Count Rossi among them, had advised him to be less imprudent. In these days Matilde, whose heart had been so long in torture, had a new affliction. Her little daughter Lauretta, whose health was always uncertain, fell ill as soon as they left Florence. One night when the child was moaning in fever she stayed up till dawn watching over her, terrified at how quickly she had got worse and waiting anxiously for Raimondo's return. At daybreak he came back. He must have been drunk. For just because, tortured by anxiety and exhaustion, alarmed by her child's illness and terrified at its danger, she dared to say:

'What a life you're leading . . .' He stared in her face, with bloodshot eyes, tightened his fists and swore at her. What did he do next? Or say? She did not know. All she remembered was that on coming round from her swoon, Stefana her maid told her that the master had gone off, in the same evening clothes in which he had come, taking only a small grip in which he had thrown a few things haphazard. She remembered what torture

298

it had been to be unable to hurry after him, to be unable to leave her poor daughter in that state; how she had sent Stefana to Florence, thinking he had gone back there; how she heard next day that after going first to a hotel in Livorno itself he had taken ship for Sicily.

The baron arrived like lightning from Turin before she had given him any news of what had happened. Then another torment was added to the many already tearing at her. Her father's rancour against his son-in-law suddenly burst out, in all its terror.

'He's gone off, has he? So much the better!' he said at first. But as she burst into tears, not knowing what to do and seeing her very existence destroyed, a violent gust of rage thrust all the blood into his head.

'So you're regretting him, are you? You'd like to defend him, would you? You'd even go running after him, would you?'

Terrified, her hands joined in entreaty, she brought out between sobs, 'What about my children . . . my little orphans?' But he interrupted with an even more savage outburst:

'Ah, his paternal love, eh?, his love for his children, eh?, the blood he poisoned on that innocent creature . . .' and in a flood of crude, rending, rushing words he told her of Raimondo's unworthy life, of what she did not know, what he himself had not known for a long time, lulled by vanity, by silly pride at connection with one of the 'Viceroys'

'You want to implore him as well, now, do you . . .? Want me to go and ask pardon on your behalf, on mine, on those innocents'! Isn't this ten years' experience enough for you, silly girl? D'you want to begin trembling before him again? D'you think I don't know what you've suffered?' And as her shoulders hunched and she gave a shiver he shouted, 'Doesn't all that matter to you? Could you still love him? . . .'

Yes, it was true. She was not weeping for her children's future, she was not indignant at the memory of her own agonies; if she had suffered in silence, if she had done no more than accuse her rival, if she had never said a word in reproval of Raimondo, the one and only reason was her love for him.

'After what he's done to you? . . . Can't you realise that he's never returned your love? That he'd ask for nothing better than get rid of you, you fool. Yet you love him like a dog licking the hand that hits it?'

Yes, yes, just like that! The love of a dog for its master, the devotion of a slave for a being of another race, stronger, taller, rarer. Yes, the submission of a dog to its master; for even after the extreme shame he had inflicted on her, in spite of his brutal revelations, in spite of her father's righteous anger, she still thought she could not live away from Raimondo, could not leave him to that other woman.

So she spent long, endless days of inner anguish; the baron treated her with open coldness, seemed not to notice her tears. But she was waiting, yearning and praying for something; not Raimondo's return, which would have been too great a joy, but at least a letter of regret from him, or a message from one of his family . . . The child had recovered; at the Madonna's feet she implored pardon for an abominable thought: had Lauretta got worse she could have called him . . .

Instead of which she herself fell ill. Seeing her weeping in her fever too, the baron burst into the railing tone he put on when yielding:

'So you won't put an end to it? He's even to have the pleasure of being begged as well? Take heed though . . .' he added threateningly, 'from the day you return together you'll have to consider me as no longer existing . . . Choose between us two. Don't imagine I can have anything in common with him!' Poor father! Rough, unbending and hot-tempered with all, yet he had always given way to his daughters, trying to put a bold face on it, making decisions dictated by his violent character but prevented by his inexhaustible goodness of heart from carrying them out in the long run. So he wrote to the duke, and after accompanying her to Milazzo, went with him to join Raimondo, whom he then led back to her.

Not a word passed between her and her husband in connection with the past; if he did go back to live with her would she ever be able to remind him of the wrong he had done? On his part he never asked pardon or said a good word to her; he came to meet her as indifferently as if he had left her the day before. Nor did she hope for more than this. What had once been a dream of love and happiness had melted from day to day; now, resigned to the sadness of reality, she asked for nothing but quiet. As long as Raimondo loved his children, as long as he did not leave them again, she was ready to endure anything.

Now, at the prince's, where they had then come for Lucrezia's marriage, leaving the children at Milazzo, his relatives were treating her better. The bride, beside herself with delight at the marriage being so near, was full of demonstrations of affection for her, asked her advice exclusively about wedding clothes and final details of the trousseau. The princess, always timid and detached, showed her more sympathy than before. Even Don Blasco and Donna Ferdinanda, who had begun coming to the palace again every day, also seemed a little subdued, for instead of picking at her they took no notice of her at all. What did that matter! They were like that; they had to be taken as they were. As long as Raimondo did not leave her once again! As long as those ghastly days of his desertion never returned! She even became almost resigned to being so far from her children!

Her little niece Teresa's company made things more tolerable. How like the prince's daughter was to her own Teresa! The same fine blonde beauty, the same grace, the same sweetness of voice and of look. Their characters were also like each other really, though her own child showed an almost restless vivacity while her little cousin was quieter and more obedient. How much of this was due to her father's authority? While Raimondo took no notice of his daughter, Giacomo watched almost too heavily over the little princess. He was educating her to mortify her desires, to repress her wishes. He made her spend whole days with the nuns of San Placido so that she should get used to obedience and monastic discipline. Poor little girl! Every time they put her on the wheel which passed her into the convent through the impenetrable walls segregating the nuns from the world, she stretched out her arms to her mother and to her aunt with a look of terror in her wide-set eyes. But the princess had orders from her husband, who considered the child as a kind of mute ambassadress to soothe the Abbess's and Sister Maria's discontent, so she would persuade her daughter to be good and not to be frightened. The little girl would say 'Yes' again and again, sending her mother kisses as the wheel turned deep in the wall and passed her through on to the other side, into the big cold grey room with a great, black, bleeding, Crucifix taking up an entire wall. Her mother, the nuns, all and everyone praised the wisdom she showed; to gain this praise, not to displease her father, she did what they wanted. The countess felt that her own Teresa, in spite of her apparent vivacity, was sweet and good at heart too. Was Lauretta not even quieter and more obedient than her own cousin? And as she thought of her little angels she longed for Lucrezia's marriage to be over so that she could get back to them soon.

All was ready. In the bride and groom's future home, an apartment next to Don Paolo Giulente's but separate from it, the last touches were being given to arrangement of furniture; all had been done with great expense and much taste. The family notary had already drafted the marriage settlement, on the basis of the prince's transactions and under his dictation. Benedetto, to ingratiate himself with his brother-in-law, had let him do what he liked and been content with five thousand *onze* for the moment instead of eight thousand, as the prince said that he had not the whole sum to hand. Gradually from that first meeting with the monk and the old spinster he had succeeded in getting them to take a little more notice of him every day, by continuing to nod like a puppet at everything they said.

As to politics, Don Blasco and his sister worked themselves up more than ever, shouting outrages and insults against the Liberals; then the young man would pretend not to hear and turn away, letting them say what they liked, as if their waves of abuse did not crash over him too. But in all other circumstances, in every other discussion, he would take their part and agree with them at all costs, watching for a look, a nod or a word.

Just at that time one of Donna Ferdinanda's debtors, a certain Calafoti, had declared himself bankrupt and let it be understood that his property had been either sold or mortgaged. The spinster was screeching like a hen plucked alive against the 'thief', the broker who had proposed the affair, and the Prince of Roccasciano, who had approved it. But Benedetto, hearing her talking, said:

' I know this man Calafoti. If Your Excellency cares I can go and have a word with him. The laws he is adducing are all null and void; by threatening to sue him we can bring him to heel.'

She did not wait to be asked again for the required permission. After a week of discussing and dealing Benedetto obtained a special mortgage. In exchange Donna Ferdinanda did not come to the palace on the wedding day. Nor did Don Blasco. Business was one thing; so was talk!; to approve, by their presence, the alliance of an Uzeda with the *Affocato* Giulente was quite another. But apart from those two not a single one of the other relations was absent, either at the Town Hall in the morning or at the cathedral in the afternoon.

The Marchesa Chiara accompanied the pair wherever they went. She was exhausted but went on moving up and down stairs and refused to call anyone in. On the afternoon of the wedding, tired by constant coming and going, she flung herself fainting on to a chair next to Donna Eleonora Giulente. Perhaps it was just over-tiredness, but she really did not feel at all well, had dull aches and sharp twinges of pain. With her elbows propped on the chair arms to keep her womb free and erect, she was pressing her lips together a little at each spasm, but when her husband came hurrying up and asked her anxiously what was the matter, she replied:

' Nothing, I am all right,' lest he called in midwives.

She got up and went round the room. There were great numbers of guests, all the relations, all the nobility, and then the duke's new friends the authorities, the Mayor, the Prefect whom he had invited to show the Liberal character of the alliance. And while the pro-Bourbon nobility was grouped in the hall or in the Red and Yellow Drawing-rooms, the Deputy held a democratic circle in the portrait gallery, where he was being complimented on arranging this fine marriage, and discussing public business. Don Paolo Giulente, finding no chance of getting into conversation with the nobles, came in to listen, open-mouthed, almost beside himself with joy at becoming a relative of the great man. His brother Don Lorenzo was wearing for the occasion the green cravat of an Order which his friend the Deputy had arranged for the Turin Government to grant, together with some substantial contracts for posts and military transport.

A good number of lesser requests to him were actually beginning to be carried out; the Honourable Member had got jobs, subsidies and Orders of St Maurice granted to patriots of '48 and '60, seen that the pension rights of old veterans of the Sicilian revolution were recognised and that Garibaldi volunteers were admitted into the regular army, and had urged on cases of damage by Bourbon troops to those noted for patriotism. Such clients, satisfied or about to be satisfied, stood listening to him as if he were an oracle, proud of having him as a friend and of being admitted into the home of the Viceroys, of finding themselves served by footmen in sumptuous liveries.

Baldassarre, in full dress, was moving around at the head of a procession of these footmen carrying trays laden with ices, iced drinks and cakes, serving the picture gallery after the drawing-rooms, but with the same etiquette, following the example of the prince, who made the same bow to all; though, to tell the truth, around His Excellency the duke there were certain types that had sprung from goodness-knew-where. They would take the little plates of ices and throw their spoons on the floor, or gulp down the crushed fruit-drink as if it were fresh water, or snatch cakes in handfuls as if they had never eaten any before that evening. With the Viceroys looking down from high on the walls! Enough; his job was to carry out his master's orders!

Just then Cousin Graziella, apart in a group with the Duchess Radalì and the Princess of Roccasciano, was saying to the young prince, who had got a special permission to stay out at night for his aunt's wedding:

'We'll have to choose the bride for him ourselves! There'll be plenty of choice!'

She did not know how to point out to the Giulente that this wedding was being forced on them against the wills of the majority of the family. But Donna Eleonora noticed nothing; sitting next to the princess and the Countess Matilde she was smiling beatifically as bride and groom passed, their faces, particularly Lucrezia's, glinting with the joy of triumph. Anyway, though Donna Ferdinanda and Cousin Graziella might snub her, the princess was all courtesy and the Countess Matilde all sympathy with a mother's happiness. Even Chiara came to fling herself down beside Donna Eleonora once more.

'Are you tired, marchesa?'

'Me? Oh no! I'm fine.' The stabs of pains were becoming more frequent, almost taking her breath away; she would have happily had her baby right there on that sofa.

Ferdinando, trussed up in formal clothes which he had put on for the second time in his life, was going round like a soul in purgatory, knowing nobody, having led a Robinson Crusoe life for so long. He had come to act as witness for his favourite sister and was longing for the ceremonies to end so as to get back home.

In God's good time the procession moved down the grand staircase, distributed itself into carriages, and moved off to the cathedral. The ceremony itself took place in the bishop's private chapel, conducted by Monsignor in person. All the guests bore torches, bride and groom stood before the glittering scented altar, Donna Eleonora Giulente was sobbing like a fountain.

'Most moving, most moving' the duke was saying quietly to the Prefect beside him. Suddenly there was a commotion; Chiara had been incapable of standing another moment and dropped on to a stool. Everyone surrounded her, but she reassured them with a smile. Even Monsignor the Bishop smiled, knowing her to be in an interesting condition. The marchese dragged her off to their carriage while the rest of the party went on to the Giulentes' house, where there was almost a more sumptuous display even than that of the prince's; endless refreshments, ices melting on trays for lack of consumers. Finally the bride and groom got into a carriage and went off to the Belvedere.

Next morning there drove up to visit them, one after the other, Giulente husband and wife, Don Lorenzo and the duke, the princess and even Chiara, looking fresh as a rose; the pains had vanished and she was determined to go to her sister's. That afternoon bride and groom were not expecting anyone else when, *drlin, drlin*, a tinkle of harness-bells and Donna Ferdinanda's carriage, covered with dust, stopped at the villa gates. The old spinster, as if she had left them the evening before, as if they had been married for ten years, gave her hand for her niece to kiss and as soon as she sat down said to Benedetto:

'A fine affair you suggested! The other creditors are opposed to ceding the mortgage!'

Benedetto was so astounded that he could find no reply, but Lucrezia turned to him, saying:

'Is there no way of getting them to agree?'

'The creditors? . . . of course . . . They can be got to agree . . .' and just restraining a smile he exclaimed, 'Your Excellency must not worry, Your Excellency's credit was privileged. We'll make 'em do the proper thing, don't doubt that!'

Next day Donna Ferdinanda came back with her defending lawyer so that Benedetto could explain things to him. And she returned again next day and the one after, until to content her he went down into town with his wife to disentangle the web himself. They were supposed to spend a month or so at the Belvedere, but this meant they stayed there scarcely a week. He did not complain, pleased at having made peace with the aunt who, after seeking him out every day in the country, now came morning and evening to visit him in town.

She would arrive at a time when the Giulente father and mother had not yet been to see their daughter-in-law, who always stayed in bed late. Benedetto, up with the sun, would give the servants orders for meals and see that his wife when she rose found the house all in order. And Donna Ferdinanda, after discussing the matter of her loan, would begin commenting on her niece's and nephew's affairs; they were dining late in order to follow that *Italian* mode brought over by that pig of a duke; if it was Friday she said they bought fish that was too expensive when they could have had stock-fish, as she did, and why give the maid full keep instead of just soup, as she herself did at home? Gradually she put her nose into all the most minute and intimate details; she went over their accounts, examined the washerwomen's bills, criticised a purchase of dusters, laid down rules of domestic economy, blamed Benedetto's open-handedness after having opposed the marriage because of the Giulente's 'meanness'.

Benedetto never seemed annoyed by this curious minute vigilance, for he thought it a sign of benevolence; in fact to ingratiate himself better, he invited his aunt to dine once a week and another to take luncheon. But the old spinster needed no begging to come and made use of her niece and nephew in any way she could, while exercising her criticism with ever-increasing authority, expecting to be listened to in all things and every way. Unable to get a rise out of Benedetto, who would stand before her like a servant, she criticised her niece for getting up late and staying in a dressing-gown till midday with hair over shoulders and feet in slippers. Eventually the latter said to her husband:

'She's beginning to annoy me, you know!'

Then to please her, and taking no notice of Donna Ferdinanda's pouts, he began spacing out their invitations; but just when he thought he was going to eat alone again with his wife he would see the spinster suddenly appear, called by Lucrezia.

Lucrezia indeed changed her mind from one moment to the next, and everyone agreed with her, not only her husband, but also his father and mother. They fussed over her as if she were a precious object, satisfied her slightest whim, gave her everything she wanted. So she would get up a little later every day and do nothing for a couple of hours, not even wash. When she was finally dressed she would go off sometimes to visit her sister Chiara, who had miscounted the months and not yet been delivered; but more often to the palace where she had sworn never to set foot again, but now stayed so long that her husband often had to pass by and fetch her at meal-times. She would also return there every evening to take part in the usual conversazione. So that, all in all, and apart from her hours of sleep, she was spending more time under her parental than under her marital roof. But the Giulente family considered it quite natural for her to want to see her relatives, nor did Benedetto see fit to remind her of her former intentions. Then one fine day when he offered to accompany her to the palace as usual, she said:

'I'll have both hands cut off before I go to that house again!'

'What's happened? What have they done to you? ...'

'What have they done to me? Just read this!'

For weeks the prince had been putting off payment of the last three thousand *onze*; now finally he had sent in a new bill through Signor Marco in a sealed envelope addressed to Benedetto. Lucrezia had opened it. There was a debit column, giving expenses for the wedding; a total of a hundred and twenty-five *onze*. Drinks, cakes, packets of candles, oil for the Carcel lamps were all noted down; to every servant a tip of an *onze*; ten *onze* for flowers, twelve *tarì* for carriages hired by Baldassarre and even fifteen *tarì* for broken plates. When Giulente read this bill he burst out laughing, so absurd did he find meanness pushed to such a point. But Lucrezia was furious against her brother.

'What d'you find to laugh about? It's disgusting behaviour! That's why his orders were so big . . . But thirty *onze* worth of cakes, whoever could have eaten that amount? A hundred *rotoli's* weight! And those few roses he had sent down from the Belvedere? And the broken plates? . . .'

Although her husband tried to calm her by pointing out that after all the prince was not obliged to spend his own money, she refused to listen to reason and began pouring out other matters which she had previously denied even to herself.

'Not obliged? And what about the income from my dowry which he appropriated for six years, measuring out my food while not letting me buy myself a pin? . . . And that transaction he forced me into, taking me by the throat, before consenting to our marriage? And stripping Ferdinando with me? I swear I'll never look him in the face again . . .'

And she did in fact give up going to the palace. The prince on his side did not come to her either; his wife, who wanted to pay her sister-in-law a visit, was rigorously forbidden. Cousin Graziella, after visiting the newly-married pair once, followed the head of the family's example, so that Lucrezia began inveighing against that other gossip too.

'She doesn't want to come to my house? The honour would be hers. Stuck-up little thing, whom my mother never even bothered about, to give herself such airs! Do they think they're hurting me by not coming to my house? Don't they know there's nothing I'd like better? That I don't want to see one of them any more?'

Don Blasco, for his part, had never once set foot in the newly married couple's house, and Lucrezia, declaring herself content, also spoke out against the monk's crazy behaviour and dirty habits. She had it against her sister Chiara too, without the latter having done anything to her, and derided her for her eternal pregnancy which was now reaching its tenth month. She attacked them all in fact, and to the Countess Matilde, who came to visit her as before :

' D'you see,' she said, ' what a dreadful lot they are! They've made you suffer, haven't they? And that rascal of a husband of yours? With all the rest of them helping him to run after that woman? . . .'

Pale then flushing at this speech, Matilde tried to put in a good word even so; but the other warmed to her theme.

' And you're defending him too? Let him be! All tarred with the same brush, they are! And there's no telling what trouble's still in store for you, you poor thing! As for me I thank the Lord that I was able to get away from them! Do they think I'm going to bow down to them again? A lot I care for them and their visits! . . .'

One day on coming home, Benedetto, who had bowed his head to these outbursts to please his wife and not from his own inclination, found her sitting beside Don Blasco, whom she was serving with biscuits and Rosalio wine. The monk, no longer seeing Lucrezia at the palace, having heard of the break between brother and sister, had appeared like an evil genius before his niece. And Lucrezia, who had been abusing him so roundly, had at once risen to kiss his hand. ' How is Your Excellency? My husband has gone out . . . If Your Excellency would care to wait a moment, he cannot be long . . .' And while they waited for him the monk got out of her the whole story. At her out-burst against Giacomo and Cousin Graziella he seemed to swell up in his chair; but he expressed no opinion of his own, lined up with neither side : he just nodded, encouraging the story-teller to go further. On the arrival of Benedetto, who could not believe his own eyes, the monk allowed his new nephew to kiss his hand, chattered away for a time about all manner of subjects, ate another biscuit, drank another glass of wine, and went off, accompanied by husband and wife as far as the landing.

From that day Benedetto could not get rid of him. He came constantly, at different times, when least expected. Preceding him would be a loud, masterful ring at the door bell, and once he was inside he would begin spinning around like a top, talking of a thousand things, peering into all the corners, groping about in all the furniture, reading all the papers, having his say on all his niece's and nephew-in-law's affairs even more than Donna Ferdinanda, but going off as soon as the latter appeared. Benedetto was no longer master in his own house, as nothing escaped the double criticism of the spinster and the monk. But he put up cheerfully with everything, pleased to find himself acknowledged by all the Uzeda, sorry only at the prince's coldness because of matters that did not concern him. For him whatever his wife did was right and she, who had taken on Vanna and so always heard what was going on at the palace, burst out to Don Blasco against her brother, accusing him of having robbed her, of having robbed Chiara, of now trying to rob Raimondo.

' He urges his brother on against the wife! He's said to have told him, " What are you staying here for?" Just to throw fuel on the fire! He must be up to something! He's not one to do anything for nothing! And Raimondo is leaving with Matilde for Milazzo, they say. She's so silly, my sister-in-law is! I tried to open her eyes, as I feel sorry for her. This will end badly for her! Why, they've even asked Benedetto's advice about dissolving the marriage! I told him not to get mixed up in it all! ...'

She did not say that Benedetto, sent for by Donna Ferdinanda, in whose house Raimondo was awaiting him, had been flattered at the confidence on such an intimate matter, and after struggling against his own conscience had gradually let himself be won over by the honour the spinster had done him of letting him in on a family secret, of asking his advice as a *relative* rather than consult anyone else. This idea had overcome his scruples. A stranger, some intriguing lawyer capable of doing anything for money, would have been far more to be feared and might have advised them to start on the case at once! Instead of which he was confident of succeeding in making peace between husband and wife; there would be time till the very last moment. Then the huge obstacles to be overcome ended by reassuring him. The dissolving of a marriage was a most difficult enterprise; but Donna Ferdinanda wanted to dissolve two, both Raimondo's and the Fersas', and reasons, even pretexts, were lacking on either side.

What harm, then, did he do by listing the necessary reasons asked for by his brother-in-law before, and in discussing with the old spinster what to do if any one of those reasons really existed? Was not the whole thing purely academic, a kind of lesson in canon law, like that of his ancestor praised by the Cavaliere Don Eugenio, Gentleman of the Bedchamber? . . . In spite of that, secretly he was uncomfortable when meeting Matilde, feeling himself already an accomplice in the web being woven against the poor creature. The countess, however, seemed more serene and confident than at the time of her arrival in the Uzeda household. Gradually she had allowed herself to be won over by hope, seeing that Raimondo no longer mentioned return to Tuscany and promised to take her, immediately after Chiara's delivery, to Milazzo to join the children and then to Turin, where her father, placated, was awaiting them. Just as her father had forgotten his severe resolutions against Raimondo, so also Raimondo could have forgotten the love of that other one, might he not? . . . Did not everything come to an end, in time? . . .

And Chiara did not deliver. The ninth month—for the second time!—was about to end and her belly did not deflate. Pains and spasms were continuous now, but with the courage of a maniac she said nothing to anyone, determined to have her child without the help of doctors or midwives. Then the tenth month was nearly over and still she did not give birth. Surely, surely she had calculated wrongly; but, to her husband, to her relatives who exhorted her to call someone she would reply stubbornly:

'I don't want anyone!' determined to have her child by herself.

'This is new!' cried Don Blasco, who wanted to put his nose even into his niece's womb. 'Whoever heard of a ten months' pregnancy? Why, it might go on for twelve with such a donkey.'

In fact, the eleventh month, according to the first calculation, had begun. And one night when she could bear no more, feeling at death's door, and no longer hid her own agonies, her husband lost his temper for the first time in eight years of marriage and yelled:

'If we don't get in a doctor I'm taking my hat and leaving.'

Doctor Lizio came, and shut himself in with the woman in labour, while the marchese waited anxiously in the drawing-room with relatives. Hearing the doctor opening the door and calling, he ran to ask in trepidation:

'Doctor! . . . Has she had it?'

'Had it? What d'you expect her to have?!' exclaimed Lizio. 'Your wife has a cyst in the ovary as big as a house. A bit longer, and she was done for!'

## 3

AT SAN NICOLA, after the new Italian government settled down, life went on just as under the Neapolitans; and that was one of the main arguments of the Liberal against the Bourbon group during the constant political discussions in the shade of the cloisters.

'Why, to listen to you one'd think the end of the world was due and the monastery about to be blown up, instead of which it's all going strong.'

'Going strong my foot!' boomed Don Blasco. 'You just wait and see.'

For the moment the monks went on playing ostrich. Meanwhile the little prince's character became worse and worse as he grew. From hectoring the lay-brothers he was now terrorising the men-servants, from whom he demanded the most forbidden things; curved knives to scoop out bamboo canes which he wound with wire and made into barrels for muskets and pistols; gunpowder to load these weapons which could easily have blown up in his hands and blinded him in both eyes; rockets and squibs to take gunpowder from, or sulphur, saltpetre and carbon to make it himself. He had an instinctive and dominating urge for the chase; in the garden during recreation, as he could do nothing else he would throw stones at birds, chancing cracking a companion's head, or clamber up the walls to destroy sparrows' nests, risking his own neck. And when the servants displeased him, did not get him nets, bird-lime, powder, he would curse them, denounce them to the Novice Master for faults that were completely invented, or put them to even harder trials by flinging about everything in his room after they had just tidied it.

Nor had the mania for smoking left him either. Attributing his nicotine-poisoning at the time of the revolution to the bad preparation of tobacco, he now tried real cigars and got more poisoned than before. On the master's discovering this too it was decided to give him a heavy punishment and forbid him to go out for a week; then the week was reduced to three days, thanks to the nearness of Christmas.

Every year when this came round one of the novices had to give a sermon, receiving in reward an *onza*, almost thirteen lire in the new money, together with a box of chocolates and two live cockerels. The Christmas sermon that year of 1861 fell to Consalvo Uzeda. It had been written for him by the Father Librarian, a literary man, so that instead of the few pages of other years this filled a whole exercise book. Consalvo, having an iron memory and a brazen face, awaited the ceremony with a calm and confidence unknown to his companions, who paid for their presents with fifteen days af anxiety and one of panic. On the day of the function the Chapter-house, in which the monks had already settled into their stalls, was invaded by the usual crowd of male relatives; the women, because of the enclosure, remained next door in the sacristy, the doors of which were left wide open. Everybody was exclaiming in whispers:

' What a fine lad! How frank and self-assured!'

Then the young prince, in a pleated white cotta climbed to the pulpit, gazed calmly down at the crowd of spectators and glanced at the sacristy, turning his little roll of manuscript in his hands and coughing a little before beginning. Under the Abbot's stall, standing with the prince, the Duke of Oragua and Benedetto Giulente, Don Eugenio was saying:

' What mastery! He might have been preaching for years!' But the amazement was almost boundless when the boy opened the exercise book, gave it a glance, lowered it and recited from memory:

' Reverend Fathers and beloved Brothers, it was a night of deepest winter when in a stall at Nazareth . . .' and went on to the end without even a glance at the exercise book, gesticulating, pausing for effect, changing tone like a trained orator or an old actor on the stage. When he finished and went down again,

314

he was nearly suffocated by all the embraces and kisses. The princess had tears in her eyes, even Donna Ferdinanda was moved, but although mute, the Deputy—whose throat tightened and sight dimmed at the mere thought of a crowd—was not the least admiring.

'What presence of mind! What frankness! . . .' And all the ladies drew him to them, hugged him, kissed him on the face. He let them, returning kisses on cheeks that were fresh and scented, wrinkling his nose at those that were flaccid and wrinkled. Apart from the monastery gifts he also put in his pockets the lire given him by his uncles and aunts. Most content at all was Fra' Carmelo; he felt himself to be author of that triumph, to have a right to part of the applause, the congratulations, the ladies' kisses. Had he not kept a guiding eye on that boy for the five years of novitiate? Had he not praised his intelligence, prophesied his success? The boy's masters complained at his not loving study; well, was he going to be a lawyer, doctor or theologian? He was with the Benedictines to receive an education suitable to his birth; then he would go home and be Prince of Francalanza!

That was the day Consalvo was longing for. From impatience at its not coming fast enough he let himself go more and more, so as to get himself sent away, putting not only lay-brothers and servants, but even his own master with their backs to the wall.

During the revolution and immediately afterwards the parents nicknamed 'Scabby' had taken their son Michelino from the monastery, the Cùrcuma their Gasparino and the Cugnò their Luigi; and no new novices had entered except for Camillo Giulente, as there was a rumour of the Government suppressing the monasteries. The only ones to stay were those whom their families destined for the habit, among them Giovannino Radalì, the 'madman's son'. On his father's death the duchess, from love of her eldest son, had destined her second to be a monk. Consalvo, who was not taking vows, wanted to leave as soon as possible, at once. Instead of which every time he asked his father, 'When can I come home?' the latter answered in his usual cold dry way admitting no reply, 'I must think it over!' He never did think it over.

The boy felt an aversion growing for this severe father from whom he had never heard a kind word. When he went home on holidays he would spend a moment with his mother, then go down to the courtyard and visit the horses and carriages, ask the names of all the harness in the stables. The monk's habit bothered him as it prevented his getting up on to the box and learning to drive. He would have plenty of time for fun later, Orazio, the new coachman, would say to him. (Pasqualino had gone off to Florence in his uncle Raimondo's service.) But Consalvo wanted to have fun at once, to get away from the monks' tutelage, do what he liked. And at the idea of having to return to that monastic prison, he even envied the servants, and Donna Vanna's son, Salvatore, who had entered service with the Uzeda as an ostler and now spent his whole blessed day on the box driving about town. Consalvo envied and admired him for his great and varied knowledge, for the curses he so freely used. And Fra' Carmelo, when the time came to take him back to the monastery, had to talk himself hoarse before tearing him away from stalls and stables.

'What have you been doing?' his mother and aunt would ask him.

'Nothing,' he would reply, slightly red in the face.

He had been listening to Salvatore telling him about the habits of some of the Benedictine fathers.

'At night they go out to visit their mistresses, and sometimes even they take them back with them into the monastery wrapped in cloaks. The porter pretends to take them for men! Surely Your Excellency who lives in there has seen them?'

He had never seen a thing himself, and these revelations all at one time astounded and disturbed him.

'But isn't it a sin?'

'Eee! . . .' exclaimed the retainer. 'If they'd been the first to do it! But they've always done it, the monks have! Aren't the lay-brothers nearly all sons of the old monks?'

'Fra' Carmelo too?'

'Fra' Carmelo? Fra' Carmelo is another matter . . . He's the bastard of Your Excellency's grandfather, and Don Blasco's spurious brother . . .'

'So he's my uncle?'

'And Baldassarre is also . . . the prince's bastard brother.

Yes, they have their fun, do the Uzeda. And so will Your Excellency when you've grown up.'

Oh, how he longed to grow up! With what impatience and resentment against his father did he see the days, weeks, months, years pass in that prison! In what a state of mind did he now hear severe sermons by the monks, after knowing about their lives! Often he would discuss these secret matters with Giovannino, tell him what he would do as soon as he was outside the monastery, and Giovannino listened to him in utter amazement, as if he did not understand. This boy was like that, frenzied at times as a devil, at others inert as a loony. He too wanted to leave the monastery, and would go off on some days into terrible rages; then he would persuade himself that his mother the duchess was right, that all the family money belonged to his brother Michele, that he would live like a lord among other lords at San Nicola. Then he would be silent, no longer dream of escape, no longer envy Consalvo's future liberty.

When the political agitation stopped it also lessened a great cause of quarrels in the Novitiate and among the monks; but another reason for quarrelling soon appeared. The rumours about the suppression of religious houses in the near future were confirmed from Rome; it could not be long before the usurpers' government laid hands on Church property. Don Blasco had his say against the Liberals, turncoats, enemies of God and of themselves, who refused to listen to him. Now, however, it was not a question of shouting but of making some arrangements in view of that event. At San Nicola all the monastery's income had been spent without a thought for the morrow in the certainty that their plenitude would last till the end of time, but with the world so upside-down and the danger of the Government really abolishing religious orders, would it not be wise to take some thought, to draw in on expenses, so that the unprovided should not be left high and dry?

The Abbot, as always, had first taken counsel with the Prior. Don Lodovico had been too modest to make any pronouncement. 'What can I say to Your Paternity? The future is in God's hands. Anything might happen in these wicked times. The enemies of the Church are quite capable of this and more. I wouldn't be surprised if they restarted the persecutions of that

hellish year 1789!' He was sincere in his bitterness towards the
new order of things, which at first he had supported from self-
interest to keep in with the new temporal powers. But the
suppression of the monasteries destroyed all his dreams of
revenge, of domination, of honours. What did he care now about
the San Nicola budget, when the whole of his future, fruit of
fifteen years of policy, was in danger, and he would now have to
think of some new line on which to strike out, another aim
towards which to direct his own activity? And this poor wretch
of an Abbot was insisting on having his opinion about a few
petty daily expenses!

'Tell me how I'd best act! What would you do in my position? . . .' For a moment Don Lodovico felt tempted to wash his
hands of him but, bowing his head with greater humility than
before, he replied:

'Your Paternity is too good! Economies always seem to me
praiseworthy. If the Lord does not allow his servants to be put
to the proof, we will have more for good works . . .'

So the Abbot pronounced for economies by agreement with the
Chapter. But the monks were all not of one mind. Among those
who did not think suppression possible, among others who feared
having to renounce luxuries which they had always enjoyed, the
party for economies found a good deal of opposition. Between
these two camps Don Blasco would not take either side, lashing
out sometimes against one and sometimes against the other. He
could not very well be against economies in the hope that the
government would never come to pillaging as he had been
prophesying this pillaging and throwing it in the face of Liberal
'traitors'; and anyway economies which could eventually be
divided among the monks in the case of dissolution were to his
liking, as long as he got his own share when he left the monastery. But he did not want to renounce the comfort to which he
was used; then the very fact that this party was led by the Abbot
and his nephew the Prior and those of the Chapter made him
take the opposite side and call them all 'filthy ragamuffins', and
shout, 'Let 'em go out and keep inns and shops! Let 'em start
selling oil, wine and *caciocavallo* cheese! That's the only thing
they're good for! Those are the jobs they were born for! . . .'
When on the other hand he heard the 'patriot party' lull them-

selves with the certainty that the government in any case would look after them whatever happened, he would come out with:

'The government'll kick you all out and put out its arse for you to kiss! Judas sold Christ but he did at least get thirty pieces of silver! You others will just get kicks in the backside.'

In his heart, though, at the idea of dividing the money and finally possessing something of his own, he was in favour of economies though struggling against them. Anyway the running expenses at San Nicola were huge, not so much from the value of things bought, as for the royal way of spending money and rewarding the smallest job of work, of letting almost anyone enjoy the rich goods heaped up in the monastery larders. With a little more order, by letting the cooks steal a little less and the lay-brothers in charge of the estates enrich themselves a little more slowly than usual, enough could be saved annually for quite a number of families to live in ease. But houses given to those protected by the monks must not be touched; Don Blasco was just waiting to see them try to lay hands on the Cigar-woman's shop and apartment!

Neither he nor others had any intention of renouncing their rights; with free board and lodging each choir-monk had three *rotoli* of oil a month, a *soma* of coal, a *salma* of wine, all of which they handed over to their mistresses. Saving money was all very well, of course, but each expected his share.

The Abbot, willy-nilly, had to let them be. Anyway he shut an eye now as they had to be propitiated. Camillo Giulente, now twenty, had expressed a firm wish to pronounce vows and pass into the formal novitiate. A vote was needed for this and opposition against the intruder broke out more violently than ever, with shouts and loud threats to prevent the sanctioning of this outrage. But the Abbot insisted personally with all the monks and recommended the boy, stressing all his excellent qualities, how well he had done at his studies, his sad situation as a poor orphan.

He got the Bishop to talk to the leading monks, whom he also approached through their relatives, and anyone else who could exercise any influence on them; one or two had bowed, others given vague promises and in the end, in spite of all the shouting and plotting, Giulente had been admitted, but only by very few votes. The news caused great excitement. Jumped-up nobles of recent date rejoiced as if they had had some good luck themselves, recognising the influence of the new era, the unprejudiced action of the Liberal monks. But purists were still outraged.

Once the trial year was over, before the novice could pronounce his vows, the Chapter had to renew their scrutiny. The Abbot, though sure of the result, treated the matter with great care and entrusted himself to Don Lodovico, explaining the new reasons which should induce the monks to say 'yes'. Was it possible after a first favourable vote to give a contrary one, if during all that time the young man had been a living example of respect, humility and religious zeal? Anyway if what was feared should really happen, if the government did suppress the monasteries, what bother would the new monk be to the old ones? It was a good thing, in fact, in these sad times to show persecutors of the Church that the monastic state answered a real social need, since, in spite of the dangers of enjoying no advantages from it, young men still asked to bear its yoke . . . The Abbot, assured by Don Lodovico that all would go as he wished, slept peacefully. When on the day of the voting the monks were put the question if they wanted Giulente among them, thirty in thirty-two voters replied no and only two agreed.

'For once people here are using their heads!' exclaimed Don Blasco, almost under His Paternity's nose.

The plot had been secretly prepared for some time. At the first voting half the voters had bowed to authority, knowing well that their vote was not binding and that they would have to do it all over again, but once they had to give it seriously no one had hesitated at all. Pro-Bourbons and pro-Liberals, supporters and adversaries of the Abbot, those for economy and those for spending, all agreed in opposing the admission of a grandchild of notaries like Giulente among descendants of the conquerors of the kingdom and of Viceroys. To them it did not matter whether the end of their period of plenty was near or far, nor did setting an example in the interests of religion; it was a matter above all of upholding principle, of keeping 'cattle in their places', as Don Blasco put it. If the young man was an orphan and poor he would be given a place to sleep and eat as would any one of the many parasites who lived on the monastery, but to be allowed to don the noble Benedictine habit? To be called Your Paternity? To sit in their refectory? . . .

Throughout the whole clientele of the monastery went long whispers of approval; that was what should have been done from the beginning! It was a fine lesson for the Abbot! . . . The young man, from disappointment and shame, did not show his face for a month. When he reappeared, pale and red eyed, no one knew what to do with him. If the Fathers did not want him he could not be sent back among the novices at his age, particularly after that scandal, as it drew on the poor wretch jeers and insults from the young prince and his companions. So the Abbot had to assign him an out-of-the-way cell at the end of a deserted corridor; and Giulente exchanged the habit of St Benedict for the humble cassock of a priest, and spent all day studying the books which his protector sent him from the library. In the refectory, as neither the Fathers nor the novices wanted him with them, he ate at the second table in the company of lay-brothers.

Don Lodovico expressed his own regret to the Abbot for this persecution. He had been very careful to avoid doing any of the propaganda with which His Paternity had charged him, first of all because his determined neutrality forbade him, then because he did not want Giulente in the monastery either. In spite of this he had been the only one to vote ' yes ', to show his own loyalty to his Superior, while certain meanwhile of the other monks' unanimous opposition. After the result of the scrutiny, he threw the blame on the deceitfulness of the monks who, after so many promises, had at the very last moment, from ' stupid ' prejudice, gone back on their tracks.

So things went on, with the usual bickering between parties, the usual more or less stormy discussions, when one fine day the whole community was abuzz with the rumour of an event as extraordinary as any during the revolution.

Garibaldi was already in Sicily recruiting, why no one knew, or rather all knew well; to march against the Pope. As he advanced, an ill-repressed quiver went up all round, in town and country, while authorities wavered about what on earth to do, at one moment pretending to oppose him, then letting him through.

When he appeared before Catania the garrison which was supposed to stop him had evacuated the town, and the Prefect went down to the port to board a man-of-war. And the General marched in with his volunteers between two rows of applauding and frantically shouting population, amid a delirium of enthusiasm compared to which even demonstrations of 1860 seemed lukewarm and dim. From a balcony of the Workers' Club, dominating the main street swollen as a torrent with people, he explained the aim of his new enterprise, and in his gentle voice gave out the call for the new war, ' Rome or death! . . .' And where should he go and set up his own headquarters then but at San Nicola!

The shouting and confusion among the monks there also left the demonstrations of '48 and '60 far behind. Don Blasco became a fanatic. The things he said about the ' Piedmontese ' for not shooting Garibaldi, and about Garibaldi for not sweeping away the ' Piedmontese ', would have made an infidel's ears burn. This was his main hope, his sustaining faith; that the two parties would exterminate each other, the brigands from Basilicata give the last tip of the whole affair, and then come a cataclysm, a universal deluge no longer of water but of fire and iron so that the world would rise purified from its own ashes. Those fools of Liberal monks, ' those milk-sops ', were still daring to clap hands while the revolution was threatening final ruin to the last most august, most sacred representative of legitimacy; the Holy Father! They were clapping hands with the agitators, the down-and-outs in search of a hand-out, the escaped galley slaves who made up the new bands! They were waggling hips fattened at the expense of San Nicola, rubbing hands which that idle life of theirs still let them keep white and smooth as women's!

' You bunch of cadgers, d'you think you've won a lottery? Don't you understand that the sooner heresy triumphs, the sooner they'll have you flung out in the street? What have you to be so gay about, who are worse traitors than Judas! Don't you realise you've everything to lose and nothing to gain?'

' Well?'

' What d'you mean—well?'

' Well, we'll get some liberty too . . .' When the monk was given this reply he went pale, then all the blood mounted to his head and his eyes seemed about to start from their sockets.

' Oh so that's what you lack, is it?' he hissed. ' It's liberty you lack, is it? . . . So you're locked into a prison, you poor wretches, are you? . . . What's the liberty you lack then, to booze like wineskins? To guzzle yourselves to death? To keep your sluts? Why, don't you know what people call you . . .?' And he spat out in their faces the nickname by which they were known all over the town, ' Hogs of Christ!'

Amid this flurry of discussions threatening to end in blows the poor Abbot was like a chick lost in stubble, not knowing what to do, not wanting to lend a hand or in any way to speed the collapse of good principles, but unable to oppose the Garibaldini's coming. Nevertheless he clung to the Prior, put himself in his hands, never left him for a second. Don Lodovico, complaining of the sad times, imploring the Lord to ease those hard trials, took over control of the monastery and prepared for Garibaldi's reception. He ordered the royal apartments to be aired, straw and forage to be got in, cellars and larders emptied. When the General arrived, he went to meet him at the very bottom of the stairs, accompanied his staff to their rooms, and presided over the Redshirts' dinner, apologising for the absence of the Abbot kept to his bed by a slight indisposition.

Don Blasco, yellow as a lemon, no longer able to shout at the Garibaldini's coming, had shut himself into the Novitiate again. Almost all the boys had gone, taken away by their respective families getting to safety for fear of disturbances. Only the young prince, Giovannino Radalì and two or three others remained, while the Uzeda had all escaped to the Belvedere, except for Ferdinando, shut up as always at Pietra dell'Ovo, and Lucrezia with Benedetto, who during those agitated days took his place among the few authorities and rare notabilities that remained. He would have volunteered to go through the new campaign with old comrades-in-arms had he not felt it his duty to remain with his wife. The day after Garibaldi's arrival he went to the monastery to pay his respects to the General, who recognised him at once, shook hands and talked to him for a time in spite of the coming and going of deputations, representatives of all kinds hurrying to greet the former Dictator. Uncertainty and disquiet, hopes and fears about what would happen next were universal. What plans had Garibaldi? What were the orders of representatives of authority? Would the struggle, if there was to be one, break out in Catania? What would the National Guard do? . . .

No one knew a thing. Some said that the Government was secretly in league with Garibaldi and only pretending to obstruct him so as to throw dust in the eyes of the great powers. Benedetto, who had begun republishing his newspaper *Italia risorta*, upheld this view, and the silence of the Duke of Oragua, to whom he had written letter after letter begging him to return to Sicily, as his presence might become necessary, tended to confirm it. However, he assured the Dictator of the unanimous support of the entire town. After taking leave he was just about to go out into the town again when he heard his name called.

' Excellency! Excellency . . .'

It was Fra' Carmelo behind him, who when he got up to him whispered in his ear with an air of mystery, ' Your Uncle Don Blasco wants to talk to you.'

Skulking in the farthest room of the farthest corridors in the Novitiate, Don Blasco insisted on hearing his nephew's voice twice before opening. Then he locked the door in the lay-brother's face.

' Now have you gone off your head too, you swine?' said he to Benedetto.

The latter had scarcely muttered a timid submissive ' why? ' when the monk started again with renewed violence.

' How d'you mean, " why "? You have the face to ask that? With civil war about to break out? The town shelled? The streets running with blood? Decent folk persecuted . . . And you ask me " why " . . . ?'

' It's not any fault of . . .'

' It's not any fault of yours? Whose then? Mine? Oh, of course! I was the one to start things off, wasn't I? I know that game! Put the blame on decent people who're guilty of sticking to their principles. I'm surprised they haven't come to arrest

324

me! Let 'em, let 'em! . . .' And his eyes glittered like a lion's.

'Calm yourself, Your Excellency . . .' stuttered Giulente.

'So I must calm myself too, must I? While my country is threatened with final ruin? When I see a creature like you clapping hands with the others, instead of working to avoid this inferno . . .'

'In what way though?'

'In what way though? By making 'em leave! Let 'em cut each other's throats, in the country, out at sea, wherever they like and not inside a city like ours, where the damage could be incalculable, involving women, old people, children, decent . . . They can go and do it where they like; the world's a big place! . . . That's the way! . . .'

Giulente stood perplexed, not daring to contradict his uncle, but not wanting either to contradict himself within half an hour.

'But what can be done? The whole town's for the General.'

'The whole town? First of all you're a fool! Who in the town? Madmen like you? And all the more reason! If the town is for him, if he's entered it to triumph, what's to be done about it? If it was a strong-point I'd understand; but a city open to the four winds? If he must start a battle, let him do it elsewhere! Let him take with him whoever and whatever he likes and good journey to him!'

The monk was gradually becoming calmer and said the last words almost in the tone of any other human being. But as soon as Benedetto observed:

'And who's to persuade him of that?'

'Oh, by the blood of Mahomet!' shouted the monk as loudly as before, with a gesture of fury. 'Am I talking to an animal or a reasonable being? Who's to persuade him? You people around him! Isn't there a National Guard? Isn't there any kind of authority? You, what the devil are you? A captain, a good citizen, and all that, aren't you? It's up to people like you to speak up frankly and clearly, after those Piedmontese rabbits of yours have beaten a retreat, leaving us in the soup! Or d'you think maybe I ought to get involved with those assassins, brigands, galley slaves, pimps . . .'

But at the sound of a step in the corridor, Don Blasco went silent as if by magic. He gulped as if his throat was itching, took a step or two through the room, paused a moment to listen; and then when the noise stopped he declared:

'If you can get that in your head, all the better; if not get this, that as far as I'm concerned I don't care a fig for you or Garibaldi or Victor Emmanuel or any of you.'

Giulente went home thoughtful and worried. As soon as he entered his wife's room he saw Lucrezia sitting in a corner, staring at the floor with red eyes.

'What's wrong with you? . . . What's happened? . . .'

'Nothing. Nothing's wrong with me.'

'But you've been crying, Lucrezia! Tell me, now! Tell me what's wrong?'

She denied it, without looking him in the face, her mouth obstinately shut, and had Vanna not come in Benedetto would have been unable to know anything.

'The mistress doesn't want to stay in town,' declared the maid. 'All her relations have gone, even the poor are getting to safety, why should she be the only one to remain in danger?'

'What danger? Lucrezia, is that what's bothering you? But there's no danger at all! What are you afraid of? Am I not here? They won't do anything to me, in any case! If there was even the remotest danger, would I keep you here? We'll leave if things look bad; do I have to promise you that?'

After he had gone on talking for a quarter of an hour she muttered:

'I want to go away to my relations.'

'But Holy God, why? You were so calm this morning! What on earth can have happened?'

This is what had happened; the wife of Orazio, the prince's coachman, had visited her former young mistress and announced, panting through her teeth, that she too was escaping to the Belvedere.

'One can't stay here, Excellency. Don't you know what happened today? The Piedmontese soldiers still in hospital marched off to join the other troops in the fort, the Garibaldini tried to make them prisoners. And then, oh Jesus and Mary, the lieutenant ordered bayonets to be fixed! I was just passing with my babies . . . I'm still atremble with the terror of it! I've made a bundle of some clothes, and tonight I'm off . . .'

If the coachman's wife was going away, was she, the prince's sister, less than the coachman's wife? This idea had not come into her head suddenly. When struggling to marry Giulente, she had sworn she would never have anything more to do with the Uzeda; all the reasons given by them for denigrating Benedetto and his family had only confirmed her more in her determination. But once she had triumphed over opposition and began to think over, in the long hours of idleness and inertia, those arguments used by her Aunt Ferdinanda, by Giacomo, by the confessor, a conviction that she had come down in the world by marrying Benedetto struggled for a little with her former obstinacy. Having quarrelled with her brother, the torture of being unable to enter the house of the Viceroys any more, of feeling herself almost exiled by her relations, had gradually begun to preoccupy her while she still went on inveighing against them. At the beginning of the public disturbances the general flight of nobles and rich had filled her cup of misery to the brim, and now she had even forgotten what she had said against Giacomo, the coldness that had grown up between them, her firmness and determination not to give way; she wanted to go off to the Belvedere if even the coachman's wife had gone . . .

Giulente was still trying to persuade her when the post arrived. Among the newspapers there was a letter from the duke at last. The duke said that he had received no more letters which, particularly in these moments of agitation, he was awaiting with impatience. The news from Sicily had made him quite feverish and he felt like packing his bags at once, but unfortunately he was prevented by many and serious matters ' all of interest to the constituency and to Sicily '. He particularly wanted to be among his fellow-citizens so as to warn them not to let themselves be drawn along by Garibaldi. ' So I tell this to you who can get the hotheads to understand; the more insistence there is on utopian principles the surer becomes a shipwreck. Anyway the Government is firmly decided to oppose such aberrations in every way. And I think they're quite right; in fact they've been losing time about it. Garibaldi should be stopped by force; one cannot allow a nation of twenty-seven million to be put in turmoil by a man who has distinct merits of course but seems sworn to get them forgotten by conduct

which . . .' And here came two whole pages against Garibaldi.
'And anyway, let's face it, even the Government isn't free and
we must not count too much on non-intervention; there's France
making a fuss, and Napoleon now says . . . Austria is just waiting for an excuse . . . all Europe watches . . .' Here came another
page of grave considerations on the international situation. 'And
so I do ask you to make these truths plain to our friends, and
even plainer to our opponents. A serious disaster to our country
must be avoided and all must be persuaded of the dangers in
the situation. I beg of you to talk and if need be write on these
lines; in fact I am certain that you in your quick-witted way
have already been doing this . . .'

Thus for the third time in three hours one of his relations was
urging him along a road that he found repugnant. The duke
was writing, language apart, just as Don Blasco was talking; the
pro-Bourbon monk was at heart in agreement with the Liberal
deputy; and his wife was shut in her room sulking and plotting
with her maid to induce him to desert his post.

That evening, at a tempestuous meeting of the National Club,
when the Garibaldino and Government parties had almost come
to blows, he got up to speak. In the embarrassment overwhelming him, the most opportune arguments seemed those suggested
by Don Blasco. Nobody could doubt, he said, his devotion to the
General, nor did his conscience allow him to agree with those
who wanted to take sides against the Liberator of Sicily, but he
should be told, with due respect, of the danger to which the
town was exposed. There were two possibilities only; either he
was acting by agreement with the Government, in which case
there was no reason for him to remain in Catania; or the
Government was opposed to him, in which case he should search
his own heart lest he inflict the horrors of civil war on a
populous and flourishing city. And such actually was the case,
for the Government had decided to oppose him . . .

This speech shocked his old friends, but, taking them on one
side one after the other when the meeting was adjourned without decision, he exhorted them to bow to crude naked truth, to
the news given him by the duke. 'Why doesn't he come himself
then?' he was asked. 'What's he staying in Turin for, when
there's a crisis here?' And Giulente justified the duke's conduct,

and announced that he would be starting his journey south as soon as possible, but meanwhile a deputation must be sent to the General asking him to evacuate the area ...

This propaganda achieved the desired effect. Till now suspicions had been mounting about the party hostile to Garibaldi, since pro-Bourbons and frightened people with no faith were with it, but now that a proved Liberal was advising not resistance, but respectful explanation of their danger, this point of view made headway. Even so, Benedetto had not quite the courage to go to the General personally to explain his new opinion; he let others go. Forced to take his wife up to the Belvedere, he returned to town alone, awaiting events and writing and telegraphing to the duke to come.

A few days passed without any change in the situation. From the top of the dome of San Nicola Garibaldi often scrutinised the horizon with a telescope, or studied his plans, bent over maps, or received the people and deputations that came to visit him. Finally he embarked with all his volunteers, for an unknown destination, maybe Greece, maybe Albania. But after his departure, a residue of discontent was left in the city, a subdued unrest which people of influence and even the National Guard could not succeed in placating. Now the movement was turning against the gentry, against the rich. Giulente harangued rioters but no one listened to him any more; and once again the duke wrote that he could not come, that he was unwell, that the heat had affected his digestion ...

One afternoon Don Blasco was risking a visit to the Cigar-woman, where he was talking away fanatically again about how he hoped Garibaldini and Piedmontese would exterminate each other, when Garino arrived, yellow as a corpse.

' The revolution! . . . the revolution! . . . They're burning the Nobles' Club! . . .'

In fact demonstration had turned to riot, and flames were licking round the club of the aristocracy. The monk, it goes without saying, went and locked himself up in the monastery again and did not leave it until the town was reoccupied by regular troops. But the excitement produced by the incident of Aspromonte, the terrors, the dangers, did not seem to have stopped. The prince did not move from the Belvedere and Giulente once again began begging the duke to show himself, to bring peace to the town. The duke did not come. Again he replied that his doctors had forbidden him to return to Sicily. 'I am in despair at not being among you as I should and would be, not only because of all that you tell me about Catania, but also of what is happening in Florence.'

Benedetto did not know what he was alluding to; at that moment it did not occur to him that Raimondo was in Tuscany. A few days later he realised what this meant, when the count and Donna Isabella Fersa arrived together and put up at the hotel, still together as if they were husband and wife.

4

T H I S event made such an impression that suddenly Garibaldi and Rattazzi, Rome and Aspromonte, all passed into second place. Count Uzeda with Donna Isabella! At the hotel together, like two lovers who had eloped to force their families' hands! What about the countess? And the baron? How ever had they all got into such a tangle? How would it all end?

Pasqualino Riso, back from Florence with his master, was besieged with questions. He looked just like a gentleman himself, did Pasqualino; a suit of latest cut, fine linen, rings on his fingers, polished shoes, and had it not been for his clean-shaven face, anyone might have called him 'Cavaliere'. In porters' lodges, stables, coachmen's cafés, in the antechambers of his master's relations, he gave all explanations asked. That the young count couldn't last long with his wife he'd foreseen for some time, as anyone could have the year before, when Signor Don Raimondo had run away from the woman who was embittering his life.

Everyone knew he loved Donna Isabella; what should the countess have done had she been anyone else? Been prudent for her children's sake! Instead of which, no sir; sobs, screams, accusations, threats, her father always on the spot; only a stucco statue could have put up with it!

But although the poor young count had lost patience once, yet he had given way—that proved he wasn't in the wrong!— forgotten the past, and resigned himself to going back to her, because of the children of course. Men can't always stay sewn to women's skirts, and the young count had done no more than all husbands. Wise women, those with the tiniest bit of brain, understand these things, shut an eye and do God's will. Instead of which that poor holy little countess, after promising to be reasonable, had began all over again. Why, worse even than before! Her husband couldn't go for a breath of air without her making a scene; whenever he went to the *Glubbo* to meet friends, or out for a drive, there were suspicions, sobs and reproofs at once. And the scenes about his drives in the *Cassine* Gardens!

The young count, on horseback, used to meet Donna Isabella in her carriage and of course stop to greet her; at that very moment clip, clop, and what should appear but the mistress's carriage! . . . Poor woman, if she was so put out, why not go to the *Popoli* Gardens which were just as pretty! . . . And why with her children? That eldest girl understood as much about lots of things as a grown-up woman. The children should have been left with the English *Missa* whom the young count had taken on for that very purpose! . . .

Then in the evening, at home, it was hell! With the young count always patient, so help me! . . . When the mistress wasn't following him around, she'd try other tactics; shut herself up in her room for a fortnight together, never put her nose outside or listen to reason or requests, never consider the youngest child, who needed air and refused to go out if her mother stayed indoors! And the count, all holy patience he'd been! . . . As it was his own wife that was putting him in this predicament, the master never said a word.

But one day what did the countess do but call her father, settle him in the house and encourage open war between father-in-law and son-in-law! She must have gone mad! She could interfere in the young count's affairs up to a point, but not her father! Who was her father anyway? An outsider, a dressed-up rustic and a busybody to boot! Things should be said frankly: first of all he'd no manners; think of it, he'd taught his daughters to call him *tu*! Then urged on by the countess, he'd become an absolute animal in spite of holy baptism, and the count had to put up with the man's impertinence in his own home! One day, just because the count said that he'd be prevented from accompanying his wife to the theatre, the rustic baron even dared threaten him with his stick! Holy God of

love, that was really too much! The young count had only said
one single word: 'Carter!' . . . just what was needed! Then
he took up his hat and went off, for ever, this time. Could
anyone honestly advise him to go back and forgive? His
daughters would have to go off to college, or if the mistress
wanted to keep them with her, the master would let her. Even
so . . . even so . . . For the oddest thing, sirs, was this; that
while the countess was playing the jealous wife she was also
amusing herself out in society! Not that anything happened. No,
in conscience that couldn't be said, nor would the master have
kept his hands in his belt if it had, but she had a mania for
going to balls and the theatre, and the grand clothes she wore
when she had a party, for men mainly, bachelors, among others
a certain Count Rossi, their landlord . . .

Pasqualino's story went round from mouth to mouth, was
repeated by coachmen to their families, by scullions to cooks,
by porters to landladies, each of whom embroidered something
of their own on it, until by the time it reached the general
public, opinion was prepared and sympathy gained for the
count's cause.

Many however shook their heads and did not let themselves
be carried away; and gradually, without anyone knowing its
origin, on information from Florence and Milazzo, from some
words let out by Pasqualino himself when alone with intimates
after a drink or two, the truth began coming to the surface.

Raimondo had sworn to break off relations with his wife at
the very moment when his uncle the duke forced him to take
them up again. As happened every time that people tried to dissuade him from some course of action, he became more stubborn
than ever. Away from both Matilde and Donna Isabella he
enjoyed an illusion of that liberty which meant more to him
than anything else; forced to renounce it, he promised himself
to regain it at all costs, and his easy submission to the duke's
advice was aimed entirely at putting his wife in the wrong by
his own concessions, the only point on which Pasqualino's
version was not entirely false. His master's ideal was to free
himself from wife and mistress at the same time, but he had not
taken sufficient account of one party concerned, Donna Isabella.

Since the very beginning of her relations with Raimondo,

333

since resisting the young man's courtship in her husband's house and showing she was attracted but prevented by duty to her state, she had often repeated to him with a bitterness which should have shown him her feelings, 'If only we'd met before when we were both free! How happy we could have been . . .' Those words which he did not believe had chilled him to the bone, or rather would have had he thought them at all sincere. Just as his wife's great mistake was loving him so much, wanting to have him all to herself and unite with him, so any such aspiration on his mistress's part would have been a mistake equally serious. Yet, determined to overcome her resistance, he too had repeated, 'How happy we could have been!' and sworn that his one dream was to live with her, for her. Afterwards he tried to draw back. But Donna Isabella, who for him had lost all family and protection, had no intention of letting him escape. To draw on this tepid lover, whose character she was beginning to realise to her own cost, all she had to do was blame his coldness on his relatives' opposition and his wife's wishes. Each of these allusions was like a spur plunged in the young man's side; in his determination to show her that he was free to do what he wanted, he did what he did not want . . .

And so the Countess Matilde's agony began all over again, more atrocious than before, increased by this new deceit and by being unable now to have recourse to her father, not from any belief in this threat of abandoning her but from a vow with herself not to confess her mistake and from her old fear of a clash between those two violent natures . . .

When she felt herself most alone and lost, her father came to join her. His blind love for his daughter and no less blind hatred for his son-in-law made all his avowals of indifference vain. He followed developments, step by step, from a distance, waiting to intervene and when things were boiling over he appeared. Pasqualino himself had heard the interview between father-in-law and son-in-law, after a few days of apparent calm. The final scene took place in the stables of Palazzo Rossi, to prevent Matilde and the children from hearing. To the baron's blunt and threatening questions:

'Don't you want to put an end to it? Don't you want to?' Raimondo had replied in his usual tone of contemptuous superiority, 'What are you talking about? Mind your own business! . . .' Yes, replied the baron, it was his own business, his daughter's peace which he cared about more than all else, which he wanted assured at any cost, even at the cost of taking her away and breaking her heart for ever . . . 'Well, what's keeping you? Go away then!' Pasqualino was crouching in a stall near by and could hear but not see his master; but that reply of the count's and the short silence which followed it, sent a chill through his bones. 'All right, we'll go . . . But before we do . . .' Then Pasqualino realised what was happening. With bloodshot eyes and raised fist, the baron had already seized hold of his son-in-law; but, even if the coachman had not flung himself between them, one word of Raimondo's, 'Carter!', would have been enough for his father-in-law to start back.

Of course the count had said that word, Pasqualino was not just imagining it; and the effect on the baron had to be seen to be believed! That great hulk of a man who could have flung his slim jaded son-in-law to the ground with a wave, broken him in his big hairy hands like a cane, seemed a boy facing his master. Young Uzeda, elegant and soft, descendant of Viceroys, had struck the peasant baron like a thunderbolt by that word, by that insult which showed the distance separating a vicious but well-bred noble from a jumped-up brutal peasant.

Yes, a carter, approved Pasqualino; among people of birth quarrels are not settled by blows. And by that word the count reminded his father-in-law of the honour done him by marrying his daughter; if the baron stood there motionless as a statue it was because he at once realised he was in the wrong. Had his connection with the Uzeda not seemed wonderful to him? Had pride at entering the Viceroys' family not blinded him for years to his daughter's sacrifice? Had a confused and almost instinctive sense of his own inferiority to his son-in-law not hampered him every time that, once his eyes were opened, he decided to reproach him with his conduct, his vices, his hardness, the blood of an innocent child? A carter, yes; the man deserved the insult for letting himself be carried away by anger and trying to settle the quarrel as if it were between coachmen. And he had openly acknowledged this out loud, in front of his son-in-law, before turning his back. For in fact the scene had not finished just then; it had had a little sequel which Pasqualino only related in strict privacy.

'I may be a carter . . . yes . . .' had stuttered the baron, 'but you're a . . .' And suddenly he spat in the other's face a word which the coachman whispered, very faintly, in one or two people's ears. Raimondo left his home straight away, rushed to his mistress, made her pack her bags, and took her off with him to Sicily.

She had needed some persuading, for in point of fact Donna Isabella was not at all sure such a journey was opportune. She saw that Raimondo wanted to take her with him to his home town so as to make an open, definite break with the Palmi family; but she also realised that it was only a reaction to insults and an impulse of hatred aroused by that stormy interview which had brought her lover to this decision, and not devotion to her. And she also felt that making a public show of their relationship down there in a provincial town would do them both harm and scandalise the more-or-less strict local morality. But as it was already too late for any comments from her to have any effect but excite Raimondo the more, and having no choice but, if she wanted to win him, to entrust herself to this very excitement, she came. The Uzeda, at any rate, would be on her side.

In fact as soon as she arrived Donna Ferdinanda, who in spite of the scarce-stilled public unrest was in town for a law-case against some debtors in arrears, came to visit them at the hotel, asked what had happened, approved of Raimondo's decision with a single but very expressive word: 'Finally . . .'

In town too were Benedetto and Lucrezia, who had at last gathered up courage to return. Raimondo paid them a visit the day after his arrival. Lucrezia repaid his visit the same evening, in spite of her husband's opposition. The latter judged his brother-in-law's conduct very severely and had he dared would have prevented his wife from making that visit; but Lucrezia declared that she could see nothing wrong in going to see her own brother; did she have to know that he was 'accompanied' by a lady?

At the hotel Raimondo received them alone. After some chatter about the journey and the weather he went and knocked at the door of the next room, and in came Donna Isabella, who shook Giulente's hand and kissed Lucrezia. No introductions, or explanations, nothing. At first Benedetto was most embarrassed, not knowing how to treat or what to call Donna Isabella. She herself gave the conversation its tone, and talked very much at her ease, as with three old friends, in fact three real relations. For the moment they were at a hotel, but of course they could not stay there long. Raimondo intended to take an apartment in the town, though Donna Isabella would have preferred a villa, thinking also of how to avoid gossip.

Giulente was about to say this was a good idea when Lucrezia exclaimed:

' What does gossip matter? If you hide they'll only say you're afraid! Let's be frank; lots of people will play the prude!' Donna Isabella lowered her eyes. ' If you yourselves begin showing they're right then that's the end of it!'

Raimondo said nothing, as he was waiting to see Giacomo, who was at the Belvedere, and he had that morning sent Pasqualino to warn of his arrival. But the coachman returned looking confused and could not get a word out.

' So he's come, has he?' the prince had said. ' And what does he want . . .?' as if someone had appeared asking for money.

' Nothing, Excellency . . . he sends to ask Your Excellency . . . he wonders when Your Excellency will be back in town . . .' The prince replied in the same tone of voice:

' I've only just come to the country, I'll be back in November . .' and he had turned away. When the scene was narrated to Raimondo he chewed his lips. Donna Isabella exclaimed:

' See what we've done! . . . Your brother disapproves of us!' And blaming only herself, she went on, ' I've put you on bad terms with your family . . .'

' We'll see,' replied Raimondo briefly.

Her forebodings were justified. Most people, without accepting or rejecting the excuses and accusations about Raimondo's second and decisive abandonment of his family, blamed him for coming with his mistress, staying at a hotel, and making such open show of their relationship, as if challenging public opinion. He might be right or wrong in his complaints about his wife; his passion for Donna Isabella could be excused; but moralists, fathers of families, ladies of varying degrees of respectability, wanted appearances saved; and although there were few people in town, public opinion was nevertheless shown by cold greetings to Raimondo, by ambiguous talk among servants.

In the country, in villas where news of the scandal reached, all discussed how to behave towards the couple on return to town. Many declared they would refuse to see them at all; others, on more intimate terms and so more embarrassed, made their own decision depend on how the family behaved.

Now the prince's unexpected severity to Pasqualino clearly showed that he was suddenly withdrawing his support. Faced with this obstacle Raimondo grew obstinate, set his teeth to win through; but when Donna Ferdinanda suggested that he should visit Giacomo, he became very agitated. He was ready to do everything except apply to that knave, who after giving him a free hand was now siding against him for some end of his own. He would not humiliate himself to a brother who he felt had hated him for years while their mother was alive. Then the thought of hostile demonstrations being prepared for himself and his mistress made him fly into a passion, making the blood rush to his head once again. And one day he took a carriage and drove up to the Belvedere. On seeing him arrive, Giacomo said, not in colloquial terms but formally, ' Good day, how are you?' without holding out his hand.

' Well, and you?' replied Raimondo.

' Very well.' And the prince stroked his whiskers.

The princess, who was busy embroidering with little Teresa beside her, replied to her brother-in-law's questions in monosyllables, feeling her husband's eye heavy upon her.

' Are you staying up here long?' asked Raimondo, red as a poppy.

' Yes, till November. I sent to tell you so, I think.'

And he let the conversation drop again. The child turned and looked at this uncle of hers whose appearance she could not remember well, who did not caress her, whom her father was treating as a stranger.

' I wanted to ask you something,' went on Raimondo hesitatingly, almost timidly, and getting angrier with himself the more his embarrassment grew. 'I wanted to ask you if there's some villa I might take . . . a little place would do . . . it doesn't matter its being small as long as it's clean . . .'

The prince seemed to search his memory.

'No,' he replied. 'Everything's taken since Garibaldi came.'

Raimondo, nervously twiddling his moustaches, went on:

'Anyway, I'll look round.'

Then his brother, in a cold voice without looking at him, said, 'Do if you want to. It's quite useless, you won't find anything.'

Raimondo went off silent, pale and trembling. He had humiliated himself for nothing! The other had declared war! He did not want him nearby!

The prince in fact had let all his relations and acquaintances know that he could find no words to disapprove enough of Raimondo's conduct. 'It's an unheard-of scandal! And he isn't even ashamed of himself! To have the effrontery to come back to his own town? When one wants to do something crazy like that one hides as far away as possible, where one's not known and can let people think what they like!'

And to his aunt Donna Ferdinanda, who drove up to the Belvedere one day on purpose to intervene and induce the prince to do the same as her, he replied, 'We're in different situations. Your Excellency is free to think whatever you like, to do whatever you like. You can even take them into your house, as you've no one to render account to. I have a wife and daughter and cannot put a scandal like this under their very eyes.'

He said these things in front of the princess and the child, showing steadfast indignation in spite of the spinster's insistence. Chiara also disapproved of her brother's action, as Federico considered it immoral; not to mention Cousin Graziella, who acted as spokesman for the prince. All the latter's remarks reached Raimondo's ears through the discomfited spinster, or resentful hangers-on, or gossiping servants. He fumed in silent rage; then Donna Isabella said with a sad smile:

'You can't see it through! The best thing is to leave me! I don't want to break up your family peace!'

And he, who felt the consequences of his false step growing, who in his heart was cursing the hour and place he had set eyes on this woman of whom he was already tired, for whose sake he had even bowed before his brother, drew closer to her still from pride, handed himself over bound hand and foot. So they wouldn't receive her? He promised her that she should see them all at her feet. They were talking against her, were they? He assured her that she would be his wife.

To get other relations on his side he searched out his uncle Eugenio. The poor cavaliere was in very low water. His dealing in old potsherds no longer brought anything in; and could Victor Emmanuel give a university chair to Ferdinand II's Gentleman of the Bedchamber? So he had left the little apartment where he had lived so long and moved to two smaller rooms in a remote district. Always in search of money, he had now founded the *Academy of the Four Poets*, of which he was president, secretary, treasurer and all, and was nominating to right and left founder members, promoting members, patrons, effective members, corresponding and honorary members. Each of these received a diploma, a bronze medal, a copy of the statutes, and a bill of twenty lire for expenses; but too often the post returned not a money order but a rejected packet. His relatives kept him somewhat at a distance, fearing requests for money; but on finding Raimondo actually seeking him out, he suddenly sniffed a fair wind. He went at once to pay a visit to Donna Isabella, declared himself on her side against the prince, and invited himself to lunch and dinner every day. His clothes looked as if they were weeping off him and his shoes, on the contrary, laughing on his feet. A few days later he put on a brand-new skin. In gleaming suit, freshly ironed shirt, and gloves, he accompanied Donna Isabella every time she went out, acted as her *Cavaliere servente*, and upheld her cause in public and in private, calling her his ' niece '.

Lucrezia, too, in spite of her husband, appeared in the streets with her and took her side, and launched violent diatribes against her eldest brother, putting his opposition down to a very simple motive.

' From morality, d'you think? To get his support paid for! Shall we make a bet on it? Didn't I have to pay for his consent to my marriage?'

' Lucrezia . . .' warned Benedetto.

' Well? Isn't it true? Didn't I have to accept that forced

transaction so as to marry you? Everyone knows that! Now you're getting it!' She turned to Raimondo. 'You see if I'm mistaken! Your uncle Don Blasco was right when he said . . . Oh, by the by, why not go and pay him a visit? And Lodovico? The more you have on your side the less will Giacomo's scruples count for. Come along, let's go together!'

And Raimondo drove up the mountainside once again, with his sister and brother-in-law this time, to Nicolosi where the Benedictines were having their country stay, in order to beg for his brother's and his uncle's support. Don Blasco knew the whole story and had almost forgotten Garibaldi; he was so busy shouting around as if possessed, against Raimondo for getting himself into this last and biggest mess, then against Giacomo, who was just as much to blame as his brother, with whom he was now playing the puritan after encouraging him. Why? To squeeze him dry! . . .

When his niece and nephew arrived it was after refectory and he was sleeping like a log. Fra' Carmelo woke him.

'What is it?' he called. 'What are you making all this row for?'

'Your Paternity must excuse me, but Your Paternity's relatives are here.'

Out he came, and as soon as he saw Raimondo opened wide eyes, still dazed with sleep. Raimondo kissed his hand, as did Lucrezia and Benedetto. He did not stop him, stuttering:

'Well, what's up? At this hour? In this sun?'

'We've come to pay Your Excellency a visit,' explained Lucrezia for both of them.

'It isn't so warm. Is Your Excellency well? I've not been here for two years. And how is Lodovico?'

Fra' Carmelo, flustered, came to say that His Paternity the Prior was conferring with the Abbot and could not come down for the moment. Raimondo went pale; now this other one was declaring war on him too. They were all ranging up against him! For this reason, when Lucrezia, by agreement with this uncle, suggested taking a turn in the garden, he said shortly:

'No, I'm in a hurry to get back. Let's go.'

At the hotel next morning, he was not yet up when the servant came to announce:

'Your Excellency's uncle is here.'

And Don Blasco appeared. For the first time in his life Raimondo saw his uncle actually move towards him, heard him ask in a tone that was almost polite:

'How are you?' The monk could scarcely believe his luck at hearing of a new quarrel in the family and having a chance once more to get his nose into others' business. Now was his chance to urge one brother against the other, to help undo another of the dead princess's works, Raimondo's marriage. He felt positively invited to play this game.

Donna Isabella appeared in a dressing-gown, kissed his hand, called him 'Excellency', as if he were already her uncle; and they all began talking about what to do next. Hearing her repeat that she wanted to hide herself away in the country, the monk broke out:

'In the country? Why in the country? Well till November at most. But you must get a place ready in town! Are you afraid of people? Then why did you come? That's logic it seems to me!'

His advice was to make Giacomo produce the accounts at once, withdraw his power-of-attorney and begin dividing the property; at such a threat the prince would soon get milder. But the very day after the monk's visit Signor Marco came down from the Belvedere to tell the count that the prince wanted to hand back the power-of-attorney and give him the accounts, once he returned home. Raimondo sent off the administrator with a violent 'I understand . . . all right . . .' and in a furious temper he refused to open his mouth all day. Donna Isabella, in consternation, kept on repeating, 'D'you see? I bring you bad luck! Let me go! God will look after me! . . .' Then he answered, 'No, I must win through!'

Just then Lucrezia, now very close with her sister-in-law (on the wrong side of the blanket), had an idea.

'As you can't stay in the hotel indefinitely, and now is the time for the country, why not go to the Pietra dell'Ovo, to Ferdinando's? He has lots of space; he can give you a couple of rooms. You'll be with a relation and that'll have a good effect.'

All approved of this suggestion. Raimondo had not gone to visit that brother, nor did Ferdinando even know Raimondo was back. By indifference, upbringing, taste, manner of life, they had become such strangers that each ignored the other's existence. Lucrezia, charged with the negotiations, went to Pietra dell'Ovo. Not having seen the Booby for some months, she was astounded at the change in him. He was gaunt as if he had been through a long illness, his eyes were sunken, his beard unkempt, his voice feeble and his gloom even deeper than usual.

'Of course . . . let him come . . . He can treat it as his home,' he replied to his sister, without expressing any surprise at Raimondo's return or at the request for hospitality.

'But there's something I must tell you . . .' added Lucrezia. 'He's not alone.'

'Is he with his wife?'

'With his wife, yes . . . in a manner of speaking.'

And she explained to him that Raimondo had left Matilde and was now living with Donna Isabella. Ferdinando stood listening to her, looking to right and left as if he had lost something, then repeated:

'All right, all right; tell him to come when he wants.'

When Raimondo and Donna Isabella arrived, they asked to visit the house, garden, and estate, and were full of praise for the excellent cultivation of the vineyards and the superb aspect of the orchards, approved changes in cultivation, admired all. But praise no longer had the same effect on the poor Booby as it once had. A transformation had taken place in his spirit; what had pleased him before now left him indifferent and a Robinson Crusoe's life had lost all attraction or he would never have agreed to let others into his house. The real master of the estate was now the bailiff, who did what he liked, cultivated things in his own way, pocketed the profits, and gave his master nothing but scraps. If, taken by a scruple, he sometimes asked Ferdinando for an order, the latter would reply:

'Let me be! Don't mention such things! . . . I'm finished . . . At most I may have six months to live. You can begin getting my coffin ready.'

This is what had happened. The bookseller from whom he had bought works on agriculture, mechanics and natural history had come across a number of medicinal booklets by unknown authors, theses for degrees by stupid doctors, old chemists' receipts, pages torn from anonymous encyclopædias, all waste paper which could only be sold by weight, and had one day suggested his buying them, giving him to understand that they were filled with the very flower of knowledge. Ferdinando paid a good price for them, and settled down to read the lot. Then he began getting worried. The description of diseases, the listing of symptoms, the uncertainty of cures, terrified him. Shut in his room, book in one hand, he would hold the other on his heart to verify the number of beats, or prod himself all over in terror of finding the tumours, muscle-stiffening, inflammations, which the doctors mentioned. Gradually, from a fit of coughing, a touch of indigestion, a headache, the slightest itch, pins-and-needles, he began to think he had every illness. The idea got into his solitary misanthrope's brain and caused devastation. Death now for him was just a matter of time; and it was the fear of dying alone, the need to see a friendly face, which had made him take his brother in.

When Raimondo saw that Ferdinando scarcely ate a thing, was shut up in his room all day and sometimes did not even rise, he began asking what was the matter, if he felt ill. At first, as if held back by some kind of shame, Ferdinando gave negative answers; then eventually, under pressure, he confessed. He had a chronic intestinal catarrh, a swollen spleen, slow bronchitis; shingle-germs were circulating in his blood, his glandular system was stopped up. When Raimondo began laughing at this list, he added, in a sad voice and almost with tears in his eyes:

'There's not much to laugh at, you know! D'you think it's all imagination? I know what I suffer . . .'

'Then why not call in a doctor?'

'A doctor? What can doctors do? Now I've got to this point?'

There seemed no way of persuading him. Then Donna Isabella entered the scene. Instead of contradicting the maniac she began by agreeing with him; she recognised the existence and gravity of his ills, the uselessness of medical prescriptions, but if doctors were out of their depth couldn't he at least try one of those empirical remedies which can do wonders at times?

'When I was a girl I had an internal catarrh which was

even longer and more stubborn than yours. D'you know I got rid of it? With lettuce salad!'

And she had a plate of it prepared for him, to go with a big red slice of roast meat. Ferdinando began to eat gingerly at first. He had no faith in the result, was sure that food would quicken his end.

'Now what you need on top of that is a good walk,' and she offered him her arm as if to a convalescent, and led him out into the garden.

Next day the sick man found himself, incredibly, waking up feeling lively and with some appetite. The salad and roast meat did wonders in a short time. But there was still the itch to be cured—he had given it the name of shingles.

'The remedy for that is even simpler: a bath in soft water!'

For months he had washed nothing but the ends of his nose and fingers, two or three times a week, for fear of catching pneumonia. So the shingles went off too. Milk, eggs, exercise, cleanliness, brought him back to life, and tears of gratitude towards Donna Isabella sprang to his eyes.

'What a woman! What a brain? What a mind!'

He had very few friends, but every time he met one of them he began talking about her as admiringly as if she were the wisest and most virtuous of women, an angel from heaven. He got in the habit of moving about more, went to visit his sister Lucrezia, sought people out on purpose to talk about her.

'She does so love Raimondo! How well she looks after a house! Words can't express what she's done for me! If it wasn't for her, I'd be dead and buried by now!'

One day he arrived at Lucrezia's while husband and wife were in the midst of a lively discussion. At his appearance they went silent.

'What were you talking of?'

'About Raimondo's position,' replied his sister, deciding to let him into the secret. 'It can't go on long like this. It'll have to be legalised by dissolving the marriages.'

This she announced with the same simplicity as Raimondo and Donna Ferdinanda had said it to her. To ask and obtain a double annulment of marriage seemed a very simple matter to the Uzeda; who could deny the 'Viceroys' what they

345

wanted? Were not their wishes a law to all? Did they not possess all material and moral means to overcome obstacles and resistance? They had dependants everywhere, among pro-Bourbons and Liberals, in sacristies and courtrooms. The noble were with them from solidarity, the ignoble from respect; all were bound to be proud and happy to render them a service. The only thing necessary for success in this matter was good advice; that was why they wanted Benedetto's help. Like the first time it was mentioned to him, Benedetto hesitated, halted by scruples, conscious of the evil they were making him do, of the difficulties, of the disapproval it would bring from their uncle the duke, who was such a friend of Palmi. But his wife persistently showed how stupid his scruples were and even how meritorious his help could be.

' Suppose a child is born tomorrow? Will it be condemned to remain a bastard? Raimondo cannot go back to his wife; that's as sure as death. Well? Isn't it better to get them straight with law and society? Aren't I right?'

Ferdinando now turned to his brother-in-law:

' You don't doubt that, do you? . . . What's your reasoning? Where's your head? . . .'

Benedetto tried to show that it was they on the other hand who were not reasoning, that children already born should be thought of before those unborn, but Lucrezia and Ferdinando talked him down, both together.

' The mother's family can think of the daughters! Our brother won't be denying them, will he? . . . As for the money side, that can be arranged as Palmi wants . . . If the marriages are dissolved already in fact why not dissolve them in right? Who's gaining from it? Just scandal-mongers!'

Such now was Raimondo's goad. The more difficulties he met on his way the more stubbornly he persisted; and the opposition of his brother, the muttering of outsiders, the almost universal blame urged him to win through in some way unforeseen to all, including himself. He no longer thought that his real passion was freedom, that Donna Isabella as a wife would weigh on him more than his other wife and that she already weighed on him as a mistress. Sticking to his purpose, blinded by opposition, by disapproval, by criticism, he was determined to triumph over

346

his adversaries, floor them with a blow which would be long talked of . . .

They were saying, were they, that the enterprise was hopeless, that the double dissolution would never be obtained, that Donna Isabella was condemned to remain in a false position, banned from society, from the prince's own home? He set his feet against the wall, determined to see it through at all costs, against everyone and everything. And Lucrezia, Ferdinando, Donna Ferdinanda, Don Blasco were helping him each for his own reasons and in his own way, plotting to win over the last resistance of Benedetto, who, at the idea of pleasing his wife and capturing the trust, esteem and gratitude of her relations, felt his remorse gradually melting away.

When winter came on and the prince returned from the country the one subject of conversation was the quarrel between the two brothers. Giacomo not only cut Raimondo when they met on the street but would not allow the other's troubles to be mentioned in his presence. For so long, while his younger brother had been in Tuscany or had come and gone to see his mistress, the heritage had remained undivided, and the prince had administered it on behalf of his co-heir and by his power-of-attorney. Now he sent Signor Marco to cut off all connection with his brother, notifying him that he was renouncing the power-of-attorney and wanted accounts handed over at once and the division reached. That little trumpet, Cousin Graziella, was spreading all this far and wide wherever she was, among relations or friends or mere acquaintances, supporting her cousin Giacomo, expressing the great sorrow caused to ' us of the family ' by Raimondo's obstinacy. How could he, anyway, ever hope to get what he wanted? Now it was being said that Donna Isabella was asking for the dissolution of her marriage on the grounds of non-consummation! Who did they think they were taking in? Just because there weren't children? But everyone knew that Fersa had been a great rip as a young man!

Or perhaps they hoped to maintain, as others said, that Donna Isabella had been forced to marry Fersa against her will? That would be a headache for Giulente to prove! ' What immorality, though, to support a cause condemned by all, bringing the family such distress! He's come and thrust himself among us, fostered family quarrels, has this lawyer of lost causes! . . .' She, on her part, foresaw a colossal fiasco . . .

To begin with, no civil tribunal could annul a marriage contracted under the Napoleonic code of 1819; it had to go to the Bishop's court. But here the whole thing fell to the ground, for Monsignor the Bishop, the Vicar-General Coco, Canon Russo and all the major prelates of the Curia were with the prince against the count, and rightly, knowing how badly Raimondo and the Fersa woman had behaved, and being unable to sanction such a scandal!

On the other hand, the count's and Donna Isabella's supporters were giving out that they were sure of success. Fersa's impotence, his violence to his wife, were affirmed by numbers of people. Pasqualino especially was ringing bells on his master's behalf. ' Yes, sir; *Cavaliere* Giulente, and not *Attorney* Giulente, had been looking into and organising his *brother-in-law's* case, rather than leave it to some money-grubbing little lawyer. Not that he had much work to do on it, for the nullity motive in Donna Isabella's case was quite plain. Apart from the fact that Fersa wasn't exactly a volcano as a man, her uncle had forced her to take him, with a knife at her throat; quite the opposite to the Signorina Chiara's version! At least the old princess, God rest her soul, had tried to influence her daughter gently, only resorting to threats at the very last after two years of persuading and begging. But how had Donna Isabella's uncle gone about it? Beatings morning and night, from the first moment the girl said " I'd rather die than marry Fersa!" '

Like Pasqualino, all the servants and minor dependants of the family were on the young count's side in spite of the prince's opposition. Raimondo, to acquire sympathy and support, no longer had his clothes sent from Florence or Naples as he had before, but distributed commissions of all kinds in the town, and the tailor, boot-maker, cravat-maker, honoured by having orders from the young Count Uzeda, would extol him to the skies, hold forth in his support, and argue with scandal-mongers. If anyone recalled Donna Isabella's love for Fersa, they would cite innumerable witnesses to the contrary: all the Pinto family servants were ready to come from Palermo and swear on the

Gospel that the little orphan girl had been hit again and again by her uncle and guardian, because he, ignoring the fact that Fersa was of ignoble birth, for all his wealth, was determined she should marry him. It was being said, was it, that the witnesses were suspect and obtained by bribery? They would list the Pinto family's friends in Palermo, Don Michele Broggi, the Cavaliere Cùtica, the Notary Rosa, all above suspicion of corruption and cited by Donna Isabella to attest to the ill-treatment she had been subjected to, her constant refusals. Why, even her uncle himself would come and confirm putting pressure on her!

'What then?' Cousin Graziella in turn would exclaim. 'Suppose they do get this marriage dissolved? Do they think they'll ever manage to get the other one dissolved too? Don't they know what Palmi said?' And she would tell how that troublemaker Giulente had written to get the baron too to consent to his daughter's marriage being dissolved and witness that he had forced her to marry Count Uzeda. She must, she said, from love of truth mention that Giulente had refused at first, as it was such a dreadful thing to do, and hoped to hand the job over to the duke, who was an intimate friend of the senator. Ah but the duke had other things to think of! He was still in Turin, looking after his own affairs, and did not want to return to Sicily for fear that his absence during the troubles of the year before might have been misunderstood, and when they wrote to him about Raimondo's business he replied that he would not dream of getting mixed up in it.

Then Giulente, to please his wife, brother-in-law, uncle and aunt, found himself in the position of having to approach the baron himself. 'D'you know how long he took to write the letter?' added Cousin Graziella, who was well up in every tiny detail. 'A week! He tore up a whole ream of paper! I assure you! How can one ask a decent person to agree to his daughter's marriage being dissolved, to his grandchildren being fatherless? . . .' But the letter, full of respectful expressions, compliments, and excuses, had finally been sent off, and Giulente was still awaiting a reply! He'd have to wait some time! For through certain persons in Messina the cousin had come to hear of what the baron, clenching his fists, had said to a friend: 'I'd rather see them all die first! . . .'

349

For in fact 'poor Matilde', at death's door from distress, indifferent now to all, realising that there was no hope left, would even have agreed to this last demand by her husband. The baron on the other hand swore terrible oaths that never, never while he was alive would his son-in-law succeed in breaking up the marriage. He realised that it was broken in fact, but he wanted Raimondo to stay chained for life and the Fersa never to be able to take before the world the place of his own daughter.

Pasqualino knew that too; but to Donna Graziella's coachman, who was taking his mistress's part and prophesying a fiasco for the count, 'One thing at a time,' he replied. 'Let the first case end! . . . When my mistress is free we can see about freeing the master too! . . . Now it's not Canons who have to decide, but civil judges. By Victor Emmanuel's law a marriage in church isn't worth a fig, the only one that matters is before the mayor. Down with Francis II! Long live liberty! . . .'

But Donna Ferdinanda, Lucrezia, none of Raimondo's supporters would be satisfied with a civil judgement; they wanted to legitimise Raimondo's and Donna Isabella's situation before both men and God. So Ferdinando, who was a close friend of Canon Ravesa, an important member of the Curia and owner of a vineyard next door, talked to him every day in his brother's favour. Every day too Don Blasco went to visit the Vicar-General Coco and drummed into him with noisy insistence the propriety, justice and necessity of annulling that marriage; and the irresponsibility, arrogance and rascality of the prince in opposing it.

But the most important person to win over was Monsignor the Bishop, who did nothing now without the approval of Don Lodovico. The latter, convinced that the abolition of religious communities was only a question of time, had lost interest in San Nicola and turned his attention to the Bishop's palace, where his birth, reputation for intelligence, learning and sanctity had flung open all doors. In a short time, as he had been the right hand of the Abbot so he became the right hand of the head of the diocese. His prudent advice, his unique position in relation to all political parties, made him indispensable in many delicate matters when the new political authorities had to be conciliated without the 'legitimate' ones being betrayed, to save appearances and serve Christ and Mammon. Now, had he said a word in Raimondo's favour Donna Isabella's marriage would have been annulled; but the Prior's answers to Donna Ferdinanda, who was badgering him to take up her protégée's cause, remained ambiguous, adducing difficulties to be overcome, the embarrassment to which they were putting him.

'Dissolving a marriage is a serious matter . . . Your Excellency knows well how justly contrary the Church is to pronouncing sentence of this kind, how it proceeds with leaden feet. There are some proofs and some reasons it cannot accept . . . These may be perhaps enough for secular judges, whose responsibility is not pledged to the Divine Majesty. I am truly pained to see Raimondo on so wrong a road . . . After this case will come a second, the scandal is immense . . . I have my duties to carry out . . . my conscience . . .'

'Conscience? . . . Conscience? . . .' Donna Ferdinanda, who was listening to him with shut mouth and set teeth, burst out. 'Let's leave conscience apart! Why not admit you haven't forgiven him for taking your place and want to make him pay now that you have him in a vice.'

The Prior suddenly went pale, glanced for an instant straight at his aunt, who was staring fixedly at him as if wanting to read his heart. Then he bent his head and crossed his arms over his chest.

'Your Excellency afflicts me cruelly . . . You know well that the passions of the world are alien to my heart . . . that I love my brother as I respect Your Excellency! . . . Tell Raimondo that; give me a chance of proving it . . .'

Donna Ferdinanda went straight off to Raimondo to tell him to go and make a personal visit to his brother and recommend himself to him. For a moment the young man rebelled. He was tired of begging and of being humiliated, of paying court to Ferdinando and Giulente to win them over to his case, of prompting Pasqualino and other rumour-mongers. He had already humiliated himself once before Giacomo with no results. He had humiliated himself before Lodovico on that other visit to Nicolosi, when his brother had not deigned to appear. Now he had to throw himself at that Jesuit's feet, ask his pardon for taking his place, beg him to grant not only forgiveness but protection

351

and support. It was too much, he could bear no more. The mortifications to his self-love stung him more than anything else,
made him clench his fists and chew his nails, almost brought
tears to his eyes . . .

But now all his relations and the nobility in general, just back
from the country, were siding with the prince. Cousin Graziella
was going round saying everywhere that the civil case would
not get through either, that the judges would themselves
bring an action for false witness against those who had tried
to prove lack of consent. Just think of the ecclesiastical case
then!

One Sunday, Donna Isabella, who had gone into town for
some shopping, returned to Ferdinando's with eyes red.

'What's the matter?' asked Raimondo, almost brusquely,
almost ready to burst out against her who was first cause of all
that had happened.

'Nothing . . . nothing . . .' and she began to cry.

He had to raise his voice to hear the reason for her sobs. His
mistress had met the Grazzeri and Cousin Graziella in the
street. The cousin had turned the other way, Lucia and Agatina
Grazzeri had not answered her greeting, pretending not to see
her.

Next day he went to San Nicola to visit the Prior.

Lodovico received him with open arms, listened to him with
benevolent attention. Raimondo, rather pale, said to him, 'I
implore you to help me . . .' He was invoking his help to get out
of the false situation in which he found himself. It was urgent
to legitimise it for a new and powerful reason which no one yet
knew, and which he confided to the Prior before anyone else;
Donna Isabella was pregnant.

With his eyes almost shut, his head slightly bent, his hands
folded in his lap, the Prior looked like an indulgent and friendly
confessor. Not a contraction of his face, not a dilation of his
chest hinted at the intimate satisfaction he felt to see finally
there before him, submissive and almost supplicating, the thief
who had robbed him, the person for whom he had been banned
from his family and the world.

'You can help me, put in a good word,' went on Raimondo,
'mention that after all, what we're asking is only justice . . .

for Isabella's will was forced; thirty witnesses can prove the truth . . .'

' I know! I know!' replied the Prior eventually. ' I wouldn't have listened to you had I not known that right is on your side!'

' Then can I count on you?'

' Indeed you can, indeed you can! But there's another matter. The present case is not a question so much of abstract justice as of worldly prudence. We have, of course, to render account only to God for our actions, but in order that our consciences should be entirely at rest we should not and cannot lose sight of the effect which our judgements may have! Now, how can you expect this step to be considered properly if in our own family the very head of our house does not recognise your reasons, and condemns you with such severity?'

' And suppose Giacomo comes round?' insisted Raimondo.

' It'll be a great step forward! Public opinion would follow him, you'll see, and all those who declared themselves your enemies till now will support you entirely. Then it will be much easier to get what you want. Giacomo too can be of more use with the judges than I can. You well know how close are his relations with the Bishopric's . . . a word from him would mean much more than one from me . . .'

This was the point he wanted to reach with all that talk. He did not like this affair of Raimondo's, all this mess of marriages to be dissolved and retied. The mute reproval of the general public was well-known to him and put him on guard against the mistake of supporting a bad cause, the triumph of which would anyway be of no help to him whatsoever.

On his return Raimondo sent for Signor Marco. Shut in a room together, they spent a few minutes in close confabulation. The administrator returned next day and then the day after, staying longer each time.

One afternoon Ferdinando had flung himself on his bed for a snooze when the baying of dogs suddenly awoke him; his agent was knocking on the door.

' Excellency! Excellency! . . . Your brother's here . . . The prince himself!'

He jumped to the ground, rubbing his eyes. Giacomo here?

353

When Raimondo was here too? Suppose they ran into each other?

'I'm coming at once. You keep him . . . but don't say a thing about . . .'

'What, Excellency? But the two brothers are chatting together! The princess is here too . . .'

Rushing down to prevent some disaster, Ferdinando entered the drawing-room and found his two brothers and sisters-in-law chatting away gaily together.

'We were passing this way,' said the prince, 'and thought of paying you a visit.'

Next day, in the Yellow Drawing-room, Cousin Graziella, who had come to luncheon early and found the princess with Don Mariano, was attacking Raimondo and his mistress with more than usual heat, narrating their latest moves, their approaches to the duke to lend his deputy's authority to obtain the dissolution of the marriages and get the good Baron Palmi to agree. The princess was on hot coals, changing colour, raising, lowering and rolling her eyes as if to invoke the intervention of Don Mariano, and coughing slightly to warn the cousin not to insist. But on she went more ardently than ever:

'If only they'd be a little patient! They'd be freed just the same, for poor Matilde is at death's door. They seem to want to bring on her end! Imagine what effect this news has on her! . . . But her father is swearing worse than ever that he'll never agree to suit their plans. His daughter implores him to keep calm, as when such news arrives he seems on the verge of an apoplectic fit . . . It's really a bit too much! There's Donna Ferdinanda's thumbprint all over it! Don't you think things have got to the point where they ought to be warned to be more prudent?'

The princess had no time to reply or hide the new embarrassment in which this question threw her when Baldassarre, entering soundlessly, announced with that fine serenity of his:

'The Signor Count and the Signora Countess.'

Cousin Graziella was turned to salt. Raimondo? The *countess*? Which countess? Then Donna Isabella appeared, went towards

354

the princess, who came to meet her, embraced and kissed her on both cheeks.

'How *are* you, Margherita? I was anxious to repay your charming visit of yesterday . . .'

They were calling each other '*tu*'! The Fersa woman had found a way of mentioning that Margherita had paid her a visit! And now the prince appeared, shaking Raimondo's hand and saying:

'Sister-in-law and cousin, will you both stay to luncheon?'

5

'THE Duke of Oragua! The deputy! The patriot! Where? Where is he? There he is . . . He's stouter! . . . He's been away nearly three years! . . . Does he come from Turin? Signor Duke! Excellency! Excellency! . . .'

And there were greetings and bows to left and right, some drawing back a pace before meeting him and baring their heads as at the passage of the Blessed Sacrament. When he had passed everyone turned round to follow him for a time with their eyes. Only a few enjoyed the privilege of being able to go up to him, shake his hand and ask his news. Very few indeed, the elect, could have the honour of accompanying him, escorting him, mingling with the group of close admirers and friends who followed him everywhere, to the Prefecture, to the Municipality, to the clubs. He would walk in the middle of the street as if he owned the place, listened to devoutly by those beside him, awaited by a throng of courtiers intent on singing his praises even when some pressing little need drew him into a corner.

At the palace there was the same coming and going as the time before, electors, petitioners, delegations of political societies returning to thank him personally, after thanking him in writing, for the good he had done the town and his fellow-citizens; thanks to him, the first railway begun in Sicily was to run between Catania and Messina, and in the port there were wharves for steamships, and the town had many new schools, an inspectorate of forests, and a stallion depot; a credit-establishment, the *Banca Meridionale,* was about to open; the Government had promised to undertake a number of public works and help the municipality and province; and one by one good

356

Liberals, sons of the revolution, were obtaining what they asked for; a job, a subsidy, a decoration.

His popularity was at its apex. Some did, it is true, blame him for his absence during the troubles of '62 and put it down to fear, revived those tales about him in '48, and accused him of having finally thought of his constituency only now when the Chamber was being dissolved and he wanted his mandate reconfirmed; but these murmurers were the eternal malcontents, the few republicans, an out-and-out Garibaldino or two, all people who could not forgive his adherence to the conservative party. In conversations about politics, he would uphold a moderate policy quite openly, 'Now we've had our revolution and reached our aim,' and praise the Government's prudent action, deplore Garibaldi's rashness, criticise discontent with the September Convention, affirm that a league of good men and true was necessary to save the nation from enemies, external and internal.

More than in his first period as deputy, he would now make great play with mention of important political friends, 'When I went to see Minghetti . . . As Rattazzi said to me . . . At the Minister's home . . .' But he no longer quoted Baron Palmi. If his nephew Raimondo's actions were mentioned he would make a slight motion with shoulders and head which could fit in with any mood of the questioner, approval, indulgence, blame. By now anyway Raimondo's and Donna Isabella's situation was legalised, and all the relations followed the prince's example and treated them as husband and wife. In less than six months, the Episcopal Court, accepting the fact that the marriage had been contracted by force and fear, had set Donna Isabella free.

Raimondo's marriage with Matilde had been rather more trouble. At first the baron was also expected to ask for his daughter's marriage to be annulled and assert that he had forced her into it. But the baron, ' a stubborn oaf ', explained Pasqualino, had said no and went on saying no until the very last moment, even though his daughter—God rest her soul—had finally set her heart at rest, particularly on learning that the first marriage no longer existed and that the count had a son to legitimatise. Donna Matilde—one must be fair!—in spite of wild ideas was quite sensible really, and knowing that she was ill, and realising that the count would be free anyway sooner or

357

later, had decided to ask her father's consent to the dissolving of
the civil marriage; not of the religious one, for she had certain
rather odd scruples about the sanctity of the sacrament of matrimony; but her husband would be content with a civil divorce.
Yes, the count and countess had none of the pigheadedness of
the rustic baron, who swore that he would prefer to see his
daughter dead rather than consent to free his son-in-law! . . .
He wouldn't do it? Then the count himself asked to be freed,
adducing that his mother had forced him to take that wife!

Everyone knew what sort of woman the old princess had
been, how she had tyrannised her children. Had she not
ridden roughshod over Chiara's wishes to give her to the Marchese of Villardita? So she had also violated Raimondo's to give
him the Palmi girl! There were dozens, hundreds of witnesses to
affirm that the young count had never had the slightest desire
to get married; first relations, the prince, his sisters, in-laws,
uncles and aunts, cousins, then his friends, then the servants,
and then the whole town.

But to obtain the dissolution of the marriage it had to be
shown that in the act of pronouncing the ' yes ' which tied Don
Raimondo for ever, he had felt grave fear. And then Don
Eugenio had come before the magistrates to witness that his
sister-in-law the princess had had her son accompanied to the
parish church by two armed rangers, who if he answered ' no ',
were to bind him, fling him into a carriage waiting near the
church, take him into the country and beat him up. Two rangers
came down from the Mirabella estate to confirm this testimony,
and the coachman also swore to his part of the story, as did
the sacristan. And so the Tribunal gave their verdict.

Certain people—Pasqualino found this really too much!—
were actually suggesting that these witnesses were false, that
the rangers had been paid and that Don Raimondo had given
his uncle Don Eugenio a tip of three hundred *onze*! As if Don
Eugenio Uzeda of Francalanza, Gentleman of the Bedchamber
to His Majesty Ferdinand II (without duties, however, as Ferdinand was no longer in this world and his descendants had been
dismissed) was capable of such an action! As if the judges were
people to accept untrue depositions! Others were hinting that,
being a man, the young count could not have been cowed by

threats and there had never been a case of a marriage annulled because of undue pressure on the husband's will. There had not yet been, now there was; well, what was there to laugh about? Not even Baron Palmi had found it laughable, for he had taken no part in the case! Gossip said that the baron had let things run on from love of his daughter, whose life was near its end, but Pasqualino just couldn't understand how some thoughts got into people's heads! What had Donna Matilde's illness to do with the baron's silence? Donna Matilde wouldn't suddenly get well from pleasure at hearing her marriage had been dissolved, would she? Instead of which she died—Heaven preserve us!—a few months after the count's marriage to Donna Isabella! So the baron must have remained silent because he knew his son-in-law was telling the truth!

Immediately after making his peace with the prince, Raimondo and Donna Isabella had been reconciled to most of their old opponents. Cousin Graziella in particular had set to work defending them even more warmly than Pasqualino himself, pointing out that passion is 'blind', that men are 'made of flesh and blood' and so are women, and that the blame for all that had happened could be attributed to the irresponsibility, 'to say the least', of the Palmi family. Even so a large part of the nobility still remained hostile to Raimondo and his mistress. But the cousin was full of assurances that gradually they would all be tamed, particularly when the tribunals had done their jobs and granted the divorces; not content with assurances, she also made active propaganda, persuaded the hesitating, faced up to mutterers.

Meanwhile, after thanking Ferdinando for his hospitality, Raimondo had taken an apartment in the Palazzo Roccasciano and set up house there with his future wife. Actually Giacomo, the Prior, the duke, had all advised them to do no such thing but stay up at Pietra dell'Ovo until the day of their legitimate union, and then go off to Naples, Milan or Turin, amid new people. But Donna Isabella had been so affronted by past insults that she wanted to get her revenge and enjoy her triumph.

Raimondo, who had pledged himself to conquer one and all, was still doing what she wanted in spite of himself. His firm intention was to go away as soon as possible, not for the reasons of prudence suggested by his relations but because he avowed he just could not live even a day or two in his native town except from extreme necessity; a few words from her were enough to dissuade him. Might not his relatives be giving that advice because in spite of making up their quarrel, they did not much want to receive her and preferred to know that she was at a distance? Weren't there still many who greeted her coldly and avoided talking to her?

And he began to splash money on his home, insisted on the wedding being celebrated with the greatest pomp, as if challenging those who had before considered his aim quite impossible. It was a sumptuous occasion which many of those who had most criticised him asked for the great honour of attending, and so Donna Isabella tasted the joy of seeing them at her feet. It was a pity that Cousin Graziella, who had contributed so much to it all, could not enjoy it too, for a few days before, her husband caught a cold which seemed at first quite unimportant but which on the very night of the wedding developed into pneumonia and three days later killed him.

All the Uzeda were at her home on that sad occasion. The prince, particularly, lost his habitual cold mien and showed himself very close to his cousin in her sorrow. She seemed quite inconsolable, and told everyone, amid sobs, how truly good her husband had been, and what an irreparable disaster his death was to her. Only the sight of ' her dear cousins ', the comforts of ' the family ' softened her sorrow; her ' cousins ' and ' uncles ' were the only people left in the world to her. She put signs of mourning everywhere and only just avoided painting her face black. For a number of months she steadfastly refused to go out, even in a closed carriage at night. The first visit she made, though, was to the prince's, where she gradually got into the habit of coming often to draw comfort. She would take Teresina in her arms and exclaim in broken tones, ' My daughter! My daughter! . . . If God had granted me a daughter like you, I wouldn't be all alone in the world! . . . May God always preserve you to your mother's affection . . . Oh, daughter! My daughter! . . .' and went on so that Princess Margherita, who was very impressionable, would begin crying too.

In time, however, her great sorrow grew calm and composed

enough for her to take an interest in worldly matters. Her husband had left her sole heir to a goodly substance, so that she had no worries about the future; but, not knowing how to lay hands on her inheritance, she had appealed to her cousin the prince to put things in order for her. And now she would come to the palace every day, some days more than once. And although there were no business matters to take her there she would often visit Lucrezia and ' Aunt Ferdinanda ', and ' Cousin Isabella '. Because of her mourning, however, she never went to the latter's home on Mondays, the day on which the countess ' received '.

This custom of receiving on a definite day was a great novelty, much discussed. Donna Isabella, not appeased by the triumph of one single evening and wanting to bend the last stubborn opponents, had introduced it and thus succeeded in giving her salon a special tone and unusual importance, so that the most restive eventually intrigued for the honour of being admitted there. So much so that scarcely three years after first arriving in a vulgar hotel room as a very illegitimate wife with everyone against her, that winter of '65 she found herself enthroned as genuine Countess of Lumera with a court of admirers around her.

' Thank you! Thank you! . . .' she would cry to Raimondo, flinging her arms round his neck and hugging him tight. ' You wished it and you achieved it! . . . Thank you! Thank you! . . .' Beneath these caresses he was like marble. With his case won, and the frenzy calmed which had borne him through difficulties and opposition of every kind, he was now adding up what that result had cost him. In a confused, mute fashion—for he would never admit his own blindness—he felt that he had been working away simply to forge a heavier and more unbreakable chain round his neck, when his own longing, his one ardent desire had been to free himself altogether. Discontented, restless, irritable, he would rein himself in before the world, but at home among his own people the slightest thing would make him lose his temper, shout and ill-treat someone. Pasqualino took the worst of the storm on his shoulders; Donna Isabella often felt it threatening her too, but managed to appease it by submission and by always bowing to her husband's mood.

361

Raimondo's unconscious rancour against himself now turned against his relations. He knew that in various ways, for various reasons, by either encouraging or contradicting him, they had all contributed to his situation, and being unable to blame himself he took it out on them. His wife, to avoid him thinking something else, also began criticising all the Uzeda. And there was no lack of material.

Chiara, for example, who had put on such a scrupulous act when they had not been legally wed, was now getting herself talked about all round town, for the shameful things she allowed in her own home. With her womb in the state it was after the cyst had been cut out she could no longer be touched by her husband. Then what did the mad woman go round complaining of? The state to which she had been reduced? The illness threatening her? Not at all; her great sorrow was being unable to go to bed with Federico! Realising that he, who had nothing wrong with him and was in fact sound as a bell, could not abstain the whole year round, what had she gone and thought of, if you please? Of selecting him a series of buxom maidservants, each prettier than the last, putting them into his bed, and almost attending them herself instead of being attended by them! 'Isn't it shameful? . . . Is she mad? . . .' Donna Isabella would exclaim, reminding Raimondo of the story of Chiara's marriage with that abhorred marchese whom the old princess had to force her daughter to take. 'And what about the other men? And the other women?' Lucrezia, for instance? Her madness had taken the opposite direction. After turning everything upside down to marry Giulente, she had gradually come almost to despise him, called him a fool on every possible occasion, detested his politics which had thrilled her before and said right out in his face, 'I wish Francis II would come back and tie up the lot of you!' And what about Don Eugenio's speculations? He, after making the Prince of Roccasciano pay through the nose for pots and shards, then took them off the latter's wife for a few cents when the gambling demon overcame her and she plucked them off the shelves . . . And the metamorphosis of Ferdinando? His passion for his country place had seemed boundless; then one fine day he left everything, dropped all his agricultural and mechanical experiments and came to live in town. He never failed to be present at his sister-in-law's on Mondays, went to the theatre every night, frequented the ladies, and in order not to have to set foot in the estate he had so loved let himself be robbed hand over fist by his agent. 'Is he mad? Are they all mad? . . .' Donna Isabella spoke of nothing else, knowing that by this she was appeasing Raimondo's humour. He was against the lot of them, yes, but his greatest grudge was against the prince.

Giacomo had not only done his brother moral harm but made him pay through the nose for his support. When going all out to win through and triumph over the immense obstacles with which the dissolution of both marriages was scattered, Raimondo had not even bothered to calculate what his peace with his elder brother was costing; so deeply was he then involved that he might have agreed to handing over all he possessed.

But now on making up accounts he found that Giacomo had taken a good third of his fortune. As he had done with Lucrezia, the prince had presented a bill for hospitality, a very long one, since it included his former wife's and his children's expenses too; then he brought out those old I.O.U.'s which had appeared after their mother's death and put half of them down to him; then in the bills under power-of-attorney Giacomo showed himself to be creditor for many thousands of *onze* on interest accumulated from advances. So he had taken two estates, Burgio and Burgitello.

But the biggest trickery had been in the division, for he set down the price of land according to his convenience and kept the best and nearest for himself. In exchange for other property he handed over worthless rents, difficult and uncertain of payment, and not content with all that also made Raimondo renounce the use of the apartment in their ancestral palace, that clause in their mother's will which had been like a mote in his eye . . .

Now that the frenzy of the struggle was over, Raimondo was animated by a deep grudge against him, but Donna Isabella did not remind him of these things when talking against his brother, realising that it was a double-edged argument and could twist back on to her. Instead she would criticise her brother-in-law's overbearing character, his severity towards his wife, his dislike of everyone, his double-dealing with his aunt and uncles. Curious by nature, watchful from self-interest, she now found something going on in her brother-in-law's house which was a weapon in her hands. 'Did you notice? . . . Did you notice? . . .' she said to her husband every time they came home from the palace. 'And to think he acted the moralist too! How he used to preach! . . . And that stupid Margherita not noticing a thing!'

The princess in fact did not seem to notice that their widowed cousin had been coming to console herself 'in the family' every single morning and every single evening for some time. The prince was now busy putting her inheritance in order, and as he had to talk to her about it would often go and see her on his own account. And sometimes he would bring her back to the palace with him. In the evening she would stay till the last in the Yellow Drawing-room when the usual society met.

None of the Uzeda, for the moment, were lacking: Raimondo's marriage seemed to have brought peace back to all their hearts. The duke would pontificate away, setting Europe to rights in a twinkle and Italian finances in less time than it took to say so, while Giulente sat listening as if he were the Messiah, letting himself be drawn ever more in his wake, deserting his own party to court this uncle in the hope of taking over his job. The duke had said to him, 'When I'm tired, I'll leave the seat to you,' and this had been Benedetto's secret dream, to be a deputy, to get into high politics. Meanwhile the duke had got him elected a communal counsellor, and would also discuss with him Town Council matters and reforms to be introduced. Although Parliament was in full session he did not mention leaving, busy as he was settling his own affairs. His patriotism had cost him a lot of money. To subsidise the persecuted, buy rifles and cartridges, offer drinks to the National Guard, he had contracted debts and mortgaged his small fortune; now he was putting things in order. Where was he finding the money? He was said to be drawing a percentage from contracts he had landed for the Giulente uncle, but such earnings, however big, could not be enough for the great operations which he was planning. On the foundation of the Southern Bank of Credit and Deposit he had subscribed for a hundred shares of a thousand lire each. It is true that he had not paid for more than a quarter, but at the same time he was talking of a big steam-navigation company, of a company to work the sulphur mines and another to fell the Etna forests. Don Blasco and Donna Ferdinanda were trying every means, each on his own accounts, to find out how he was setting about it. It was the Marchese Federico who put them on the right path.

With what remained from his large income the marchese used to make some purchase every year. Recently he had bought a villa at the Belvedere in order to be in his own home during country stays, and he still had in hand a small sum which he did not know what to do with. It was too small for buying land; he did not want to lend it; what was to be done with it? 'Buy public utilities!' the duke advised him, explaining the advantages of this and offering to send for some from Turin. 'Has Your Excellency bought any then?' asked the marchese. 'I've bought 'em, sold 'em . . . according to the market . . . you understand . . .' then, almost regretting having given this hint of speculations on information picked up in ministerial antechambers during his five years in Turin, he had changed the subject.

The marchese hesitated for a time, partly from loyalty to the Bourbon principle, much more from fear of losing his money, both interest and capital, with the idea that Italy was always on the point not only of failure but of bankruptcy. Finally one day, meeting the duke on his way from drawing his half-yearly dividends and tucking away a fat roll of banknotes, he made up his mind. The evening he announced his purchase at the palace, Don Blasco had to be heard to be believed!

'Ah, you turncoat! You as well? With Italy now too, are you? Have you gone mad also?'

'Why?' the marchese tried to reply. 'In '66, 7½ per cent was paid on capital . . . Dividend coupons are paid punctually when due . . .'

The monk listened with staring eyes, as if waiting to see just how far the enormities spouted by this creature would go. Eventually he burst out:

'You'll be wiping your arse with your coupons! . . . That's where you'll get 'em paid, you donkey! . . .' And turning to

365

Chiara, with hands in hair, 'Stop him . . . he wants to ruin you! Interest at 7 per cent! . . . It's not worth it even as alms!' and sweeping round a glance full of bitter irony, 'A safe investment, my dear sirs! . . . When Neapolitan income was at 110 . . . It won't take long for the dirty paper to come down to five . . . Then on 5 lire capital we'll net 5 lire a year! And all get rich! Long live the millennium! Long live the great King Victor!'

The duke was in a corner with Benedetto, explaining his ideas about the development of the Bank, which under Don Lorenzo Giulente's management was to 'come to the help of industrial and commercial development' and 'co-operate with the protective work of the Government'. At his brother's outburst he smiled imperceptibly and shrugged his shoulders. Chiara, taking her husband apart, said:

'Don't listen to that madman! . . . You've done fine. Buy some more.' And a little later she took him away before the evening broke up, as she had for some time, without letting anyone know the reason for her great hurry to get home.

The reason was this. Rosa Schirano, a new maid whom she had taken on for Federico, a fine-looking lass from Piana, white and apple pink, was pregnant by the marchese; and instead of Chiara throwing her out she was beside herself with joy. That, in fact, was the secret hope which induced her to pop so many fresh young girls into her husband's bed. As she wanted a child by him and was unable to bear one, she would content herself with another's. So it seemed quite natural to fuss over this other girl whom Federico had put with child, and envy her fate. She had herself made the girl confess, and the trembling Rosa had been astounded to find her mistress, instead of flinging her downstairs, saying, 'Don't worry now! I'll see to your child!' From that day Chiara thought of nothing but the maid. A certain sense of human respect prevented her from having the girl round in her own rooms with her belly swelling all the time, but down in the courtyard, in rooms which the coachman's wife had been forced to give up, she visited her three or four times a day, sent her the best titbits from her table, kept her in cotton-wool.

When this became known, all her relatives, particularly those ember-blowers Don Blasco and Donna Ferdinanda, began to raise the devil and shout that the slut should be kicked out of the house. But Chiara pretended that Rosa had been with someone outside and excused her, declaring she could not bear to see her suffer.

' There are so many temptations for these poor girls! Let's hope he'll marry her, whoever it was . . . I know what pregnancy means . . . I just haven't the heart to throw her out on the streets . . .'

But the oddest thing was that the marchese himself became irritated and also a little ashamed at this clandestine parenthood. Chiara never mentioned the matter to her husband. When Cousin Graziella also put her nose in and came to suggest she send that girl away, she went scarlet, not knowing how to reply there and then. But as soon as the other left she burst out, turning to Federico:

' Just listen to her! I do what I like and want and you're the only one with the right to give me orders in here. So she's being scrupulous is she, that . . . I won't say what! After stealing Giacomo from his wife! Only someone as stupid as my sister-in-law would notice nothing . . .'

Actually a number of people were now beginning to murmur, and among the servants of the two houses there was already an exchange of winks and comments which made Baldassarre feel he was swallowing barrels of poison. Could his lordship the prince not do an act of charity and survey his cousin's intricate affairs without viperish tongues finding something to say about it? Was it because there'd been some talk of their marrying years ago? But the master had carried out the old princess's wish, God rest her soul, and now he considered his children, respected his wife and had quite other things to think of than gallantry! Had he wanted to pay court to his cousin he would have done so long ago without waiting for her husband's death, for that poor good devil Cavaliere Carvano was not one to frighten a soul. Anyway, hadn't they taken a look at the princess? She had most interest in knowing the truth, and if that malicious gossip had had any foundation would she have kept so calm? . . .

The princess was calmer than ever, always obedient to her husband, always awaiting the instructions that he would often impart with a mere glance. Cousin Graziella was now almost domiciled in the palace, giving the servants orders as if she were paying them and expressing her opinion about all household affairs, heeded perhaps more by the prince than was his wife. Donna Margherita not only never complained but breathed more freely, for Giacomo left her in peace, no longer expected her to agree with him about everyone and everything nor reproved her if things did not go as he wanted. So that if the widowed cousin did not turn up some days she would send for her before the prince noticed her absence and keep her at home all day, confide Teresina to her, treat her like a sister. This intimacy also gave her another precious advantage; it spared her the horror of touching keys, furniture or objects. When linen had to be put out or cupboards rummaged, or things set back in chests, Cousin Graziella would do it all herself, coming and going round the house with keys at waist, changing everything round to such a point that in her absence no one could find a thing and she had to be sent for.

'They might at least take the child away!' said the scandalised Donna Isabella to Raimondo. 'They're making it watch a fine show!'

Don Blasco and Donna Ferdinanda were already beginning to make comments too; but when Rosa Schirano bore the marchese a fine male baby, pink and white and plump, war amid the Uzeda became general again.

Chiara, beside herself with joy, brought the maid back near her, sought out a nurse for her, gave the infant all the baby-clothes she had once prepared for her own children. She kept it in her arms morning, noon and night and held it out for her husband to kiss, saying 'Look how pretty he is . . . He's like you, isn't he? . . .' When alone she would bring down from the top of the wardrobe a dusty bottle containing the monster she had borne herself, embrace with a single look the horrible yellow tallow-like abortion and the plump baby waving its little fists, and two tears would form on her lashes. 'May God's will be done!' Then putting back the bottle she would turn all her care and thoughts to Rosa's son, whom she had even had called Federico . . .

But Giacomo now began calling his sister mad. Chiara, stung, criticised her brother for having a mistress in the house and handing his daughter over to her. Lucrezia, who had made her peace with Giacomo at the time of Raimondo's wedding, now changed sides again and accused him only because Benedetto was agreeing with him in blaming Chiara's oddities. Donna Isabella, to distract Raimondo, who was falling into blacker and blacker moods, loaded her charges more against the prince, Chiara, or Lucrezia. Don Blasco and Donna Ferdinanda each fanned the flames on his own, forming league now against Chiara, now against Giacomo, now against Donna Isabella. And all, young and old, brothers and sisters, aunts, uncles, nephews and nieces, once more flung at each other accusations of irresponsibility and madness.

Amid all this the Prior bore himself with his usual serene indifference for all things of this world, after having paid his court to the Bishop and canvassed the coadjutor, Vicar-General and canons. Ferdinando, now most elegantly dressed, talked of nothing but clothes and foreign tailors. The duke, listening to all and answering none, exchanged telegrams with stock-brokers playing the market on his behalf and was busy arranging his banks and companies. The Cavaliere Don Eugenio had dropped his *Academy of the Four Poets* and was now concentrating entirely on a deal in sulphur which looked very lucrative —with the 300 *onze* from bearing false witness, evil tongues said. And the princess was happy to keep her hands white and gleaming away from all contacts and to use them only for embracing her children.

Teresa, now nearly twelve, was her pride, both for beauty of person and goodness of soul. Never a worry did that child cause; even the prince, who seemed on some days to be searching round minutely for excuses to lose his temper, never caught her in default. All that needed saying to her was 'Teresina, your father wouldn't like that,' or 'your father wants this,' for her to bow her head without a breath. By her exemplary obedience, by her gentleness of heart, she gathered praises and prizes everywhere. As she grew older she was no longer put on the wheel to be passed through the wall among the nuns at San Placido, but often taken to the convent parlour. She, who as a child had to control her fear of staying shut in the thickness of the wall and her terror of the black Crucifix, still in her heart preferred pleasant drives in the open air, but as her parents liked her to go and see her aunt the nun, she herself would often suggest those visits behind the grilles.

Then came stronger trials. Every year on the eve of All Souls' Day the family would go to the catacombs of the Capuchins to visit the mortal remains of the Princess Teresa on orders of the prince, who himself stayed at home for fear that the sight of the dead might bring him bad luck. The child would tremble from head to foot with terror at all those corpses ranged along the walls, shut in coffins, dressed as in life with shoes on their feet and gloves on their hands; some with mouths twisted as if screaming in agony, others as if roaring with laughter; her grandmother, all black in the face, dressed as a nun, in her glass coffin with her head on a tile and her hands desperately gripping an ivory crucifix! . . . She would tremble all over, the poor child, with the terror and horror of it, and at night dream that all those dead people were dancing around her. But she hid her terror as her confessor had told her that corpses can do no harm, that it is our duty to visit them, and that we must think of them continuously as one day we too shall die and go before the eternal Judge.

In most churches, if it came to that, she had a sense of cold fear. At Our Lady of Graces there was a wall covered with votive gifts: legs, heads, arms, wax breasts on which were painted horrible purple weals. At the Capuchins, in the Chapel of Blessed Ximena, was exposed the coffin containing her body. She was said to be preserved as fresh after centuries as if she had died an hour before. On every centenary of the beatification the coffin was opened, and Teresa thought with horror that the third centenary would fall in twelve years, 1876. But as she always made a great effort to control herself, gave no signs of fear, and was seen spending long hours on her knees in those churches praying, all praised her piety. Some even said, ' She is growing up to be like the Blessed Ximena; another saint!' Such praises flattered her; to gain them she would endure all without a word. She too longed for friends of her own age, fine new clothes, gaily coloured and richly decorated, her first ear-rings and finger-ring; but her father said that such things spoilt girls; and instead of sobbing and screaming, as so many others did, she would bow her head, comforted by her mother who promised into her ear, ' You just see, my darling, when you're grown up . . .'

Consalvo had not the same character as his sister; quite the contrary. But the princess would excuse him and exhort him to be good. These exhortations did not bear much fruit. Hoping in vain to get home as a result of the disturbances of '62, he had seen the years pass one after the other without his father keeping his promise to take him away from the Novitiate. Every time the boy came to the palace he reminded the prince, but the latter invariably replied, ' Later . . . in the spring . . . in the autumn . . . it's not for you to think of . . .' So he gnawed at the bit, waiting for spring and then autumn, which always found him still in his prison, fretting and restless. Then suddenly he flung his lot in with the Liberals in hoping for the suppression of the monasteries. He was converted by Giovannino Radalì who, since his mother persisted in wanting him to take vows, was also nurturing this only hope of returning to secular life; but the announcement of the suppression was rather like the prince's promises; it was always being repeated and never confirmed by facts. So, constantly irritated by his father's obstinacy, full of envy for companions who were returning one by one to their families and enjoying their liberty, he became the torment of masters, lay-brothers, and servants, of the whole monastery. He also refused to visit his home, or if he went, greeted no one, did not talk and sulked the whole visit. Now that at the palace not a chair was moved without Cousin Graziella's consent, she upheld the prince, sure that for the moment the boy was all right where he was, and she would say to him in tones of maternal affection, while he quivered with hatred of her :

' Don't worry, you'll come away in good time; now you must study. Why, my god-daughter is being put in college too.'

Signorina Teresina in college? In the courtyard, among relatives, as soon as this news got round it was the subject of endless comments. ' Why, though? . . . Isn't she all right at home? . . . The duke wanted it . . . What has the duke to do with it? . . . No, it was the prince . . . No the cousin . . . The princess

sobs from morning till night . . .' Each gave his own opinion,
some murmured that maybe the decision had been taken because
one day the Signorina had entered the Red Drawing-room unexpectedly and surprised the prince and her godmother in too intimate colloquy . . . But Baldassarre, in that authoritative tone of
his which cut short all gossip, gave a frank, genuine version; all
the great families of Palermo and Naples nowadays put their
young ladies into college, *chic* colleges as they called them, to
learn Italian and also French; Baron Cùrcuma had done so with
his girl, so the Prince of Francalanza's daughter must also go to
such a college. The duke knew that the Convent of the Annunciation in Florence was the most *chic* of the lot because it was
the most expensive. And Signor Don Raimondo and Countess
Donna Isabella, who were at home in Florence, said the same
too and approved of the young princess receiving a proper
education! . . .

He did not say that Donna Ferdinanda, at the news of this
decision taken without her knowledge, had burst out violently
against the prince and even forgiven Chiara for her tending that
little bastard in order to go and tirade with her against these
silly new-fangled Florentine colleges, when in her day girls of
the nobility learnt to weave silk at home and never thought of
all this Italian and foreign nonsense. He did not say that Don
Blasco was stamping round his niece's and nephew's homes
preaching a crusade against the things happening up at the
palace.

For Baldassarre the prince was God, and everything his master
did was well done. He also respected all the relations, and so
these rumours of family quarrels were most distressing to him.
He wanted them all to agree for the good name and prestige
of the family. And he denied tiffs, avoided giving too much importance to big ones, imposed silence on the lower servants,
while having an ear ever cocked for spicier bits of news, attributing the malicious gossip circulating among their own servants to
the envy of other less noble houses. Those must at all costs never
reach his master; if the latter asked why some scullion or other
had been dismissed he would find a good excuse or say that it
had been done by Signor Marco. Actually he had a high regard
for the administrator, who was, like him, jealous for the family's

good name and full of respect towards the prince and his just severity towards dependants.

Anyway the envious tired of talking badly in the long run. First some of the relations left, and so reduced motives for quarrelling. One fine day Count Raimondo, without a word to anyone, packed his bags and departed with his wife for Palermo, leaving Pasqualino to sell the furniture bought a year before. Then the duke went off to Florence, taking with him the young princess, Teresa, to put her in college as arranged.

As the little girl left she cried and cried at leaving her home and entering a college in distant Florence, where not even on Sunday, not even through a grille as at San Placido, would she be able to see her dear mother. Her godmother, though, said to her, 'Don't cry like that, can't you see how much you're distressing your mother?' So she swallowed down her tears and composed herself.

On the day of departure the princess sobbed convulsively and embraced her daughter frenziedly. Cousin Graziella had red eyes too, but was encouraging everyone with: 'Teresina will be back in a few years, and we'll all go and visit her every autumn, won't we, Giacomo? . . . I'll come too, would you like that? . . . Then you'll see when you return properly educated, trained, how you'll be the envy of all! . . . Margherita you'll see too, how proud you'll be of my little god-daughter! . . .' Then the child bowed her head, dried her eyes, and said to her mother, now serious and composed again as usual. 'Don't worry, mother dear, we'll write to each other every day, we'll see each other soon . . . You see how reasonable I am? . . .' An adorable daughter! Fine blood of the Viceroys!

Then the Cavaliere Don Eugenio left for Palermo too. The reason for this departure was not very clear. The cavaliere had said that some great families of Palermo had invited him to join them in some new, large-scale speculations that would earn a lot of money in a short time. But evil tongues, which are never silent, hinted that he had run away because, having spent the money obtained from the sulphur company on credit by I.O.U.'s which he could no longer pay, he was in danger of getting into very deep water. Whatever the reasons, the fact is that after all these left, peace reigned in the family once more.

Cousin Graziella, always affectionate, came morning, noon and night to keep the princess company and lend her a hand, and Donna Margherita was most grateful for so much attention. Other relations also came, no longer as bitter as before. They would complain, it's true, every now and again; Don Blasco, for example, at the suppression of the monasteries announced in the programme for the new parliament, or Donna Lucrezia against her husband and all liberals; but nothing very positive. The prince, for his part, looked after his affairs without tiring himself too much on them and without those former interminable sittings with Signor Marco.

One day, on the 31st December 1865 to be exact, Baldassarre hurried to answer a call by his master, who was in his study with the notary.

'Take the notary to Signor Marco and hand him this letter,' the master said to him.

'Excellency,' replied Baldassarre, 'he went out half an hour ago.'

'Good; then put the letter on his table. If you, notary, would be so good as to wait a little . . . Go and get a piece of cardboard with "To Let" written on it like the signs for shops; there must be some down in the storeroom. And hang it out on the balcony of Signor Marco's sitting-room.'

Baldassarre, in spite of his habitual passive obedience, stood there a moment staring.

'A "To Let" sign on the sitting-room balcony, d'you understand?' repeated his master, who did not like having to say things twice.

'At once, Excellency.'

The major-domo rushed off to fetch the board, ran up the stairs to the offices four at a time, entered Signor Marco's little rooms and, leaving the note on the table, opened the window and began to attach the 'To Let' sign. He had no very clear idea what this order meant, or what was happening, but he felt worried. Just as he had finished tying up the board, down in the street appeared Signor Marco. He stopped a second to look up, then began to gesticulate and ask the butler what the devil he was doing. Baldassarre answered by pointing at their master's windows to show he was obeying orders. Suddenly Signor Marco broke into a run, and arrived a few minutes later, pale and panting.

'What are you doing? Why " To Let "? Who the devil told you to . . .?'

'The prince, the Signor Prince . . . there's a letter too . . . there, on the table.'

When Signor Marco read the note, his hands and his lips began trembling as if he were about to have a stroke. Baldassarre, alarmed, drew back a little, ready to call for help. Then, tearing the paper with some difficulty, the other shouted with a break in his voice.

'Me . . . Dismissal? . . . Like a scullion? The end of the month? Dirty thief! Pig of a prince!'

'Don Marco! . . .' stuttered Baldassarre in terror.

'Dismissal? . . . Me to hand over to the notary? . . . Does he think I wanted to take some of his money? . . . All the money he's stolen from his brothers and sisters? Or his papers? The proofs of his thefts? Of his deceit? Thief, thief, thief! The more pig I for having helped him! Now he's sending me packing as he's no one else to fleece . . .'

With hands to head, Baldassarre was begging, 'Don Marco! . . . Signor Marco! . . . Please! . . . They can hear you!' But the other, quite beside himself, trembling with rage, was spewing out all he had in him against his master and the whole brood.

'Ten years! . . . ten years of trying to rob his relations! Those other crafty mad rogues! He couldn't eat, drink or sleep for studying how to snare them, playing the moralist, pretending affection, respect for his mother's wishes; more Jesuitical than that Saint Ignatius of a Prior, dirtier than that other swine Don Blasco! D'you think people don't know what a pig he is, with his mistress in the house now he's no one else to rob, with his mistress under his wife's eyes, under his daughter's eyes too till the other day.'

'Don Marco!' cried Baldassarre, now at last driven to threats too, in an attempt to stop this flow of vituperation which no begging gestures and show of alarm had been able to stop. And Signor Marco looked at him, almost out of his mind, as if just noticing his presence.

375

'I'm amazed at you!' went on the major-domo firmly and coldly. 'Will you stop now once and for all!'

Then the other gave a bitter sneer.

'Be quiet, you! Taking your brother's side, are you, you bastard?'

At that moment appeared the notary from the prince's apartments.

'Signor Marco . . .' but the other did not let him say a word.

'You've come for the hand-over, have you?' he began booming again. 'What d'you want handed over? Your master's false papers? The extorted deeds, the forced transactions? Here they are, take 'em!' and he began to fling in the air all he found in the desk, on the shelves. 'Are you afraid I'll take them away? I don't need them. Everyone knows what a cheat, thief and forger your prince is! You know he robbed his sister the nun and the convent by that quibble about royal approval, and his mad sister by consenting to her marriage, and the Booby because he's a booby, and the young count by backing him during those other scandalous goings-on! . . . You yourself know better than I all the plots he laid, those old I.O.U.'s paid off by the mother and repaid twice over, first by the legatees, then by the co-heir; and the presumed debts; the extorted power-of-attorney . . .'

'Please, Signor Marco . . . control yourself!'

'Control myself! I'm quite under control, I assure you! Or d'you think I'm sorry to lose my job? . . . I'll find another, don't doubt that! . . . I'll be treated better anywhere than by these harlequins and false princes here . . . Or maybe they're afraid I've been stealing from them, eh? . . . That I've enriched myself at their expense? . . . That swine of a monk said so once; d'you think I wasn't told? . . . I who had to pay up out of my own pocket? For if they found themselves one cent out, they'd complain a whole month . . . A truly munificent family to set up a nest in!' and, flinging open cupboards and drawers, he went on, 'Here! Take it all, I'll hand you over the lot! Come and look under the bed to see if the pot's still there! . . . Search me in case I'm taking anything away . . . Here, catch these; they're the keys of the cupboards and chests. Tell him to . . .' and he dropped them on the floor. Suddenly he noticed in the open cupboard, hanging on a brass hook, the key of the princess's

376

catafalque, except for snuff-boxes, the only legacy from his defunct mistress after nearly thirty years of service. In a second he seized it and flung it against the wall.

'Take this with the rest!' he shouted with a swear word strong enough to make the dead woman blush down in the Capuchin catacombs.

# 6

ALONG dusty roads, under a fiery sky, drove endless rows of carts crammed with household goods. Wheels squeaked, bells tinkled, and carters sitting on shafts or crouching on top of loads would turn their heads every now and again if a more frequent clatter or livelier tinkle announced a carriage passing. Then the row of carts moved right over to the side of the road, and the carriage passed amid clouds of dust and cracking whips while at the windows appeared terrified faces of refugees.

' The scourge of God! . . . Punishment for our sins! . . . More than ten years we've been left in peace! . . . Those murderers in the Government!' The poor followed on foot, drawing hand-carts with a few thin palliasses and one or two broken-down chairs; and in short halts to regain breath and dry the sweat pouring down their grimy foreheads, they exchanged comments on the cholera, its origins, the universal flight emptying the city.

Most believed in evil spells or poison spread by orders of the authorities, and would rail against the ' Italians ' who spread such poisons as much as the Bourbons. In '60, the patriots had hinted that there would be no more cholera, since King Victor Emmanuel was no enemy of the people like King Ferdinand. And now here it was starting all over again! Then what was the use of a revolution? Just to have pieces of dirty paper in circulation instead of the fine gold and silver coins which were at least a pleasure to eye and ear under the other Government? Or to pay income tax and death duties, unheard-of diabolic inventions of the new Parliamentary thieves? To say nothing of conscription, the flower of youth torn from their families, dying in war, although Sicily had always been exempted by ancient privilege

378

from military tribute? Were these then all the advantages brought by a united Italy? And the most discontented and enraged cried, 'How right the Palermitans were to take to their rifles . . .' But the Palermo revolt had been defeated. In fact, according to the few with no belief in poisoning, it was thence the pestilence came, borne by soldiers hurriedly brought in to pacify the rebellious city . . .

And on heaps of stones by the roadsides, in narrow shadows thrown by walls from whose tops sprouted the spiky crests of prickly pears, refugees sat and discussed these matters, while past them filed carriages, carts, and pedestrians who were not yet tired out.

The poorest of these had loaded all their things on donkeys, and men, women and children followed the slow patient beasts on foot with bundles of rags on their heads or under their arms or thrust on sticks. Acquaintances would stop each other, strangers exchange news and comments with the solidarity of danger in common misery. The womenfolk repeated what they had heard said by priests: cholera was a punishment for the sinful times. Had the excommunicated not warred on the Pope? Was the Church not persecuted? And, to fill the measure, now came a law despoiling convents and monasteries! The end of the world! The year of calamity! Who would ever have thought it! So many poor monks flung into the middle of the street? Holy places desecrated? Where would it all end?

All nonsense, judged the menfolk on the other hand, 'The monks had been spoilt and done nothing! Except eat! If monastery walls could speak they would have some fine tales to tell. It was high time their frolics were put an end to! The one good thing this government has done! . . .' But think of all the saintly Fathers—and there were some—forced to live on a lira a day! The Benedictines, for instance, would be hard put to make do on a lira a day, after having led the life of kings! 'Ah yes, but what about the splitting up of the monastery funds, eh?'

News of this had been circulating for some time and people gave details as if they had been present themselves; savings made during recent years, in expectation of the law, had been distributed variously all round; every monk had drawn no less than four thousand *onze* in gold and silver coin. Then they had

379

divided up the table silver and all other valuables and, when the moment to leave drew near, sold the vast quantities of provisions accumulated in the storerooms: big barrels of wine, huge jars of oil, great sacks of corn and vegetables. So much the more money in their pockets—and even so the storerooms still seemed full! 'They'd done right! Why should they leave cash as well to those Government thieves?'

And the little caravans would start off on their march again, heads whirling at the thought of the millions of *onze* that would go into Victor Emmanuel's pocket from selling the contents of San Nicola and all the other communities. Many beggars took advantage of the great mass of people surging by, stretching out hands from heaps of stones on which they were lying. Ragged children with them ran behind carriages in case some passenger dropped a coin into the dusty road. Those on foot recognised fleeing nobles, repeated their names, horror-struck at the emptying town. 'The Prince of Roccasciano! The Duchess Radalì! The Cùrcuma! The Grazzeri! There won't be one left! . . .'

Towards evening, when the heat of the day lessened, three big family coaches, one behind the other, raised great clouds of dust on the road from Catania to the Belvedere. In the first was the Prince of Francalanza, Donna Ferdinanda and Cousin Graziella, the latter invited to the family villa as she could not be alone at La Zafferana. The young prince Consalvo was on the box. He was brandishing a whip triumphantly though still wearing a Benedictine habit, as his father had decided to bring him home at the very last moment when the monks were dispersed; Don Blasco and the Prior had also asked for hospitality at the palace. In the second carriage was the princess, without anyone sitting beside or opposite, just her maid in a far corner. Contact with a shoulder would have given her convulsions, so she had declared herself only too pleased for the prince to travel with his cousin. But the other carriage was crammed; there was the marchese and Chiara, Rosa with baby, and finally Don Blasco. The latter had refused the prince's hospitality in the country and accepted the marchese's, so as to avoid his sister Ferdinanda. His aversion did not cede to the danger of cholera and made him prefer even the little bastard's company.

The Prior, on the other hand, had stayed in town at the episcopal palace, where Monsignor the Bishop had received him with open arms. All his relations' begging and invitations had been unable to make him take flight; his place, he said, was by the beds of the sick, with Monsignor. The one to insist most had been the prince, who maintained, as always, that in grave and solemn moments the family should keep together, so he was sorry to leave one of his relations in the midst of danger. What would people say? That he thought of nothing but himself? . . . But just as he had not succeeded in moving the Prior, so he had also failed with Ferdinando, who, having acquired a taste for town life, would not hear of taking refuge even at Pietra dell'Ovo. Lucrezia had already left for the Belvedere that morning with her husband, father-in-law and mother-in-law. As for their uncle, the duke, he was in Florence near his niece Teresina, and since the cholera did not rage there or terrify people as much as in Sicily he was quite serene. To the Cavaliere Eugenio, still in Palermo, no one gave a thought.

At the Belvedere began again the gay country life of autumn, so much so that the alarm spread by the first news of the pestilence soon seemed unjustified; in the city there had been a suspected case now and again. The young prince, having finally doffed his habit for clothes like everyone else's, began tasting the enjoyments which he had yearned for. First of all he went shooting with a real gun on Mounts Elce and Urna, exterminating rabbits, hares, partridges and even sparrows, if he found nothing else. Then every day he had horses harnessed to learn driving, and soon his gig became the terror of those on country roads, always running into carts and carriages, rushing at full tilt to pass all other vehicles, at the risk of overturning, crashing or killing someone. When not driving he would be in the stables watching horses being groomed and learning the special language of coachmen, ostlers and farriers, criticising the horses of other nobles who had taken refuge at the Belvedere or near by, or so-and-so's recent purchase, or someone else's carriages. And Donna Ferdinanda, hearing him speak with ever-growing competence on such gentlemanly subjects, would say to him admiringly, ' Those are the things to learn ! . . .'

The princess too, though still sorrowing at Teresina's departure so far away, was proud of her son's progress; Graziella, even prouder, was prodigal of caresses to the boy, though Consalvo never replied with equal effusion but did his best to avoid her. He had not forgiven her for opposing his return to the paternal roof earlier, and now on seeing her as much at home there as one of the family and taking his mother's place, his antipathy grew. Donna Graziella really was behaving more as mistress of the house than as guest, particularly in the evenings when there was company and she did the honours of the house, all the more if the princess felt indisposed. And this often happened. Without having any definite illness Donna Margherita, after her daughter's departure, felt a bout of dim malaise coming over her, headaches, and difficulties in digesting. And, glad to avoid a crowd, infectious contact, contagious handshakes, she would go off to bed leaving her guests in the drawing-room conversing animatedly, gambling and playing charades. Leaving the Giulente villa, Lucrezia was now helping her cousin in running the house. She who at home never even put a finger into fresh water came to lend a hand from pride at having a place again in the home of her brother the prince.

Chiara was busy spoiling the little bastard, fussing over him much more than did the marchese, who always felt uncomfortable and ashamed at recognising his parenthood publicly, while his wife almost gloried in it. If the princess or Donna Ferdinanda or some other relation did not put themselves out to be nice to the baby, Chiara would look offended and might even not set foot in the villa for a week if she got it into her head that anyone was criticising her adoption of the child.

Vice versa, she was now of one mind with her uncle Blasco, who, as he was staying with her, implicitly approved.

At the news of the law for suppressing monasteries, the monk, during his last period in the cloister and first months at his nephew's, had been frenzied, like a devil loosed from hell. The newly coined swear-words, curses, imprecations against the Government that he spat out at San Nicola, the palace, the Cigar-woman's, in pro-Bourbon chemists and even in the streets, were beyond counting; his vituperations against his brother the Deputy, who had voted for the law, were far more violent than anything else that had ever come from his mouth.

As if this monstrosity were too big, too stunning, he soon reduced himself to fuming silence, from which he was roused only by rumours repeated in his presence about the division of the monastery's savings and the four thousand *onze* due to each monk. Then he would begin thundering, ' Division, my foot! Due, my backside! Not a sausage is there for distribution. And if there were, no one would touch it! Us become accomplices of those thieves? Of that refuse of the galleys? Of those out-and-out brigands?'

So he spoke before strangers, people of no consequence, and servants; in the family, among intimates, he would admit the division but reduce his own share to a few hundred *onze*, a couple of spoons and a pair of sheets, just enough to avoid destitution. He had come away from San Nicola with two chests, the keys of which he never let out of his possession. The prince in town had glanced them over as if weighing and judging them, with a new respect for this uncle, who now owned something; but all efforts to get a look inside the chests had been in vain, as the monk bolted himself into his room every time he rooted about in them.

At the Belvedere, even Chiara and Federico often talked to each other of all this money that Don Blasco must now have. The marchese, fearing its being wasted on the Cigar-woman, would have suggested means of making it secure, of using it to get income, had the monk been anyone else, had Don Blasco not attacked him every half-year when his dividends fell due, and, nagged and prophesied the shares' collapse. The inflation, the war, the cholera, every public calamity, had been causes of jubilation for the monk, who would rub his hands together every time and shout to his nephew, ' Goodbye to your dirty paper! It's done for, your Government is! You wouldn't listen to me; all right! . . .' But the marchese always drew his dividends to the very last cent on the day arranged. When the danger of cholera had stopped entirely, one day he went down into town on business and also to draw his half-yearly payment. On his return to the Belvedere, when taking his walk on the terrace after dinner, as Chiara played with the little bastard, he mentioned to his uncle what he had done that day.

' I drew my money from the coupons too . . . Now they pay

in advance, because of the exchange. If I sent them to Paris I'd draw as many Napoleons again . . . I've ordered another lot of shares. We'll take them with a number of friends . . . as today there's no other way of laying out money . . .'

He wanted to insist on what a good chance this was, but fell silent as Don Blasco suddenly stopped and stared at him hard, as if about to burst:

'Can you let me have ten thousand lire's worth?'

At first the marchese thought he had not heard properly.

'Let you have . . . How d'you mean? For Your Excellency?'

'I'm asking if you can sell me ten thousand lire of shares, d'you understand or don't you?'

'But I think . . . of course . . . ten thousand lire of capital you mean . . . Yes, Excellency, I can write another letter at once, to make quite sure, if Your Excellency wishes.'

'When will you write?'

'Tomorrow.'

'And will they come at once?'

'By return of post.'

The monk turned his back and walked off a little, then returned, planted himself there in front of him again and went on:

'Listen, while you're at it, ask for twenty thousand lire's worth.'

'Yes, Excellency, however many Your Excellency likes . . .'

As soon as he was alone the marchese rushed off to his wife and said, agasp with amazement:

'D'you know what? . . . d'you know what? . . . Uncle wants to buy shares!—twenty thousand lire's worth of shares! He's commissioned me! I can scarcely believe it! I must be dreaming.'

Chiara replied calmly, with a little shake of the shoulders:

'Why are you so amazed? Don't you know my family's all mad?'

Once again, in whispers behind each other's backs, the Uzeda were all calling each other mad. Was not Chiara mad for treating her maid like a sister and the girl's bastard like her own son? Wasn't Lucrezia mad for maltreating that poor devil Benedetto in every way? And what about Donna Ferdinanda, who, with no advantage to herself, interfered in the affairs of the whole family? And what was to be said of the prince, who, after having forgotten his cousin Graziella for so many years, now linked himself to her right under his son's eyes. Perhaps that was the reason which made Graziella more and more antipathetic to Consalvo. He contradicted her on everything, in front of other people. He avoided remaining alone in her company, and affected to treat her like an intruder when servants mentioned her. This, though, was the only feeling he showed, for he was at home as little as possible, rode out on horseback when he was not driving his carriage, straddled every peasant's donkey, and held converse with every carter. The cook, from the kitchen window, whence the gardens were in sight to the end of the olive groves, would see him going after women collecting bundles of old vine-twigs. One afternoon the factor nearly caught him in the hayloft with the wife of a farmer, Rosario Farsatore. He did not seem in the least put out, and when the matter came to Donna Ferdinanda's ears it raised him in the old spinster's esteem. The prince pretended to know nothing; he seemed to have decided to let his son run wild a bit, as if to make up for the last years of enclosure in San Nicola.

'What about Fra' Carmelo?' Donna Ferdinanda or the princess, or Lucrezia would ask every now and again. 'What news of him?' But the young prince neither knew nor bothered to find out what had happened to his former protector. At San Nicola, while he gnawed at the bit and awaited the suppression law as his only salvation, it had amused him to torment Fra' Carmelo by predicting the disbandment of the monks and the closing of the monastery, but the other used to shake his head and smile incredulously, not understanding how any monks could believe such a thing. 'Send them away? Sell the estates? Words, gossip, today as before! Who would dare to? What about the Pope's excommunication? The Catholic powers? The reaction of the whole of Christendom? . . .' And nothing could shake his security, neither the news in the papers, nor the preparations for evacuation, nor the novices' departure. After that Consalvo had no more news of him.

One morning, at the Belvedere, while the family was rising from table after luncheon, Baldassarre came and announced:

'Excellency, Fra' Carmelo is here.'

'Fra' Carmelo?'

No-one recognised in the figure advancing towards the prince with arms raised, the lay-brother of the fat pink and white face, jovial air and round tummy.

' They've thrown me out . . . they've thrown me out . . .'

In a few months he had lost half his weight, and in his yellow flabby face his eyes which had once been laughing, now had a strange expression of disquiet, almost of fear.

' Excellency, they've thrown me out! Excellency, they've thrown me out! . . .' and he looked at all the gentlemen, at all the ladies, as if trying to arouse reaction to the horror of it.

' So it was true! Is there nothing to be done about it? You who've power . . . You let those rascals rob St Nicolas, St Benedict, all the saints in paradise . . .'

' What can we do about it? . . .' exclaimed Consalvo, rubbing his hands. And Donna Ferdinanda added :

' You wanted a Liberal government, didn't you? Now enjoy its fruits!'

' Me? . . . Me, Excellency? . . . As if I knew a thing about Liberals or non-Liberals! . . . I minded my own business! . . . Sixty years I was in there! . . . No-one had dared touch it in all the revolutions I'd seen, '37, '48, '60 . . .'

' A fine trio of lottery numbers!' exclaimed the young prince, and as Baldassarre had come to tell him his gig was harnessed, he got up, exclaiming under the lay-brother's nose :

' Now there's the law, my good man . . .'

' But is it a just law? The property of the Church? . . . Can I come into Your Excellency's house and take anything I like? Can a law be made like that? . . .' and he began a confused account of what had happened at the actual spoliation . . . ' That delegate, for the hand-over . . . The Abbot refused to be present, and he was right; a shameful thing like that! The man went and slept in His Paternity's bed, the rascal; beyond belief . . . The Prior came and gave him all the keys, Excellency; of the church, the sacristy, the storerooms, the museum, the library . . . everything has been sold at public auction; tables, chairs, plates, wool, wine, beds, as if they were no-one's . . . And the candlesticks in the choir, that robber thought they were of gold and took them away by night! They tied 'im up, those others, even bigger robbers than he! Now there's nothing left!

. . . Just walls! They've thrown me out! . . . they've thrown me out! . . .'

The princess tried to comfort him with gentle words; the prince offered him a drink; but he refused and began going over the same story again, getting more confused than before. Then he went off to the marchese's villa, to Don Blasco, and began once more:

'They've thrown me out . . . and Your Paternity's doing nothing? . . . Your nephew, the Prior? Monsignor the Bishop? . . . Why don't they write to Rome? . . . Must it end like this?'

Don Blasco, who had drawn his dividends the day before, boomed:

'How do you expect it to end? When I yelled at those ruffians, "Mind your own business! Don't play with fire! You'll pay for it! . . ." they called me mad, didn't they? And they just hid their heads in the sand, the fools did, saying the Government wouldn't touch them or would give them a good pension if it did. And what about those companions of yours playing the revolutionary? That pig Fra' Cola, for instance, distributing bulletins to the novices? That other twister, my nephew, making up to Bixio and to Garibaldi? That clumsy fool the Abbot scratching his mangy pate, not knowing what to do, like a chick in stubble? . . . Now what d'you expect? . . . You've been your own enemies . . . The Government is a thief, and had to do its thief's job; why's that a surprise? The fault is with those blockheads who helped it on and suggested, "Come along and rob me!" and even opened up the doors . . . Didn't they once tell me they wanted some liberty? Well, they've got it now! The lot . . . No one'll stop 'em! . . .'

'And they've thrown me out! They've thrown me out! . . .'

When the Uzeda family returned to town at the beginning of the New Year 1862, a letter from the duke to Benedetto announced that the Chamber of Deputies would soon be dissolved. This time he did not even trouble to come, but charged his friends with working for him. Business affairs prevented him from leaving Florence, and these affairs, after all, were actually more the electors' than his own. So votes should go to him as the city's natural, legitimate representative; it was absurd to think of anyone trying to oppose him. As for rendering any account of how he had exercised his office, explaining his own political convictions or studying the needs or listening to the wishes of his electorate, an exchange of letters with Giulente, uncle and nephew, with some others of importance, was enough.

The usual malcontents began making their silly accusations again, trying to dig up old stories. The republicans, the left, blamed the duke for his servility to the Government, and tried to put up a nominee of their own, but they met strong resistance on all sides and had to beat a retreat. A satirical little weekly rag called the *Ficcanaso* (or Nosey-parker) made people laugh by saying that the Honourable Member Oragua had done as much in the Chamber as Charles in France without ever opening his mouth, but the paper *Pensiero italiano*, successor to *Italia risorta*, declared that the country had too many talkers, and preferred responsible citizens who voted without listening to any other voice but that of their own conscience. It never named the duke without calling him the 'eminent Patriot', the 'distinguished patrician', the 'illustrious Deputy'. At the proclamation of the dissolving of the Chamber it began a panegyric of him.

Among the many merits of the 'conspicuous Citizen', not the least was that of having played a large part in the institution of the Southern Bank of Credit, and Don Lorenzo Giulente, in his director's office, would recommend the duke's election to those who came to draw money. 'There's no need to remind you . . .'

But in view of the indications of opposition, the Deputy's friends wanted to achieve a shattering victory; in fact they put together almost three hundred votes. The duke, in gratitude, arranged for a heavy fall of Orders of St Maurice and St Lazarus on his constituency. Benedetto was among the first to get one, and was certainly pleased, although already a 'cavaliere' by birth. But from the day of its announcement his wife gave him no respite. 'Cavaliere! . . . Listen, Cavaliere! . . . What are you doing, Cavaliere? Cavaliere, shall we go out? . . .' she would say either alone with him or before strangers, in season and out of season. And if there were others there she would invariably add, 'Now, you know . . . my husband's a cavaliere, yes, sir! A knight without a horse . . .'

388

The real origin of the harshness with which she had treated him for some time was the conviction now firmly fixed in her mind that he was not noble enough for her. Little by little, day by day, she realised that her relatives had been right in denigrating the Giulente; and forgetting her accusations against the prince, she made peace with him, making the first move herself lest it be said that the Uzeda refused to have anything to do with her. And the more submissive Benedetto was to her, the more she felt that she had granted him a special grace in marrying him. The Liberal opinions which she had once admired now exasperated her as proof of his vulgarity. Pure nobles were all Bourbonists; her uncle the duke and one or two others only played the Liberal as a speculation. If her husband's patriotism had brought him great honour or lots of money it wouldn't have been so bad, but those down-and-out's principles of his, aired with no constructive profit, showed up both Benedetto's low origin and his stupidity. Now, to boast of an Order like that, of a title of cavaliere that was given to absolute nobodies, really showed him up as descendant of petty attorneys! Benedetto laughed about this a little, but it hurt him, and once when they were alone he said to her:

'You might drop this joke.'

'Joke? What joke? They made you a cavaliere, have they or haven't they? Is that true or not?'

And to boast of her severity, not content with making him look a fool by calling him that, she would say before Donna Ferdinanda or Don Blasco:

'Anyway he needs no Order! He's already nature's cavaliere!'

But the odd thing was that Donna Ferdinanda would not listen to her now, in fact sided quite openly with Benedetto, who was being useful to her just then because of the famous law on compulsory inflation. As years went by the more her hoard increased the meaner she became; now she lent her money at thirty or forty per cent, and called a thief any poor devil who was a day or two late in payment. Now she refused to have anything to do with 'dirty paper', as she called banknotes, and recognised no other money but old Sicilian coin. If her clients, when debts fell due, came to pay interest in paper, she refused to renew the loan, demanded her capital back at once, and got her nephew *the lawyer* to suggest ways of eluding the law and obliging people to pay in silver coin . . .

As for Don Blasco, he too had other things to worry about, and the Giulente were beginning to enter his good graces. On returning from the country he had taken a small apartment by the Trinità, to be free and near the Cigar-woman just as when at San Nicola; but he now needed to furnish his little home. And spitting curses against the 'Piedmontese' who had flung him into the streets with a pittance of a lira and a half a day, he asked each of his relations for a piece of furniture; a sofa from the prince, a pair of armchairs from the marchese, a wardrobe from Benedetto. Having bought some lengths of linen, he distributed it round his relatives for them to have it sewn up; once it was sewn, he asked for some embroidery to be added. And everyone made it a duty to please him, even rivalling each other in rendering him those services and ingratiating themselves, now that he too had a little nest-egg of his own. Exactly how much he had no one knew, but when the first half-year for his shares fell due and he found that the coupons were paid punctually—in paper, it's true, but paper as valid as money—he told the marchese to buy him another ten thousand lire's worth. And while shouting against the thieving Government, he kept its share certificates under his pillow.

At the beginning of summer, although the Chamber was still sitting, the duke arrived. The usual demonstrations by friends and admirers began again. He pontificated more solemnly than ever and commented on the work of Parliament. The suppression of religious houses was the greatest fact of modern times; he enumerated and illustrated its immense advantages. Before all else the estates brought under direct cultivation would redouble and improve their products ' to the advantage of agriculture, industry and commerce, chief source of social riches'. In the second place, all, even those with no capital, could own land by being assigned small allotments to be paid for with produce. Finally the Government, with the proceeds of the sale, would reduce taxes ' to the relief of public and private finance'. It was like another 'agrarian law'; he cited the Romans, Servius Tullius. And those who did not understand clapped all the same in expectation of the Golden Age.

Meanwhile he was preparing to buy up some of the sequestrated land—some said in fact that was why he had come—and he advised the prince, Benedetto, and the marchese to do likewise. When Don Blasco heard of this, he went blind with rage.

' The goods of the Church to this family of unbelievers and damned? So you're holding the sack open for the thieves, are you? Aren't you afraid of the after-life? It's no surprise that swindler '—that was now his only name for his brother the Deputy—' doing such a thing after he'd voted for the theft. The first shall be last and not even can the Lord God Himself save him from eternal fire! But what about you others? Woe to you! Fire and brimstone be on your heads! Burning souls!'

Donna Ferdinanda on her part was all against it from religious reasons, and she too threatened the buyers of Church lands with infernal punishment. The princess, whose health was worsening, supported her aunt, and one day the Prior came to the palace on purpose to warn his relations against such purchases in language of evangelical persuasion.

' Do not let yourself be drawn into temptation. They will tell you that it's a propitious occasion to make material gains, but the health of the soul is the highest of goods. The Lord will compensate you in another way and give you elsewhere what you are renouncing now . . .'

The prince listened to both sides without expressing an opinion of his own. The marchese, though, judged such scruples excessive, and Chiara, so as to follow her husband, refused to listen to her confessor's warnings. Lucrezia on her side urged Benedetto to buy, to enrich himself, for now she considered him not only ignoble but poverty-stricken too; he did not own a single country estate, while the Francalanza had sixteen!

Meanwhile Parliament was discussing another law ' to the advantage of the public and private increment ' as the duke explained, although he did not go to the capital. This concerned the freeing of lay chaplaincies and livings, and very quietly the prince began conferring with his notary and legal adviser, and preparing documentation so as to obtain ownership of all his ancestors' religious foundations, particularly of the chaplaincy of the Sacred Lamp. Then one fine day in came Don Blasco, who had not set foot in the palace for some time.

'Careful, now! If the chaplaincy is freed, its property is divided among all descendants!'

'Your Excellency is mistaken,' replied the prince. 'The property re-enters the primogeniture.'

'Balls! Primogeniture indeed! Where are primogenitures now? They've been abolished for forty years. I've read the deeds myself!'

'But the right of patronage has been in my hands.'

'Patronage? As if you were some private company?'

Don Blasco was now talking like a treaty of jurisprudence.

'It's a simple inheritance *cum onere missarum*; must I explain the Latin to you? Or shall we go back over all your tricks to avoid paying out the legacy to the convent? In short, we must reach an agreement here and now; otherwise I file a suit, and then we'll see what the law says!'

The prince finding himself caught out, felt bile coming back to his throat, and exclaimed:

'Did Your Excellency not forbid us to touch the goods of the Church?'

'Swine!' broke out the monk. 'What has the Church to do with it? Masses will be said as before, in fact better than before! Did you think you could put the whole income into your pocket?'

But before there was time to go deeper into the matter or decide anything, one August evening, as a crowd of guests were watching from the palace the procession of the image of St Agatha, the duke arrived, yellow as a corpse, and announced:

'The cholera! The cholera! Again! ...'

This time it was the real thing; those poisoners had finally hit on the right dose, for before twenty-four hours had passed the germ spread. And once again the country roads were full, day and night, with jostling refugees, and a terror infinitely more contagious than any plague seized the bravest at the announcement of the disease's rapid progress, and urged them up towards the hills, into the Etna woodlands. There with the assurance of immunity, the rent of every shack amounted to a fortune!

The Uzeda arrived at the Belvedere a few hours after the duke's news, he himself in the first carriage, such was his panic.

Once again Cousin Graziella was with her cousins. Her presence had now become all the more necessary as the health worsened of the poor princess, who, perhaps from fear of cholera or from discomfort at the sudden flight, went to bed as soon as she reached the villa. Partly from this, partly from the general gloom produced by hearing of the massacre caused by the epidemic in the town, there were no more receptions, gambling or late nights.

During the day they walked on the estate. Consalvo, Benedetto and one or two others risked going out on the roads, but the prince wanted everyone home by Angelus and had all doors and gates bolted. Don Blasco, at the marchese's villa, prudently kept to his own room and never even went over to quarrel with Giacomo, partly to avoid the company of that 'swindler', the duke. But suddenly one dreadful day consternation fell; cholera had broken out at Belvedere. The maid of some people who had come from town three days before was dying of it; the bell of the Last Sacraments could be heard in streets deserted as those of a dead town.

'We must get away! Let's be off! At once! . . . to Viagrande, to La Zafferana . . .' Lucrezia left at once for Mascalucia with the Giulente. The duke, more dead than alive, would have liked to perch on the peak of Etna to be quite safe, but for the moment the marchese's opinion prevailed, which was that they should all go up to Viagrande, where they were almost sure to find a house to hold the whole family. But someone must go ahead to find one. The duke, longing to get away at once, offered to accompany the prince. Giacomo said to his wife:

'D'you want to come too?'

For some days the princess had been suffering from bad stomach trouble, could no longer digest and dragged herself agonisingly from bed to armchair; and for that very reason all agreed that she must be got to safety before others. So husband and wife left at once with their uncle and Baldassarre. The others stayed to load the carts of luggage, for this time, as they were not going to their own house, beds, linen and objects of daily use had to be taken. That night the major-domo returned to tell them that lodgings had been found, and next day at dawn they all rushed away from the Belvedere, where cholera was already raging. The house at Viagrande had been found

393

thanks to the Prince of Francalanza's money and connections. Even so it was a bug-run of three fair-sized rooms and two tiny ones all on the ground floor, the poor home of a cooper, where the ' Viceroys ' were only too glad to be able to roost. Thanks to the Uzeda name they were allowed entry into the village, though coming from an infected part, but once there, the prince, the duke and Don Blasco began shouting that no one else must be let in, or it would mean the ruin of Viagrande.

In fact not only had the epidemic decimated the population which had stayed in town, where as many as three hundred deaths a day could be counted and there was no longer any civil organisation, powers, deputies, counsellors or anything; but it was now beginning to spread for the first time with extraordinary violence through the Etna woodlands, which had till now escaped all other cholera epidemics. It was at the Belvedere, it was at San Gregorio, at Gravina, at La Punta, it was reaching scattered houses, did not spare cottages right out in the country; and not only the poor died, but people of property too, gentry who took every kind of precaution. So terrified crowds were fleeing from one hamlet to the next as best they could, on carts, on horseback, on foot. Anyone with the germ of the disease on them fell by the roadside, writhed in the dust and died like a dog; the unburied corpses, under the torrid summer sun, exuded pestilential smells, making the horror all the worse. Fugitives who arrived safe and sound in places still immune were greeted by shots from the terrified peasantry, lest they succeeded in finding a refuge and gave the disease to the healthy.

Drought made those conditions even more desperate; all cisterns were dry, nothing could be washed, there was scarcely enough water to relieve thirst. At Viagrande the prince paid a lira for every jug of water; and the princess might have been a well she wasted so much, washing herself every hour in those rooms with greasy floors and walls and bedaubed doors, the very sight of which gave her the shivers; and she was devoured by thirst. Her intestinal pains never left her. At times she seemed to have cholera cramps, so that the duke in terror thought of escaping farther off. But his fear was misplaced; those pains, that tendency to vomit, the princess had been suffering from for more than a year, not with the same intensity as she did now, it was true, but with the same symptoms. The prince, when reassuring his uncle, showed other fears.

'Margherita would never let me call a doctor . . . but I'm very much afraid . . . I'm told she may have cancer of the stomach . . .'

But the duke was not listening. Just now he had his own skin to think of, for cholera might break out any moment at Via-grande; in fact there had already been some scares.

'Let's go! . . .' he insisted, 'let's go farther off, to Milo, to Cassone, on the mountainside . . .' and when finally the first sure case appeared in the village, while all repeated, 'Let's go . . . get farther away . . .' terror gave him diarrhoea.

This time the difficulties in finding a house were much greater. The duke went to look for one around Milo. The prince made ready to leave for Cassone.

'D'you want to come too?' he repeated to his wife.

She had spent a ghastly sleepless night, tormented by nausea and vomiting, and had just managed to dress, pale and haggard, when Chiara said:

'No, leave her . . . she'll come when you find the house . . .'

Even the servants said it was not wise to expose her to the discomforts of a search, and that it would be much better for her to leave when they knew where she was going. But Cousin Graziella, hearing that cases of cholera were multiplying rapidly in the village, was of a contrary opinion.

'I say, take her off at once . . . in her condition she might well have less resistance to contagion . . . Giacomo is bound to find some sort of house . . .'

Donna Ferdinanda was also of this opinion, but Consalvo, holding his mother close, whispered to her:

'No, don't go yet . . . it's better here . . . we'll all go later . . .'

She caressed the boy with her thin cold hand, and glanced timidly at her husband, waiting for him to decide.

'D'you want to come or don't you?' he asked her curtly, in the tone he adopted when decisions began to irk him; and the question, which had a literal meaning to everyone else, took on another meaning for the princess, who understood his intentions and gestures and divined what he implied.

'No, I'll go with you . . .'

395

Just as she was about to set off, the young prince said insistently:

'Mother, stay here . . . or take me with you,' and the lad, ordinarily so gay and thoughtless, now showed a kind of frightened disquiet.

'There's not room for everyone!' cried the prince brusquely. The princess hugged her son and said to him:

'Stay here . . . Stay here . . . we'll all be together tomorrow . . .'

She got into the carriage next to her husband, holding a piece of camphor to her nose, Baldassarre mounted the box and the carriage left.

Till nightfall there was no news. At ten o'clock arrived an express message from the duke at Milo, telling them that he had found a hut up there in which there was only just room for himself; so that left them free to join Giacomo.

At Viagrande meanwhile there was growing frenzy as panic became contagious. They were already beginning to accuse Giacomo of having forgotten them like that egotist the duke. Don Blasco was talking of getting on a horse or a donkey and going off anywhere, when at dawn next day arrived Baldassarre, pale, overwhelmed and trembling.

'Excellency! . . . Excellency! . . . The mistress, the princess! . . . Caught cholera! . . . Died in three hours! . . .'

# 7

AT THE prince's wedding to Cousin Graziella, celebrated three
months after the epidemic ceased, only relatives and a few
intimates were invited; the widower was still in mourning and
the bustle of a reception would have been inappropriate. Anyway, as the prince himself explained, the marriage was one of
simple convenience; both he and the bride had many an autumn
on their shoulders and were linking their destinies without
youthful fancies and only in order to be able to ensure each
other mutual help. Cousin Graziella needed a man to look after
her interests and give her back a position in society, the prince
was finding a new mother for his children. That union, foreseen
by some since the princess's bad health had made her life uncertain, was expected daily after her sudden death hastened on
by cholera, and it aroused almost universal approval. The confessor, the Vicar-General, all priests frequenting the house
thought it proper and provident. Preparations for the nuptial
ceremony were modest not only because bride and groom were
both in mourning; there was scarcely a family not in mourning
for some dear one after that fearful epidemic. Benedetto Giulente
had lost father and mother in one day, at Mascalucia; the
Princess of Roccasciano had been widowed and the Duchess
Radalì lost an uncle, the Cavaliere Giovanni Artuso. But this
had not caused very great sorrow as the cavaliere was rich and
childless, and had left his whole fortune to the Radalì family;
the income to the duchess and the property to Giovannino, his
godson. The mother was perhaps a trifle sorry that the inheritance had not gone to her eldest son, for whom she had sacrificed
her life. The suppression of monasteries had already upset her

plans, as Giovannino could no longer be professed and had returned to the lay world; now this inheritance evened the two brothers' situation, that is diminished that of the elder. She loved them both, but for the duke she also felt a kind of instinctive respect as head of the family, as heir and successor to his father's name and honours. And so the closing of the monasteries and her uncle's error did not upset her plans, as long as Giovannino remained unmarried. She was working to this end, letting the young man free to gad in his own way, encouraging all his tastes for shooting, horses and all pastimes, so that he should feel no temptation to change his life.

That Donna Graziella would act as mother to the prince's children was of course beyond all doubt. Baldassarre had mentioned to his dependants, who were repeating them everywhere, details of letters exchanged between the bride and the young princess. The girl had heard in Florence of her mother's death. What sobs! What convulsions! The headmistress had been at her wit's end to know what to do. Poor girl, how right she was! Alone, far from home, unable even to give her a last embrace! Mama! Poor Mama! They were really worth reading, those letters, for the young ladies at the Convent of the Holy Annunciation received what was called a ' comi fo ' education, and the young princess was clever and studious and always getting first prizes.

But eventually, when her godmother sent her dead mother's prayer-book, rosary and a lock of her hair, with a promise that the prince would have her home as soon as possible and a hint that she should write him no more of such harrowing letters in his affliction, poor thing, then the young princess gradually calmed down. 'You are right, dear godmother. I was forgetting my poor father's sorrow and thinking too much of my own, and that's not just . . .' What were these letters to the prince like? ' Don't torture yourself, dear papa; think, as I do, that mother is in paradise and looking down at us all and watching over us and wanting us to be glad that she is among the blessed and that we shall all be joining her one day, with God's grace . . .' Really amazing for a girl of fourteen to write like that! . . .

The prince then sent her his great news. He was inconsolable for the loss of that saint and would mourn her till the very last

398

day of his life, but his children needed someone to replace her as a mother, and for that reason and that reason alone he was taking the advice of all his relatives who were begging him to remarry; he was therefore wedding the cousin who had given so many proofs of affection during the 'great disaster' and who was the most suitable, being a relation, to carry out the delicate functions of second mother. Cousin Graziella added a postscript of her own under her confessor's dictation. 'Dear daughter, you will understand, from what your father has told you, that henceforward I shall have more right to call you by the name which I have always given you in my heart. My greatest ambition is to soften the loss of your saintly mother, not to make you forget her, which will be impossible not only for you but for us all. Through this even closer link between us I shall always be by your side, to watch over you and your brother as your saintly mother asked on her deathbed. I yearn to hold you close to my heart; if your studies prevent your returning home just yet we ourselves will come and see you shortly . . .'

But it was a long time before any reply came to this letter. What had happened? Had the post been up to its tricks? Or was the Signorina unwell? Or had she, maybe, taken the news of the marriage badly? . . . Baldassarre did all he could to dissipate this last doubt. He was also trying his best to hide from people the young prince's ill-humour, but not succeeding, as from the first announcement of the marriage Consalvo had taken a firm stand against his father and future stepmother.

Naturally, while waiting for the wedding, Cousin Graziella no longer came to the palace now there was no mistress of the house to receive her, but the prince visited her and wanted his son to do so too. Wasted breath; the young prince was deaf in that ear, and when he met his father's future bride at relations' houses would scarcely greet her, reply with mortifying coldness to her effusive 'my son', or even avoid her, showing clearly the aversion with which she inspired him. The prince, to the great and general amazement, seemed not to notice and to have changed character, as if wanting to ingratiate himself with his son. He was generous with money, let him do what he liked, bought him carriages and English horses; but Consalvo was cold with his father too, avoided him, spent weeks at a time in the country shooting, so that gradually the prince's rage mounted. The major-domo, man of peace that he was, noticed this, was pained and tried to get the young prince into a better mood. Consalvo let him have his say; then all of a sudden cut him short with an icy, 'Don't bore me any longer. Look to your own job. And don't bore me . . .' Youth! Youth! One had to be patient with them, let them have their way before they reached an age of judgment! But what about the young princess? Could she possibly turn against her father and stepmother too? A girl so wise, so obedient, brought up at the Holy Annunciation? . . .

After keeping all waiting more than a week, finally the Signorina's reply arrived. 'Dear father, dear mother,' it said: 'I have not written earlier because I have been unwell; nothing of importance, so do not worry. Now, thanks be to God, I can tell you of the great joy with which I learnt of what you are doing for our sakes.' And so on for two pages full of warm expressions, ending with 'your most affectionate and grateful daughter, Teresa.' She also wrote to her brother in the same strain, but the young prince in replying to her never mentioned his stepmother or made any allusion to the coming wedding, as if he had never heard of it.

Two days before the ceremony he went off shooting with Giovannino Radalì and other friends, saying he would be away twenty-four hours, but on the day of the ceremony, when his father and stepmother and their guests went to the Town Hall, he had not got back. He did not even arrive that afternoon when the bride and groom returned from church. Great scandal was in the air, with servants gossiping, dependants on tenterhooks, the bride forcing a smile and Lucrezia repeating every quarter of an hour, 'Where's Consalvo? . . . Why don't you send for him?' in spite of its having been explained again and again that the youth was out in the country.

The prince, rather pale, said that the group of sportsmen must have had an accident, for none of Consalvo's companions had returned and the Duchess Radalì and her son the Duke Michele were sending home every half hour, worried about their Giovannino. Had their boat overturned on the Biviere? Or their carriage upset? Or a gun exploded, God forbid?

Donna Ferdinanda however was calmness itself, well aware that her protégé must have arranged it all to avoid being present at the marriage ceremony; and in her heart she approved. How silly of Giacomo to hint all round that he was getting màrried so as not to leave his children motherless! His children were no longer babes in arms! And then it wasn't as if their mother had ever had great authority over them. The prince had never let her do the least little thing for them. Now, on the other hand, what would be seen? This scandal-mongering cousin acting the mistress at the Francalanza palace!

The old spinster whispered these things into the ears of Chiara and Lucrezia, who repeated them to the marchese, to Don Blasco, and all realised that Giacomo was marrying Graziella only because as a young man he had got it into his head to do so. His mother had been against it and so he had bowed to her iron will. He even seemed to have forgotten about it, and treated his cousin coldly, as if he had never given her a thought, and was interested only in business affairs. But as soon as he arranged these he went back to his old love.

Now, after all these years, no longer young, with two growing children to look after, his first thought on being freed was to marry her, widowed, ageing, ugly, simply for revenge, to undo his mother's handiwork. Had he not also undone it in other ways by eluding the terms of her will and despoiling legatees and co-heir? What remained now of the dead woman's work? Had Raimondo not also undone the marriage willed for him by her? And Lucrezia, who was to stay at home, had she not married too? . . . 'Wild! Stubborn! Mad!' They exchanged the same accusations; but this time all were agreed in blaming the prince and joining against him, the only exception being the Prior. Worldly interests, family troubles, touched him much less than before, now he was about to leave for Rome.

After the suppression of the monasteries all at the Curia had recognised that the learned and holy Benedictine should go ahead in other ways. He had been offered a bishopric and only had to choose, but aiming higher, he had asked to go to Propaganda. In those very days he had been called to the great Congregation, with nomination as Bishop *in partibus*. What did he care about his brother's wedding, his mother's Will, and all the

petty family intrigues? He was preceded in Rome by such a reputation and so many useful recommendations that he was sure,
with his talents, to reach the highest rank of the Hierarchy in
a short time.

As with the Prior, so too in Don Blasco the dissolution of the
religious Orders had aroused other desires, other ambitions.
Having converted into good income from government shares his
money from the monastery, the monk had at last seen the dream
of his youth come true: to own his own property, to be a capita-
list. He had almost forgotten his hatred for his rival and
nephew and bothered no more about him or anyone else.

But appetite comes with eating, says the proverb, and Don
Blasco was not content with a few thousand *onze;* he wanted
to get really rich and find out how to make money. For one
thing he wanted to try to acquire some of the property of the
chaplaincies and benefices. On finding that Giacomo was trick-
ing him and starting the law-case on his own in spite of his
promises, he became the leading spirit of the family league
against him on the system already used against his brothers.
Tit for tat, says another proverb, and the prince, who had made
Raimondo and Lucrezia pay him for his support, now had to shut
his uncle's mouth, for the latter, who never hesitated to use his
tongue, had begun saying around that the princess's death was
not as above board as it might be, and that Giacomo having
made 'poor Margherita rush on to Cassone while she was so
ill and actually showing first symptoms of cholera had been due
to his desire to rid himself of her, after forcing her to make a
Will which left all to him and nothing to her children, that
Consalvo's coldness had its reasons, and that . . . and that . . .

The prince then recognised his relative's rights to share the
benefices and calm was restored. A calm only in appearance
though, as rumours were bubbling beneath the surface. Giacomo
did not want to quarrel with the monk and fall out with him
now that he had money; nor with his aunt Ferdinanda for the
same reason; least of all with the duke, whose authority as
Deputy was useful against rapacious tax-gatherers. But he
would inveigh furiously against everyone else. The agent of
taxes, a man called Stravuso, was his particular bane. This man
had a reputation not only for rapacity but for a terrible Evil

Eye, and the prince, on joining battle, was even afraid to name him; he just called him 'God save us!', gripping an amulet in his closed fist, a bit of iron twisted into the shape of fingers making the sign against the Evil Eye.

'*Me* talk to "God save us!"? . . .' said he to his uncle on the eve of the wedding. 'I'd be mad to! . . . Get him sent away! . . . Get him moved, he's a thief lying in wait to strip us bare! . . . Not content with making me pay 20 per cent on the freeing of the benefices, he's after doubling the death-duties for outsiders! If we were outsiders we wouldn't inherit at all! The property comes to us just because the founders were our ancestors!'

The duke, who was praising the new laws to the skies, advised him not to complain; even with that 20 per cent deducted, the rest was all gain. The important thing, in the legislator's view, was that all property and income be taken from the monks and used for the enrichment of private citizens, and therefore for the increase of public prosperity. And so, while waiting to take his share of the released benefices, the duke had contracted for two properties of the Abbey of San Giuliano, Carrubo and Fontana Rossa, of which he would be taking possession within a few days; and he incited his nephew to do likewise, choose himself some good tract of land to be paid for by the year from its own produce and improved so as to multiply its value. But the prince said:

'Excellency, I can't. My confessor won't let me. He's given me scruples, and on this solemn occasion of my marriage I intend to respect them. That doesn't mean Your Excellency has done wrong; our two cases are different . . .'

The duke stared him straight in the eyes to see if he was serious or joking. Then he brought out the same objection made by the prince to Don Blasco:

'Then why are you putting in for the property of the benefices? Don't those belong to the Church too?'

'No, Excellency,' replied the prince. 'The Church was merely administrator according to the founders' intentions. The incomes only must be put to sacred use, and for that we are all responsible.'

While they were having this discussion the young prince's

absence was keeping other relatives gossiping behind the back of the new princess, who was making a great show of being worried and of fearing, like her husband, that the youth might have had an accident. She talked of sending messengers up to La Piana to find what had happened. In spite of her disquiet, however, she saw to the service of refreshments, whispered orders to Baldassarre, pressed guests to more cakes and ices, and carried out for the first time the duties of mistress of the house.

Don Blasco did not need much asking; now chains were up at San Nicola he could be as late as he liked. And as he munched away, he was making good use of his time to gather information on solvent signatures, for he too was now lending out money. Every now and again he also went up to a group amid whom the duke, having finished his talk with his nephew, was discoursing on public affairs.

The matter worrying the Deputy at the moment was the Town Hall. Things were going badly there, and the great man's friends were begging him to take over and give this further proof of devotion to his home town. But he declared that he lacked not will but strength. He was already Deputy, Provincial Councillor, member of the Chamber of Commerce and of the Agrarian Council, President of the Administrative Board of the Credit Bank, Councillor of the National Bank and the Bank of Sicily, and if that were not enough, he was always being put on all Watch Committees, all Commissions of Enquiry. At each new nomination he protested that it was too much, that he had not even time to scratch his head, that room must be made for others; but after long polite discussion he eventually had to yield to his friends' insistence. His adversaries, Republicans, malcontents, complained of this concentration of so many offices in one person, and the duke used this as a reason to refuse the office of Mayor. Benedetto, who after agonising private sufferings was just beginning to take an interest in public affairs again, pressed his uncle-in-law, and repeated the invitation in the name of the Town Council, adducing lack of capable persons.

' You're not suggesting, are you,' replied the Deputy, ' that I'm the only one who can act as Mayor? Why don't you take it on yourself?'

'Because I haven't Your Excellency's qualifications!'

'Just say you accept and you'll be nominated within a fortnight.'

Benedetto continued to ward him off, smilingly pretending that he did not think this a serious offer, but longing for it in his heart. There was one great difficulty, though, his wife's opposition. She became more and more irritable whenever she heard talk of public posts, elective offices, Liberal policy; and threatened to have kicked downstairs anyone who came to see him in his position as Town Councillor or President of the National Club, and tear up any such papers addressed to her husband before he read them. If she made so much fuss about so little what would she do if he was Mayor? So from fear of her, Benedetto parried the renewed offers of his uncle, who, as an irresistible last argument, now said, 'The day I retire you'll find the ground well prepared . . .'

While the Deputy was insisting, and Lucrezia speaking ill of her husband to Chiara, and Donna Ferdinanda ill of the prince to the marchese, and the parasites paying court to the new princess, and Don Blasco flitting from group to group, came the rattle of a carriage driving in at full tilt, and all exclaimed:

'Consalvo! . . . the young prince! . . .'

Baldassarre rushed downstairs to meet him. The youth looked in excellent trim, with boots as clean as if he were about to go out, but to the major-domo, who asked him anxiously what had happened, he replied:

'I'm only alive by a miracle.'

As he entered the drawing-room all crowded round him. He began to describe a most complicated incident, losing his way on the Biviere and starving for twelve hours and a sinking boat. 'Jesus! . . . Jesus! . . . Holy God of Love! . . .' people exclaimed all round. The princess particularly was repeating again and again, 'Oh this passion for shooting . . . Oh, dear boy! . . . How alarming! . . .' As the prince himself made show of believing this story, everyone was careful to pretend delight at his son's escape. Only Donna Ferdinanda curled her thin lips in an ironic smile, knowing well that her protégé had run no danger at all . . . Meanwhile Benedetto was whispering to his wife about

405

the offer of the Mayoralty made by her uncle and of his refusal. Lucrezia turned, looked him in the face and spat out, 'Must you always be an idiot?'

The title of Mayor, it occurred to her, might ennoble her husband in some way and confer on him the authority, lustre, and importance which he lacked. But after the duke obtained Benedetto's nomination she realised that he remained more a Giulente than ever, a kind of clerk, a wretched paper passer, a public servant. And when they called her *Mayoress* she flushed like a poppy, as if they were insulting her, as if the complimentary tones concealed hidden irony. Now she gave Benedetto no quarter. After urging him to accept the office she flung its pointlessness, boredom, and perils in his face. When he had so much work that he returned home later than usual, tired out and famished, she would greet him with a long face and half the table laid with a dinner gone cold. When people came and asked for the Mayor, she shouted to the maid, 'He's not in! There's no one in! Send away those bores . . .' so that the bores heard and felt no wish ever to return. When Giulente in spite of this received such people from prudence or necessity, she threw a shawl over her head and went round to relations or friends with outbursts of:

'I can bear no more of it! I'm going mad! What a hellish life! If only I'd known! . . .'

When others tried to show she was wrong and pointed out Benedetto's affection and respect, her resentment got worse; she began to imagine herself ill-treated and to attribute every kind of evil to her husband. As the Giulente had never had a grant of estates she considered him poverty-stricken, but being unable to hint at this with any show of reason she accused him of meanness. He left her free to spend what she liked, but once she had got it into her head that he was mean the notion took on more reality for her than any fact, and with the air of a victim resigned to her destiny, on the verge of tears, she would refuse to buy any new clothes, hats or jewels, and would go around dressed like a servant. Her husband could get no explanation from her for this slovenliness, but she had her say against him at the palace. If the prince or Donna Ferdinanda reminded her of her frenzied determination to marry him she counter-attacked with:

'Why didn't you open my eyes then? What could I know! It was for you to warn me!'

'Oh! Oh! Surely you haven't forgotten all you did?'

'How could I know? You should have been firmer about preventing me from doing such a silly thing!'

This new idea became so nailed into her head that she would burst out to anyone she was with, complaining of her own unhappiness to people she had scarcely spoken to before, and adding to excuse herself:

'My family betrayed me. That man wasn't the right husband for me. They forced him on me. I've been sacrificed! . . .'

She also ran Giulente down in another way, ridiculing his patriotism, attributing it to ambition or saying it did not really exist.

'The fool has played the Liberal in order to become somebody. But he's become nothing and done less than nothing. Wounded on the Volturno indeed! Look at his leg, it's healthier than mine!'

Often she said even worse things quite shamelessly, partly because she could not realise their unseemliness, partly because she thought she could say whatever occurred to her. She never rose before midday, and remained without dressing for two hours or more, with a skirt thrown over her night-gown, neck and arms bare, and feet in slippers. She would show herself in this state to valet and cook, and even receive visitors. If Benedetto was present and exclaimed, wringing his hands, 'But, Lucrezia! Please . . .' she looked at him in amazement, with staring eyes. 'What's the matter? They're intimates, aren't they? Should I put on a ball gown for them? One of those you had me sent from Paris? . . .' If he then told her to order clothes and spend whatever she liked, she shrugged her shoulders. 'Me? What for? To celebrate what? I don't go anywhere nowadays, or see anyone of my own class! Save your money, do!'

At times he would get desperate and lose patience; then she threatened to leave.

'Ah, so you're taking that tone, are you? Be careful or I'll leave you flat . . . Don't you give me ideas about going or wild horses won't hold me back . . . you know what we Uzeda are like when we get something in our heads! Raimondo turned things upside-down to leave one wife and get another! Giacomo swore to marry Graziella, so killed off that other poor wretch before her time . . .'

' Quiet now. What are you saying!'

Yet he put up with her frenzies, whims, contradictions, reproofs, ironic jeers. But his wife's fierce enmity did him no less harm than the duke's protection. The latter had not yet left for the capital and was now spending all his time on his own affairs, seeing to his estates, improving the properties that he had bought from mortmain, speculating on contracts, using his credit with public offices to recoup what he had spent during the revolution. And with the air of advising Giulente, he persuaded him to do whatever he wanted. Officially his nephew was Mayor; in fact he himself was. Not a chair was moved in the Town Hall without his approval, but it was especially in the nomination of employees, the concession of public works, the distribution of honorary, but indirectly or morally profitable jobs, that he made his will prevail. He protected faithful followers however inept, advanced men from whom he hoped for something in exchange, and gave no quarter to those of opposing parties, whatever their qualifications or whoever recommended them. All this with a convincing show of utter disinterest, urging his nephew to do what he himself wanted as if it had nothing to do with him at all.

Thus by dint of open injustices and flagrant violations of the law, the Town Hall became an electoral agency, a factory for clients. Benedetto, from respect and timidity, above all from hope of gathering his uncle's political inheritance, did not dare contradict him. When he hesitated a moment about some more than ordinarily grave wrong the duke conquered his scruples by adducing needs of political strife, or promising to make it up later, or simply by hinting that after all he had put Giulente in the job, so the latter should do what his uncle wanted. In exchange he guaranteed him support by Government and Prefecture, sustained him in the Council, even praised him in the family and contradicted Lucrezia, who abused him in front of all. To please her uncle she replied that the little good her husband ever did was when he followed his advice. But when alone with Benedetto, she flung at him his blind obedience to the duke.

' Swine! Idiot! Fool! Don't you see he's squeezing you like a lemon? He wants you to take the chestnuts out of the fire without getting burnt himself! . . . At least if you got a share . . .'

And she advised him to participate in the Deputy's dubious affairs, sell his own authority, get himself paid for actions which it was his duty to do. She would say this with no scruples, as if it were the most natural thing in the world, something the Viceroys had done at the time of their power .

So, partly for his wife's sake and partly for the uncle's, Giulente committed all sorts of injustices, though refusing to be paid for them, risking his fine reputation as a disinterested Liberal and ' wounded hero of the Volturno '. But ambition blinded him. He wanted to play a part in politics, and the goal for which he endured the Town Hall was Parliament. When the duke retired sooner or later he wanted to take his place. While other relatives all had eyes on the money being made by the Deputy, he aspired to the political inheritance; a seat in the Chamber of Deputies would be confirmation, recognition of his patriotism, of his capacities.

Even so his wife's contempt grew. She did not understand that public office could be exercised for the pleasure of exercising it, without speculation and with a loss of time, a putting aside of all other occupations for it and a disregard of private affairs. For he never went to the country and let agents and factors do what they liked! As if he was in a position to allow himself such a luxury! As if he were the young Prince of Mirabella!

Consalvo could do and did do whatever he liked. He never bothered about domestic matters—for his father thought of those —and only came home to sleep, when he did sleep there. He gave up the room he had occupied on returning from the monastery, and arranged a small apartment on the first floor, over-looking the inner courtyard, in the process breaking down walls, blocking up windows, opening new stairs, disorganising the plan of the palace a bit more. The prince let him be. Not content with being entirely segregated from the rest of the family with servants exclusively for his own use, he was now eating alone, declaring that his father's hours did not suit him. The prince accepted this too, to the great amazement of those who knew his overbearing character and need of absolute command.

The young man led a fine life: horses, carriages, hunting, fencing, gambling, and the rest. The Nobles' Club having ended after a fire in '62, he, together with a dozen or so companions, founded another club, a smarter, richer resurrection of the old. Though only authentic nobles were admitted, Consalvo had got in two or three young men who were not of the same class but useful to him as pimps. His protection and friendship he granted only to those who were of use to him and who admired and courted him. As at the Novitiate, now too he derided those less noble and rich than himself; one of his complaints against his father was that the latter's grasping avarice led him to hold out a hand to the newly enriched.

The outward luxury of the Uzeda, which seemed unique before 1860, was now beginning to be equalled if not surpassed by new people. While the palace furniture of fifty years before was falling to pieces and liveries of the previous century being eaten by moths, there were now families spending fortunes to set up houses and carriages in the modern taste. But shabby furniture and liveries were a kind of additional title of nobility in the prince's eyes; all might now have porters at their gates while twenty years before the only one in town was at the Uzeda palace, but who else had a pike-rack in their hall?

Consalvo, anyway, did his best to destroy the effects of parental meanness. When, from high on a brake or stage-coach in elegant clothes sent specially from Florence, he drove a team of four horses like an expert coachman, stopping to pick up friends whom he met on his way, overtaking all other carriages, whipping coachmen who dared cross his path as his ancestors had, people would stop to admire and repeat his name and title with pride, as if some of his lustre was reflected on those who could greet him or at least knew him by name in the very town where he was born. If he bought or sold a pair of horses, if he dismissed or re-engaged a servant, if he won or lost at the tables, news of these events was the small-change of every conversation. His dislike of his stepmother was generally praised and explained by his respect for his mother's memory. All were either self-interested or enthusiastic about finding him a wife, and every now and again the rumour of a possible marriage would go round everywhere until, repeated before him, it made him burst into roars of laughter. For the moment he wanted fun; there would be plenty of time to shackle himself later. And his assiduous visits to this or that lady, the showy presents which he made to singers and actresses explained that reply. For Pasqualino Riso the high old days of Count Raimondo were back. His young master made him earn his keep.

His energy had another outlet, less elegant but just as widely known. He and some of his wildest friends had formed a group which was the terror of half the town by night. Armed with swordsticks, revolvers or sometimes just daggers, they meandered round with street-women, singing at the tops of their voices, putting out gaslamps, starting quarrels with passers-by, forcing taverns and brothels to open by yelling and flinging stones at the windows, playing *tocco* and *briscola* with pimps, ordering suppers ending with every plate broken; innkeepers let them be, since they were usually ready to pay for any damage they did.

Sometimes, however, from a whim or the pleasure of bullying and of exercising the Viceroys' hereditary power, the young prince refused to pay up or paid in blows. While squandering sums on women he was also capable of taking for fun off one or two poor wretches the few coins they had in their pockets, compensating them later but meanwhile leaving them sobbing or blurting out strings of oaths which made him double up with laughter.

Often he and his band went down to the port and caused uproar in taverns where English sailors got drunk like savages. He would jump on to a table, holding the floor boldly, preach on the rule of St Benedict, repeat his uncle's and Giulente's political opinions. Without knowing a word of English he held long, serious discussions with the sailors, making up for his own use and consumption a language no one understood. Such evenings often ended with a boxing-match, bruised ribs and broken crockery . . . What would Fra' Carmelo have said? The lay-brother still appeared now and again at the palace, looking thinner and wilder every time, to sing his usual chant of, 'They've thrown me out . . . they've thrown me out . . .' Nothing else could be got from him.

When Consalvo happened to go near San Nicola on his nightly excursions, he was always meeting the Brother, wandering round the local streets like a soul in torment, or standing still and staring at the dark mass of the monastery walls. The young prince would alter his voice and call out mockingly, amid the others' laughter, 'Father Prior! . . . Father Abbot! . . . Where are the pigs of the Lord?'

He was life and soul of the group, their acknowledged and obeyed leader. Often Giovannino Radalì would go with him, but though he was now free, rich and a baron, his moods were uncertain; sometimes he did wild things, at others reining in his companions; usually he took part in these excursions with a deep frown and a false laugh. Now and again he vanished, went off to Augusta, to the estate left him by his uncle, where no-one could get at him until, in a sudden change of mood, he decided to return. Then Consalvo would drag him off on his revels.

One night the band came to blows with a group of townees, barbers and shop assistants, about some women. Staves fell, knives flashed, but luckily the police arrived and all took to their heels. Those beaten up, tricked husbands, victims of bullying, dared make no complaint; anyone threatening to go to the police was dissuaded as the culprits were nobles: the Baron Radalì, the young Prince of Mirabella, the young Marchese Cugnò! And the police, if anyone did have recourse to them, arranged matters; a few bank-notes and all was smoothed over. But such was the prestige of those names that few dared complain. Most considered themselves honoured to deal with such nobles, admired them and talked of them with deepest respect.

In carnival time, the favourite disguise for urchins and carters was that of 'baron'. They would go round dressed in ragged trousers, mended shirts, an old swallow-tail coat, a huge paper collar and a paper top-hat high as a chimney-stack, calling each other, amid laughter from passers-by, by the names of real 'barons'. 'Bye-bye, Francalanza! . . . How're things, Radalì? . . . Just off to the theatre, Marchese! . . .'

What could workers have done, such thought, without those

412

nobles whose luxurious way of life, pleasures, even follies, were chances for poor folk to work and earn?

And the young prince was a regal spender. His father paid for his horses, carriages, guns and dogs, and allowed him a hundred lire a month for small pleasures. But Consalvo sometimes lost in one night his allowance for the entire year, and next day he would go round to the moneylenders, who gave him whatever he wanted against his signature on an I.O.U. As for his relations, they either encouraged him to squander or ignored his extravagance, or were taken in by his wiles, as he knew how to get round each one of them by encouraging them in their various whimsies. Benedetto alone realised that this manner of life must be costing a great deal and suspected his debts, but the young man won him over by playing on his vanity as a patriot, ' a wounded hero of the Volturno ', a future deputy; and when Benedetto told his wife of his fears to be passed on to the prince, Lucrezia jumped at him.

' What are you putting your nose into? Let him be! D'you think my nephew's a beggar who can't allow himself such a luxury? He can pay his own debts, anyway! '

Donna Ferdinanda for her part would go into ecstasies at her protégé's success and show her pleasure by every now and again giving him a five-lire note, which the youth thanked her for profusely, then left as a tip to a café waiter.

The duke, deep in his own affairs, heard rumours of his grand-nephew's debts, but the youth only had to call the Deputy ' saviour of his country ', ' great statesman ', and prophesy a ministerial post, to quieten him down. A little later, to ingratiate himself more with Donna Ferdinanda, Consalvo would agree with her complaints of the duke's treachery; and in this he was sincere, for though he took no part in politics he was all for absolute government, which protected nobles and kept the mob in order. These sentiments, however, did not prevent him from being pleasant to his Uncle Giulente, though he did not call him ' Excellency ', but simply *Voi*. Later he sympathised with his Aunt Lucrezia if she complained of her ' swine of a husband '.

So in spite of his cold relations with his father, he followed the latter's example and treated each Uzeda according to his particular fixation. His Aunt Chiara would talk to him about adopting her maid's bastard, and he approved her decision. His Uncle Ferdinando, who had thought himself to have every conceivable disease when full of health, now that he was visibly wasting away thought himself robust and could not endure being advised to see a doctor. Consalvo would congratulate him on looking so well.

Don Blasco had not shown himself at the palace for some time. Since he had lived in his own home and dealt with his own money, his mania for criticising the whole family had gone; when he happened to be with his relations he chatted of this or that and soon left. So as not to be alone at home he had brought in the Cigar-woman, her husband and daughters. Thus he was served hand and foot and needed for nothing. For some time he was not to be seen at all.

'What's uncle doing? . . . what's Don Blasco doing? . . .' But no one knew a thing. The prince, the marchese, Lucrezia, and to some extent even Benedetto, were trying to ingratiate themselves with him because of the money he must have tucked away; but he evaded them all and if he heard them make smiling allusions to his riches, started shouting as before, 'What riches or poverty? . . . What . . .?' and out came more newly-coined swear words.

One day, though, when Benedetto was reading in the Prefect's Announcements the list of latest purchases of Church lands, he came across the name of Matteo Garino.

'Isn't that the Cigar-woman's husband?' he asked his wife.

'I think so. Why?'

'He's bought the "Cavaliere", one of the best of the Benedictines' properties.'

Without an instant's hesitation, Lucrezia exclaimed, 'Garino? It's Uncle Don Blasco who's bought it.'

Shortly after the truth came out. Garino was a cover-name for Don Blasco, who had put up the money and was already in possession of the estate. A monk, a Benedictine monk, one who had made a vow of poverty, buying land from his own monastery and so flouting Divine Law! The scandal was tremendous; Donna Ferdinanda was all vituperation of her brother. The duke smiled sceptically, remembering the furious threats of eternal damnation spat out by the monk. And the prince himself, although not wanting to get on the wrong side of an uncle who could buy such estates, shook his head. And all zealous Catholics, supporters of the Curia, homeless monks, pro-Bourbons who had once been Don Blasco's close friends, turned against him. But if anyone mentioned these critics he would shout:

'Yes, sir, the "Cavaliere" was bought on my account; and why not? Who's criticising? My sister who's been a money-lender for fifty years? My nephew who 'as robbed all his relations? Are they scrupulous and fearful of wrong doing? . . . I've no scruples about it at all! If I myself hadn't bought the "Cavaliere", someone else would have. Anyway it would never have stayed with the monastery, for the good reason that the monastery no longer exists! . . . In fact, it's the same in my hands as if it were still with San Nicola. Why, I've had the chapel restored, and say Mass in it every day when I go there. If it had gone into anyone else's hands, it would be used as a pigsty by this time . . .'

Actually he only said Mass now and again, as he was so busy ploughing up the enclosure, tearing away old trees, scooping out a well, enlarging the farmhouse and adapting it as a villa to stay in, moving the surrounding wall so as to tidy up his boundaries; then he had to keep a watchful eye on builders and diggers lest they steal. In the country, to be ready for wind or rain, he wore a shooting jacket and half-length boots; back in town he put off his habit and scapular, but designed himself a black suit like a Protestant clergyman's, with a waistcoat buttoned to the top and a clerical collar. He disapproved, though, of two or three of his former colleagues who had stripped off everything and plunged without reserve into secular life, like the revolutionary Father Rocca; and of those who without putting off their habits gave cause for gossip by their conduct, like Father Agatino Renda, who spent all day with the widow Roccasciano, gambling from morn till night. Father Gerbini had gone to Paris, where he had been made rector of the Madeleine; others who had stayed in Catania were leading priest's lives. But Don Blasco proposed himself as a model to the lot. Fra' Carmelo, who often came to visit him as he did the prince, seemed not to notice the change in His Paternity as he repeated with desperate gestures his eternal refrain, 'They've thrown me out! . . . they've thrown me out! . . .' Don Blasco would give him money, a drink, comfort him with fine words. But whenever the madman had taken drink, he would be less sane than ever and begin reviling the devil worshippers who had stripped the monastery.

'Assassins and thieves! Thieves and assassins! The biggest monastery in the kingdom! . . . And those thieves went and took its property! To hell with them! To hell with them, they're excommunicated . . .'

Once, more delirious than usual, he fell on his knees declaiming and making great signs of the Cross. 'In the Name of the Father, of the Son, of the Holy Ghost! In God's name I adjure you . . . Restore your ill-gotten gains to San Nicola! Thieves! . . . Swine! . . . Are you Christians or Turks! Think of your souls! Of hell-fire!'

Don Blasco finally lost patience, took him by a shoulder and pushed him out.

'All right, all right, we understand. But be off for the moment. I'm busy . . .'

And he banged the door in his face as Donna Lucia appeared.

'He's beginning to interrupt my devotions, that old loony. If he comes back again, just throw him downstairs, d'you hear?'

8

ONE NIGHT, while Lucrezia was snoring away in bed and Benedetto studying the Council accounts at his desk, a sharp ring at the bell made husband start and wife awake. Benedetto went to open the door, and found himself facing the young prince, who was white as a sheet.

'Can I wash?' he asked his uncle, drawing from his jacket pocket a hand red with blood.

'Consalvo! What's happened? What's the matter? . . .'

'Nothing, don't shout . . . To open a window . . . I broke a pane . . . and cut my hand . . . Let me wash! . . . It's nothing.' But it was a deep wound, beginning from the back of the hand, twisting under the thumb-joint and ending at the wrist. It had been treated with lint, but must have opened again as the handkerchief wound round the hand had not a white corner on it, and blood was dropping, marking suit and shirt.

'I couldn't go home in this state . . .' the youth explained as he kept his hand immersed in a basin of reddening water. But suddenly he lost the confidence that had sustained him till then and began to tremble, his forehead covered with cold sweat, staring round with a stunned look in which Giulente could now read shock at sudden aggression, fear of death glimpsed in a blade flash.

'Tell the truth. What happened? . . .'

'Again? . . . A broken pane, I told you . . . Now go and call Giovannino, who went to the chemist's with me. He's waiting down below . . .'

Consalvo's friend, even paler, confirmed his story. The truth came out next day. For some time Consalvo had been after the daughter of Gesualdo Marotta, the Belvedere barber. She made a living as a ladies' hairdresser, and although always in the streets, took no notice of men for fear of her brothers, who did not jest on matters of honour. But when the young prince got a whim into his head he would not rest till it was satisfied, and in spite of pleading and the Marotta brothers' warnings he set every pimp in town on to the job of overcoming the resistance of the young woman and her family, promising to take her off the streets and away from her wearisome job that exposed her to perils, and set her up in a dressmaker's shop, and also assure her the custom of all his relatives and friends. It had all been useless. Then, seeing he could achieve nothing by fair means, one day he had the girl kidnapped and kept her with him for three days up at the Belvedere. For a time the brothers were silent, as if in the dark. Then one night, as the young prince was leaving the Café de Sicilia in the company of Giovaninno Radalì, he felt a slash with a sharp blade on the hand he put out instinctively to defend himself. ' We'll meet again! . . .' the aggressor called as he ran off at Radalì's cry.

The prince said nothing when he saw his son with a bound hand. He made show of believing the story of the broken pane and even tended him together with the princess, who watched beside Consalvo's bed as devotedly as a real mother. The youth scarcely bothered to hide his irritation at these unwelcome attentions, and greeted as liberators the friends who visited him morning and evening. The danger he had been through, the blood lost, filled these comrades-in-play with admiration; but on recovering he never put his nose outside the gates.

The Marotta brothers had let him know that they were ready to start again when they next saw him by night or day, and that the second time he would not get off with just a scratch, and that they were waiting to do their own justice as well as denouncing the matter to the law.

The Uzeda, worried about the heir's life, had recourse to the duke; he alone, with the authority which came from his political position, could get Prefect or Questor or magistrates to see the rascals left the youth in peace. The duke, on hearing of the incident and what was wanted of him, instead of siding with his grand-nephew, unexpectedly flew into a rage, all the stranger as it was not in character.

'Serves him right! These are the consequences of the life he leads! Why don't you put him under lock and key? Are you proud of his exploits? What d'you want from me?'

No-one had ever seen him so put out; he looked almost like his brother Don Blasco. The fact was that his adversaries were trying every means of attacking him again, and Consalvo's silly imbroglio played right into their hands. The Deputy had not been to the capital for two years and had quite abandoned public affairs in favour of his own. What a great patriot, eh? Such unselfishness he showed, such love of his homeland! When he had irons in the fire at Turin and Florence he used the excuse of public affairs to keep away from Catania, even if the Chamber was locked and ministers scattered; nothing could have torn him from Turin during the troubles of '62. He had only come home to be re-elected. The last time he had not even bothered to do that, considering his constituency as a feudal right which no one could take from him. Now that he wanted to settle his own affairs, although most serious matters were being discussed in Parliament, he did not move. But even if he did go what would he do there? What had he done in all his eight years as a deputy? He had raised and lowered his head like a puppet, to say yes or no as he was bid! Why, if he'd opened his mouth just once! His excuse was that the public put him off. But the truth was that he hadn't the shadow of an idea in his noodle and could not even write a line without several mistakes, and he thought to hide his supine ignorance by an air of presumption and self-confidence! And a person like that was entrusted with all the affairs of the town and province, allowed to dictate his opinions on every kind of question: public education, engineering, music, ships . . . Not content with exercising so much personal power he also got his adherents in everywhere to play his game; so that Giulente uncle had been given charge of the Bank and Giulente nephew been made Mayor.

All these accusations by his enemies circulating round town were gaining credence, becoming a threat. Giulente took up his defence, but people did not listen to him now as they had at one time; the Deputy's discredit was beginning to spread to him. He was called a hypocrite for trying to keep old friendships after becoming a mere executor of the duke's abuses and injustices. A hypocrite only? The bitterest said that he got his share of the Deputy's spoils too; some share must be coming to him from their illicit profits, from fruits of their trafficking.

This subject of the Deputy's earnings excited his enemies more than any other. The duke, they said, used his public offices to his own advantage. The money he had spent on the revolution was bringing him in a thousand per cent! That explained his 'patriotism', his play-acting conversion to liberty while the Uzeda family had always been a nest of Bourbonists and reactionaries, and in '48 he had actually sat and enjoyed the spectacle of the city in its death agony through a telescope as if he were at the theatre! It was partly explained by fear too, a need to prove his Liberalism and democracy to avoid getting shot—and some fools had let themselves be taken in by that abolition of fine-quality bread for about a fortnight. But greed had overcome fear. Well-informed folk told how once, in the first phase of the new government, he had made a most significant remark that revealed the hereditary avarice of the Viceroys, the rapacity of the Uzeda of old: ' Now that Italy's made, we must make our bit . . .' If he had not said those exact words he had certainly put the idea into action; that was why he was so loud in praise of the new regime and its beneficent effects. Laws were good when they were good for him. That suppression of the religious communities for instance! According to him the release of Church lands would result in lighter taxes and make everyone a property-owner. Instead of which taxes were growing heavier all the time, and who had those properties gone to? To the Duke of Oragua, the rich folk, the capitalists, those who already ruled the roost . . .

So the opposition to the Deputy was merging with the general discontent, the disillusion that followed the hopes aroused by political changes. Before, when things went badly, commerce languished and money was scarce, the fault was all Ferdinand II's; when the Bourbons were sent packing and Italy made one, everyone would be suddenly swimming in gold. Now after ten years of liberty things were going from bad to worse. People had been promised a reign of justice and morality, but favouritism, cheating and thieving were as rife as before; the powerful and arrogant were all in their places still. Who called the tune under the old government? The Uzeda, the rich, the other nobles with their hangers-on. The very same people who called it now!

These ideas, which were making headway everywhere and also harming Giulente, were attributed by the latter to envy by the inept, to enemies' bad-faith, and particularly to the propaganda of his former friends the revolutionaries. The duke's great fault was upholding the cause of law and order, of moderation and prudence. If instead of supporting the Government he had flung himself into the arms of those fanatics of the Left, he would have been applauded by them. But Giulente might as well have been preaching to Turks; the only people to listen, approve or encourage him were the duke's partisans. These were still numerous, but above all they were more authoritative, more influential than the anonymous mob of his accusers, among whom actual voters could be counted on the fingers of one hand. They were faithful too, deaf to accusations, and tied all the closer to the Deputy, as his fall would ruin them too . . .

Now with public opinion in this state, this silly pickle of his grand-nephew's was a greater bother to Don Gaspare. About the danger to which the young man was exposed he did not care a rap. He had none of Donna Ferdinanda's tenderness nor the other relatives' interest in the heir to the princedom, nor did he really fear losing his seat at the next dissolution of the Chamber or his hold over the town. But he wished to avoid being a subject of controversy and to retain intact the prestige of that first period; for that reason Consalvo's misadventure put him into a real fix, for if he helped to support an abuse and to persecute the kidnapped girl's relations, he would rouse more clamour against himself than ever, while if he renounced his nephew's defence it would be attributed to fear of rousing more opposition against himself. After hesitating a little between the two lines, making Consalvo feel the weight of his displeasure but defending him before outsiders, he took the bolder course.

One day the most troublesome of the girl's two brothers was sent for by a police inspector, who advised him to desist from his threats for his own good or he would be formally cautioned. At the same time witnesses of the kidnapping turned their coats and declared that the girl had gone to Villa Uzeda of her own free will. Then two peasants were found who said they had seen her there at other times, and a number of other villagers came forward to affirm a local rumour that this was not the girl's first escapade. The girl's family cried vengeance, but were persuaded by neighbours to desist and make the best of things, and the young prince, though absolved from all responsibility by the best witnesses, to avoid other trouble, declared himself ready to put up three thousand lire for the dressmaker's shop.

One fine day, as news was expected any moment that the incident had been settled, partly by threats and partly by promises, and that the young man was no longer in any danger, the prince, who had not rebuked his son at all till then, entered the latter's room red in the face as a tomato, and brandishing a piece of paper.

'Now you! ... What's this letter mean?'

It referred to a debt of six thousand lire which Consalvo had guaranteed with an I.O.U. renewed a number of times every four months. The creditor, wanting to get paid and profiting by the youth's confinement to the house, had written to the father to tell him of the I.O.U. falling due and asking to be paid.

Consalvo at first was taken aback, but as his father, spurred on by this silence, asked for explanations and began shouting louder than ever, he replied coldly and calmly:

'You needn't raise your voice. What have they written?'

'You can read, can't you?' exclaimed his father, thrusting the sheet of paper under his nose.

But the young prince drew quickly back, as if threatened by some dirty contact. During the long days spent in an armchair, with his slung arm in enforced inertia and with no possibility of using his right hand, quivering at the sight of blood still oozing from his wound and soaking the bandage, there had gradually risen and grown in him until it became irresistible the same sense of disgust which had tormented his mother, the same repulsion for all physical contact, the same revulsion from things handled by others, the same fear of contagious dirt. The nearer

422

his father came holding out the letter, the more he edged away with his hands behind his back to avoid taking it.

'All right . . . all right . . .' said he, twisting round to glance sideways at the writing, 'I've seen . . . It's Don Antonio Sciacca.'

'Ah, Don Antonio, is it?' shouted the prince 'Then it's true? You don't even bother to pretend? . . . You have the face . . .'

Consalvo suddenly looked straight into his father's eyes and stared at him fixedly with a hard expression, like a challenge; then dropping the formal *lei* said:

'What d'you expect? . . . I needed money . . . You don't give me much! . . . So I took it . . . you have the money and can pay . . .'

The prince looked as if he had been struck by lightning. He turned on his son a stare no less fixed or hard, and gasped:

'Not a cent . . . will I pay . . . It's my money, isn't it? I'll get you condemned and tied by the Courts, you little swine! D'you understand? . . .'

Even colder than before Consalvo replied:

'Fine. Then don't bore me any more . . .'

'So I bore you, do I? I bore you . . .' And suddenly, like someone who finally manages to vomit after many vain efforts, he let himself go. For two years he had been working up to it; for two long years he had allowed his son every liberty. During all that time he had repressed and suffocated his imperious need to command, to see all bow to his own will as head of the house, as master, as absolute arbiter of the family destinies; he, who had martyrised all his family and done whatever he liked with them, had forced himself to loose the bridle on the neck of his son, who was the most legitimate subject of his power. For two years, while pretending to be tolerant, indulgent, affectionate, he had been smouldering inside, hiding his aversion for Consalvo while returning the hatred which he felt his son had for him. Now finally he burst his bonds.

As long as it was a matter of the young man's wild life or his coldness towards his stepmother, the prince managed to rein himself in. But now Consalvo was wounding him in the strongest of all his feelings, no longer attacking his moral authority but his purse. His whole life through, ever since reaching the age of reason, the prince had struggled to accumulate in his own hands as much money as he could by taking it from his mother, brothers, sisters and wife. More than all the other Uzeda he had been a representative of those avid Spaniards, intent only on self-enrichment, incapable of understanding any power, value or virtue greater than that of money. And now that he had succeeded in his intention and foresaw a serene enjoyment of the fruits of his long and patient labours, here was his son beginning to dispose of his fortune as if it were the boy's own!

Had Consalvo asked him for the six thousand lire he would have given them; but the idea of a contracted debt, of a signed I.O.U., of interest paid in advance to money-lenders, caused a revolution in the father's head, made him see his own wealth as irreparably endangered. For that I.O.U. could not be the only one; his son's natural inclination to squander money now seemed obvious, and the wretch was daring to take a haughty line as if he had merely exercised a right! And now the boy was telling him not to be a bore into the bargain! Answering his father back in that tone!

' I'll just show you if I bore you or not! I'll see to that! I'm the master here; get the idea well into that cracked head of yours! Here it's my will that's to be done in all and by all. Why d'you think I've been so good to you till now? I'll just show you, you imbecile . . . With everyone, all my relations, the whole town, talking about your filthy life! Your life of taverns and brothels! D'you think I don't know of your scruffy little adventures? Why aren't you blushing with shame? Why haven't you hidden yourself away from decent people? The dignity of our name trampled in the company of dirty swillers! Not to mention money wasted, flung away as if it were stones! Does anyone spend more than you on whims and silly amusements? . . . And it's not enough for me to let you be, say nothing, put my hand in my wallet all day long . . . You dare to complain you haven't enough! And instead of excusing yourself, of asking pardon, you want more into the bargain! Who d'you think you're dealing with, imbecile? . . . Not a cent will I pay! It's time we came to an understanding, you know! . . . As we're at it, once and for all . . . You'll have to change your tune . . . As long as you're in my house you must do what I like, behave as among civilised people. This isn't a tavern to visit only for bed and board! I

424

can't make you like me, and don't care whether you do or not; but I demand the respect that's my due; I demand the respect you owe to your mother . . .'

Consalvo had not said a single word, not made a gesture during the prince's tirade. The latter stopped for a second, after a question or exclamation, as if to give his son time to reply and justify himself. Standing beside the window, the young man was looking down into the service courtyard at carriages drawn up outside the coach-houses and ostlers intent on cleaning them; had he been alone in his own drawing-room he could not have remained more impassive. But at the prince's last words he turned slowly round:

' My mother? . . .'

There was an indefinable expression on his face, of curiosity, of surprise, of doubt, dominated by a very faint smile in his eyes alone.

' My mother? . . . my mother's dead. You know that better than anyone.' The prince was silent and looked at him. Suddenly there was a rustle of skirts and in came the Princess Graziella, warned by a maid who had heard raised voices.

' What is it? What's the matter?'

Consalvo thrust his hands into his pockets and without saying a word passed into the next room. The prince was led away by his wife.

For weeks father and son never exchanged a word. The affair of the debt, when known by relatives, divided the family in two camps. The duke, who still had not forgiven his grand-nephew for the embarrassment in which he had put him, upheld the prince, incited him not to give way but let the I.O.U. come to court. Giulente also considered it necessary to give the young man a fright, or nothing would stop him on the road of debt if the prince decided to pay up the first one. But Lucrezia, to contradict her husband and give a lesson in munificence to this beggarly husband who judged everyone by his own standards, exclaimed that Consalvo had the right to amuse himself, that six thousand lire for a Prince of Francalanza was like ten lire for a Giulente, and that it was quite impossible for the Uzeda family to have the scandal of an unpaid I.O.U. Donna Ferdinanda of course attacked the avarice of the prince, who by not giving his son enough was forcing him to have recourse to loans. Chiara agreed partly with one side and partly with the other according to Federico's mood. As for Don Blasco, who had been invisible for some time, one fine day he came to the palace and began attacking not only Consalvo for his debts and scandalous conduct but also the prince and princess, to whose weakness he attributed Consalvo's wild life.

'It's all your fault! That's not the way to educate him! Why pay his debts? Cut off his supplies, that's what he needs!' And without naming her he burst out against Donna Ferdinanda, calling her every name under the sun, as by spoiling him she had first started the young prince on the wrong path.

Donna Ferdinanda heard of this speech by the monk at the same time as her agent was giving her an amazing piece of news. Don Blasco, not content with having bought the San Nicola estate, had acquired from the Crown Lands just about that time one of the houses belonging to and near the monastery—the south one, former home of the Cigar-woman—and done it so cleverly he had got it for a song. Then the heavens opened.

'A house too?' screamed the old spinster. 'Haven't I always said he's a real swine! Telling others what they're to do, with all he has on his conscience! For outsiders to buy up monastery property is quite understandable; they've no obligations. But him? Who would have starved if he hadn't become a monk, who's fattened himself at the community's expense? . . .'

'Wasn't it he,' they said to each other at Timpa the chemist's, 'who wanted to slaughter all free-thinkers and launch a new crusade against excommunicated usurpers and restore everything to the Pope and Francis II?'

But nowadays Don Blasco did not care a fig if the King was called Francis or Victor; now he was settled in the San Nicola house he was his own pope. He had let the shops at good rents, and also the first floor to a teacher who gave lessons at the technical school now in the monastery. He felt no scruples; indeed if all the monks had imitated his example and bought up monastery land instead of squandering the money they had been given, the San Nicola property would never have fallen into the hands of strangers.

'That was the real way to deal with the suppression, not just useless and ridiculous complaining. If all the monks bought back the property, they'd have got the better of the Government!'

He still had his say against this Government, particularly because of the taxes it made him pay; but when those faithful to the cause of reaction prophesied an end of the Liberal spree and return to old conditions and restitution of ill-gotten gains from the Church, the monk would protest:

'What d'you mean? Ill-gotten gains? I paid for the "Cavaliere" land and for that house with good money down, didn't I? I'm quite above board, d'you understand? Was I given them or did I steal them, that they can be taken back?'

'You shouldn't have bought them, knowing where they came from! The day will come for making up accounts, for the *Dies irae*; don't doubt that!'

'Eh? Who? What must come?' shouted the monk then. 'I don't care a fig!'

'The hand of God reaches everywhere. The ways of Providence are infinite!'

Quarrels would start again every afternoon. The Bourbonists and clericals received broadsheets giving the revolution's end as certain and imminent. These articles, read out aloud, listened to as if they were Gospel truth, applauded at every phrase, would make the Benedictine furious. One day when the group, after one of these readings, was criticising him more sharply than usual, Don Blasco got up, made a very expressive gesture, shouted, 'Go and get . . .' and left, never again to set foot in that chemist's shop. When passing by it in the afternoons he hurried his step, looking straight in front of him, and if people were sitting outside, crossed the street on to the opposite pavement. He did not even set foot in the palace, where that money-lender of a sister of his was also inveighing against the purchasers of Church property as if they were so many thieves, and where that other Jesuit, Giacomo, was making up to him now that he knew him rich, though without disagreeing with Donna Ferdinanda.

'He'd like me to leave him the "Cavaliere",' he would shout to the Cigar-woman, to Garino and his daughters. 'He'd have no scruples in taking it from me at second-hand! All I'll leave him is thirty-seven bundles of cauliflowers, the Jesuitical thief!'

The Cigar-woman, Garino and the girls approved, and laced the dose by running down all his relations to the monk, so that he should leave everything to them. And they served him like a god, rushed to his slightest sign, walked on tiptoe when he was resting, sat up with him late at night if he was not sleepy, accompanied him to the 'Cavaliere' land, praised the viti-culture, the buildings, the success of all his speculations.

One of these, however, went slightly amiss. The 'Cavaliere' land bordered to the east on another property, in the hands of the Public Trustee and still unsold, whose boundary consisted of an old hedge of prickly pears with big gaps in it. Don Blasco was having a fine high wall built covered with flints and broken bottles, and he appropriated a number of little pieces of land; in a corner where there were no traces of hedge he annexed to the 'Cavaliere' a fair-sized slice of this other land. This had now been discovered by the Intendancy of Finance, who poured out summonses, which set the monk baying and yelling against Italian thieves, as in the old days. He almost got to the point of reconciliation with the reactionaries at the chemist's.

'Accuse me of encroachment? Surely the San Nicola property stretched as far as the vineyards? Are they trying to teach me what the monastery property is, those thieves who've stripped a kingdom?'

Garino added the rest. But as no talk could return summonses by the Public Lands Department, and an enquiry on the spot would prove them right, the ex-police informer, seeing the monk so worked up, suggested one day:

'Why doesn't Your Excellency say a word to your brother the Deputy?'

Don Blasco did not reply. He had already been to the duke.

For years he had not spoken a word to his brother, for even longer he had been abusing him in public and private. So Don Gaspare was astounded at seeing him appear. The monk entered his brother's study with his hat on his head as if in his own home, said 'Morning to you' in the tone of one seeing a person from the day before, and sat down. The duke, after the first moment of amazement, smiled subtly and answered in the same tone, 'Well, what's up?'

The monk at once plunged into his subject.

' You know I've bought the " Cavaliere " land of San Nicola? There's no boundary line and I had a wall put up. Now the Public Lands people are accusing me of encroachment . . .'

The duke went on smiling from ear to ear, enjoying it all. Then the monk was silent, thinking there was no need to add more, but his brother wanted the satisfaction of hearing this man by whom he had always been reviled asking for help and said :

' Well? . . .'

' Well? . . . Can't you talk to someone?'

It was not exactly what he had hoped, but the duke was a good old man at heart, not of the same stuff as the prince and the Prior, and he contented himself with that.

' All right. Come back with the papers tomorrow.'

So, to the amazement of all their relations, the two brothers were seen going together up and down the steps of the Intendancy, the Prefecture, the Civil Engineers and the Public Lands Department.

In a few days things looked like being arranged, but the duke now suggested a more radical solution to the monk.

' Why don't you just buy the other estate?'

' Where'll I get the money?'

' Oh, we'll find the money!'

He got it from the banks on whose board he was. With it he speculated in public lands, redeemed properties taken from mortmain and purchased some of them anew. Now to be under his own roof as well he was building a fine new house in the Via Plebiscito. Through him, Don Blasco was allowed a discount at the *Bank of Credit and Deposits*, and signed an I.O.U. for twenty-five thousand lire. The ' Cavaliere ' land, increased by almost double, thus became a good-sized property, ' a real feudal estate ', as it was called by Garino, who was now for ever exalting the duke, his talents, the position and power he had reached through his own abilities. But the gossips at the pro-Bourbon pharmacy were harder at it than ever prophesying the day, now imminent, when Don Blasco and other committers of sacrilege would have to restore their ill-gotten goods. The monk let them be and no longer even passed the street around the pharmacy, a glimpse of which even from a distance made him want to retch.

But as time went by, lack of conversation began weighing on him, and one Sunday, meeting his tenant, the teacher, on the stairs, he invited him in.

The teacher said he had been a Garibaldino, described the Aspromonte affair, talked of nothing but conspiracies and threatened the end of the world too, but only if Italy did not occupy Rome.

'So you think this Government will last?' asked Don Blasco in trepidation.

'If it does its duty! Otherwise we'll kick it out as we have the others! We aren't frightened by police! We've seen firing! We know all about revolutions!'

'Some people, though, think we might return . . .'

'Return? We must go forward! Integrate national unity! Smash the last stronghold of theocracy, the last bulwark of obscurantism . . . Humanity never returns! We've buried the Middle Ages! The State must be lay, and the Church return to its origins; as that great man Jesus Christ said, " My Kingdom is not of this world "!'

His tenant's conversation, though from time to time it did make a quiver run down his spine, pleased Don Blasco a good deal, and one day, as he was passing in front of Cardarella's pharmacy, old meeting-place of Liberals, the teacher, who was inside deep in discussion, called him in. They were talking about the suppressed religious orders, and the teacher refused to believe that some years the income of San Nicola had been beyond a million lire.

'Yes, sir,' confirmed Don Blasco. 'It was the richest in Sicily, maybe in the whole former kingdom.'

Then the teacher burst out against monks, priests, parasites of a society ' which, thank heavens, was finally being organised on different basis '.

From that day Don Blasco got into the habit of frequenting the new chemist's. To this shop came rabid Liberals, shouting as much as those other retrogrades against the Government but for a different reason: because it was a government of rabbits, of France's lackeys, of Napoleon III's boot-lickers; because it persecuted true patriots and played the Jesuit in the Roman question. Aspromonte and Mentana would come up, but Rome must be

Italian at all costs, or they would go down into the streets and begin shooting again. 'Rome or death!' shouted the teacher, who always had news of wars and revolutionary movements ready to break out, and Don Blasco, among the others' shouts, would boom:

'The Holy Father should think it over quietly, while there's yet time and remember '48. If he hadn't listened to the reactionaries then, now he'd be respected President of the Italian Confederation!'

'Quietly?' cried the teacher. 'Holy cannons is what they need! The blood of Monti and Tognetti is still steaming! It takes guns to break down the stronghold of fanaticism.'

One day he entered his landlord's apartments with an air of glory and triumph.

'This is it, at last! War!'

Don Blasco, disturbed by the news, as he feared a war might threaten the Italian state, was reassured when his tenant told him that the election of a German Prince to the throne of Spain had been considered by France as a *casus belli*. 'Our duty . . .' But as he was explaining what Italy's duty was a servant appeared from the Uzeda palace. The prince asked for news of his uncle and at the same time warned him that Ferdinando was very ill and they ought to pay him a visit. Don Blasco, longing above all else to hear the words of his new friend, answered:

'All right, all right; I'll be up tomorrow . . .'

# 9

FERDINANDO had been failing for a year. His haggard face, yellow eyes, white lips had long been signs of hidden illness, inner suffering; but while when perfectly well he thought he had every disease under the sun, now that something was really decaying in him, if people asked what was wrong he replied irritably:

'Nothing! Why should anything be wrong? D'you want me to fall ill to please you?'

And he gave the prince a rude reply when the latter one day advised him to go up to Pietra dell'Ovo for a time and breathe healthy country air. He no longer wanted to hear his country house even named. The books which had cost so much were gathering dust and moth on the shelves, implements were rusting and breaking, but the estate was prospering now that he no longer experimented with novelties. Stubbornly he denied his sufferings, his stomach pains, his intestinal disturbances, and attributed them to fantastic causes: undercooked bread, sirocco, evening chill. But he was falling into deep funereal hypochondria. For long, long days he never said a word, never saw a living soul. Shut up in his room, flung on the bed, he lay motionless, following the flight of flies. When the crisis passed, he gobbled indigestible food. One summer night his manservant, terrified by black vomit and blood-speckled diarrhoea, sent a son over to the palace to warn the family.

At the prince's arrival and suggestion of sending for a doctor, the sick man cried that he wanted no-one and had quite recovered. But now all realised that his condition was serious. Lucrezia, his childhood companion, tried vainly to convince him that he must see a doctor; he threatened to lock himself in his room and see no one at all. But his pulse showed that fever was raging. To conquer this obstinacy, they had recourse to a trick, as if he were a child or madman; by pretending that a surveyor had to come to draw the plan of the house they got a doctor into his room. The doctor shook his head; the patient's condition was much more serious than they thought. At the age of thirty-nine he was dying. The old and impoverished blood of the Viceroys was festering inside him, no longer nourishing the flaccid fibres. To try to combat his blood-condition a most severe diet and cure were necessary. But the maniac would listen to no-one, least of all his relations. If they insisted he shouted, 'Oh, stop it, won't you?' As he was convinced that he was perfectly well, their suggestions that he was ill could only mean they wanted his death, were expecting it. Why? To get his inheritance! He confided this to his servants, and when the Uzeda left, said:

'D'you think those come here for love of me? They're after my money! Another time tell 'em I'm not here.'

But actually his money had gone already. First in wild experiments ruining the soil, then in mad expense on books and implements, later in cheating by the factor when he had refused to set eyes on his property even from a distance and begun to incur debts. Without surprise or wondering why, he found himself surrounded by people offering to lend money, within reason of course. And he signed I.O.U. after I.O.U., all of which ended up in the hands of the prince, who with his eyes on the property at Pietra dell'Ovo, and realising this madman would never make a Will, was getting a hold on it that way. The maniac, incapable of totting up money borrowed and thinking himself still master of his own property, was convinced that his relations were waiting round him for his death. As soon as they appeared he turned his back on them all, except his nephew Consalvo.

The latter's debts had been finally paid, which was widely attributed to Donna Ferdinanda. But in fact the old spinster had not herself paid a cent. She would have died of a stroke if she'd had to pay out sixty lire, let alone six hundred, or six thousand! The money had really been paid by the prince, whom Princess Graziella, with a generosity that edified all, had persuaded to pardon her stepson. Surely the Prince of Mirabella's signature could not be cited? That would never happen while she was alive! Why if Giacomo was stubborn enough to go on saying ' no ' she'd pay out of her own pocket! Yes, for Consalvo as for Teresina, she felt a true mother's love, though she had not borne him in her womb and her stepson repaid her so ill! ' But what can I do? No-one commands the heart, do they? Ah well, one day or other he'll realise I should not be treated like this . . .' She had induced the prince to pay the I.O.U., and also found the expedient of hinting that it was the spinster's generosity, lest Consalvo presume on the paternal weakness in future.

Aversion between father and son was meanwhile growing daily. To avoid the prince's company and at the same time seem victimised, Consalvo deserted the paternal house. But instead of going with friends to café or club, he went to his uncle Ferdinando's where he bought papers and read out the political news. The sick man took a passionate interest in the threatened war, which was the only subject that could loosen his tongue. Don Blasco, on finally coming to visit his nephew, also discussed this subject with him passionately, repeating the teacher's arguments; but the duke assured everyone that it was all a false alarm and there'd be no war, with as convinced an air as if this had been secretly confided to him by Napoleon.

When the news of the declaration of war did finally burst on them, the great man exclaimed that Bismarck and William must have lost their heads. Or were they joking? To attack Napoleon? The French Army, the first in the world, would rout, mince, pulverise the Prussian, and take Berlin in two weeks at the most. Instead of which came cables announcing German victories.

Then the Deputy's adversaries began to ridicule him with more zest. That nincompoop with the air of a reborn Cavour was not even capable of understanding the most obvious things. Contradicted by facts, he held stubbornly to his silliness, announced new French plans, then imminent retaliation, intervention by the Powers.

Ferdinando, from deep in the armchair which he now never left because his legs did not hold him, would listen to those speeches as anxiously as if his health depended on them. Trembling with fever, his forehead aflame, he let a new obsession

434

overwhelm his weakened brain now: Napoleon's victories, which he yearned for. Buying a map of the Rhine, he spent his days sticking big pins in all the French positions and small pins in the Prussian ones. War bulletin in hand, he studied the operations of the two armies, changed his signs according to the real changes, and as the small pins advanced and the big pins withdrew his illness got worse. In raucous, cavernous tones he explained what the French should have done to regain their lost positions. He improvised strategic plans, plotted out every day numerous *theatres of war*, disposed divisions and regiments arbitrarily, exclaiming, 'This one here, that one there . . .' until, exhausted, overwhelmed, he fell back with hands dangling and head awry, eyes shut and mouth open as if on the point of expiring.

Meanwhile the duke, feeling the opposition to him growing and the ground shrinking beneath his feet, had realised he must do something in order to restore his prestige, and was preparing an unexpected move. Fear of war was increasing general discontent; the Government's adversaries were taking advantage of this to shout and threaten louder. Members of the opposition, drawn from different parties and social orders with varying roots and opposing aims, were momentarily agreed on demanding Rome. The worse the situation of France became, the more accusations of weakness and cowardice poured on the Government from all sides; threats of taking over power seemed about to become action at any moment. Now, while those with nothing to complain of were keeping malcontents at bay, advising prudence and steering between two currents, one night the duke, who had been away on his estates, went to the National Club where battle was joined day and night, and expressed his opinion unhesitatingly; the moment had come to act! If the Government let this chance escape it would never be excused in the nation's eyes! He had always opposed the impatience of the progressive party, for though it might be warm-hearted, it could do the country great harm. But now times were ripe and any delay would be an inexcusable fault. If those in Florence didn't do their duty he threatened ' to go out into the streets with a rifle, as in '60 . . .'

435

'Ah, the buffoon . . . ah, the old fox . . .' they exclaimed in the enemy camp. But in spite of his denigrators the duke's new opinions, so frankly professed and repeated daily to whoever wanted to listen or not, did sustain his shaky credit. Benedetto Giulente had been amazed to hear them as, foreseeing his uncle following a temporising policy till the last, he had done so himself. He was even more surprised when the duke came to see him and said they must begin republishing the news-sheet *Italia risorta* to urge the Government along the road to Rome; the time was ripe, by not following the current they risked being overwhelmed by it.

Benedetto, though spending all day at the Town Hall, got together an editorial staff of municipal clerks and elementary schoolmasters, and published the news-sheet. Lucrezia ranted against this husband of hers who now wanted Rome, if you please, ' as if he could put it in his pocket or carry it off to sell at a fair!' But Benedetto's inflamatory articles, announcing that the duke was on the people's side and ready to leave for Florence if the Government refused to listen to the country's voice, obtained a new wave of popularity for the Deputy.

The day when the news came of Victor Emmanuel's letter to the Pope, there also arrived an unexpected guest from Rome, Don Lodovico. He had sent news of himself to his family only once a year or so, intent as he was on the duties of his office and the forwarding of a career which was now well advanced. Already, in little more than three years, he was Secretary of Propaganda, Archbishop of Nicea, and held in high esteem by Pius IX. To the prince, who looked at him at first as if he had dropped from the moon, he said in a tone of gentle reproval:

' Ferdinando is at death's door, and you merely wrote to say he was unwell! Had it not been for Monsignor the Bishop, I'd not have known the truth!'

And he went and settled by his sick brother's side. The latter no longer left his bed; when he shut his eyes his green, emaciated face was like a corpse's, but he refused all treatment more obstinately than before. As his body decayed the last gleams of his obscured reason dimmed too; now he sent out every day for dozens upon dozens of boxes of pins and reams of paper and packets of pencils. These were for tracing plans of campaign,

436

putting in signs for forts, encampments and headquarters; but he forgot what he bought them for, and went on ordering more and more and shouting and raving if he was not obeyed. With evangelical patience, with untiring zeal, with admirable abnegation, Don Lodovico watched over the sick man and complied with his every mania. Meanwhile—this was driving Baldassarre to despair—evil tongues were saying that he had come to Sicily not for the love of the Booby, to whom he had never given a thought, but to avoid being in Rome at such a critical moment, and take council later from events! . . .

These events were moving fast. Italian troops got orders to advance into the Roman States. There was a feverish wait for news. The duke was now at the Prefecture all day, opening the Prefects' telegrams and then spreading the news in them as if he had received it direct from Lanza.

'It's the end of the world!' cried the old spinster at Ferdinando's, where the whole family were now meeting in a room far from that of the dying man, who refused to have anyone near him. The prince shook his head and the Princess Graziella made the sign of the Cross, while Monsignor Don Lodovico murmured with eyes to the ground:

'We must forgive them for they know not what they do.'

Lucrezia was viper-like against her husband, and no-one mentioned the duke, whose conduct was so shameful. But Donna Ferdinanda, unshakable in her faith, launched out particularly against Don Blasco, who was now booming more loudly than ever round the pharmacies:

'I always said so. Pius IX' (he no longer called him 'The Holy Father') 'should have seen it in time when he was master of the situation. What does he expect now? He's made his bed and must lie on it!'

He had joined the Reading Circle and went there every day with his teacher friend to get news and reassure himself about the chances of having to hand back the San Nicola land. He would also bawl abuse at the tepid of heart, vigorously support his brother and read Giulente's fiery articles out loud, approving them, admiring them.

437

'Ha! How well my nephew writes! That's what I call writing!'

But Don Blasco's recent apostasy, the duke's longstanding betrayal, did not withdraw the esteem of purists from the Uzeda; with the Curia, particularly, their conduct, loyalty to sane principles, constant devotion to the good cause made them favourite children. One day in spite of bad weather Monsignor the Bishop went to visit Ferdinando in order to repay a visit made by Don Lodovico, to have news of the sick man and console the afflicted family. All went to meet the prelate and kiss his hand. The princess had tears in her eyes from emotion.

'What news of our dear sick?'

'Not good, Monsignore,' replied Lodovico, sighing sadly. 'We've even had to send a message to our brother Raimondo.'

'But is there no remedy whatsoever?'

'We've tried everything; Lourdes water, Loretto medals . . .'

'Good, good. But have you called a doctor? What medicines have you been giving him?'

'Alas! . . .' Lodovico seemed to mean by opening wide his arms, 'our poor brother's life is no longer in the hands of man . . .'

He did not say that Ferdinando had gone completely off his head. Mute distrust of his brothers, secret suspicions that discounted any possible connection between their over-zealous care of him and any affection, were growing daily and had so taken charge of his mind that he could accept no other idea. He, who for thirty-nine years had given such proof of disinterest as to be called 'Booby' by his mother and let everyone rob him, suddenly revealed his Viceroy side by absurd, mad suspicion, now that he had nothing more to leave. As his body grew weaker and his brain darker, his suspicion grew, until with the arrival of his brother Raimondo it became raging certainty.

The count arrived with his wife and young son. She looked thirty years older, did poor Donna Isabella; unrecognisable as once her predecessor had been unrecognisable too. In the five years they had been away, in Palermo, Milan, Paris, wherever her husband's whims had taken them, rumours had from time to time reached Sicily that she was paying bitterly for the harm done to the first countess, that Raimondo, thoroughly tired of this woman whose acquisition had cost him so much, and unable to consider breaking this second chain which he had so stupidly put round his own neck, had taken to gadding more than before, bringing fresh girls into his marriage bed, maltreating in every way his new wife, whose prudence, patience, submission and humility, were never enough to avert the rancour, spite, almost hatred, of her husband. But although these rumours were not incredible in view of Raimondo's character, they had as yet found little credit, for they might have been put around by people envious of Donna Isabella, by the count's enemies or by the usual evil tongues.

With Raimondo's arrival, no more doubt was possible. He stayed at the hotel as he had seven years before after finally leaving his first family, but this time he was accompanied by four or five women, governesses, *bonnes*, and maids, all young, each prettier than the last, Swiss, Lombard, English, an international harem. He had a room apart from his wife, and when relations came to visit they heard him calling her *voi*, and could read Donna Isabella's expiatory sufferings in her face. She had changed, not only in appearance but in manner. She talked slowly, avoided looking at her husband, seemed afraid of displeasing him even by her presence. And Raimondo did not hide his own feelings towards her. That *voi* had been eloquent enough, but he affected not to address a word to her, not to hear what she said. When he went to visit his sick brother he said to her in front of all his relations: ' You needn't come too.'

Now the Booby, already out of his mind, went into panic-stricken frenzy at sight of his brother. With eyes starting from his head, hair all tumbled over his haggard terrifying face, he shrieked:

'Murderers! . . . Murderers! . . . Help! . . . The Prussians! . . . They want to poison me!'

He shouted in delirium the whole night through. But when the crisis was over the same idea remained, fixed and irremovable. Such was his persecution mania that he refused to open his mouth for fear of poison. Every time anyone came near him with food he clenched his teeth, screamed, and found enough strength in his scraggy arms to thrust off attempts to make him swallow a sip of milk or soup.

'Help! . . . Bismarck! Murderer!'

Lucrezia sat beside him, took him by the hand and asked:

'But what are you frightened of? Don't you recognise us? . . . D'you think I want to poison you? or Giacomo? or Raimondo? . . .'

The madman smiled incredulously, but when they tried once more to get him to take a mouthful, prolong his life for a day or two, avoid his dying of hunger, he began shouting again. 'Murder! . . . Help! . . . Murderer!'

One night, as Don Blasco was about to leave home in the teacher's company the prince's coachman came up, panting hard.

'Excellency, they're waiting for you at the Cavaliere Ferdinando's . . . they're all there . . . The Signorino's having the Last Sacraments . . .'

The monk was in a great hurry to get to the Reading Circle and hear the latest news, of which the last to come was of Italian troops before Rome. Curiosity was universal and highly excited. Don Blasco was in a positive frenzy. Even so at this announcement of death he was just about to answer that he would come at once, when suddenly up rushed another messenger, this time from the duke.

'His Excellency expects you at home immediately . . . It's most urgent.'

'I'm coming.'

The teacher, declaiming against the Tribunal of the Holy Office, accompanied him to the duke's new house, where the latter had been living since the first of the month. On reaching the gate the monk asked permission of his companion, who walked up and down and waited for him. Two or three minutes later Don Blasco reappeared at a run, pale in the face and waving a piece of paper.

'It's ours! . . . it's ours! . . .'

'Who? . . . What? . . .'

'Come on! . . .' exclaimed the monk, speeding his pace and panting hard.

'To the Reading Circle! . . . Rome is ours! . . . The breach is open!'

'What? . . . Wait! . . . Show me!'

' On . . . On . . . my brother got the dispatch. The troops are in. To the Circle!'

He rushed in like a bomb among members sitting on the pavements in the cool.

' It's ours! It's ours! It's ours . . . Rome is ours!'

All got up, surrounded him, talking together, and gesticulating. He spread out a piece of paper on which the duke had copied the telegram sent to the Prefect in order to hide its official character, changing the address to make people think it had come to him. People hurried over from the end of the room, passers-by stopped, the crowd grew from moment to moment. All wanted to read the news, but Don Blasco did not let any of them handle the dispatch, which in the excitement risked being torn to pieces.

' Read it! Read it! . . . We want to hear it!'

Getting up on a chair the monk read out in his booming voice:

' Florence, 5 p.m., to Honourable Oragua, Catania. At ten this morning after five hours' gunfire national troops opened breach in walls at Porta Pia . . . white flag raised on Castel Sant'Angelo ended hostilities . . . Our losses twenty dead, about one hundred wounded . . .'

A yell went up all round. But Don Blasco, dominating the shouts, called:

' To the Hospice . . . For the band . . . Stop! . . . flags! . . .'

In a second, every flag in the Reading Circle was brought by waiters dazed at the shouting. Don Blasco seized one, opened a way amid the crowd and yelled out again:

' To the Hospice! . . . to the Hospice!'

On the way shouts of ' Hurrah for Italy!' . . . ' Hurrah for Rome!' echoed all round, demonstrators grew and grew in numbers. Those still ignorant of what it was about were calling out to know what had happened, and all cried back:

' Rome taken by our troops! . . . A dispatch has reached the Deputy, the Duke of Oragua! . . .'

When the band of the Hospice, collected in a rush, began playing, the noise became deafening. Meanwhile musicians and bandleader were asking:

' Where to? . . . Where'll we go?'

' To the Deputy's! . . .' replied ten, a hundred voices. ' To the duke's.'

In the Deputy's house every window was lit up, a flag as big as a ship's sail fluttered from the central balcony, and the Deputy in person answered and waved his handkerchief to the cries of ' Hurrah for Rome! Rome, Italy's Capital! Hurrah for Oragua! Hurrah for the Deputy!'

Suddenly, while some shouted for silence expecting a suitable speech, the duke vanished. To avoid the danger of having to speak, as Giulente was not there to help him, being with his wife at the dying Ferdinando's bedside, the duke now came down to meet the demonstrators and mingle in the crowd.

' Hurrah! . . . Hurrah! . . . to the Prefecture!'

And the march began again. Don Blasco, holding the banner at the slope, his top-hat slightly askew, his clerical collar damp with sweat, was walking in the middle of the demonstration arm-in-arm with the teacher, who had run across him again and now did not let him go.

' On with your lights! . . .' shouted his followers at every step, and applause or whistles alternated as windows were lit or stayed closed and dark as before. The flood of demonstrators stopped a moment in front of a draper's shop, ' Torches! . . . Hand-torches!'

All those found were distributed and lit at once. The smoky, guttering gleams, reflected on houses, lit up their fronts, struck gleams in window panes; handkerchiefs and hats waved over the sea of heads; the band raised general enthusiasm by playing at full blast the Royal March and the Garibaldi Anthem. Shouts echoed loudest, longest, thickest around the Deputy.

' Hurrah for Rome! Hurrah for Italy! Hurrah for Oragua!'

Suddenly the demonstration stopped again as if held up and a muttering arose.

' Still here! . . . On . . . on! . . . Down with! . . . Death to! . . . What is it? . . . What is it? . . .'

From an alley had appeared a friar. At sight of the habit the demonstrators leading stopped and shouted to the unfortunate man:

' Down with priests! . . . Down with habits! . . . Hurrah for our own Rome!'

The friar, livid-faced with starting eyes, glanced a moment at the screaming and threatening crowd. Suddenly he raised his arms and wailed:

'Eh! ... Eh! ...'

'It's the mad one ... Let him go!' exclaimed some. But few heard this and the crowd began moving on shouting:

'Death to priests! ... Down with the Temporal Power! ... Down! ... Death!'

Don Blasco craned his neck and recognised Fra' Carmelo, another of the mad Uzeda, a bastard who in spite of his christening was showing himself one of the family too. Meanwhile, at sight of the habit, the teacher quite lost control like a bullock at a red flag.

'Death to crows! ... Down with tricorns! ... Hurrah for lay thought! ... Down with ultramontanes!'

In the fantastic light of the torches, the madman went on gesturing frenziedly, shouting, 'Hey! ... hey! ...' without recognising His ex-Paternity, Don Blasco. The latter, not to be outdone by the teacher yelling away by his ear was also shrieking:

'Down! ... Death! ... Down! ...'

# BOOK III

# 1

' M o s t honoured Signor,

' A knowledge of the origins and history of our island nobility should never be underestimated, particularly in these times when the value of that nobility is at last being appreciated at home whereas hitherto naught but the foreign was admired. It might seem superfluous to undertake such a narration after the works of Mugnòs, Villabianca and other famous and immortal writers had torn aside the veils of history, but that those distinguished and authoritative authors stopped, by nature's law, at the times in which they lived. Apart however from the need to prolong their accounts into our own days there is another reason for re-telling; and that is the rarity of those distinguished works, which few have means to acquire. Wherefore, that all may have access to a new and modern version, we decided to embark on this enterprise. Lest we be accused of pride for undertaking so vast a task we would not mention that we learnt the doctrines of heraldry with our mother's milk, being ourselves descendants of not the last among armigerous families of Sicily, acquiring thus a suitable ground-work of such knowledge. Therefore we nurture a hope that thanks to our indefatigable studies and our patient examination of important archives rich in documents on which we alone have had the opportunity of setting eyes, we can bring to conclusion the task which we have set ourselves, in the words of the Poet " From infamy secure, perchance with praise ".

' You, most honoured and illustrious Signor, as a cultivator of historical studies and a lover of Sicilian glories, will not, we are sure, deny us your much desired assistance by associating yourself with our enterprise; so we hope and trust that your noble self will deign to put your signature on this form, already subscribed by numerous persons of importance. No low ideas of profit move us, since, thanks be to God, we are not in need of money, only of your noble support in order to provide for simple expenses. Thus we can assure all being well.

SUBSCRIPTION FORM

FOR THE WORK

of the Cavaliere Don Eugenio Uzeda of the Princes of Francalanza and Mirabella, Dukes of Oragua, Counts of La Lumera, etc. etc.; formerly Gentleman of the Bedchamber (with functions) to His Majesty King Ferdinand II; decorated with the Ottoman Order of Nisciam-Iftkar by His Highness the Bey of Tunis, Member of various academies, etc. etc., entitled:

THE SICILIAN HERALD

consisting in the documented history of the origins, fates and stories of noble Sicilian families from remote antiquity until present times: in three volumes, of which the first contains text, the second genealogical trees, and the third coats-of-arms. To appear by instalments every month. The price of every instalment: two lire; of subscription to the complete work: fifty lire. N.B. Anyone arranging for six subscriptions will have the right to publish his own genealogical tree. Anyone arranging for twelve will be granted a full-page of his coat-of-arms in colour.'

This circular, distributed in many hundreds of copies, proved to the Cavaliere Don Eugenio's fellow-citizens that he was still among the living. There had been no news of him for some years. At first he had written to his relations asking them to lend money for some important and safe speculation, but as they all flatly refused, he had finally given up. What he had done all that time, where he had been, no one knew. None of those who went to Palermo ever saw him, none heard tell of him, and in fact so ignorant were people about him that many supposed he had passed quietly on to the next world. Before the post had finished distributing the leaflets on *The Sicilian Herald*, the author arrived in person.

He had been away for a long time and was now nearly sixty;

but he was also strangely disfigured, in fact almost unrecognisable. On his thin, emaciated face his nose seemed to have lengthened like a trumpet or snout, a flexible proboscis perfectly adapted for rooting in muck. Loss of teeth, by making his mouth fall in, also contributed to the ignoble, almost animal aspect of his whole face. The filth of his shirt and tail-coat, which was too long and too wide, worn with a waistcoat that had once been white, and a greasy hat that seemed to be sweating from heat, made him look like a waiter in a cheap restaurant or a croupier in a billiards and gambling saloon. The gout that tortured his feet gave him a twisted dragging walk. He put up in a third-class hotel; but the first people to whom he revealed his identity—as no one recognised him—were told that he had found no rooms free at the Grand Hotel, and that having left Palermo unexpectedly he had been unable to bring his trunks with him.

The first visit he made was to the head of the family, but on reaching the palace gates he was amazed to find them shut and only the wicket open. When he made himself known as the master's uncle to the new porter, who was looking him up and down, he was told there was no one there. Neither the prince nor the princess, nor Consalvo; they were all away. The young prince had been travelling for nearly a year, the master and mistress were away collecting the signorina from college and showing her some of the world. Not quite convinced, used to being turned away, the cavaliere was looking up at the windows as if trying to see through the walls, when he heard himself greeted:

'Excellency? ... Your Excellency here?'

It was the coachman, Pasqualino Riso. He too had gone down in the world and no longer sported smart uniforms, rings and golden chains as once upon a time.

'All away, Excellency ... the house is empty!'

'When will they be back?'

'We don't know, Excellency; perhaps the master and mistress, for the vintage ...'

'And the young prince?'

'Ah, the young prince, not for the moment ...'

And Don Eugenio, eyes glittering with curiosity in his

famished face, sat down on the backless chair which the porter
kept at the door of his little room, and asked:

'Why? What's the news?'

Gradually Pasqualino revealed the truth. The young prince
could no longer live at home, at least for a time, because of
the constant friction with his father. From all these upsets the
Signor Prince had fallen ill. As for Don Consalvo, he could not
be said to be afflicted enough to fall ill, but the quarrels and
disagreements had made him lose weight too. So it was best
for them both to be apart for a time . . . thus the prince had
had time to calm down and persuade himself that after all his
son had not actually murdered anyone! Perhaps they were
accusing him of taking no interest in the administration of the
property, of ill-treating his stepmother? 'But Your Excellency
knows what the Signor Prince is like; he'd have both hands cut
off rather than hand over the account-books and strong-box
keys to others! It's true the Signorino is not as fond of the
princess as he was of his mother. But one has only one mother,
hasn't one, Cavaliere? A stepmother should be respected, and
he does respect her . . .' The real reason for the friction was in
fact different. The Signor Prince did not want to have money
spent, and the young prince on the other hand spent it like a
lord . . . So the Signorino had signed one or two I.O.U.'s, and
every time creditors presented one to the prince, good God, he
nearly had a stroke. He even wanted to have him arrested, as if
such a thing could be said in the Francalanza palace even as
a joke!

Pasqualino made a gesture of indignation, brought out another
chair from the little room and sat down next to the cavaliere,
who, nodding his head gravely, took from his pocket a half-
smoked cigar and asked the coachman for a match. 'Then,
Your Excellency will allow me? . . .' and he lit his pipe and went
on with what he was saying. For whom, then, had the Signor
Prince amassed all those riches? Not for himself, as he got no
pleasure from them; not for his daughter; for once married the
Signorina Teresa would take her dowry and that would be
that; so for the son, surely! Then why keep him short of money?
A young man like the Prince of Mirabella needed so many
things; he had to spend a lot! . . . The master did not under-

stand that, for he himself as a young man had lived like a monk . . . 'But we're not all made the same way are we?' And then times had changed. The gentry had to spend if they wanted to be respected; otherwise some newly enriched shoemaker would be more respected! . . .

And Pasqualino, in his bitterness at being unable to get as much as he once used to for private household expenses, boldly qualified the prince as swinishly stingy, capable of denying his own son for a lire, and for the cavaliere's benefit, he hinted that if the head of the family had been different he would have helped relations not as rich as himself. Don Eugenio, smoking and spitting, his thin Don Quixotish legs crossed, bowed his head, agreed with the coachman and with himself too. 'I said . . . it couldn't last . . . my nephew has such a way of behaving!'

The conversation went on in the cool of the vestibule. Master and servant discoursed intimately, as equals, mingling smoke of pipe and cigar; in fact though Pasqualino was no longer smart as before, yet he seemed the master and Don Eugenio the servant. The head porter, part-scandalised and part-envious of the confidence granted by the cavaliere to the coachman was walking dignifiedly up and down before the entrance, his hands behind the back of his frogged overcoat.

'Who is that old rag-bag?' asked the estate-clerks as they came out after work.

'The Signor Prince's uncle, so he says!'

All in all, that was the best greeting poor Don Eugenio got. Next day he began to do the rounds of relations who were in town. First he went to his brother, Don Blasco.

The monk now looked on the point of exploding. His great belly was swelled out with blubber, his head bigger than ever and his chin sunk into a gelatinous mass of neck. He was now so huge and his legs so weak that he could not move. Beside him Donna Lucia, Garino's wife, seemed light and slim.

'Why've you come back?' he said to his brother by way of greeting, immediately he saw him enter. He had in fact received the circular of *The Sicilian Herald*, and realising from it that the author must be in sore need of money was making the first move to avoid requests for subsidies.

451

'I've come only for a little visit,' replied Don Eugenio. 'First of all to see you all again, and then to associate you with the work which I sent you a leaflet about.'

And he began to enumerate distinguished subscribers: His Highness the Bey of Tunis, the Vizirs of the Regency, the chief grandees of Palermo, the Prince of Alì, the Marchese of Lojacomo, the Duke of this and the Count of that.

'Well?' exclaimed the monk, as if to say 'Why come to tell me all these lies?', without even asking his brother. 'Have you been in Tunis? What were you doing there?'

'I also have subscriptions by twenty Town Councils, thirty Societies and eight Libraries. It's superb business. When all is said and done, and expenses of printing, paper, postage, etc. deducted, even with only the subscriptions gathered so far it's a sure gain, but I've still half Sicily to go round for subscribers. If we reach three hundred there'll be ten thousand lire net profit.'

'Well . . .?'

'I'd like to suggest our printing the book together.'

The monk stared him in the whites of the eyes.

'Are you mad?'

'Why? Or don't you think there's profit in it? I'll tot it up for you in a minute and show you the signatures I've gathered.'

'I don't want to see a thing! Whatever you say I believe; thank you very much; but keep the ten thousand lire for yourself.'

The cavaliere persisted for quite a time in the wheedling insinuating tone of some agent or middleman, with a fine flow of words to show the beauties of his proposal in the best light but to no purpose; Don Blasco went on refusing, first dryly, then raising his voice, then shouting for this nagger to get out of his hair.

'Then . . . if you don't want to run the business risks . . . do me a favour . . . Subscribers don't pay in advance, I need a sum down to begin printing. Lend me a thousand lire or so . . .'

'I haven't got it.'

'I'll hand over the surest signatures, you can choose them yourself.'

'I haven't got it.'

The cavaliere did not allow even this to discourage him. He reduced his request from a thousand to eight hundred and then to five hundred lire, and as the monk went on replying almost in a whine of impatience; 'I haven't got it . . . I . . . have . . . not . . . got . . . it . . . How am I to din that into you? . . .' Don Eugenio ended calmly:

'Then I'll wait till it's convenient for you. I'm in no hurry; I must get all the subscriptions first . . . Then I'll bring the application forms, enquiries, and leaflets to show you.'

Hoping to succeed better with his sister, the cavaliere went and renewed his efforts with Donna Ferdinanda. The old spinster, dry and green as garlic, seemed to defy time; the years passed over her without effect. She was now sixty-two but looked no more than fifty. Only her hands had become covered with wrinkles and were worn thin and calloused from counting money, as if from working iron or hoeing land. She too had received *The Sicilian Herald* circular; on seeing her brother she began to ask news of his health, of Palermo, of the people she knew in that city, listening with interest to the interminable speeches of the cavaliere, who, encouraged by this friendly reception, named great numbers of people with whom he was, he said, like a 'brother', telling stories about them with as much interest as if they affected him personally. 'The separation of the Duke Proti, such a dear friend . . . that mad baroness simply *refused* to listen to me . . . As I told the prince, my dear Emanuele, I said, do think it over well . . .' His gossip went on a long time because Donna Ferdinanda was giving him a lot of rope, which the cavaliere did not even need, so happy was he to mention his grand connections at Palermo.

'And d'you know the best of the news? Palmi's daughter is married!'

'Yes? Who to?'

'To my friend Memmo Duffredi, Duffredi of Casaura, Ciccio Lojacomo's nephew, one of the first nobles of Palermo. He's worth millions!'

'Really?'

'Such luck for the girl! That intriguer the baron arranged it all and pinned Memmo down. Of course, as a relation I couldn't quite say it, otherwise I'd have gone to Ciccio and

453

warned him, 'Your son can find a better match . . .' And that girl *has* a certain way about her . . . Anyway, I didn't say a word, particularly as when it was all being arranged I was in Tunis . . .'

'Oh, so you've been in Tunis, have you? And what were you doing there?'

'What was I doing there? Nothing. Just a trip . . .' and he coughed a little, even so, embarrassed and almost confused. Donna Ferdinanda went on asking him questions about Tunis, if it was a fine city, how long he had been there and so on, until the cavaliere, as if finally making up his mind, said:

'I also went there to gather subscriptions for my new book, you know . . .'

'Book?' exclaimed the old spinster, looking amazed. 'What book?'

'D'you mean to say you never got the leaflet?'

'I never got anything.'

'*The Sicilian Herald?* . . . the history of our nobility?'

'A book! So you're printing a book, are you? . . . ha, ha, ha,' and she broke out into one of those rare laughs of hers which caught people on the raw. Don Eugenio, who had sustained scatheless all the monk's refusals, was quite riled by his sister's hilarity.

'Why not?' asked he, trying to re-erect his own dignity which Donna Ferdinanda was demolishing with that nasty laughter of hers.

'Why shouldn't I be as good at writing as anyone else?'

'Ha! ha! ha!'

On and on went her laughter. But when the old man explained what book it was he had written she became subtler, more ironic, more cutting. A history of the nobility after those of Mugnòs and Villabianca? To slip in all the new rich who called themselves 'Cavaliere' and 'Marchese'? Genuine nobles were all in the old books! . . . Then the cavaliere tried to show what a good speculation it was at least, but the old spinster gave him no quarter. Make money with dirtied paper? Who on earth valued soiled paper except cheesemongers? And whoever would think of buying a book from him? They'd all start laughing like herself! Signatures? Given to get rid of him! The point was how many would pay up later! . . .

'At least, lend me a couple of hundred lire, won't you?'

'No, you'd never give them back.'

And all insistence was useless.

When he went to repeat the attempt with his niece Chiara, Don Eugenio was not even able to see her; the maid said that the marchese was out and the marchesa shut in her room with a headache.

'Tell her her uncle is here.'

'Your Excellency must excuse me, when she has a headache, nobody can talk to the Signora Marchesa.'

On the cavaliere making a gesture of impatience, the woman muttered, looking around, 'Excellency, there's trouble.'

'What trouble?'

'The Marchesa . . . but please, Signor Cavaliere, don't lose me my job . . . Mad for her husband, wasn't she, Excellency? All one they were. Whatever the Signor Marchese wanted was law for her . . . and the master never took advantage of it; love and accord in every possible way. But now? . . . now there's no more peace, because of that son of . . . I know who! A little devil he is, Excellency, and the mistress dotes on him, lets him do what he likes, takes his side against the master. They quarrel every day . . . the Signor Marchese wants to correct him, teach him manners, make him study, but Your Excellency's niece takes against the master for maltreating the lad. Yesterday things came to a head; they haven't talked for twenty-four hours . . . The Signor Marchese left the house at dawn. I wonder if he'll come back!'

And Don Eugenio for all his insistence could not persuade the maid to face her mistress's ill-temper by taking the message.

Then he went to knock at the Giulentes' door. He reached it at about dusk, after a day hurrying to and fro. Benedetto was not there; and Lucrezia was unrecognisable she had become so hideous. Her body had become a sack of flesh in which neither breast nor waist nor hips could be distinguished. Her face, from continual acrimony and incurable discontent at her own condition, looked hard and sour, unexpectedly like the prince's. The

455

first remarks she made to her uncle on seeing him after all those years were against Benedetto.

'He's not here; he's never at home. Now he's not mayor any more he's got himself nominated President of the Provincial Council. For love of country, of course, Your Excellency! The older he gets the more of an ass he becomes. He's mad! But the awful thing is he makes me mad too. After twenty years . . .'— she calculated time in her own way—' any man who was less of an ass would have realised he ought to stop sucking up to people. Instead, he's like an egg on the boil; the longer he's at it the harder he sticks! He wants to be a deputy: what for, I ask? If he were a deputy, what would he get out of it? All he got from being mayor was that not a soul could ever see him, not even those he'd been crazy enough to help. Serves him right! . . .'

Towards her own family she still had that mixture of resentment, envy and respect, according as pride at being part of it, regret at having left it, or suspicion of being rejected by it was uppermost in her mind. When talking of the prince's journey now, she kept on mentioning that her brother and sister-in-law wrote to her every two days, and quoting from their letters announcing an autumn return. Then she began criticising and pin-pricking:

'They were right to collect Teresina from college themselves and carry her off travelling . . . My sister-in-law's another mother to that girl! . . . She loves her so much she kept her two years more than necessary in college so as to turn her out a lady of letters. Graziella knows such a lot about belles-lettres!'

Then she at once added, 'Your Excellency hasn't seen Teresina's latest portrait? . . . No? Wait, you'll see what a beauty she is. They sent it me two months ago . . . But as to Consalvo,' she went on after showing her uncle the portrait, 'there's no news whatsoever . . . he might not be their son at all. Without the letters he writes to his aunt we wouldn't know if he was alive or dead. He's said to be in Paris now . . . he's been in Berlin, London, Vienna . . .'

The cavaliere was not listening to her but mulling over his best approach. As soon as his niece paused, he explained the speculation he proposed and its combination of sure

financial gain with nobility of purpose? But Lucrezia replied:
'The history of our nobility? Where's there any nobility nowadays? What history does Your Excellency intend writing? Boot-lickers are the rage now, not nobles! Nowadays to get any respect one has to come from nothing! Why not write the history of jumped-up peasants and notaries? There's money to be made there!'

Imperturbable, Don Eugenio started again next day. At the Radalì-Uzeda's he found the Duke Michele and the Baron Giovannino; the duchess was out. Michele, at twenty-five, was losing his hair and seemed twice that age. Giovannino on the other hand was more graceful, slim and elegant than before. When they heard their relative's request, they both replied that only their mother could give an answer. And next day the cavaliere went back and talked to the duchess, who said in surprise, ' Me print books? However did such an idea get into your head? As if I could know a thing about it!'
So Don Eugenio had a walk for nothing.
But he did not lose heart. From distant relatives he passed to friends, mere acquaintances, people he met in the street whom he stopped under pretence of seeing and greeting again. He would begin by recounting as if he'd had it directly the news of the prince and of Consalvo learnt from Lucrezia, regret the quarrel between father and son, announce the return of the young princess, whom he said he had seen in Florence. ' What a beauty! . . .' Then he talked of his sojourn in Palermo, described the apartment of ten rooms in which he lived on the Cassaro, all the while draped majestically in filthy ragged clothes which told only of poverty, hunger and squalid promiscuity. He would also mention his journey to Tunis, the decoration he had received from the Bey, without explaining quite why he had obtained it and what precisely he had done at His Highness' Court. After thoroughly bemusing people with all this he would ask point blank:
' Did you get my leaflet?'
And again he explained the scope of the book, enumerated the subscribers he had got. These grew in numbers every time; the signatures of private citizens went up from two to three

hundred, to four, five hundred; those of Town Councils from fifty, to sixty, to ninety; libraries multiplied from one moment to another. A thousand subscribers were already certain, another thousand more or less definite. And he would offer a part share, ask for less and less money down, and finally declare that he would be quite content with twelve signatures, with six, even with one. To get away from him people made ambiguous promises. But he noted down their names in a grimy dog-eared notebook, stuffed only with circulars and application forms which he redistributed, thrusting them into the pockets of anyone who made to refuse them, and asking them to put them around and fill one up as soon as possible. After a day of work, just as he was about to go into his hotel again, he met Benedetto coming out.

'Excellency! . . . how are you? . . . I came to visit you; I'm so sorry for not being at home yesterday.'

Somewhat embarrassed, Don Eugenio invited him up to his room. It had a sagging floor, two strips of white cotton acting as curtains on the window, a basin on a chair and a jug on the floor.

'I had to come here as the Grand Hotel was all full up. How uncomfortable one is in this town. At Palermo I had a twelve-roomed apartment. The staircase was really superb! . . .'

And in spite of Lucrezia's refusal he pulled the circulars from his pocket and got down to business at once.

'Didn't your wife tell you? . . . I've come to get my book printed. I won't hand it over to anyone, not for twenty thousand lire. But I haven't the money to start printing. Shall we do it together? Let's split the profits, like good relatives and friends.'

Giulente hesitated a little, then asked: 'What did Lucrezia say?'

'Your wife? She said "yes", as long as you were sure it was a good thing. Just look here,' and beside himself with delight at having finally found someone who did not refuse him he thrust some signed forms in front of him. 'All right, all right, if Lucrezia approves . . .'

'Even if she changes her mind, after all, we don't need her consent!'

Benedetto hesitated a little, then said:

458

' No, it's necessary . . . for now she keeps all the money!'

' What! The money? Haven't you a thousand lire or two to dispose of?'

' No, Excellency. Public affairs have been taking so much of my time that I've handed over all accounts to her . . .'

# 2

T H E prince's return with his uncle the duke, his wife and his
daughter, at the beginning of winter, gave new food for public
curiosity. Everyone was longing to see the face of this little
princess whose beauty had been so much talked of. But though
exaggerated advance praise had made people rather sceptical,
yet the reality left imagination far behind. The girl's white skin
and fair hair, her delicate, exquisite, almost vaporous beauty
were unparalleled in the family of the Viceroys. The old Spanish
race, mixed in the course of centuries with island stock part
Greek, part Saracen, had gradually lost its purity and nobility of
form. Who, for example, could have distinguished Don Blasco
from any fat friar of peasant stock, or Donna Ferdinanda from
any old spinning woman? But just as in the preceding generation there had been the exception of Count Raimondo, so now
Teresa too seemed to have come from some old cell of pure
Castilian blood left intact.

Tall, narrow-shouldered, with a waist round which her
hands could almost reach, making the curve of her hips more
pronounced, Teresa had a natural elegance, a noble grace of
bearing, not wholly freed from the awkwardness of a college girl
who had been in an ill-fitting uniform a few months before. At
first when she drove out in a carriage with her stepmother,
people would stop on the pavements or wait by the palace gates,
to stare at her open-mouthed. She seemed not to notice this
blatant curiosity, and never in fact looked at anyone.

At home, naturally, the first to come and visit her were her
uncles and aunts. Lucrezia now almost hung round her niece's
skirts, accompanied her everywhere, gave her advice, enjoying a

chance to exercise her own mania for authority. Her the princess let be, but she did not even return Chiara's visit, because of the little bastard. How could a girl like Teresa, just out of school, go to a house where such things went on? To all and sundry, servants, relations and acquaintances, she would say with elaborate gestures and rolling of the eyes, ' Can I allow my daughter to know such things? I can't help it if Chiara takes offence.' And Chiara did take offence. She had now broken off connection with all her relations from love for the maid's son, who had become so spoilt that he ordered her about as he liked, called her *tu* and even hit her when he felt like it. But she let him be, and if the marchese said a word of protest there would be shouts, threats, hell let loose. On hearing of her sister-in-law and cousin's scruples she railed loudly against her, particularly when by Giacomo's orders Donna Graziella took Teresa to kiss the hand of her uncle Don Blasco. So she could go to the monk's, who kept that Cigar-woman and his three daughters at home, could she, and not to her? ' Yes, of course, it's because they're hoping the monk will leave 'em something . . .'

Don Blasco lived like a lord nowadays. Apart from his house and two estates, he had also put aside quite a bit of money, and the prince paid him respect because of this. The Benedictine let him visit as he did Lucrezia and Chiara; he never went out to anyone as he could no longer get upstairs. But he laid down the law to nieces and nephews, used them in every way, and if any of them made him angry would take out a sheet of paper like Donna Ferdinanda and tear it to pieces. ' Not a cent from me! . . .' His niece Teresa's visit gave him much pleasure; his daughters did not appear, and the princess explained to the girl that Donna Lucia was her uncle's ' housekeeper '.

Such precautions were anyway quite wasted on Teresa. She had no improper curiosity and when she realised that her elders had something to say to each other would move away, go to tidy her room or look after her own little affairs. Not only was she quite outstandingly beautiful, but also full of talents and more accomplished than a good many men. She could draw and paint, speak French and English fluently, write verses and compose music; with all this she was remarkably modest, simple, good and affectionate. On returning to her childhood home where she had left her mother who was now no longer there, she had to be supported and her eyes were two springs of welling tears; but her cult of her dead mother did not prevent her respecting and loving her father and stepmother. She was devout too, with some prayer-book always in her hand when not working at her embroidery, drawing or music. They were gilt books, covered in velvet and scented leather; Months of Mary, Litanies of the Blessed Virgin, lives of saints, holy pictures at every page, all prizes from the Convent of the Annunciation.

But this devoutness and piety did not prevent a love of worldly pleasures and the latest fashions proper to a girl of her years. When she had to dress for making visits or receiving them, or for driving or the theatre, she would linger like other girls before her mirror, and she had a way all her own of wearing the simplest dresses which made her look as if she were going to a ball. When stuffs or trimmings or ornaments had to be chosen at a milliner's or dressmaker's, she would show great taste in selecting the most elegant, sweetly influencing her aunt Lucrezia, who since keeping the money keys got herself a new dress every fortnight, each worse chosen than the last, though expecting her taste to be praised. The princess on the other hand let her stepdaughter do as she wanted and choose what she liked, even referring to her for her own clothes. 'What taste that girl of ours has! What a model daughter!' She praised her particularly for sweetness of character and goodness of heart, kissed and embraced her in front of everyone even at parties, and watched over her like a real mother.

She was very scrupulous too, and did not allow her stepdaughter to read anything but religious books in case she got ideas in her head, or let certain things be talked about in front of her, for fear of words contaminating thoughts. So she was on tenterhooks when her sister-in-law Lucrezia gossiped about mistresses, conjugal separations, illegitimate births. She would begin coughing then to give that tactless woman a hint, and if coughing was not enough would change the subject brusquely in a way all her own, which seemed done on purpose to call attention to the very things she wanted passed over. But Lucrezia noticed nothing at all, and was even tactless enough to keep on saying to her niece, with or without any connecting thread but

462

most often when complaining of Benedetto, 'Take care who you marry, dear, won't you? . . .' or 'Keep your eyes open when you're married, won't you? . . .' The princess would change colour, raise her eyes to the ceiling, making heroic efforts to contain herself, not to say what she thought to this mad-woman whom the Lord had quite rightly deprived of daughters if that was how she thought girls should be brought up. 'Sister-in-law! . . . Lucrezia! . . .' But nothing was of any use, and once the princess put her cards on the table.

'Excuse me, cousin, but such subjects seem quite out of place. Teresa will get married at the proper time, her father will see to that, don't you worry. I don't care for these modern fashions of talking about such things to young ladies.'

Teresa, with eyes lowered and hands in her lap, did not seem to be listening. Lucrezia was speechless and left shortly after without bidding anyone goodbye. But there was another person also who often talked scandal and had to be kept under control by the princess: the Cavaliere Don Eugenio. As soon as the latter heard of his brother's and niece's arrival, he hurried off to them to begin all over again about *The Sicilian Herald*. The duke, without Don Blasco's shouts or Donna Ferdinanda's play-acting, had given him a straight answer. 'My dear fellow, no one has ever made money with books; you'll make even less than others, as you've never learnt how to anyway. If you want to print the book no one can prevent you, but I haven't the money to throw away on such schemes.' Don Eugenio accepted the reproof with bowed head, as if recognising he deserved it, bearing himself flatteringly and humbly before this intriguer who mouthed pompous judgements after enriching himself at public expense, when all was said and done, by manipulating State grants in all sorts of underhand ways!

'At least,' insisted Don Eugenio, 'you'll see the book is bought by the State libraries, won't you? That won't cost you anything, you're so influential . . . All you have to do is say a word.' To this praise the Deputy listened with half-closed eyes, basking in it. Yes, the good days had returned for him. Since his new attitude about the Roman question he had taken on a new lease of life; the election of November '70 had been another triumph. A word from him would certainly have been enough to help his brother. Even so to the other's importunity he replied that he would see, would have to think it over as he had scruples on the matter. 'What would people say? That I'm using my influence to get favours for my family? . . .'

Then Don Eugenio turned to the prince. The latter had avoided as best he could saying anything at first, but eventually found it difficult to insist on a crude refusal, for he was not familiar enough with his uncle to send him packing, nor could he plausibly adduce lack of money. So he let a promise be squeezed from him to advance a couple of thousand lire, waiting until subscriptions had reached a hopeful stage before paying out.

Meanwhile Don Eugenio, elated by this promise, began coming to the palace almost every evening, to the great mortification of the princess, who could not endure the sight of his famished face and wretched clothes, and felt like a soul burning in purgatory when he began telling stories about Palermo society. ' Sasà is marrying off his daughters . . . Cocò's wife has had another of her . . . Nenè's son ran off with a dancer . . .' Cocò was the Prince of Alì, Sasà the Duke of Realcastro, Nenè the Baron Mortara, and nobody could name anyone in Palermo without Don Eugenio's assurance that this person was ' like a brother ' to him . . . Every time he described his apartment the number of rooms grew; it had now reached fifteen and as he could not reasonably increase them any more he began adding ' Apart from stables and coachhouses . . .' The prince let him talk on, but made him pay for his attention and promise of money by using him as a servant, sending him here and there with letters or messages, though still from a certain human respect calling him ' Excellency '. He never mentioned any of his own affairs or made him any sort of confidence. The cavaliere was curious by nature and yearned to know whom they thought of marrying Teresa to, and what Consalvo was doing, when he would be back, but he never managed to learn a thing, particularly about the young prince, who only wrote to Donna Ferdinanda.

News about the young man got back to the palace through Baldassarre, who wrote to the prince every two days with details of his young master's life. These letters would draw ringing laughs from Teresa, written as they were in a fantastic language peculiar to the major-domo. ' His Excellency be well and is enjoying himself . . . today we went to the *Buà di Bologna*, where there was great passing of carriages and gentlemen and ladies on horseback . . .' Every day the major-domo announced the programme for the next, ' Tomorrow we go to the *Ussaburgo* . . . tomorrow we leave for *Fontana Bu* to see the Royal Palace . . .' Donna Ferdinanda was awaiting the account of a far more important visit: that to His Majesty Francis II. Before Consalvo left she had made him promise when he passed through Paris to ' kiss the King's hand ', and as soon as she heard that her nephew was in the French capital she reminded him to keep his promise at once.

Father Gerbini, now Chaplain at the Madeleine in Paris, who frequented the houses of all the legitimatist nobles and had access to the ex-King as one of his intimate circle, requested an audience for the young Sicilian, laying timely emphasis on the loyalty of most of the Uzeda family to the Bourbon cause. In a long letter, which Donna Ferdinanda read out amid a circle of relations, Consalvo described the affectionate greeting of their former sovereign, the concern with which he had asked after the whole family and the gift he had made before dismissing him after a long conversation: his own portrait with an autographed dedication. ' Her Majesty the Queen was unwell, so he had been unable to be received by her too, but the " King " had told him he would like to see him again before his departure! . . .'

Then too came a letter from Baldassarre describing the visit to ' *So Maistà Francisco Secundo*, together with *So Paternità don Placido Gerbini. So Maistà* talked to *So Eccellenza* about *Sigilia* and the *Sigilian* gentry he had met in Naples and *Pariggi. So Eccellenza* kissed his hand and *So Maistà* gave him his portrait, saying that we must come back another time to be presented to *So Maistà* the Queen.' In fact before master and servant left Paris both announced this second audience, but this time the major-domo's letter to his master contained a detail of which there was no word in Consalvo's letter to his aunt. ' *So Maistà* made a great fuss of *So Eccellenza*, and when they shook hands he said who knew when we would meet again; and *So Eccellenza*, as *So Paternità* told me, answered, " *Maistà*, we'll meet again in Naples, in *So Maistà's* palace!" . . .'

From Paris the young man finally returned to Italy, stopped for a short time in Turin and Milan, and passed on to Rome, the last stop on his journey. There he remained some time. But after a couple of letters to his aunt no more was heard from him. Donna Ferdinanda had also recommended him to 'kiss the Pope's foot', and Baldassarre had at the beginning announced that 'Monsignori Don Lotovico' was to take his nephew to the Vatican, but then did not say if the visit had taken place. One day, quite unexpectedly, he announced by telegraph their imminent return.

Met at the station by Donna Ferdinanda and by Teresa—for the prince had stayed in the palace and ordered his wife to do so too—Consalvo made a kind of triumphal entry between two rows of servants and estate employees, who admired their young master's excellent bearing, hailed his return and did all they could to help Baldassarre unload the great quantity of trunks, suitcases, portmanteaux and hat-boxes which filled the carriage and a hired cart. The prince, part-dignified and part-affable, was waiting in the Red Drawing-room and gave him a hand to kiss. And the princess did the same, but with more demonstration of loving concern, 'Have you had a good time? Was the sea calm? Have you all your things? Your rooms are quite ready.'

Travel weariness, bemusement on arrival naturally explained Consalvo's lack of loquacity in those first few hours. In fact that evening, after sending to his father's, sister's, and stepmother's rooms various presents, he chattered away, described his impressions, told some comic anecdotes about Baldassarre, who knowing no language abroad had often got into trouble, and started quarrels with people at whom he mouthed Sicilian swearwords; once in Vienna he had nearly spent the night on a guardroom floor.

Next day Consalvo went on talking about his journey, particularly about Paris; but gradually, as this subject came to an end, the young man took no further part in the conversation. If the princess told some story, or the prince discoursed on family affairs, he just sat and listened and replied with a 'Yes, Excellency' or a 'No, Excellency,' now and again. At table he would sit with his nose in his plate and never look at anyone, often without uttering two consecutive words. The prince for his part began sniffing and dropping into silences, though he sometimes made remarks which did not augur well at all. The princess raised her eyes to the ceiling in consternation, and Teresa, tortured by the chilly atmosphere, even began losing appetite. As he got up from table when his son left the prince burst out with:

'Here we go again! You'll just see, we'll have it all over again! What's wrong with the young fool? He's been travelling for more than a year, had everything he wanted and this is his thanks, sulking, ruining my meals day after day! . . .'

It could not be said that the 'young fool' was mute from lack of desire to talk, for in the presence of strangers he would go on and on telling of his travels, of the great things he had seen, of novelties not even a rumour of which had yet reached Sicily. With Benedetto Giulente in particular and with people more or less in public affairs, he discoursed to their amazement about the organising of city police, maintenance of public gardens, systems of watering streets or illuminating theatres. Why on earth did he bother about such things? To show people he had been abroad? No, not at all; for as well as talking on quite different subjects from before, he was even changing his way of life. He scarcely saw his old wild companions, no longer sought them out, seemed in fact to avoid them. His passion for horses seemed to have quite passed; he never went into stables, never talked to ostlers. No women, no gambling; now he spent his time shut in his own room, where no one knew what on earth he was up to. When he went out he made frequent visits to his uncle the duke and talked to him of serious matters, or was seen in company of people whom before he had avoided like the plague: pundits, politicians of the Reading Circle, frequenters of pharmacies, public place-holders, all the Deputy's retinue. Every day the post brought him a pile of Italian and French newspapers, and every week arrived a big packet of books chosen and ordered by himself.

'What other nonsense is he getting up to now?' the prince said to his wife in ever more acid tones.

'What are you complaining of?' she would reply in conciliatory tones. 'He's quite unrecognisable, he might be a different boy. Let's bless that journey for changing him from black to white!'

Some days Consalvo did not come to table at all; to the lackey sent to call him he replied from behind the door that he was busy. Then the prince flung down his napkin, ground his teeth, almost burst out in front of the parasites present at the meal. At a sign from the princess, Teresa went to visit her brother, and insisted with gentle voice and loving persuasion on his opening the door.

' Why don't you come, you know father gets annoyed.'

' 'Cause I'm busy, I'm writing, I can't lose the thread . . .'

' Stop writing then, to please him, dear! You have so much time to study! Otherwise it would look as if you were doing it on purpose, had something against him . . . or against mother.'

' I haven't anything against anyone. Can't you see I'm writing.' In fact the writing-table was covered with sheets of paper and open books.

When finally he did come to table the prince slowly swelled with rage at seeing his son taciturn and pensive as a new Archimedes.

' I'll eat alone rather than see that funereal face! Frowning like that all day long! He has the Evil Eye! My food will go down the wrong way! It'll choke me! . . .'

Teresa, as the only one capable of exercising an influence over her brother, would go to Consalvo again, take his hands, beg him to be good, talk to him of his filial duties, and he, mute and motionless, let her have her say. But once when among other arguments she produced that of gratitude owed to his father and stepmother he replied with cold and cutting irony:

' A great deal, in truth . . . My father has always loved me, hasn't he, since he kept me shut up for ten years in the Novitiate, as he kept you at college for six? We both of us ought to be grateful, oughtn't we, for his not letting six months pass after our mother's death before putting another in her place? . . . She too, from paradise, must be grateful to him for the respect, love and care with which he surrounded her . . .'

' Quiet! Quiet!' exclaimed Teresa.

' Why should I be quiet? You know, don't you, what they

made the poor thing suffer? But you were in Florence, you couldn't know anything . . .'

'Quiet, Consalvo!'

'Well, what d'you want? Tell me what I must do to please him! When I was out of the house all day, amusing myself in my own way and spending money, it was "no, sir, you must change your life!" Now that I'm always indoors, studying, is he going to badger me still?'

Consalvo was studying political economy, constitutional law and administration. People who did not know what he was doing but could see a radical change in him, attributed it to his lengthy travels, to the common sense which all young men must get into their heads one day sooner or later. The journey in fact had been the origin of the young prince's conversion, his great lesson.

The struggle with his father had disgusted him with his home and also with his native town, where lack of money and weight of paternal authority prevented him doing all he wanted; so he had greeted with joy the idea of leaving and seeing a bit of the world. But the first impression he felt as soon as he got out of Sicily was that which a real king must feel on his way into exile. The day before, although he could not gad as he liked, he had yet been an important person, the most important person in his own town, where everyone from high to low doffed their hats and took an interest in him and his affairs; quite suddenly he woke up to find himself a nobody in the midst of a crowd which did not notice him. Had he seen no-one it might have been better, maybe, but the letters of introduction with which he was furnished put him into touch at Naples, Rome, Florence and Turin with the other nobles of those parts, and he then realised that there were people even more important than he was. The name of the young Prince of Mirabella had lost its virtue, become that of a noble among thousands. The real luxury, as opposed to his father's mediocre one, the sumptuous taste and elegant splendour of which he had been unable to form an idea in that corner of Sicily away from the highways of the world where he had lived, forced him to recognise his own inferiority. The Club at Catania was almost a family affair with himself enthroned there. In Naples or in Florence he could obtain a membership card for only a few days; had he stayed longer he would have had to expose himself to a vote, to being recommended, to run, why, even risk of blackballing! A revolution had taken place in his head.

Suffering deeply in his pride, in his ' Viceroys'' vanity when he went to pay visits in palaces four times as big as his ancestral one, in which, instead of shops let out were galleries vast as museums and full of art treasures, he had ceased to frequent such acquaintances and refused to make new ones. To assert his own wealth in some way he flung money about on hiring carriages, in cafés, theatres, or shops, where he would buy quantities of useless things simply in order to leave his address, the Prince of Mirabella, Hotel such and such—the most expensive in town. It was not so bad in Naples, where Spanish tradition equal in every way to that of Sicily drew an ' Excellency ' even from unknowns who professed themselves his ' servants '. But in Florence, in Milan, he just got a plain ' Signore ', and in vain did Baldassarre, who was always beside him, lavish his Your Excellency, or dialect *Voscenza*; people would smile or look amazed at the major-domo's extravagant expressions.

To avoid these mortifications the young prince left Italy much earlier than he had intended. In foreign countries the greater riches and power of members of his own caste did not wound him so much. But another discomfort awaited him. With his poor, ill-pronounced French he felt quite an outsider in Vienna, Berlin and London, while in Paris he made people smile as Baldassarre had done in Italy. But meanwhile Sicily, his native town, his own home, where his former consideration and primacy still awaited him, were becoming ever pettier and more squalid in his eyes. How could he resign himself to returning there after having seen the great life of big cities? And how could he hold a mediocre position in a capital? He must be first among the first then.

And once Consalvo got this idea into his head he began to consider ways of carrying it into effect. Would his father consent to his going away for ever? That was doubtful enough; but one thing was quite sure—that he would allow him as little. money as possible, and even that with humiliating bonds such as on this journey, when all expenses had to be paid out personally by the major-domo! So he would not be able to achieve his aims while his father was alive; and the prince might live to a hundred like so many of those Uzeda, all tough as leather unless the old blood disintegrated before its time . . .

Then Consalvo, coldly reasoning, taking all factors into account and calculating about his father's death as an event necessary to his own happiness, considered another side of the matter; that the whole of his paternal inheritance, on the day when he was its only master, would not be enough to give him the satisfactions he was seeking. Great for Sicily and anywhere else too for one without immoderate desires, the Prince of Francalanza's fortune was to Consalvo little more than mediocre —for Rome. His father's death was therefore useless to him; he would have to seek another means. And there, in the capital as he passed through on his way home, he found it.

His uncle the duke had among other letters also given him some for colleagues in Parliament. On his first way through, he had seen for a moment the Honourable Deputy Mazzarini, a young lawyer from the province of Messina, who was in politics while carrying on his profession at the same time. On his way back Consalvo was thinking of everyone except this man, for whom he felt deep class contempt, when one evening the Deputy came up to him in the street.

' In Rome again, prince? On your way back of course? Why didn't you tell me of your arrival? I'd have come to visit you, it would have been a pleasure. You've had a good time, there's no need to ask you that!' He was talking away, gesticulating, calling him by the confidential *voi*, even touching him. And Consalvo, chilly towards demonstrations of intimacy, drew back, disgusted at the contact. But the Deputy, although he kept on saying how busy he was and had in fact left a circle of people surrounding him, kept him talking, and before leaving him said, ' We'll meet tomorrow; I'll come and visit you at the hotel.'

So astounded was Consalvo that he had no time to put him in his place. And next day Mazzarini came to fetch him, invited him out to dine and dragged him off to the Morteo café. Numbers of other Deputies were there, surrounded by groups of clients. Mazzarini himself, before sitting down, had to rid himself of four or five people awaiting him, and for the whole length

471

of the meal he talked of all the things he had to do, of political combinations, of public business. A telegraph boy brought him two wires for which he signed the receipts as he chewed, marking inkstains on the napkin which he wore tucked into his collar. People crossing the café greeted him, and he replied, interrupting himself and calling out, ' Cavaliere! . . .' or an ' Ah, my dear Commendatore! . . .' By the fruit course he had a little court round him, to whom he was talking with great animation, of Rome, of what must be done to make it worthy of its destiny, affirm its Italian status, keep the Vatican in check. When lunch was over, a little tipsy, he took the arm of Consalvo, who trembled at the contact. But the Deputy, with a smile which was intended to be discreet and was actually beaming, exclaimed, ' A tough life, politics, particularly if one has to earn one's living too, but when all's said and done it does have its satisfactions . . . And you, prince, haven't you ever thought of taking up public life?'

Words thrown out at random just to go on talking; but Consalvo was dazzled. Tired, bored, revolted by the Deputy's chatter, by the presumption with which the man was treating him, by the squalid luncheon which he had to swallow down in spite of himself, he suddenly saw opening before him, straight and easy, the way he was searching for, one which made a little busybody like Mazzarini into an important, revered and courted figure; which would let him reach fame and supremacy, not only in one region or over only one class but throughout the whole nation and over everyone. A deputy, a minister—' *Excellency!*' ' President of the Council ', a true *Viceroy*! What was needed to obtain such posts? Nothing, or not much. Mazzarini had talked of his hard struggles in his constituency, but did the Duke of Oragua not possess a feudal constituency which he would naturally pass on to his nephew? The attorney, to get himself known, had had to create a clientele round him patiently and carefully; the Prince of Mirabella had one ready-made. As to knowledge or capacity he did not give that a thought; if an ignoramus like his uncle could be a deputy, he considered himself capable of ruling the nation's destinies. A clear memory, facility in speech, self-assurance before a crowd, qualities whose lack had tortured the duke all his life and increased his poverty of mind, all these were possessed by Consalvo. At San Nicola, before gorging monks or crowds listening to Christmas sermons, later in city streets, in taverns, surrounded by every kind of person, he had made play with his eloquence. Looks fixed on him, the silence of an expectant audience had never worried him. What else was needed?

He had promised his aunt to kiss not only Francis II's hand but also the Holy Father's feet. The second visit he suppressed, as it suited him to change not only his ways but also his ideas. Till that moment he had been a convinced pro-Bourbon and so pro-clerical, though not a believer and in fact so sceptical about matters of religion as not even to go to Mass—another ground for accusation by his bigot father. Now to embark upon and succeed in his new life he would have to be a Liberal and a priest-eater like Mazzarini. He did go to visit his uncle Lodovico, however. Monsignore Lodovico greeted him with his usual unctuousness and cold expressions of sentiment borrowed for the occasion. The former Prior of San Nicola seemed preserved in vinegar, bone-thin, with a smooth face and not a single white hair; no one would have guessed him to be over fifty. When his nephew asked if he would be returning to Sicily his eyes glittered as he replied quietly and modestly:

' Not for the moment. My new duties will keep me even more in Rome . . .'

' What duties, uncle?'

He lowered his lids and said:

' The Most Holy Father wishes, from no merit of mine, to raise me to the Sacred Purple.'

A sly one, that! He got where he wanted by slyness! . . . Consalvo decided to take him as model. Now instead of avoiding Mazzarini he sought him out, got him to act as guide round the Chamber and Senate in order to examine his field of future action at once. He then realised that if all he lacked to occupy a Deputy's seat now was age, he needed something more to get higher. That was why, when he got back home, he seemed changed beyond recognition. Convinced he ought to study, he began to buy book after book, of every kind and size. He devoured them from beginning to end, or took nibbles at them, making notes, full at first of good intentions, ready to take it all really seriously. All this material required no teacher; all he needed was the superficial preparation he already had and his natural intelligence. The monk's Latin, whose study he had loathed now stood him in good stead. Later, with the fervour of a neophyte and the presumption of an Uzeda who recognised no obstacles, he bought Spanish, English and German grammars and readers to learn those languages by himself.

The news of his conversion soon spread. Amazed, suspicious, or pleased, his relations, his former friends, even his servants said he was spending all day at his desk. He joined the Reading Circle. He, founder of the aristocrats' club, went to discussions on politics and administration, criticised or praised men and ideas, named authors and quoted books. One evening when Giulente and the duke in the latter's house were discussing consumer taxes and if it was better for the Commune to farm them out or collect them on their own, Consalvo produced an opinion with a great show of erudition. Benedetto when leaving exclaimed on a bantering, patronising note:

'We'll make you Town Councillor as soon as you're old enough . . .'

'What? Why? No! . . .' exclaimed he. 'Oh! And how does one set about it?'

'Why? To take part in representing your country! As to " how " that's quite simple.'

First of all he introduced him to the National Club. Some members there made a few difficulties. Was he a Liberal or a reactionary Uzeda? Some were sure he was as pro-Bourbon as his aunt Ferdinanda, that in Paris he had even gone to visit Francis II. But Giulente stood surety for his nephew's Liberal sentiments. He had paid a visit to the ex-King, it was true, but only because forced by his parents; the visit was a pure formality anyway and did not involve him in any way. Till that moment he had been a mere boy not responsible for any ideas he might have expressed; now if he was asking to join the club, that meant that he approved of its programme. Anyway, it wouldn't do to refuse him, as otherwise he might throw his lot in with the reactionaries.

The hesitant contented themselves with these assurances, murmuring even so that according to one version of his audience

474

the young prince had told the dethroned King that he hoped to see him back in the Royal Palace at Naples. When Consalvo heard this rumour was going round he protested vehemently that it was an out-and-out lie, whose origin he didn't understand. But when alone with the major-domo, the only person who could have put the rumour about, he bawled at him:

'You idiot, it was you wrote home that I told Francis II I hoped to meet him in Naples! Wasn't it, devil take you?'

Baldassarre, embarrassed and confused, replied:

'Yes, Excellency . . .'

'And who told you such a silly tale?'

'I was told by Father Gerbini, who heard Your Excellency say it . . .'

Raising a threatening arm, Consalvo went on:

'Another time you repeat such nonsense you'll feel the weight of my hand, d'you understand?'

He was elected to the club unanimously. Donna Ferdinanda was worth hearing then! Already getting wind of this apostasy she had seized her nephew by an arm and shouted at him, 'Take care or I'll never look you in the face again! Take care or you'll never have a cent from me!' And Consalvo had pretended ignorance, protested his own innocence, 'What *has* Your Excellency been told?' But one fine day Lucrezia came and brought her the news of her nephew's election to the club. She too was fuming with indignation; but really she was denouncing Consalvo to his aunt in order to wrench him out of her old heart, and talking ill of him to enter the old woman's good graces herself and revenge herself on the princess.

'Ah, what a race! . . . Ah, what Jesuits! . . . He told me it wasn't true! . . .'

What the old woman could not tolerate, she said, was the little popinjay trying to deceive her so barefacedly.

'Oh, the devil take them! I'd like to see them dead, the lot of 'em!'

And as she had ten years ago at Lucrezia's marriage, she went to fetch the usual sheet of paper which she kept in a wardrobe, and tore it into a thousand pieces in her niece's presence.

'Not a cent! Like this!'

Chiara too, as her husband drew gradually closer to Liberal

ideas, breathed fire at her nephew and husband. Don Blasco, on the other hand, by now a Liberal of almost ancient date, approved his nephew's conversion. Consalvo let all those mad folk have their say and made his maiden speech in the club one evening when the assembly was discussing commercial treaties. In the narrow hall people were crowded together and chairs were touching. To avoid contact Consalvo pulled his chair out of a row, ruining its order. He was listening with an air of grave attention, chewing his moustaches. But when the chairman announced, ' If no one wishes to speak, I will put the sub-committee's conclusions to the vote,' the young prince got to his feet.

' I wish to speak.'

Deep silence fell at once, and all eyes were turned towards Consalvo. With his shoulders against the wall and facing so that the audience was to one side, the platform to the other, he began.

' Gentlemen, I must first of all ask you to excuse me for the hardihood of which you will accuse me at seeing the last to arrive among you dare to speak about a grave matter, the object of much careful examination on the part of members whom, wishing but unable to call my colleagues, I must and wish to call my masters.'

The laborious phrase was produced with such confidence, came out so smoothly, was so able and opportune, touching the vanity of preceding orators, coming so unexpectedly from the mouth of a young man till that moment known only for his prodigality and vices, that many murmured ' Bravo! . . Good! . . .'

He went on. He said that if his hardihood could be judged great he knew that the indulgence of his audience was no less. Then, qualifying the sub-committee's report as 'a model of its kind ', he called it ' truly worthy of a Parliament '. He cited two or three paragraphs almost word by word. This feat of memory raised a long admiring murmur. But maybe the indulgent assembly was waiting for him to express his own opinion? This he would do ' with the humility of a disciple but the boldness of an apostle '. He was for liberty; for liberty ' which is the greatest conquest of our times '; which ' can never be abused ' for it is ' self-correct-

476

ing '. The advantages of a Liberal régime were infinite, ' as the celebrated Adam Smith says in his great work . . .' and is also ' the opinion of the great Proudhon . . .' though perhaps ' the famous Bastiat does not admit it ' yet ' the English school is of the opinion . . .' The wonder and delight on all sides matched the performance. Benedetto enjoyed it as a personal triumph, and seemed to be saying, ' D'you see? Didn't I guarantee it to you? . . .'

Again and again salvos of applause interrupted this speech which all thought improvised, so confidently was it pronounced. A real triumph followed the peroration, on the necessary correspondence between economic and political liberty, ' the greatest guarantees of well-being and happiness, the reason for this, our young Italy's existence, reunited as a free and strong nation by virtue of its people and its King!'

3

O N E night, while all were asleep in the palace except Consalvo, bent over his volume of Spencer, loud bangs were heard on the door. Garino, husband of the Cigar-woman, had come rushing over to call the prince as Don Blasco had had a stroke.

The monk, flabby as a deflated wineskin, was in his death throes. The night before, after a tremendous blow-out and booze-up, he had been undressed and put to bed by Donna Lucia and fallen asleep at once. But in the middle of the night a dull thud made all rush to him, and there lay Don Blasco stretched full length on the floor, senseless. The Cigar-woman, her daughters and a maid kept on telling everyone within sight, while Garino, after leaving his message for the prince and calling a doctor, rushed home, frowning and silent. As the doctor was declaring that there was nothing he could do with a lightning stroke of this kind, and the women went on moaning and invoking the Blessed Mother and all the Saints of Paradise, Garino took the prince by the arm as soon as he arrived and drew him into a far room.

'Excellency, we're done! I've searched high and low and not found it! Your Excellency's done and so are we! After serving him so many years! And the girls too! Never should His Paternity have played such a trick on us!'

'Have you looked really everywhere?'

'Turned the house upside down, Excellency. As soon as it happened, I took the keys and searched high and low . . . In Your Excellency's interests . . . But who could have thought such a thing? After His Paternity had promised the girls twelve *tarì* a day! It's betrayal! I'm done! And so's Your Excellency . . . I thought the Will must have been written years ago, that other time he had a dizzy turn.'

' Could he have given it to the notary?'

' There isn't a notary! His Paternity wouldn't hear of one, in fact when Notary Marco mentioned it to him . . . from friendship for us . . . he answered sharply that he'd make his Will by himself and lock it in his strong-box! . . . but there's nothing in the whole place . . . If only I'd thought of such a thing . . .' And he was silent, looking at the prince.

' What would you have done?'

' I'd have written out the Will according to his intentions . . . to give him it to sign . . . He'd have put his signature to it in half a minute. I could also . . .'

But at that point he was called inside. The doctor, just to content ' the family ', had ordered the sick man to be bled and have leeches applied to his temples. Garino rushed off to carry out the doctor's orders, and the prince began going round the house.

By the time the blood-letter came it was dawn. The operation had scarcely any effect; the eyes of the dying man just opened for a second, but not a muscle moved, not a word came from his tightly shut mouth. With the day came the princess. The other relations knew nothing yet and began arriving later, one after the other. They entered the room of the dying man for a moment then passed into the next-door room, where they lounged about and waited for a chance to take the prince aside and say in his ear :

' Is there a Will?'

' I don't know . . . I don't think so,' the prince would reply. ' Who can think of such a thing now?'

Actually they were all thinking of nothing else, devoured by curiosity and by greed for the monk's money. Don Blasco was the first Uzeda with money to have died since the old princess. Ferdinando had not counted; he had very little, and the little he had was already in the prince's hands. But the Benedictine, what with two farms, a house and savings, was leaving nearly three hundred thousand lire, and everyone hoped to get some scrapings. If there was no Will, then his two brothers Gaspare and Eugenio and his sister Ferdinanda would be heirs; and the old spinster, after a life of enmity, was waiting to grab her share. All the others on the contrary were hoping for a Will naming them. The prince whispered into his uncle's ear that he did not hope for anything for himself but something for Consalvo, and every half-hour he sent one of the family's servants, who had come with their masters, to the palace to call his son. But the young prince's first answer had been that he was in bed, then that he must have time to dress, then that he was just coming, and the last messengers could not find him at all.

He had gone off to the National Club for the meeting of a sub-committee charged with studying town-planning. Eventually he arrived when the leeches were being set on the dying man. The prince did not even say a word to him, and instead took aside Garino, who was just back for the fourth or fifth time. Then the Cigar-woman's husband entered the dying man's room, which his wife and the girls had never left for a second. Instead of helping, the leeches hastened the end; putting his head out of the door Garino announced:

' The Lord has called him!'

All entered the dead man's room. He lay motionless, rigid, with shut eyes, his temples dotted with leeches' bites. The room stank with the nauseating smell of blood, like a butcher's shop. On floor and furniture was an appalling confusion of clothes scattered here and there, basins full of water, bottles of vinegar. The Cigar-woman, who had at once opened wide the windows so that the Benedictine's soul could fly straight to heaven, was arranging, between sobs, two candles on the bedside table. The girls were weeping like a pair of fountains, and Lucrezia looked as if she had lost her second father; but the sobs and prayers gradually ceased; then, drying her eyes, Lucrezia said quite calmly:

' Now that uncle is in paradise we can see if there is a Will.'

Amid the general silence, the prince, as head of the family, made a gesture of assent. But Donna Lucia, who had just finished lighting the candles, turned and said:

' There is a Will, Excellency. The dear departed was so good as to consign it to me. I'll go straightway and fetch it.'

The very flies could be heard as the woman handed an

open envelope to the prince and the latter, from respect, passed it to his uncle the duke. The duke glanced at the sheet of paper on which were written only a few lines, and without reading it out aloud, announced the contents of the short sentences as he ran over them.

'Universal heir, Giacomo . . . Executory legatee . . . a legacy of two hundred *onze* a year to Don Matteo Garino . . .'

'Nothing else? . . . nothing else? . . .' everyone was asking.

'Nothing else.'

Donna Ferdinanda got up and began reading the piece of paper, taking it from the hands of the prince, to whom the duke had passed it. But Lucrezia came and stood beside her and said:

'Would Your Excellency let me look?'

The prince seemed quite disinterested. The two women, bent over the document, exchanged a few whispers. Then Lucrezia announced out loud:

'This Will is false.'

All turned. The prince, looking astounded, exclaimed:

'What do you mean, false?'

'False?' cried Garino, who was standing in a doorway.

'I said—it's false,' repeated Lucrezia, giving a push to her husband, who was also trying to read the sheet of paper. 'This isn't uncle's writing; I know his writing.'

'Let me see . . .' and Giacomo scrutinised the letters carefully, while all the others crowded round examining it too.

'You're mistaken,' said the prince coldly. 'The writing is our uncle's.'

None of the others expressed an opinion. In a subtly ironic tone Lucrezia replied:

'Then I'd like to know when he wrote it. Last night? There's still sand on it!'

The Cigar-woman intervened.

'Excellency, His Paternity wrote the Will the day before yesterday as, poor man, his heart spoke and told him his end was near . . .'

'And why didn't you say anything?' asked Donna Ferdinanda.

'Excellency . . .'

481

'I was told of it,' affirmed the prince.

'But you told us you didn't think there was any Will.'

'You could have let us know,' went on Donna Ferdinanda.

'Nonsense!' cried Lucrezia, giving another push to Benedetto, who was making some prudent remark in her ear. 'It's a false Will, that can be seen by the freshness of the writing and also by the signature. Uncle used to sign *Blasco Placido Uzeda*, with his second name in religion . . .'

Then Garino thought he ought to put in a word.

'Then Your Excellency thinks? . . .'

'You be quiet!' cried Lucrezia contemptuously, proud of performing an act of authority in front of the whole family.

'Your Excellency may be mistress,' the tobacconist went on, regardless, with a show of dignity, 'but you cannot insult a gentleman. Are you suggesting *I* concocted it, this false Will?'

All of a sudden the Cigar-woman burst into tears.

'The insult! . . . Most Holy Mary! . . .'

The duke, the marchese, Benedetto, all intervened together:

'Whoever said that? . . . Keep quiet at such a moment . . . Silence, I tell you; what behaviour!'

'You accept the Will then?' insisted Lucrezia, turning to her brother.

'Of course I do!'

'Then we'll see what the courts say. And now call in the authorities to put up seals . . .'

Across the room the Cigar-woman was tearing her hair and kneeling before the dead man.

'Talk! Tell them if it's true . . . such an insult . . . after all the years we've served you . . . Speak from heaven with the voice of truth! . . .'

Then broke out a struggle more ferocious than any previous one. Donna Ferdinanda was not inclined to take lightly being deprived of her part of the inheritance, but Lucrezia was implacable at the chance of revenging herself on Graziella, who had treated her badly, and also partly at the hope of her uncle's inheritance setting her household accounts in order, for since she had kept them there was never enough money. The easy-going marchese wanted to avoid scandal, but Chiara, so as to do the opposite of what he wanted, took sides against Giacomo with her aunt. Gradually all her love for her husband had turned to the bastard, and as Federico was ashamed of his clandestine parentage and refused to recognise it, her old hatred was reborn for a husband imposed on her. In her sterile Uzeda head she had conceived and brought to birth a plan: to leave Federico, adopt the little bastard and take him away with her. And as she needed money for this she pinned her hopes on her share of Don Blasco's inheritance. So she, Lucrezia and Donna Ferdinanda really let fly about that forger and thief Giacomo, who was trying to lay hands on the monk's property just as he had snatched poor dear Ferdinando's land; and about that police-spy Garino, who had suggested the trick and carried it out, for in the days when he plied the honourable trade of spy he had made a practice of imitating the writing of decent people to embroil them with the police. But the funny thing was that one thief had robbed another; for Garino, who was to have inherited only twelve *tarì* a day, had overdone it and brought his legacy up to two hundred *onze* a year! And the prince couldn't breathe a word about it or he'd be digging his own grave!

Garino and the Cigar-woman swore and perjured themselves that it was all an infamous lie invented by relations who had never been able to get on. Whom did they expect the poor man to leave his money to? To his sister and brothers who had loved him about as much as dogs do cats? The natural heir was the prince, the head of the family! As for themselves, it was surely quite natural that the holy man should want to repay their services; in fact to tell the truth two hundred *onze* seemed a paltry sum after all they'd done for him, didn't it?

Anyway Donna Ferdinanda sent off the first official plea impugning the Will and asking for a legal enquiry. The prince shrugged his shoulders on receiving this. Nothing 'saddened' him more than a family quarrel, and to all he met he would express his deep regret at his aunt's and his sister's conduct. But what could he do about it? Could he renounce the inheritance? It was they who were obstinate, overbearing, mad! At home, however, he became more irascible than ever. Reserved in the presence of strangers, he let out his ill-temper and bitterness to wife, children or servants. Teresa, actually, never gave him any pretext, being always docile and obedient; the princess also bowed her head to the storm. But he attacked his son continually, attributing Donna Ferdinanda's harshness to the latter's political apostasy.

'He's now quarrelled with his aunt who was so fond of him, the idiot! He'll lose her fortune just to go and talk nonsense at that club and in the streets. Now he's got me into a legal case. I ask you, could a worse disaster ever have happened to me than a son who's such a fool and rascal?'

But apart from that he had many other reasons for complaint. Imbued more than ever with his new ideas, determined, with the stubbornness of his family, to persevere on the road he had chosen, Consalvo was now spending enormous sums on books. He sent for them every day, about every subject, on a mere suggestion by a bookseller, with quantity as his only criterion. It was the same mania for show and for doing things on a grand scale which before, when smart clothes were his only thought, had made him buy walking-sticks by the dozen and cravats by the box. It was humanly impossible not only to study, but even to read all that printed paper pouring into the palace, subscription copies, huge encyclopaedias, universal dictionaries. Every new parcel made the prince more furious.

'D'you see? . . .' Consalvo would answer Teresa, when his sister came to talk the language of peace and love. 'D'you see? He's got it into his head to go against me in everything. What harm am I doing? Is there anything more commendable nowadays than study? Knowledge? No; but even that! . . .'

And when the prince faced him and directly reproved him for falling out with his aunt and wasting money, 'I make up my own mind,' replied the son coldly. 'Everyone's free to think as he likes. My aunt can't impose her ideas on me . . . and if I spend something on books do I ask for anything else? . . .'

Every Sunday there was another quarrel about Mass. It bored Consalvo to attend it, and he would smile an ambiguous smile at his father's religious zeal. When forced to go to confession he recited to the old Dominican a rigmarole of clownish sins. He would also jeer at his sister for her fervour in devotion, and turn his back on the black cassocks always rustling around the house.

In the Milo cemetery the prince had had a monument of bronze and marble erected over the tomb of his first wife. On anniversaries of her death he would go up there with the princess and Teresa, have many Masses said for the repose of her soul and place huge wreaths on the tomb. Consalvo always refused to go with the family; he went either a day before or a day after. At every excuse his son put forward the prince looked at him fixedly, then he let himself be led off by his wife, who was doing all she could to keep the peace and avoid quarrels. By now there was more ill-feeling between son and father than between stepson and stepmother; Consalvo bowed more to a word from the princess than to the prince's injunctions.

One day he announced that he had taken on a tutor of German and English. The father, after looking him straight in the face, asked:

'Will you explain once and for all what the devil you think you're doing?'

Consalvo stared back.

'What I feel like doing,' he replied.

Suddenly the prince went scarlet as a lobster, leapt from his chair as if thrust by a spring and rushed at his son, shouting:

'Is that the way to reply, you carter?'

Had the princess and Teresa not flung themselves between them and Consalvo not left the room at once, it would have ended badly. From that moment the break was final. By the prince's order the young man no longer came to eat with the family, which pained the princess somewhat and his sister more, but pleased Consalvo a lot. He saw his father for a minute every day to say good morning or good night, and the latter no longer complained of his son's silence and solitude and even avoided a meeting himself. Before the young man had gone on his travels, at the time when his bad habits and debts had given the prince bilious attacks, nervous tics and real illness, an awful thought had occurred to the father: perhaps his son had the Evil Eye? This thought was now growing, although he did not dare show it. Why, for instance, every time he started a discussion with his son did he either get a headache or a bilious attack? Why during Consalvo's long absence had he felt so well? Or, following another train of thought, had that political conversion which so enraged Donna Ferdinanda and seemed almost to justify this impugning of the Will, not been another proof of his evil influence? Delving into his memory the prince found other reasons for believing in that dreaded power; a sale gone badly when his son had said, ' It'll be hard to get a good price '; an earthquake shock just after the young man had remarked ' Etna's smoking '. So he was pleased now to see little of him. If he met him on the stairs or on his way through the rooms, he answered his greeting with a nod and hurried on; if he had to be close to him in the drawing-room during visits, he talked to him as little as possible and got away as soon as he could.

The only way to bring peace back to the family was for the young man to marry and set up house on his own. Anyway he was now twenty-three, and heirs to the Uzeda princedom married young. Hangers-on, gossips, the curious, all those who took as much interest in Francalanza affairs as if they were their own, were impatiently awaiting his and Teresa's marriages and discussing possible matches. For Consalvo there was almost too wide a choice; the Baron Currera, the Baron Requense, the Marchese Corvitini, the Cùrcuma and numbers of other families had richly dowered daughters of marriageable age. For Teresa things were more difficult. The only young men both rich and noble enough to marry her were the two sons of the Duchess Radalì. The duchess, who had sacrificed her best years for love of her elder son, was very possessive and had not yet got him married as she could not find a good enough match for him. She kept him sewn to her skirts as if someone might steal him; but Giovannino she let free lest the young man should feel like marrying. His uncle's inheritance had made him as rich as his elder brother; but there were differences between the two to be considered. Michele was not of very winning appearance, at twenty-six he had little hair and was too fat; but he was the elder and bore all the family titles. The second son, who only had the untransmissible title of baron, was one of the most graceful and elegant young men in town. Though they had been to the Uzeda palace very little ever since there was a girl of marriageable age living there—in fact because of that—rumours of a possible marriage found credit. But if the prince was asked

486

what truth there was in this he would declare that Consalvo had to marry first, and the princess would be quite annoyed. ' I do dislike all this gossip, as it might so easily come to Teresina's ear, and I'm so careful of her. My system is that girls shouldn't hear these or any other remarks . . .'

Teresa never seemed to hear either this or anything much else that was said, and dreamt open-eyed through the days. She devoured the few novels and books of verse which the princess allowed her to read, and painted pictures of battlemented castles rising from bright blue lakes, of troubadours with guitars slung from their shoulders, or more often of chatelaines kneeling and praying, or of a Madonna with the Divine Child in her arms. The princess preferred the austere and particularly the sacred compositions, so the girl stopped drawing more frivolous subjects. She never relaxed this constant submission to the will of others, this sense of dutiful obedience. The more trouble Consalvo gave the family, the more she thought it her duty to avoid causing her parents the slightest distress. The poetic tales in the books would arouse her fancy and quicken her heart, but if the princess judged she was spending too long on frivolous reading she stopped at once. Often when she heard a novel or play or book of verse praised she longed to read it, imagining how lovely it must be and the pleasure it would give her, but she put it out of her mind if her stepmother said, ' No, Teresina, it's not for you.' Sometimes such books were in the possession of Consalvo, who, though he only pursued positive studies, also bought lighter reading to show himself *au fait* with everything. So all Teresa would have had to do was borrow the book from her brother and read it in secret, but this idea never even entered her head, for the same reason that in college she had refused to read certain books which her companions contrived to get hold of, and had not listened to the talk of her frustrated friends on forbidden subjects. Both confessor and headmistress had told her there were certain things she should never mention, and she had rigorously abstained. Just as in her childhood the thought of praises and prizes to be obtained won over the temptations of curiosity, so now aspiration to be an example to others made her forget what she was depriving herself of.

Now she was often taken to the theatre; in summer to

comedies, in winter to melodramas; and she did not know which of the two she liked most. Now and again she herself would compose a waltz or a mazurka, or nocturnes, symphonies, wordless fantasies with titles like ' Yearning!' ' Enchantment!' ' A tale of melancholy!' ' For ever! . . .' and her acquaintances, relatives and friends would all buzz with admiration at hearing them. Even her music-master, an old man chosen on purpose by the princess so as not to put ' tinder next to fire ', was full of praises. Don Cono, the old family hanger-on, called her ' Bellini in skirts ' and once even exclaimed, ' I consider that the orchestra of warriors might fittingly rehearse her music and then execute it in public!' ' The orchestra of warriors ' meant the local military band, which had the reputation of being one of the best in Italy. Teresa parried this, while the princess could not make up her mind between pleasure at showing everybody ' my daughter's talent ', and loathing for publicity. The prince, as no money was involved, showed complete indifference. But Don Cono held fast his idea, and one day came and said that he had already spoken to the band-master.

Then Dono Cono brought the latter to the palace. Dark hair, light moustaches, pink cheeks, he was young and handsome as the Archangel Michael. As soon as the princess set eyes on him she began sniffing and making signs to Don Cono to say that she'd never expected such a thing from him, to bring a man with those looks to the house? . . . Meanwhile the band-master was playing the young princess's compositions on the piano with a touch and expression which made them unrecognisable to the composer herself. At every piece he expressed growing admiration and when there were no more said he would prefer not to choose as each was lovelier than the other; being unable to take them all he left it to the ' princess ' herself to choose. Teresa gave him ' A tale of melancholy ', but when, after scoring it, the band-master appeared a week later at the palace gates to show her his work, the porter told him that his master and mistress were no longer receiving.

' To bring a man like that to the house? Never did I think you'd do such a thing . . . It's obvious you've no daughters!' Donna Graziella had said to the old hanger-on in her worry. But she was exaggerating as she did in everything else; would the young Princess of Francalanza ever glance at a band-leader?

' A tale of melancholy ' was played one Sunday on the marine parade by the regimental band. The concert was one of their best, and Teresa's composition seemed like part of a real opera with some of the singing parts rendered by a French horn as soft as a human voice, and organ effects which made people think they were in San Nicola listening to Donato del Piano's instrument. Teresa listened in a closed carriage under the plane trees, her heart beating fit to break, with a sob in her throat and a face pale as a white rose, then suddenly flushed scarlet when at the end of the piece there was a burst of applause.

Her own music, the music of others, plays, poetry, swept her into ecstasy, high away into a blue ether where she could no longer feel her body and breathed and drank in the purest of happiness even amid tears. But none of the emotions, sweet, ardent or sad, tender or desperate, always ineffable, swelling her heart with joy or gripping it with anguish, were known to the world. She never betrayed herself; even when her mind was most perturbed, thinking of love, waiting for love, or when she was in the company of men, of handsome youths like her cousin Giovannino Radalì; while her imagination was painting in bright outline her own future, her joys and sorrows, fortunes and disasters, she remained calm, composed, and serene. It needed no great effort to disperse those fantasies by turning her mind to the petty or thankless calls of reality.

The meeting with the regimental band-master, his praises, his playing of her music, had loosed a tempest within her. But when the young man did not return to the palace because of the princess's veto, she never gave him another thought. Don Cono, still taken by his idea, and encouraged by success, spoke one day to the controller of public entertainment so that the conductor of the municipal orchestra should also arrange for one of the princess's compositions to be played. This controller of entertainment was Giuliano Biancavilla, son of Don Antonio and one of the Bivona. He was about thirty, with a dark skin and hair black as an Arab's, but slim and elegant and with the gentlest of eyes. As soon as he heard Don Cono's suggestion he at once gave the appropriate orders, and the princess agreed to her daughter having all the necessary interviews with the conductor, who was about sixty. But how many ways the devil has of getting his tail in! Donna Graziella, with all her precautions, could not prevent the young controller from setting eyes from afar on Teresa! In the theatre he would stare at her without stopping for an instant; at the parade, his carriage would always follow the Uzedas'; even in church he arranged to be on their way. As soon as the princess realised what was going on, she referred the matter to the prince, who let fall only three words:

'Mad, poor man.'

Then his wife's tongue began working. A Biancavilla pretending to the hand of a Princess of Francalanza? Maybe because an Uzeda had married a Giulente? Poor man, he thought he had another Lucrezia to deal with! Noble? Oh yes, the Biancavilla were noble and rich too, but their riches and nobility did not make them equal to the Viceroys. 'What daring and impertinence! To set people gossiping about my daughter! ...' And she never seemed to realise that by all her talk she was spreading the news quicker.

In a short time it was the sole subject of conversation in town. 'Will they give her to him? ... Won't they give her to him? ...' But all recognised that Biancavilla had set eyes too high. Baldassarre, particularly, was beside himself. Of course he wanted the young princess to marry someone suitable for her, at the very least a baron rich enough to keep her regally, and while waiting for the prince to make his choice in his heart he had destined his young mistress to her cousin Don Giovannino. One thing, anyway, he was sure of: that the Signorina Teresa would never even notice Biancavilla's existence.

Instead of this, as time went on the young man's looks had drawn hers as by some magnetic force, and now made her quicken and suddenly catch her breath. She would look at him too every now and then, and find her view blurred by her own emotion. After a glimpse of him however distant she would return home happy and smiling and begin improvising on the piano, atremble from head to foot, as if he could hear all the secret thoughts of love she was confiding to the instrument, the divine hopes of eternal happiness. At college she had sometimes composed a few verses on feast days of mistresses or birthdays of

490

friends; now she wanted to write one for him, set it to music only for him:

> *Were I but the pallid*
> *little ray of light*
> *that in the dusky night*
> *the moon lays on thy brow;*
> *Were I but the zephyr*
> *gently breathing air*
> *fondling thy hair . . .*

She could get no further, but began composing a ballad on this theme, called ' Were I . . .' weeping sweet tears when no one was watching as the passionate notes flew from the keys.

That winter some balls were given by Baron Cùrcuma. Till then Donna Graziella had not taken Teresa out in society, firstly because she did not want young men to approach too near her ' daughter ' and also because she considered no house worthy of being frequented by the young princess. The Cùrcumas', though, passed muster, and the prince also wanted the whole family to go. But Donna Graziella had a presentiment; and the very first evening who should be there but Giuliano Biancavilla . . . Had that presumptuous youth known a little of the world he would have kept quietly to his place; instead of which he actually introduced himself and asked Teresa for a dance! . . . She trembled in his arms; not a word did he say except ' Are you tired? . . . Thank you . . .' But she felt in heaven, while the princess on tenterhooks was making her husband signs to alert him about the danger. But the prince was deep in conversation with his host. And suddenly the young thruster reappeared to ask the signorina for a mazurka. Then Donna Graziella intervened.

' Excuse us, cavaliere, my daughter's tired.'

With a tightening of the heart Teresa noticed her stepmother's opposition. Inflamed at having held her a moment in his arms, Biancavilla now began following her through the streets like a shadow. The princess puffed and sniffed with rage. Once at the door of the Minorite Church, as he passed in front of them she exclaimed quietly, but loud enough for those around to hear, ' What a bore! . . .'

Teresa mourned long, hiding her tears, foreseeing all her hopes dashed if her parents would not have him. The Biancavilla family also knew that the Uzeda would never consent to the match. But the young man, quite beside himself with love, kept on and on imploring his mother and father to make the request; so much so that one day Biancavilla's father took his courage in both hands and went to talk to the duke. The latter, with much use of ' greatly honoured ' and ' what a pleasure it would be for me ', told him he would speak to the prince. Giacomo repeated to his uncle the same three words he'd said to his wife, with one small variation, ' Mad, poor things!' Then the duke with many a fine turn of phrase answered Don Antonio that there was nothing to be done, ' as the prince wanted Consalvo married first '.

This was not an excuse. The prince had started negotiations with the Cùrcuma and gone to their house to arrange a match between the young baroness and his son. The match had been accepted blindly, and Consalvo's assiduous attendance at the baron's balls was taken as the start of his courtship to the daughter of the house. But he knew nothing of his father's arrangements, and went into society nowadays just to talk politics and philosophy. All the gold in the world would never have got him to dance a waltz; he would hold forth among the men, and if any ladies or girls came up, talked to them about municipal accounts, school regulations and the yield from consumer taxes, with many quotations of statistics and Latin proverbs. Repeated from mouth to mouth, the news of his own marriage eventually reached him. Then he burst into a cordial laugh and said even more laconically than his father:

' Mad!'

Take a wife, marry a gold-draped doll like that young baroness, tie himself still more closely to this town which he yearned to leave, create binding family duties, when what he needed was to be free as air, to dedicate all his energies to achieving his aim? Mad, yes, they really were! The matter seemed so absurd that he did not even stop his visits to the baron.

At this point Giuliano Biancavilla left, having lost all hope. Some said he had gone to Rome, some to Paris, some added that he would never return home again, careless of his sorrowing family. The duke, charged by the prince who was afraid of speaking directly to his son, announced to Consalvo that it was time he took a wife and that the whole family was agreed on the young baroness.

'Of course, Excellency,' replied the young man. 'There's one difficulty though.'

'What's that?'

'I don't want her!'

'And why don't you want her?'

'Well, I just don't! Is it I or Your Excellency who's to marry? It's I, isn't it? So it's up to me to show my own wishes. And I don't want her.'

At the moment when the duke referred this reply to the prince Giacomo was already in a furious temper, having just heard that the expert charged by the Court to examine the late Don Blasco's Will had pronounced against the genuineness of the signature. On hearing of his son's decisive refusal he burst into a raucous shout.

'It's his Evil Eye! He's doing it on purpose. To kill me. I'll see him die first! Tell him that he can choose who the devil he likes. Marry the first slut he wants, one of those tarts he went round with before he got it into his head to be literary. Marry whomever he likes and go to the devil, because I don't want to have any more to do with him and his Evil Eye!'

'Excellency,' replied the young prince to his uncle, who had brought him this second message, 'I wish neither to marry the Cùrcuma girl nor any other. I'm still young and there's lots of time for shackles later. Anyway it's quite certain there's no point in talking to me about marriage for the moment. I'm not a woman like Aunt Chiara, whom my grandmother forced into marriage . . .'

The new storm blew up with a rumble, lightning flashed from the prince's furious eyes, thunder boomed in his harsh voice.

'Holy God of Love!' cried the princess to Teresa. 'How dreadful this quarrel is, how shocking! However will it end? . . . But you . . . You haven't given anyone the slightest worry . . . Blessings on you! . . . May you always be such a saint . . .'

Teresa let herself be embraced and kissed by her stepmother, relished the praise, deplored the quarrel between her father and brother, implored Our Lady to stop it. What could she offer the Virgin to obtain such a grace? Her love for Giuliano? . . . No, that was too much, it was what she had most at heart . . . She no longer saw the young man, knew nothing of the request and its refusal. Even so she realised that her parents did not look favourably on that match; but hope was still alive in her. Some day or other her father and stepmother might think it over and consent to her being happy . . .

One day, though, the storm brewing between her father and brother did break. The latter had ordered on his own initiative, without consulting anyone, four large bookcases to take his books. When the prince saw this furniture arriving he sent for Consalvo and asked him excitedly:

'Who gave you permission to order things for my house?'

The young man replied, with the studied coldness which particularly infuriated his father: 'I needed the furniture.'

'Here it's I who give orders; I've told you that often enough,' replied the other, making violent efforts to control himself. 'Not a nail is to be put in without my permission! If you want to act the master, you can leave. Nobody's keeping you here . . . Take a wife and be damned to you!'

'Already,' replied Consalvo, more coldly than ever, 'I have told uncle that I don't want to get married . . .'

'Oh you don't want? . . . You don't want? . . . Then I'll kick you out of the house, you swine! Carter! Animal!'

'All the better,' rejoined the young prince, cold as ice. 'You'd be doing me a favour . . .'

Suddenly the prince went pale as if about to faint, then purple as if about to have an apoplectic fit, and finally broke into a bark like a dog.

'Get out! . . . Out of my house . . . Now this instant, throw him out! . . .'

In rushed, pale and terrified, the princess, Teresa and Baldassarre. Frothing at the mouth, the prince was dragged off by his wife and the major-domo.

Teresa then went up to her brother, clasping her trembling hands and exclaimed in a voice of anguished reproof:

'Consalvo! . . . Consalvo! . . . how *can* you do such a thing!'

'D'you defend him?' replied the young man, still calm but in a voice that was slightly strident. 'Go on then, defend him, defend them, our mother's murderers.'

'Oh!'

She hid her face in her hands. When she looked round she was alone. Servants were rushing to and fro throughout the house. A doctor was called, ice-packs applied to the prince's forehead. She fell on her knees before the statue of the Blessed Virgin. After that horrible scene, after her brother's terrible words, remorse was seizing her for not having offered her love, her hopes of joy as sacrifices, so that the violent quarrel and terrible accusation could have been avoided. She asked the Virgin to forgive her for her selfishness, begged for comfort and help, trembling with fear, swaying as if the floor were shifting beneath her knees. She was still kneeling when she was surprised by the princess coming to call her to her father's bedside.

'Daughter! Daughter! . . . what a daughterly heart! . . . Yes, beg Our Lady for peace to return. She alone can do that miracle now . . . Your father won't see him any more, won't have him in the house; and he doesn't budge . . . But you no! You no! . . .'

And between kisses and tears she talked of someone else, of him, and gave her the news that he had left.

'It was the best thing for him to do. You may have found him attractive; I don't blame you for that; we've all been girls in our time and know how these things are. But you'd never have been happy with him, and your father, whose one thought is your happiness, did not want him . . . I'd never have talked to you of this but for all this trouble, and if I didn't know you were sensible enough to realise that your father only wishes what is for your own good. Isn't that true, my daughter? . . .'

The first time that the prince heard his son's name after that scene he yelled:

'Don't mention that name again, he's got the Evil Eye! Don't ever mention him again. Or I'll send the lot of you away . . . !'

The break was definite. The duke, on being told of what had happened, came to fetch Consalvo and took him off for some weeks to the country. On their return it was decided that the young prince should go and live in a house belonging to his father down by the sea. The young man asked for nothing better. He did up an apartment to his own taste and moved in, happy as a king. Now he could be his own master, no longer went to Mass, saw whom he liked, invited home big-wigs from the club to show them two large rooms full of printed paper. The advantages were legion. At the palace he had been unable to show his Liberal leanings by putting out lights and flags for patriotic celebrations. Now on the 14th March and on Constitution Day he put out a flag as big as a curtain and had the balconies arranged with rows of lamps which shone out sadly in the dark and deserted quarter. Now he could stay in his study as long as he liked and take his meals at any unusual hour. He was studying the *Popular Encyclopaedia,* memorising articles about questions of the day, and then astounding the Assembly with his erudition by saying ' So-and-so and so-and-so have written on this subject, etc., etc.' As once he had thrust his four-horsed carriages into the mob so now he crushed it with the weight of his knowledge. And people who had drawn aside at one time to avoid his horses' hooves while still exclaiming ' What a fine turnout!', now listened to him, bemused by his eloquence, muttering, ' What a lot he knows!'

The native Spanish arrogance of his ignorant and overbearing stock, the need to adapt to democratic times, were thus linking up inside him all unknown to himself. Nothing would stop him from reaching his goal, the hardiest enterprises never deterred him. He read the heaviest books, even a treatise on advanced calculus, as if they were novels. From all this study he drew mediocre profit—the only one possible; he acquired a smattering of information about many things, all sorts of odds and ends, contradictory ideas, much heavy and indigested knowledge. But amid the ignorant mass of local nobles he gained the reputation of being ' well-informed ', and when working folk heard the young Prince of Mirabella named they would all say ' You mean the one who's gone literary?'

One fine morning, amid the printed matter which the post brought him in cascades, he received from Palermo the first instalment of *The Sicilian Herald, an Historico-Noble Work by*

*the Cavaliere don Eugenio Uzeda of Francalanza and Mirabella.*
Besides him, all relations, subscribers and clubs were sent copies.
The ' *Historico-Noble* ' work began with *Short amplified notes*
about the dynasties which had reigned in the island: the Royal
Norman House, the Royal Swabian House, the Royal House of
Anjou, and so on till the Royal House of Savoy—for the cavaliere had recognised the new monarchy in order to sell copies of
his book to the State libraries. The *Short amplified notes* amused
Consalvo, the Royal House of Savoy infuriated Donna Ferdinanda, although the old woman was already in a permanent
state of rage because of the still undecided law case. But her
fury against the prince's family was a natural growth, since the
advances given by the prince to Don Eugenio had made the
printing of that ' filth ' possible.

Having promised two thousand lire, however, the prince had
only given five hundred, for which his uncle had had to give him
an I.O.U. with a blank date. But after Don Blasco's death financial relations between uncle and nephew soon took a dangerous
turn. Don Eugenio, first amiably, then threateningly, wrote to his
nephew asking for more money, otherwise he would join Ferdinanda in impugning their brother's Will. The prince, on his
side, tried to keep his uncle in hand by using the I.O.U. When
the printing of the book was under way one day the cavaliere
suddenly appeared from Palermo, looking more sordid and starving than ever. After long negotiations the prince handed out
another two thousand lire, against which Don Eugenio renounced
by signed deed all that would be due to him in a division of the
monk's property and agreed to his nephew becoming owner of a
thousand copies of the book.

The prince had realised that this publication was not as crazy
an enterprise as everyone else thought. The first instalments,
beginning the story of each family, went like hot cakes. Don
Eugenio, in truth, restricted himself to transcribing Mugnòs and
Villabianca and scattering about a few remarks out of his own
head. But those books were unprocurable or very expensive, and
anyway almost impossible to read with their out-of-date print
and dry, yellow, dusty paper, while Don Eugenio's edition was
most handsome, and the pages with coloured coats-of-arms
stood out in red-lead and gold. Furthermore the compiler had

497

recourse to the simple artifice of suppressing certain details, so that three, four or five families which happened to bear the same surname without any relationship at all could believe that the story of the only one authentically noble was their own. In Palermo, Messina and the whole of Sicily, he thus found numbers of would-be gentle families and so of subscribers. Some hinted that he was also taking bribes to add here and there ' a branch of this armigerous family flourishes in the ancient town of Caropepe, etc. . . . '

Donna Ferdinanda, however, was going purple with indignation, and Consalvo too had a deep contempt for this relative of his who not only prostituted himself so but discredited the whole family.

But, contrary to his aunt, the young prince kept his feelings to himself, and only showed them when they were useful. He was trying to behave in politics as he had seen his father do at home, keep in with all, and accept the madnesses of all except for a kick or so at those who could no longer harm him. He now adopted this method and made himself pleasant to all parties. That of his uncle the duke was still in power. Actually, during the four years that had gone by since the solving of the Roman Question, popular favour had gradually begun to veer away from the Deputy, as the latter, forgetting the danger he had been through, sure of having consolidated his own position and no longer fearing revolts and sudden changes, had begun to show a partisan side again, to look after his own affairs and those of his friends rather than of the town, and treat his parliamentary seat as his own private property.

But if lesser folk were beginning to mutter, the greater ones on the other hand, such as the heads of the *Camarilla* were all for their Honourable Member and no-one else, because of his sane moderate principles. In November of that year, '74, he was re-elected with no demonstrations but no opposition, unanimously. And so, when with this uncle and his friends, Consalvo would praise their solid faith and the good conservative principles ' on which the health of Italy depends '; but when he happened to be with any of their adversaries, he would affirm the need for progress and for the Left to try its hand at governing too. For ' as the celebrated So-and-so said, Parties in power should alternate'. If with two people of opposing opinions he would be silent or agree with both and disagree with neither. Except in the great aristocratic principle of deep contempt for the mob, in the certainty of being truly made in another mould, in his compulsive urge to order the human flock about as his ancestors had done, he was ready to concede anything at all. He had no scruple even in saying the very opposite to what he really thought, if it was necessary to hide his own ideas and express others. The words 'republic' and 'revolution' sent quivers of terror down his spine, but in order to be in with the current fashion for democracy and get his rank forgiven he ingratiated himself with the extremists.

At the National Club a good number of members, though accepting current institutions, honoured Mazzini and Garibaldi above all men of the Risorgimento. Other associations, particularly popular ones, celebrated the 19th March, St. Joseph's day, in their honour. On that occasion he too put out his big flag and lights and sought out the most noted republicans in order to tell them, 'I don't understand why some people are so exclusive; without Mazzini the sacred flame would have gone out; and without Garibaldi, why, Francis II might even be in Naples still!'

He had no belief in the sincerity of other people's faith either. Monarchy or republic, religion or atheism, for him they all just depended on material or moral advantage, immediate or future. In the Novitiate he had seen many an example of out-and-out licence by monks who had vowed before God to renounce all; at home and in the outside world he had seen everyone trying to feather their nests above all else. So to him there was nothing apart from self-interest, and to satisfy his self-love he was ready to use every means at hand. The hereditary sense of his own superiority prevented him from recognising the evil of this sceptical egotism of his; the Uzeda could do what they liked! Count Raimondo had ruined two families; the Duke of Oragua had enriched himself at public expense, Prince Giacomo by robbing his own relations; the women had done wild things that were on the verge of madness; and if sometimes he realised himself to be wrong according to the morality of most, he would think that after all he did less harm than all those others.

4

I t  t o o k Prince Giacomo some time to recover completely from
the stroke brought on by that last discussion with his son.
Threatened by cerebral congestion, in his terror of sudden death
he condemned himself to a starvation diet which affected his
blood. Weak, irritable, he became more than ever the terror of
the household and, attributing his own illness more and more to
his son's noxious influence, would not even hear him named. At
first, if Baldassarre or any of the hangers-on or servants happened to mention the young prince, he would seize that ignoble
amulet of his, grip it tight as if about to drown, and exclaim:
  'God help us! . . . God help us!', imploring them to be
silent, to stop at once, red in the face as if dying from suffoca-
tion. Hearing him talk of his supernatural terror, of his un-
natural aversion, they would make the Sign of the Cross. Teresa
suffered more than anyone else. As her brother could not come
to the palace any more she went to visit him herself, in the
company of the princess, for whom Consalvo now felt an indifference that was almost serene and urbane, little removed
from affability. Without the prince knowing, the stepmother
sent the young man much of the produce brought by their
agents from the country, and although she herself controlled very
little actual cash she put her own purse at her stepson's disposal. Consalvo thanked her but refused to accept anything;
his father made him an allowance, and Baldassarre would bring
round the money on the first of every month. It was not much
but he did his best to make it suffice by suppressing his expensive
habits and mortifying his luxurious tastes. And he did not
suffer, or if he did, it was like a painful and necessary cure to

regain health. As for the prince, his son did not seem to exist for him any more; if forced to mention him, he no longer called him 'my son' or 'Consalvo' or 'the young prince', but 'God save us!' He would say, for instance, to Baldassarre, 'Take his monthly money to "God save us!" Or in some rare moment of good humour he would ask the princess, 'What does that swine "God save us!" have to say? ...'

Teresa no longer thought of Giuliano, forgot her own sorrows in her horror of this dreadful hatred. She no longer read, no longer sat at the piano, with that gloomy thought always preying on her mind. Her brother's exile weighed on her. But why had he roused their father's anger? What had he dared blame him for? Suppose Consalvo was right to blame him? Suppose it was true . . .? Then she would hide her face in her hands as she had at that ghastly moment of revelation, so as not to think, so as not to remember. Could she not recall her stepmother acting as mistress in her poor mother's house? Did she not remember her pain at the announcement of her father's marriage to another woman a few months after her sainted mother's death . . . No! No! To switch her mind away from her memories, to overcome her dreadful thoughts, she made the Sign of the Cross, prayed and felt fortified by prayer. It was blameworthy to dwell on such thoughts, to continue that enquiry; all she owed her father was respect, obedience and love. And thinking it her duty to make up to him for Consalvo's rebellion, she obeyed blindly and served him humbly.

The prince showed no gratitude for that inexhaustible goodness of hers. If at times she felt sad and to raise her oppressed spirits for a moment sat down at her piano, the sounds would irritate him and he told her to stop. Concentrating more than ever on money, he would quarrel about the price of her clothes. Teresa accepted it all. But from a mere whim to criticise, to exercise his authority regardless, and also from a kind of envy aroused in him who had always been clumsy, by the ability with which she made a modest little dress look like a luxurious robe, he would carp at her continually about her dressmaking and her patterns.

One day, unlike his usual behaviour, he noticed his daughter's dress not to reprove its elegance but to say it was too simple.

' Haven't you something prettier to wear today?'

It was a Sunday in summer, and the princess and Teresa were about to drive out as usual to take ices and then pause a little by the gates of the public gardens to watch the crowd of pedestrians entering, in their middle-class way, while the concert was in progress. But just after leaving the palace Donna Graziella, still buttoning her gloves, said to Teresa:

' Let's go and visit Aunt Radalì. Today is her Saint's day.'

It was some time since she had been taken there, but the princess and the duchess greeted each other as if they had met the day before. Her two sons, the duke and the baron, were there, and other relations; refreshments were served, and the party broke up very late.

The duchess returned the visit together with her sons, and the two families began seeing much more of each other than before. The duke Michele, half bald, fat, asthmatic, careless in his dress, was awkward and unhappy in company. Giovannino, on the other hand, cut a very good figure. When he greeted his cousin and sat down by her to chat, he did it all most gracefully and also, apparently, eagerly. The elder son, grosser and more ignorant, only opened his mouth to talk of quails and rabbits, fishing in the Biviere and Pantano rivers, dogs and shot-guns. Teresa, polite and friendly to both, gradually felt a growing admiration for her cousin's looks. She had forgotten Biancavilla, but there was a void in her heart; it was filled by the thought of Giovannino. After long mortification her soul was opening again to love. Song flowered on her lips once more, the piano became her confidante, poetry books her inspiration.

The intimacy between the two families became closer and closer. There was a constant exchange of presents, and rumours of Teresa's engagement to one of her cousins gained fresh credence, but neither the prince nor the princess let out a word. Baldassarre, however, was triumphant; the match destined by himself for the Signorina Teresa was the one preferred by his master and mistress themselves. And to his intense pleasure and delight he saw mutual attraction between the signorina and the baron growing day by day. The duke Michele would give quantities of game to the Uzeda family, but Giovannino, whose main interest was floriculture, sent huge bouquets of flowers which all ended in Teresa's room, or rare and delicate plants which she would lovingly tend. The elder son was a great trencherman and always slightly bemused from food and drink; if any of the company danced he would doze away in an armchair, while Giovannino took the floor with Teresa. One of the things which gave the young princess most pleasure was hearing her brother mentioned in that house where he was never named; to hear his praises sung, his intelligence and the earnestness of his conversation lauded, were the best means to his sister's heart. And Giovannino, remembering the days of the Novitiate and their pranks at San Nicola, would prophesy the best of futures for Consalvo and pay him visits on purpose to tell Teresa that he had found him intent on study.

'You know, cousin,' he said to her one evening, 'Consalvo . . .'

'Ssh . . .' exclaimed Teresa in a low voice, clasping her hands, 'Papa . . .'

In fact the prince was at that moment passing near them on his way to Giovannino's mother.

'They want Consalvo as Town Councillor,' went on Giovannino in his cousin's ear. 'You'll see he'll turn out one of the first . . .'

Benedetto Giulente had carried out his promise and been the candidate's sponsor, never suspecting that he was preparing the ground for a rival. To him it seemed that a job in civic representation would be enough for his nephew's activity and ambition; at the most Consalvo might take part, later, in municipal administration, be elected Assessor, even perhaps Mayor one day. That he actually aspired to Parliament, Benedetto neither suspected nor thought possible. First of all his uncle the duke had assured him, Benedetto, so many times that on retiring from active politics he would hand him over his seat. This retirement, in view of the Honourable Member's age, could not be very long delayed; perhaps the seat would be vacant by the next parliament, when Consalvo would not even be legally of age. Anyway, the boy lacked so much else, chiefly experience of public life or repute for patriotism. In the eyes of Benedetto, who had been yearning for so many years to get into the Cham-

503

ber of Deputies, the fact of having taken part in the battles for unity and independence, of having paid tribute in blood, was the best title for aspiring to public office. Now Consalvo had not only been a child when he himself was battling on the Volturno, but until two years before had been quite open about his affection and regret for the old régime. Believing his nephew's conversion to be in great part due to himself, Giulente was naturally proud of it, thinking himself destined to guide the Uzeda heir in public life for a long time still; and the young man's flattering attitude confirmed him in this.

His eyes were not opened by the results of the administrative elections. He was a candidate himself, having finished his five years' term, and Consalvo was presenting himself for the first time. Consalvo was elected second, immediately after his uncle the duke, who still headed the poll, and Giulente tenth . . .

At the first meeting of the re-elected Council the young prince was severely dressed in a frock-coat of English cut with dark cravat and top-hat. When all were seated he was still moving round the narrow meeting hall greeting acquaintances, chatting with the Mayor, questioning the Secretary and turning now and again to half-a-dozen bystanders near the door. On finally sitting down in a corner to avoid neighbours, he began turning over the budget report in gloved hands and taking notes, sending ushers hurrying around with messages to right and left, as he had seen done in Parliament at Montecitorio. As soon as there was a chance to speak, he seized it. The matter in hand was street-sprinkling, which was done with too primitive methods. He asked to speak and explained what he had seen abroad. He recommended the London system, and suggested the Mayor should write to ' the " Lord Mayor "'—as the highest civic dignity in the English capital is called.' While at it he added that the Town Council might also consider organising a fire brigade. ' In my travels I never saw a town, however small, without an institution of the kind, the need of which I do not have to put forward to my honourable colleagues on the Council.' Even so, to illustrate how useful this service was, he enumerated the number of houses burnt in Constantinople on an average every year. ' Of course—we are not in Turkey . . .' and he paused briefly to give his colleagues time to laugh at his little joke, ' but just think, honourable members of the Council, of the great sulphur deposits heaped all round us within the town precincts.' Then he explained that sulphur ' is a highly combustible substance and even part of gunpowder itself, and its precipitation, slowly, with oxygen, in factories, is much used in industry and commerce under the name of sulphuric acid. A too speedy precipitation would send our town up in flames . . .'

This speech was a great success. Few observed that this fledgling had talked as if he were lecturing them; almost all admired his facility of speech and considered that the young Prince of Mirabella was really a very ' well-informed ' young man. He went on talking every day. In the debate on the budget he made thirty harangues, each more amazing than the last; on the matter of the grant to the Municipal Theatre he brought in Sophocles and Euripides, the Odeons of Greece and Circuses of Rome; when speaking on the hospital he gave a little medical course distinguishing all diseases which needed separate wards; on fishing he cited Darwin and *The Origin of Species* ' as the moon-fish which is served at our tables and the sardines which feed our people all descend from the same protozoa '. At a meeting about the cemetery he risked the idea ' I would really not be against the concept, more aesthetic historically and more rational scientifically, of cremation . . .' but unanimous and lively protests from pro-clerical councillors made him realise he had taken a wrong turning.

There and in the town altogether the pro-clericals were a force to be propitiated. They had already noticed that the young prince, having put out flags and lit up his house for all constitutional and democratic celebrations, took no notice of religious festivals, particularly the Feast of St Agatha. This was always celebrated twice a year, in February and in August, but the new free-thinking majority on the Council, judging that one spree was enough, had suppressed in their budget an allotment for the summer festa. This was the signal for a kind of civil war. From pulpits, in confessionals, in sacristies, the priests rallied the faithful to counter-attack. The Liberals held stubbornly to their proposal, the indifferent were forced to take sides, and things were threatening to go badly. The Town Council was called in to decide. Unusual crowds attended the tempestuous meetings:

sacristans, vergers, contractors and petty tradesmen interested in the festa for what profit they could get from it; self-appointed journalists were busy taking down verbatim reports on the debate for spreading around later.

The Liberal champions made a great show of eloquence but were whistled down, while the pro-clericals, though mostly poor orators, received ovations. The Duke of Oragua did not speak, for he never spoke, but it was known that he would be voting in favour. Giulente in his heart was contrary, but to flatter the duke would vote with him. Which side would the young prince be on? Curiosity was great, so the day he spoke a crowd three times bigger than usual crammed the little hall and strained to hear from outside. He began speaking amid a deep silence. His preamble increased curiosity, consisting as usual in laudatory repetition of everything said by ' my distinguished predecessors '. Then he went on. ' But, gentlemen of the Council, allow me to leave aside the question under discussion for a moment and ask myself a question which may not seem to have direct bearing on it, but in fact has.' (The journalists noted down: *Signs of attention.*) ' The question is this: do the representatives of the town come to the Council Chamber to sustain any ideas which happen to pass through their heads, however provident and just, or to carry out the mandate given them by the sovereign people? . . . Surely to look after the interests and satisfy the needs of those they are representing. Now take this matter we are dealing with now, has the city any wishes on the matter? Yes, and what are they? . . . Gentlemen of the Council, it would be vain to hide it; the city or at least the great part of the city wants the festa!' The religious silence kept till that point was broken by a shout of approval. ' *Hurricanes of applause,*' noted pro-clerical journalists, while free-thinking councillors shook their heads, made signs of protest, asked leave to speak.

Calm amid the tempest, glancing at some papers in front of him, he went on, his strident voice dominating the hubbub. ' Let us consider for the moment as certain that the city is for the festa; what other obligation have we, its delegates, but to translate it into action? My colleagues in those seats (pointing at the most advanced Liberals) must excuse me, but I can understand all others rebelling at this concept except they, who take the

506

Categorical Imperative as one of the more salient points of their programme! . . .' And in the silence now re-established he then began a lesson on free will, quoting the 'celebrated Aristotle', the 'illustrious Scottish school', and naming great English, German or French authorities every half minute. The audience was quite crushed by the weight of this speech, but now he had already gained the mob's heart, his erudition could not but be another reason for admiration. Even so to soothe representatives of radical ideas, on finishing his lesson, he added, 'Nor does anyone invested with a mandate abdicate his own principles by carrying out the will of the mandator. I have heard the cry of clericalism raised in this hall against all those who will vote for the festa; but gentlemen of the Council, who could dare to read the conscience? Or do we wish to return to the unhappy days of Torquemada? You know that here there are sitting men whose patriotism is above all discussion '—the flattery was aimed at his uncle the duke—' men who, by voting for the festa, in no way intend to cancel out a past which history has written in letters of gold on imperishable annals! . . . I will vote for the festa too. *(Formidable burst of applause)* But my vote will not affect my principles. *(Renewed applause)* For those I am responsible before my own conscience, and I do not compound with my own conscience! *('Excellent')* Nor would I ever advise my honourable opponents to compound with theirs. But, gentlemen of the Council, there may in this hall be Clericals, Catholics, Atheists, Protestants . . . Jews, Turks, if you will *(laughter)* —and are you quite certain I do not myself follow the doctrines of Mohammed? *(renewed laughter)* I have read the Koran, which is the Gospel of Islam, and if a paradise of houris really does exist then many of us would be quickly converted to the Ottoman faith! *(Burst of general laughter)* But even a Turk, you can be sure, if he came into this hall on a mandate from our citizens who want the festa, would vote for it too! . . . If I tell the agent who looks after my estates to carry out a certain job, I'd find it odd, to say the least, if he refused because it was against his principles! *(laughter, applause)* If he did refuse, d'you know what'd happen? I'd send him packing! And if we refuse the festa, d'you know what the town will do? Elect other Councillors who will re-establish the grant!'

By now every sentence was greeted with a hail of applause, and when he began describing the various ' legitimate, proper, and honest ' reasons why all classes of the population wanted the festa, ovation changed to triumph; the pro-festa party nearly carried him shoulder high through the streets; even his opponents were forced to recognise his ability. For the festa his balconies were lit bright as day and, as the Saint's procession happened to pass right under his house, he arranged for a number of rockets and squibs to be let off.

The day before this the Council elected him Assessor.

For this same festa prince Giacomo gave a big reception. Among the first to arrive were the Duchess Radalì with her sons; and Giovannino, taking Teresa aside, gave her the news of her brother's nomination. She could not enjoy it because the prince was in a terrifyingly black mood. That morning the Courts had given out their decision about Don Blasco's Will; this, as the result of expert examination, was declared to falsify the last wishes of the Benedictine—God rest his soul. This setback, coinciding with Consalvo's becoming Assessor, had seemed to the prince a new proof of the necromantic powers of ' God save us!', and he had been in a frenzy all day. Now, lest people say he was taking it too hard, he was trying to show indifference and talk of other subjects. But however he twisted and turned everything he said ended in an outburst against corrupt experts and rascally judges. ' They've been paid to declare black as white. Had I bribed them by now the decision would be the opposite . . .'

Teresa was helping her stepmother serve the guests. The Duke Radalì did not need to be asked twice, always ready as he was to eat and drink, but Giovannino was waiting for Teresa to finish in order to serve her himself. She had scarcely touched the ice offered her by the young man. With her father in such a mood she had no heart to amuse herself, to enjoy the party or Giovannino's company. The latter never took his eyes off her, and seemed to be looking for a chance to stay by her.

' What's the matter, cousin? . . . Aren't you happy? . . .' he said to her as the crowd of guests began looking out of the windows to watch the procession pass.

508

' No, it's nothing . . . why?'

' There's a look about you . . . No fault of mine, I hope?'

' Of course not! . . . Come along and watch the procession.'

Thus she broke off every time conversations which threatened to take a dangerous turn. It was her duty to do so, not that her cousin's tender words and loving looks displeased her. The other brother, less sensitive and with no kind word, was apt to paw her and embrace her, turning it into a joke afterwards and making people laugh, thus preventing any complaints from her. But Giovannino's secret and timid attempts perturbed her like something forbidden, a real sin.

On the balcony crowded with ladies, she could scarcely get a peep at the procession. Giovannino came and stood beside her, also pretending to look.

From the street came a buzz like a beehive, so vast was the crowd, and the great bell of the cathedral with its slow, grave stroke seemed to beat time for the bells of the abbey, and of the Collegiate and Minorite churches. ' *Hurrah for Saint Agatha!*' . . . All the ladies knelt. Teresa, prostrate, her head low, her eyes fixed on the Saint, made the Sign of the Cross. Then began fireworks paid for by the prince. In the midst of smoke as from a battlefield gleamed sharp and frequent flashes like shots from a regiment of soldiers, the shouts of ' hurrah!' were lost amid crashing explosions, and all that could be seen were handkerchiefs waving over the sea of heads like swarms of frenzied doves. Teresa wept hot tears in her emotion, praying the glorious Martyr to give peace back to her family, to compose all their quarrels, to bring happiness to her father, to her brother and stepmother, her uncle and aunts—to them all, them all . . . Suddenly she felt her right hand taken and pressed. It was Giovannino, kneeling beside her. She had not the heart to break away. The Saint seemed to be blessing this union, promising them all her help. And the crackle of rockets and squibs, the clamour of bells and human cries became more deafening. Amid this din she seemed to hear gentle words, *his* voice murmuring:

' Teresa . . . Teresa . . . do you love me?'

All of a sudden the fireworks ceased and ' hurrahs ' filled the sky. Then, sweetly, slowly, after giving Giovannino an answering

squeeze, she freed her own hand . . . In the silence gradually
re-establishing was heard a voice calling:

'Have you all gone deaf?'

It was the Cavaliere Don Eugenio, that moment arrived. He
seemed even more starving than when he left. His suit, all
blotched and mended, drooped over him, his shoes had seen
no wax for ages, and his cravat was like a piece of string. At
the sight of his uncle, the prince's face, already dark, went quite
black. First that adverse court decision, now this scarecrow!
And Don Eugenio had in fact journeyed from Palermo in order
to ask for more money.

'I have an idea; since the *Herald* . . .'

'You want some more money, do you?' . . . shouted the prince
in his face, dropping the 'Excellency'. 'That's cool! Isn't all
you've had enough? Now instead of paying it back, you're asking for more, are you . . .?'

'I've nothing to pay back: your only right is to the copies!'

'Well, I want those!'

'After my renouncing those rights?'

'Many thanks for the renunciation! The Will's been judged
false, d'you understand? Go off and draw your share now, go
on . . .!'

The money scraped together from *The Sicilian Herald* had not
helped the cavaliere much. First of all the people he sent around
to collect the money for the instalments kept a good half for one
reason or another, and certain of them even made off with the
whole price. When he tried collecting on his own all his earnings went on travelling expenses. The paper-makers, the
engraver and printer had been paid only in part. They had
therefore arranged to have all copies of the book sequestrated
and freed only on payment, so that if Don Eugenio sold a copy
he had to pay for it at cost price and make only a lira or two's
profit. The sums paid by 'cadet branches' of 'noble families'
had gone in a day or two of good living, and now he was again
flung into indigence. To raise himself he tried another coup:
*The New Herald or a Supplement to the Historico-Noble Work.*

Having less shame and more hunger now than before he
intended putting in it not only forgotten families, but also new
nobles, those who were not to be found in Mugnòs or Villa-

bianca, people who got themselves called 'Cavaliere' without having any real title, who made a great show of more or less imaginary coats-of-arms. But for this he needed more money . . . Seeing that he could expect nothing from the prince he went to Consalvo, who might give him help in his quality as Assessor. But the young prince had now taken another step forward in his political ideas.

On the 16th March of that year, 1876, after sixteen years the party of the Right had finally collapsed, to the amazement of the local moderates and the utter delight of the progressives. In the crash, the enemies of the duke prophesied that the great patriot, following his usual tactics, would turn against his own friends in favour of the new winners; but the prophecy did not come true. The duke, who had not been going to the capital for some time, was not aware of the reasons and importance of this Parliamentary revolution, refused to believe in its success and duration, and so stuck to his own ideas more than ever. This was his salvation, for the triumphant progressives had no voice in affairs as yet, while almost the whole of the governing class of the country were against the vaunted novelty.

On the dissolution of the Chamber, a lawyer called Molara dared to put up against the duke, with a near-revolutionary programme which mentioned the 'fifteen years of misgovernment', of rights 'trampled underfoot', of 'imminent' vindication, not to speak of 'redde rationem'. The duke's supporters all drew close around him, feeling themselves threatened with him. In reply to Molara's 'challenge' Oragua produced, after five legislatures, a 'Letter to my electors'. This was written by Benedetto Giulente, who was still waiting for a chance to make a programme of his own. It enumerated the reasons why the right wing could expect the gratitude of the Italian nation, whose unification was all due to that party; if errors had been committed those had origins in circumstances and not intentions. Don Gaspare was thus re-elected with over two hundred votes; Molara could scarcely scrape together a hundred. One of the Reparation Ministers passing through Catania was greeted with whistles.

But while the duke was quite giddy with his new triumph, Consalvo had sniffed the wind and realised the change taking place in the whole of Italy, and the imminence of Liberal reforms. So without participating in the electoral campaign he declared the Right to be dead and buried. Keeping people at a distance so as to avoid contagion, he began to declare himself 'democratic'. And here was his uncle, Don Eugenio, choosing this very moment to come and suggest this business of a 'New Herald! . . .' He let the scarecrow wait a good while in his ante-rooms; then, after listening to the request, shrugged his shoulders.

'Heralds and Trumpeters indeed! What's the point of them? Such things have had their day! The Commune can't spend public money on supporting publications based on class-divisions! There's only one class, that of free citizens!'

This reply, heard by his clerks, repeated throughout the offices, brought him applause from good democrats. The cavaliere went straight off to report it to the prince, to gain a mark by showing his son up in a bad light. But neither informing nor persistent begging brought in a cent; Giacomo even asked for the money back that he had advanced before, and accused him in addition of stupidity for letting his creditors impose sequestration on him.

The cavaliere made another attempt with his sister Ferdinanda. When he appeared at her house the door was shut in his face. Even so, he sent a message to the old spinster asking for a small loan, which would be nothing for her and would assure him of a meal. The old women replied that even if she saw him dying of hunger she would never give a cent towards printing that 'filth'.

This road being closed too, Don Eugenio fell back on his niece Chiara. He found the marchese alone; his wife, who had given him no respite for some time, had one day ordered horses harnessed secretly and driven off with the little bastard to the Belvedere, from which she never returned. The cavaliere tried to explain his plight to his nephew, but the latter could talk of nothing but his own troubles and all that mad-woman had made him suffer. So that the unfortunate ex-Gentleman of the Bedchamber left empty-handed once again.

Not knowing where to turn next, he went to Giovannino Radalì. With the keen nose of a starving hound he had noticed the tenderness between the two cousins, particularly from Baldassarre's remarks. The major-domo was more pleased and satisfied than ever with the turn things were taking. The growing intimacy between the two families was an indication that the prince approved of the match 'since His Excellency never did a thing without a double aim '—and the mutual love of the two young people assured their union. If it was not actually talked of openly yet, that must certainly be due to the prince's disappointment about that Will; as the master always dealt with one matter at a time he naturally had to wait for the case to end before deciding to get his daughter married. Breaking the reserve which he scrupulously maintained on all matters concerning his employers, Baldassarre then assured his intimates that once the quarrel was settled the match would quite certainly be arranged.

So the cavaliere began winking at Giovannino and praising him in the presence of Teresa, who would flush all the colours of the rainbow. 'As if one didn't know he'll be your husband . . .' he would murmur in his niece's ear; and in the young man's, 'As if one didn't know she'll be your wife . . .' He encouraged them both, gave them news of each other, carried greetings and messages to and fro, until eventually he asked Giovannino for a small loan of a thousand lire. The young man gave it at once, and Don Eugenio made off.

5

'MAYOR at twenty-six? . . . Whoever heard of such a thing!
. . . He'll need a tutor at the same time! We'll be ruled by wet-
nurses! . . .' But sarcasm had no effect, so enthusiastic were
Consalvo Uzeda's supporters. In the year since the young prince
had become an Assessor, had there not been more continual improvements to the city than his predecessors had carried through
in eighteen years? The town-criers, who before went round in
greasy slovenly rags, dragging rusty sabres like old spits, now,
at his suggestion, were in splendid new uniforms, all facings,
frogging and pom-poms so that they looked like admirals to a
man. And the fire brigade, with gleaming helmets and red
plumes like Roman soldiers of the Holy Sepulchre, wasn't that
all his work too? . . . 'Make way for the young! Make way for
the young and learned like the Prince of Mirabella!'

Now he studied no longer, judging his preparation as sufficient, and realising too that in a chief branch of knowledge,
that of throwing dust in people's eyes, he was already a past-
master. He knew that his family's great popularity depended on
its outer splendour, on showy liveries, gleaming carriages, majestic porters, and although people said that times had changed,
he knew that all these things, visible signs of richness and power,
had never, could never lose their value with changing times.
So the improvements made by what he, although only an Assessor, already called 'my administration' had been chiefly connected with things that showed and could be appreciated at once
by the crowd. Thus he had taken the greatest trouble about
training and dressing the municipal services, watchmen, crossing-
sweepers, dog-catchers, of which he was head and which he

would review like a general. When he left the paternal roof one of his minor sufferings, endured in patience like all the others, had been no longer to have clusters of valets, scullions, coachmen and attendants who bowed as he passed; now he had a little army at his command.

Direct contact with things or people was still a torture for him. He would receive them with his hands deep in his pockets so as not to have to shake those of others, or shake them wearing gloves which he would then throw away. He signed papers with a pen in two fingers while a clerk held the sheets so that they did not slide away beneath, and on leaving the Town Hall had his chair locked away in a cupboard lest anyone should sit in it. One day when the key could not be found he stood up for six hours. Some scruffy clerks, with long hair and black nails, were a horror to him. He would snort and exclaim, ' Don't push on top of people ' as they talked to him of business or reported on their duties, and instead of answering their questions would suddenly burst out with ' Do get that quiff cut off!' or ' Clean your nails a bit!'

' As if we could all spend our days in front of the mirror as he does!' those rebuked would mutter, calling him aristocratic, proud and a fraud, for to hear him anyone would think all men were brothers on the same bench . . . But such complaints were lost amid the chorus of praise from the other employees for whom he had created jobs or put up salaries, arranged bonuses or granted holidays or condoned shortcomings; all those stood before him humbly and called him ' Your Excellency ' like servants. Thus the party wanting to raise him to the highest office was strong in the town and very strong in the Town Hall. Even so he wavered, adducing his immature age and inexperience. And to Giulente, who was playing into his hands with even greater trust, he confided that he was afraid of coming a cropper and ruining his future. ' You won't fall,' Benedetto assured him protectively, ' we'll all sustain you, the whole of your uncle the duke's party.' But he did not yield even when the Prefect asked him, and thanking ' from the depths of his heart ' the deputations come to invite him, he declared that the weight was too heavy for his shoulders. He continued to hold off, knowing that there was a current running against him of inevitable complainers, envious malcontents, all those who wanted to break with these ever-present nobles, these eternal Uzeda. When the municipal employees repeated, as they did every day:

' Your Excellency should be Mayor; the city wishes it . . .'

' How do I know?' he replied once. ' The city has said nothing to me!'

Then a demonstration was formed, with music and flags, to go and acclaim him as head of the town. He allowed a half-promise to be torn from him: ' If the Prefect proposes my nomination . . .' The demonstrators went and shouted ' Long live Mayor Mirabella!' under the balconies of the Prefecture. Then when the decree of nomination was ready, he posed another condition: that every faction of the Council from Bourbonist pro-clericals to Republicans should be represented on the Electoral Committee. They let him dictate the list of Assessors himself. At the top he put Benedetto Giulente. The latter protested in vain, but Consalvo said to him:

' If you don't accept, it's no go. I'll be Mayor in name but in fact we'll do everything together. I realise that I'm asking a sacrifice of you, but you have made many others! . . .'

Lucrezia's reaction to this can be imagined. She was beside herself.

' Mayor to Assessor! He's making a prawn's progress! One of these days he'll be nominated usher! The job for which he was born! And he lets himself be taken in by that little Jesuit! To serve as his footstool! To act as his servant! There's nothing else he's good for.'

She went and unbosomed herself to her aunt Ferdinanda. Both of them were on tenterhooks just then, as they were awaiting a decision any moment from the Court of Appeal about Don Blasco's Will. The day this was announced in the prince's favour, annulling the first expert opinion and establishing a new one, the aunt and niece, green with bile, screamed and ranted so much that poor Giulente, worn out by all the shouting and railing, escaped from home in despair. The prince, who had recently been in bad health again, recovered suddenly as if by a miracle, and showed his pleasure by speaking to people almost urbanely, even asking news of ' God save us!'.

Some weeks later, in spite of the heat of the season, the

princess went out with her daughter and bought quantities of house-linen. Then she called seamstresses to sew and embroider sets of all kinds. 'We're working for the young princess!', they would say in positive tones aimed really at eliciting some confirmation. But the princess said nothing, though she embraced her stepdaughter more often than usual, and looked at her with an air as if to say 'Wait and see! ...' Teresa asked no questions, but realised that the day of her happiness was near. Baldassarre was beside himself with delight and announcing the wedding without reticence; it was almost certain now; wasn't the prince going to the duchess's every day to discuss settlements? It might be only a matter of weeks before all the relations received news of the happy event.

In fact, one day, in connection with some bed covers which she found it difficult to choose, Teresa said to her stepmother, 'Let Your Excellency choose, to me they're all pretty ...'

'Why, d'you think I'm to use them? Don't you realise they're for you?' replied the princess.

Teresa's forehead went scarlet. She held her breath and lowered her lashes.

'Come here! ...' and drawing her to her heart, Donna Graziella began, 'It's for you, for your marriage. The moment has come to make you happy ... D'you think your father hasn't been thinking of you? He has so much business, so many cares! But now we'll do everything quickly, you'll see ...' And imprinting a kiss on her forehead, while holding her head in both hands, she exclaimed, 'Are you pleased to become a duchess?'

For a moment Teresa thought she had misunderstood. She fluttered her lashes, looked her stepmother in the eyes, and repeated like an echo:

'Duchess? ...'

'Duchess Radalì, of course, and also Baroness of Filici, as your second son will bear that title! Duchess, and with lots of ducats too! One of the richest! Your father will treat you well, as Consalvo has behaved so badly. He's already arranged everything with your aunt ... and in time my things will go to you too, won't they? Well? Are you pretending not to know? ... Why are you looking at me like that? ... What's the matter?'

'Mamma ... Mamma ...'

Ever paler as her stepmother said those words, more and more shaky and trembly, as if at a glimpse of some horror, she now put one hand to her forehead and with the other seized the princess.

'Mamma, no . . . I didn't think . . .'

'What? . . . My dear girl! Confide in me! . . . You didn't think what? . . . But I was sure though . . . He's been coming here almost every day! Anyway you know now . . . Don't you . . . No? . . . You say " no "? . . . Why? For what reason? Isn't your father making sacrifices to ensure this match for you! . . . 30,000 *onze*, d'you understand? He'll give you 30,000 *onze*! . . . And Michele has four times that again. And you say no? . . . Why? . . .'

'Because I thought . . . I didn't think . . . that it was him . . .'

'Who then? . . . Another? . . .' and the princess seemed to be searching about in her mind. Then suddenly, as if it had that moment occurred to her, 'His brother maybe?' she added.

Dropping on to a chair, Teresa hid her face in her hands and burst into tears. From the first moment she had realised, with a tightening of the heart, that all her refusals would be vain; they had decided to give her to the elder son, she had at all costs to accept him. And her stepmother's honeyed words as she said with clasped hands, 'If I'd known! . . . Why didn't you speak? . . . Now that your father's arranged everything . . .' confirmed her in that wretched certainty and made the tears flow more than ever. Speak? To whom? With what purpose? In a family where there was no trust, where all were quarrelling with everyone else, caring only for their own interests? As they had first made her used to giving way about everything and then lulled her into confidence that they would make her happy. Could she ever suppose they would have chosen by themselves without consulting her, and one day come and say 'Well, you must marry someone you don't like . . .?' But why? Why did they want to give her to the other one and not the one who had her heart?

'For your own sake!' exclaimed the stepmother. 'We've decided this way for your own sake! He's the elder son, you'll be a duchess, your sons will have two titles to choose from, while with the other there won't be a single one left . . . And he's also

518

richer; not by much, it's true, but there's still a difference! And a daughter of the Prince of Francalanza can't marry an obscure younger brother as if she were a nobody!'

What did that matter? As she had given her heart to Giovannino? As it had never crossed her mind that the other brother, so gross and ugly, could be her husband?

'But don't you know,' went on the princess, 'that your aunt the duchess won't ever agree to Giovannino's marrying even if we did, as I'd like to in order to please you? Don't you know our aunt wants only her elder son to marry? Such is the rule in our families; in fact if times hadn't changed it would not even occur to Giovannino to approach a girl like you, knowing he could not marry her!'

'No, no! . . .' broke out Teresa then amid her tears. 'Don't blame him; it was me too . . . I love him too . . .'

'Oh come!' exclaimed her stepmother with a smile full of indulgence. 'Just passing children's fancies . . . aren't they?' she went on in another tone, seeing Teresa's mute sobbing beginning again. 'Are you determined to cause your father pain? With all the other troubles he has? Then go and tell him you don't want to!'

'Me, mamma? . . .'

'Why d'you expect me to tell him this *pleasant* news? Come now! I'm upset by your refusal too, you know, but, but . . . I'm not your mother . . . And it's not as if you, or your brother, care whether I'm upset or not . . .'

'Oh, mamma! . . . Why do you say that? Don't you know I've always respected you and loved you as if you were my own mother?'

'All right! . . . all right! . . .'

Oh, why did she not have her real mother by her in that sad hour when her need of sincere affection, of true protection was more necessary than ever! Her mother would never have left her alone, sobbing, as her stepmother did, with only these words for comfort:

'All right; I'll tell your father. After all, it's he who'll have to deal with it! . . .'

The princess never mentioned the marriage again to Teresa, just as if they had not discussed it in the first place. Nor did the prince say anything to her. But from her father's changed bearing she realised he knew all, and what he wanted from her. From one day to another he never said a word to her, never called her by name, never seemed to notice her presence. The air of content which had come over his face at the good news of the court decision vanished again, and he went round frowning worse than ever and losing his temper again about the slightest thing.

The news began to filter out among the family. Most of them thought Teresa silly to prefer the baron to the duke; some supported her, Consalvo among them. About his sister he did not care a fig, and he took her part to show off his culture and democracy. 'You see the force of prejudice?' he would exclaim. 'They want to give my sister to a cousin,' and then came a long lesson on marriage between close relatives. 'But of the two, they give her the one she doesn't want, not the one she wants. Why? For a difference of words! Duke or baron! . . . It would be different if behind these titles there was a real duchy or a real barony!'

Aunt Ferdinanda's and Lucrezia's aversion now had new fuel. So that silly girl preferred the younger son to the elder! Opposed her father's will! And to think the father had been unable to educate her to blind obedience! . . . Her uncle the duke, with a foot in both camps as always, leant a little this way and a little that, but in his heart he was for the match chosen by the prince as more worthy of the family; and anyway the duchess herself did not want her younger son to get married, did she?

The duchess, in fact, was in a great state. After sacrificing her whole life for love of her elder son to ensure great riches for him and his descendants, after waiting so long to get him a wife, as there was no one she considered worthy, now that she had found him his cousin Teresa and was on the eve of crowning the work of thirty long years along came a love-affair with Giovannino to destroy all her plans at one blow. She had never suspected such a thing, so obvious had it seemed to her that Giovannino must feel obliged to remain a bachelor in order that only the eldest son should continue the family. 'When Michele gets married . . . When Michele has children . . .' Giovannino himself had talked of nothing else but Michele's, the duke's marriage.

The two brothers were fond of each other, and had always been close, so if now Giovannino seemed to be putting a spoke in the wheel it was her fault for not having told him of the match she had in mind. The fault was also Michele's. Lymphatic, incapable of excitement, fond only of shooting and good food, when his mother let years pass without finding him a wife, he had never asked for one. Now that his cousin Teresa was suggested, he was prepared to marry her, without any desire, without any urge, as he would have married any other girl. He treated his cousin with the familiarity justified by their relationship, joked with her as he joked with all, rather grossly; he was incapable of saying a tender word to her. How could anyone suspect then that he was the girl's future husband? It was not even suspected by Baldassarre, who was astounded at hearing that the bridegroom was not to be his favourite but the other brother. What? The prince wanted to give that other one to the young mistress? Suppose the signorina didn't want him! Hadn't he himself, Baldassarre, announced to all that the bridegroom was the young baron Giovannino? 'Oh, come on! The prince doesn't know that the young mistress loves the younger! When he sees she's really in earnest he'll come round . . .' Instead of which Teresa's eyes were always red with tears because of the aversion her father showed her and the coldness with which her stepmother also treated her, because of this new quarrel broken out in the family which she longed to see at peace. And one day the princess said to her:

'Well, can you tell us what's the matter with you?'

'Nothing, mamma, there's nothing the matter with me.'

'Then why all this continual gloom? You're holding stubbornly to your idea, are you? Well, now it's time to speak frankly. Your father has declared that you'll either marry Michele or no-one. I didn't want to tell you before, thinking he might change, but you know him better than I do . . . D'you want to cause him great pain just at this moment? Don't you know he's ill, much more seriously than he seems? And not only your father but the duchess too? Two families! You've disturbed two families! . . . Now that you know how things are, persist if you wish. Of course nowadays parents' wishes have not the effect of law on children. If you want him at any cost you can even elope, as girls do who have no respect or shame . . .'

When she used these arguments Donna Graziella's voice sweetened, as if she could not believe in the hypothesis she was enunciating. 'You can marry him too, but on other conditions, of course, and without your parents' blessing. If you think you could be happy like that, go ahead.'

Teresa wept no more now; she had poured out so many tears in secret, soaking her pillow every night. She looked ahead of her fixedly, seeing nothing, with a nervous trembling of her jaw, an infinitely bitter twist on her lips. The princess now stopped being severe and reverted to quiet persuasion, saying lovingly that the best judges of what suited her were her own parents, and that by herself she could make a mistake, as had for example her aunt Lucrezia, who had wanted to marry Giulente at all costs, and how did she speak of him now? Certainly the cases were not the same, for there was not so much difference between Michele and Giovannino to make one worthy of her and the other not. But there was a serious reason which had decided them to give her the elder, a reason she should be told.

'If Michele isn't as handsome as Giovannino, he has iron health, while his brother is delicate, sickly. Apart from another even more serious thing : his overwhelming restlessness . . . Don't you know his father was mad when he was born? May God disprove the prophecy, but suppose one day his brain went too? That would be nice for you! . . . So you see your father has reasons and not just fancies. To flout him means giving him pain which can be fatal to him, particularly as we are not sure what his illness is. I cried so much a few days ago when the doctor confided to me that his health has to be taken very seriously. I didn't want to say anything to you but you should know what your responsibility would be if you oppose his wishes, which are only for your own good.'

She began again the next day and then the one after, on and on, cajoling, producing reasons against which Teresa would never pronounce the opposing reasons crowding to her mind. For example hadn't her aunt Lucrezia just changed her mind from sheer caprice, as everyone said? . . . And if they were so afraid for Giovannino's mental health, why were they urging her to give him such a heavy blow as this, by refusing to allow her to marry him after he had told her that he loved only her? No, she did not say either these or any other things she thought, for had she done so she would have had to say that her father wanted to sacrifice her to a stupid prejudice, that her stepmother was pretending all that fondness in order to induce her to do what the prince wanted; she would have had to say that in no other family was a father's illness a reason for making his daughters unhappy; she would have also had to say that Consalvo's rebellion now seemed justified and that she should rebel herself . . . But this was sin! The confessor had warned her, recommended prudence, obedience, self-denial, all the Christian virtues of which she had such luminous examples in her family: Sister Maria of the Cross, who had been at San Placido since childhood, who had renounced with exemplary vocation this sad world to give herself to her Celestial Spouse and was now, as just reward for her Christian virtues, Abbess of her convent; Monsignor Lodovico, who had also spurned the rank awaiting him in secular life in order to embrace the monastic state. And Blessed Ximena in the past. That very year occurred the third anniversary of her exaltation among the Elect; would her descendant show herself degenerate just as that saint was looking down from paradise with particular love and fervour? The same arguments were repeated by her aunt the Abbess, at San Placido, where the princess now took her every Sunday by her husband's order.

The Abbess, with a waxen face amid white veils, was well into her second childhood, and from behind the parlour gratings did nothing but repeat to her niece what had been impressed on her, saying, 'You must carry out your father and mother's wishes. Our Lord orders it, Our Immaculate Virgin orders it, our protector St Joseph orders it . . .' Her voice had taken on the lilt of recitation of a Litany. And there among the convent walls, Teresa remembered her distant childhood, the old fear she had felt when they put her on the wheel to take her into the impenetrable convent. But she also remembered the nuns' praises when she helped to deck the altars with flowers and light the candles before the Crucifix. 'A holy little nun! A holy little nun! . . .' And the instinct of sacrifice, the urge of humility, the thirst for rewards which had preoccupied her as a child, awoke in her again. Her confessor suggested a further scruple: that of urging another soul to sin; for she did not now know it, but so it was—the younger Radalì had threatened to rebel openly against his mother.

This was untrue. Giovannino had no idea of rebellion at all; at the announcement of his brother's intended engagement he just lost his gaiety. Baldassarre, more determined than ever about arranging the second son's marriage, no longer understood what was happening. 'Had Giovannino paid court to his cousin or not? Had the signorina shown she liked him or not? Was the duke Michele totally indifferent to his cousin as he was to all other girls or not? Was he very fond of his own brother or not? Then who was all this muddle due to? To the prince, stubborn like all the Uzeda . . .' Baldassarre at one point put a hand over his mouth so as not to repeat people's opinions about the family ' and of the duchess, who was not part-Uzeda for nothing . . .'

The centenary of Blessed Ximena was celebrated with unusual pomp. For the triduum the church of the Capuchins, all red drapery, gold fringes and flowered carpets, was lit up like broad day. Bells rang festively; Masses said continuously on every altar drew huge crowds of faithful of all kinds. The Saint's descendants also came, but at different times, to avoid each other, so much did they love one another.

The princess and Teresa, the first day, lingered to beg their glorious relative to heal prince Giacomo, who for two weeks had been kept to his bed by mysterious ailments. But the greatest solemnity was reserved for the third day, when after Pontifical High Mass the people would be admitted to contemplate the relics.

Already the Father Guardian, helped by Father Camillo and Monsignor the Vicar-General, had produced a little volume entitled ' On the tercentenary of the canonisation of Blessed Uzeda', printed with much display of margins and colours. All the relatives had received a copy, and Teresa, who had gone to Confession and was waiting to go to Holy Communion on the day of the great feast, meditated over her own copy. The legend of the Saint, which she had heard repeated piecemeal and in differing versions, was narrated consecutively in that booklet.

'Ximena, of the illustrious stock of Uzeda,' so began the first chapter, 'was daughter of the Viceroy Consalvo and of the noble Caterina born Baroness of Marzanese. From her tenderest years she was an example of edification to her family, delighting in sacred images and the Divine Offices. Although her natural choice was to dedicate her life to her Celestial Spouse, yet her father was persuaded for political reasons to marry her to the Count of Motta-Reale, a mighty Spanish noble, but a man of cruel mind and with no fear of God.' There followed a narrative of Ximena's refusal, her long weeping, and the conflict between her filial and her celestial love. But one day when the girl was fifteen a singular miracle occurred; an angel appeared to Ximena and said to her, 'The Lord has chosen you to redeem a soul; obey.' Then the girl accepted the match.

The second chapter described the count's castle, set on an eminence, 'astride many trade routes', and narrated the wickednesses of her lord. 'He attacked travellers, left them naked and tied to trees by the roadside, or took them prisoners, or murdered them amid cruel torments.' His life was an orgy; 'he abused women, guzzled and drank from morn till night, cursed God and the Saints, and laughed at the Ministers of Heaven'. And the torments he inflicted on his bride were the subject of the third chapter. 'Jeered at all day for her devout practices, forced to hear the coarse talk of that evil man and his henchmen, to observe their wickedness, to be present at their rascalities, Ximena made of her faith an ever-stronger shield, praying for the Almighty's forgiveness for these fallen souls. But that wretched husband of hers in his iniquity, exacerbated by such exemplary sanctity, maddened by the protection his wife gave to the poor creatures who had fallen into his clutches, put Ximena to such a proof that the very pen blushes to narrate it. One night, drunk from all the wine swilled, he let his friends penetrate into the nuptial chamber where Ximena was reposing after a day spent in prayer and good works. The wretched girl awoke all of a sudden, and, terrified by the drunken men's shifty eyes, leaped from the bed and fell at the feet of a sacred image of the Blessed Virgin of Perpetual Succour which she always kept with great devotion above the bed. Then a new miracle

525

occurred; the frenzied crew stopped as if some magic ring were preventing them getting any nearer to the woman, and coming suddenly to their senses, they made the Sign of the Cross before the image, then left the room.'

When one fine day the count set off for his estates in Spain and his wife remained in Sicily alone, all suddenly changed in the castle of Motta-Reale. 'Where before there had echoed obscene songs and clash of swords and sounds of shot, savage cries and sad laments, now only the praises of the Most High rose to heaven. That place, once the terror of passers-by, became a hospice for the derelict and sick drawn there by the countess's great reputation for charity. She lodged pilgrims, adopted orphans, helped the needy, cured the sick, tended wounds and sores with her own hands and healed them most wonderfully. On the spots where so many wretches had fallen victims to the count were raised altars and crosses in expiation of old crimes and for the conversion of unbelievers. All Ximena's fortune was divided among churches; she herself lived a frugal life, saying " little is too much, a lot alarms me ". Not content that the poor should come to her, she would go to the poor herself, facing storms and perils, visibly protected by Heaven . . .'

There was no news meanwhile of the count. What was he doing? Where was he? 'One stormy night, while lightning flashed and thunder crashed, the countess got up, woke her maid, and said to her, " Go and open the gate, someone is knocking." The woman replied, " No one is knocking; 'tis the thunder." And a second time the countess got up and said to the woman, " Go and open, someone is knocking." And the woman replied, " No one is knocking, 'tis the wind." And a third time the countess got up and said to the woman, " Go and open, someone is knocking," and the woman replied, " No one is knocking, 'tis the rain." But when she was ordered to waken the servants, the maid herself rose. When the castle gate was opened, a beggar was found, asking for the mistress of the house. This was an old man, ragged and barefoot, whose face was stamped with the stigma of vice; the terrible disease which is the just punishment of the dissolute had corroded away his features and his eyes were closed to the light of day. He was dying of hunger, could scarcely stand, and would have been at the mercy of any small child. Who was this old man? It was the Count of Motta-Reale!

'Having squandered all his riches in dissipation and gambling, lost his health, been abandoned by his former comrades in debauchery, rejected by all from horror of the disease destroying him, he had dragged himself from one place to another, blaspheming and cursing; till, having returned to Sicily, he heard of the great charity of a woman who greeted and tended all the sick, even those with leprosy. And as he climbed up to the castle and entered it, his dead eyes had been unable to recognise his old lair or his dulled ears to distinguish his consort's voice. But she had recognised him. And, after restoring him with food and drink, dressing his wounds and washing his feet, Ximena put him to rest in her own bed . . . And the wretch, who till a few hours before had cursed and despaired, felt for the first time a gentle sweetness in his veins and a fire of gratitude melt his stony heart . . . But now his hour had sounded, and God had arranged to give him not the ephemeral health of the body, but the true health of the soul . . . The old man, cared for by the Blessed Ximena, entered his death agony amid the gentle murmur of her prayers. But his end had nothing dreadful about it at all; in fact he seemed completely healed, and to hear ineffable music and breathe sweet perfumes when a short time before he had been rotting and suppurating all over . . . And a smile of contentment played about his mouth as his lips murmured, "Who art thou who dost not reject me and who grantest me back life?" . . . And the Blessed Ximena replied, "Look me in the face."

'Then came the greatest miracle. The blind man's eyes opened; he recognised his wife, the woman he had maltreated and offended and who alone was protecting him now in his wretchedness and infirmity; and at the instant when his soul, forgiven and redeemed, rose to heaven, from his lips came the words, "A Saint, O Lord! a Saint! . . ." '

Teresa's eyes were bathed in tears of emotion; but the little book was not finished. The last chapter narrated new, greater, clearer proofs of charity and sanctity given by the Blessed Ximena after her husband's death. At the end it told of her death and her miracles. 'She had not yet expired when flights

527

of little birds came and settled on the roof of her house, perched on her balcony, entered her little room like celestial messengers come to meet her lovely soul. Sweet scents of roses and jasmine and hyacinths spread like incense from her body, and a great number of sick, brought to look at her for the last time on her death-bed, were miraculously healed on kissing the hem of her robe.

'By divine prodigy the earthly remains of this chosen soul were preserved from corruption; after all the centuries the Blessed Ximena's flesh still keeps the freshness and colour which it had in life, so that she seems deep in some divine dream. During plagues and other private and public calamities Blessed Uzeda has operated innumerable miracles, proved before the Sacred Courts of Rome. And for this reason, we hereby publish for the first time the cause for her canonisation, which we have been able to procure thanks to the noble intercession of his Most Eminent Cardinal Lodovico Uzeda, the Blessed Ximena's distinguished descendant.'

The reading of this story, the solemnity of the centenary, the harangues by her confessor, her stepmother and her aunt the nun, her father's illness, even the raising of her uncle Lodovico to the supreme dignity of the Church in those same days, all united to bend Teresa's heart like wax.

After all, was she being forced to marry a monster as the Saint had been in her time? Michele was no monster; he was a good young man. And her parents were not forcing her, they were just trying to persuade her, showing her the virtue of obedience, speaking for her own good, for the peace of two families, for the health of her father, made ill—it was said—by all his rebuffs. They were warning her not to follow Consalvo's sad example, and promising her every reward, earthly and celestial.

Then that solemn ceremonial of the centenary, particularly on the third day, the adoration of the relics! She had gone to the altar steps for Holy Communion, had received the Sacred Host, while the smoke of incense and the scent of great masses of flowers were wafted in the air and bells rang festively and the organ played, grave and potent. How many brows had been bowed, how many prayers murmured before the Saint, to whom she had been compared herself! But for years and years she had been terrified at the idea of actually seeing the dead woman's centuries-old corpse, as if by some new and ghastly miracle the lifeless body might raise itself in its coffin, break the glass and grasp the living amid the nauseating stench of rotten balsam . . . With the crowd opening respectfully to let them pass as she advanced towards the glittering chapel, her terror grew, turned her to ice, her legs felt as if they were giving way, cold shivers ran down her backbone. Ah, that coffin!

With eyes tight shut she fell on her knees, overwhelmed, trembling, beside herself with terror. A voice beside her murmured:

'Pray to her for your father . . . promise her that you will be good like her . . .'

And from fear, to get away at once, to avoid seeing that horror, she replied, with tight-shut eyes:

'Yes . . .'

More time passed. The prince's health improved and relapsed, the duchess came to the palace with her elder son, the network of advice, persuasion and inducement grew tighter round Teresa. Her stepmother told her that Giovannino, so as not to be an obstacle to his brother's happiness, had given an example of obedience and gone off to Augusta where he had settled to look after his properties. Teresa considered herself as bound by her vows to the Saint; and she consented. Only one condition did she make. To her stepmother she said:

'I'll do what you wish on condition that father promises me one thing. That he'll make peace with my brother and agree at least to see him, even if he doesn't want him to live here again. That he'll end the quarrels with my uncle and aunt and come to an agreement. It won't be difficult to conclude if each gives way in something. With your permission, I will talk to my aunt and uncle myself.' Her voice was grave, her eyes lowered.

'What a saint!' exclaimed Donna Graziella. 'Your dear mother must be inspiring you! Thus shall we see peace return among us! . . . I'll talk to your father at once and we'll obtain what you wish.' Next day in fact she announced:

'Your father agrees. Consalvo will come here on the day when your future husband does. We will go and invite your uncle and aunt ourselves. And let's hope for a settlement of the quarrel.'

Three months later the duchess came to present the duke Michele to the home of his future bride. Consalvo was already at the palace, and Teresa, taking him by the hand, led him to her father's room.

'Father,' she said, 'here is your son coming to kiss your hand.'

The prince, keeping his left hand in his pocket, held his right out to be kissed, and at his son's question, 'How is Your Excellency?' he replied, 'Very well,' dropping his voice a little and not asking 'And you?' in reply. But before they had exchanged four words Donna Ferdinanda's carriage clattered noisily into the courtyard. The princess kissed the old woman's hand and embraced her sister-in-law Lucrezia, who was wearing a most elegant robe: apricot satin with pistachio trimmings. She had told everyone that the quarrel with her brother was being made up and that she would now be giving her dressmaker many orders for the wedding of 'my niece the young princess with my nephew the duke'. She was heavily in debt with her dressmaker, her modiste, her jeweller. Her administration of her husband's affairs was getting more and more chaotic, but the portion of Don Blasco's inheritance due to her would settle things up.

Then all the other relatives arrived: the Duke of Oragua, Giulente, the marchese, without his wife, who refused to leave the Belvedere, where the little bastard, getting older and more and more spoilt by her upbringing, was now hitting her freely. The prince greeted his relations, looked at Consalvo out of the corner of his eye, and never took his left hand from his pocket. Finally the bridegroom-to-be arrived with his mother. The duke was almost elegantly dressed and did not put up too bad a show, and seemed truly happy. His mother had explained that Teresa was in love with him and that Giovannino's glooms derived from the boy's getting a fixed idea about marrying his cousin, without either the girl or her family or she herself, his own mother, who ought after all to count for something, agreeing. So he had gone off to Augusta; there he would realise how much he was in the wrong. Consequently the duchess was triumphant; the work of

530

her whole life was being brought to a happy conclusion: her elder son was marrying and continuing the family. The younger son, after and because of that failed love of his, would surely not disturb her any more. As to the princess, she was aglow with satisfaction; Teresa's wedding was all her own work. The girl, it was true, had been most submissive and she kept on kissing her every quarter of an hour before the whole company, but it was she herself who had given good advice and found persuasive reasons, was it not? She had done so for her dear daughter's happiness, for her husband's satisfaction, for the family peace . . .

Even the prince looked quite amiable in spite of disquiet inspired by his son and traces of recent illness. The arrangements about Don Blasco's inheritance were reasonable; the house was to go to Donna Ferdinanda and the income to the duke, who had made two big gifts of money to Lucrezia and Chiara; one hundred and twenty *onze* a year would go to Garino; and the Cavaliere estate, with its new land—biggest and best mouthful —to the prince himself.

So there was general peace, and only Donna Ferdinanda looked askance at Consalvo because of the apostasy with which he had stained himself. But Teresa, after having reconciled her brother and her father, now took Consalvo by the hand and led him before their aunt.

'Aunt,' she said, 'Consalvo wishes to kiss your hand.'

He bowed quickly to take the wrinkled hand and hide the laugh rising in his throat. This old woman, who had no scruples about laying hands on Church property herself after inveighing against others as sacrilegists, was against him because he had changed his politics in words and nothing else. And as he made a great effort over himself to bring her hand close to his lips she was drawing it back, thinking to do something disagreeable, and grunting a cold 'All right, all right . . .' He turned his back on the mad old woman. But what to call Teresa then? Consalvo laughed to himself at the zeal with which she was bringing the recalcitrant relations together. To sow peace among those who would begin quarrelling again next day, to show her obedience to that rascally father and stepmother and be called a model daughter, she had renounced Giovannino's love, was marrying that oaf of a duke!

531

'Are you pleased?' he could not prevent himself asking, when they were alone a moment.

'Yes,' she replied, and on her brow the veil of sadness for her sacrifice melted to serenity at duty done.

As this happened in the Yellow Drawing-room, Baldassarre, alone in the antechamber, was talking to himself in a fury.

'Well, fancy that! I'd never have thought it. Now she too! Are they all mad then? . . . No, they oughtn't to have done this to me . . .'

No, till the very last he had refused to believe that the whole city had said, 'It's the duke! She'll marry the duke!' No, he had answered everyone with a pitying smile, like one who sees farther than others. Now, seeing all those people reunited, the duke Michele sitting next to his young mistress, his young mistress receiving compliments from all, his head began to spin. The Uzeda blood awoke in him again. After fifty years of unlimited devotion, blind obedience and suppressed will, he had expressed an opinion, announced an event. Everything had made him think it inevitable, and when the prince opposed it he had trusted the young people's wishes. Instead of which the baron had gone off to Augusta and the young princess was smiling at the young duke. Did that mean that because of a whim of theirs, because of their madness, his, Baldassarre's word, meant nothing? Was he worth less in that house than the handle of a broom?

And he went on talking to himself, never heeding the ring of bells, forgot his orders, made mistakes in the service; but when people began leaving, he was suddenly animated by a febrile impatience. He almost pushed the guests out by his glances, could not keep still a moment, and finally, when he thought there was no-one left, entered the Red Drawing-room.

'Excellency . . .'

The young prince was still there. On seeing the major-domo enter, Consalvo got up and kissed his father's hand. No sooner had he turned his back to join Teresa and the princess, than the prince at last took his left hand from his pocket where he had always kept it the whole time, and made the sign against the Evil Eye. But Baldassarre's voice called him again.

'Excellency.'

' Yes, what d'you want?'

' Excellency,' said the major-domo, ' I'm leaving.'

' Where for?' asked the prince, thinking that he had given some commission which he had forgotten.

' I'm going away, I wish to offer Your Excellency my resignation.'

The prince looked at him a moment, thinking he had not understood.

' Resign? For what reason?'

' For no reason, Excellency. I've been in Your Excellency's home forty years, and now I wish to leave. Your Excellency can't keep me by force, what? In your own house Your Ex-cellency can give what orders he likes, who can complain of that? . . . And I'm master in my own house too. Your Excellency can find himself another major-domo better than me . . . There's no lack; I'll be off on the first of the month.'

' Have you gone mad?'

' There's no lack . . . Your Excellency is master in his own house . . . Do as you wish. I'm off . . . on the first of the month.'

# 6

ONE of the first measures by the young Mayor, immediately after his installation at the Town Hall, was building a 'hall' for meetings of the Town Council. The previous room was now exchanged for a grand hall with two banks of seats gradually sloping up from floor-level to form an amphitheatre, with three rows of seats in each bank. At the end of the hall was what looked like a huge high pulpit holding, below to the right, places for the Council, above for the Scrutators and the Prefect's arm-chair, to the left places for secretaries, and in the middle on a high dais a gilt and sculptured mayoral throne, with a cushion which the usher took away and locked up when the young prince adjourned a meeting and left. In the middle of the hall was a big bench for deputations, beyond, tables for 'the Press', and opposite the mayor's pulpit the public gallery.

'A parliament in miniature!' said those who had been to Rome, and the meetings of the Town Council, under Consalvo's presidency, now took on a truly parliamentary character. The Order of the Day, which before was just written out and tacked on a door, was now distributed in print to all councillors. A series of rules laid down by the Mayor gave the procedure to be followed in open debate. Orators were not to speak more than three times on the same subject. The Secretary was rigorously forbidden to speak, even to answer Councillors' questions, and if any of these happened to complain about filth in the streets or dogs without muzzles, the young prince would call from his throne, 'Notice of that question is required.'

The new administration turned its attention first to public works. The Mayor, in a speech which referred to the Appian

534

Way 'linking Rome to the Adriatic', showed the great need for attending to the streets. The city was flung into confusion, and considerable sums spent on indemnifying owners who suffered damages, but the striking results brought considerable praises to the young Mayor.

As well as streets the Mirabella administration, as everyone called it, set about building a big market place, a big theatre, a big slaughter-house, a big barracks and a big cemetery. New buildings sprang up everywhere and work never ceased, the town was transformed, praises for the young prince rang to the skies. Some did timidly observe that all these things were fine, but what about money? Was there enough? . . . Then Consalvo answered that the budget of a city in constant development 'presented such elasticity' as to allow not only those expenses but even greater ones.

Being so popular, he did what he liked with the Assessors; if they showed any hint of contradiction he would stifle it by arousing dissension among those united in opposition; or if matters became more serious, by threatening to resign. That would quieten everyone. For whatever went well he took all the credit himself; for what obtained no popular approval he threw the blame on the Council. The meetings of the Council had become a spectacle to which, thanks to the public gallery, people came crowding as to a play or a show of juggling. The members of the Nobles' Club, the young prince's ex-companions in his revels, would go up every now and again with the intention of making fun of him; but Consalvo's serious, weighty, authoritative mien was so imposing that they scarcely even risked a quip to each other. Did anyone still remember the first phase of his life? His success made him proud, his power astounded him. Was he not almost certain now of getting wherever he liked?

'He'll be a deputy, they'll send him to Rome when he's old enough; there's the makings of a minister in him!' they were beginning to say in town. But if he heard such things, he shrugged his shoulders with a smile half pleased and half modest, which almost meant 'Thanks for your good opinion of me, but I need more than that!'

So he kept on good terms with all, and gathered praises from all sides. Those who realised what he was up to and denounced him were either not believed or suspected of envy or malice, or if they found anyone to believe them would get a reply of 'It's what all do in these days of cut-throat competition! The young prince has the advantage of being rich and not having to make his money out of us!' But there were livelier opponents too.

As the town was transformed materially, so it also took on a new direction morally. The old duke's popularity was melting away from day to day; the National Club, which he had always dominated, lost more and more credit. The new popular societies had not any yet, but would get it from the reforms promised by the Left. Meanwhile there now took part in discussions on public affairs classes and persons who would have been incapable of understanding a thing about them before. The Press was bolder too, if not freer, and treated its ancient overlords with little regard. The young prince sniffed the wind and to the democrats made a great show of his ideas on democracy. According to him the liberty and equality written in the laws were still myths; people were lulled by the idea of ancient barriers being broken down, but privileges still existed and were merely of another kind. They had broadened the right to vote, and that had seemed a revolution; but how many enjoyed this right? So a new revolution, a 'legal and moral' one, must take place to extend the right to all.

The word 'revolution' set his lips aquiver and his heart atremble, and his deep, sincere and ardent desire was for double the number of police to citizens. But as the wind was blowing from another direction he sought out the best-known radicals and said to them, 'A republic is the ideal régime, the sublime dream which will be a reality one day since it presupposes perfect men and adamantine virtues, and the constant progress of humanity makes us look ahead to the day of its fulfilment.' And he would declare, 'I am a monarchist from necessity in this transitional period. But can millions and millions of free men voluntarily acknowledge and boast of being subjects of a man like themselves? I have no master!' And in this he was sincere, for he wanted to be master of others.

The duke and his reactionary friends, stubbornly supporting the Right and awaiting the return of Sella and Minghetti like that of Our Saviour, had created a Constitutional Association,

536

of which, however, the Honourable Deputy himself refused to be head. He too in his heart now realised that it was a cul-de-sac; but he was now nearing seventy, he was tired, he had nothing more to do. In under twenty years he had put together a fortune of some millions, the administration of which would absorb the whole of his remaining activity. Though he had now decided to withdraw from public life he had one last ambition, to be named senator. So in order to keep in with public opinion, till the end, he considered it best not to abandon brusquely the Party to which he had linked himself ever more closely since 1876, and not to come out too openly against the Left Wing from which he expected to receive a seat at Palazzo Madama. So he had Benedetto Giulente made president of the Constitutional Association, with himself as only a simple member.

Meanwhile, in opposition to this there had been formed a Progressive Association, of which Consalvo became a member. ' Uncle and nephew in opposite camps? Youth rebelling against age?' they said in the squares. But the usual malicious tongues hinted that it was in friendly agreement, that the duke was pleased at his nephew being in the opposite camp, just as the young prince took advantage of his uncle's credit with the Conservatives. Anyway, although a member of the Progressives, he declared to them that the Left had not yet any ' financier of Sella's calibre ' or as ' eloquent an orator as Minghetti '. But to those who showed their disillusionment with the Constitutional régime he freely declared that ' the mistake was ever to think it could yield good results. Flocks have always needed shepherds, sticks and sheepdogs . . .' He even agreed with the few who regretted the old days of Sicilian autonomy. ' Let's say it frankly between ourselves; maybe we'd be better off today.' He would have had no difficulty in conceding to his aunt Ferdinanda that the Bourbon Government was the only decent one, but as the old woman could be of no use to him he let her talk on. In fact he made use of her opposition as well as of the break with his father. He knew that many were laughing incredulously at his proclamation of democratic faith, and exclaiming, ' He, Prince of Mirabella, future Prince of Francalanza, descendant of the Viceroys? Oh, come off it! . . .' So he would affirm, ' For this faith and these principles of mine I have quarrelled with my father, renounced my aunt's inheritance, and would endure even greater adversity!'

In the Council a quarrel would sometimes break out between aristocratic conservatives and progressive radicals. Then he would exclaim, 'We mustn't talk politics here . . .' But once when the discussion became too lively, he was dragged in. Rizzoni, an extreme radical, cried:

'Let us ask the young prince if the future is not ours, if he isn't a democrat too . . .'

'My nephew? . . .' replied Benedetto Giulente, 'Aristocracy incarnate? . . .'

When forced to reply, he smiled, stroked his moustaches, and said:

'The ideal of democracy is aristocratic.'

'What's that? Listen to this! . . . Really new! . . . What the devil! . . .' all exclaimed.

He let them have their say, then repeated:

'What, in fact, does "democracy" mean? That all men are equal! But equal in what? In poverty and subjection maybe? Equal in their duties, in their strength, in their power . . .' And as after a second of amazement exclamations broke out again, he quickly changed the subject by saying, 'Now we can move on to the next item on the agenda: a petition to the Government for the construction of a dry-dock . . .'

Nowadays Consalvo paid occasional visits to his father. He no longer felt any aversion to him; the zeal, the enthusiasm with which he busied himself with public affairs, the concentration of all his energies on achieving his new aim, left no place for any other feeling either of hatred or love. As for the prince, his son's visits made him quiver with terror, and as soon as he heard him announced by the new major-domo (for Baldassarre, stubborn as a true Uzeda, really had left) he would plunge his left hand into his pocket and only draw it out to spread it open in the sign against the Evil Eye behind his son's back as the latter was leaving. Their talk was always of indifferent matters, as between strangers. The prince pretended not to know that Consalvo was the highest civic magistrate. But on the whole now they were behaving civilly to each other.

Teresa, now Duchess Radalì, saw this as the compensation of her own sacrifice. Except for the very first period, when the memory of Giovannino was not quite dead in her heart and his superiority over his brother seemed greater to her than ever, she had not suffered as much as she had feared. The duke Michele not only treated her well and left her full liberty, but showed her in his own rather gross way a lively and sincere affection. His mother too, from pleasure at seeing her own plans fulfilled, made a great fuss of her and even let her take part in the running of the house. The baron was at Augusta, busy with rustic pursuits, and wrote two or three times a month to his brother or mother, ending his letters with ' greetings to my sister-in-law '.

The calm reigning at her new home, the peace re-established in her old one, her husband's affection, Consalvo's triumphs, the praises gathered by herself—for she had at once taken first place among the young matrons of the town—made smiles come more and more readily to her lips. It was true she no longer felt like composing music or poetry, but she still often sat at her piano for exercise, and maybe took even more trouble about her appearance than she had before.

Now she was free to read the books she liked most, and when she had nothing to do, devoured novels, plays and poetry. But the stimulant of this reading never prevented her from attending to her religious devotions with zeal and fervour. To the Radalì palace came Monsignor the Bishop himself, the Vicar-General and the same prelates who frequented the prince's; all pointed to the young duchess as a model of domestic and Christian virtues.

Soon pregnancy made her entirely forget her past dreams and drew her closer to present reality. She suffered little discomfort, and time flew by fast amid all her many cares and thoughts. The birth went off well; all expected a son and a son was born, a big, florid baby who might have been a year old. ' How could it be otherwise?' said everyone. ' With a daughter and wife as good as her, protected by a Saint in heaven? . . .' Preparations for baptism were sumptuous. The duke wanted his brother to be godfather. His mother approved; Teresa, on her nuptial bed, where she stayed more from contented indolence than from any need, said that of course there could be no better choice.

Giovannino was rather tardy in replying, but when begged by the duke in the name of his mother and also of his wife, arrived on the eve of the ceremony.

He seemed a different man; he had become stronger, the sun had bronzed him, his beard gave him a more manly air, as attractive as his old one but in a different way. He shook his sister-in-law's hand, asked most solicitously for news of her health, and wanted to see his little nephew, whom he found a darling and kept on kissing again and again. She, even calmer and more serene than he, greeted him like a friend whom she had not seen for a long time. After the ceremony of baptism, to which were invited all relations close and distant, all acquaintances, half the city, Giovannino announced that he was going back. They all did their best to hold him, but he declared that there was a great deal for him to do in the country and went off promising to return soon and see his little godson again.

At the baptism, many of the guests who had not frequented the Uzeda before asked about a haggard flabby-looking old man in a brand-new suit, worn-out shoes, a filthy old hat and with silver-knobbed cane.

It was the Cavaliere Don Eugenio. The printing of the *New Herald*, a supplement, had brought him another moment of prosperity. He had spent money wildly and still had a little left. But the scandal he had made was appalling, for he had attributed titles of nobility and coats-of-arms and coronets to whoever paid him; grocers, shoemakers, barbers were making great show in their shops of gilt-framed pictures with, beneath crowns, helmets and multi-coloured draperies, shields containing lions, eagles, snakes, cats, hares, rabbits and every kind of beast and bird; and also castles, towers, pillars, mountains; and stars of all sizes, and silver moons, full and crescent; golden suns and comets; all the colours of the spectrum, all the metals, all the mantles. No scruples or difficulties had stopped him; one with a name meaning 'baker' was given a blazing oven 'on a field *or*' one meaning 'cauliflower' a big bunch of greenery 'on a field *argent*'. And so his enterprise brought him in quite a good sum, but, as at other times, most of this had gone on the way. He had however bought back the edition of the first *Herald* which the printer had sequestrated, and had returned to his home town with a thousand copies of this to sell and live by.

But he made his calculations without the prince. The latter, once the law case was settled, had regretted their agreement and complained of being defrauded, of being left empty-handed while Don Blasco's inheritance should all have gone to him. The ill-humour, the lack of appetite, the weakness he had suffered from before, began tormenting him again. In dumb irritation, unable to say he was ill from a superstitious fear of his ills growing by admitting them, he blamed his daughter for imposing the transaction on him and declared he had been stripped like a piece of wood. As soon as he saw his uncle Don Eugenio return and heard that he had a little money, he asked him forthwith for the repayment of his loan. When Don Eugenio mentioned his renunciation of rights on Don Blasco's Will, he shouted:

'What rights, what wrongs? I've been stripped! Everything! I gave you money; give me it back now that you have some.'

Seeing things look bad, Don Eugenio confided:

'I haven't any! I swear to you I haven't any! Just a few cents to live on; if I give you two thousand five hundred lire, how do I eat?'

'Give me the copies then,' replied Giacomo promptly.

'But they're my only revenue! If you take them away where can I lay my head? What does a bit of dirty paper matter to you? . . . You who are so rich. It's bread and butter to me . . . I'll sell them off gradually and so just manage to rub along.'

Inflexible, the prince insisted on having the whole edition of the *Sicilian Herald* and of the *Supplement* as security for his loan.

Although half Sicily was flooded with this publication, Don Eugenio would often manage to place a copy or two, whereupon he went and fetched them from the palace, promising the prince to bring him back the money and divide it. But no money ever came, and one day the nephew lost patience and declared:

'The joke seems to me to have gone on long enough. From now on, if you want more copies you'll pay for them beforehand.'

541

So when the money brought from Palermo came to an end, the ex-Gentleman of the Bedchamber's difficulties began once more. Like a bookshop tout he climbed up and down stairs, his feet swollen with gout, dragging himself painfully, to offer his *Herald* and show specimen pages; and when he managed to find a buyer he ran and begged the prince to hand him over a copy, swearing and forswearing himself that he would return at once with the money. But the prince would say harshly, ' Bring the money beforehand!' Not knowing where to turn, the old man stopped relations and mere acquaintances in the street to lend him the thirty lire required. Having scraped these together, he took them to his nephew, who let the copy go only after having pocketed the money. But, once handed the price from the buyer, Don Eugenio forgot to pay off the debts, so that the operation became more difficult every time. Recently too the cavaliere had found the market much harder; people to whom he had never suggested the *Herald* now replied, ' What, again? I've got it already!' Were they saying that to send him away? . . . One day, just to make sure, he asked one of these how he had got it! ' How d'you think? I bought it, of course! Some- one came on behalf of your family; aren't you the prince's uncle?'

The old man banged his forehead. That rascal Giacomo! . . . Not content with taking nine thousand lire's worth of property off him in exchange for the two thousand five hundred of the loan, not content with having made his own sales impossible by demanding the price beforehand, he was now selling copies on his own account! ' Ah, thief! . . . Ah, the thief! . . .' But com- posing his features into his usual look of amiability, he hurried to the palace.

' If you've sold copies too, let's make up our accounts,' he said to the prince.

' What accounts?' replied the latter, as if in amazement.

' You've been selling the book! By now my debt must be paid off!'

' If only it were! We'll do our accounts when I've time.'

Don Eugenio returned assiduously, but his nephew either said that he was busy or had a headache or was just going out. His uncle did not lose patience; he came back every day to remind him of his promise. Then one bad morning, flinging himself on a chair, he said:

'Listen, we can make up our accounts at your convenience, but today I've nothing in my pocket and am tired out. Lend me something.'

'What? You want change?' exclaimed the prince, going pale. 'D'you think we're quits? Half a dozen copies or so have been sold! And you have the face to ask for more money?'

'I don't know what to do!' confided the cavaliere, looking famished and staring him straight in the eyes.

'And you come to me? What right have you? Why should I give you money to eat? Why have you spent everything? Why haven't you ever thought of the future?'

'I need something to eat, d'you understand?' repeated the cavaliere in the same tone of voice, and his eyes seemed to be eating his nephew up.

'Go to your brother, to your sister ... they have an obligation to help you ... why come to me?'

Then, alarmed by the old man's expression, he turned his back.

When he heard him go, he called the porter and ordered him never to let the old man in again.

This order had the unanimous approval of the servants; that cavaliere was really no honour to the family, not so much for what was said about him as for the state into which he had fallen. The new major-domo confessed, 'I'm ashamed every time I have to announce him to the master ...'

All the old man's attempts to get into the palace were vain. He could go on declaring, 'My nephew is waiting for me, he told me he'd be at home,' or, 'I saw him coming in,' or, 'There he is behind that window ...'; the porter, the ostlers, the retainers all said in his face, 'Your Excellency had better go, it's just a waste of time.' They called him 'Excellency' as in carnival time they did the street-sweepers dressed up as barons. He tried to force his way in, but then they seized him and pushed him out. 'Excellency; so roughly? ... Those are not ways for Excellencies like you! ...'

One day, he sat down in the porter's lodge and declared he would not move until his nephew passed. At first the porter joked about it; then he tried friendly persuasion and touching his pride. 'This isn't the place for Your Excellency . . . a gentleman like Your Excellency sitting with a porter! Aren't you ashamed?' But the old man did not move, did not reply, sat there grim and hungry as a wolf. Then the porter began losing patience and suddenly stopped the 'Excellency'. 'Are you going, yes or no? . . .' and as Don Eugenio sat nailed into his chair the other finally lost his temper, even stopped calling him *Lei*, and seizing him by the shoulders, pulled him to his feet and kicked and pushed him outside, yelling:

'Out with you, I say, the devil take you!'

Donna Ferdinanda thrust him out as if he were a mangy cur; the duke gave him a small sum, making him realise that he could rely on no more alms from him. The best thing to do was find him work, which he himself wanted; so Benedetto Giulente, who had also given him money, mentioned this to Consalvo.

'What job d'you suggest?' answered the young prince. 'He's an old fool, can't do a thing. D'you want the Mayor's uncle to act as usher or dog-catcher?'

It was clear that there was nothing doing in the Town Hall because of the young prince's understandable pride. Giulente went to the duke and suggested he should be put in some office at the Provincial or Prefect's headquarters; then the duke, to avoid other demands for financial help, arranged a post for him as copyist at the Provincial Archives, the best that could be found. But when the old man was told this he went red as a poppy.

'Me a scribbler's job? Who d'you take me for?'

'But you see . . .' Benedetto suggested respectfully, 'Your Excellency has no academic degrees . . . and is not so young . . . Public administration is demanding work . . .'

'And you suggest making me a copyist?' cried the cavaliere, 'me, Eugenio Uzeda of Francalanza, Gentleman of the Bedchamber to Ferdinand II, author of the *Sicilian Herald*? . . . Why don't you take on the job yourself, you little donkey?'

So the old man began asking for money again. But the duke, to punish him for refusing that post, shut the door in his face, and Lucrezia, after judging him worthy of the highest offices simply to put her husband to shame, refused to have him sniffing round her house either. One day the cavaliere, in ever more wretched and bedraggled condition, went to his niece Teresa. The porter did not recognise him and would not let him pass. When he eventually reached the young duchess, who wrung her hands at seeing him in such a state, he began complaining:

'You see how your father's reduced me? He stole my book, the rascal? He's a thief who . . .'

'Uncle, please!' exclaimed Teresa. And she emptied her purse into the hand of the old man, trembling with greed at sight of the money. He appeared again and again at the Radalì palace, but the dowager duchess, to avoid the servants' comments, declared that Teresa could help him if she wished, but was not to let him into the house again.

And so that door was shut on him too.

What he expected was a post as professor or accountant paid enough to live a gentlemanly life and do no work, but as this was not forthcoming he took to stopping people he knew in the street and giving them an account of his circumstances.

'They've despoiled me, reduced me to poverty, they have! My brother the Benedictine left me five hundred *onze*, and they tore up his Will and made a false one! My nephew the prince stole my great work the *Sicilian Herald*! . . . And they shut their gates in my face! On me, Eugenio of Francalanza! Gentleman of the Bedchamber! President of the Academy of the Four Poets! . . . Do they know who I am? If you come to my house I'll show you my medals and diplomas—a whole shelf full . . .'

His megalomania grew from day to day, with his wretchedness, his difficulties and humiliation. He would announce:

'The Government has invited me to Rome for a Chair in Dante Studies. But I'm not going! I'd be mad to! I'd far rather go to Germany where they know all my famous books and where learning is respected! . . . The Prefect told me that the King wants me to be his son's tutor. Me, a pedagogue? What do they take me for? If he's called Savoy, I'm called Uzeda. Ah, Don Umberto, don't you know . . .?' Then, in a whisper, 'Could you lend me five lire? I've left my purse at home . . .'

He would be given two or one, even a half-lira; and he accepted anything. His relations, warned of this scandal, shrugged their shoulders or said, 'We must see to it' without doing anything. Giulente and Teresa did, secretly, help him as best they could, but he had now got into the habit of seeking alms; it was pleasant and easy and the passage of money from others' pockets to his own seemed quite natural to him. Also a deep instinct of revenge against his relatives urged him to go on putting them to shame.

And one day the news went through the city:

'Have you heard? The Cavaliere Don Eugenio is begging in the streets!'

He was now literally begging. Even if he had a few lire in his pocket he would go up to unknown passers-by, hold out a hand and say:

'Please will you give me a little money? Just a cent to buy myself a cigar?'

He snatched at the money as if it were prey, thrust it into his pocket and then went up to another:

'Please, a coin?'

Teresa, accompanied by her husband, went to visit him in the garret to which he had been reduced, and threw herself at his feet.

'Uncle, we'll give you whatever you want, as long as you don't do this any more! A person like you to lower yourself so!'

'Yes, yes . . .'

And he took the money they offered him. And next day began again. Now it was an obsession; the habit had become a disease and ended by bemusing his weak Uzeda brain. Ragged as a real beggar, his dirty white beard straggling over his haggard face, his feet in floppy cloth slippers, he went around leaning on a stick and asking:

'A coin, please! . . . just this once! . . .'

And to earn his money he would make a show of madness. Some asked who he was, wasn't he the Cavaliere Uzeda? Then he would cry:

'Eugenio Consalvo Filippo Blasco Ferrante Francesco Maria Uzeda of Francalanza, Mirabella, Oragua, Lumera, etc., etc. . . . Gentleman of the Bedchamber (with functions) to His Majesty, a real King! . . .' and he doffed his hat. 'Ferdinand II; decorated by His Highness the Bey of Tunis Nisciam-Ifitkar; President of the Academy of the Four Poets, Corresponding Member of numerous scientific-literary-volcanological societies, of Naples, London, Paris, Caropepe, Petersburg, Paulsburg, New York and Forlimpopoli, author of the celebrated, historico-heraldic-blasonic-noble-chronological work entitled the *Sicilian Herald* with supplement . . . Please . . . a coin to buy myself a cigar . . .'

7

T E R E S A's second child, another boy, was born a year after the first, and everyone said to husband and wife 'So you're losing no time!' She had suffered little at the first birth, and this one she scarcely noticed; worthy reward for her purity. The baptismal ceremony was a modest one this time partly because it was for a younger son, a little baron, and partly for another more distressing reason. The prince, scratching the nape of his neck one day between the shoulder blades because of a strong itch, had broken the skin and drawn a little blood. At first he took no notice of it, but after a time just where he had scratched there formed a kind of tumour which grew until it irked his movements and prevented him from lying on his back in bed. Everyone attributed this to excessive scratching. Even so, as the uncomfortable growth did not go, a surgeon had to be called.

The doctor confirmed that it was of no importance, but added that it would not heal without a small incision. At this announcement the prince went pale and refused to submit to the operation, But, ever since Teresa bore her first child, the tumour had grown more and given so much trouble that he had consented to its being cut. The operation lasted longer than was expected, and the prince was confined to house for many days. Meanwhile, the baptism of the little Baron of Filici took place without pomp. Mayor Consalvo was godfather and Giovannino came from Augusta for the ceremony. During the year he had made two or three visits to his godson, according to his promise; brief visits, of one or two days. It was said that at Augusta on his estate of Costantina he had a farmer's daughter, a well-set-

548

up pink and white peasant girl, for whose sake he never stayed very long in Catania. The duchess his mother was very pleased about this, as the surest guarantee against his marrying. The duke Michele was pleased to hear of his brother enjoying himself. And Teresa, in spite of being prevented in honesty from approving that relationship, yet showed her brother-in-law sisterly affection and always made a great fuss of him. When he sent commissions from Augusta for his mother to do she would often carry them out herself. Usually he asked for linen and objects of domestic use, but every now and again also for lengths of cloth for women's dresses, corsets and silken kerchiefs . . . Were they for the farmer's daughter?

Every time he returned to his maternal home his face was browner, his beard shaggier, the skin on his hands harder. But in that face like a desert Arab's the white of his eye was very gentle. Teresa would thank the Lord for the wisdom inspired in him, for the health accorded him, but in her heart she asked herself how a young man who had been so elegant, so avid of pleasures, of fine rich things, could resign himself to leading a tough country life, to living with a peasant girl amid peasants? . . . Was she herself not the cause of that transformation? And at once, as if to exculpate herself in her own eyes, she thought, ' I'm quite changed too! . . .' Where, in fact, were those poetic inspirations, those winged fantasies of hers now?

She had been married for two years and was already starting her third pregnancy. When she had dreamt of Giuliano Biancavilla, of Giovannino, did the thought ever occur to her of becoming a mere machine for producing children? . . . And she struggled hard against thoughts which must surely have been suggested to her by the spirit of temptation. Biancavilla, back from his travels, had also forgotten and taken a wife. One day she met him face to face; for a moment she quivered, but an hour after the meeting had forgotten it. Giovannino was her brother-in-law; no, nothing more remained of those old dreams. Was she sorry? No! she thought. ' What do I lack for happiness? I'm young, pretty and rich, everyone loves me, everyone praises me, I have two angelic little sons. What have I to complain of?' Had she not done the right thing in the measure of her own ability. Would her mother up there not bless her?

Would the Blessed Ximena not be pleased with her distant descendant?

The spirit of temptation used subtle means to disturb her in this serenity. Perhaps it was books, poetry, novels which, at certain times when she felt most calm and sure and was smiling with greatest content, suddenly produced a sort of cloud in the clear sky of her mind and gave her an obscure sense of discomfort, a faint rancour at happiness lost before she had been able to reach it. Was it a sin to read those books, to allow those visions? Her confessor, the priests who surrounded her, said it was, that they were dangerous; but maybe they recognised at the same time that such a danger was more distant for her, with her upright soul and healthy mind and pure conscience? And then . . . she had renounced so much: if she ever renounced living in her imagination what would she have left?

Giovannino read a lot too. Every time he came from Augusta he would ask her, ' Sister-in-law, have you any books to lend me?' and take cases of them away among the household things he had come to fetch. Was that how he killed time when there was no work to be overseen on the land, no vintage, sowing, or harvest? . . . Whenever he came to town he also laid in a stock of sulphate of quinine. Malaria reigned at Costantina, and on his land at Balata and Favarotta. During the dangerous season, it was true, he would go off to Melilli on the Hyblean hills, where the air was healthy; but it was a good thing never to lack that sovereign remedy either for himself or for his workers.

One fine summer evening Teresa and her mother-in-law, leaving the little heir at home in custody of a nurse-maid and taking the younger boy with its nurse in their carriage, were going for their usual drive. The unweaned baron, rocked by the gentle movement of the carriage, was sleeping amidst a cloud of gauze on his nurse's lap. Teresa was wearing for the first time a sumptuous robe which had arrived from Turin a few days before. She saw all the ladies whose equipages crossed hers turn round and look her over in admiration. The carriage drove on up to Our Lady of Graces. There mother, daughter-in-law and nurse alighted, entered the narrow chapel and knelt before the altar. Teresa's eyes were lowered to avoid the sight of the walls covered

550

with those horrid *ex-voto*, of the charnel-house which disgusted her now as it had horrified her in childhood. But, gazing at the statue of the Virgin she poured out all her gratitude for the graces showered on her. For some time now she had been feeling so calm; almost happy! It was long since anything had perturbed her; she had no favour to ask of the Madonna. Yes, her father's still uncertain health, the black mood that gnawed him after his surgical operation. Glum, grim, taciturn, impelled more than ever to get at someone, he had begun turning over in his head again the idea of finding Consalvo a wife. Though he did not speak to and seemed to take no notice of that Evil-Eyed son of his, he was plagued by the thought of his family ending if the fellow did not take a wife. And he had sought out a new match in Palermo, a match said to be quite outstanding. But Consalvo said no once again, and the prince broke off relations with him more violently than ever.

Teresa prayed longer because of this; then she crossed herself and rose to her feet. Her mother-in-law had already got up. The nurse, a humble peasant holding in her arms the fruit of Teresa's womb, ended her prayers. The baby, awakened by the clatter of feet and the muttering of blind beggars, was staring at the flaming altar half delighted and half bemused. After distributing to the poor all she had in her purse Teresa got back into the carriage. The old duchess ordered the coachman to drive on as far as the Café di Sicilia.

There the waiter had not yet brought them out their ices when an excited cry was heard behind the carriage.

' Teresa . . . Mamma . . .'

It was Michele, unrecognisable, his shirt awry from sweat, pale as a corpse. They asked in consternation :

' What is it? . . . Michele! . . . What's the matter? . . .'

Michele turned to the coachman.

' Home!' he ordered, ' Drive home at once . . .' and he opened the door, got in and flung himself down next to the nurse.

' My father? . . . the baby?' Teresa was exclaiming already, seizing one of his hands. But he cried :

' No, no . . .'

And while the whipped-up horses started amid sparks from the cobbles he finally explained.

'Giovannino . . . a telegram from his agent . . . pernicious malaria! . . . I rushed to the doctor then to the railway station . . . I've been searching for you everywhere . . . I'm leaving to-night by special train . . .'

At the first moment, Teresa felt almost a sense of relief. Stunned at her husband's aspect, terrified by his obscure words, she had thought of the ghastliest catastrophies: her father's death, a sudden threat to her other son. Assured that none of her own blood were in danger, she did not take her brother-in-law's illness very seriously. Now with Michele losing his head, and her mother-in-law suddenly full of tenderness for the son she had so neglected, frantically talking of leaving, of rushing to call other doctors, she felt that her duty was to keep her head. On reading the agent's telegram her confidence was reaffirmed. The telegram read: 'Your Excellencys' brother found in bed high fever stop Fearing pernicious malaria immediately given quinine stop Request member family with doctor.' Michele had paid no attention to the doubt in the wording of this communication. She encouraged them all, offered to accompany them, but the old duchess, who kept exclaiming every two minutes 'My son! . . . my son! . . .' wanted her to stay. Then she prepared her husband's and her mother-in-law's baggage, forgot nothing, asked them not to leave her without news, and assured them that even with malignant fever the quinine already administered and the care of the Catania doctor would surely triumph.

At seven o'clock in the evening Michele and the duchess left. When she was alone in the house her confidence began waning. Had things not been serious the telegram, the request for another doctor, the calling of relatives would have been unnecessary. And why had he not signed the telegram himself? . . . Holding her children tight against her breast she prayed in her heart, 'Oh Lord, oh Lady of Graces, please may there not be a tragedy . . .'

And why by dawn, when Michele and the duchess must have reached his bedside, why was there no news? . . . She said to herself to give herself courage, 'No news is good news!' . . . and tried to imagine her husband's and mother-in-law's happy faces at finding Giovannino smiling at them, reassuring them. Then why did they not reassure her too? Did they not know that she was worried also? . . . How she regretted now the cruel selfishness which had almost made her rejoice at hearing it was her brother-in-law in danger! Was he not almost a brother to her? Did she not love him with sisterly love? The memory of that other love she had nourished for him was lost and cancelled now! Now he remained only a friend, a relation, one who had held her baby at the font of redemption.

There was still no news. People came to ask, relations, friends; she could give none. The marchese Federico, shaking his head, mentioned having heard that the imprudent young man had slept some night on the Balata land in the middle of the malarial zone. 'I'm afraid this is the serious kind; worse than a whiff of grapeshot!' Princess Graziella protested. 'Nonsense! New diseases come with the wind! . . . If he's taken quinine in time, there's no danger!'

By midday nothing had come. She wanted to send a telegram herself asking for a reply, but when she suggested doing so to her stepmother, the latter replied that it did not seem necessary, that it was better to wait.

In the afternoon she was alone again. Sad thoughts assailed her once more. To combat them, to thrust them out, she began praying. And as she prayed she thought of the Blessed Ximena, of the votive lamps burning in her chapel. In the clothes she was wearing, throwing only a shawl over her shoulders, with her maid she had herself driven by closed carriage to the Capuchin convent. Beneath the altar lay as usual the centuries-old coffin, object of her terrors. She gazed at it, joined hands, begged her saintly ancestor for poor Giovannino's health, and told the sacristan to light a perpetual votive lamp. On getting home, she found nothing, but a ring at the bell made her start. Perhaps it was the telegram? But no, it was a messenger from the Town Hall sent by Consalvo, for the latest news . . . She needed air, and opened a window. On returning to her room, she fell on to a chair with her face in her hands. He must be dead. Michele was not giving her the news because of her condition. And suddenly the past all came back to her memory; she saw him again as she had known him, as she had loved him. She heard his gentle tone when he asked her, 'Teresa, Teresa, d'you love me? . . .' and with arid eyes, with a catch in her throat, she

553

acknowledged, 'Yes, it was I who killed him! . . . For me he changed his life . . . went to bury himself down there . . . to find death!'

She rose to her feet. Had anyone heard her? The babies were asleep and she was alone. And the torturing, terrible thoughts assailed her once again. It had not been she alone, it had been all those others even more! Her stepmother, her father, his mother, all those hard, ruthless, implacable people, all those who had kept happiness from him, and from her too. For she had not been happy, no, never! And they praised her for loving her husband. But not for a second had she loved him. He came near to revolting her! She despised his ignorance, his vulgarity! And they had sacrificed her from pride, caprice, worship of titles, idolatry of vain words. Mad and malign; Consalvo was right. He had done right to rebel. It was she who had been stupid in obeying blindly. Her fault! Hers too! Just in order to obey, to respect, to content; whom? 'Our mother's murderers! . . .'

With eyes starting, she held her breath. Had the baby heard? . . . He was looking at her, with his clear, calm eyes gleaming like stars in the evening twilight . . . She did not rush to him. In the half-darkness the silver of the Crucifix, the glass on the picture of Our Lady were gleaming too. Why then did They allow such things? Did They not know? Did They not see them? Could They not prevent them?

The door opened; her maid came in exclaiming:

'Excellency, the telegram!'

She read. 'Doctors assure final attack overcome stop Recovering consciousness stop We feel calmer.'

Then she burst into tears.


Michele returned a week later. His brother was then convalescent, but the day of their arrival they had found him at his last gasp. In a fit of delirium he had tried to throw himself off the balcony; four men had scarcely been able to hold him back: it was a real miracle he was saved. As soon as he was in a fit state to travel he would be brought home to ensure his recovery by a change of air.

In fact a few days later the dowager, who had stayed at his

bedside, wrote calling her elder son to help her transport the sick man. When Teresa saw him arrive, bent, thin, with a straggly beard on his yellow face, she scarcely recognised him. Now peace had returned to her soul. For a second she had despaired of Divine help, and just as she was doubting, as she was almost accusing the Lord of forgetting her, the poor man had been saved by a miracle. She recognised the intervention of Blessed Ximena, and she raised her most fervent thanks to heaven. Now the votive lamp burnt day and night in the chapel, and the news of the miraculous intervention increased the Saint's fame.

All trace of the storm had left her. Before Giovannino's weak, haggard trembling, she felt nothing but great compassion and prayed for nothing but his recovery. As she looked after him in every way, like a nun, she was thinking, ' How ugly he's got! He's unrecognisable!' And he let himself be tended like a child, without strength, without will, without memory. The terrible blow had dazed him, blood was gradually flowing back into his fibres, but his mental faculties took much longer to return. The strong doses of quinine had taken away most of his hearing; often he thought himself still in Augusta and called people in his household there. Only rarely did words come to his lips. At moments his tired, fixed stare seemed like a blind man's.

A month later the doctors advised his removal to the mountains. His mother went with him to Tardarìa. During their absence, which lasted three months, Teresa had another baby boy. In November, as it was too cold to stay up in the woods any longer, the old duchess returned with the convalescent. Giovannino was now completely recovered, his face full of healthy colour; but his mind was still weak. His slight deafness made him restless and irritable. One moment he longed to go out and see people, the next he shut himself into his room and avoided all. Often he would lose his temper, speak rudely at some little contradiction or unimportant observation by his mother or brother; sometimes he screamed with hands to head, ' D'you want to send me mad? . . .'

Only Teresa seemed to exercise a pacifying influence on his sick spirit. As if by virtue of some finer sense he always understood all that Teresa said, almost read her words in her looks, in the movements of her lips. And very gradually, through her beneficent influence, he grew better, recovered, took up his former habits again, began to dress with care once more, to take an interest in what he saw and heard. One day he had his beard cut off. It was a transformation, like one to be seen in a theatre; in a second he was young again and the handsome young man of before reappeared.

'That's the way!' said Consalvo, who often came to visit him when his duties as Mayor left him free.

The latter was now at the apogee of popularity; everyone talked of his intelligence and shrewdness, the good he was doing to the town; the Government had nominated him Commendatore of the Order of the Crown of Italy. Often he would get into discussion with Giovannino, for the latter observed that this system of spending money freely on works of varying utility would expose the once flourishing finances of the Commune to the risk of collapse.

'When there's money spend it!' replied Consalvo. '*Après moi le déluge* . . .'

'They'll get into debt if you go on at this rate . . .'

'Someone'll pay up. My dear fellow, I'm out to make myself popular, and I use whatever means I find. D'you think this mob realises what I'm worth? One must throw dust in their eyes!'

Teresa and Giovannino would talk about him constantly and agree entirely in their judgment of him. That contempt of his for all and sundry grieved them. It was, of course, a sign of strength in a way, but would it not do him harm in the long run? Teresa, in particular, believed true strength to be more modest, more considerate, more timid. Giovannino agreed with her judgments, but he would excuse Consalvo and attribute all that was least fine·in him to the political system. What caused her most sorrow was that her brother had no firm faith, agreed with all and laughed at all. He no longer practised his religion and this was an infinite sorrow to her; but she would have preferred a frank negation to the subterfuges which he used. On the Feast of Saint Agatha he attended Pontifical High Mass at the head of the Town Council, in black suit and decorations, before thousands crammed into the cathedral. Afterwards he declared, 'The masquerade's over.'

'Why d'you go then?' his sister asked him. 'Isn't it better to stay at home, if you think it's a masquerade?'

'It is indeed better,' agreed Giovannino.

'If I stay at home, though, I lose the support of the sacristans and bigots.'

'But the free-thinkers who see you going to church,' added his cousin, while Teresa nodded approvingly. 'What do they say?'

'They say as I do: " One has to pay for popular favour ".'

No, no, she wished her brother were not like that. And she had lively discussions with him, during which he called her a sentimental devotee and a clerical, ending with 'Now don't you go and put your Monsignori against me!'

But even the prelates who came to visit the young duchess were full of praises for her brother. They shook their heads a bit, it's true, at his scepticism, but recognised his good qualities; and 'when the basis is good, there's no need to despair'. Her frequenting of these ecclesiastics, her listening to them, did not bring Teresa to any renunciation of her ideas on religious politics. A devout believer but no bigot, she could not for example condemn the suppression of the religious Orders when she heard stories—now that she was married—of some of the Benedictines' scandalous lives. And why ever was the Pope so stubborn in upholding the Temporal Power if Jesus had said, 'My Kingdom is not of this world . . .'?

Such opinions, which would have brought excommunication down on any other, were tolerated in her by the spiritual advisers who surrounded her and took advantage of her piety and her influence over her brother the Mayor. If they wished to get boys into the orphanage or old people into the almshouses or sick into hospital; if the Sisters of Charity needed help to prevent their ejection by atheists; or land was to be acquired cheaply for Catholic Homes; if disputes arose between Town Hall and Curia, Teresa served as intermediary, often obtaining what she asked from Consalvo. But she was deeply hurt by the jokes, witticisms, sceptical declarations made by her brother, who told her he was granting these favours in order to get a return in time. Once when she reproved him for his lack of character, he replied smiling, 'My dear, d'you remember the story of the man

557

who saw a mote in others' eyes and not the beam in his own? Just think a bit of what you've done yourself!'

They were alone. She bowed her head.

'You wished to marry Giovannino and you took Michele, whom you didn't want; is that true or not? And it was a serious action, the most serious of a lifetime, one of those which decides a whole existence. I could say, just to follow your example, that you did that from lack of character. But instead I'll say you did it because it suited you! Character, get well into your head, is doing what suits us.'

She was still silent. It was the first time her brother had ever spoken to her of these intimate things. Then, as if trying to correct any wounding effect of his words, Consalvo went on:

'Anyway, I'm not blaming you. Maybe it was better for you. Poor Giovannino since his illness isn't quite right in the head.'

'Why?' she asked. 'How can you say that? It doesn't seem so to me . . .'

'It doesn't seem so to you . . . it seems so to all who talk to him. Don't you see he's always in the clouds? Look how he walks alone in the streets, he bumps into passers-by, doesn't see carriages; just the very same as his father.'

'Are you sure?'

'The other day if it hadn't been for the town guards he'd have ended under a cart. Sometimes he doesn't reason and makes me repeat things two or three times before he can grasp them. Talk about it to your husband, get him looked after, take care before there's some disaster.'

She was deeply perturbed. Her brother-in-law had seemed to her entirely recovered; nothing had made her suspect that his unbalanced state of mind was lasting. Now, waiting for him to come home, she almost felt afraid, as if a madman really was about to appear before her. But on seeing him enter, serene, smiling, with a parcel of cakes for the babies and a quantity of little news items for her, she was sure Consalvo was mistaken or at least exaggerating.

'You know,' she said to her brother the first time she found herself alone with him, 'your fears are quite unjustified. Giovannino has nothing wrong with him . . .'

Consalvo shook his head. But as Teresa insisted and told

him how the young man aroused no suspicion at home, how he talked to her perfectly reasonably, he let out, with an air of gallantry:

'I can well believe he's all right ... with you.'

Suddenly, at these words, before she had even realised their meaning, a flush rose to her face. She wanted to reply, to tell him that was an improper and unworthy jest, that his words hinted at a foul and injurious suspicion, to ask him to explain them, force him to deny them ... but all these ideas passed like flashes through her mind and she remained mute, stifled, blushing furiously, hearing no more of what her brother was saying.

When she was alone she tried to think it out. What had Consalvo meant? Could he be suspecting her? And even if he did entertain a suspicion of that kind, would he tell it to her face? ... No, it was a joke, a thoughtless but innocent allusion to what had once been ... Why had she not replied at once, though, and declared those words out of place? Why was she still so perturbed, why was her disquiet lasting even now that she had taken her head in her hands and asked herself all those questions? Had she been silent because she had been caught in the wrong? So her brother-in-law was restless away from her and did not reason because of her? Then by what virtue was he serene and smiling before her? And she, what had she done to make that possible? She had tended him, she had shown her sisterly love for him, she had used her ascendancy over him to heal him ... What then? Nothing else ... nothing else! ... The Lord was her witness ... Nothing; he was just like a brother. Why then those words of her own brother? ... Because there had been something between them, once upon a time, long, long ago? Because Giovannino was not her brother by blood? And a ghastly doubt passed through her mind: 'Is what Consalvo said being repeated by others? ...'

That storm of doubts and fears and protests going through her head was now stilled by surprise. How, if she was innocent in act and thought, had Consalvo been able to think evil or bring up a past which she thought dead and buried? How? ... Why? ... Then seeing Giovannino come home, hearing him chatter as he sat beside her at the same table, she understood; because they were now living under the same roof, because they

559

were together all day, because they drove out in a carriage together, because she would meet him at her father's, her aunt's or uncle's, wherever she went. No, she had not realised that their intimacy had reached such a point, or rather she had not understood how that intimacy could arouse a dreadful suspicion. But now her mind was beginning to clear; yes, he was not her brother, he was a stranger, a man whom she had loved before . . . He must leave then, go far away from her, as in the first years of her marriage, as before his illness. Yes, he must leave. And suddenly she realised the most terrible thing of all: that this was impossible, because she loved him. At the idea of not seeing him again, at the thought of breaking that sweet and dear communion of souls, she felt her heart torn asunder. And now that no longer intermittent flashes, but a crude harsh beam was lighting up her thoughts, she realised that she did not love only his spiritual company but the whole of him, body and soul, as before, as always.

Her husband was becoming ever grosser and clumsier, losing his last few hairs; that shiny cranium of his disgusted her. At the idea of passing her hand over Giovannino's thick, scented locks she trembled . . . Why were they so harmonious in their judgments, their tastes, their opinions? Because they loved each other. Why had she alone been able to quieten his restless spirit at the time of his suffering? Because they loved each other! . . . They loved each other; that meant they were infamous. The more worthy of eternal damnation the more sacred the bonds which they should have respected . . . She, the saintly! . . . the saintly!

And it seemed to her terrified mind that sin had been committed, that there was no way out. Every time Giovannino neared her she trembled as before the witness and accomplice of her own sin. She avoided him, she never looked him in the face, she fretted when he held his little nephews in his arms, and kissed them long and avidly, as if kissing her, part of her flesh. 'What's the matter with you, Teresa?' he would ask her. And her embarrassment, her coldness grew, as he no longer called her 'sister-in-law' but by her own name, and she herself called him by his name, so close had become their intimacy. Michele, her mother-in-law, also began noticing her changed humour and could not think to what it could be attributed, or put it down to some indefinable illness of which she complained. If they knew! . . . If they found out!

When her terror reached a climax it dissolved like fever. What could they find out? What acts? What words, what glances of understanding? Had anything ever happened between them, for a day, an hour, a minute, which could make either of them blush? Where was the sin except in thought? And was she quite sure that he was nurturing sinful thoughts like her? What direct proof had she? On the contrary, her alarm now, the repulsion she was showing him, might they not be the only indications to give her away? And gradually, forcing herself to reason, she grew calmer. He would leave, time would once more quench the embers suddenly ·flaming in her heart like volcanic fires.

A sudden worsening of her father's condition helped her to forget. The tumour, which for a time had vanished from where the surgeon's knife had passed, reappeared again farther over, in his right armpit. As soon as the sick man noticed the new malignant growth he had such a fit of impotent rage that terror froze all those around him. She hurried to him, spent entire days at the poor wretch's bedside, endured patiently all the outbursts of his bile, soothed her stepmother's agonies. At the opportune moment the doctors got ready to cut and cauterise. This time too the sick man screamed that he would not have it. 'They're trying to kill me! They're not doctors, but butchers! You're paying them to kill me to rid yourself of me . . .' In his delirium he suddenly flung off the mask of zealous God-fearing Catholic and from his mouth came foul and horrible curses. The princess stopped up her ears, Teresa raised her eyes to heaven; but the Monsignori affirmed, 'It's not him talking, it's the poison in him. He doesn't know what he is saying.' At the sight of black cassocks, though, the sick man yelled, 'Hey, you black crows, what d'you want? Sniffing human flesh, are you? . . . Get out of here! . . . get out! . . .'

The crisis ended in an outburst of tears. He promised Masses for the souls in purgatory, candles and votive lamps to every Madonna and Crucifix, asked his family to forgive him, begged them never to leave him. Teresa, kneeling by his bedside, persuaded him to let himself be operated on once again.

'Do it . . . do what you like . . . But don't leave me! . . . Please, by your mother's soul . . . Don't leave me . . .'

She was present at the butchering . . . At first, the sight of her father under the chloroform and the felt mask, throwing himself about, laughing and mouthing incomprehensible words, then growing quiet and pale, seeming dead, froze the blood in her veins. She tried hard not to be a nuisance to the doctors, and by extraordinary concentration of will-power she conquered her own fears. But at sight of the knives, at the whiffs of carbolic acid mingling with the smell of anaesthetic, a chill came over her heart, a nausea rose in her throat, and suddenly everything seemed to be going round.

'Go away! Go away!' the surgeon said to her when she came to. But she shook her head; she had promised and she stayed.

She did not see the wound but saw the circular gesture of the operating surgeon's arm, the blood squirting on to his aprons and his assistants', marking bed and floor, making the smell even more revolting than ever. How much blood! How much blood! Basins filled with it, were emptied and filled again . . . She was on the other side of the bed, holding one of her father's hands, cold as a corpse's. She could neither pray nor think, overcome by horror. Only one idea occupied her mind: 'When will they end? . . . Will they never end? . . .'

They would never end, it seemed. Like a craftsman struggling to reduce an inert material to a prescribed form, the surgeon went on cutting, snipping, scraping. He put aside one instrument, took up another, then went back to the first, calm, cool, very watchful. An incident prolonged the wait, retarded the operation. A drop of putrid blood fell on a scratched hand of the assistant. To prevent the man being poisoned the cauteriser was lit, and red-hot platinum passed over the hand; there was a sizzle of burning flesh, the air became pestilential.

An hour later all was over. Marks were washed off, the wound bound up, instruments put back into their cases, the prince was awakened. Her father's first look, still blind, still dead, increased Teresa's horror. Despite this she waited for his return to life. She said to him, smiling and squeezing his hand:

'It's all over . . . it went splendidly . . . didn't it, doctor? . . .'

But suddenly all her strength left her. Her husband, who had just come in with the princess and other relatives, took her off to a far room. The doctor came and said authoritatively:

'Will you or won't you go home now? . . . You must rest; there's nothing more to be done here.'

She had not the strength to re-enter the sick man's room even for an instant, but she asked Michele to stay so as to bring her the news later. She swayed as she went down the stairs, leaning on the doctor's arm, then let herself drop on the carriage seat. And as the horses galloped off and a swirl of air refreshed her breast, her spirit was finally liberated from its long oppression. She thought, 'What agonies! What misery!' Of what use to her father were the riches, the power that he had clung to so grimly? Would he not exchange them all for health? And he was condemned! That operation had been almost useless; the growth would reappear elsewhere . . . And it was against that poor corroded life that she had, one day, rebelled one moment, in her heart—not in words, Lord, only in thought; but such a thought was equally blameworthy—it was against that poor life she had rebelled. Why? How could she have? If he had done wrongs now he was paying for them by ghastly torture. And if he had done wrongs, was it for her to judge him? He had made no effort to see her happy; could she judge him for that? . . . And where was happiness? Would she have been any happier otherwise? Who knows what other agonies there might have been! What other miseries . . . Always before her eyes was that gesture of the surgeon cutting living flesh.

Did her father think of these things? Did he realise he had been deceived? She must not judge him; but why then did all the accusations which she had heard repeated against him return to her mind? Of his having been hard, false, violent, of his robbing sisters and brothers, and falsifying the monk's Will, and leaving his uncle to die a beggar, and embittering the life and hastening the end of his wife, of her own mother? . . . Were these things true? Had he been so bad? . . . If he had been calumniated by envy and malice, was not the world much worse? What a sad and horrible world, in which hatred could thrive between father and son! . . . He still refused to see Consalvo; so her sacrifice had been in vain. He would die without seeing him, cursing and sobbing. What a world of sorrow, what a world of misery! . . . Then, quickly, as if the horses drawing her were transporting her backwards in time, she thought of the convent, where she had felt oppressed when a girl, as a secure refuge, a port sheltered from storm. Blessed indeed was her aunt the nun, who spent days, every one the same, amid her prayers and the simple cares of that holy house, out of sight of evil, safe from temptations, errors and faults. She thought, ' Why was I afraid of the convent? . . . If only I had entered it for ever! . . .'

Now her aching mind realised that the truth was there, in that silence, in that solitude, in that renunciation. ' Would you enter it now?' she asked herself, and replied, ' Now, this instant!' What was life but a waiting for death? Why should she have any repugnance for the solitude, renunciation, silence of cloistral life if she now felt so alone, terrifyingly alone, if she had renounced so many things close to her heart, if the world was now all sadness and pain. ' If only I weren't born? . . .'

A chill quiver shook her as the carriage stopped in the courtyard of her home. What about her children? Had she forgotten her children? When she pressed them tight to her her long agitation of spirit melted into tears. And at that second she heard a voice, a bright, sweet, pitying voice.

' Teresa, what's the matter? . . . How did it go? Is he bad?'

She could not answer; sobs prevented her.

' Teresa! . . . For the love of God, don't torture yourself so! You who are so strong . . . Wasn't the operation a success? Yes? . . . Well then? Come, Teresa, be reasonable. He'll recover, you'll see. Oh, you poor thing . . . How right . . . But enough now! Enough, Teresa. Listen to me . . . tell me . . . Didn't Michele come with you? . . .'

She replied with shakes of the head. She wanted to tell him to be quiet, as that sweet voice, those gentle words increased her storm of sobbing, as that sweet pity laid bare her own misery. No, she was not strong; she was weak, timid, fragile; she could give no help to others; she needed help and support herself.

And the warm voice said again:

"Poor little thing! Poor little thing! . . . Take courage.

Here are your children, look how lovely they are . . . for love of these little angels, do not fall ill yourself . . . And my mother isn't here ! . . . Would you like your brother? Would you like me to send for him? . . . Tell me what you want; here I am . . .'

And his arm went round her, his temple brushed hers. She was still crying, but from tenderness, not pain. After the horrors she had seen, after the gloom of her thoughts, her mind needed comfort, and those comforting words slid into her heart as sweetly as balsam. She, who had thought herself alone in the world, with no one to understand her, now abandoned herself with the trembling enjoyment of weakness to that strength, this sympathy. He dried her eyes, smoothed the disordered locks on her forehead. His hand was trembling.

' Like this . . .' he murmured . . . ' There . . . like this.'

His arm went around her waist again, and he took one of her hands. The sobs racking her agonised breast made their embrace closer. He kissed her on the forehead.

She freed herself from the embrace and rose. The dowager was arriving.


From that moment each read blame in the other's eyes. They avoided looking at each other but the thought persisted. If the hand or clothes of one brushed those of the other, their foreheads flushed and their minds clouded. She no longer thought of her father, who was dying, or of her children. Of temptation only, always. She went to throw herself before the Blessed Ximena; the votive lamp burnt ceaselessly, like the flame in her heart. Prayers were no use; no one heard her. Nothing was any use. She thought, ' It will be today . . . or tomorrow . . .'

Her husband once said to her :

' Giovannino rather worries me . . . he's gone strange again, as after his illness, have you noticed?'

She had seen nothing. She was amazed no one had yet noticed her own confusion of mind.

' He doesn't speak, he doesn't laugh; it must be that fixation tormenting him again . . . what can we do?'

What could they do?

One day, at table, Giovannino announced :

' I'm leaving for Augusta.'

This is salvation, she was thinking, salvation, while the dowager and Michele exclaimed:

' Again? To have a relapse? At this season? . . . We won't let you leave here!'

This is salvation, she was thinking. And when Michele asked her, ' It's true he can't leave, isn't it?'

' It's unwise . . .' she replied.

He raised his eyes to hers. They had not looked straight at each other for so long. Then she was afraid: those staring, flaming, terrible eyes, those eyes of a madman, were repeating to her, ' D'you want to send me insane then?'

And he stayed. But he became wild. She noticed his madness at once, for it was turned against her. He avoided her, never said a word to her. When the babies were handed to him he pushed them away, as if he were touching herself in touching the flesh of her flesh. A terrible misanthropy assailed him, he no longer left the house. One day, when made to go out, he never came home. Next day he returned. No one knew where he had been.

The same day she was called at dawn by the princess. Prince Giacomo was in his death agony; the poisoned blood was gradually spreading gangrene over the whole body. The morning before, to everybody's amazement, he had sent for Consalvo. He wanted to make a last effort to induce him to take a wife; fear of the Evil Eye ceded before the supreme necessity of ensuring a descendant. To his superstitious mind, weakened still more by illness, his son's marriage was now the only means of wresting that dreadful power from him. Married, established in a home of his own, master of a bank-account and of his wife's dowry, he would have no reason to wish his father short life.

Consalvo came at once, asked anxiously after his health, and sat at his bedside. The prince explained:

' I've called you to say something . . . It's time you took a wife.'

' Your Excellency must think of recovery,' exclaimed Consalvo. ' Then we'll talk about such matters.'

' No,' insisted the prince. ' You must take a wife now . . .' He did not add ' because I'm going to die '.

566

Consalvo controlled a movement of irritation.

'But what does Your Excellency fear? That our family will die out? Don't worry about that . . . I'll take a wife, I promise you that. But leave me a little time. Would you like me to give you a written assurance?' he added smiling. 'I'm ready . . . Will that please you?'

The sick man was silent a moment. Then he went on in a sharper tone:

'I want you to lose no time. It must be done now.'

'Now, at once, this minute?' . . . replied Consalvo in the same jesting tone.

'Now . . . or you'll regret it.'

Consalvo had great difficulty in hiding a movement of rebellion.

'But by God's goodness, why is Your Excellency in such a hurry? It isn't as if I were a girl getting older and running the risk of not finding a husband. I'm just twenty-nine; I can still wait, make a good choice. In Your Excellency's time boys of eighteen were given wives—now ideas are different. I don't say that by the old system they turned out bad husbands and fathers . . . but I suppose it's thought today, and I myself think, that one should have acquired a wide experience, be in the prime of life oneself before giving life to others. I may be mistaken, but if I took a wife now I can assure you I'd make my partner unhappy and be unhappy myself. I'd regret having listened to Your Excellency. I would like to please you, but that obedience to your wishes might bring consequences too grave to me and others.'

While his son was speaking, showing off his eloquence, the prince said not a word. When Consalvo left he seized the bell and rang furiously. The princess, the servants hurrying in, found him in a state that terrified them. Pale as if already dead, with taut cheeks and contracted jaw, the counterpane tight in his emaciated hands:

'The notary! The notary! The notary!' he was bellowing. At every word from his attendants asking him what was the matter, trying to calm him, he bayed like an angry dog:

'The notary! . . . The notary! . . . The notary! . . .'

In this state Teresa found him. He would not calm down until the notary came. Then he disinherited his son. Only under the impetus of fury, to take revenge, had he been able to force himself to dictate his last wishes. And cutting short with raucous cries the remarks of the old notary, who could not believe his own ears and was trying to recall him to reason and prevent this monstrous act, he dictated:

'I nominate universal heiress of all my patrimony, of all my patrimony, my daughter Teresa Uzeda, Duchess Radalì . . . with the obligation that she give her children my family surname and call them Uzeda-Radalì of Francalanza . . . So for all her descendants for ever . . .'

'Excellency . . .'

'Write! . . . I leave to my wife Graziella, Princess of Francalanza, my ancestral palace . . . with the express obligation, express, express, write, express, that she live in it alone during her natural life . . .'

'My lord Prince! . . .'

'Write! . . .' and he continued to dictate legacies to servants, to relatives for mourning expenses, to churches for Masses, to priests for charities; and not a single word, not a hint of that son. He ordered that his funeral be celebrated with the pomp proper to his name, that his body be embalmed. But gradually as he expressed these wishes his voice became hoarse and his vital energies left him; when he ended, the notary thought that the last moment had come. Then the sick man revived, took the sheet of paper, read it word by word and signed it. When the last formalities were done and the Will was sealed, that violent agitation of his suddenly ran down. He had spoken of his own death! He had dictated his last wishes! He had made arrangements for his funeral! He had cast the Evil Eye on himself! Nothing now remained for him but to die! No one got another word out of him. Motionless, grim, he shut his eyes, waiting.

The notary had already hurried off to the Duke of Oragua.

'The young prince is disinherited! Put out of his home! His daughter sole heiress! The palace to the stepmother! Was ever such a thing seen? Is the House of Francalanza at an end? . . . Do something! . . . Prevent the scandal! . . . Persuade that madman . . .'

The duke was very busy in those days; the Thirteenth Parliament had ended and electoral committees were to meet on the

26th May. Though he had decided to retire once he obtained nomination as senator, he was presenting himself for re-election again because the nomination did not come through. And what with the devotion of old friends, and the disillusioned indifference of those who pinned their faith on the promised electoral reform to get rid of him, his candidature was going no worse than at other times. Giulente, who had thought himself on the point of obtaining the post, went back to canvassing for the duke. In spite of his preoccupations, on hearing the notary's news the duke hurried off to the palace, but the prince had left orders that not a soul was to be allowed inside. Then he went to search out Consalvo. The latter was at the Town Hall, where he was presiding in the Council Chamber over a meeting of engineers for some new public works he had thought up, the building of big aqueducts destined to supply the town with water. On hearing that his uncle was calling for him, he asked those present to excuse him and went to receive him in his private office.

'Do you know what's happened?' exclaimed the duke in a low voice but with an air of grave disquiet. And he told all.

'Well?' replied Consalvo, twirling his moustaches.

'What d'you mean "well"? . . . Go and throw yourself at his feet! . . . Ask his pardon . . . Surrender just this once . . .'

'Me? . . . Why? . . .' And with an ambiguous smile he added, 'Can he take from me what is mine by law? No, he can't. He can do what he likes with the rest!'

His uncle stood there looking at him, in amazement, not understanding. Was it really true then? Was this Uzeda here different from all the others? When the others were quarrelling and scuffling with each other, riding roughshod over all scruples and laws so as to make money, did this one here remain indifferent, even smiling at hearing himself disinherited?

'But you don't realise what you're losing! . . . The palace left to his wife to prevent your having it! Don't you understand that? Aren't you sorry? . . .'

Consalvo let his uncle have his say. Then he answered:

'Has Your Excellency finished? May I say that my portion by law, that is a quarter of the patrimony, is enough for me, in fact too much? As for the palace . . .' He was silent for a moment as that did really rather bother him; the prince had known where to get his blow in. 'As for the palace, there's no lack of houses, and with money a finer one than ours can be set up. Now if Your Excellency will allow me; the deputation is waiting.'

The news spread throughout the city. And with one voice the prince was blamed by high and low. Antipathy, hatred for his son, there might be. But surely not to such a point? One's soul to God and one's property to whoever had the right to it! . . . Did he not remember that his mother the old princess had hated him too but even so had treated him as she did her favourite? . . . Such a thing was only possible in that cage of madmen. Mad the father and mad the son! But the young prince's partisans exclaimed: 'You see how disinterested he is? . . . Though being a man of character and not budging, he loses a fortune and doesn't care a rap!'

But if all, universally, blamed the prince, real consternation reigned amid servants, retainers, and hangers-on. The House of Francalanza at an end! The money to the girl! The palace to the wife! Had the end of the world come? . . .

One person only found difficulty in hiding her joy: the dowager Duchess Radalì. The fortune now concentrating in her elder son's hands would be huge! The young duke would have an immense income! If Giovannino did not marry—and she was there to see he didn't—the duke's riches would be enough to make one's head reel! . . . She almost felt her own reeling and could not understand how Michele remained indifferent to that announcement, how he could say:

'Mother, I'm not thinking of that. I'm thinking of Giovannino . . . Can't you see? He's grim, taciturn, there are days when he terrifies me . . .'

She saw nothing, sure that Michele was exaggerating. Her joy could be read in her eyes, showed at her every act, in her every word. Teresa looked at her and did not understand. Alone among them all she knew nothing of her father's Will. She did not hear the mutters of her relations, did not understand people's allusions. A flame was burning in her breast, an enclosed flame which was gradually consuming her. Why had she not let him leave? Why had she not warded off the temptation? And his eyes were always saying, 'So you want to send me mad? . . .'

She was incapable of hearing or understanding anything, under the weight of the tragedy she felt growing all around her. There were moments when she prayed for her father's death agony to last, for only that agony, that terror of death detached her from her corroding thought. What would happen after her father's death? Then, seeing the prince's atrocious torture, she blamed herself for her inhuman wish.

The prince was dying piece by piece, amid curses and prayers, raging and tears. At one moment he was afraid of being alone, at another the sight of healthy people made him furious. Having named his daughter his heiress, he thrust her away from him too, for as she was to inherit she must be hurrying on his death by her thoughts. No one talked to him either of the Will or anything else. He himself insisted on starting any subject of conversation. Most often his door was shut; no one could penetrate to him.

And one night a servant hurried off to the Radalì palace: the prince was dying. The news was told to the baron Giovannino for him to pass on to his brother, who was asleep with his wife.

'What am I to do? . . . What am I to do? . . .' he stuttered, in prey to extraordinary confusion.

Finally he went to call his mother. The old dowager hurried into the marriage chamber. At her sudden appearance Teresa, who had been lying awake a long while, felt a great chill creep over her body. 'My father? . . .' and with a cry she fell senseless on the bed. The old duchess shook Michele to wake him from his heavy sleep, and ran to find a cordial. The lady's maid and nurse also rushed in.

In the room next door the baron seemed stunned. His brother was calling him, the servants were saying to him as they hurriedly passed to and fro, 'The poor young duchess! . . . Come in too, Your Excellency . . .' But he was staring at the threshold of the marriage chamber with fixed dilated eyes, as if seeing some horror there.

'Giovannino!' suddenly called Michele.

He entered. She was lying on the bed with bare arms and naked breast, her golden hair spread over the pillow, her lips open and eyes turned up. 'Help me to raise her . . .'

571

She was rigid as a corpse. He raised her by the armpits. As if his hands were burning he began rubbing them together. He was trembling. They were all trembling, for the night was icy cold.

'She's coming to her senses,' announced the dowager.

Then he moved away, and went into the window-embrasure in the next room. Half an hour later they all three came out, Teresa supported by her mother-in-law and her husband. Michele said to his brother:

'You go to bed . . . It's cold . . . I'll be back as soon as possible.'

At the prince's were gathered all the relations. Consalvo was in the Yellow Drawing-room with his uncles and aunts; at the dying man's bedside were only the princess and his uncle the duke. Teresa went and knelt beside her stepmother.

'The sooner it's over the better' they were saying in the Yellow Drawing-room. 'He's suffering so . . .'

Consalvo said nothing. He was thinking with terror of this fearful disease which could one day gnaw away and destroy his own body at that moment so full of life. The impoverished blood of the ancient race was making, after Ferdinando, another premature victim, for his father was scarcely fifty-five years old. Would he too die before his time, before achieving his truimph, killed by those terrible ills which struck down the Uzeda while they were still young? His father would have given all his riches to live a year, a month, a day longer. What would he not give himself for the vivid healthy blood of a peasant to flow in his own veins? . . . 'Nothing!'

It was the corrupt blood of his old race that made him what he was: Consalvo Uzeda, today Prince of Mirabella, tomorrow Prince of Francalanza. It was to that historic name, to those sonorous titles that he felt he owed his place in the world, the ease with which avenues opened before him. 'All must be paid for!' thought he. But rather than give a thing for the long strong life of an obscure plebeian he would have given all, at the cost of any ill, for a single day of supreme glory . . . 'Even at the cost of reason?' The only danger really terrifying him was that other obscure one weighing on all of his race. But then on considering the lucidity of his own spirit, the rightness of his judgment, the acuteness of his views, he felt reassured; those poor in spirit, those monomaniacs called Ferdinando and Eugenio Uzeda may have lost their reasons; he was not threatened . . . And at that moment, under the influence of those thoughts, of those fears, he almost came to judge himself severely for the long quarrel with his father. Were the stubbornnness and obduracy which he had shown not disturbing symptoms, signs that one day he might lose his way like those others? Though resisting his father's impositions, and even judging him according to his deserts, could he not have kept a certain restraint, respected forms, saved appearances? Why this present scandal? Might he not even have done his father wrong? . . . And now he felt almost disposed to change his attitude and ask the dying man's pardon.

In the sick-room they were reciting the prayers for the dying; the prince had reached his death rattle. In the sight of death fear again froze Consalvo's heart. He felt pity for his father, for all his family. Wild, hard, bullying maniacs; were they responsible for their own awful qualities? 'All must be paid for!' and they were paying for their great name, their ostentatious style of living, their much-envied wealth. But that blank face of his father, that blind gaze, that ghastly rattle . . . The young man bent his knees, sensed things which he had denied. He who had made a jest of his sister's religion, accusing her of bigotry, realised now what a refuge for her were prayer and faith. Kneeling with joined hands, immobile as a figure on a tomb, she saw nothing, heard nothing. Consalvo almost envied the unfailing comfort to which she could have recourse in her sorrow.

Suddenly the priest watching over the dying man raised his arms. A sound of sobs came from the princess, of groans from the serving women, of sighs from the marchesa and Lucrezia.

Teresa did not weep; nor did the Duchess Radalì or Donna Ferdinanda in truth. All filed before the body, kissing the hands. Then the women were led away, except for daughter and wife. In the Red Drawing-room the old duchess kept repeating that perhaps it was best the poor man had died: his was no life recently. The Duke of Oragua with the major-domo and Benedetto Giulente were making the necessary arrangements, while the servants put up all the shutters, closed all the gates. Michele came up to Consalvo, shook his hand and murmured, 'Courage! . . .' The other was about to reply when he heard a voice say:

'Excellency . . .'

It was the porter making a sign that he must speak to him.

'Excuse me,' he said to his cousin, and went up to the servant thinking some order was wanted.

'Excellency . . . come here . . .' whispered the other, drawing him into the next room with an air of mystery which Consalvo, in spite of the sad moment, considered faintly absurd. 'Excellency!' he suddenly exclaimed, when they were alone, in a voice of horror which caused the young man a quiver of apprehension, 'Excellency . . . A tragedy! . . . Your cousin the baron . . . the young duchess's brother-in-law . . .'

'Giovannino?' he exclaimed, not understanding.

'He's killed himself, he's dead! . . . Just now—yes, just now, the duchess's man came . . . I've left him down below . . . Dead from a pistol shot. To warn Your Excellency first . . . Someone should be sent . . .'

A gasp of panic and horror escaped from Consalvo. 'The madman's son', madness, violent death! . . . Then all of a sudden he shook himself and gripped the servant's arm.

'Not a word to anyone, d'you understand? I'll go myself. Wait for my return. Don't say I've left . . .'

He felt a need for action. And that urge, the clarity of his perception, the speed of his decision, gave him a real sense of relief, of confidence, as if he had come out of an unpleasant dream and just that second realised himself to be awake and safe . . . Yes; in his cousin's madness and suicide Teresa was somehow involved; he did not know how far, but he was sure it was not just heredity, not just illness that had overwhelmed Giovannino's brain. So the suicide must be hidden from Teresa, the family, from the people. And as soon as he reached the Radalì palace, as soon as he entered the room where the corpse lay on the floor beside a sofa beneath a trophy of weapons, he exclaimed to the consternated servants:

'Oh these accursed weapons! He thought the revolver wasn't loaded . . . Poor Giovannino! What a tragedy! . . .'

574

No-one dared reply. Before representatives of the law arrived he took away the weapon gripped in the dead man's fist, extracted the five remaining cartridges, and put it back into the corpse's hand. And to the magistrate, who had heard of Prince Giacomo's death and was saying in sorrowful tones:

'Your Lordship the Prince! . . . What tragedies! . . . Two at once! . . . It seems incredible.'

'It does indeed . . .' he agreed in a clear and completely steady voice.

That 'Your Lordship the Prince', which the magistrate was the first to call him, was a reminder of a new era opening for him. The firmness he had shown, the promptness with which he had seen what must be done reassured him. He had no fear of falling into the Uzeda madness: all he had inherited from his family were its riches and its power. And this deception of justice by him was another reason for self-congratulation. He said to the police magistrate:

'My poor cousin was alone in the house. He had a passion for firearms . . . And thought this revolver was unloaded. Instead of which, look, there was just one forgotten cartridge . . .'

8

FOR a month the two duchesses lay between life and death.
The mother's sorrow was terrible, for in the ghastly tragedy she
saw the hand of God. That death had been permitted in order
that she should realise her own error and measure the sin she
had committed by not loving, not caring for, that poor boy.
She had almost calculated on his death, for the other brother to
enjoy the fruits! She had not even heeded the first threat, when
the poor wretch had been on the brink of the abyss! So before
the bleeding body she collapsed as if a hand had felled her. On
recovering her senses she wept on and on, and at the sight of
her other son's mute, inconsolable sorrow, she was almost
suffocated by sobs.

As for Teresa, all were amazed at the extraordinary strength
she showed in the first moments. The two disasters which threw
two families into mourning hit her more than anyone, as she was
part of both. And yet in the first hours, when the others lost
their heads, she showed incredible fortitude. That she should
seem untouched by the baron's death was thought almost
natural, as she had just closed her father's eyes and so was
under an even greater sorrow. Consalvo alone could not understand how the new disaster, which affected the others by its
tragic coincidence with the first and even more by its unpre-
dictable suddenness, had neither shaken his sister nor caused her
to show any sign of surprise, as if she had foreseen it. Torn
herself from the prince's deathbed, she alone was able to tear her
husband and mother-in-law from Giovannino's corpse, she alone
induced them to leave their house and move with the children
to the Francalanza palace. She was up all night with never a

576

tear, drying the tears of others, moving from stepmother to mother-in-law, children to husband. Only with the new day, when the sound of the deathbell rang from San Martino de' Bianchi, did she put her hand to her heart and fall to the floor.

Pity for her was immense. 'Only God could give her such strength,' said priests, 'another would have been burnt out on the spot.' And womenfolk, servants, the humble exclaimed, 'To think that she saw the dead bodies of her father and her brother-in-law all within two hours! . . . It's a wonder she didn't go mad!' Donna Ferdinanda, Lucrezia, and Chiara with perfect calm took turns at the bedside of the three sick ladies, for the princess too had to take to her bed. Consalvo was often with his sister, keeping Michele company. At night, he had the register open to the public at the porter's lodge brought upstairs, counted the hundreds of signatures arranged in columns, and looked at the hundreds of visiting-cards heaped on two large salvers. He read the obituary notices all ending with 'our deepest condolences to the inconsolable son', the motions of sympathy passed by the Town Council, the Chamber of Commerce, political groups. Those were all a documentation and measure of his popularity and credit, for big and small, known and unknown, the whole population of the town passed through the palace gates.

After the funeral, celebrated with extraordinary pomp, he began to receive visitors. From two till six in the afternoon, from eight till eleven at night, the drawing-rooms were crowded. Assessors, Town Councillors, municipal officials, the Prefect, the General, the Questor, relatives, friends, acquaintances, admirers and partisans of every kind, representatives of all parties and of all dependants filed continually by. All talked ceaselessly with an air proper to the circumstances about the incredible double tragedy. He would discourse a little on his father's illness and his cousin's 'accident', then to save people embarrassment change the subject, ask the Assessors and the Prefect for news of affairs, comment with others on the results of the general elections and on his uncle the duke's renewed success. A fortnight after the two deaths he was back in the Town Hall; now he could not live away from it, feared things might get into a mess without him, being in the hands of Giulente, who, as senior Assessor, had taken over control.

Engulfed anew in the sea of public affairs, when he returned to the palace, when he dined, when he went to bed, he thought of nothing else. Anyway there was no one to disturb him. The sick women were slowly recovering, tended by the widowed princess, by Lucrezia (delighted at the chance of acting as mistress of the house once again), by the other relations, and by the usual monsignori. The dowager was the first up; she was little over fifty and looked like a decrepit crone. It was Teresa who worried the doctors most; her illness clung on stubbornly, as if fed by some mysterious poison sapping all her strength. Gradually she too grew better, but on the first day she tried to rise she fell back, senseless. Then she came to again. One morning when Consalvo, before going out, visited his sister to ask if she needed anything, he found her with her stepmother, her mother-in-law and Michele. As soon as he entered they all turned towards him, silent and grave. Teresa, her head raised on a heap of pillows whose whiteness made her emaciated face look waxen, said in a slow faint voice, as if tired:

'Listen, Consalvo; sit down a moment . . . We have to talk to you.'

He sat down and waited.

'Listen; we have been discussing a matter that concerns you. Our father . . . our father, as you know, in a moment of anger . . . tried . . . tried to put me before you . . . I do not believe that could have been his real wish. Had God not taken him, he would certainly have changed it. I have told Michele and our mother that in all conscience I cannot accept . . . what was given me in such conditions . . .' she was silent a moment then added, 'You say it : . . I can't.'

A moment of silence. The old duchess's eyes were full of tears, and she shook her head bitterly. Consalvo said:

'Why talk of these things now?'

His sister's words, this renunciation of her inheritance, left him quite indifferent. He had now become used to the idea of getting nothing from his father but his legal portion. But he was rather surprised for a time at Teresa's magnanimous disinterest, approved by his brother-in-law and aunt.

'One day or another,' said Michele, 'we must talk it over. My mother and I are in full agreement with Teresa. We do not wish to profit by that Will to take from you what is yours. We are rich enough . . . too rich . . . and will give . . .'

He turned his head to hide eyes red with tears. His mother was sobbing.

'But why now?' replied Consalvo. 'There would have been time. Aunt, do calm yourself! All right, all right; I thank you . . . You know that I don't have certain prejudices . . . I mean that for me all children, male and female, eldest sons or . . .' then noticing the old woman's humble almost supplicating attitude, he did not finish the phrase. Instead he said, ' Anyway, if Teresa renounces the Will, we'll divide everything equally. Will that be all right?'

'Yes, as you like . . .'

Teresa, who had remained motionless with eyes shut, now seemed to wake up.

'Another thing,' she went on, 'our late father in the same moment of crisis . . . decided to leave our mother this house . . . It is not right that you . . . the heir of the name . . . the only one of our name, should have to move . . .'

He felt an indefinable emotion; it was pleasure at triumphing over his father's wishes, pride at being able to stay in the home of his ancestors, fear of owing something to his stepmother in exchange. But Teresa was continuing:

'Our mother renounces the house . . . she'll take another property instead . . . or compensation in money . . .'

'For myself,' exclaimed princess Graziella, 'it's all the same! I want all to be done by agreement, so that the family is always united . . .'

'But,' went on Teresa, 'she should not have to leave her husband's home herself . . . You will grant her an apartment for as long as she lives . . . Its ownership will be yours.'

She was silent a second time. She might have been on the point of death, with a soul already detached from the world, dictating last dispositions to ensure the peace, well-being, and happiness of those remaining behind.

Donna Graziella, under the influence of the generosity and disinterest shown by all, in order not to do less than others, in case it were said that she alone was putting obstacles to the general accord, had agreed to the exchange, but nothing would have induced her to move out of the palace.

'That's only right . . . Fine . . .' said Consalvo. 'Thank you. We'll settle it all.'

From that day Teresa got rapidly better. On every side rose a chorus of praise for what she had done, for the noble renunciation in which she had taken the initiative and that she induced all the others to accept. The Bishop in person came to visit her as soon as she was in a fit state to receive him. While she kissed his ring with tears in her eyes he said to her, 'My daughter, I have heard. May you be blessed now and for ever for the good you do.' She shook her head, murmuring, 'It's so little . . .' Then in her mother-in-law's and husband's name as well as her own she begged him to distribute ten thousand lire in alms. Already other prelates had been given stipends for Masses to be said for the repose of the prince's and the baron's souls.

The Radalì family had arranged to leave the Francalanza palace and move to Tardarìa as soon as Teresa was in a fit state to travel. Since that ghastly day only Michele had set foot in the house marked by his brother's blood, but in connection with preparations for departure one or other of the women would have to go there. As this would have been a harsher trial for the mother, Teresa went with her husband. She climbed the stairs leaning on his arm, but on entering the antechamber she was forced to sit down and sniff her smelling-salts. When she recovered strength she did what had to be done with her old firmness. The dead man's rooms were all locked up.

Next day they left for the country and stayed there the whole summer and autumn.

Meanwhile Consalvo established himself in his ancestral home. He left to the princess the apartments looking south and reserved for himself the main reception-rooms, but only for seeing guests, as his own living-rooms he fixed on the second floor. With his stepmother he had very little in common. They ate separately because they had different meal-times. Each had separate servants and carriages. They would meet from time to time about matters of administration. Consalvo knew nothing of the state of the house while the princess was well informed, and so if the administrator wanted orders or explanations he left word for his stepmother. Not only did he feel more drawn by public affairs than by his own, but he considered that the latter were not worth bothering about as long as the family property remained undivided.

This division began on the Radalìs' return. The two women had entirely recovered their health. The mother-in-law seemed even older, and the daughter-in-law was pregnant. All articles of the contract were settled by mutual consent, with the same disinterest of which everyone had given proof at the start. Teresa wished all the historic estates to remain with her brother, contenting herself with recently acquired property and odd bits of income, capital and credits. In exchange, Consalvo asked for this wholly moral difference to be taken into account in the valuation of the lands. The princess renounced the palace in exchange for the estate of Gibilfemi and the farm of Oleastro, which were worth twice as much.

During these negotiations, Consalvo had been to see his sister nearly every day. Having got into this habit he continued it. After all he ought to show gratitude for her renunciation, which had doubled his part of the inheritance from a quarter to a half. But in spite of this duty of his, in spite of the sorrow of mourning, he found it difficult to avoid needling his sister for her fervent, growing piety.

Now the Vicar-General, her confessor, Sisters of Charity, seemed to have taken up residence in her home. With these the new churches of Our Lady of La Salette and Mercè, the miracles of Lourdes and of Valle di Pompei, and missionary work were the usual topics of conversation. The disbanded Capuchin friars had reunited in spite of the law and bought a house with the offerings of the faithful.

Consalvo learnt that his sister had contributed to this purchase. Had she not formerly considered the law dispersing the same community to be quite a proper one? How could she go every Friday to pray in the Blessed Ximena's chapel, where burnt the lamp lit for the health of Giovannino, of whose madness and suicide she had been partly the cause? Did she know that the young man had killed himself and not died by accident? . . . This stubborn faith of hers, so resistant to disillusion, was it sincere or was it maybe a form of the family's hereditary mania? Consalvo inclined to this last hypothesis, partly because he had no faith at all himself. But never an act or a word revealed what was in his sister's heart. When he began making ironic allusions she said:

'Listen, Consalvo; each of us is responsible to God for our own actions. Your scepticism may make me suffer, but I don't reprove you for it. So I should like you to respect my beliefs, or if you like to call them so, my superstitions. Am I asking too much?'

He bowed his head, first because the argument was valid, but also because Teresa's connections in the clerical world could be useful.

In fact the time so long awaited was rapidly nearing. Electoral reform was the order of the day; after voting on it the Chamber would dissolve. And he now realised that his own election was not as certain as it had seemed that first day in Rome during his conversation with the Honourable Deputy Mazzarini, and later at the start of his term as Mayor. Because of the broadening of the franchise and the scrutinising of the lists, it was no longer his uncle's few hundred votes which could send him to the Chamber; now it needed thousands. And though he felt sure of the city, he did not know how much he could rely on the rural wards.

Already the old duke had sniffed the wind and told his intimates that he would accept a seat in the Senate. Sure of being swept away like a dry leaf he was finally retiring in good order, pretending to renounce spontaneously so as to avoid the shame of a defeat. And while Consalvo was thinking of his own situation, worried by this change and by the 'moral revolution' invoked by himself but come rather too soon, Giulente saw nothing, noticed nothing. He still hung round the old duke's feet as if the latter were the oracle of twenty years before, waiting to gather his inheritance, still swearing by the Right and by Cavour, sure that the new electors would throw out the Government of Reparation and restore the principle of moderation. And, thinking over such matters day and night, he left control of his household more and more to his wife, who had got into such a muddle that she too was now waiting for his election—without saying a thing to him, in fact still deriding him about it—to avoid giving him the accounts, until he made money like her uncle Gaspare . . .

Consalvo did not bother about him; he despised him to such an extent that at times he almost pitied him. Realising the need of getting to work soon, he put forward the actuation of a resolve already in his mind for some time: to resign from his office as Mayor. He needed to be free, and he wanted to avoid the danger of a prolongation in office losing him the advantage obtained and changing it into irreparable harm. The whole edifice was beginning to creak, in fact. His wild expenditure had exhausted the exchequer, and the last budget had closed with a considerable deficit which he had only been able to hide by a series of artifices. But the situation was no longer tenable. Either taxes had to be imposed or debts contracted, and he did not want to have to face the unpopularity of such provisions. So he seized the first excuse to beat a retreat.

One day the Council accountants were discussing again how to get dues paid, as the contract system had not produced good results. In private conversation, he declared that he considered a return to direct payment a mistake and that it was a matter of correcting the current system's defects and of not abandoning the system itself. He did not breathe a word of this at meetings and let the majority give their opinion. The majority voted to change the system. That same night on going home he wrote two letters, one to the Prefect resigning his office, the other collectively to all the Assessors announcing that 'for reasons of delicacy' he had already sent in his resignation to the Prefect.

It was a thunderbolt from a clear sky. 'Delicacy? . . .' exclaimed Giulente, whom all the others asked for an explanation. 'What delicacy? I don't understand! . . .' And the Town Council in a body went to call on him, while the news rapidly spread throughout the civic offices.

'Can you explain?' said Benedetto to him on behalf of his colleagues. 'What does this letter mean?'

'It means,' replied the prince, looking in the air, 'that I did not wish to exercise pressure, and as your way of seeing things is contrary to mine I am resigning in order to leave your hands free.'

'But about what? . . . The dues? . . .'

'About the dues and other things . . .'

Knowing that these people were come to induce him to withdraw his resignation he cut short any chance of their insistence. He said that for some time, in a number of matters, in hundreds of little daily affairs, he had observed that there were no longer the same good relations between them all as before. Now he could neither renounce his own ideas nor impose them on others; so the best thing was to go.

'You might have said so before! And not leave us in the lurch! What a way of doing it! . . .'

In a confused way they realised the trick played on them, the mess in which he was leaving them. Giulente alone insisted:

'Well, we can set things to rights, we'll go back on our decisions; the Council itself has not yet examined them. We'll do as you wish . . .'

'It's useless for you to insist,' declared Consalvo. 'My decision is irrevocable. And please realise that I'm not made of iron. I have worked for a number of years on behalf of my city; now I need a rest. Anyway, it's time I gave a little thought to my family affairs, now that I have them to look after . . . Thank you for your concern,' he added to the fuming Assessors, 'but believe me, I can't. No-one is necessary. You have as much experience as I; I leave the administration in good hands . . .'

Benedetto went to ask the Prefect to intervene; wasted breath. The Town Council met in Giulente's house to deliberate. Some of them, wanting to avoid embarrassments, maintained that the Mayor's resignation should be followed by that of all the Assessors; but would that not seem like desertion? Would that not show up their incompetency and give credit to those who called them puppets moved by the Mayor as he liked?

'It's a betrayal!' cried the most outspoken. 'A black betrayal! We've let this rascal trick us!'

'Calm, please! . . . Why a betrayal? . . . What interest would he have? . . .' said Giulente.

'What interest?' they bawled at him. 'Don't you realise? . . . Don't you realise he wants to be a Deputy, and that he's dropping us now he sees the whole edifice is in danger, after he's made full use of the situation? Now that he has other interests with elections imminent?'

Giulente went pale, looked round with an air of bewilderment, as the truth dawned on him. Just recently he had actually realised that his nephew also had ambitions to become a Deputy, but he was sure that Consalvo was not presenting himself at once and would step aside at least the first time. In any case how could he ever have suspected such a trick, to be left with a mess of taxes, debts and hatred on his hands? He ceased to protest against his colleagues' recriminations and ejaculations against the ex-Mayor. 'Deceit . . . Betrayal . . . Cheating! . . . Deserves a knife in the ribs . . .' the words echoed in his thoughts. He realised they were justified, understood at last that this knave whom he had himself initiated into public life was snatching from him the post he had awaited so long, and giving kicks as thanks. What about the duke? The duke, who had so often promised to leave his political inheritance to him when he retired? . . . The duke, to whom he hurried, said:

'It's true I promised you my support, but in other times, when I could not foresee actual development . . . Now that Consalvo is presenting himself as candidate you can surely understand what an embarrassing situation I'm in . . .'

'So it's true? He's a traitor too, worse than his nephew, is he?' thought Benedetto. But out loud he said:

'Your Excellency must surely be aware that Consalvo is of the Left and belongs to the Progressives, while Your Excellency . . .'

'Still thinking of Right and Left, are you?' laughed the duke, who had in his pocket a formal promise of a seat at the Senate. 'Don't you see that the old parties are finished? There's a revolution, don't you know? Who can say what the voting booths will say now they've let in the mob? A real leap in the dark! If I presented myself for election,' now, at last, in self-justification he acknowledged the truth, 'I'd be left far behind.

D'you expect the electors to listen to what I say? The support I could give is purely idealistic . . . it could be a stone round the neck which would sink the candidate.'

Then Giulente hurried to Consalvo, in a state of violent exasperation. With the old man he had not dared drop his former respect, but he felt the need to let himself go, to tell this knave what he thought of him.

'You've done . . . you've done what you've done for your own ends, to leave me holding the bag, haven't you? . . . To ruin me? . . . To take my job? . . .'

Consalvo gave him an ambiguous smile and pretended not to understand. 'What's the matter? . . . Calm yourself! I don't understand . . .'

'Is it true you're putting up as candidate?'

'Perhaps, if there's any chance of my getting in . . .'

'And didn't you know . . . don't you know it's my seat? That I've been waiting for it all these years? That your uncle promised it to me?'

'Seat?' exclaimed Consalvo with the same air of simple amazement. 'What seat? With the revision of the electoral register there won't just be one seat, but three.'

'So you're laughing at me too? Jeering at me too? After taking my seat by treachery!'

The smile vanished from Consalvo's face.

'I must observe that you are over-heated and not thinking of what you are saying.'

'Aha, not thinking, aren't I?'

'This isn't a matter of seats in a theatre, where anyone sits who's paid for a ticket. I've taken nothing from you, for the very simple reason that you have no seat to take. If you think that you can get in there's nothing to prevent your putting up. If I happen to think I can, I'll put up too. We're not such close relatives as to make us incompatible. There is no pledge between us; each is free to do what he wishes.'

'And you're also free to leave us in the lurch, now that you see the abyss yawning in front . . .'

'There's no abyss. There are some difficulties to be overcome. That means you will have a chance of showing your abilities.'

The blood rushed to Benedetto's head.

'You're all the same, you lot!' he shouted suddenly. 'A bunch of arrant scoundrels!'

Consalvo looked him for a moment in the whites of the eyes. Suddenly he let out a laugh in his face, turned his back and vanished.

As Giulente left he did not answer servants' greetings, did not hear what the major-domo said to him. They thought he had gone mad, seeing him rush off, flushed in the face, with arms raised and fists clenched, talking to himself. 'Cheats, liars, traitors . . . The revolution! A leap in the dark! . . . They fall on their feet though . . . the uncle's arranged things for himself! . . . Now the nephew! . . . A leap in the dark . . . Pro-Bourbon to the bones! . . . He should have been strung up in 1860! . . . And I, like a fool, have served them both! . . . Those good wishes to Francis II! . . . Now he's on the Left! . . . A fool I've always been, a fool!'

Bitterly, torturingly, there suddenly awoke in him a realisation of how he had been used and kept under, of the contempt with which they had treated him. 'We're not such close relatives!' That little swine had spat that out in his face! . . . Relatives? Had they ever been relatives to him? All, yes all of them had looked at him from above, as an intruder, as unworthy of them! First they had despised him for his studies, the ignoramuses, for the 'ignoble' degree he had obtained. And they had been the only ones for whom he had exercised his profession at all in order to help their intrigues; the old woman, the prince, Raimondo . . . 'Who are they anyway? . . . A bad brew of Spanish adventurers enriched by robbery. I'd like to wipe my feet on them!' But actually what he had done was serve them, court them, flatter them. Had he not magnified their presumption, encouraged their madness, approved their rascalities? 'Fool! Fool! I've always been a fool!'

He reached home without knowing how he got there. He tore at the bell, entered like a man possessed. Lucrezia, who was lounging in an armchair with her hands in her lap, looked at him with some curiosity and then said:

'What's the matter?'

He stood there in front of her, with eyes starting from his head.

'What's the matter? . . . What's the matter? . . . The matter is that you're all a bunch of filthy traitors . . .'

'Who?'

'Who? Your uncle, your nephew, your relations, that evil race. Cursed be the hour and the day . . .'

She was still looking at him as if he were a strange ridiculous object. More amazed than angry, she interrupted:

'What the devil are you saying?'

'What am I saying? What I've got to say. Are you defending them? Or taking their part?'

'What an imbecile you are!' she exclaimed, rising to her feet. Then Benedetto lost his temper. He seized her by an arm and yelled:

'It's true, isn't it? . . . You're right to say so! . . . I am an imbecile! . . .' and he gave her a terrific slap which caught her full on the cheek and rang like a bullet shot. Then suddenly he left her to go and lock himself into his room.

The servants, having seen their master enter in that unusual state, had been listening; none of them dared let out a breath. When the scene was over the maid peeped every now and again through the door which was still open, to see what her mistress was doing. Lucrezia was standing motionless by the window, her cheek flaming red and swollen. She was still in the same position an hour later. Then suddenly she began walking up and down, looking in the air as if to catch flies, at the ground as if to search for some lost object, stopping suddenly in the middle of the room as if taken suddenly by an idea, then starting to pace again as if following someone. When servants came asking for orders she gave brief though not angry answers. Her cheek had become less swollen and was gradually whitening. From time to time she touched it with her hand.

'Excellency,' they came to ask her, 'shall we serve dinner?'

'Wait,' she replied, and went and knocked at her husband's door.

Benedetto had flung himself on the bed, with clothes unbuttoned and head still aflame. Seeing his wife enter, he said nothing. Lucrezia went up to him.

'How d'you feel?' she asked him.

'All right,' replied Giulente, without looking at her.

'D'you want to dine?'

'As you like.'

'Or d'you think it's early?'

'As you think.'

'Then shall I tell them?'

He nodded indifferently. Lucrezia gave orders for the meal to be served. Then she went back to her husband's room.

'Why are you staying in bed? Is anything the matter?'

'No, nothing.'

He got up, but only to fling himself into an armchair. He had regretted his brutality, but could not express his sorrow. And he was continually ruminating his rancour, considering possibilities open to him, uncertain which to try.

'What did you decide in the Town Hall?' asked Lucrezia again.

'I know nothing . . .' he burst out. 'I never want to hear another word. They can all go to the devil! If a single one of your family comes here I'll throw him headlong down the stairs.'

'You're right,' replied his wife.

The day before, from behind the door, she had realised from the Assessors' discussion the trick played on her husband by Consalvo, and she had realised that Benedetto could not be a Deputy. At once there had sprung up in her again the old aversion for her nephew, for these Uzeda who seemed sworn to thrust her aside and take everything for themselves. But she did not know yet quite whom to blame. Was it really Consalvo's fault and not that ass Benedetto's? Was what the Assessors said true? Would the duke not set things to rights? . . . She had not been convinced by her husband's distraught air on coming home or by his violent words against Consalvo and the duke; he could have talked for a whole day without convincing her. What had converted her was the slap. As if her torpid brain needed a material shock to function properly she had at once said to herself, 'He's right!' During the two hours she had spent in the other room, looking at the street without seeing it, walking up and down like a caged animal, she had repeated mentally, 'He's right! . . . It's Consalvo . . . It's uncle . . . They want to crush me! . . . What do they think they are? . . . Masters of every-thing?' And now at Benedetto's last outburst she repeated,

'You're right! You're right!' During dinner they were both silent. Giulente scarcely tasted the food and left his knives and forks on his plate. 'Are you feeling ill? . . . Would you care for something else? . . . Would you like to go to bed? . . .' She was prodigal with every kind of attention, stopped eating when her husband ate no more. Suddenly Benedetto got up. He felt really ill, his head was going round, and he went to bed. She helped him undress, shook up his pillows, prepared his coffee.

'Would you like to be alone? Would you like to rest?'

'Yes.'

She went away. But scarcely had she shut the door when she re-opened it.

'Don't torture yourself,' she came back and told her husband. 'There'll be more than one Deputy. You put up as well. We'll see who's stronger, him or us!'

9

THE situation in the constituency was this. Now that the business and conservative stronghold that had supported the Duke of Oragua for twenty years was dismantled, the Constitutional Association dispersed, and even the Progressive group in dissolution, the flourishing and belligerent workers' societies at last found, in the vote, a weapon with which to enter the lists. While among the middle classes the former moderates, admirers of Lanza and Sella, were forced to hide, new phalanxes of electors spoke freely of more liberty and radical reforms, of republic and of socialism. But such words, terrifying timid progressives and pushing them into the conservative ranks, gave new life to the all but expiring moderates. Thus the most advantageous position was between Progressives and Radicals. This Consalvo of Francalanza took up at once. His adherence to the party of the Left, his break with his uncle after the 'Parliamentary revolution' of 1876, legitimised, as it were, the ultra-Liberal programme which he announced.

Immediately on relinquishing the Town Hall he set to work outside the city, in the rural wards. Out there peasants and villagers were awakening to politics. There were workers' societies, agricultural clubs, ordered and disciplined democratic groups, with which he must come to terms. Nobles, middle-class and the well-to-do were won over at once. Accompanied by friends or admirers who came forward spontaneously, he began touring the constituency. The local mayor, the chief landowner or the most influential person in each place would give a dinner or reception in his honour and invite other leading characters. Elections were not mentioned, but the prince was affable to all,

591

informed himself about local needs, listened to everyone's complaints, took notes in a notebook and left people enraptured by his polite ways, dazed by his eloquence and pleased as if he had actually written a decree for the construction of a railway, the repairing of a road, or the transfer of a local police chief.

But after a banquet or refreshments, after a visit to notables, Consalvo would go and visit local workers' groups. There, in squalidly furnished rooms, crowded by poor men with calloused hands, he went through torture. He shook those gloveless hands, mingled with those humble folk, sat among them, accepted the refreshments they offered him, and did not by the movement of a muscle reveal the agony of this propinquity. Briefed beforehand, he made long speeches about village needs, about the wine crisis, or fruit crops, or the tax-load, promised laws to protect agriculture, guaranteed tax reliefs, scattered promises of rewards and incentives of all kinds. His theory was of progress; 'neverending progress . . .'

When he saw portraits of Garibaldi, of Mazzini on the walls he would insist on the urgency of 'ampler liberties demanded by the spirit of the times'; when he saw those of the royal family, he recognised the need 'to move with leaden feet'. Nearly always he found someone to act as guide. But sometimes there was no one to introduce him to more intransigent circles, and then he would just appear, ask for the 'president', announce that he happened to be passing by and much wished to visit 'this group so worthy of the village'.

Almost everywhere he gained sympathies and votes. The very fact that Don Consalvo Uzeda, Prince of Francalanza, was paying them a visit, disposed these humble folk in his favour. His handshakes, homely speeches, resounding phrases and promises converted the most restive. Even though there were a number of recalcitrants, he achieved the effect of creating schism where before had been accord. A dozen societies elected him on the spot as their honorary president. And he thanked them for 'the great honour of which I would be unworthy were it not a pledge of my limitless devotion for the workers, whose improvement, welfare, and happiness have been and will aways be the aim of my life'. After official speeches he added, 'When you need me, when you come to town, remember that my house is yours . . .'

And still he never mentioned the election. Having carried out this first part of his programme he went on to the second, an accord with other candidates. For three seats there were a dozen or so aspirants. Apart from those whose claims were absurd, such as Giulente, there were, apart from his own, four serious candidatures: Vazza, a lawyer with a very wide clientele who presented himself under a 'liberal' programme without indicating any parliamentary party; Professor Lisi, formerly president of the Progressive Party, and thus of left-wing tendencies; Giardona and Marcenò, Radicals. Consalvo got in touch with the first of these latter two, the milder one, with a view to common action. Did the other's watered-down Radicalism and his own advanced Liberalism differ so much that they could not come to an understanding? Even so, Giardona's supporters wanted explicit promises. He bound himself to vote for all the reforms, particularly social reforms, demanded by the other's Party. He went among them and said, 'I am a socialist. After a study of Proudhon I am convinced that all property is theft. Had my ancestors not robbed I would have had to earn my living by the sweat of my brow.'

Yet those declarations were not found completely satisfactory. Advanced radicals supporting Marcenò turned against him. A little news-sheet called *The Rasp* came out with an attack on him, called him 'The noble prince, *Sire* de Fancalanza' alluding to his pro-Bourbon relatives, and affirmed that an aristocrat like him, descendant of Viceroys, could not be sincere in such show of democratic faith. Then he had a news-sheet published called *The New Elector*. Every number, from beginning to end, was full of him, of his achievements as Mayor, of his claims on the town's gratitude. The daily papers also bore leading articles exalting 'The young patrician who is a democrat in deeds not in mere words.'

Having made his pact with Giardona, he now had to choose between Lisi and Vazza to form the triad. He wanted to go with the latter, who was the stronger, but Giardona threatened to spoil this, as Vazza, who proclaimed himself ambiguously 'liberal', was the most moderate of the lot and well thought of even by the Curia. An alliance with Lisi, who was nearer their

593

ideas, was the only natural one and he recognised this as suitable. Agreement was reached, but each set to work on his own account.

The electoral reform law was still before the Senate when already people were flocking to the prince's every night: noble relatives, civic employees, elementary schoolmasters, lawyers, brokers, contractors. It was like a subscription ball. The state apartments were opened to the public. He did not relegate his electors to the dark little administrative offices as his uncle had done; he flung open the grand Yellow and Red Drawing-rooms, the Hall of Mirrors, the Portrait Gallery. All were animated by the liveliest enthusiasm. Petty tradesmen, who came to the palace for the first time and sat on satin armchairs under the Viceroys' immobile gaze would have let themselves be cut to pieces for this candidate who promised them earth and heaven, general and particular good to each single voter. A land surveyor composed a pamphlet entitled, *Consalvo Uzeda Prince of Francalanza, Short Biographical Notes* and presented it to him. He had it printed in thousands of copies and distributed throughout the constituency. The absurdity of this publication, the crudeness of the praise filling it, did not bother him, sure as he was that for one elector who would laugh at it a hundred would believe in it all, like articles of faith. He felt an infinite contempt for that mob, and a violent rancour against whoever tried to bar his way.

As excitement grew, attacks by *The Rasp* news-sheet became sharper, and a quantity of broadsheets and manifestoes and electoral bulletins, supporting this or that candidate, or speculating on the curiosity that induced people to fling money away on bits of dirty paper, began attacking him morning and night, belabouring him with every kind of insult. He laughed at these before others. But inside he raged. Had he been able he would have put a gag on those libellists, banished, imprisoned them.

But the accusation that wounded him most and made him really bleed was one beginning, 'Electors, the candidate we present to you has no feudal estates or coats-of-arms, no gold with which to corrupt consciences; but you, citizens, can·show your conscience to be a treasure too big for a handful of money to buy '. It was untrue, for he had spent money only on printing, postage and transport. But this lie could gain more credence than the others; and he wanted to be elected because of his proved aptitude for public life, because of the culture he had tried so hard to acquire.

Then, remembering his determination to keep calm, to let people have their say, he shrugged his shoulders, dominated his gusts of anger when touched on the raw, and said to himself, ' What does it matter if they do elect me for my coats-of-arms and my estates? As long as they elect me!' And to his intimates, who grew angry on his behalf at seeing him thus attacked, he said with a smile, ' They're right! My chief title for election is that of prince!'

What he said in jest was in fact true. ' Prince of Francalanza ': those words were the passport, the talisman that worked the miracle of opening all doors. He knew that declarations of democracy could do him no harm with electors of his class, as the latter did not consider them sincere and felt sure of having him on their side at the proper time. On the other hand he felt that accusations of aristocracy did him no great harm with the majority of a people brought up for centuries to respect and admire nobles and even to take pride in their scale of living and their power. For him such people as let themselves be won over from the Viceroys had been perverted by false doctrine and silly flattery. He was sure that if he had a heart-to-heart talk with those crying out most for ' Liberty and Equality ' and said to them, ' Now, if you were in my place, would you shout that?', the proud republican would be in a fix. The point was, said some, that such eminent positions and privileged situations should not now exist. Then Consalvo would smile pityingly. As if, even admitting the possibility of abolishing all social inequalities by a stroke of the pen, they would not be created anew next day, men being naturally different and the clever being always, at all times, under whatever régime, sure to down the simple, the bold to override the timid, the strong to subdue the weak!

Even so he bowed down and conceded all, in words, to the spirit of the new times. The angry little news-sheets lunged at him tenaciously with accusations of ' Spanish ' arrogance, of

' ingrained ' pride. To the electors who called him ' Your Lordship the Prince ' all the time he said, ' I'm not called Lordship the Prince, I'm called Consalvo Uzeda . . .' He seemed now almost eager to denude himself of all that could offend feelings of human equality, no longer spoke of ' my travels ' or ' my estates ', seemed to be trying to excuse himself for his title and riches, to be almost ashamed of the great coat-of-arms over the arch of the palace gates, of the arms-rack in his vestibule, of the portraits of his ancestors, as marks and proofs of unworthiness. But this he did at suitable times and places, before sincere radicals and pure republicans. Most of the time he knew himself to be amid those who by calling him ' Prince ' and appearing in his company believed they were in some way partaking of his lustre.

He worked very hard paying visits, writing letters, directing his canvassers, presiding over committee meetings. At night he could scarcely get to sleep; his hand was burning so with the contact of dirty, sweating, rough, calloused, infected hands, his mind inflamed so with anxiety about the outcome. Would he succeed? At moments he had an intimate and definite certainty of it; the Government was for him; Mazzarini, who had reached power and was now Minister of Public Works, had sent from Rome copies of all his letters recommending him to the Prefect. But he was not content with mere success, he wanted outstanding success, to be first among those elected, to assure himself a stable constituency with a unanimous, plebiscite-like vote. The agreement with Giardona had certainly helped him, but that with Lisi may have been an error.

Vazza's situation on the other hand was very strong, and according to many he would come out top. He was gathering adherents everywhere, and the clergy in particular, without upholding his cause in public, were working for him secretly but very efficaciously. Consalvo had made a real mistake in renouncing this alliance and preferring Lisi. To compensate for this and take advantage of the sacristy influence he thought of having recourse to his sister.

It was some time since he had seen her, but he knew that her severe almost austere life, her total renunciation of worldly occupations and pleasures since her mourning, her edifying piety, had put her even more into the good graces of the Monsignori. So he went to visit her. When just about to enter her drawing-room he heard a high-pitched voice saying:

' I've said it to all, and I'll never tire of repeating it! May Samson fall with all the Philistines!'

It was his Aunt Lucrezia. He stopped to listen.

' Your Excellency must forgive me,' came Teresa's gentle tones, ' but to say such a thing against your own nephew . . .'

' My nephew? . . . No nephew of mine! . . .' cried the other. ' Then how could he allow himself to treat my husband so? But it'll be tit for tat, as they say. Benedetto won't get in, but neither will he. We'll see! But I must say I'm rather surprised at that pig the Bishop! . . .'

' Aunt!'

' That pig the Bishop refusing to support my husband. Instead of playing Vazza's game he should be supporting Benedetto, who's always been a moderate and so much closer to the clergy! And I'm even more surprised at you refusing to say a word on your uncle's behalf! . . . But I'll talk to him! I have a tongue in my head and can talk on my own! If all abandon Benedetto, I'm still here! I won't abandon him! I've only him in the world! . . . Do you know it's given him a bad liver? Those murderers, they'd like to kill him off! But he laughs best who laughs last!'

Containing his laughter, Consalvo entered. As soon as she saw him, Lucrezia got up.

' Well, goodbye, I've things to do,' she said to her niece. And without looking at him, as if she had not noticed him, but raising her voice and passing by him with a haughty stiff air, she repeated, ' He laughs best who laughs last!'

Consalvo burst into a roar of laughter.

' That mad-woman has it in for me! . . . What the devil did she expect? What wrong has she been done?'

' Poor thing, don't talk ill of her,' replied Teresa with pitying indulgence.

' Anyway it's lucky you don't agree with her! Does she want me to renounce my own future just for the sake of her husband? Now all of a sudden she's afire with love for the husband whom she did nothing but revile before . . .'

Teresa made no reply, but gave a gesture of deep compassion.

'And what did she want from you? Was she talking to you about the election?'

'Yes.'

'She wanted your vote, ha ha.'

'No, she thought I could help them.'

'And what did you reply?'

'That I can do nothing.'

'For me either?' added Consalvo quickly.

'For no-one, brother. I take no part in such things.'

'What about your Monsignori?' he exclaimed with a smile.

'Neither they nor I speak of such things.'

'What do you speak of then, tell me?'

At Consalvo's slightly mocking tone Teresa shut her eyes a moment, as if gathering strength to meet contradictions, as if praying for the unbeliever.

'We have been talking in these last few days of a great miracle permitted by the Lord. Have you heard no mention of the Servant of God?'

He knew something, vaguely, about an alleged miracle that had occurred to a peasant woman of Belpasso. But Teresa went on without awaiting his reply:

'She's a humble peasant girl who lives in a hut with her father and mother, out in the country at Belpasso. She's always been very religious, but signs of Grace have shown in her recently. Every Friday, after she's been on her knees three hours, there appear on her body Our Lord's stigmata; she exhales an odour of sweet incense and from her lips . . .'

'Is that what you call signs of Grace? They're hysterical phenomena!'

Teresa was silent a little, with the expression of indulgence one accords to poor ignorant sinners.

'If they were hysterical phenomena, doctors would be able to cure her. Instead of which none of those who've seen her have been able to explain these manifestations, and all the remedies they've tried have been useless.'

'Then they've merely called in stupid doctors.'

'No, the most reputable! . . . On her forehead appears a red mark in the form of a cross, and on her side one in the shape

598

of a lily . . .' In a low voice she added, ' His Lordship the Bishop is about to visit her.'

' Will he visit her side?'

She drew back with a look of contemptuous reproof.

' Consalvo! You know that you grieve me by talking like that . . .'

' Oh nonsense! Can't one make a joke? . . . But you seriously believe it, do you?'

' I believe it,' she replied shortly.

He considered her a little. What he wanted to say was, ' Who d'you think you're talking to? . . . Are you off your head like all the rest of our family?' But he had not come for that.

' So you never talk of the elections, you say?'

' No. I don't understand such things; and then the Church takes no part in these struggles.'

' Neither elected nor electors, eh? And yet your spiritual Fathers are making a great deal of fuss about a certain lawyer . . .'

' The Holy Father has ordered Catholics not to vote *as a party* . . .'

' Aha . . . Then you know there's a distinction between an organised party and single citizens?'

' It's not difficult to understand that.'

' All right, all right! And as single citizens, what are Catholics doing?'

' They sometimes support whoever is closest to them.'

' That being?'

' Whoever believes.'

The two words meant, ' You're not among them and that's why I can do nothing for you.' But Consalvo pretended to be ingenuous and replied:

' Whoever believes in what?'

' In the eternal principles of truth, first of all!'

' And then?'

' In the Church's triumph.'

' Do you too? . . .' began Consalvo, on the point of protesting, of saying what he thought to this silly woman. But he held himself in once more. What did such nonsense matter? The impor-

tant thing was to know if he had any chance at all of her intercession. 'Oh, fine! . . .' he went on in a different tone. 'The
Church's triumph . . . Over whom is it to triumph, may I ask?'

'Over its enemies and persecutors.'

'And who are they? Where are they? In Italy? In France?
Go on, tell us. What must we do? Restore Rome to the Pope,
eh? Give him all Italy, all the world? Let's hear, let's have an
explanation once and for all, so I know where I am and see how
far we can agree . . .'

She said, seriously:

'It's useless for you to take that tone. Sooner or later right
will triumph.'

'How? When? Where?'

She raised her head and half shut her eyes, as if inspired.

'There will be born,' she said, 'a great monarch, in direct
descent from St Louis of France, who will be called Charles. He
will make seven kingdoms in Europe, and put the Holy Father
back on the Chair of Peter . . .'

This time Consalvo could not restrain his laughter .

'Ha ha ha . . . So he's to be called Charles, is he? Why not
Philip, or Ignatius, or Epaminondas? Where the devil d'you get
such nonsense from?'

'If it's nonsense why bother about it? I'm sorry you laugh at
such things . . . I've told you many times that we each have our
own convictions . . .'

'Yes, yes . . . But where d'you get this one from? Where have
you heard that all these nice things are going to happen?'

She stretched out an arm towards a shelf full of books and
took down a small volume bound in black leather with gilt edges.
Consalvo read on the frontispiece, 'Liberated Europe, or The
Triumph of the Church of J.C. over all Usurpers and Heretics.
Echo of the Prophets and the Fathers . . .' Suddenly she turned
her head, hearing a lackey announce from the threshold as he
drew back the door curtains:

'Father Gentile, Excellency.'

In came a tall, thin, priest, with strong glasses on a beaked
nose.

'My brother, the Prince of Francalanza,' Teresa introduced,
'Father Antonio Gentile . . .'

The priest gave a deep bow. Consalvo looked him over from top to toe. Another one! This house was becoming a positive sacristy!

'Father,' added Teresa, turning to her brother, 'is good enough to direct my children's education . . .'

'I am very happy,' replied the ecclesiastic, 'to be able to serve the duchess.'

'You're not a Sicilian, are you?' asked Consalvo, to say something, so as not to seem to be leaving at once, but impatient to get away since realising he had already wasted too much time.

'No, sir, I am Roman,' replied the Father.

'You've been here some time?'

'Only a few months.'

'Such a pleasure . . .' muttered the prince, getting to his feet.

The priest rose and bowed a second time. Teresa excused herself and accompanied her brother.

'Well?' insisted Consalvo. 'What must one do to obtain the duchess's support?'

'But I'm worth nothing!' protested Teresa with a quiet smile.

'Must one swear loyalty to Charles, to the Great Monarch? Is there no other way? But he's still to come, isn't he? Anyway, goodbye for now . . . And this one here, where did you fish him from? Who is he?'

'One of the most cultivated priests of the Society of Jesus.'


'Time wasted! Time wasted! . . . There's nothing to be done with these Uzeda! The best, those who seem the wisest, suddenly show they're mad as the others! Now this one is calling Jesuits into her home, believing in silly prophecies and alleged miracles, and becoming a blind instrument of priests! Where was the girl of once upon a time, so graceful and sweet, gentle and poetic, pious but not bigoted, believing but not blinded? Even physically she had lost her elegance of carriage, was growing fatter, unrecognisable. Madness was gaining on her too, taking a religious form, becoming mystical hysteria! All the same, the lot of them!' He alone esteemed himself wise, strong, prudent, immune from hereditary taint, master and judge of himself and others . . . And when the decree closing the Parliamentary session appeared in the *Official Gazette,* he flung himself head first into the struggle.

Night and day his home became like a public square, a public market, where delegates called from the rural wards and town electors came and went, discussing, bartering, yelling, with hats on their heads and staffs in their hands. On his instructions, his canvassers dragged up to the palace, luring them with marsala, cigars, and curiosity at entering the Viceroys' palace, individuals of all classes, puffed up with sudden importance, shopkeepers, clerks, ushers, innkeepers, barbers, and people humbler still, servants, scullions, all the scum who, by writing a signature before a notary, now held in their hands a fraction of sovereign power. He shook all their hands, greeted them all with a ' thanks for your support ', called everyone *lei.* They went off enchanted, alight with enthusiasm, protesting, ' And they called him proud! Such an easy-going gentleman! ...'

One evening as Consalvo was going round the rooms he saw a new face which seemed very like ... like whose ? ... Like Baldassarre, their former major-domo! But the mutton-chop whiskers had vanished, and instead on his former servant's shaven lips now grew a great pair of dyed moustachios the hue of riding-boots.

' Thanks for your support,' said Consalvo to him, shaking his hand.

' Not at all! ... Duty ...' stuttered Baldassarre.

On leaving the prince's the major-domo had gone into politics, embraced the democratic faith, and now presided over a workers' mutual aid society. Since the young prince—Baldassarre still adopted the diminutive for his former young master—was presenting himself on a democratic programme, he had induced his fellow members to support him. Thus he re-entered the palace which he had left a servant, with all the importance of a bearer of a big block of votes. Seated on one of those satin chairs which once he had moved forward for the gentry, he looked around and listened with the gravity of a former major-domo, more serious and imposing than most others there. A country mayor sitting beside him said to him:

' With us it's a foregone conclusion. And how do things go here, professor?'

'Excellently!' said Baldassarre with a nod of the head. That evening members of the committee were giving the names of friendly electors whom they had induced to write their names on lists. The former servant went up to Consalvo.

'Prince'—from democratic reasons he no longer used the 'Excellency'—'our society has fifty electors' names written down. They're all ours!'

'Thank you. I don't know how to thank you.'

'Not at all, please, my duty! We're sure to win! Victory is ours!'

'Thank you with all my heart for your good wishes.'

Baldassarre, forgetting the wrong done to him by the dead prince, now made such efforts to ensure the young prince's triumph that in a short time he became one of his chief lieutenants. He reported to Consalvo, received his instructions, sometimes gave him advice. Master and servant vanished, they sat side by side at the same table, the prince passed pen and paper to his former dependant, and they called each other *lei* like two diplomats drafting a treaty.

Meanwhile the struggle was sharpening. Consalvo made tentative approaches to the clerical leaders, but the latter replied that his alliance with Lisi and Giardona ruled out any accord. Giulente was gasping for breath. To save the Town Council he had been forced to impose new taxes, increase old ones, dismiss employees, stop public works not yet finished, reduce all expenses; and complaint was unanimous against him for unpopular taxation and systematic meanness. That long aspiration of his to the old duke's political inheritance, even his liver complaint were thought a bit ridiculous: his wife completed his ruin by vaunting his patriotism after having derided it. 'He nearly lost a leg on the Volturno! . . .' and by asking everyone she saw, shop assistants, hawkers, 'Aren't you an elector? . . . Then go and write your name . . .' And she had finally handed over the accounts of her administration, in worse confusion than the Town Council's.

The other candidates however did not admit defeat, the ones with the least chance being the most stubborn, falling back on every available means, bargaining for votes and loosing violent accusations against their luckier rivals, particularly the prince.

' *We* have no nephews being educated by Jesuits, or uncles who are Cardinals of Holy Church, or reactionary relations. *We* don't rely on support from all classes, nobles to mob . . .' Consalvo ignored them, hurried into the country, returned to town, enlarged his circle of adherents.

Baldassarre's agents, on their side, went about preaching the prince's democracy in taverns, buying drinks for all who promised a vote. One night, though, there was a nasty discussion between the prince's supporters and opponents who called him ' Demagogue, Jesuit and traitor '. Words turned to blows, chairs and bottles flew, knives gleamed, serious threats were uttered. Then Consalvo fell back on his former companions in revelry, on those with whom he had once gadded in taverns and brothels. Cut-throat faces, pallid pimps with scar-marked visages, kept guard on his palace and person. They spread around in places of ill repute, threatened, warned . . . ' Francis II's candidate has loosed the Mafia in the constituency to terrorise honest citizens,' denounced opposition news-sheets. But in the heat of battle even the most ferocious accusations had lost all reality, were attributed to partisan hatred, to bitterness by those feeling ground giving way beneath their feet. The name of Francalanza was on all mouths, no one doubted the prince's election now. He began preparing his electoral speech.

The event was announced by great multi-coloured placards stuck all over the town: 'ELECTORAL MEETING. Citizens! On Sunday, 8 October 1882, at 12 Midday, in the Gymnasium (ex-Benedictine Monastery), the PRINCE OF FRAN-CALANZA will announce his political programme to voters of the first constituency.' Then followed signatures of his Committee: that of the chairman, a retired magistrate well thought of by all parties and so put in that position by Consalvo, and of six vice-chairmen, more than five hundred members, eight secretaries and twenty-four assistant-secretaries.

Such programme speeches were a novelty. Elections could no longer be arranged on the quiet, in the family as it were, as in the Duke of Oragua's day. Each candidate had to present himself to the electors, render them an account of his ideas, discuss questions of the day. 'At least it's certain that only those with the gift of the gab will go to Parliament . . .' But to hear the Prince of Francalanza making a speech in public like a travelling quack would be a truly extraordinary spectacle. The other candidates gave their speeches in theatres, but for Consalvo's there was so much anticipation, such a deluge of requests for seats, such masses of representatives coming in from the country, that no theatre seemed sufficient. The Gymnasium, which was actually the inner cloister of the San Nicola monastery, was big as a public square, and had, with its arches, columns and terraces, a certain air of an amphitheatre; it was the vastest, noblest, and best-adapted setting to the greatness of the event. Consalvo, who had made this choice, knew what he wanted.

He went to direct preparations personally. But while decorators were busy putting up clusters of flags and festoons of ivy and curtains and portraits, the prince looked round in a daze, suddenly swept by memories of boyhood. The vast, noble monastery, the grandiose home of festive monks, the aristocratic college of his youth was unrecognisable. The corridors which had once stretched as far as the eye could reach had vanished, shut off by walls and gates, converted into school-rooms. The refectory was transformed into the Technical Institute's art-studio, cluttered with easels, hung with prints and plaster casts; the night Choir was full of nautical equipment; over the doors of rooms, in the place of great pictures were stuck placards inscribed 'CLASS ONE', 'MANAGEMENT', or 'HEAD-MASTER'. Down in the courtyard, store-rooms were transformed into barracks. Generations of soldiers and students succeeding each other since 1866 had devastated the cloisters, broken the benches, damaged the balustrades. The walls were covered with obscene figures and remarks, and inkpots hurled as missiles from exasperation at failed exams or delight at promotion had printed great splotches of ink all over the walls.

Faced with this devastation, Consalvo now felt a sense of regret at the death of that monastic world which he had witnessed with such glee. But then—how well he remembered!—he was fifteen years old and impatient to take the place awaiting him in the world. Had he been told then that one day he would return to San Nicola to make a speech there about social

605

equality and lay thought! . . . No, he could not accustom himself to the democratic ideals against which his upbringing and his very blood protested.

There at San Nicola, perhaps more than at his own home, he had been infused with the pride of nobility, become used to consider himself of different clay from the common herd . . . Where was his room? He looked for it in the Novitiate, and could not find it. Perhaps it was where there was a notice 'PHYSICS ROOM'. A janitor, acting as his guide, was describing the magnificence of the monastery, the sumptuous fêtes, the number of guests, the nobility of the Fathers, and regretting the sight of present ruin. 'Here lived the novices, all sons of the very top barons! Fine times! Now cobblers' sons come.' The prestige of nobility and wealth must really be undying if this poor devil spoke thus of a reform advantageous to his own class. Consalvo wanted to reply, 'You're right . . .' but the hammering from the courtyard reminded him of the need to hide his own feelings, to play the part he had assumed. There, in those walls, he had joined the 'rats'' party, whose tails Fra' Cola had wanted to cut off. Might someone not blame him for that remote past . . . Bah! Who ever remembered a boy's monkey-tricks? Giovannino was dead, he could not return from the next world to contradict him! And even if he did?

Preparations were nearing completion. On the Sunday of the meeting all was ready. The courtyard looked magnificent. Two thousand seats had been arranged neatly in the arena, and there still remained space for standing spectators. On the southern part of the arcades reserved for committee and associates stood a big table surrounded by armchairs and flanked by smaller tables for press and stenographers. The other three sides were for guests: authorities, nobles, representatives. The whole terrace, like the arena, was for ordinary spectators. To protect their heads from the sun great awnings of tricolour muslin had been stretched across. Clusters of flags covered the columns, with a portrait in the middle of each cluster. To right and left of the balustrade from which the candidate was to speak were portraits of Umberto and Garibaldi, then Mazzini and Victor Emmanuel, then Queen Margherita and Cairoli; and so on, round with Amedeo, Bixio, Cavour, Crispi, Lamarmora, Rattazzi, Bertani, Cialdini, the family of Savoy and of Garibaldi, Monarchy and Republic, Right and Left.

By ten o'clock crowds were beginning to throng but the doors were well guarded by numbers of committee members, recognisable by great tricolour cockades pinned on their chests. Down in the outer courtyard workers' societies were gathering around their flags and banners to receive the candidate and accompany him to the Gymnasium. Three bands arrived one after the other, with numbers of hangers-on and crowds of curious spectators behind them, and a buzz rose to the sky as torrents of people flowed through the wide-open doors of the Royal Staircase. Band instruments glittered like mirrors in the gay autumn sunshine, pennants and flags waved in the breeze, multi-coloured placards shone bright on monastery walls.

Baldassarre, in frock-coat and tall hat with a cockade as big as a mill-wheel, was coming and going, sweating and puffing, as he had done twenty-eight years before when he had organised the aristocratic ceremonial for the old princess's funeral. Then he had been a wage-earning servant, now he was a free citizen at a democratic meeting, lending his support to the prince not for money but for an ideal. To the crowd, trying their best to enter, he was saying, with raised hands, 'Gentlemen, please, a little patience, there's plenty of time . . . another hour . . .' Could this mob be let in before the guests? . . . But by half-past eleven further resistance was impossible. He gave his dependants orders to defend reserved places at least, and allowed the terrace and arena to be opened. In a second the human wave swept over all. These were still an anonymous crowd of ordinary people, but gradually more respectable folk began appearing, elegant ladies and gentlemen before whose carriages another crowd in the outer courtyard opened way. In the arena Baldassarre was pointing ladies to their places, while turning round now and again towards his companions. 'Tell the bands to come here, and take their places! Or there'll be no music at the candidate's arrival . . .' The fools could not get hold of a single one of them! It was impossible to fetch the bands, even after shouting for an hour. In the end he had to run round calling them himself, 'What are you doing there? That isn't your place! Come on inside! . . .' He was no longer a major-domo, but could not bear seeing things badly organised. Had one of the Committee not said that the band must play at the prince's arrival? He bawled, ' He's being received in the Gymnasium, not in the courtyard. D'you want to teach me? . . .' And he put the bands in their places and ordered them to play the ' Royal March ' and the ' Garibaldi Anthem ' . . .

Now the Gymnasium offered a truly extraordinary spectacle. The arena was a sea of heads, the rows of chairs full, the standing spectators packed like sardines. On the terrace was a multi-coloured crowd, above which flowered the sunshades of many ladies who had found no place down below. But the most splendid aspect was that of the arcades. There all the best society was gathered, ladies in front rows, men behind, with a buzz like a beehive rising all round of elegant chatter, prophecies on the election results and political gossip, but also exclamations of impatience, sporadic impatient clapping as at the theatre, which made all turn their heads and take out their watches.

It was already midday, and the great bell of San Nicola was ringing the first chimes, when there came a distant clamour. ' He's here! He's here! ·. . . He's coming! . . . It's starting!' Now could be distinctly heard the cry, ' Hurrah for Franca-lanza! . . . Hurrah for our Deputy! . . .' and outbursts of clapping which grew, echoed around the passages, made the window panes quiver and awoke all the dimmed echoes in the monastery. Those in the Gymnasium had risen to their feet, necks outstretched, eyes fixed on the entrance arch. Suddenly as the first flags appeared, the first notes of the ' Royal March ' rang out, played by the three bands, and a great shout, a hurricane of applause, of hurrahs, of confused cries rose from the vast enclosure and re-echoed tempestuously amid the other crowd surrounding the candidate.

Consalvo advanced, very pale, thanking with slight nods, deafened, dazzled, overwhelmed by the spectacle. Behind him new torrents of people were pouring on to the terraces, under the arcades, into the arena, overcoming resistance by first occupants. And meanwhile thousands of other hands were applauding, waving handkerchiefs and hats; the ladies stood on chairs, saluting with fans and sunshades, forming picturesque groups against the dark background of the great masculine crowd. The ovation was prolonged, shouts and sharp cries went up as the march started again, and hand-claps crackled like a violent hailstorm on tiles. Here and there little groups of opponents and indifferents remained silent, but from above all that multitude seemed but a single mouth shouting, two arms applauding, 'One . . . two . . . two and a half . . . three minutes . . .' some counted, watch in hand, and others could be seen with tears of emotion in their eyes. Many lost their voices. Tired of waving handkerchiefs, they tied them to red, sweating necks.

'Enough . . . Enough . . .' Consalvo was saying in a low voice with a sense of real alarm before that yelling sea; and from far away Baldassarre, unable to cross the living wall now tight all round him, made desperate signs to the music. Finally the players understood, the music stopped, applause and shouting died down. But, suddenly, as the President of the Committee moved towards the balustrade to introduce the candidate, out rang the notes of the 'Garibaldi Anthem', a new quiver ran through the crowd, frenzy started up again.

Consalvo, overcoming his second of fear, was now distributing thanks to left and right more frankly and smiling, sure of himself, his heart aswell with pride and confidence. The music stopped once more, the crowd went silent. Flags propped against the columns of the arcade formed a new decoration; officials, journalists and stenographers sat down at their tables, secretaries pulled paper out of their briefcases. One of these rose to his feet, and amid a solemn silence began to read out in a strident voice the list of adherents' names. But people got bored, the words were lost in general mutter. A group of jesting students were now animatedly discussing if the candidate would begin with the aristocratic 'Gentlemen' or the republican 'Citizens'. Affirmed one, 'What's the betting he says "Gentlemen and citizens"?' But enthusiasts were sending severe glances towards these sceptics and demanding silence. Finally the litany ended. One hand on the velvet-draped balustrade, Consalvo waited, turned aside. At a sign from the Chairman, he turned round to the crowd.

'Fellow citizens! . . . If kind friends have led you to think that I possess gifts of oratory and brought you all here with promises of hearing a real speech, I am sorry to have to disappoint you . . .' The clear, steady, confident voice reached every-

609

where, faint but distinct, even in the remotest corners. ' I declare to you, fellow citizens, that I am no orator such is the tumult of impressions, of feelings, of emotions overwhelming me at this moment.' *(Shouts of ' Good!',* wrote the stenographers.) ' I feel that never till my very last days shall I cancel the memory of this indescribable moment, of this immense current of sympathy surrounding me, encouraging me, warning me, inflaming my heart, and returning to you as warm and vital and sincere as it flows from your hearts to mine. *(Prolonged applause)* But this is too small a restitution and not enough to repay my debt; my whole life dedicated to your service would scarcely be enough. *(Applause)*

' Fellow citizens! . . . you ask a programme from one requesting the honour of your votes. My programme may lack other merits, but will at least have that of brevity; it can be summed up in three words: Liberty, Progress, Democracy . . . *(Loud and enthusiastic clapping)* It makes me almost superstitiously pleased to hear you, free citizens, crown not me but these sacred words with your applause, here among old walls which were once a stronghold of sloth, of privilege, of theological obscurantism . . . *("Excellent!", unanimous outburst of loud approval)* Here amid these walls, once a den of ignorance, today a beacon vivid with the radiant light of victorious thought! *(New outbreak of frantic clapping, the orator's voice inaudible for some minutes)* Fellow citizens, my faith in these great human ideals is not new, does not date from recent days when all make show of them, as gallants vaunt the graces of the lady they desire . . . *(Laughter)* protesting that they don't want her favours . . . *(more laughter)* but are satisfied with sighing from afar . . . *(shout of general laughter)* My faith dates from the dawn of life, when class prejudices which I knew and do not regret having known, as I am now better able to combat them . . . *(Good!)* shut me forcibly here amid these walls.

' Allow me to tell you an anecdote of those far-off times. Those were the days when Garibaldi the Liberator was coursing triumphantly from one end to the other of the feudal Bourbon domains, to make of them a free province of the free Italian Fatherland . . . *(Hurrah! Good!)* I was a boy then, and to my inexperienced and ignorant mind Garibaldi's name sounded like that of a formidable warrior who knew no other law but the harsh, violent one of war. Then one day came a rumour. Garibaldi was at our city gates; the Benedictine monks were making ready to entertain him . . . being unable to subdue him and his red devils . . . *(Laughter)* And I was almost afraid of looking at that thunderbolt of war, lest by his glance alone he might burn me up. Then one day my companions pointed out to me the Hero of Two Worlds. And I saw that blond Archangel of liberty intent on . . . d'you know what? On tending roses in our garden! From that day came the revelation of that vast and generous heart in which leonine strength was coupled with gentle sweetness . . . *(Crashing applause)* of that man who, after conquering a kingdom, had, like Cincinnatus, to fall back on cultivating the sacred rock where today hovers the magnanimous spirit of him who was rightly called the " Knight of Humanity " . . .'

Stenographers stopped writing, such a hurricane of applause and shouts burst out. Shrieks of: ' Hurrah for Francalanza! . . . Hurrah for Garibaldi! . . . Hurrah for our Deputy! . . .' In the universal clamour the prince's words were lost and all that could be seen was his mouth opening and shutting as if he were chewing, and his arm swirling to finish his anecdote, which was about his mistaking Menotti Garibaldi and the father, the substitution of himself for his dead cousin . . . ' Silence! He's still talking . . . Hurrah for Garibaldi . . . Hurrah for the young prince . . .' Pulling his own handkerchief out of his pocket he began waving it and shouting ' Hurrah for Garibaldi! Hurrah for the Hero of Two Worlds . . .' Then, as he waited for silence, he mopped the drops of sweat on his brow.

' Fellow citizens,' he went on when calm was restored, ' I am young in years and life can teach me many things, show me the fallacy of many others, and give me the experience and mature good sense which I may not yet have. But whatever may be the experiences and trials which the future holds in store for me one thing I can affirm from this moment, sure that no passing of years or varying of fortune could ever change it: my faith in democracy . . . *(Outburst of enthusiastic applause)* This faith is dear to me as a banner won in battle is dear to a leader . . . *(Outburst of clapping)* A mountain-dweller who spends all his days amid mountain peaks may find the grandiose spectacle says little or nothing to him; but a climber from the plain who has gradually conquered the sublime and arduous peak finds his heart swell with joy and just pride as he contemplates the horizon he has earned. *(General and prolonged ovation)*

'Citizens! I do not wish to disturb the solemnity of this occasion by mentioning the petty competitions of small minds, but you know that an accusation was launched against me; you know that I was called . . . aristocratic . . .' The stenographers did not know whether to note down *deep impression,* or *silence,* or *general stir;* but already the orator was sweeping on. 'This accusation is founded on my birth. I am not responsible for my birth . . . *(No! No!)* nor you for yours, nor others for theirs, considering that when we come into the world our opinion is not asked . . . *(Loud laughter)* I am responsible for my own life. And my life has all been spent on a task of redemption; redemption from social and political prejudice, moral and intellectual redemption. And this nothing has stopped; neither easy living, nor derision, nor harmful suspicion, nor, more serious to my heart, opposition on my own family hearth . . . *(Good! Bravo! Applause)* You see that this is a faith I can no longer renounce. It is the dearer and more precious to me the more it costs me . . .' *(Outbursts of loud and prolonged clapping. Shouts of ' Hurrah for Francalanza ' . . . ' Hurrah for democracy ' . . . ' Hurrah for liberty ' . . . Orator forced to silence for some minutes)*

Pleasure, admiration was general, among friends who saw his triumph assured, adversaries who recognised his ability, even ordinary folk who understood nothing but exclaimed, 'What a lawyer he is! There's no lawyer can talk like that!', while ladies enjoyed themselves animatedly, as at a theatre, exchanging observations on the prince's artistry and his looks as if he were a leading actor playing a role.

'But you, fellow citizens,' he went on, 'may consider that if this faith involves a programme, it is proper for a legislator to trace a clear line on all questions affecting politics, public administration, economics and so on. Allow me then to tell you my ideas about those things. Now that the old political parties have dissolved, the new ones are not yet defined. I look forward to their formation, and will follow the fate of that party which gives liberty with order at home and peace with honour abroad *(Excellent! Applause)*, of that party which will carry out all legitimate reforms, while preserving all traditions *(Bravo! Good!)*, of that party which will restrict useless outlays and expand productive ones *(lively applause)*, of that party which will not try to fill the coffers of the State by emptying the pockets of private citizens *(general laughter, applause)*, of that party which will protect the Church as a spiritual power, and control it as an element of civil discord *(approval)*, of that party, in fact, which will ensure in the fairest way, by the directest route, in the shortest time, the prosperity, greatness and strength of our great common homeland.' *(General applause)*

Actually the applause was not general at this passage, in fact a cough or two from a corner made many heads turn.

'You may say to me,' went on the orator, 'that this programme is too vast and too eclectic, as, according to a proverb, one can't have a full barrel of wine and a drunken wife. *(Laughter)* A full barrel would be useless riches if one could not touch the liquor inside, and it might just as well contain water or any other fluid. But as for a drunken wife, that would be almost too good to be true; I appeal to all husbands. *(Outburst of very loud laughter, lively and repeated clapping)* From a barrel one should draw just enough wine to quench the thirst and raise the spirits. The French say, " Si jeunesse savait! Si vieillesse pouvait!" That which is impossible in the life of one man is not only possible but necessary in the collective life of a people. The legislator should possess the audacity of youth, coupled with the wisdom of old age. The law should keep count of all interests, all beliefs, all aspirations so as to fuse and harmonise them. It must be regulated by experience of the past, but one cannot and should not clip the wings of the future! *(Ovation)* So how enviable and envied are our institutions, which by careful balance between Parliament and executive power, allow the ideal harmony to draw nearer. But, like all human things, such institutions are not perfect, though perfectable, and to this work of continual improvement I will dedicate all my strength, devoid as I am of either fear or fetishes. The Constitution can and

613

should be improved. That necessity is realised by all, from the people claiming its complete Sovereignty, to the King who recognises his as coming from the people. *(Approval)* Luckily today in Italy people and King are all one *(applause)* and the democratic monarchy of the House of Savoy is a legal expression of the democratic-monarchist sentiments of all Italians. *(Excellent!)* While loyal Princes and upright Kings sit on the throne, disagreement will be impossible, fortune secure! *(Outburst of prolonged applause, shouts of " Long live the King! Hurrah for Italy!" . . . Voice of orator swamped by clapping)* But the tutelage of popular sovereignty and the well-being of workers should be the legislator's principal aim, and this will be impossible to achieve unless the rightful, the direct representatives of the people sit in the Chamber. May I therefore express my hopes for the election of many working-class candidates? Many are opposed to such candidates, quoting the English proverb about " *The right man in the right place* ". But they forget that this quotation is a two-edged sword, that when Parliament occupies itself with working-class matters, " *the right men in the right place* " will be the working-class citizens themselves! *(Good! Bravo!)* Once upon a time a wig-maker set up as critic, and the celebrated Voltaire, annoyed at his presumption, said to him, " *Mastro Andrea, go and make wigs.* " *(Laughter)* But if wig-making had been under discussion and Voltaire had tried to air his opinion, Mastro Andrea could have given the famous poet the answer, " Monsieur Voltaire, go and make tragedies!" *(Loud laughter, prolonged applause)* Fellow citizens, the social question, let us frankly admit, is more urgent at this moment than any other. Is it new? No, indeed not. Let us just glance over its history . . .'

' Now we're for it!' muttered his adversaries the students here and there. But angry voices shouted, ' Silence!' while the orator, beginning with Adam and Eve, Cain and Abel, galloped through Babylonia, Egypt, Greece and Rome, skipped over the Middle Ages, plunged into the French Revolution, halted at Prince Bismarck and academic socialism. The public's attention was beginning to wane, yet many made an effort to follow this wild race of his. ' Is the State therefore to be the incarnation of Divine Providence? *(Laughter)* No, what the State cannot achieve must be supplied by individual initiative; hence trade unions, scrutineers, co-operatives, liberty to strike. Does this solve the social question then? No, it takes more than that!'

Some of the ladies were yawning behind their fans, people who dined at one were creeping away. But eventually, declaring that social problems 'are Gordian knots which no sword can cut, but which loving study and industrious patience can unravel' the orator passed to foreign policy. 'The state of Europe, it would be vain to hide, is still influenced by the Holy Alliance.' The unity of Germany should please Italians, but maybe pan-Slavism was a phenomenon not devoid of danger. 'I believe that Prince Metternich was merely guessing when he said . . . Yet it did not escape the acute eye of Count Cavour . . . And certainly the concept of the famous Pitt . . .' Past filed every statesman, past and present, in were dragged Machiavelli, Gladstone, Campanella, Macaulay, Francis Bacon. The orator asked himself, 'What is England's historic mission? . . . And if Spain hears the call of blood? . . .' All this on the betrayal of Tunis! 'No, it was not the France of Magenta and Solferino; it was the France of Brenno and Charles VIII . . .' The audience stirred a little; the stenographers noted ' *Loud applause* '. But racial antagonisms would be made up one day; then would rise the United States of Europe. 'As Camillo Benso di Cavour once so aptly said, " Peace must be sought in trusty alliances and strong battalions." *(Good!)* There is a great argument nowadays between the supporters of big and those of small warships; I consider both to be necessary for modern naval warfare. Caius Duilius destroyed the Carthaginian fleet by turning a naval battle into an infantry battle at sea. *(Bravo! Applause)* So one not too distant day, when we have our natural frontiers again *(lively applause)*, and joined in one group the peoples who speak the tongue of Dante *(outburst of applause)*, established our colonies in Africa and maybe in Oceania too *(Good!)* we will rebuild the Roman Empire!' *(Ovation)*

He then passed straight on to matters of finance.

'Here be sighs, wails and woes! . . .' *(Laughter)* But the woes were not impossible of solution. 'Now let us not compare ourselves, from patriotism, to the United States of America . .' First of all the tributary system must be reformed. 'As Paul

Leroy Beaulieu says . . . according to the famous Smith's opinion . . .' Quotations and figures came crowding on each other's heels. Few were now following him in these elucubrations, more were leaving, ladies yawned openly. 'Now let us pass to commercial treaties . . . Let us consider Agrarian Committees . . .' At every announcement of a new subject, little groups of bored spectators drifted away. 'A fine speech but too long . . .' Those leaving forced crowds to draw aside, the faithful hissed 'Silence!', and Baldassarre was in tortures at seeing the public's bad manners. 'Administration of justice . . . Justice in administration. Decentralise by centralising, centralise by decentralising ' . . . As for the Merchant Navy, the system of prizes was not devoid of anomalies. Then came ' postal and telegraphic reform, legislation on telephones; nor must we forget the hydra of bureaucracy . . .'

Now big empty spaces were to be seen in the arena and under the arcades, particularly on the terraces where the sun was roasting people's heads. 'This isn't an electoral programme, it's a ministerial pronouncement . . .' muttered some to each other. The audience was crushed by weight of erudition, by monotonous use of names; the over-bright light, the silence of the monastery was hypnotising; the Chairman slowly lowered his head, overcome by drowsiness, but at an outbreak of the candidate's voice he would raise it quickly and look around in bewilderment; musicians yawned, famished. Every now and again Baldassarre gave a signal for applause and encouraged the faithful, who were also dejected and overwhelmed; he was desperate at seeing all the orator's fine remarks pass unobserved. The latter had been talking for an hour and a half, he was all of a sweat, his voice hoarse, his right arm numb with continual gesticulating, and refusing to do its duty. Still he went on, determined to see it through in spite of his own and the public's exhaustion, as he wanted it said that he had talked for two hours together. At one moment chairs overturned by people escaping made a great noise. All turned, fearing an incident, a quarrel; for a moment the orator was forced to stop. When he started talking again his voice came raucous and faint from his gullet; he was near collapse, but had reached his peroration.

'These and others are the reforms I long to see: but I must

616

not abuse your patience.' Sighs of relief from oppressed breasts. 'Fellow citizens! If you send me to the Chamber, I will dedicate the whole of myself to carrying out this programme. *(Fine! Bravo!)* I do not presume myself infallible, for I am neither a prophet nor a prophet's son *(laughter)*, but I will gladly accept, in fact I beg my fellow citizens to put forward, whatever ideas, suggestions, proposals they may think right and useful. *(Excellent)* Let our motto be: *Fiat Lux! (Applause)* The light of science, of civilisation, of constant progress. *(Outburst of applause)* May the thought of our homeland be at the very core of our hearts. *(Approval)* Our homeland is this Italy which Dante divined, and which our fathers gave us at the cost of their blood! *(Lively applause)* Our homeland is also this island blessed by the sun, where was born the *dolce stil nuovo* and whence have sprung so many glorious initiatives. Our homeland, finally, is this dear and lovely city of ours where we all form, as it were, one single family. *(Acclamation)* It is said that Deputies represent the nation and not single constituencies; but what are national interests but the sum of local interests? *(Excellent! Applause)* And so when turning my mind to the study of the larger questions of general politics, I promise to bear as close to my heart as if they were my own matters that regard Sicily in particular, this constituency, my native town, and each one of my fellow citizens. *(Great acclamation)* In gratitude for listening to me so indulgently, may I end by inviting you all to give three ringing cheers for Italy! *(Outburst of applause, shouts of " Hurrah for Italy!")* Long live the King. *(General loud clapping)* Hurrah for Liberty!' *(Whole public stands up to applaud and acclaim, handkerchiefs waved, shouts of ' Long live Francalanza! Hurrah for our Deputy!' Chairman embraces orator. General emotion, indescribable enthusiasm)*

Consalvo was at the end of his tether, exhausted, overwhelmed, drained by his histrionic efforts. He had been speaking for two hours. For two hours he had made the public laugh like a comedian, moved them like a tragic actor, yelled like a charlatan selling pomade. And as the 'Royal March', played on Baldassarre's orders, spurred public enthusiasm, the group of jeering students asked each other:

'Now he's talked, can you tell me what he said?'

In the final days Consalvo's anxiety grew feverish. He could scarcely fail to succeed, but wanted to be first. His supporting committee now included the whole city, the whole constituency, electors and non-electors. Posters with the words 'VOTE FOR THE PRINCE OF FRANCALANZA: ELECT CONSALVO UZEDA OF FRAN-CALANZA. PRINCE CONSALVO OF FRANCALANZA CANDIDATE FOR THE FIRST CONSTITUENCY' grew bigger and bigger, covered huge areas of paper with letters a foot high; the very walls seemed to be shouting his name . . . First! First! He wanted to be first! . . .

On the eve of polling day there was real pandemonium in the palace; all were asking, 'The prince, where's the prince? . . .' But his household replied he was with his uncle the duke, who was not well. Despite this all work went on as intensely as if he were there. Giardona's and Lisi's representatives had come to make up final lists of election officials. Meanwhile invigilators over the rural wards were making ready to leave. At midnight the prince arrived. The meeting went on until two in the morning, when the first carriages left for outlying wards.

And next day, when booths were opened and voting began, together with the news of the prince's victory—for electors were declaring for him in thousands, returning specially from the country, hauled to voting booths on chairs if they could not go on their own feet—a rumour, first vague, then ever more insistent, went round among Lisi's followers: 'Betrayal! Betrayal! . . .' In the last hours of the previous night, it was affirmed, the prince had come to an agreement with Vazza. Some gave details, 'We saw him entering the lawyer's house towards eleven o'clock . . .' and there, they asserted, had been plotted their betrayal, agreement with the clericals, abandonment of Lisi, perhaps also of Giardona. 'What? When? What the devil are you saying? The prince was at the old duke's and didn't move from there! . . .' replied his supporters in their glee at victory already assured.

Towards dusk the first telegrams from provincial wards reached the palace. But those results were not all equally favourable; some local candidates had strong majorities, in first counts the prince's place oscillated between second and third. Consalvo, very pale, was all atremble. But as the results of the urban wards came in his position consolidated. There was no mention of third place now; he was with Vazza between first or second. When the last telegrams and last messages with the definite figures arrived, there was no more doubt; he was first with six thousand and forty-three votes; Vazza came just after with five thousand nine hundred and eighty-nine votes; then Giardona with four thousand nine hundred and fourteen votes; the radical Marcenò was out with three thousand three hundred and nine votes; Lisi dropped to fewer than three thousand votes; the others were all a thousand votes or so apart, with two thousand, or even scarcely a thousand. Giulente had only seven hundred!

It was late at night, but the Francalanza palace was all lit up, with every window aglitter. An endless throng poured in to congratulate 'the first elect of the people'. There was an incessant buzz on the stairs; it was impossible to breathe in the rooms. Consalvo, radiant, moving with difficulty amid the compact crowd, was seizing every hand, embracing all, healed as if by magic from his mania about isolation and contagion in his wild delight at the magnificent triumph. When a great torchlight procession, a vast demonstration with music and flags, frantically acclaimed him, he went on the balcony, harangued the crowd and gave himself up once again to their curiosity, like a tribune.

For three days the town was in constant ferment. Every night the demonstration was renewed, the enthusiasm grew instead of cooling. In the slums a little song to the tune of 'Mastro Raffaele' was all the rage:

> Long live the prince,
> Who pays our drinks,
> Long live the prince
> Who fills our bellies.

Groups of drunks went round shouting 'Hurrah for Victor Emmanuel! Hurrah for the Revolution! Hurrah for His Holiness! . . .' and things even wilder. For three days the palace was invaded by people coming to congratulate him, an incessant procession from ten in the morning till midnight, with scarcely two hours' pause for lunch and dinner. He made an attempt at talking modestly about the general results, about the 'fine experiment ' of the new law, about the good sense shown by Italians, but they would not let him have his say, insisted on talking only of him, of his resounding, richly deserved victory.

On the fourth day he went out into the streets. His arm nearly broke with all the hat-doffing and handshaking. Joy was written all over his face, showed in all his actions and words, in spite of his studied attempt to hide it. Tired of seeing the populace, to taste another flavour of triumph he thought of visiting his relatives. He began with the old duke, who was quite genuinely ill, after eighty years of machinations and intrigues.

' Is Your Excellency pleased with the results?' Consalvo asked him.

But though the old man had recommended his nephew everywhere so that power should stay in the family, he could not even so prevent himself feeling jealous of this rising star, while his own had not only set politically but he felt himself to have a very short time to live.

' I've heard . . . good . . .' he muttered shortly.

' Have you seen how well things have gone in the rest of Italy? The world seemed to be falling about our ears and yet there are scarcely a dozen Radicals in. The Right has also gained . . .'

He was flattering his uncle a little, for he hoped to be his heir. In Rome he would need money, a lot of money; the richer he was the sooner he could win a place in the capital. He was not worried by the coolness shown by the duke; to whom else could the old man leave his fortune but to the heir of the Uzeda name? To Teresa's children, maybe?

On leaving his uncle's, he went on to his sister's. Though owing her gratitude for her generosity at the time of their father's death, he had not yet forgiven her refusal to help him during his struggle, and he wanted now to show her that he had been able to win through on his own. But Teresa was not in. The porter told him that the young duchess had driven out in her country coach, together with Monsignor the Vicar-General. He went upstairs even so, and found the old duchess with Father Gentile.

' Teresa has gone to Belpasso, to visit the Servant of God . . . you know, the peasant girl of the miracles . . . His Lordship the

Bishop had allowed no-one to pay such a visit; but made an exception for your sister alone . . .'

'The duchess's sanctity,' said the Jesuit with compunction, 'explains and sanctions this exception.'

Consalvo thought he should bow his head a little in sign of thanks, as if for a courtesy addressed to himself.

'And when will she be back?'

'Tonight for sure.'

'His Lordship the Bishop,' the priest explained, 'has prudently taken such measures to prevent this sight from feeding the crowd's unhealthy curiosity; but the Christian sentiments animating the young duchess and distinguishing her among others . . .'

The conversation, always on the same subject, continued between the Jesuit and the old dowager. Consalvo noticed a printed piece of paper on the desk by which he was sitting and read it out of the corner of his eye. FORMULA OF OATH. 'In the presence of the Most Holy Trinity, of the Most Holy Virgin Mary and of all the Saints who were born or who lived on the soil of . . . In the name of the towns of . . . represented here, and before our venerated pastor, guide and spiritual head; I, delegated to this effect, declare to be formed the Christian province of . . . under the special patronage of Saint . . . In the name of this new province I freely and solemnly recognise Jesus Christ, Son of the living God, true God and true Man, in the Most Holy Host exposed on this altar, as our Lord and Master and as Supreme Head of . . . At the feet of Jesus Christ we place our belongings, our families, our persons, our lives, our honour, in a word all that is closest to the heart of man . . .'

Barely suppressing a smile, Consalvo rose to his feet.

'D'you know that Ferdinanda is ill?' the dowager said to him.

'What's the matter with her?'

'A chill. But at her age anything can be serious . . . Why not go and visit her?'

He heeded this advice. Something might come to him from there too, half a million or so. Had he been more farseeing he would have dealt better with the old woman, without of course renouncing any of his own ambitions. The obstinacy and harshness with which he had treated her had been silly, worthy of a crazy Uzeda, not of the Honourable Deputy Consalvo of Francalanza, of the new man he wanted to be. On reaching the old woman's house, that house to which he had so often come as a child to look at coats-of-arms, hear tales of the Viceroys and drink in aristocratic hauteur, a quiet smile came to his lips. Suppose his electors knew!

'How is my aunt?' he asked the maid, a new face.

'So so . . .' replied the woman, looking curiously at this unknown gentleman.

'Say that her nephew the prince would like to see her.'

The old woman was quite capable of not receiving him; he awaited the reply with some anxiety. But Donna Ferdinanda, on hearing Consalvo was there, answered the maid in a voice made hoarse by her chill, 'Let him in.' She had heard of the latest outrages committed by her nephew, that speech made in public like a mountebank, the denial of his class principles, the praise of liberty and democracy, the Francalanza palace invaded by a mob of rascals, Baldassarre admitted to the table where he had once served; it had all been described to her by Lucrezia, in order to avenge herself, to ruin Consalvo's chances for the inheritance. Donna Ferdinanda had felt the old Uzeda blood boil with indignation and rage. But now she was ill, her humours tempered by the egotism of old age and infirmity. And Consalvo had come to visit her; so he was humiliating himself, giving her this satisfaction denied her for so long. After all, in spite of his apostasy and outrages, he was still Prince of Francalanza, head of the family, her protégé of long ago . . . 'Let him in.'

He came respectfully towards her, bent over the little iron bedstead, that one of years ago, and asked:

'Aunt, how are you?'

She made an ambiguous gesture of the head.

'Have you fever? Let me feel your pulse . . . No, just a little heat. What have you taken? Have you called a doctor?'

'Doctors are all donkeys,' she replied briefly, turning her face to the wall.

'Your Excellency is right. They know very little . . . but they do know a bit more than us . . . Why not get one in early . . .'

The old woman replied with an outbreak of cavernous coughing that ended with yellowish phlegm.

'You have a cough and take nothing! I'll bring you some pastilles which are quite miraculous. Will you promise to take them?'

Donna Ferdinanda gave her usual nod.

'I knew nothing or I'd have come before. But I was only told that Your Excellency wasn't very well at the Radalis' a few moments ago . . . Do you know that today my sister has gone to see the Servant of God, the one whom people say all those things about? She's the only one to have permission and has gone with the Vicar-General. It seems a most unusual favour . . . Does Your Excellency believe all that is being said?'

No reply. But he still went on talking, realising that the old woman must enjoy hearing gossip and news, seeing someone near.

'I don't believe any of it, with all due respect. Is that a sin? Even St Thomas wanted to see and touch before believing . . . and he was a saint! But frankly, certain stories! . . . Teresa's quite infatuated now . . . Ah well, each of us has his own conscience to deal with . . . And what has my Aunt Lucrezia against me? What did she expect me to do? . . . She goes round everywhere talking against me as if I was the foulest of creatures . . .'

The old woman did not breathe a word, her back still to him.

'All for the great love for her husband which has burst all of a sudden in her breast! . . . Before she used to declare Giulente's attitudes ridiculous '—he did not call him *Uncle*, knowing that would please her—' now all those who have not suported him are infamous!'

A new outbreak of coughing made the old woman shake like a bellows. When it calmed she said in a feeble tone but with bitter contempt:

'Infamous times! . . . Degenerate race!'

The shaft was directed at him too. Consalvo was silent a little, with head bowed but a mocking smile on his lips, as the old woman could not see him. Then in a gentle humble tone he went on:

'Your Excellency may blame me too . . . If I've done anything

623

to displease you, I ask your pardon . . . But there is nothing for which my conscience reproves me . . . Your Excellency cannot regret that one of her name is again among the first in the land . . . Maybe you are pained at the means by which this result has been obtained . . . Believe me it pains me more than you . . . But we do not choose our period for coming into the world; we find it as it is, and as it is we must accept it. Anyway, if it's true that things aren't too good nowadays, were they all so very wonderful before?'

Not a syllable in reply.

' Your Excellency judges our age to be infamous, nor would I say that all nowadays is for the best; but surely the past often seems fine only because it is past . . . The important thing is not to let oneself be overwhelmed . . . I remember how in '61 when our uncle the duke was elected deputy for the first time, my father said to me, " You see? When there were Viceroys, the Uzeda were the Viceroys; now that there are deputies, our uncle is in Parliament!" Your Excellency knows I was not on good terms with my dead father; but he said then a thing which seemed to me and still seems very just . . . Once the power of our family came from kings; now it comes from the people. The difference is more in name than fact . . . Of course it's not pleasant to depend on the mob, but lots of those sovereigns were not exactly saints. And one man alone who holds the reins of power in his own hands and considers himself invested by divine right and makes a law of his every whim is more difficult to win over and keep on good terms with than the human flock, numerous but servile by nature . . . And then the change is more apparent than actual. Even the Viceroys of long ago had to propitiate the mob; otherwise ambassadors went and complained in Madrid and had them recalled by the Court . . . and even beheaded! . . . You may have been told that nowadays an election costs money, but remember what Mugnòs wrote about the Viceroy Lopez Ximenes, who had to offer thirty thousand *scudi* to King Ferdinando in order to keep his job . . . and wasted the money! How right Solomon was when he said there's nothing new under the sun! All complain of present corruption and refuse to trust the electoral system because votes are bought. But does Your Excellency know Suetonius, the celebrated writer of antiquity? He tells how Augustus, on election days, would distribute a thousand sesterces a head to the patrician order of which he was a member, so that they should not take anything from the candidates . . .'

He was saying these things for himself too, to affirm the justice of his own views, but as the old woman did not move he thought that maybe she had dozed off and he was talking to the wall. So he got up to look; Donna Ferdinanda's eyes were wide open. Then he went on, walking up and down the room.

'History is monotonous repetition; men have been, are and will always be the same. Exterior conditions change. Certainly there seems an abyss between the Sicily of before 1860, still more-or-less feudal, and this of today, but the difference is all on the surface. The first man to be elected by near-universal suffrage is not a member of the working class, or a bourgeois or a democrat; it is I, because I'm called Prince of Francalanza. The prestige of nobility is not and cannot be extinguished. Now that all talk of democracy, do you know what is the most sought-after book in the university library where I sometimes go for my studies? The *Sicilian Herald* of poor old Uncle Don Eugenio, peace be on his soul. It's been so much handled that it's had to be rebound three times! For just consider: before being noble meant the enjoyment of great prerogatives, privileges, immunities, and important exemptions. Now if all that is over, if nobility is something purely ideal yet sought after by all, may that not mean that its value, its prestige, have grown? . . . In politics Your Excellency has been loyal to the Bourbons, and that is most proper if they are considered as legitimate sovereigns . . . But what does their legitimacy depend on? On the fact that they were on the throne for more than a hundred years . . . Eighty years from now Your Excellency would also recognise the Savoy dynasty as legitimate . . . Of course absolute monarchy did look after our class interests better, but it's been overwhelmed by a superior force and an irresistible current . . . Must we too set their feet on our own necks? Our duty, it seems to me, instead of despising the new laws, is to use them! . . .'

Swept away by oratorical fervour in the exaltation of his recent triumph, feeling a need to justify himself in his own eyes, to re-establish himself in the old woman's good graces, he was

625

improvising another speech, the true one, in confutation of what he had said before the mob. And the old woman lay there listening, without coughing now, subjugated by her nephew's eloquence, entertained, almost lulled by his emphatic and theatrical declamation.

' Does Your Excellency remember our readings of Mugnòs? . . .' went on Consalvo. ' Well, let us imagine that historian to be still alive and wanting to bring up to date his *Genealogical Theatre* at the chapter *On the family of Uzeda*. What would he say? He'd say more or less, " Don Gafpare Vzeda " ', he pronounced the ' s ' as ' f ' and the ' U ' as ' V ', ' " was promoted to highest ranks during the great changes resulting in the passing of Sicily from King Don Francis II of Bourbon to King Don Victor Emmanuel II of Savoy. He was elected Deputy to the National Parliament of Turin, Florence and Rome, and was eventually raised by King Don Umberto with singular despatch to the rank of Senator. Don Consalvo Uzeda, Eighth Prince of Francalanza, held power as Mayor of his native town, was then Deputy to the Parliament of Rome and after that . . ." ' He was silent a moment, with closed eyes; already he saw himself on the Ministerial bench at Montecitorio. Then he went on, ' That is what Mugnòs would say if he were alive today; this is what the future historians of our family will say in different words. The old Uzeda were Knights of St James, now they are Knights of the Crown of Italy. The two things are different, but through no fault of theirs! And Your Excellency considers them degenerate! Why, may I ask?'

The old woman did not reply.

' Physically, yes; our blood is impoverished; and yet that does not prevent many of us reaching Your Excellency's enviable age in health and sanity . . . By nature they're often stubborn, excessive, unbalanced, and even . . .' He wanted to add ' mad ' but passed over that. ' They're never at peace between themselves and always at each other's throats. But let Your Excellency think of the past! Remember that Don Blasco Uzeda was nicknamed in the Sicilian tongue *Sciarra* which may be translated as *Quarreller*. Remember that other Artale Uzeda, nicknamed *Sconza*, which means *Rotten*! . . . I and my father did not see eye to eye, and he disinherited me, but the Viceroy Ximenes imprisoned his son and condemned him to death . . . Your Excellency can see that in some aspects times have changed for the better . . . And remember the felony of the sons of Artale III; remember all the quarrels between relatives, about confiscated property, about dowries . . .

'Even so I have no intention of justifying what is happening now. We're too voluble and too pig-headed at the same time. Look at my Aunt Chiara, first willing to die rather than marry the marchese, then one mind with him in two bodies, then completely broken with him. Look at my Aunt Lucrezia, who, vice versa, acted the madwoman to marry Giulente, then despised him like a servant, and is now all one with him to the point of quarrelling with me and pushing him into a ridiculous electoral fiasco! Look, in another way, even at Teresa. From filial obedience, to be thought saintly, she married someone she did not love, so hastening poor Giovannino's madness and suicide, and now she goes and kneels all day in the Chapel of Blessed Ximena, where the lamp burns which she lit for her poor cousin's health! And what was Blessed Ximena herself if not divinely pig-headed?

'I myself, since the day when I decided to change my life, have lived only to prepare myself for the new one. But our family history is full of similar sudden conversions, of stubborn addiction to good or evil . . . I could try and amuse Your Excellency by writing out all our contemporary family history in the style of old authors. Your Excellency would soon realise your judgment to be mistaken. No, our race has not degenerated; it is the same as it ever was.'